Soul Flame
Domina
Childsong
Yesterday's Child
The Magdalene Scrolls
Hounds and Jackals
Night Trains (with Gareth Wootton)
The Watchgods
Curse This House
Vital Signs

Green City in the Sun

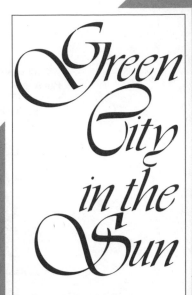

Green City in the Sun

BARBARA WOOD

RANDOM HOUSE
NEW YORK

Library of Congress Cataloging-in-Publication Data

Wood, Barbara.
Green city in the sun.

1. Kenya—History—Fiction. I. Title.
PS3573.05877G74   1988   813'.54   87-26527
ISBN 0-394-55966-5

Manufactured in the United States of America
98765432
First Edition

DESIGNED BY DEBBIE GLASSERMAN

*This book is dedicated to my husband,
George, with love*

ACKNOWLEDGMENTS

I would like to thank the following Kenya people for their kind assistance:

In Nairobi:
Professor Godfrey Muriuki and his wife, Margaret, both of the University of Nairobi; Philip and Ida Karanja; Rasheeda Litt of Universal Safari Tours; Allen and Gachiku Gicheru; Dr. Igo Mann and his charming wife, Erica; John Moller, who explained about hunting; Valerie and Heming Gullberg, coffee growers; and the staff of the Kenya National Archives, for smoothing the way.

In Nyeri:
Satvinder and Jaswaran Sehmi, who became our good friends; Mr. Che Che, manager of the Outspan Hotel; Irene Mugambi, for sharing her invaluable insight into Kenya women.

In Nanyuki:
Mr. and Mrs. Jacobson; Mr. Edmond Hoarau, general manager of the Mount Kenya Safari Club, for making our stay there so pleasant; Jane Tatham Warter and her friend Mrs. Elizabeth Ravenhill; and P. A. G. ("Sandy") Field, for a delightful afternoon of talk.

Thanks also to Terence and Nicole Cavaghan, for an invaluable introduction; Tim and Rainie Samuels; Marvin and Sjanie Holm, who gave us that first, critical introduction; and, finally, Bob and Sue Morgan of Survival Ministries, for taking us into their home in Karen, for sharing their lives and love with us, for introducing us to their Kenya friends, and for coming to our aid in a dire moment.

And to Abdul Selim, surely the most patient and cheerful driver in all of East Africa, a special *asante sana.*

All Kikuyu and Swahili words and names are pronounced as written.

The name of the African family Mathenge is pronounced Ma-THEN-gay.

Kenya was, until 1963, pronounced Kee-nya. After independence the *e* was shortened and the pronunciation became officially Ken-ya, as in "pen-ya."

FOREWORD

Kenya came into existence by accident.

In 1894 the British were anxious to get to Uganda, a strategic military point at the headwaters of the Nile in the heart of Africa, so they built a railway from the east coast of Africa inland six hundred miles to Lake Victoria, the gateway to Uganda. As it happened, that train crossed a stretch of land inhabited by wild game and warring tribes, a land that appealed only to intrepid explorers and missionaries. When, after its completion, the Uganda Railway proved to be a financial drain and a white elephant, the British government sought a way to make the railway pay for itself. The answer, it was soon seen, lay in encouraging settlement along the line.

The first to be offered this "vacant" territory were the Zionist Jews, who were at that time searching for a permanent homeland. But the Jews declined, wanting to go to Palestine. So a campaign was launched to lure immigrants from all over the British Empire. Treaties were drawn up with the local tribes, which had little concept of treaties and were somewhat perplexed by what the white man was doing here; then the government offered, cheaply, huge tracts of "unused" wilderness to anyone who would come and settle and develop it. The central highlands of this country, being at a high elevation, were cool and fertile and lush; many Britons from England, Australia, and New Zealand, looking for a new home, a place to make a fresh start and build a new life, were attracted.

Although the Colonial Office staunchly maintained that the area was just a protectorate and would one day be returned to its black inhabitants when they had been taught how to run it, in 1905, when two thousand whites were outnumbered by four million Africans, the British commissioner for the East Africa Protectorate declared that the protectorate was a "White Man's country."

Green
City
in the
Sun

D r. Treverton?"
      Deborah awoke with a start. She saw the Pan Am flight attend-
ant smiling down at her. Then she felt the shuddering of the plane
which meant it was beginning its descent to Nairobi. "Yes?" she said
to the young woman, shaking off the lingering effects of sleep.

"We have received a message for you. You will be met at the
airport."

Deborah was breathless. "Thank you," she said. She closed her eyes
again. She was tired. The flight had been a long one—twenty-six hours
almost nonstop, with a change of planes in New York, a refueling in
Nigeria. She was going to be met. *By whom?*

In her purse was the letter that she had received the week before at
the hospital and which had taken her by surprise. It had come from
Our Lady of Grace Mission in Kenya, which was requesting that
Deborah come because Mama Wachera was dying and asking for her.

"Why go back," Jonathan had said, "if you don't want to? Throw
the letter away. Ignore it."

Deborah had not replied. She had lain unable to speak in Jonathan's
arms. He would never understand why she had to go back to Africa or
why it frightened her to do so. It was because of the secret she had kept
from him, the man she was going to marry.

After Deborah had claimed her suitcase and gone through customs,
she saw, in the crowd waiting on the other side of the guarded exit, a
man holding a chalkboard with her name written on it. DR. DEBORAH
TREVERTON.

She stared at him. He was a tall, well-dressed African, Kikuyu,

Deborah judged, the man the mission had sent to meet her. She walked past him and hailed one of the taxis lined up along the curb outside. This, Deborah hoped, would buy her additional time. Time in which to decide if she was really going to go through with it, go back to the mission and face Mama Wachera. The mission driver would report that Dr. Treverton had not come in on this flight, and so they wouldn't be expecting her. Not yet.

"Who *is* this Mama Wachera?" Jonathan had asked as he and Deborah had watched the fog roll into San Francisco Bay.

But Deborah hadn't told him. She had not been able to bring herself to say, "Mama Wachera is an old African medicine woman who put a curse on my family many years ago." Jonathan would have laughed, and he would have chided Deborah for the seriousness of her tone.

But there was more. Mama Wachera was the reason why Deborah lived in America, the cause of her leaving Kenya. It all was tied up with the secret she kept from Jonathan, the chapter in her past which she would never talk about, not even after they were married.

The taxi sped through darkness. It was two o'clock in the morning, black and chilly, with the equatorial moon peeping through branches of flat-topped thorn trees. Overhead the stars were like dust. Deborah withdrew into her thoughts. *One step at a time,* she reminded herself. From the moment she had received the letter asking her to come, Deborah had moved only one step at a time, trying not to think of what lay beyond each of those steps.

The first thing she had done was arrange with Jonathan to take care of her patients. They were in practice together, two surgeons sharing an office; they had become business partners before deciding to become marital partners. Then Deborah had canceled her speaking engagement at the medical school and had arranged for someone else to chair the annual medical conference in Carmel. The appointments for next month she had let stand, confident that she would be home long before then.

Finally Deborah had obtained a visa from the Kenya Embassy—she was a United States citizen now and no longer carried a Kenya passport—had purchased malaria pills, had received last-minute shots for cholera and yellow fever, and had, twenty-eight hours ago, miraculously, finally boarded the plane at the San Francisco airport.

"Call me the instant you get to Nairobi," Jonathan had said as he had held her tightly at the departure gate. "And call me every day while you're there. Come back soon, Deb."

He had kissed her, long and hard, in front of the other passengers, so unlike Jonathan, as if to give her an incentive to return.

The taxi followed the dark, deserted highway and took a curve at high speed, its headlights sweeping over a roadside sign and briefly illuminating the words WELCOME TO NAIROBI, GREEN CITY IN THE SUN.

Deborah felt a pang. It rocked her out of the numb state the long flight had lulled her into. She thought: *I have come home.*

The Nairobi Hilton was a golden column of light rising from the sleeping city. When the taxi drew up to the brightly lit entrance, the doorman, an African in maroon coat and top hat, hurried down to open Deborah's door. As she stepped into the cool February night, he said, "Welcome, madam," and Deborah found herself unable to reply.

She was suddenly remembering. As a teenager she had accompanied her aunt Grace on shopping trips into Nairobi, and Deborah had stood on the sidewalk in those days gawking at the taxis pulling up to the fronts of fabulous hotels. Out of those cars *tourists* had stepped, amazing people from faraway places, decked out in cameras and stiff new safari khakis, surrounded by heaps of luggage, laughing, excited. Young Deborah had stared, fascinated, wondering about them, envying them, wishing she could be part of their wonderful world. And now here she was, paying a taxi driver and following the doorman up marble steps to the polished glass doors he held open for her.

It made Deborah feel sorry for that young girl. *How wrong she had been.*

The people behind the front desk all were African and young, dressed in smart red uniforms and speaking perfect English. All the girls, Deborah saw, wore their hair in tight cornrow braids, twisted into intricate birdcage styles. She also saw what they chose to ignore: their receding hairlines. By middle age these young women would be nearly bald—the price for high Kenya fashion.

They welcomed Dr. Treverton warmly. She smiled back but spoke little, taking refuge behind her facade. Deborah didn't want them to know the truth about her, didn't want to give herself away with her British accent. The desk clerks saw a slender woman in her early thirties, looking very American in blue jeans and western shirt. What they did not know was that she was not American at all, but pure Kenyan like themselves, who spoke their native language as easily as they spoke it.

There was a basket of fresh fruit waiting in her room, and the bed had been turned down; a chocolate mint in silver foil lay on the pillow. A note from the management said, *"lala salama,"* "sleep well."

As the porter pointed to the bathroom, the minibar, and the TV, Deborah went through the money she had obtained from the cashier downstairs, trying to recall the current exchange rate. She tipped the man twenty shillings and saw by his smile that it was too much.

And then she was alone.

She went to the window and looked out. There was not much to see, just the dark shapes of a city folded up for the night. It was quiet, with not much traffic and not a pedestrian in sight. Nairobi, which Deborah had said good-bye to fifteen years ago.

On that day an angry and terrified Deborah, just eighteen years old, had vowed never to set foot in this country again and had walked onto the airplane determined to find herself a new home, a new place in the sun. She had worked hard in the following years to create a new self and to put behind her this Africa, which was in her blood. Deborah had found an ending at last in San Francisco, in Jonathan. There she had found a place where she could belong, a man who could be her sanctuary.

And then the letter had come. How had the nuns found her? How had they known the hospital where she worked, that she was even in San Francisco? The sisters at the mission must have gone to a lot of trouble and expense to find her. Why? Because that old woman was dying at last?

Why ask for me? Deborah mentally asked her reflection in the window. *You always hated me, Mama Wachera, always resented me because I was a Treverton.*

What have I to do with your final moments on earth?

"Urgent," the letter had said. "Come at once."

Deborah rested her forehead against the cold glass. She was remembering her last days in Kenya and the terrible thing the medicine woman had said to her. With the memory came all the old pain and sickness Deborah thought she had rid herself of.

She went into the bathroom and turned on the bright light. After running hot water into the bathtub and scenting it with the Nivea bath foam the Hilton provided, she turned to look at herself in the mirror.

This was Deborah's final face, after so many, and she was satisfied with it. Fifteen years ago, when she had first arrived in America, her skin had been darkly tanned, her black hair curled short under the ears, and her clothing had been a simple sleeveless dress of Kenya cotton and sandals. Now the skin was pale, as white as she could make it, from years of pointedly avoiding the sun, and the hair was ironing-board straight, gathered in a gold clasp and flat down her back. The shirt and jeans had designer labels, as did the expensive running shoes. She had worked hard to look American, to look white.

Because she *was* white, she reminded herself now.

And then she thought of Christopher. Would he recognize her?

After her bath Deborah wrapped her long, wet hair in a towel and went to sit on the edge of the bed. She found she was not ready for sleep; there had been enough of that on the plane.

She picked up her carry-on bag, which she had not let out of her sight since leaving San Francisco. Besides containing her passport, return ticket, and traveler's checks, the bag held something more precious, and Deborah drew it out now and laid it on the bed beside her.

It was a small package of brown paper and string. She picked open the wrapping and separated the contents: an envelope of faded photographs, a bundle of old letters tied with a ribbon, and a journal.

She stared at them.

This was Deborah's legacy, all that she had come away with in her flight from Africa, all that was left of the once proud—and infamous— Treverton family. The photos she had not looked at since collecting them into this envelope and sealing it fifteen years ago; the letters she had not read again since that awful day when Mama Wachera had spoken those words to her; and the journal, an old and battered leather volume begun sixty-eight years ago, Deborah had never read. Stamped in gold on its cover was the name TREVERTON.

A name that was magic in Kenya. Deborah had recognized the expressions on the faces of the young Africans downstairs when she had checked in: the brief, startled look when she had said her name, then the moment of staring at her, of being enchanted for an instant, followed by the inevitable shuttering, the retreat behind a fixed smile to mask the hatred and resentment because of the *other* things the Trevertons had stood for. Deborah had been used to those looks as a child; she was not really surprised to find them here still.

There was a time when the name Treverton had been worshiped in Kenya. Deborah's hotel stood near a wide street that had once been Lord Treverton Avenue. Today it was Joseph Gicheru Street, named for a Kikuyu who had been martyred for independence. And the taxi had passed what had once been Treverton High School, and Deborah had seen the new sign which said MAMA WANJIRU HIGH SCHOOL.

It's as if, Deborah thought, *they are trying to erase our memory from the face of the earth.*

But no amount of "Kenyanizing," Deborah knew, was going to obliterate the Trevertons from this country. They were too ingrained, too much a part of its soul, its destiny. The mission where Mama Wachera lay dying was called Our Lady of Grace Mission, the name the Catholic sisters had given to it when they received it from Deborah's aunt many years ago. But before that it had been simply Grace Mission, named for the woman who had founded it, Grace Treverton, famous pioneer of public health in Kenya.

Dr. Grace Treverton, a legend as large as her flamboyant brother the earl, had founded the mission sixty-eight years ago, in the wilderness of the Central Province. She was the woman who had reared Deborah in the place of a real mother, and she had gone to her grave with formidable secrets locked in her heart. Aunt Grace had lived through it all, Deborah knew; she had witnessed and been part of every Treverton triumph and shame, had seen Kenya rise and fall and rise again.

Deborah reached out and touched the items on the bed; she was almost afraid of them. The photos—she barely remembered who the people in them were. *Christopher as a youth. But not as a man. I regret that.* And the letters—Deborah recalled in them only the few, devastating lines. Lastly, the journal, all that was left of Aunt Grace's legacy.

Deborah had never read the journal. At the time of Grace's death she had been too grief-stricken to open it; later she had turned her back on the family and the past this book represented and contained.

She picked it up now and held it between her hands.

She imagined she felt an energy emerge from it. The Trevertons! In public a beautiful people, rich beyond imagining, members of nobility, gay polo-playing society leaders, primary movers in East Africa; but in private tormented by secrets, by a poor boy's affliction that was the family disgrace, by a sensational trial that had made headlines around the world, by forbidden loves and lusts, and by darker secrets yet— rumors even of human sacrifice and murder.

And of superstitions—Mama Wachera and her curse.

And Christopher, Deborah wondered. *My handsome, gentle Christopher. Were we, too, victims of the Treverton family's fate?*

Deborah opened the envelope and drew out the photographs. There were seven of them, the one on top having been taken back in 1963, just before Kenya's independence and the end of the world as she had known it. It was a group snapshot, taken with an old Box Brownie. Four children had been arranged according to height: Christopher was the tallest, being the oldest—eleven. Next to him was Sarah, his little sister, the same age as Deborah, who was eight and who stood in the middle. Last came Terry Donald, ten years old and even then a robust little boy in khaki hunting outfit.

Tears blurred Deborah's vision as she peered closely at the smiling faces. Four barefoot kids, dirty and happy, standing in the middle of goats and chickens, seeming to be without a care in the world, unaware of the storm of change that was gathering around them, that would shatter their world. Four children—two African, two white, and all the best of friends.

Sarah, my dearest friend, Deborah thought sadly. *We grew up together, played with dolls together, discovered boys together.* Sarah, black and beautiful, had shared her dreams with Deborah. They had been as close as sisters, had planned their futures together, only to be torn apart by the old medicine woman. What had become of Sarah? Was she still here in Kenya?

Deborah picked up another photo. It was of Aunt Grace, taken back in the 1930s. Looking at the sweet oval face, the smile, the softly marcel-waved hair that seemed to glow like a halo about her head, Deborah could not believe that Grace Treverton had once been accused of being "mannish." This remarkable woman was known for another great achievement besides the founding of the mission: She had written a book titled *When* You *Have to Be the Doctor*. First published fifty-eight years ago and periodically revised and updated, it was one of the most widely used health manuals in the third world.

The next picture was of a darkly handsome man riding a polo pony. Valentine, the Earl of Treverton, Deborah's grandfather—a man she'd never known. Even in this small and slightly out-of-focus shot she could see what everyone else had seen in him—a strikingly attractive man, with a resemblance to Laurence Olivier. On the back was written: "July 1928, the day we had lunch with His Royal Highness Prince Edward, the Prince of Wales."

The fourth photograph bore no date, no inscription, but Deborah knew who it was—Rose, Countess of Treverton. It looked like a candid shot; Rose was looking over her shoulder in surprise. There was a timeless quality to the picture, in the simplicity of her white gauze dress, the careless angle of her white parasol, the hair worn down about her shoulders, like a girl's, even though, at the time of this picture, she must have been around thirty. Deborah was drawn to her eyes; there was a haunted look to them, a strange melancholy that made one wonder what pain had afflicted this woman.

Deborah could not bring herself to look at the last three pictures. The room was becoming crowded with ghosts, and some were the ghosts of people not even dead. Where was Sarah, for instance, at this moment? Sarah, who had had such dreams, such ambition! Gifted with an artistic talent that had made Deborah amazed and envious, Sarah had dreamed of designing a whole new "Kenya look" in clothing. She had dreamed of fame and riches, and Deborah had left her, abruptly, on that fragile brink.

Sarah Wachera Mathenge, Deborah thought. *My sister . . .*

Then Deborah thought of Terry Donald, a ruddy, handsome boy whose bloodline stemmed from the early adventurers and explorers of the Dark Continent—the last in a line of white men born in Kenya, with the savannas and jungles and the hunt in their very bones.

And finally, Christopher . . .

Deborah put the pictures back in the envelope.

Was Christopher still in Kenya? Fifteen years ago she had left him without explaining to him why or even that she was going. They had made plans to get married; they were in love. But she had deserted him, as she had Sarah, without a backward look.

Suddenly Deborah knew she had come back to Africa not because a dying old woman was asking for her, but in the hope of finding herself, her people, again.

It all came clear. There was Jonathan, back in San Francisco, waiting for her. But Deborah knew that somehow she had hesitated to make that final commitment to him and to the family they hoped to have together, before she had first reconciled the present with the past. Jonathan didn't know much about Deborah's past, about her search for identity. He knew nothing of Christopher, or of the painful truths Deborah had learned about him. Nor had Deborah told Jonathan of the discovery she had made fifteen years ago, when she had found out that Mama Wachera, the African medicine woman, was, in fact, her grandmother.

Deborah picked up Aunt Grace's journal again, suddenly anxious to read it. She felt a powerful draw to its pages. She trembled to think of the revelations she might read here, yet perhaps there would be answers, too, and a key to her peace of mind.

As her eyes settled on the first page, on the faded ink and the date, "February 10, 1919," Deborah thought: *Perhaps those were the best days, so many years ago; then Kenya had been young and innocent; visions had been crystal clear; people knew where they were going; their hearts were earnest. The men and women who came to Kenya were bold and adventurous, not just ordinary people, but people driven by a pioneering spirit to create a new land for themselves and for their children.*

They are part of me, no matter how hard I've tried to run away from them; they live in me still. But there are others also, those who were already here, living on ancient ancestral land, when the white strangers came. They are part of me, too. . . .

PART
ONE
1919

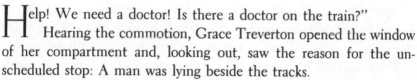

Help! We need a doctor! Is there a doctor on the train?"
Hearing the commotion, Grace Treverton opened the window
of her compartment and, looking out, saw the reason for the un-
scheduled stop: A man was lying beside the tracks.

"What is it?" said Lady Rose as her sister-in-law Grace reached for
the medical bag.

"A man is hurt."

"Oh, dear."

Grace paused before leaving the car. Rose wasn't looking good. Her
skin had taken on a disturbing pallor in the last hour. They were only
eighty miles out of Mombasa, the seaport where they had boarded the
train, and they would not arrive at Voi, their dinner stop, for several
more miles. "You should eat something, Rose," Grace said, giving a
significant look to Fanny, Rose's lady's maid. "And drink something.
I'll just quickly see to that poor man."

"I'm quite all right," Rose said a trifle breathlessly. She dabbed her
forehead with a perfumed handkerchief and rested her hands on her
abdomen.

Grace hesitated a moment longer. If there was something wrong,
especially with the baby, Rose could not be depended upon to admit
it. Giving another look to Fanny, which said, *Stay close to your mistress,*
Grace hurried out of the carriage.

The desert sun and dust engulfed her at once. After weeks of being
cooped up on board the ship and these past eighty miles confined to
the tiny train compartment, Grace felt momentarily dizzied by the vast
African sky.

When she reached the stricken man, a group had gathered around him, talking in a mixture of English, Hindi, and Swahili. Grace said, "Pardon me, please," and tried to push through.

"Stay away, miss. 'Tain't no sight for a lady." A man turned to stop her, and his eyebrows shot up.

"I might be able to help," she said, sidestepping him. "I'm a doctor."

The other men now looked at her in surprise, and when she knelt next to the fallen man, they all fell silent.

They had never seen a woman dressed so strangely.

Grace Treverton wore a white shirt with a black tie, a black tailored jacket, a dark blue skirt that reached her ankles, and, most curious of all, a wide-brimmed black velour tricorn hat. These colonial men, living out of touch, on the fringes of the British Empire, did not recognize the uniform of an officer in the Women's Royal Naval Service.

They watched in astonishment as she examined the man's wounds without the slightest flinch, with no sign of fainting. The man was positively *bloody*, they were thinking, and this queer female was as calm as if she were pouring tea!

The men began to murmur. Grace ignored them, trying to do something for the unconscious man, who was a native dressed in skins and beads and who appeared to have been the victim of a lion. While she worked with the antiseptics and dressings from her bag, Grace heard the low voices of the men standing around her, and she recognized the drift of what they were saying.

Some were shocked, scandalized at her behavior, others were amused, and all were skeptical. No proper lady, Grace had heard since she first entered medical school back in London, would involve herself in such unpleasantness. Her behavior was downright improper! But these men could have no idea that the wounds of this poor African were nothing compared with the injuries Grace had treated on board the hospital ship that had assisted in the evacuation of Gallipoli.

"We must put him on the train," she said at last, when nothing more could be done for him.

No one moved. She looked up. "He needs proper help. These cuts need to be sutured. He's lost blood. Well, good heavens, don't just stand there!"

"He's done for, that one," a voice grumbled.

"Don't know who he is anyway," said another.

"Masai," said a third, as if that were supposed to explain something.

Grace stood up. "Two of you pick him up and put him on the train. At once!"

They shuffled uncertainly. A few men turned and walked away. The rest looked at one another. Who was *she* to be giving them orders? They looked at her again. But she *was* awfully pretty, and she did appear to be a lady.

Finally two men lifted the native and deposited him inside the brake van. As Grace turned back toward her compartment, she heard a few snickers, and two men looked at her with undisguised contempt.

But at the carriage another man was waiting, sunburned and smiling, to help her up the impossible steps. "Don't mind them," he said as he touched the brim of his hat. "They're behind the times by ten years."

Grace smiled in gratitude and paused on the small platform to watch him stride back to the second-class carriage.

She returned to her seat to find Rose fanning herself and staring out the window.

Grace reached across and touched her sister-in-law's thin wrist. She counted a strong and steady pulse. Then she felt the abdomen beneath the gauze of Rose's summer dress.

Alarmed, Grace sat back in her seat. The baby had descended into the pelvis.

"Rose," she said cautiously, "when did the baby drop?"

Lady Rose brought her gaze away from the window and blinked, as if she had been far away, out on the plain among the thorn trees and waterless scrub. "While you were outside," she said.

Grace tried not to let her sudden worry show. Above all, Rose must be kept quiet and untroubled. And this journey wasn't helping!

Grace opened the flask of mineral water, poured some into a silver cup, and handed it to her sister-in-law. While Rose drank, spilling a little when the train gave a lurch and started to roll again, Grace tried to think.

The baby had descended too soon. It wasn't time yet. The due date was more than a month away. Did that mean there was something wrong? And how far off, then, could the birth be? *Surely we have time!* she thought, reflecting on this deplorable little train with its individual carriages that separated the passengers from one another. Once the train was moving, there was no way to stop it, to get help.

Grace was angry with herself. She should not have allowed Rose to travel. She should have put her foot down. Rose wasn't a strong woman to begin with; the rigors of the journey from England had taken their toll. But Rose would not be dissuaded. "I want my son to be born in our new home," she had persisted in her maddeningly illogical way. Ever since Valentine, Rose's husband and Grace's brother, had written eloquent letters describing the magnificent house he had built in the central highlands of British East Africa, Rose had been obsessed with having the baby there. And to weaken further Grace's stand that Rose wait to travel until after the child had been born, Valentine had written insisting that they come, agreeing with his wife that his son should be born in their new country.

Grace had written angry replies, but both brother and sister-in-law had preferred to set aside common sense and act out their impractical dream.

And so the two women had left England and Bella Hill, the ancestral mansion in Suffolk, with all their possessions and the company of six servants, to brave the safe postwar seas and come to the recently demilitarized, exotic, and alluring British East Africa Protectorate.

Lady Rose leaned forward and fussed for a moment over her rose-bushes. Although the five other servants and the family dogs rode behind in the second-class carriage, these rosebushes accompanied the countess as if they were children. Grace eyed them in annoyance; those plants had created more than one episode of inconvenience since they had left England! And then she softened when she saw how her sister-in-law fretted over them.

Soon now, Grace thought, *she will have the baby to center her life on.* The baby that Rose had so desperately wanted, even after the specialists in London had pronounced her incapable of childbearing. The baby, Grace reminded herself now, that she hoped would make her brother settle down.

She sighed and gazed out the window. Valentine was a restless man; this untamed country suited him. Grace could see why he had been smitten by East Africa, could understand his decision to leave Bella Hill in the care of their younger brother and come here to carve a new empire out of the wilderness.

Perhaps this land will tame him, Grace thought as the train rocked her to sleep. *Perhaps Valentine will be a new man. . . .*

GRACE WAS STILL thinking of men when the train pulled into Voi station and the passengers made a dash for the dining hut. She had dreamed of the hospital ship again, and of Jeremy.

Because of her sister-in-law's condition, it was not proper for the two women to dine with the other passengers, and so a supper was brought into the private carriage and served by an elderly, respectable-looking African. Grace touched little of the boiled beef and cabbage as she looked out the window at the dining bungalow, brightly lit against the desert night. She watched the men inside, eating at tables covered with proper white tablecloths, using china and silver, being waited on by wine stewards and white-jacketed waiters. The night air was filled with the rumble of men's talk and laughter and with the smoke from their cigars. Grace envied them.

Rose sipped claret out of a crystal stem glass and spoke quietly of her plans for the new house. "I shall plant my roses where I can always see them. And I shall have an At Home every Wednesday and shall invite all the suitable ladies from the neighborhood."

Grace smiled indulgently at her sister-in-law. There was no need to disillusion Rose yet; she would learn soon enough the reality of her new life when she saw the plantation and discovered that her nearest neighbor was miles away and that the "ladies" Rose spoke of were going to be hardworking farm wives with little time for afternoon teas.

Something outside the window caught Grace's attention. It was the man who had earlier helped her up the carriage steps. He was overseeing the transfer of supplies from the train to some wagons, and the supplies, Grace saw, were guns and camping gear. *So,* she thought, *he is a hunter and is leaving the train here at Voi.*

Curious about him, Grace watched him. He looked very fetching in his khakis and pith helmet. When he turned suddenly and met her gaze, Grace's heart skipped a beat. He smiled, and then, as he swung himself up onto a horse, he saluted and rode away.

As she watched him disappear into the night, she realized that this was the way it always was with Grace and men—and how it would always be. She confounded them, like those that afternoon who had not known how to act around her, or she brought out in them some inexplicable resentment, or she received their highest compliment, like the hunter's; that they regarded her as being as good as any man and therefore worth treating as a fellow.

Grace recalled the men on the hospital ship, the wounded ones who were brought aboard each day. How wonderful they were with her at first, flirting, thinking she was a nurse. And then how abruptly their attitude changed when they discovered she was a doctor *and* an officer: the sudden deference and arch respect, the creation of an invisible barrier that she didn't know how to cross.

The day she had been accepted into medical school, nine years ago, Grace had been counseled by an elderly woman doctor. "You will find that your new title will be a curse as well as a blessing to you, " Dr. Smythe had said. "Many male doctors will resent your intrusion into their jealously guarded fraternity, and many male patients will judge you incapable of practicing medicine. You will not have a normal social life because you will not fit into any of the accepted feminine roles. Some men will place you on a pedestal and make you unreachable to them. Others will see you as a curiosity, a freak. You will intimidate some, amuse others. You will be entering a man's world without being accepted as a full member, and you will receive few of the privileges of that world."

Dr. Alice Smythe, in her sixties and never married, had spoken truly. Grace Treverton was now twenty-nine—and a spinster.

She rested back in her seat and closed her eyes.

This was the "price" she had been warned about years ago, when she had announced her intention to pursue the study of medicine. Her father, the old earl, had refused to support her, and her brothers had laughed, predicting she was going to give up her femininity. Something of their prophecy had come true. She had indeed made sacrifices. There was little prospect now of marriage and babies, and she was, at nearly thirty and despite two years at sea working among thousands of soldiers, still a virgin.

But not all men were like her brothers or those rough men in the dining hut. There was the hunter who had noticed her, and back in Egypt, where she had been stationed during the war, Grace had encountered officers, cultured gentlemen who had respected the stripes of rank on her sleeve and the M.D. after her name.

And there had been Jeremy.

In truth, Dr. Smythe's forecast had seemed extreme when Jeremy had placed the engagement ring on Grace's left hand. But that dream had gone down with the torpedoed ship, and with Jeremy, in the cold dark waters of the Mediterranean.

The supper dishes were cleared away, and the women were asked to stand on the carriage platform while their beds were made up. Grace supported her sister-in-law by the elbow as they stood at the rail, breathing in the fresh night air and marveling at the splendor of the stars. Soon the full moon would be rising over Mount Kilimanjaro.

England seemed a galaxy away now, almost as if it had never existed. How long ago it seemed, the departure from Southampton. And then the three weeks' steaming eastward, each day taking one farther from familiar sights and deeper into the unknown. Port Said had seemed strange to Grace now that the war was over and tourists were beginning to come back. Peasants had come aboard the ship with their trinkets and "guaranteed" ancient artifacts; vendors had circulated with food and strong Egyptian wine. Then there had been the Suez Canal, surrounded by harsh, barren desert, and Port Sudan with its stately trains of camels and Arabs in burnooses. From Aden, that bleak oasis in the wilderness, the steamer had carried them along the exotic Somali coast into the sultry Indian Ocean, where sunsets streaked the sky in crimson and gold. Finally Mombasa, the coast of British East Africa, with its bleached white buildings, coconut palms, mango trees, brilliant flowering shrubs, and Arabs hawking everything anyone could desire. Where were the mist of Suffolk, the dignified old stones of Bella Hill, the Elizabethan pubs along country lanes? They belonged to another world and in another time.

Grace stared at the men sitting on the veranda of the dining hut, with brandy and cigars, waiting for their berths to be made up and for the journey to resume. What dreams had brought them to this wild and virgin territory? Which ones would survive; which, fail? What lay ahead for each of them at the end of this train ride? Nearly a whole day must be spent on the rails before Nairobi could be reached. After that, for Countess Treverton and her retinue, there would be many days yet in an oxcart, on the dirt track to Nyeri in the north.

Grace trembled to think of it. Her dream, the dream she had shared with Jeremy during their cruelly brief time together, lay at the end of that savage road. It was Jeremy who had spun the glorious vision in her head, of a haven of hope and mercy in the wilderness; he had planned to come to Africa after the war and bring the Word of God to the heathen. They were going to work together, Jeremy healing the spirit and Grace, the body. They had filled their shipboard nights with talk of the mission they were going to establish in British East Africa, and now the moment was close at hand. Grace was going to build that hospital, for Jeremy; she was going to carry his beautiful light into the African darkness.

"Dear me," said Lady Rose, leaning against her sister-in-law, "I believe I must lie down."

Grace was startled when she looked at her; Lady Rose's face had gone as white as her muslin dress. "Rose? Are you in pain?"

"No . . ."

Grace struggled with indecision. To continue on or to stay here? But this desert station was no place for a woman about to have a baby, and Nairobi lay only a day away.

Grant us time, Lord, Grace prayed as she and Fanny put Rose to bed. *Don't let it happen here. I have no chloroform, no hot water.*

There was no sign of distress on Rose's face; her expression was dreamy, as if she were far away. "Are my roses all right?" was all she said.

After waiting for her sister-in-law to drift off to sleep, Grace removed her navy suit, brushed it out, and hung it up. Many women doctors were accused of adopting masculine traits, and Grace's continuing to wear her uniform, despite the fact that she had been discharged from the navy a year ago, was looked upon with suspicion. Which was nonsense. Grace was simply a pragmatic woman. The suit was good quality; the stripes had been removed from the sleeve; there was no reason it could not be worn for years to come.

"Our little sailoress" Valentine had called her. Even though their father had fought in the Crimean War, and even though Valentine had enlisted to fight the Germans in East Africa and had served as a regimental officer, Grace's joining the navy had been met with great disapproval. But Grace had the Treverton stubborn streak and had followed the dictates of her conscience. Just as she was following it now, here in Africa, determined to fulfill a dream that had been born on a warship in the Mediterranean.

Valentine didn't approve of her plan to build a hospital in the bush, bearing as he did a deep-rooted contempt for missionaries in general, and he had informed his sister that in no way was he going to assist in such a folly. But Grace did not need Valentine's help; she had a small income from her inheritance, a little support from local churches back in Suffolk, and she was possessed of a backbone as stiff as any man's.

A moan came from Lady Rose's berth. Grace turned sharply. Her fragile sister-in-law lay breathing deeply with her hands on her abdomen.

"Are you all right?" Grace asked.

Rose smiled. "We are fine."

Grace smiled back, comfortingly, to mask her fear. So many miles, so many *days* to go yet—and the worst of the journey still ahead!

"Is he kicking?" she asked, and Rose nodded.

It had been decided that the baby would be named Arthur, for the younger brother who had been killed in France in the first year of the war. The Honorable Arthur Currie Treverton, one of the first brave boys to sign up when England went to war.

The whistle blew, and the train began to roll. Grace looked out the window and saw the reassuring lights of Voi station fall behind; then there was night all around. The train chuffed across a bleak and sterile landscape, following an old slave route to Lake Victoria. This modern year of 1919 was but an eye's blink from the days of Arab caravans, when chained Africans had trudged this way to the slave ships on the coast and thus to their doom. The policing of this route, to stop illegal slaving, had been part of the way the British government's propaganda had explained the embarrassment of a railway that had cost so much and seemed to go nowhere. As golden sparks from the engine flew past her window, Grace imagined the camps of those slavers, squatting under the stars, their prisoners moaning in chains, bewildered. What had it been like for those innocent Africans to be taken away on terrible ships and forced to serve masters on the other side of the world?

Grace made sure the windows were tightly closed. She had heard stories of man-eating lions that pulled people from train windows. This was a wild and uncivilized country, the night more treacherous than the day. Never had she felt so vulnerable, so isolated. There was no communication between the first-class carriages; they were like a string of little boxes hurtling through the night with no way to contact the passengers in the next cars, no way to stop the train. Grace prayed that they would make it to Nairobi in time.

She tried to relax, keeping an eye on Rose, who appeared to be sleeping, and thinking of what she would do tomorrow. *We will stay in Nairobi,* she decided. *We will not continue on until after the baby is born.*

Valentine would be petulant, of course, because delay in Nairobi could mean a delay of three or more months, as the long rains were due to start soon and all travel into the Central Province would then be impossible. But Grace would deal with her brother. She was no less anxious than he to have his wife established in the big house he had built, but for the safety of mother and child Grace was going to insist that they wait.

Knowing that she would not be able to sleep, Grace decided to begin writing in her new journal. It had been a gift from one of her professors in medical school, a handsome volume bound in Moroccan leather with gilt-edged pages. She had waited until now to start it—waited for the first day of her new life.

She had just written "February 10, 1919" on the opening page when Rose screamed.

The baby was coming.

2

She was furious with her brother.

Black clouds hung over the hills, threateningly, like vultures. And here they were, two women, six servants, and fourteen Africans, inching their way up a perilous dirt track in five wagons loaded with all their worldly possessions. What protection were the canvas covers going to be against a sudden torrent? What was Valentine going to say when he saw the ruined Aubusson carpet, the sodden paintings from Bella Hill? How was he going to soothe Rose when she saw that the lace tablecloth and silk gowns were destroyed by rain? This was a preposterous undertaking, bringing all this useless clutter into a wilderness! Valentine was insane.

Grace looked at her sister-in-law, who was bundled up in a fur coat and staring ahead as if she could see what lay at the end of this trail.

Rose was still very weak; she was shockingly pale. But she had refused to stay in Nairobi, especially after she had received the message from Valentine telling her to come ahead. Grace had tried to stand her ground, but there was Rose, the next morning, giving orders to her English servants to have the wagons loaded. Grace could not dissuade her sister-in-law from going, and so now here they were, in the middle of a wild land, hacking their way through mango trees and banana plants, fighting insects and being kept awake at night in their tents by the roar of lions and cheetahs. And the heavy rains about to break!

The sound of the baby crying made Grace turn around and look at the wagon behind her. Mrs. Pembroke, the nanny, produced a feeding bottle and quieted it.

Grace frowned. The way that baby had survived was a miracle.

When the lifeless little form had appeared on the sheets, Grace had thought certain it was dead. She had not found a heartbeat, and its face was blue. But she had blown into its mouth all the same—and it lived! A small, weak baby girl, but alive and growing stronger every day.

Grace thought about the young woman at her side. Except for the episode at the Norfolk Hotel, when she had insisted they continue on to Nyeri, Lady Rose had been silent since the birth of the baby. No, Grace reminded herself now, there had been one other exception: When pressed to give the child a name, Rose had said simply, "Mona." Grace had not known what to make of it until she had seen the romantic novel Rose had been reading on the journey. The heroine's name was Mona.

Grace had had no choice but to allow it to stand as the baby's name because her brother had made no provision in the event the baby should be a girl. In his vanity and single-minded obsession to found a dynasty, Valentine had never dreamed that he would produce anything other than a son. Grace had the baby baptized and had then sent word to her brother.

His response had been: "Come at once! All is ready!"

In the ten days since leaving Nairobi, Lady Rose had spoken not one word. Her eyes, large and dark and looking feverish, remained fixed ahead while her small white hands worked themselves inside the ermine muff. She sat inclined forward as she rode in the wagon, as if urging the oxen on. When spoken to, she did not reply; when the baby was put in her arms, she regarded it vacantly. The only interest she had shown, besides her determination to see the new house, was in her rosebushes, which rode beside her in the wagon.

It is the trauma of the birth that has caused this, Grace decided. *And the shock of so many changes all at once. She'll be better once she's in the new house.*

Before meeting Valentine on her seventeenth birthday, three years ago, Rose had lived a sheltered life. And even after her engagement to the young earl Rose had been exposed to little social life; she married him three months after the first meeting and moved into Bella Hill to be swallowed up by its Tudor shadows.

It was a mystery to everyone why Valentine had chosen shy, dreaming Rose when he had his pick of every eligible young woman in

England. Valentine was dashing, handsome, wealthy and had recently inherited a title. Granted, Rose was beautiful, in an insubstantial way— she reminded Grace of the tragic maidens Poe wrote about—but she tended to live in another world, and Grace feared she was no match for a force like Valentine.

Yet he had chosen her, and she had accepted him at once. And she had brought her incandescence into the dark, stately halls of Bella Hill.

Grace was anxious to see what her brother had accomplished in these past twelve months. People had voiced skepticism, declaring that he had taken on what looked to be an impossible task. But Grace knew that her brother was capable of incredible things.

Valentine Treverton was a passionate man with a restless nature, a man of such appetite for life that he had pronounced England stifling. He longed for a virgin world that he could make his own, where he would be the law, and where there were no traditions and precedents to tell him what to do.

Anyone who had ever met Valentine was dazzled by him. He walked with a long stride and greeted people with arms held wide as if for an embrace. His laugh was deep and honest and spontaneous. And he was so handsome that even men were charmed by him. But Grace knew his other side: his temper; his moods; his utter conceit and belief that nearly everyone else was inferior to himself. Grace had no doubt that he was going to stamp this wilderness beneath his boot.

The first raindrops made everyone look up at the sky. In an instant the Africans were shouting to one another in rapid Kikuyu and gesturing wildly. Grace didn't have to understand the language to know what they were saying. If heavy rain fell, this road would turn into an impassable bog.

"Che Che!" she called to the Kikuyu headman.

He came back to her wagon. "Yes, memsaab?"

"How much farther is it to the estate?"

He shrugged and held up five fingers.

Grace gave him an impatient look. What did the man mean? Five miles? Five hours? God forbid, five *days?* She looked up at the sky. The clouds were low, the color of charcoal; banana fronds stirred in an ominous wind. "We must hurry, Che Che," she said. "Can't we go faster?" The lead wagon seemed to Grace to creep at a snail's pace; the two men with rifles, riding lookout for wild animals, appeared to be dozing; and the natives dressed in goatskins and carrying spears merely strolled alongside.

The headman nodded to Grace and walked ahead to the first wagon, where he shouted orders in Kikuyu to the driver. But the wagon moved no faster.

Checking the urge to jump down from her wagon and prod the oxen herself, Grace wished now that she had listened to the advice of a gentleman she had met at the Blue Posts Hotel in Thika. He had explained to her that her headman's name Che Che meant "slow" in Kikuyu and that no doubt there was a good reason for his being called that. But Grace had not been inclined to hire a different headman in the middle of a journey, and as a result, here she was, between the town of Nyeri and her brother's estate, in the prelude of a storm.

She turned around and saw that Mrs. Pembroke had wisely retreated under the cover of the wagon's canvas roof, the baby in her arms, with Fanny, Rose's personal maid, sitting next to her, looking miserable. All the men were walking beside the wagons and carrying guns; even old Fitzpatrick, the butler who had come with them from Bella Hill, was looking out of character in his khakis and sun helmet.

Grace realized she might almost think this a comical parade if she weren't so anxious, so angry.

When she looked at her sister-in-law again, Grace was surprised to see a faint smile on the pale lips. She wondered what Lady Rose was thinking.

In fact, Lady Rose was concentrating on the sanctuary that lay at the end of this horrible trail: Bella Two, the home Valentine had built for her. He had written in a letter five months ago:

Our estate lies in a valley forty miles wide, between Mount Kenya and the Aberdare Range, just thirty miles south of the equator. We stand at over five thousand feet above sea level, and there is a deep, lush gorge on our property down which the Chania River tumbles and churns. The house is unique. It is of my own design, something new, for this new country. I have decided to name it Bella Two, or Bella Too; you can choose which. It is a proper house complete with library, music room, and nursery for our son.

Valentine had not needed to say more; Rose had at once pictured the new house, the house that was going to be *hers,* not a place where she felt like an outsider, surrounded by the grim portraits of Treverton ancestors. It was a house where she was going to be sole mistress at last, with the keys hanging at her waist.

Since the birth of the baby four weeks before, Rose had thought of nothing other than the new house. She had found that if she concentrated very hard and focused all her energy upon Bella Two, she would not have to think about the "other thing."

She was fantasizing now about the hours she was going to spend directing the installation of draperies, the placement of chairs and tables, the arrangements of flowers. And most important, Rose was going to see that the correct etiquette was followed for her At Homes: the polishing of the tea service that had been given to her grandmother by the Duchess of Bedford; the baking of scones and sponge cakes; the making of clotted cream; teaching the staff the proper way to make finger sandwiches, that they slice the cucumber *just so.* And Rose herself would hold the key to the tea caddy, carefully measuring out the Earl Grey and Oolong.

Just because one was in Africa, she had decided, there was no reason for one to stop being civilized. One must hold to decorum at all costs. Rose knew that her sister-in-law did not approve of, as Grace had put it, the "monstrous collection of baggage" Rose had brought with her, but Grace did not understand social obligation. That was because Grace was not going to be mistress of a five-thousand-acre plantation or the countess of Treverton, who had a responsibility to set high standards. Grace had come to Africa with but two trunks—one for her clothes and books, the other containing medical supplies!

Rose now walked in her mind through the rooms of the new house, seeing them as Valentine had described them, with their polished wood and stone columns, the beam ceilings, the fireplace as large as a theater stage. She saw the music room, where she would play the grand piano which was now traveling in the last wagon. The legs had been removed to be shipped separately from London. She saw the billiard room with its Savonnerie carpet, the type the royal family used, and there was even, in the first wagon, a carefully packed crystal chandelier for the dining room.

But when Rose's fantasy brought her to the door of the bedroom, she stopped short.

Grace, sitting beside her in the wagon, did not see the sudden stiffening of Rose's body, the smile turn into a thin line. She did not know of the thumping heart, the fresh anxiety. Rose kept it all to herself, for it was something no one must ever know.

Valentine came into her mind and she shivered. Rose already knew how he was going to react to the baby: He would pretend that nothing had happened, that little Mona hadn't even been born. He would give Rose that familiar look, that *wanting* look, and then he would start making those demands on her body again.

How overjoyed she had been, last year, to be told she was pregnant. As propriety demanded, Valentine had immediately removed himself to a separate bedroom, and Rose had luxuriated in seven months of freedom. Had the baby been a boy, Valentine would have been satisfied. But now he would renew his efforts to produce an heir, and she shuddered to think of it.

Rose had gone to Valentine a virgin and ignorant of the ways of men with women. Her wedding night had shocked her, and then revulsion had set in. It had gotten so that she would lie in bed, tense, hardly breathing, listening for his footsteps. And he would come, under the cover of darkness, and use her like an animal. But Rose had learned to take herself out of the act. When she sensed this was going to be one of his nights, she would drink laudanum before retiring and then retreat into a fantasy while he did his work. They never spoke of it, not even in the crucial moments, but Rose had once considered speaking to Grace about it. Then she had changed her mind, remembering that even though her sister-in-law *was* a medical doctor, she was still a maiden lady and therefore would know nothing about these matters. So Rose let the matter rest, assuming it was like this between all husbands and wives.

There was a sudden commotion up ahead; men at the front of the line shouted excitedly, and Che Che came running, for the first time in his life Grace had no doubt, to announce that they had reached the Chania River.

Grace's heart leaped. The Chania! Farthest frontier of Kikuyu territory! And on the other side of it, her brother's plantation!

Everyone hurried now, even the animals, as if sensing they were near the end of their long trek. The men pushed and heaved the wagons across the river, which was low in these last days of the dry season, and up the grassy slope that marked the beginning of Valentine's land.

Rose came to life. She clutched her sister-in-law's hand and smiled. Grace was almost delirious. The end at last! After weeks on the ocean and in trains and wagons, of sleeping in tents and being eaten by insects, their destination lay just over this rise. A proper house, real beds, English meals . . . But more, the finish to all her wandering and travels; the place where she and Jeremy had planned to begin their life together. Perhaps, if he wasn't dead, as she thinly hoped, he would find her here, at last.

When a sign, TREVERTON ESTATE, tacked to the trunk of a chestnut tree came into view, the company cheered. Even old Fitzpatrick, the staid butler, threw his sun helmet into the air. The baby began to cry; the wagons creaked and lurched; the Africans slapped the animals and goaded them on.

They crested the rise and were met by a breathtaking sight: majestic Mount Kenya rising into a crown of mist. Just as Valentine had described it! And over there, to the southwest, at the edge of the cleared forest, exactly where he had said he had built it, on a gently rising hill that commanded a view of the mountain and valley—

Everyone fell silent. A cold wind whistled down from the snowy peaks, tugging at skirts and hats, making the wagon canvas snap loudly in the silence. The only sound to be heard as everyone stared was the cry of baby Mona.

Grace blinked in disbelief. And Rose whispered, "But . . . there's nothing here! No house, no buildings . . . nothing at all . . ."

3

Hello there!"

Everyone turned to see Valentine riding up. He wore Hessian boots, jodhpurs, a white shirt with the sleeves rolled up and the top buttons undone, and he was bareheaded. *As if it weren't a cold day,* Grace thought in annoyance. *As if it weren't about to rain!*

"You've arrived!" he shouted as he jumped down from his horse and strode over to his wife. Valentine swept Rose into his arms and kissed her hard on the mouth. "Welcome home, darling."

He turned to Grace, his arms held out. "Ah, and here's the blessed little doctoress!" But when he tried to embrace her, Grace pulled away.

"Valentine," she said sharply, "where is the house?"

"Why, it's right there! Can't you see it?" He waved toward the hill that had recently been cleared of trees and brush. "At least, it *will* be there. Come now, you look like a rainy day."

"It *is* a rainy day, Val, and we're tired and hungry. Do you mean to tell me the house isn't even *built* yet?"

"Things move slowly in Africa, old girl. You'll learn that soon enough. We have a tent camp down by the river."

"Valentine, you can't possibly expect us to—"

"Here," he said as he took her arm, "let me introduce you to our nearest neighbor. He's very good at polo. Has a handicap of six. Grace, please meet Sir James Donald. James, my sister, Grace Treverton."

He had come riding up with Valentine and was pragmatically dressed in rugged pants and safari jacket, with a pith helmet on his head. When he dismounted, Grace noticed that he walked with a slight limp.

Sir James was smiling before he reached her; it was a shy, almost self-conscious smile, and she saw that he couldn't be much older than she, possibly thirty-one or thirty-two. He surprised her when he held out his hand to shake hers, something an English gentleman would never do with a lady. Then he said in a cultured voice, "Val tells me you're a doctor," and Grace said, "Yes," defensively. But when he said, "That's bloody marvelous. We desperately need doctors here," Grace suddenly noticed how handsome he was.

They stood silently for the moment, their gazes held, their hands still clasped, and then Valentine said, "Let me show you around the new homestead."

Grace watched Sir James return to his horse. He was a tall, slim man, and he carried himself very straight, almost stiffly, as if to compensate for the limp.

Lady Rose had stayed back by the wagon with a lost look on her face. When her husband called to her, she said in a timid voice, "Valentine, dear, don't you want to see the baby?"

A shadow briefly crossed his handsome face; then he said exuberantly, "Come along now! Take a look 'round your new home!"

Mrs. Pembroke followed Lady Rose into the pony wagon and sat between the two sisters-in-law. Grace moved the blanket from Mona's face and saw that the baby was strangely quiet.

The wagon, driven by one of Valentine's Africans, took them to the gentle hill that rose from the forest. As Grace stepped down to the red earth, she asked her brother again why the house wasn't built.

"With limited labor available I had to establish priorities. It was more important to get my seedlings transplanted before the rains than to have the house built. In fact, the seedling nursery was the first thing that went up. Once the planting is done in the fields, I'll have the workers start on the house."

"Why did you tell us the house was finished?"

"Because I wanted my wife here with me. If I had told her she must live in a tent for another year, she would not have come."

When they reached the crest of the hill, Grace received a shock. The forest was gone; a magnificent vista stood before her. After weeks of cutting her way through dense growth, Grace was breathless to see so much sky. She felt as if she floated in space. The valley below, sweeping away to the foot of Mount Kenya, had been cleared of all trees and bracken.

Valentine ran his hands through his thick black hair. "What do you think, old girl? Can you see it? Acres and acres as far as the eye can see of rich green coffee trees covered with white blossoms, as if a wedding party had passed through. And bright red berries waiting to be picked!"

Grace was impressed. Her brother seemed to have worked a small miracle in this wilderness that stood at the back of beyond. The forest ended abruptly at the edge of newly tilled soil, and great rows of holes marched in a straight and orderly fashion to the misty ends of the valley—surprisingly large holes, Grace thought, knee-deep and as wide as a man, accompanied in their parade by neat lines of banana trees.

"There will be six hundred coffee bushes to an acre," Valentine explained, his voice filled with pride. "And that's five thousand acres, Grace! In three or four years our first harvest will be in. Those banana trees are for shade—coffee requires shade, you know. I've also planted imported jacaranda trees, which will stand along those borders." He waved an arm. "In years to come they'll be flowering with lavender blossoms. Can you see it? *This* will be the view from the front of the house.

"Over there," Valentine said, pointing to an enormous flat area down by the river, "is the seedling nursery. There's a furrow from the Chania to irrigate it. Those chaps down there are uprooting the weak seedlings. That's the secret of a successful crop, Grace. Some growers make the mistake of leaving the weak ones in for another year, thinking it'll strengthen them, but the trick is just to pull them out and plant new seed. The world doesn't know it yet, Grace; but someday there is going to be a great demand for Nairobi coffee, and it's all going to come from the Treverton Estate!"

"How do you know so much about growing coffee, Val?"

"The padres of the mission where I bought the seeds have been helpful. Plus there're some decent blokes in Nairobi willing to share tips. And Karen's taught me a lot."

"Karen?"

"The Baroness von Blixen. She has a coffee estate out by Ngong. We're using the bronze-tip variety here. The best arabica seeds in the world, Grace. I planted them a year ago when I came back from German East Africa." He looked up at the pearl gray sky. "As soon as the rains begin, we'll transplant the seedlings."

Grace stared in fascination at the regiment of African women in the fields, dressed in soft brown hides, with babies on their backs, bent straight-legged and tamping the dirt inside the holes with their hands. "Why are there mostly women and children working, Val? Why are there so few men?"

"Those chaps down there are the ones that felt like working. The rest are no doubt sitting under a tree down by the river, drinking beer. It's bloody difficult to get them to work. Have to keep after them all the time. Once my back is turned, they're off into the bush. You see, by Kikuyu tradition, all farm work is done by women. It is beneath a man's dignity to tend crops. Men were the warriors; they did all the fighting."

"Do they still fight?"

"We put a stop to that. The Kikuyu and Masai were constantly at war, raiding one another's villages, stealing cattle and women. We took away their spears and shields, and now they simply do *nothing.*"

"Well, you can't force them to work."

"Actually, we can."

Grace had heard about the Native Labor Act back in England when the archbishop of Canterbury had attacked the practice loudly in the House of Lords, calling it modern slavery. Kikuyu men, once warriors but now idle and without employment, were being forced to work on white settler farms, the rationale being that the labor gave them something to do and that their tribe benefited from the food, clothing, and medical care they received in return.

"The war with Germany nearly did us in, Grace. British East Africa is headed for certain bankruptcy if we don't find a way to generate revenue. This can be gotten only through agriculture and export. The white farmer can't do it single-handedly, so if we all work together, everyone—natives and Europeans—will benefit. And I'm going to fight to make this new country work, Grace. I didn't come here to fail. Others like me, like Sir James, we're bloody struggling to bring East Africa out of the Pleistocene and into the modern age. And we're dragging its people with us, kicking and screaming if we must."

She looked down at the cleared fields, at the hundreds of rows waiting for their seedlings, and said, "There are more natives here than I expected. I had understood from the Land Office that we had purchased vacant land."

"We did."

"Then where did all these women and children come from?"

"Across the river." Valentine pointed, and Grace turned around. On the opposite bank, through cedars and olive trees, she could see clearings, small native plots with round thatched huts and vegetable gardens. "However," Valentine said, "that's our land, too. It extends quite a bit in that direction."

"People are living on your land?"

"They're squatters. It's a system the Colonial Office worked out. The Africans can have their shambas—that's their word for 'farm plot'—on our land if in return they work for us. We take care of them, settle their disputes, bring a doctor 'round if they need it, provide them with food and clothing, and they work the land for us."

"It sounds very feudal."

"As a matter of fact, that's exactly what it is."

"But . . ." Grace frowned. "Weren't they already here before you bought the land?"

"Nothing was stolen from them, if that's what you're thinking. The Crown made an offer to their headman that he couldn't refuse. It made him a chief—the Kikuyu don't have chiefs—and gave him all sorts of authority. In return, he sold the land for some beads and copper wire. It's all legal. He put his thumbprint to a deed of sale."

"Do you suppose he understood what he was doing?"

"Don't go 'noble savage' on me, old girl. These people are like children. Never even saw a wheel before. Those chaps down there were hauling logs on their heads. So I managed to lay hand on some wheelbarrows, and I explained that they were for the logs. Next day I saw them carrying the logs inside the wheelbarrows all right, with the wheelbarrows on their heads! And they have no notion of property, no notion of what they can do with land. It was going to waste. Someone had to step in and do something with it. If we British hadn't, then the Germans or the Arabs would have. Better us taking care of these people than the Hun or the Mohammedan slavers."

He strode away from her toward Mount Kenya, with his hands on his hips, as if he were going to shout at the mountain. "Yes," he said in a deadly even tone, "I'm going to do something with this land." Valentine's black eyes blazed as the wind whipped his hair and cut through his shirt. He had a wild, challenging look, as if daring Africa to defeat him. Grace sensed something barely harnessed within her brother, an energy only just under control, an obsession and a madness that had to be kept under constant rein. It was a strange power that drove him, she knew, a force that had propelled him out of dull, old, law-burdened England and into this untamed, lawless Dark Continent. He had come to conquer; he was going to sweep his hand across this primordial Eden and leave his mark.

"You see now, don't you?" he cried into the wind. "You understand now, don't you, Grace? Why I stayed here? Why I couldn't go back to England when I was discharged from the army?"

His hands curled into fists.

"Feudal" she had called it. Valentine liked that. Lord Treverton, *truly* an earl over a domain of his own creation, not like Bella Hill, where obsequious cap-lifting peasants lived on mediocre farms and looked up at the big house as if it were a Christmas pudding. Suffolk revolted him in its tiresome tradition and done things and eternal sameness, where men's imaginations stretched no farther than tea time. When Valentine had come to British East Africa to fight the Germans, he had suddenly come alive. He had looked around himself and had *seen:* what he had to do; where he belonged. Destiny filled him; purpose flooded his veins. It was as if Africa, a slumbering, clumsy giant waiting to be wakened and prodded into productive life, had been waiting for him and for men like him.

Valentine trembled in the wind, not with cold but with vision. He lifted his dark eyes to the ominous clouds and hoisted a mental saber. He felt as if he rode a warhorse and faced an army. He felt clad in armor and backed by a host of thousands. Ancient fighting blood was stirred from dormancy; ancestral Trevertons shouted silently in his brain. *Conquer,* they said. *Subjugate . . .*

He turned abruptly and looked at Grace as if having forgotten she was there. Then his face warmed into a smile, and he said, "Come, let me show you *your* small piece of Africa."

A trail had been hacked through the forest from the hilltop to the ridge overlooking the river. Valentine brought his sister to the grassy edge, just a few yards from where her oxcarts were being unloaded, and pointed down to the flat banks of the Chania. "There's your land," he said, describing the boundaries with a sweep of his hand. "It begins up there, just beyond that clump of gum trees, and tumbles down here to the river. Thirty acres, set aside for you and God."

Grace filled her eyes with the sight of the cedar trees, the brightly blooming snapdragons, the mauve and yellow orchids. It was paradise. And it was hers.

I've come at last, Jeremy, whispered the secret voice of her heart. *The place we dreamed of. I shall build it exactly as we planned, and I shall never leave it because, God willing, if you are still alive, you might find me here one day.*

"Is that down there yours, too, Val?" she asked, pointing to the area a hundred feet below her.

"Yes, and wait till you hear the plans I have for it!"

"But . . . someone is living there." Grace counted seven little huts standing around an old fig tree.

"They'll move. That's Chief Mathenge's family. His three wives and grandmother live there. They don't belong on this side of the river actually. You see, this whole area was set up as a buffer zone between the Masai and the Kikuyu in an effort to get them to stop fighting. It's sort of a no-man's-land. Neither tribe is allowed here."

"But the white man is?"

"Well, of course. Now those down there—it seems that some years back there was an epidemic of some sort across the river where the main tribe lives. This group broke off and came here to get away from the evil spirits or some such. Mathenge's promised me he'll herd them back across."

Valentine turned to look at Rose. He saw her back on the hill, where she stood like a statue in the middle of the cleared land as if calmly waiting for her house to be built up around her. He walked toward her.

"Valentine tells me that's *your* land."

Grace looked up. Sir James had joined her. He had removed his pith helmet, and his dark brown hair was rumpled in the wind, glistening in places from occasional raindrops. "Yes," she said. "I'm going to build a hospital."

"And bring the Word of God to the heathen?"

She smiled. "Minister to the body, Sir James, and the spirit will follow."

"Please, just James. We're in Africa now."

Yes, she thought. *Africa. Where gentlemen shake hands with ladies and an earl goes about with his shirt unbuttoned.*

"You've carved a big slice of work for yourself," Sir James was saying as he stood close to her, looking down into the wide ravine. "These people are plagued with malaria and influenza, yaws and parasites, and a host of diseases we don't even have names for!"

"I shall do my best. I've brought medical books with me, and plenty of supplies."

"I must warn you, they have their own medicine people, and they don't like the *wazungu* to interfere."

"*Wazungu?*"

"White folks. That family down there, for instance, in those huts 'round the fig tree. They're the family of a very powerful medicine woman who practically runs the clan that lives across the river."

"I thought they had a chief."

"They do, but it's his wife's grandmother, Wachera, who is the real power in these parts."

"Thank you for telling me." Grace looked up into his attractive face. "Val told me about you in his letters. He said your ranch is eight miles north of here. I trust we shall become friends."

"I've no doubt of it."

A draft suddenly blew up from the river and swept Grace's sun helmet off her head. Sir James caught it, and as he handed it to her, he saw the glint of gold on her left hand. "Your brother didn't tell me you were engaged to be married."

She looked down at the school ring that had been given to her by Jeremy the night before the ship was torpedoed. She had been rescued from the freezing waters and had wakened after a bout of pneumonia to find herself in a military hospital in Cairo. Lieutenant Junior Grade Jeremy Manning, she had been informed, was listed as missing.

She would never give up the hope of someday finding him. Their shipboard love had been brief but intense, the sort of romance that war creates, compressing years into minutes. And she refused to believe he was dead. No one, not even Valentine or Rose, knew of the messages

Grace had left for Jeremy in the past year, starting in Egypt when she had entrusted a letter with the Colonial Office. She had left subsequent notes in Italy, France, the length of England. Coming to Africa, she had left word of her whereabouts at Port Said, Suez, Mombasa, and, lastly, the Norfolk Hotel in Nairobi. She dropped the letters like a trail of breadcrumbs, hoping that Jeremy had somehow survived, had been rescued, and was alive at this moment, searching for her. . . .

"My fiancé was lost at sea during the war," she said quietly.

Sir James saw the awkward flutter of her hands, the attempt to cover, protect the ring, and he checked the impulse to offer her a comforting arm. "My sister's a doctor," Valentine had told him. "But she's not as mannish as some." James was incredulous. Surely this soft-spoken woman with gentle, pleasing features and an endearing smile was not the same one who had written such large and brave letters to her brother. The plans Grace had described for her hospital had been painted in bold, sweeping strokes; she had sounded almost Amazonian. Sir James had not quite known what to expect, but certainly not this attractive young woman with enchanting eyes.

Back on the hilltop, buffeted by the rising wind, Lord Treverton strode toward his wife with a searching look. Why the devil didn't she answer him?

"Rose?" he said again, louder.

She was staring in the direction of an unusual cluster of gum trees down the rear slope of the hill. They were incongruous with the surrounding forest of chestnuts and cedars; there appeared to be a clearing in the heart of them, a protected glade perhaps, a place where one could be safe.

This new world frightened Rose. It was so wild, so primitive. Where were the ladies who would be calling on her? Where were the other houses? Valentine had written that the Donald ranch was eight miles away. Rose had pictured a country lane and pleasant Sunday drives. But there was no road, just a dirt track cutting through a land of naked savages and dangerous beasts. Rose was afraid of the Africans. She had never met a person of color before. On the train she had shied away from the smiling stewards; in Nairobi she had left Grace to deal with the native staff.

But Lady Rose did so want to be useful in this new land. She desperately wanted to make Valentine proud of her. She despised her own frailty, her inability to charge into life as her sister-in-law did. During the war Rose had timidly suggested she might join the Volunteer Aid Detachment and nurse wounded soldiers. But Valentine would not hear of it. So instead, she had rolled bandages in her parlor and had knitted scarves for the men in the trenches.

She had come to the Dark Continent in the hope that African life would make her more substantial, that the demands of settler life would erect a steel framework within her soft shell. She had once thought that marrying Valentine would color in her transparent places, but instead, she seemed only to fade beside the brilliance of his glory. And then she had thought: *Pioneering woman.* Rose liked the sound of that; it tolled like a cast-iron bell. It meant a woman who brought civilization to the bush, a woman who set standards and who led the way. Rose had also placed her hopes in *motherhood,* which sounded so firm, so important. She would be solid at last, in British East Africa, and people would no longer look through her.

"Rose?" Valentine said, drawing near.

Valentine, I love you so! I wish I could make you proud of me. I'm sorry the baby wasn't a boy.

"Darling? Are you all right?"

He would try again for a son, and the thought of it made Rose shudder. Their love for each other was so beautiful, why did Valentine have to spoil it with that messy bedroom business? "Those gum trees," she murmured. "Don't cut them down, please, dearest."

"Why not?"

"They feel . . . special somehow."

"Very well, they're yours."

He studied her. Rose was so pale and thin she looked as if the wind would carry her away. Then he remembered her ordeal on the train. "Darling," he said, stepping close to her to shield her with his body, "you're not well yet. You need to get your strength back. Wait till you see the camp. We have a proper cook, and we always dress for dinner. And the house will be wonderful, you'll see. Just as soon as the seedlings have been transplanted, we'll start building."

He laid a hand on her shoulder and felt her stiffen.

So, he thought darkly. It was going to begin again. His nights alone in bed, when he was driven mad by desire for his own wife, and then his taking her, closing his eyes to the look on her face. Rose would lie there afterward like a wounded deer, silently reproaching him with her violated body, driving him to undeserved feelings of guilt. He had thought she would come around in time, that she would learn to enjoy their lovemaking; instead, she seemed to grow to dislike it more each time, and he had no idea what to do.

"Come along, darling," he said. "Let's join the others."

Rose went first to Mrs. Pembroke and took the baby from her. Cradling Mona between her ermine muff and the soft fur of her coat, Rose followed her husband to the grassy slope where the others stood talking.

From this overlook Rose could see, a hundred feet below her, a cluster of huts on the wide, flat riverbank. A little girl tended a small herd of goats; a pregnant woman milked a cow; there were other women in the little vegetable plots, preparing for planting. *What a delightful scene,* Rose thought.

"You'll never guess what I plan to do with that bit of ground," Valentine said. "That's where the polo field is going to be."

"Oh, Val!" Grace laughed. "You won't be happy until you've turned Africa into another England!"

"Is there room for a polo field?" asked Sir James.

"Those huts will have to go, of course, and that fig tree will have to be pulled up."

They fell silent and listened to the light rain begin to patter in the foliage around them. Each pictured the great coffee plantation that was going to fill the valley and the hospital Grace was going to build down by the river. Lady Rose, holding her baby in the warmth and dryness of her ermine coat, stared down at the native village.

A figure, a young woman wearing hides and great necklaces of beads, came out of one of the huts. She crossed the compound, and Rose saw that she carried a baby in a sling on her back. The African woman stopped suddenly, as if she sensed being watched, and looked up. High on the ridge above her an apparition in white was looking down.

The two women stared at each other for what seemed like a long time.

4

When the young woman entered the hut, she said respectfully, *"Ne nie Wachera,"* "It is I, Wachera," and handed her grandmother the gourd of sugarcane beer.

Before she drank, the older woman poured a few drops of beer onto the dirt floor for the ancestors, then said, "Today I will tell you of the time when women ruled the world and the men were our slaves."

They sat in the watery light that came through the open doorway, there being no windows in the mud and cow dung walls of the round hut, and listened to the rain patter on the papyrus thatch roof. Following Kikuyu tradition, the elder Wachera was passing the legacy of her ancestors on to her son's eldest daughter, and they had been at it for many days. The instruction had begun with lessons in magic and the healing ways because the grandmother was the clan's medicine woman and midwife; she was also the keeper of the ancestors and guardian of the tribe's history. One day the girl, a young wife carrying her first child on her back, would also become these.

While she listened to her grandmother's words, recited in the smoky air of the hut as former grandmothers had done all the generations back, young Wachera wrestled with impatience. She wanted to ask a question, but it was unthinkable to interrupt an elder. She wanted to ask about the white spirit on the hill.

The old woman's voice was dusty with age; she spoke in chanting fashion, her body swaying, causing the great loops of beads on either side of her shaved head to rattle softly. Every so often she leaned forward to stir the soup simmering on the fire. "Today we call our husbands 'lord and master' after Kikuyu custom," she said to her granddaughter. "We are owned by men; we are their possessions to do with as they please. But always remember, my son's daughter, that our people call themselves the Children of Mumbi, the First Woman, and that the nine clans of the Kikuyu are named for the nine daughters of Mumbi. This is to remind us that we women were powerful once and that there was an age in the mists when *we* ruled and the men feared us."

While the young woman listened and committed every word to memory, her hands worked quickly and nimbly on a new basket. Her husband, Mathenge, had brought her the bark of the *mogio* shrub, but then he had promptly left, for it was taboo for a man to engage in basket weaving.

Young Wachera was proud of her husband. He was one of the new "chiefs" recently appointed by the white men. It was not the Kikuyu way to have chiefs—the clans were governed by councils of elders—but the *wazungu* saw a need, for some reason beyond Wachera's comprehension, to appoint individual Kikuyu chiefs over their own people. Mathenge had been chosen because he had once been a famous warrior and had fought in many battles with the Masai. That was before the white man said the Kikuyu and Masai must no longer fight.

"In the mists," the aged voice was saying, "the women ruled the Children of Mumbi, and one day the men became jealous. They met secretly in the forest to discuss a way to overthrow the domination of women. But the women were cunning, the men knew, and would not be easily vanquished. Then the men remembered that there was a period when women were vulnerable, and that was in their pregnancy. So the men decided that their revolt would be successful if launched when the majority of the women were pregnant."

Young Wachera had heard this story many times. The men had conspired to impregnate all the women of the tribe, and then, months later, when many of their wives and sisters and daughters were heavy with pregnancy, they had launched their attack. And they had been triumphant in overthrowing the old matriarchal laws and setting themselves up as lords over the subjugated women.

If there was bitterness in the old woman's heart over this ignominious history, she never betrayed it, because of the tribal code of etiquette and manners: Kikuyu women were brought up to be docile and shy and uncomplaining.

It was because of this upbringing that young Wachera had never questioned the wisdom of her husband's decision to work with the white man or her brothers' choice to run north with their shields and spears to seek employment on the white man's cattle shamba. Indeed, the wives of those few Kikuyu men who had gone to work for the white man were now envied in the village because their husbands brought home sacks of flour and sugar and a much coveted cloth called americani. Thus were the two Wacheras wealthy because of Mathenge; they owned more goats than any other women in the clan.

Wachera missed her husband terribly now that he was the "headman" on the white man's shamba. She had fallen in love with Mathenge Kabiru because of his flute playing. During the season when the millet was ripe and had to be protected from birds, the young men would go through the fields playing their bamboo flutes, and Mathenge, tall for a Kikuyu because of Masai ancestry, and handsome in his *shuka* and long, braided hair, had traveled through villages, delighting the people with his melodies. But Mathenge's flute was silent now because white man's duties called him away.

"It is time now," the grandmother said as she stirred the banana soup, "for you to hear the story of your famous ancestress, the great Lady Wairimu, who was taken as a slave by white men."

The Kikuyu had no form of writing, and therefore, their history was an oral tradition. From early age every child was taught the lists of generations and was called upon to recite them. Young Wachera knew the history of her family all the way back to the First Woman. "The earliest generation was called the Ndemi Generation," she would say, "because they were unruly and waged war; their children were called the Mathathi Generation because they lived in caves; *their* children were called the Maina Generation because they danced the Kikuyu songs; after these came the Mwangi Generation, so called because they wandered. . . ." And years were counted not in numbers but by descriptive names so that when the grandmother said that Lady Wairimu had lived during the *Murima wa Ngai,* "the trembling sickness of heavenly origin," Wachera knew to place her ancestress in the year of the malaria epidemic five generations back.

She listened in breathless wonder to the heroic account of how Wairimu, having been stolen from her husband and taken in chains to a "great field of water on which giant huts floated," had escaped from the white slavers and made her way back to Kikuyuland, fighting lions and subsisting on the boiled stumps of banana shoots. It was Wairimu who had first told the Children of Mumbi about a race of men with skin the color of turnips, and that was how the word *muthungu* came to mean "white man," because in those days it meant "strange and inexplicable."

Young Wachera remembered when she had first seen a *mzungu*. It had been two harvests ago, while she was still pregnant with her son. The white man had come into the village, and the women had run in terror, Wachera fleeing into her grandmother's hut. But Mathenge had been unafraid. He had gone forward and spit on the ground in greeting. While the women had watched from their hiding places, the two men had conducted a strange business which involved the receiving of beads and americani on Mathenge's part and in return his pressing his thumb to what looked like a large white leaf. Later, around the fire and drinking sugarcane beer, he had told Wachera and the other two women he owned about something called a "land sale" and a "deed" which he had marked with his thumb.

The white men baffled young Wachera. Since that first meeting she had seen them but a few times—they were clearing the forest from the hill above the river—but this morning she had seen the arrival of many more, and it had startled her. Then she had seen the apparition in white, looking down at her, and now, as she listened to the end of Wairimu's remarkable tale, Wachera began to wonder if it had not been a spirit at all but a white *woman*.

She said, *"Ee-oh!"* "hurrah," when the story was over, but the elder Wachera stayed her with sad words: "Unfortunately Wairimu was captured a second time and taken away upon the field of water which stretches to the end of the earth, and she never returned to Kikuyu-land."

The girl was spellbound. What must it have been like for poor Wairimu? What strange fate had awaited her on the other side of the great water?

Feeling the baby stir against her back, Wachera laid aside the basket she was weaving and reached up to bring him down to her breast. His name was Kabiru. In Kikuyu tradition, the souls of forebears lived on in children, and so the firstborn son always received his grandfather's name. In this same way grandmother and granddaughter were both called Wachera. The name meant "She Who Visits People," and it had been handed down through the generations from the first Wachera, who had visited people as the clan's medicine woman.

The grandmother smiled as she watched the young mother nurse. The old woman knew the ancestors were pleased with this young Kikuyu woman who was receiving the clan's secrets and accumulated knowledge, for she was quick and bright and respectful. Elder Wachera's son had raised his daughter well; young Wachera was a model Kikuyu wife: She kept Mathenge's hut clean, tended a bountiful garden, was always cheerful, and never spoke unless spoken to. Everyone enjoyed the sweet Wachera; mothers pointed her out to their daughters as an example to follow. During her circumcision, they would say, when she was sixteen years old and all the women of the clan had looked on, young Wachera had not flinched under the knife. It had come as no surprise, therefore, when the handsome and brave Mathenge Kabiru had approached old Wachera to buy her granddaughter. Sixty goats he had paid for her, a price still talked about among the people.

The grandmother's heart swelled. Young Wachera had gotten pregnant almost at once. Surely this granddaughter was going to produce many children for the perpetuation of the ancestors. Sad was the Kikuyu family with fewer than four children, for then one grandmother or grandfather would not gain immortality.

Elder Wachera lapsed into thoughtful silence as the rain pattered on the roof. The air in the hut became thick with the smells of wet earth, cooked bananas, smoke, and goats. Timelessness descended upon the two women. They formed a tableau identical to those of their ancestors because the Kikuyu were governed by tradition, the customs and laws set down by Ngai, their god who lived on Mount Kenya, and change was abhorrent to them. By her bare foot lay elder Wachera's divination gourd. It had been hollowed and dried and filled with magic tokens in an age so remote that not even she knew which ancestress had made it. The gourd was the symbol of Wachera's power; with it she read the future, healed sick bodies, and communicated with the ancestors. Someday the gourd would be passed on to the younger Wachera, and in this way the grandmother would live on, as her own grandmother now lived in her.

While the rain fell, elder Wachera's thoughts went to the rest of the clan across the river.

Forty harvests ago a terrible curse had fallen upon the Children of Mumbi. Drought had struck first, followed by starvation, and then a sickness had swept through the Kikuyu and Masai people, killing one in three. In that time elder Wachera had lived with her husband and his other wives across the river in a large settlement. Wachera had been unable to save the clan from the sickness, but the ancestors had spoken to her and told her that she could save her own small family by moving to the other side of the river, where the ground was blessed by Ngai and where there were no evil spirits of sickness.

The rest of the villagers had scoffed at the folly of such a move. In numbers there was safety, they had argued, but Wachera was by then a widow, the sickness having called her husband to his ancestors, and so she had turned her back on the village, which she knew God had cursed, and had brought her co-wives and children to this new ground. Here she had found *mugumo,* the sacred fig tree, and she had known that her visions had been right. While the rest of all the tribes in the land today remembered that year as *Ngaa Nere,* the year of the Great Hunger (and the white man called it the smallpox epidemic of 1898), the survivors in the old village and their descendants referred to it as the year Lady Wachera Moved Across the River.

She was thinking of them now. There was her sister, poor childless Thaata, whose name meant "barren" and who subsisted on the living she earned from making pots. And then there was Nahairo, who must certainly be near her time. Although Kikuyu women did not believe in preparing for childbirth, for it was considered bad luck and also a waste of time if the baby did not live, Wachera nonetheless had her birthing knife sharpened and ready.

Lastly, the medicine woman thought about Kassa, her brother, who was one of the tribal elders. She had received news that he had run north toward Mount Kenya and had obtained employment on the white man's cattle shamba. Kassa was now a counter of cows, and Wachera was greatly troubled. She sensed that some calamitous change was about to overtake the Children of Mumbi. Change had already come, but only in vague, subtle ways. Certainly tribal life went on the same as it was in the days of the ancestors. Perhaps a few women were carrying their babies in americani, and there was old Kamau who had accepted the white man's god and was now called Solomon. But in all, the old ways continued to be strictly observed.

Wachera's gaze drew inward.

And yet there was evidence of change right here in her own little family. Mathenge was supposed to be a warrior, but because the white man had forbidden the Kikuyu to carry spears, he no longer conducted raids against the Masai. Wachera remembered with nostalgic yearning the old days when Masai raided Kikuyuland for cattle and women. And some of the women did not protest because the Masai warriors were reputed to be superb lovers. . . .

Wachera's heart grew hard. She had known the white man was coming with his changes long before he had set foot in Kikuyuland.

It was many harvests ago, before young Wachera was born. Elder Wachera had been visited in her sleep by Ngai, the God of Brightness, and he had taken her up to his mountaintop kingdom and had shown her future events. When she had revealed these to the clan, they had been shocked and frightened because Wachera spoke of men who were going to come out of the Great Water and their skin would be like that of the light-colored frog, and their clothes would resemble butterfly wings. These *muthungu* were going to carry spears that produced fire, and they were going to ride a giant iron centipede across the land.

An emergency council had been called to consider Wachera's prophecy, and it had been decided that the Children of Mumbi would not go to war against the newcomers but would treat them instead with courtesy and study them with suspicion.

Soon the white men did come, and the Children of Mumbi had seen that they were peaceful and intended no harm and wanted only to pass through the land of the Kikuyu. Many members of the clan believed the *wazungu* were searching for a permanent homeland and that, before many harvests had passed, they would be gone from Kikuyuland and never be heard from again.

Wachera calmed her troubled heart with a proverb that said, "The world is like a beehive: We all enter by the same door, but we live in different cells."

A clap of thunder brought both women out of their thoughts. They did not raise their faces or turn to the open doorway, for it was taboo to look upon the god working, so the elder stirred her soup and the younger returned the baby to its sling on her back.

When the thunder subsided, young Wachera gazed out through the rain at her husband's hut, which was two spear throws from her grandmother's hut, and the terrible aching came over her again. It was a yearning that was like an insatiable hunger: to lie in Mathenge's arms; to feel the warmth of his warrior's body; to be solaced by his deep laugh. But it was taboo for a husband to lie with his wife while she was nursing, and so Wachera would have to be patient. She picked up her basket and began to weave again, filling her head with plans for her maize plot, with contemplation of the rain, with fantasies about her own future, when one day she would sit in a hut exactly like this one and pass on her knowledge to her granddaughter.

Ironically, thoughts of the future suddenly brought her mind back to the present, as if there were some mystical connection between the two, and Wachera found herself thinking once again of the white woman on the hill.

5

When Grace heard the whispering sound, she thought the rain had started again.

She was in her tent unpacking and setting things out while the men were in the dining tent for a "sundowner," even though dusk had long since winked out and night was upon them. Grace was in the process of getting ready for dinner, having put on her navy uniform, when she paused to look at the Distinguished Service Cross in its velvet case, the honor she had been awarded for valor in the war—a poor compensation, she thought, for Jeremy's life.

Hearing the gently sibilant sound beyond her tent walls and thinking the rain had begun again, Grace went to the canvas doorway and looked out. There was no rain, only a heavy mist. She searched the compound, seeing the ghostly shapes of tents, the halos of lantern light, and she listened. With the setting of the sun the forest had come alive with bird sounds, crickets, the warble of tree frogs. Then she realized that what she had thought was rain was, in fact, someone weeping. The sound was coming from the next tent.

After putting on her heavy navy coat, she hurried along the planks that had been laid in readiness for the mud and stopped at her sister-in-law's tent. "Rose? Are you all right?"

She found Rose sitting at a dressing table, bent over with her head in her arms.

"What is it, Rose? Why are you crying?"

Rose sat up and dabbed at her eyes with a lace handkerchief. "It's all so terrible, Grace. Those camps—after we left the train at Thika, I had thought we had seen the last of all that. I had *so* looked forward to a proper house."

Grace looked around Rose's tent. It was more elegantly furnished than her own, with a gilt-edged mirror over the dressing table and satin pillows on the bed. Even the sheets were not merely white but shades of antique rose and teal blue, the Treverton colors. Grace saw that her brother had gone to a lot of trouble to please his wife.

Then she realized that Rose's personal maid was not present. "Where's Fanny?"

"In her tent. She says she wants to go back to England! Grace." Rose's voice dropped to a whisper. "Please tell *him* to leave."

Grace looked over at the African who was standing by the tent door holding a water bottle and a linen towel. He wore a long white kanzu that came to his bare feet and a Turkish fez on his head. "What's the matter with him, Rose?"

"He frightens me!"

The man spoke. "My name is Joseph, memsaab. I am a Christian."

"Please leave us," Grace said.

"Bwana Lordy told me to take care of the memsaab."

"I'll explain to Lord Treverton. You may go, Joseph."

When they were alone, Rose turned to her sister-in-law with a pleading look and whispered, "Grace, you must do something for me!"

Grace studied Rose's face. The ivory cheeks were flushed; the lips, trembling. A few strands of moonlight-colored hair had escaped from combs and framed Rose's face. "What do you want me to do?" Grace asked.

"It's . . . Valentine. You see, I can't—I'm not ready to—" Rose turned away and fumbled for her silver hairbrush. "You're a doctor, Grace. He'll listen to you. Tell him it's too soon after the baby. . . ."

Grace was silent. She didn't know what to say.

"Help me, Grace. I can't face it. Not yet. First I must get used to"—she waved her hands—*"all this."*

"Very well. I'll talk to him. Don't worry about it, Rose. Come along now. The men are waiting for us."

Both women received a shock when they stepped from the cold night into the dining tent.

"Valentine!" Grace said. "How on earth did you manage it?"

"It was a bit dicey, old girl, what with the war and all. Sometimes it comes in handy to be filthy rich!" he said as he strode across the tent

in a black tuxedo and starched white shirt. Lord Treverton kissed his
sister on the cheek, then received his wife with a beaming smile. "Well,
my darling, what do you think?"

Rose's eyes moved over the Chippendale chairs, the Belgian lace
tablecloth, the silver candlesticks and china place settings. A gramophone played a waltz; lamplight made the crystal and champagne
glasses sparkle; the air was scented with wild jasmine. "Oh, Valentine,"
she breathed. "It's *lovely.* . . ."

"Let me introduce you to our guest," he said, indicating the new-
comer among them. He was District Officer Briggs, a portly man in his
sixties who wore a pressed khaki uniform and polished Sam Browne
belt. Valentine poured aperitifs, and they all drank a toast to British
East Africa.

"I had hoped to meet your wife, Sir James," Grace said as she took
a seat next to him at the table. She thought him quite attractive in his
smartly cut white dinner jacket.

"Lucille would love to have been here. It's been months since she's
seen a white woman. But I'm afraid her condition made the journey
down from the ranch impossible. She's expecting our third child in a
few weeks."

"I say," said DO Briggs as he took a seat across the table. "What
a blessed sight you two ladies are! Every white man in the district will
be thundering up here just to get a look at you!"

Lady Rose laughed and tossed her head. The rhinestone band around
her hair glittered; the single osprey feather brushed the air. Valentine's
wife was wearing the latest postwar fashion: a slim-line Poiret gown
with long ropes of pearls and a square neckline cut daringly low.

The dinner was served in eight correct courses by silent Africans in
long white kanzus who appeared from the back of the tent with silver
platters. "Not as good as I'd wanted," Valentine said as he poured the
champagne. "We've got terrible shortages here in the protectorate
because of the war."

Officer Briggs took a spoon to his soup as if it were the last he was
ever to have. "Bloody Germans! Ran us like hounds after a fox. Farms
being left to rot, crops unharvested, railway getting blown up, and no
medical supplies. We lost fifty thousand men, Dr. Treverton. It wasn't
just you lot in Europe who had it bad, you know."

"I wasn't in Europe for the war, Mr. Briggs," Grace said quietly. "I served on hospital ships in the Mediterranean."

Suddenly all was silence, except for the forest sounds out in the cold mist. Then Sir James said, "We can only hope the rains do come. We're in the middle of a depression; can't afford to add famine to that."

"But I thought it *was* raining," said Rose.

"You mean that bit this afternoon?" said Officer Briggs. "That was a drop in the bucket! If that's all it does, we can say good-bye to all the farms hereabouts. In East Africa, when we say rain, Lady Rose, we mean *rain.*"

"You see," Sir James said, "we have no seasons here, just wet spells and dry spells. In Europe you plant and then you harvest. In British East Africa you plant, but you don't necessarily harvest."

"You know a lot about this country, Sir James. Have you been here long?"

"I was born here. In Mombasa on the coast. My mother was a missionary; my father was something of an adventurer. They were as different as night and day, and I've been told that their courtship was something of a legend."

Grace looked at him. Sir James had a striking profile with a large, straight nose and square, hollow cheeks. "It sounds romantic," she said.

"My father was an explorer. He met Stanley when he was in the Sudan and had been in London during David Livingstone's funeral. Something about those two men infected my father. He came to Africa with a dream to open up the Dark Continent."

"And did he?"

Sir James reached for his champagne glass. "In some ways, yes. He was one of the first white men to set foot in this country. That was just over thirty years ago. When the natives saw him, they ran away, frightened. They had never seen anyone with other than dark skin."

"How did your father overcome that?"

"He was clever. In 1902 he made a safari up into this area, and the local Kikuyu barred the way, saying he could go no further unless he brought rain with him. He replied through an interpreter that he thought that reasonable payment and retired to his camp to wait. Presently the rain did come, and my father got all the credit for it."

Grace laughed. "Did you go on such journeys with him?"

"Not as a boy. He was too busy searching for immortality to be bothered with a child. My father claimed to have been the first to discover the Great Rift Valley, but that honor went to someone else. He dreamed of having something great named for him, but fame always eluded him. And so he turned hunter, and *that* was when I joined him on safari."

Lady Rose said, "Sir James, I've been wondering. Why is it called 'safari'? What does that mean?"

"It's the Swahili word for journey."

While the gazelle cutlets were being served, Grace found herself thinking of the man at her side. Sir James intrigued her; he represented something mysterious and exciting. "Have you ever been out of East Africa, Sir James?"

He gave her another of his shy smiles, as if he were self-conscious about something. "Please call me James," he said, and Grace recalled one of Valentine's letters in which he said that James Donald, who owned a cattle ranch up toward Nanyuki, had received a knighthood for his war actions.

"I went to England only once," he said. "That was back in 1904, when I was sixteen. My father died, and I went to live with an uncle in London. I stayed for six years but had to come back. I found England too tame, too safe, and too predictable."

"And a jolly good thing he came back, too," Briggs said as he ran his bread around his plate. "It's because of Sir James's knowledge of the bush and the natives that he was so invaluable in the campaign against the Germans."

"Oh, no war stories, please!" said Valentine suddenly.

But Briggs went on. "Any story about one man saving another man's life is worth telling," so that Grace recalled another of her brother's letters in which he had written: "I've decided to buy land near James's ranch. He's the bloke I met up with during the campaign."

Grace knew nothing about her brother's involvement in the East African phase of the war. He had come down as an officer with General Smuts, had fallen in love with the country, and had decided to settle here. Grace realized now, sensing a moment of awkwardness at the table, that the friendship between Valentine and Sir James must have had its genesis in an episode of valor and sacrifice. Since neither man would speak of it, she was left to ponder her brother's inexplicable annoyance at the raising of the subject. Was it because he hated to be reminded of his monumental debt to Sir James?

"So you're a doctor, Miss Treverton," Officer Briggs said. "You'll be kept plenty busy, I can tell you that. Your brother tells us you're planning to set up some sort of mission. Seems we have enough of that kind of thing in the district. Never could understand why everyone's so hot to educate the wogs."

Grace smiled coolly and turned to Sir James. "I take it that you are very familiar with the natives in this area. Perhaps you will be able to illuminate me on how to win their trust."

Valentine answered for his friend. "No one knows the Kikuyu the way James does. His father was made a blood brother of Chief Koinange's tribe. Got to witness some secret ceremonies. They called him Bwana Mkubwa, which means 'big boss.' They even have a nickname for James."

"What is it?"

"They call him Murungaru. It means 'straight.' No doubt for his looks *and* his character." Valentine signaled for a servant to clear the dishes away. "So the natives know *him* as well as he knows *them!*"

"Are they friendly around here?"

"We have no trouble with them," Sir James said. "The Kikuyu used to be a very warlike people, but we British have put a stop to that."

"That spear over there," said Valentine, pointing to the wall, "was given to me by Mathenge, the chief in these parts. He's my headman now."

"Are they truly pacified?"

Sir James tilted his head. "I couldn't say. Outwardly they appear to be quite accepting of our rule over them. But one can never tell what an African is thinking. When men like my father came here, the indigenous tribes were like a Stone Age people. They had no alphabet, no wheel, only rudimentary farming, carrying on just the way their forebears had for centuries. Amazingly, these people had never even developed the lamp, not even the simplest kind used by the ancient Egyptians. Now the missionaries are trying to rush them into the twentieth century. The African is suddenly being taught to read and write, to wear shoes, to use a knife and fork. He is expected to act and think like the Briton who has two thousand years of development behind him. Who knows what will come of it? Perhaps fifty years down the line we will regret having pushed the African through such a compressed tuition. Maybe one day millions of educated Africans will suddenly resent the domination of a handful of whites and there will be terrible war with a lot of blood spilled."

Sir James paused, slowly turning his wineglass on the lace tablecloth. Then he said more quietly, "Or perhaps it will happen sooner than that."

Everyone stared at the revolving glass, its facets glinting in the candlelight, the pale yellow champagne undulating.

Then Valentine said abruptly, "It'll never happen!" and waved his hand for dessert to be served.

Plates of fruit and a block of cheese were brought. District Officer Briggs was the first to help himself, saying, "They're a strange lot, the wogs. Got different notions of pain and death from us. Nothing bothers them. They're taught from birth not to show weakness. And they're so bloody accepting of things. Sickness, death, famine—it's all *shauri ya mungu,* the will of God."

"They believe in one god?" Grace asked, directing her question to Sir James.

"The Kikuyu are a very religious people. They worship Ngai, creator of the world. He lives on Mount Kenya, and he's not too much different from some versions of Jehovah."

"Blasphemy," murmured Valentine.

Sir James smiled. "The Kikuyu aren't polytheistic. They don't have to give up much to become Christians, and they stand to gain a lot. Which is why the missionaries are so successful."

"The Kikuyu sound like a simple people."

"On the contrary, they are not. And that is where a lot of white men make their mistake. The Kikuyu are complex in their thinking, in the structure of their society. Just to tell you all their taboos would take hours."

"Then don't bother," said Valentine as he reached for the third bottle of champagne. His eyes seemed to burn, and they settled often upon Lady Rose.

"James, you told me this afternoon about the medicine woman in this area, Wachera. Is she a chief?" Grace asked.

"Good Lord, no. Kikuyu women aren't leaders. They're barely regarded as people. They're possessions of men. Their fathers sell them, and their husbands buy them. In fact, the Kikuyu word for *husband* actually means 'owner.' And the word for *man, murume,* means 'mighty,' 'object of great prize,' 'lord and master,' while the Kikuyu word for *woman* is *muka,* which means 'person in subjection,' 'cry for nothing,' and 'given to panic.' *Muka* also means 'coward' and 'object of no value.'"

"That's terrible!"

"Look out," said Valentine. "Next, my sister will be trying to turn them all into suffragettes."

"Kikuyu women don't see their lot as a terrible one," Sir James said. "They think it an honor to serve men."

"A lesson, old girl," said Valentine, "you could do with learning." He placed his hands on the table. "Now then, I trust you ladies will forgive us if we have our coffee here? I'm afraid we haven't the room for the gentlemen to retire with cigars."

"Oh, dear," said Lady Rose. "You're not going to smoke, are you?"

He gave her hand a squeeze. "We're not savages, my love. In Africa one must be prepared to make sacrifices. We will forgo the cigars."

From her place across the table Grace saw Rose respond to Valentine's touch. She saw the dilated pupils, the red cheeks. When Valentine started to lean away, Rose laid her hand over his, and there was desire in her eyes. "Darling," she said a little breathlessly from the effects of the champagne, "do you think we might go back to Nyeri town and stay at that quaint little hotel?"

"The White Rhino? Not on your life, my love. The walls are so thin you can hear the bloke in the next room change his mind!"

"But if you only knew how I'd *much* rather stay there until Bella Two is built."

"Can't be done, my dear. These monkeys have to be watched every minute or else they won't work. The minute my back is turned they run off into the woods for a beer drink."

The doubtful look evaporated from Lady Rose's face when the silver coffee samovar was brought out and the bone china cups were distributed. She smiled approvingly at the African servant who wore white gloves and called her memsaab. The table was kept immaculate, the correct spoons had been set out, and the gramophone played Debussy. The champagne had made Rose giddy. She had been warned about the altitude but had forgotten and taken too many glasses. But she didn't mind. Rose relished the warmth inside her, the delicious stirrings in her body. Impossible now to imagine her bedroom fears. She hoped Valentine would visit her tent tonight.

Her husband was saying, "Did you know that the word *coffee* comes from the Arab word *qahweh,* which originally meant 'wine'?" While Sir James turned to Grace and said, "When can you come to the ranch? Lucille is anxious to meet you."

"At your convenience, James. I shall be getting to work right away building my own house down by the river."

"We'll see how the weather holds. Perhaps I'll call back for you next week."

"I would be glad to deliver the baby for you if you'll send someone 'round."

"You can be certain of that!" He gave Grace a long, considering look, then said, "I wish I didn't have to rush off at first light in the morning. Meeting someone new is always such a treat here. But I've some cows I'm worried about, and I can't figure what's ailing them."

"Is there no veterinarian?"

"In Nairobi, but I haven't seen the man in weeks. He has a terribly large territory to cover. I shall have to send blood samples down to Nairobi for microscopic analysis."

"I brought a microscope with me, if that would help."

Sir James stared at her. "You have a microscope? My dear woman!" He took hold of her hand. "You are an absolute godsend! May I borrow it for a few days?"

"Of course," she said, looking down at the strong, sunburned hand that held hers, covering Jeremy's ring.

A howl tore through the night, making the forest explode in a cacophony of squeals and shrieks. "What the devil was that?" cried Valentine as he shot to his feet.

Another unearthly howl suddenly sobered the company in the dining tent. Valentine flew out, with Briggs and James close behind. The two women remained at the table and listened to the dogs barking, the Africans shouting, and, thinly, a baby crying.

"Mona!" said Grace, rising and going to the tent flap. But when she looked out, she saw that the action was at the opposite end of the camp from where Mona and the nanny were quartered.

She squinted through the mist. Men were running; lanterns were being lit. And the dogs—they yelped in a chilling frenzy.

"What is it?" Rose asked behind her.

"I don't know. . . ." Then she saw Valentine striding toward his tent with a thunderous expression on his face. He went inside and emerged with a whip.

"Valentine?" she called.

He ignored her.

Grace tried to see through the mist, tried to make out what was happening. The dogs were wild; sharp commands failed to calm them. Beneath it all, Lord Treverton's voice was low and strong, giving orders.

Grace stepped out of the tent. The men's voices died down until all that was left was the whining of the dogs. She moved forward, shivering in the mist, her breath a steam jet before her. Then she heard a crack in the air, like a gunshot, and she realized it was the sound of the whip.

Now she hurried, unaware that Lady Rose followed. When Grace rounded the supply tent, she stopped.

The men—Africans in khaki shorts, servants in kanzus, and the three white men—were in a circle and in the center, tied to a tree, was a Kikuyu boy, his back exposed to the descending lash. He didn't flinch, didn't make a sound as the whip laid a red stripe across his flesh.

Grace stared in horror.

Valentine's face was stony as he raised the whip again. She saw the muscles of his shoulders strain the fabric of his dress shirt. He had removed his jacket; his back was damp with mist and perspiration. The whip fell with force. The boy embraced the tree, as unmoving as if he were carved from its black wood. Valentine widened his stance, raised his arm, and briefly his dark eyes were illuminated in lantern glow. There was a strange passion in the look, Grace saw, a power that frightened her.

As the whip came down, she cried out.

He didn't acknowledge her.

Up went the *kiboko,* and down it whistled, laying another red slice.

She bolted forward. "Valentine! Stop this!" When she seized his arm, he shook her off. Sir James caught her, and she turned on him. "How can you stand for this?"

Briggs answered: "It was the boy's duty to watch the dog compound. But he got drunk and fell asleep. A leopard got in and snatched one of the hounds."

"But . . . it's only a *dog!*"

"That's not the point. His duty could have been to guard you or the nanny and the baby. What then? A lesson has to be taught. Without discipline one might as well pack up and go back to England."

The last stripe cracked the air, and Valentine coiled his whip. Retrieving his jacket from Sir James, he said to his sister, "It's what has to be done, Grace. We'll all perish in this godforsaken country if we don't have law and order. And if you can't accept that, then you've no business being in Africa."

As he walked away, a servant rushed to the boy with a washbowl and cloths, and the circle broke up. Grace said, "Brutality and cruelty aren't necessary."

Sir James said, "It's the only language they understand. These people think kindness a weakness, and they despise weakness. Your brother did a strong thing, a manly thing, and because of it, they will respect him."

Angry, Grace turned away and was startled to see a figure standing in the mist by the supply tent. Lady Rose stood as if frozen, her eyes two smudges on her pale face. "Go back inside, Rose," Grace said, taking her arm. "You're shivering."

The champagne warmth was gone. The face had returned to cold ivory. "Remember your promise, Grace," Rose whispered. "He mustn't touch me. Valentine mustn't come near me. . . ."

What had the Children of Mumbi done to make Ngai angry? The Lord of Brightness had withheld the rains so that there was drought in Kikuyuland, and soon there would be famine, which would bring the evil spirits of sickness.

Because the day was unseasonably hot, young Wachera sweated as she toiled in the forest. She was not alone in her work. A spear throw from her, elder Wachera was also bent over, collecting medicinal herbs and roots, her body creating music with its hundreds of bead necklaces, copper bracelets, and anklets.

The two women were collecting lantana leaves and thorn tree bark. The former was used to stop bleeding; the latter, for stomach ailments. Elder Wachera had taught her granddaughter how to recognize these magic plants, how to collect and prepare them, and how to administer them. The process was exactly the same as it had been in their ancestors' time, when medicine women had gone into the forests and searched and collected, as these two were doing today. The grandmother had taught young Wachera that the earth was the Great Mother and that from her sprang all that was good: food; water; medicines; even the copper that adorned their bodies. The Mother was to be revered, and that was why, as they worked, the two Wacheras chanted holy spells over the earth.

Outwardly the grandmother appeared to be at peace. She was a graceful, elderly African woman modestly clad in soft goat hides, her head shaved and gleaming in the hot sun, her nimble brown fingers moving quickly through leaves and twigs, sorting, rejecting, plucking, her wise old eyes instantly recognizing good medicine from bad. Her sacred chants sounded like a song, a mindless hum that would make the casual observer think her a woman with not a care in the world, not a thing on her mind.

But the truth was, elder Wachera's thoughts were running a complex course, examining and rooting out problems in the same way her fingers traveled through the plants: how to cure Gachiku's barrenness; which recipe to use for Wanjoro's love potion; preparations for the upcoming initiation rites; organizing the ceremony to call down the rain. In good times the God of Brightness was thanked and praised, but in bad, a path was beaten to the medicine woman's hut.

Only that morning Lady Nyagudhii, the clan's pottery mistress, had come to complain that her pots were breaking, inexplicably. Wachera had produced her Bag of Questions and had thrown the divining sticks at the woman's feet. She had read in them that a taboo had been broken, that a *man* had visited Nyagudhii's molding place. Pottery making was strictly women's work because the First Woman was called Mumbi, which means "She Who Makes Pots." From start to finish the digging of the clay, the molding and drying, the burning of the pots, and lastly their marketing were solely in the hands of women. For a man to touch any material associated with this work, or for him to be present during any stage of its progress, was forbidden by Kikuyu law. The mysterious breakage of Nyagudhii's new pots could only mean that a man, either intentionally or unwittingly, had trespassed upon the taboo ground. Now a goat would have to be sacrificed at the sacred fig tree and the pottery work area be ritualistically cleansed.

But the heaviest thought weighing upon Wachera's mind was the drought. What had caused it? How to propitiate Ngai and bring the rain?

She looked at the meager collection in her basket: a few brittle leaves; grass as dry as straw. Their medicine would be weak, and sickness would again strike Kikuyuland. The soil beneath her bare feet was parched and dusty. The Great Mother seemed to gasp for water. Back in the village the maize plots had withered and dried, stored grain turned to powder, branches shed their leaves and drooped in sorrow. She thought again of the ceaseless work being done on the ridge overlooking the river. Great metal monsters pushed down trees and uprooted stumps; oxen drew giant metal claws which wounded the earth; the white man on his horse showed his whip to the sons of Mumbi as they toiled beneath the rainless sky like women! Wachera could hear the ancestors weeping.

It had occurred to her that there might be a *thahu* upon her people.

Thahu meant "badness" or "sinful thing." It was a curse that befouled the ground and the air; *thahu* could make a man sicken and die; it could destroy crops, render cows and ewes barren, make women dream bad dreams. The forest was populous with spirits and ghosts; the Children of Mumbi knew to watch their steps lest they offend a tree imp or the spirit in the river. They knew that devils clung to the black cloak of night and that the good manifestations of Ngai rode the wings of morning. There was magic everywhere, in every leaf and branch, in the cry of the weaverbird, in the mists that hid the God of Brightness. And because there was this second Unseen World with its own laws and punishments, the Children of Mumbi were careful to honor it. One never harvested the last tuber from the earth, or drained the well dry, or maliciously broke wood, or overturned a rock. If one transgressed against the spirit realm, one apologized or placated with an offering. But if someone were careless and gave offense without the proper apology, then *thahu* would result, and its scourge would fall upon the Children of Mumbi.

But what had brought on the "bad thing"?

Thahu was the most powerful force on earth, the Kikuyu knew, and to call down a curse on a clan member was worse than committing murder. People who perpetrated *thahu* were burnt alive on a woodpile, and those who were the victims of *thahu* had little hope of relief. Elder Wachera had seen a member of her own family run mad with insanity after a man, jealous of her uncle's large goat herd, had put a *thahu* on him. Wachera had been a little girl and had witnessed the complex ritual of the witch doctor as he had tried to lift the curse. But to no avail. The *thahu* was stronger than human medicine; once invoked, a curse was rarely broken; that was why the Children of Mumbi did not take curses lightly.

When their search for medicine was exhausted, the two women then gathered firewood, tying dried sticks into enormous bundles and hoisting them onto their backs and attaching them by straps across their foreheads. The loads were so heavy that the grandmother and granddaughter were bent nearly double, their faces pointing to the ground. With the elder in the lead, balancing her burden with the practice of seventy years, the two trudged the dusty track back to the village, which lay many spear throws away, a distance which the white man called five miles.

As she walked, young Wachera thought about her husband. Would Mathenge come to the village tonight? She had last seen him when third wife had given birth. By Kikuyu law the husband could not see the baby until he had given his wife a goat. Mathenge had come, so tall and slender in his single red blanket knotted over one shoulder. He no longer carried a spear because white man's law now forbade warriors to do so; in its place he carried a walking stick, which made him look important.

In the course of her daily work—fetching water from distant pockets in the dried-up river, harvesting puny onions and withered maize cobs from her garden, milking the goats, curing the hides, sweeping the huts, repairing the roof—Wachera had espied her husband up on the ridge. He often sat in the shade of a tree talking with other Kikuyu men; sometimes she heard him laugh with the white man. And when he did come home, he would sit in his bachelor's hut, where women were forbidden to enter, and regale his brothers and male cousins with talk of the *mzungu*'s new shamba.

Wachera's curiosity about the strangers was growing. She had paused on several occasions in her work to watch the strange *mzunga* who was erecting a mysterious structure downriver. It was but four posts with a thatch roof. And the white woman wore baffling attire. Not an inch of flesh was open to the air and sun; she appeared to be bound up, like a baby in its sling, with only her black skirt being loose and dragging in the dirt. Impractical clothing, the Kikuyu woman thought, for such hot weather.

The *mzunga* gave orders to the men who worked for her, members of Wachera's own clan, men who had once been warriors but who were now building a white woman's hut and calling her Memsaab Daktari, "Mistress Doctor."

Wachera wondered what age-group the *daktari* belonged to. Her own age-group was called Kithingithia because they had been initiated in the year of the Swelling Sickness, which the white men called "flu" and said had occurred in 1910. Since they appeared to be close in age, Wachera wondered if the *daktari* had been circumcised in the same year. And if so, did that make them sisters in blood?

The memsaab further puzzled Wachera in that she was clearly one of the white man's wives and yet she had no babies. All the village commented on how wealthy Bwana Lordy must be, considering the size of the shamba he was clearing, and that he had no fewer than seven wives. The Kikuyu did not know that their tally took in Lord Treverton's sister, his wife's personal maid, Mona's nanny, two parlormaids, a seamstress, and a cook, all brought out from England. So many wives, the Africans declared, but only one *toto*, one baby, among them. And not a belly on any of the women! Were the wives barren? Why didn't he sell them back to their fathers? Such useless creatures. Surely there was bad luck here. Bwana Lordy would be wise to find another witch doctor.

One thing puzzled young Wachera even more about the new bwana. She knew that there had been a big war between two *wazungu* tribes and that it had lasted eight harvests. Bwana Lordy had come back from the war to erect his cloth huts and drive metal monsters to clear the forest. And now his wives had come; most likely some of them were women captured in raids during the war. But . . . where was the cattle? What kind of warrior returned from war *without* the enemy's cattle?

Finally Wachera's thoughts moved away from the white man and returned to her husband.

How could she get him to come back to her? Even though the harvest was meager and the goats skinny, Wachera would prepare for him a feast. She would give him the last of her good beer and be uncomplaining and submissive. If only he would come! She considered asking her grandmother for a love potion to give secretly to Mathenge but knew that the elder had more important things to deal with.

There was going to be a rain sacrifice at the sacred fig tree.

Wachera remembered the last time such a ceremony had been conducted because she had been chosen to take part in it. Only clean and blameless members of the clan could participate: elders who had outlived their worldly desires and thought only of the spiritual; women who were past childbearing and were therefore no longer perpetrators of lust; and children under the age of eight because they were pure in heart and untainted by sin.

The ceremony had taken place at the foot of the very fig tree which was the heart of Wachera's little village. It was reckoned to be a very ancient tree and had proved its blessedness by saving the family from sickness and hunger in the year Wachera Moved Across the River. Young Wachera had no doubt that when the rain ceremony was conducted this time, the ancestors who lived in the venerated fig tree would send the rain.

The two women reached the river and followed its trickling bed toward their village on the north bank. When they came through the trees, elder Wachera let out a cry. A gigantic iron monster with a man riding its back was pushing down third wife's hut.

Elder Wachera shouted to the man riding the monster, a Masai in khaki shorts who dismissed the old woman but eyed the young one with interest. As the iron beast chuffed and belched and ground the hut beneath its feet, the grandmother placed herself in its path until the Masai driver halted the animal and stilled its roar.

"What are you doing?" she demanded.

He replied first in Masai, then in Swahili, and finally in English, none of which the two women understood. Then he said, "Mathenge," and gestured up to the ridge.

There the tall and handsome warrior stood looking down. At his side, also watching, stood the white bwana.

I f Memsaab Daktari will pardon," the Kikuyu headman said, "a *square* house is bad luck. Evil spirits will live in the corners. Only a *round* house is safe."

Grace gazed at the clearing where work was finally, after seven months, beginning on her cottage and said patiently, "It's all right, Samuel. I prefer a square house."

He walked away, shaking his head. Although Samuel Wahiro was a Christianized Kikuyu and one of the few who wore European clothes and spoke English, he was completely baffled by the ways of the white man.

Grace watched him go, thinking what walking paradoxes these converted Africans were. Outwardly they appeared to have been completely Westernized, but their minds and souls were still rooted in Kikuyu superstition.

She looked at the bare beginnings of her little house and felt a thrill of excitement. She had not thought, back in March, when she had settled into her tent in Valentine's camp, that it would be so long before she had her own home. But everything seemed to have conspired against progress: the drought, which had required the full work force to concentrate on Valentine's coffee fields; frequent Kikuyu festivals and beer drinks that had called the workers away for days at a time; and then, when they did work, a slow pace that was maddeningly un-British. But at last her little clinic was up—four posts and a thatch roof, plus a large, square mud hut for patients whom she wanted to monitor—and now her house could be started.

She had sketched a simple plan for the workers to follow, and she came down every morning from the tent camp to see that they got started. As a result, the early quiet around the river was disturbed by the incessant clamor of hammer and saw, as beams were cut and shaped, foundations laid, doors fashioned. Up on the hill, Bella Two already stood one story tall, and now a team worked almost night and day on the second level. The noise from the two construction sites was such that Grace almost believed the two work crews were competing to be the louder.

She looked up at the dirt track that came down from the ridge. Sir James had said he would pick her up in his new truck shortly after dawn, and it was nearly seven now.

Grace was going into Nairobi to meet with the Principal Medical Officer, to see what could be done about educating the Africans in nutrition and hygiene. Seven months ago, upon her arrival with Rose and the baby, Grace had gone out with an interpreter to take a look at the local people. What she had discovered—the poor health, the custom of sleeping with goats, the overwhelming *flies*—had shocked and dismayed her. Grace had come to British East Africa with a trunkful of medicines, bandages, and sutures, but these were of little use, she had realized, in the face of such severe malnutrition, endemic disease, and generally appalling condition of the people.

Here, she decided, was where her work among the Kikuyu would begin—not in her clinic with its tongue depressors and thermometers but on the homesteads and around the cookfires. The Africans had to be taught that it was their way of life, not evil spirits, that was the cause of their illness and suffering.

Although Grace had been told in a letter from the Principal Medical Officer that there weren't enough trained men to go around and that she was on her own in this area, she was going into Nairobi to try to get help.

She heard the grind of a motor and saw the dust trail behind Sir James's truck. Four Africans rode in the back; they would hack a trail for the truck, maneuver it through bogs and over obstacles, and guard it in Nairobi's lawless streets. With luck they should reach Nairobi, ninety miles away, by sunset.

As Grace climbed into the cab next to Sir James, she saw the young

African woman—the medicine woman's granddaughter—standing at the edge of the new clearing, watching her.

THE HORSES BURST over the hill at a furious gallop, hooves thundering, riders arcing high in the air with a skillful handling of rein and stirrup. Lord Treverton was near the front, a dashing figure in scarlet Savile Row jacket, white riding breeches, and black top hat. He felt as if he were riding over the roof of the world. The morning was cool and sharp; dew lay like a sparkling blanket on the biscuit-colored grass. His pulse raced; he was *alive.* He felt invincible.

Brigadier Norich-Hastings, master of the hunt, was in the lead, following a pack of forty hounds; next to him rode the huntsman, a Kikuyu named Kipanya who, although dressed in red shirt and black velvet cap, clung barefoot to the stirrups. Kipanya controlled the hounds by his voice, having been trained by Norich-Hastings in the ancient "cheers" of the sport, and by his copper horn. Three whippers-in kept the dogs together. These men were also African, wore the prestigious red and white uniform of the hunt, and rode shoeless. Behind them came the guests of Brigadier Norich-Hastings, the "smart set" of British East Africa, who raced across the Athi Plains outside Nairobi as if it were an English countryside. Indeed, the hunt was in every detail true to tradition, down to the grooms, second horsemen, terrier men, and earth stoppers, with the small variation that they chased not a fox but a jackal.

They had begun at dawn, with a meet on Brigadier Norich-Hastings's front lawn, where hot tea and scones had been served. On command from the master, the hounds had moved out to search for the quarry; they had given out a cry when the jackal was scented, and Norich-Hastings had shouted, "Tally ho!" The cream of British East Africa society had galloped off behind the pack, some cursing the extra bottle of champagne the night before, but all in excellent spirits and secure in the certainty of their supremacy over all of creation.

Valentine rode Excalibur, his imported Arab stallion. Next to him was His Excellency the Governor, who was followed by Count Duschinksi, a Polish expatriate. Rose was not at the hunt; in fact, she had not come down to Nairobi at all this time but had asked to be allowed to stay home, where she could escape, she had said, the fierce September heat. Valentine had very much wanted her to come with him but had not insisted. Even back in England Rose had not enjoyed riding to hounds, her sympathy always going to the poor fox. Rose's excessive fondness for animals was beginning to extend to forest orphans, such as hyraxes and monkeys, which she had turned into pets.

The horses and ponies gathered speed across the plain. The thrill of the chase mounted; the element of danger became intense. Only last Sunday the hounds had treed a snarling leopard, and the master, who always carried a revolver, had had to shoot it. And although there were no Suffolk hedges or treacherous streams to cross, African fox hunting was still fraught with hazard; last May Colonel Mayshed's horse had stumbled in an unseen pig hole and had sent its rider flying headfirst to meet his death.

It was nearly nine o'clock now; the sun was rising and growing hot over the yellow, scorched plain. Lack of rain had turned the protectorate into a bleak, God-abandoned land of bleaching skeletons, starved cattle, withered crops. But the hunt was good, the company lively and witty, and a grand breakfast awaited them at the end.

All of a sudden the hounds stopped running and dropped back. When the horses drew up, rearing and whinnying amid the pack of confused dogs, the riders saw a large cock ostrich emerge from the dry bush. He fanned out his wings and ran toward the dogs, which retreated with yelps. Kipanya and the brigadier tried to control them, but the ostrich, making threatening feints toward the pack, had them cowed.

"Look!" cried Lady Bolson. A small flock of baby ostriches stumbled from the bush. Lady Anne's husband, the viscount, reached inside his jacket and produced a vest-pocket Kodak, with which he promptly took a snapshot.

A moment later the female ostrich appeared. The two parents rounded up the babies, and the family cantered off, leaving behind a knot of milling hounds and laughing riders. The hunt was over.

Tables had been set on the veranda of Brigadier Norich-Hastings's large sisal estate house; china and crystal and white tablecloths shone like beacons to the exhausted but happy riders. Norich-Hastings's staff of Africans, overseen by his wife, Lady Margaret, stood ready in long white kanzus with scarlet sashes around their waists. As the guests climbed the steps of the veranda, wiping their foreheads and laughing over the ostrich incident, the servants immediately started to draw back chairs, assist with napkins, pour the tea. The food was then brought out of the house—silver trays laden with slices of pawpaw and banana, bowls of steaming porridge, platters of fried eggs and crisp bacon—and the company broke into animated conversation.

"I was charged by a buffalo last week," came the booming voice of Captain Draper of the King's African Rifles. "One of my Wakamba chaps told me it meant that my wife had a lover. So I replied that it must be bloody dangerous to go on safari during Race Week in Nairobi as surely the whole country is full of rampaging buffalo!"

Those at his table roared while at the next a more sober dialogue was taking place. "All this pushing for giving the Asians the vote. And the bloody gall of them to demand the right to settle the Highlands! I maintain that the protectorate is a white daughter of the Crown and not an Asian granddaughter. They've got India. Let 'em go back if they're not happy with the way things are run here. To my mind British East Africa is exactly *that:* a place where British ideals, civilization, traditions, and way of life must prevail. I say, keep the Highlands white!"

Valentine was only half listening. His pulse had not slowed from the furious ride; he could barely sit still. He was anxious to be starting the ninety-mile journey homeward, restless to take his surprise to Rose. The segment of population that had come out in 1896 to build the Uganda Railway, laborers imported from India, and that had stayed on afterward as shopkeepers and office workers, did not interest the earl. The Asians were pressing His Majesty's government to grant them an equal vote with the whites in the protectorate and for the right to settle in the Highlands, East Africa's choicest land, which stretched from Nairobi to well past the Treverton Estate. The handful of Europeans were fighting to keep them out.

"The answer is to press for colonial status," said a young man wearing a soft terai with the side brim turned up and pinned with an official badge. "Lord Delamere's right. If we were to be made a colony, then we would be formally annexed to Britain, which would endow the Crown with legal authority to dispose of the land however it wished.

As a protectorate we're practically orphans. But as a colony we would have to be listened to."

Valentine reached for the marmalade and spread it generously on his toast. Fresh butter, cream, and cheese were on the table; even Nairobi coffee and Darjeeling tea! Back in England serious postwar rationing was in full force; here in the protectorate prices had gone very high, imported goods were scarce, and the average farmer was struggling by on a day-to-day subsistence. But Brigadier Norich-Hastings's sisal estate was doing well, and so the retired officer could afford to deck out his tables in lavish style.

Valentine wished Sir James had come with him. His friend could do with a holiday and a chance to taste some decent food. Life on Kilima Simba, the Donald farm, was plain and hard. There was Lucille, managing two little boys and a baby girl, toiling from sunup to past sundown, making her own yeast, boiling jams to sell for a few extra rupees, mending clothes that Valentine thought should go for rags, while her husband spent the day in the saddle, inspecting his large herd, battling against an increasingly diminishing water supply, supervising cattle dips, constantly on the alert for tick-borne diseases, and making sure his chaps worked and didn't sneak off for a beer drink. Sir James was not wealthy by Lord Treverton's standards, but he was the most honest and hardworking man Valentine had ever met. If death had claimed James in that ghastly incident near the German East Africa border— and the army surgeons had declared it a miracle that he had survived— if James had died, it would have been a keen loss to East Africa. A knighthood had been James Donald's compensation for valor beyond human expectations; it seemed to Valentine not nearly enough.

"This bloke captained the Eldoret cricket side, you see," came Norich-Hastings's voice, "and there was a one-day fixture against Kisumu. He won the toss, chose to bat, and went in to open the innings. By teatime he was still making the runs."

Valentine listened to the story and laughed with everyone else. He was in excellent spirits because of the appointment he had with Dr. Hare in Nairobi later that afternoon. The physician had gladly agreed to open his office for a private consult, even though it was Sunday, and Valentine was confident that the man would have a solution to Rose's problem.

As he helped himself to deviled kidneys and scrambled eggs, half listening to talk around the table of coffee growing, Valentine reminded himself that, really, it was his fault that his and Rose's sexual relations were strained.

After all, he decided, it could not have been easy for a lady of her delicacy and breeding to give up a life of comfort and social prominence for a tent camp in the bush! Unlike Grace, who seemed to relish each challenge Africa offered, Rose was afraid of everything about this country. And there were no other ladies of her own kind to offer support. Lucille Donald had little time for Rose's sort of socializing; besides, the two women were as different as night and day. Hyenas in the henhouse were of no concern to Rose, nor how to make homemade glue out of buffalo hooves. And Lucille had not the faintest interest in fashion or style, was not curious about hemlines or where the royal family was vacationing.

Still, despite being left alone most of the time, since Valentine had to be out on the estate all day to make sure the tender young coffee trees were being properly cared for and since Grace had *her* hands full with trying to get the local Africans to come to her clinic, Rose seemed to have adjusted rather well. In fact, Valentine realized now as he laughed when another funny story was told, Rose seemed almost to welcome being left alone.

"I've got five hundred acres of coffee in bearing," said a man from Limuru, "but because of lack of rain, the beans are small, there are too many defective berries, and the coffee's got a blasted dull look to it." He turned to Valentine. "How goes your crop?"

"It's going rather well, actually."

Those at his table were not surprised. The earl's great luck and continued prosperity were the talk of East Africa. Everything he touched, it seemed, turned to gold.

"I hear you dammed the Chania."

"Yes. When it looked like the rains weren't going to come, back in March. Then I dug a furrow, so my fields are being irrigated."

"Must've surprised the darkies to see the river tampered with! They don't think ahead, you know, have no concept of tomorrow. They never grow more food than they can eat today, never wonder what they'll do if a drought hits. It's all *shauri ya mungu* to them."

"Bloody wogs," interjected a man with a sun-reddened face and bushy blond beard. "Can't get 'em to work for love or money! They sit on their black arses and expect americani and sugar and oil to be handed them, without for a moment considering that one must work to earn it!"

"You can take the monkey out of the jungle," said the Limuru man, "but you can't take the jungle out of the monkey!"

As Valentine stirred his tea, he stole a glance at his watch. His long legs shifted restlessly under the table.

"Did you enjoy the hunt, Your Lordship?"

He looked up into Lady Margaret's smiling face. She reminded him of a Pekingese dog, but with a better temperament. "And how is your charming wife, the countess?" she added before he could reply. "We need to see more of Lady Rose in Nairobi!"

Those were the times when she came to life, Valentine realized, those few occasions when Rose did come down to Nairobi. There had been the grand ball at the Muthaiga Club, given in honor of the king of Sweden, and then that pompous planting ceremony in front of Government House, to which Rose had donated a cutting of her precious roses. In Nairobi Rose was gay and lively, the center of admiring attention; if it weren't for the long journey from the Central Province, riding in wagons and stopping every night to camp, Valentine knew that she would come down more often.

"You must thank her for the tea," Lady Margaret said. "I found it be be an exciting blend."

Rose had brought with her from England a special private blend of Mysore and Ceylon tea that had been in her family for generations. When the supply had run out, instead of sending to her London tea broker for a fresh supply, Rose had had a firm in Nairobi substitute for the Ceylon a locally grown tea, cultivated in the cooler regions near Lake Victoria, and had found it produced a unique, pleasing flavor. When Rose had remarked upon it the last time she was in Nairobi, at a gala supper in honor of the King's birthday, and Lady Margaret had expressed interest, Rose had sent her a packet of the tea.

"Would the countess mind," the brigadier's wife asked, "if I ordered the blend for myself? I think I shall go off Lady Londonderry's altogether!"

He was about to reply when she went hurriedly on: "I have a small gift for Lady Rose in return. I *finally* received my order of Belgian embroidery floss. I sent off for it nearly a year ago! And there is the most delicious green that I know will go perfectly into her tapestry."

Back in April, wanting to give Rose a treat and a rest from the tent camp, Valentine had taken her on safari up the slopes of nearby Mount Kenya. He had tried to make the traveling as gentle as possible for her, rigging a hammock between two poles and having her carried in it by Africans, and she had responded by falling in love with the rain forest. In fact, she had been so taken with it that she had returned to the plantation with the scene perfectly imprinted on her brain. Rose had immediately taken a length of Irish linen from her cedar chest, unpacked her needles and yarns from a trunk, and launched upon what was promising to be a most impressive tapestry. It was only embryonic now, but one could already see how skillfully the rain forest was going to translate onto the linen: the rich shades of green dotted with bright orange and yellow and blue wildflowers; the long, ropy vines that hung from damp, twisted trees; the emerald moss and giant ferns and elephant's ear palms; even the low-hanging mountain mist had been outlined in delicate pearl blue silk thread, and off to the side Rose was leaving a space where an imaginary golden-eyed leopard would lurk.

This was what she did with her time. Stitching the tapestry was all she did. She sat in the little glade that was at the center of the eucalyptus trees, in the protection of a gazebo which Valentine had built for her, sheltered from the tropical sun in the company of pet monkeys and parrots and Mrs. Pembroke with baby Mona.

"Can we offer you a shakedown for the night, Lord Treverton?" Lady Margaret asked. With such great distances between neighbors and hotels nearly nonexistent, the strenuous travel in British East Africa had produced the custom of providing shelter for overnight guests, friend or stranger.

But Valentine was in a hurry. There were two things he must see to in Nairobi—Dr. Hare and arranging Rose's "surprise"—and then he would be striking northward, for home.

There is one possible cause for your wife's reluctance, Your Lordship. The medical term for it is *dyspareunia*. It means"—Dr. Hare tapped his pen on the desktop—"ah . . . the woman experiences pain during sexual intercourse. Does Lady Rose have pain?"

Valentine regarded the physician with a blank expression. Pain? He had not thought of that. Was it possible? Was that why she shied away from his embrace? *Did* she feel pain? Valentine sat back in the chair, oblivious of the glorious Sunday sunlight slanting through the window and illuminating Dr. Hare's cramped office. Grace hadn't said anything to him about Rose's having pain. She had been delicate in her wording, mentioning the strain of Mona's birth, the awkward train car, the lack of proper facilities.

Valentine experienced a sudden rush of hope. Could that be the answer? Could it be that simple? That Rose was afraid of pain? Because if that were the case, if it were due to a physical problem and not, as he had feared, a problem with their relationship, then surely help could be found!

"What causes the pain, Dr. Hare?"

The man shrugged. "I need to examine your wife to determine that."

Valentine would have to think about that. It had not been easy for *him* to come to this man; how could he subject Rose to a stranger's examination? Valentine had chosen Dr. Hare because the few medical men in East Africa were part of the "crowd" and gossip risk was high. Dr. Hare was new, just out from America, and not yet given to talk.

"She had a baby seven months ago," Valentine said. He would not allow himself to remember that Rose's reluctance had begun long before Mona's birth; he did not see that he was grasping at straws.

"That could be the cause," the doctor said, studying the earl's face. He saw fear on it, plain as day, and worry. Dr. Hare had engaged in many such private consultations during his twenty years of medical practice. They were all the same, like textbook chapters: wife unresponsive or even resistant to sexual advances; husband plunged into morass of self-criticism and sudden doubts about manhood.

Hogwash, Dr. Hare wanted to say. Women these days! With their talk of birth control and the vote. Why were they so set on denying their one purpose on this earth—to bear children? They made such a fuss of it, giving birth, when that was the very thing they were created for!

"Can you do anything for her?" Valentine asked, praying that the answer would be simple.

The doctor began scribbling on a pad. He would like to tell the earl what *he* would do if it were his own wife: exercise his legal right as a husband and ignore her protests. Instead, Dr. Hare said, "I prescribe a mild bromide. It will relax her. Most of these cases stem from tension in the, ah, pelvis. Usually a dose or two of this will clear up the problem." He snapped off the page and handed it to Valentine.

When Valentine emerged from the clapboard and corrugated tin building and paused to shield his eyes from the bright equatorial sun, he drew in a deep breath. He felt like shouting for joy.

He drank in the unique light of East Africa, a lumination that, for Valentine, sharpened outlines, details, and colors. Because of the altitude, the fact that Nairobi was five thousand feet above sea level, the air was crystal pure; no industrial pollution soiled it, and the few motorcars that rattled along Nairobi's dirt streets coughed negligible fumes.

When Valentine had first arrived with the 25th Royal Fusiliers, to fight the Germans down near the border, he had been spellbound by the light. It was not only bright, he had realized, but light in the sense of having no weight. Luminosity, he decided, could have density, like any object. The sunlight of England, for instance, was bogged down by smoke, river mists, fog, and salt air from the sea, but the sunlight of British East Africa was unsullied and buoyant, weightless, lending an almost supernatural crispness to shapes and textures. Even the most mundane object took on a certain glory. The grizzled old prospectors on their bony donkeys, the dusty black Africans whiling away the noon, and the prosaic old wood and tin buildings, weathered and coated with grime—all seemed washed in an inexplicable splendor.

Valentine Treverton loved Nairobi. Having once been blinded by the light of this infant town in the sun, he knew he could never live in England again.

But there was more to Nairobi than its light. It was a living, breathing, pulsating town with, Valentine was certain, a brilliant future. Although the end of the war had sent the king's troops home, ending the four-year boom, a new wave of fresh population now washed up on East Africa's shores—ex-military men flocking to the Highlands with land grants from the Crown, under the new Soldier Settlement Scheme; Boers from South Africa in their covered wagons and long mule trains; shifty-eyed hustlers and their counterpart suckers all looking for a quick way to make money; the turbaned Indians with their dusky wives and parade of children trailing behind; the white settler who came to make a new life; the strutting young officials in clean, pressed khaki uniforms, wearing big cork helmets with shiny badges in front and long, sweeping rear brims like otters' tails—and finally, in the middle of them all, serene and of blank expression, with seemingly nothing more to do than squat in the dust and stare, was the African, who had been here long before the others had even thought of coming.

Nairobi was a rough place where nearly every man carried a gun, where fires were constantly breaking out, where the Indian bazaar was overcrowded and filthy and the source of epidemics. It was a crude town crowded with oxcarts, riders on horseback, rickshas, and the occasional Model T. And it was the only town where Valentine, the earl of Treverton, felt he truly belonged.

As he took a cheroot out of his shirt pocket and lit it, wondering where he was going to find a *duka la dawa,* a druggist's shop, open on a Sunday, Valentine watched a safari column muster on the street.

It was one of the old-fashioned variety that was slowly being replaced by the automobile and would soon vanish from East Africa. A hundred natives were receiving their loads. In less than an hour the column would file out of Nairobi like a black centipede; at the rear the professional white hunter and his sweating millionaire clients would follow. The porters carried their loads on their heads because to carry them on their backs would be humiliating; that was the way women carried things. And there was a limit to the weight of their loads: 60 pounds. There was even a limit to the amount a donkey could carry: 120 pounds. But for an African woman there was no restriction on the weight of her load.

As Valentine turned and headed down the street toward the King Edward Hotel, he thought how amazing it was to remember that fifteen years ago there had been nothing here but tents and a swamp. And before that, just an insignificant river and some scattered Masai. Nairobi had been born just a few years after Valentine was; he was certain they would grow old together.

MIRANDA WEST PUT down her spoon, wiped her hands on her apron, and went to the window and looked out. Lord Treverton had said he would be stopping by today before heading back north to his plantation.

She was in the kitchen of her small hotel, getting ready for Sunday afternoon tea, a project that took almost the whole afternoon because of the care and quality she put into her preparations. Miranda West enjoyed a good reputation as far away as Uganda, and many were the settlers who came miles by oxcart to sit at one of her tables. Today she would be filled to capacity again, serving on the veranda and even out on the street. If the earl did not come soon, she would not have a chance to be alone with him. And that was all Miranda West lived for.

The dreams and ambitions of East Africa were as numerous as the immigrants who brought them. Everyone arrived with a scheme. Whether it was to make money in farming, to make money in mining, to make money in elephant ivory, to make money performing some special service for others, the idea was always to make money. There was no end to the variety and ingenuity of the schemes. For example, the Irish twins Paddy and Sean had made a brief fortune raising ostriches to fill the demand for plumes in England and America. And then, just like that, the automobile became popular and women couldn't wear big, feathery hats while motoring and so the fashion changed to tight-fitting caps, and Paddy and Sean had to return their worthless birds to the wild. Then there was Ralph Sneed, who had bragged up a storm about the mint he was going to make growing almonds in the Rift Valley. He had spent very cent of his savings on buying and planting almond trees only to discover that because of the absence of seasons in East Africa, the trees bloomed all year round and never came to fruit. Ralph Sneed had gone back to South Africa, embarrassed and penniless. Finally, there was Miranda's own feckless husband, Jack West, who was last seen heading off with a sleeping bag, a change of clothes, and a bottle of quinine—going to Lake Victoria, he had said, to find hippo skeletons and pulverize them into bone meal fertilizer, which he was going to sell to farmers at a phenomenal profit. That had been six years ago, and Jack hadn't been seen since.

So everybody in Nairobi had a plan. Miranda West's had, until now, been to capitalize on homesickness.

Back in 1913 Miranda Pemberton had responded to an advertisement in a Manchester newspaper. The ad had been placed by a gentleman currently residing in British East Africa who was looking for a well-placed woman to marry and help him in his various "ventures of a financially promising nature." Miranda, a general cook and maid of all work to a penny pincher in Lancashire, England, had written at once on a bit of fancy notepaper stolen from her employer. She shaved five years off her age and tripled the figure in her bank account. The advertiser, a prospector named Jack West, had chosen her letter out of sixty and had sent her the fare to come out.

He had met her at the harbor at Mombasa, where, after experiencing an initial shock—he was shorter and younger than she—they decided they might as well get married and make a go at it.

But the enterprise had failed. Miranda was appalled at the sight of ragtag Nairobi and the tent her new husband expected her to live in, and Jack felt cheated when she turned over her small savings. They struggled for a few months, trying to earn a living by buying produce from local Africans and selling it at a profit to wealthy parties getting outfitted for hunting safaris, until Jack took off in the middle of the night with the last of their money and Miranda's fake jade earrings.

By great good luck Miranda heard of a Scotsman named Kinney who needed a European woman to "help around" his boardinghouse near the railway station, and while he actually meant she would do *all* the work, it was at least a roof over her head and ten rupees a month.

Miranda's advantage lay in her white skin, which was why Kinney had hired her. He catered to a middle-class immigrant clientele that stayed in his house while looking for prospects or waiting for farm deeds to come from the Land Office. The wives of his boarders liked having a white maid instead of an African one, and when she demonstrated a skill for baking scones and concocting English trifle, for which his homesick settlers paid a high price, Miranda became indispensable.

In a town where women were greatly outnumbered by the men, where most of the men were bachelors, and where newly arriving women, many not even young or pretty, were snatched up, Miranda became something of an oddity. She was married, yet her husband was absent, and even though she was friendly and liked to share a whiskey and a joke, she gently deterred the frequent advances from Kinney's boarders.

Eventually old Kinney took a liking to Miranda and slowly gave over more and more of the running of the house to her. Where she saw waste she trimmed it; she balanced a tighter budget; she scrimped in places the customers wouldn't notice; and she had the boldness to double the price of a room, declaring that white people would pay for English cleanliness, and she had proved herself right. The value of the house went up.

Then war broke out. Kinney joined the East African Mounted Rifles and promptly got himself killed. To her surprise, Miranda found that having no family or other friends, he had left the house to her, and so she borrowed from the bank and set about turning the place into a proper hotel. Before long troops began pouring in from England, and Nairobi was transformed into a military camp. The soldiers flocked to Miranda's place, which she had given the rather pompous name of the King Edward Hotel, to devour her scones and talk of home.

The war came and went, and she never heard from her husband again. So Miranda's cunning and opportunistic mind surveyed the situation; she had seen what she must do to ensure her survival.

A woman needed to be taken care of, but Miranda was no longer interested in marriage. She had seen the handsome earl of Treverton in his Royal Fusiliers uniform, and she had decided that he was going to be her next ambition. It was not her plan to slave for the rest of her life in this hotel, sweating in the kitchen, trying to cater to the whims of petulant settler wives who came to the protectorate with notions of higher stations for themselves. Miranda was going to snare the earl and be taken care of by him.

Such an ambition would have been unthinkable back in England, where social strata were firmly set with locked gates at every level. But in British East Africa the ladders were there for anyone with nerve and determination to climb. The first thing Miranda had done was dress herself in a suitable guise. "Widow" rang with respectability. She could put the title on like a hat and wear it with no questions asked. There were many false pedigrees in Nairobi—Colonel Waldheim, the German dairyman, had never seen military service; Professor Fredericks, the local schoolmaster, held no college degrees—and to be the widow West was but a harmless masquerade. Titles were adopted the minute one touched ground at Mombasa, the port where all seekers of new lives cast off old identities and class restrictions. Miranda West, no longer downstairs maid in sooty Manchester, was now the dignified widow of a man who had lost his life on the shores of Lake Victoria; she kept her name out of the gossip column of the *East African Standard* and herself out of men's beds; she held a calculating eye on Lord Treverton and hoped that Jack West would never reappear.

She saw the earl now, going into the Indian druggist's across the way. She felt a catch in her throat. Lord Treverton was the most beautiful man Miranda had ever seen. He was such a contrast with the farmers and cowboys in their wrinkled khakis and pith helmets; like a young god he looked in his well-cut jodhpurs, white silk shirt, and band of leopardskin around the crown of his hat.

Miranda had to hurry. She had promised him a batch of Devonshire biscuits, which she now slipped into her Dover stove between a tray of Cornish splits growing golden brown and a tray of jumbles, which were light brown and ready to come out. The biscuits, Miranda knew, were for Lady Rose. Valentine Treverton never left Nairobi without a gift of some edible sweet for his wife. The countess was partial also to macaroons, which were cooling on a rack.

Miranda returned to the clotted cream, which she had begun the day before and kept cool overnight, and skimmed off its crust with a spoon. She wasn't going to give it to the earl to take with him; it would never travel the ninety miles. She had made it in the hope he would stop for a few minutes and try a few of her brandy snaps with clotted cream. The best way to a man's heart, she told herself . . .

Customers were starting to wander into her dining room, which had been neatly and tastefully set with white tablecloths and a small Brown Betty teapot on each table. It was Miranda's attention to such detail that these expatriates appreciated—the harrier cake made with *just* the right amount of treacle and the light touch with which she sugar-dusted her sponge cake. The story was that Miranda West had been cook to a famous marchioness who had been known for her kitchen. It was a lie, but the result was the same. Whether she had learned from the French chef of nobility or from recipes torn out of the *Times* of London, Miranda's skill with English pastries was almost uncanny. And the cleanliness, of course, was the most appreciated feature of her dining room. Every memsaab who had to get after an African house girl could attest to *that.*

As she covered the cream and hurried to the sideboard, where a kitchen boy was cutting crusts off finger sandwiches, Miranda glanced again out the window and saw Valentine emerge from the druggist's, tucking a small envelope into his shirt pocket. He would be coming here next. Whipping off her apron, Miranda rushed from the kitchen up the back stairs to her private apartment and combed her hair with an anxious hand.

VALENTINE PAUSED TO look up and down the street. In front of an Indian dry goods *duka* his Africans were loading his donkeys in preparation for the trip northward. A large package was strapped to the last animal; it contained the legs to Rose's piano, come at last on the latest boat from England. That was going to be her first surprise. The second was to be a tin of Miranda West's excellent pastries, which Rose declared were as good as those served at Ascot. The third surprise, which made Valentine want to mount Excalibur right now and gallop off home, lay in the envelope in his pocket. A teaspoon of the white powder in Lady Rose's evening chocolate, Dr. Hare had said, should do the trick.

Valentine saw a truck parked behind his string of donkeys. It was one of the new Chevrolets that were so hard to come by in the protectorate, and it belonged to Sir James. It was only two months old, and already the vehicle was worn and battered. The argument against having motorcars in British East Africa was that they wouldn't last long; the argument *for* them was that they were immune to tsetse fly and foot-and-mouth disease. Sir James was proud of his new acquisition, and Valentine liked to tease him about it, asking why an automobile manufacturer would call itself "milk goat."

And there was Grace, coming out of the Indian *duka*. Valentine was not surprised to see his sister; she was spending more and more time with the Donald family, particularly with Sir James. The microscope was one reason, Grace gladly sharing it with him for the detection of cattle diseases. The other was that Grace had become friends with Lucille Donald. The two were members of the East African Women's League and were involved in such projects as delivering sacks of maize to starving Africans. Valentine knew why Grace was in Nairobi today; it was to meet with the Principal Medical Officer to argue once again for a second District Medical Officer to be assigned to the Nyeri area. Grace had her finger in every possible pie, campaigning for the women's vote in British East Africa, joining Lord Delamere in his petition to His Majesty's government to grant colonial status to the protectorate, taking collections of what food and clothing the settlers, themselves already strained by the drought and failing economy, could spare for the Africans, who were worse off. Until now Valentine had not known his sister was so industrious, so *capable*. In these past months he had come to regard her in a new light; he was starting, in fact, to admire her.

Where, he wondered, had Grace gotten such a backbone? Valentine thought of their mother, Mildred, the countess, with her enormous bosom counterbalanced by an equally enormous bustle. She had moved about Bella Hill like a steam locomotive, the ruling force in the family, and her death had left a great vacancy within those ancient walls. Grace was like their mother, Valentine realized now—meaning that she was like himself. And that somehow pleased him.

How strange it seemed to Valentine to see Grace this way, dressed in that eyebrow-raising costume she had designed for herself: a khaki skirt divided modestly into wide-legged pants for horseback riding, a tailored white blouse, and a pith helmet broader than her shoulders, draped with a long white veil that cascaded down her back to her waist. Curious now to remember that this woman had once been the shy girl who had "come out" in London only eleven years ago and had been presented at court by their aunt, the countess of Longford, lady-in-waiting to the Queen. Grace had been so solemn in her white gown and long train, so demure and ladylike, timidly accepting the arm of a handsome young Guards officer who had gallantly swept up the end of her train with the tip of his sword. Two years later she was in medical school dissecting cadavers!

Grace was such a familiar sight in Nairobi now that one might almost think she had been born here. The eight-day journey down from the plantation did not deter her; she had taken to the bush and the camping life like a native. And she had no trouble finding accommodations along the dirt track from Nyeri to Nairobi. Grace would travel with two Kikuyu and three mules and would stop at isolated farms to spend the night. She would be welcomed with open arms because she was a doctor and always carried her medical bag. Only last month she had stopped at a farm miles off the trail and had ended performing an emergency appendectomy on the kitchen table.

The only thing that mystified Valentine about his sister was her seeming indifference to men. Even now, as he watched, a good-looking officer of the King's African Rifles in a pressed tunic with shiny buttons and a swagger stick under his arm paused to exchange greetings with her. Grace was always polite and friendly, but she discouraged further involvement. The only man she had really made friends with was Sir James.

A Nairobi tea broker was capitalizing on the Treverton name. When word got around that Lady Rose had a special blend made for herself and that Lady Margaret Norich-Hastings was ordering it, those who could afford such a luxury placed their requests. Just as the popular Earl Grey had been named for the private blend of Sir John Grey back in 1720, so now was Countess Treverton's tea becoming popular in the protectorate. A small, neatly lettered sign in the window of the King Edward Hotel advertised the fact that the blend was being served there.

Valentine removed his hat when he stepped inside the dining room. All heads turned. Miranda West's establishment catered to the respectable middle-class settler. There was a special children's section, where banana and cream sandwiches were served, and a long table exclusively for bachelor farmers who came in for lardy cakes and egg and bacon pie. But the aristocracy went to the Muthaiga Club or the Norfolk Hotel.

"Your Lordship," said Miranda as she came smoothly forward. She was wearing her best dress and had pinned a sprig of lilacs below her throat. "How are you today?"

"I'm at the top of the world, Miranda! I've a mind to buy out your entire stock, I'm in that good of a mood!"

Her eyes couldn't get their fill of him. Lord Treverton seemed unable to keep his hair combed; a black forelock fell over his brow, and it made him marvelously fetching. "I've some clotted cream today, Your Lordship, if you care to—"

"Haven't the time today, Miranda. You know how it is. I've been gone for over a week, and it'll take me nearly a week to get back. Who's made sure my chaps worked in my absence? I shall no doubt have to spend two days rounding them up in the forest."

Miranda tried not to let her disappointment show. But she was a realist. She harbored no illusions that when Lord Treverton looked at her, he saw anything other than the paid servant she really was. But Miranda had a plan. All East Africa knew that the earl's marriage was a troubled one; it was whispered how his wife was unable to produce a son and how desperately Treverton wanted one. Miranda West had decided that she was going to give him that son. In return he would take care of her for the rest of her life.

The earl didn't mind going into her kitchen, that was how human he was. Lord Treverton had no need to put on airs or act the snob; he was nobility to the marrow and a gentleman with every blink of the eye. A great man such as he would surely know to keep a mistress in style, Miranda thought as she preceded him through her dining room like a duchess, her head held high while her customers stared. All she needed was one night with him and she would give him a son. Many was the lord back in England who kept a mistress and illegitimate child; Treverton would be no different, Miranda was certain.

"Let me know when the house will be opening," she said as she handed him the cake boxes and biscuit tins. "I'll whip up my best Cornish black cake for the occasion."

"I'm hoping for December. The chaps are working on the second story now, and the flagstone terrace is already in."

"December!" she said. "You've never tasted a Christmas cake like mine. With marzipan paste and royal icing all over!" Miranda turned to the cooling table, picked up several Hundreds & Thousands triangles, wrapped them in paper, and handed them to Valentine, saying, "These are for your little girl. Mona, is it?"

"I'll keep you in mind for the celebration dinner, Miranda. I plan to make it a gala occasion. Our first night in the big house. There'll be at least three hundred guests, so start baking now!"

"I shall write the name of the new house on the cake."

"Bella Two," he said. "T-W-O. I've got a Swahili chap in Mombasa carving the stone that will go over the gate. He's promised me delivery by Christmas."

In the end Valentine tasted one of her brandy snaps with clotted cream and then ate two more. He liked Miranda West and wondered why she had not remarried. It wasn't for lack of opportunities. It couldn't be for age; if the mid-thirties was considered spinsterhood in the rest of the world, in British East Africa it was almost an asset, proving her to be a "salted" woman and not likely to go crying back to England. And it couldn't be for looks; she was pretty, Valentine judged, in a garden-flower way, with all that red hair and an attractive round face that hadn't been spoiled by the equatorial sun. And she managed the best kitchen in East Africa. Miranda West would be snapped up soon by some lucky fellow, Valentine had no doubt.

He finally left the King Edward Hotel, anxious to be starting for home. As Valentine swung up onto his Arabian stallion, Miranda West watched from her window.

9

The cheetah crouched low with ears flattened and tail swishing softly from side to side. It looked up at the window with golden eyes; in the gray-blue light of dawn it could see the raised sash, the curtain fluttering. Inside, in the safe darkness of the cottage, Grace Treverton slept deeply.

A growl rumbled from the cheetah's throat. Its muscles were tense and coiled; the cat sprang and was up on the sill, perched for an instant and then over, to land silently on the other side. It halted to sniff the air, to listen to the rhythmic breathing of the woman in the bed. Its tail swept back and forth, back and forth. In the black night that was still trapped within these walls, even as the sky began to fade outside, the beast could make out the angular forms of tables and chairs. Its nostrils picked up scents: of animal hides on the floor; of food in tins, of the human in the bed.

The giant cat waited, watched, and listened. Feline sinew tightened beneath a yellow coat spotted black. The cheetah's small head widened into a thick neck; a short mane went down between the ears and into the curve of the back that was slung between sharp points of shoulders and haunches. It was a young female. And she was hungry.

Suddenly the cheetah sprang. She flew through the air in a perfect arc and crashed onto the bed with a growl.

Grace cried out. Then she said, "Oh, Sheba!" and put her arms around the cat's neck.

Sheba gave her mistress a few licks, then jumped down to the floor, purring for breakfast.

"Surely it isn't time to get up yet." Grace sighed. "I was having a dream. . . ." She remained on her back and stared up at the thatch ceiling, troubled. The dream had been an erotic one, and it had been about Sir James.

This was not the first time Grace had dreamed about him, but it was the first of such a disturbing nature. And it had seemed so *real*. As she recalled the vivid details—they had been making love in a tentless camp beneath the stars—Grace felt her body respond. It dismayed her, this betrayal of Jeremy, whose memory she must keep alive, and of Lucille, Sir James's wife with whom Grace had become friends. The graphic content of the dream was distressing, but what worried her more were the continuing effects upon waking: the desire; the indescribable wanting.

I mustn't, she thought as she forced herself to sit up and face the chilly morning air. *I cannot allow this. He is a friend, nothing more.*

Grace washed and dressed with care, making sparing use of the water in her *debe,* a four-gallon drum that had once stored paraffin. Months ago Valentine had dammed the river, creating a small reservoir which he and the nearby Kikuyu were using in the drought. But even that supply was growing low. If the rains did not come soon . . .

It had baffled Grace at first that the temperature could be so low on the equator. While it was hot in Nairobi, only ninety miles to the north one had to dress warmly. It was due, Sir James had explained, to the high altitude and being surrounded by snowcapped mountains and rain forests. The Central Province was wetter and cooler than anywhere else in the protectorate, with heavy mists in the "summer" and daily showers during the two rain seasons. Or so she had been told. Grace had yet to experience real rain, the drought continuing to plague East Africa. She had also marveled at the uniformity of day lengths. There was no shortening of winter days or lengthening of summer ones; the length of daylight never varied throughout the year: twelve hours of light; twelve of dark.

Grace washed with her own homemade soap and then put on clean clothes. Life in this wilderness meant a constant battle for personal cleanliness and neat appearance. Especially during a water shortage. So many women seemed to give up the fight. They appeared in Nairobi in limp dresses that had once been white but were now gray and in sun helmets thick with red dust. Grace scrubbed her own helmet every night; she washed and pressed her blouses with care. It was a ritual that took up most of her evenings, but Grace had her standards. The effect was that she stood out in crowds, looking, to everyone's envy, as fresh and crisp as if she were at a Devon tea.

And it was not that she had the spare time for such industry. With so many shortages in the protectorate Grace had resorted, as other settler women had, to making her own household products. From Lucille Donald she had learned to make homemade butter in old chutney bottles, candles out of mutton fat with a bicycle pump, and potato yeast the Kikuyu way. She had even been shown by the enterprising Lucille how to save old tea leaves and use them as glass and wood polish. These tasks took time and were performed when she wasn't watering and weeding her vegetable garden, chasing antelope and hyenas off her land, keeping after Mario, her houseboy, and trying to instill in him a sense of British cleanliness and order, and finally, traipsing into the Kikuyu villages in the hope of earning the Africans' trust and friendship. Grace also tried to spare some moments for personal pursuits: writing in her journal, reading six-month-old issues of the *Times,* and sending off regular letters to friends in England, the Mission Society of Suffolk, the government. The most valuable lesson medical school had taught her, Grace had come to realize, was the skill of being able to do several things at once.

The day was coming alive with bird sounds. Thrushes and robins filled the morning with their song, larks and warblers found reason to greet the sun, and the curious red-chested cuckoo sat on its branch saying, "Fish like hell," over and over. It was because of the birds that Grace had named her house Birdsong Cottage.

She had chosen the site for her home with the same care with which she approached every endeavor. Knowing that low-lying ground held dangers of malaria and that high ground meant carting water uphill from the river, Grace had chosen, at the edge of her thirty acres, most of which were still dense forest, a spot where the wide, flat bank of the river lifted into a barely perceptible slope. It was solid ground with good drainage and easy access to the Chania. There she had built a bungalow that looked like a hybrid of African hut and Suffolk cottage. It was long and low, with a thatch roof and a veranda that went all around. To the front lay a small lawn bordered by daisies, poppies, and salvias. Inside were the few pieces of furniture she had brought with her from England: a handsome old dresser, a four-poster bed, a kitchen table, and two Morris chairs set before an enormous stone fireplace. The floor, which was hard-packed earth and was sprinkled with Jeyes's fluid to discourage white ants and jiggers, was covered with zebra and antelope skins. On the wall above the fireplace hung the pelt of a leopard Valentine had shot—the cat, he believed, that had been carrying off his foxhounds.

The "chairs" around her dining table, where she now read a book of Kikuyu grammar while eating breakfast, were, in fact, packing crates. And behind her stood the medicine cupboard, its shelves lined with neatly labeled tins, bottles, and boxes, few of which she had yet had occasion to use.

It was a quiet life—in some ways maddeningly so. Grace had not come to East Africa to spend her days making bread or putting up soap. She was here to heal, to teach, to light a lamp in the Stone Age darkness. But in order to heal, one needed patients; to teach, one had to have pupils; and to illuminate darkness, one required fuel for the lamp.

Why were the natives staying away?

"They are willing to work for my brother," she had said to Sir James. "Why won't they come to my clinic?"

"Valentine is the bwana," James had explained. "That is a status they understand. He has also earned their respect by beating them. But to the Kikuyu, Grace, you are not a woman who has proven herself. You have no husband, no children. In their eyes, what good are you?"

"They go to the missions in Nyeri."

"In order to obtain new names. The African sees that the power in this country lies with men who have names like George and Joseph. They've discovered that they can receive such names by going to the Christians and being baptized. The natives are lining up for *mzungu* names in their eagerness to be made the equals of white men. But you, Grace, don't preach or baptize. You don't have a cross on your roof, and you don't give them new names. They see no reason to come to you."

That was to have been Jeremy's side of the mission, the sermons and baptizing. He and Grace were to have been a team: doctor and preacher. Without Jeremy, Grace realized, she was lost.

"I'll give you my best advice," James had said. "Win over Chief Mathenge. Once you do that, the rest will follow."

Mathenge! A man barely one evolutionary rung above the wild beasts of the forest! A warrior who regarded the changing world with scorn while he sat in the shade and watched his women break their backs in the hot sun. "If I could win over Mathenge," Grace had said, "then I should be able to make the rain come!"

James had laughed then, the sunburned skin around his eyes folding into creases. He had a beautiful voice, Grace thought. It was cultured and genteel, the sort one expected to hear on a Shakespearean stage. James . . .

Sheba had been a gift from him. He had found the animal when he had gone hunting for a cheetah that had been killing his cattle. His bullet had made an orphan of the cub, and he had brought her to Grace as a pet.

She blinked down at the page of Kikuyu grammar she was supposed to be studying and realized her mind had wandered again. Must all thoughts lead to James? she wondered. Was that how it was going to be? With Jeremy it had been so different. They had met in the operating theater of the hospital ship and had fallen in love almost on sight. Wartime did not allow for drawn-out romances or courtships. There had been no daydreaming over him. They were in love at once and within days had been making their lifetime plans together.

But in the end, Grace asked herself now, just how well had she known Jeremy? On board the ship they had talked and talked, but what had they talked *about?*

Grace frowned as she tried to remember. Even his features were growing vague in her memory. But with Sir James she recalled every word he uttered, could picture his attractive face clearly. And she knew much more about him than she ever had of Jeremy Manning.

The first time Grace had visited Kilima Simba, the Donald ranch eight miles to the north, had been in May, when she had delivered Lucille's baby girl, Gretchen. Sir James had come for Grace in a cart drawn by a Somali pony, and the two boys, Ralph and Geoffrey, had come with him. Grace had discovered that morning that the Nyeri forest ended shortly beyond the Treverton Estate and gradually gave way to vast stretches of savanna that spread like a wheaten sea to the foothills of Mount Kenya. The endless lion-colored plains were dotted with broad-leafed trees and evergreen shrubs; the air was dust-dry, and the sky a darker, deeper blue. The dirt track passed small herds of native cattle being watched over by young men who leaned on long sticks and whose hair was greased into hundreds of tight braids. They wore *shukas,* blankets knotted over one shoulder, and their pierced earlobes were weighted down with wooden cylinder inserts. Overhead, hawks and vultures described circles; gunmetal clouds were stacked around the peaks of the greedy old mountain that refused to send the rain; and there was a silence overall. . . .

Grace had glanced frequently at the man riding by her side, his whip flicking the ears of the pony. James was cut of a rugged leanness that was very appealing; his skin was permanently tanned. He was stamped out of the pioneer mold one found in the Australian outback or American West, as African as the warriors leaning on their sticks, but with a gentleness not known to the warlike heart of the native.

Kilima Simba, he had explained, meant "Lion Hill," *simba* meaning "lion" and *kilima,* "little hill." It was a Swahili place-name, and many such were found in East Africa, the most famous being that of the continent's tallest mountain, "Little Hill Njaro."

The Donald ranch was even more isolated than Bella Two, which at least was near the small outpost town of Nyeri. It stood in the middle of yellow savanna, eight thousand acres of waterless ground and parched grass, with a large herd of crossbred Ayrshire and Boran cattle, three hundred imported Merino sheep, and a lonely farmhouse at the center.

Lucille's hunger for the company of a white woman was evident the minute Grace stepped down from the cart. There was Lucille—actually, Lady Donald since her husband's knighthood—holding the front door open while clutching her abdomen through a contraction.

Sir James came in and out of the house all afternoon, overseeing the innumerable projects on the ranch, while Grace took care of Lucille. Ralph and Geoffrey, aged four and seven respectively, played in the garden with the dogs and later came in noisily to gulp a supper of tinned ham, cornbread, and jellied preserves. Then James came in, washed and changed, and stayed by his wife's bedside until little Gretchen made her appearance at midnight. The instant the baby came into her waiting hands, Grace had thought: *She will be best friends with Mona.*

While Lucille slept with Gretchen in the crook of her arm, Grace and James had sat in the cozy living room, where a pine log fire staved off the cold night. They had talked of many things that night, of the late rains, the shaky economics of the protectorate, problems with the natives; he had asked her about medical school, about the war, about her future plans in British East Africa and in turn had talked about his boyhood in Mombasa, safaris with his father into unexplored regions, the shock of having to go to England when he was sixteen, and the awful yearning that had been like a sickness to return.

Because of the intimacy of the fire and the cold night, with the African stillness beyond the shuttered windows, Grace had wanted to ask him about his limp, the wound received in the war, and about how he had saved her brother's life. But then Grace remembered the night her ship had gone down and the hours spent adrift hearing the drowning men calling out for help in the darkness, and she had realized that just as she could never speak of that episode to anyone, so must Sir James wish to keep that chapter of his life private.

Nonetheless, she continued to wonder about it, about him and what terrible ordeal he and Valentine had suffered near the Tanganyika border.

Grace stared down at her book as morning sunlight crept over it. Her breakfast scones had gone cold; her Kikuyu lesson unlearned. It was uncharacteristic of Grace Treverton to allow her mind to drift. Discipline was what got one through medical school, what made a woman succeed in a man's world. And now here she was in an untamed corner of Africa expecting to make friends with a warlike tribe that had only yesterday laid aside its spears, and instead of concentrating on the vital lesson at hand, she was daydreaming about a man who could never be anything more to her than a friend.

She was working on Class II Kikuyu nouns. "The lion," the grammar book explained, "is in a class where it would not normally belong, the one just below humans but above other animals. The reason for this is the Kikuyu fear that if the lion overheard himself being spoken of in Class III, where he really belongs, he would take offense and kill the man who had dared to insinuate he was inferior."

Grace sighed and flipped the pages. What a language of paradoxes this was! Complex in the extreme when it came to verb tenses, there being approximately five present tenses and several future, and a riddle of past tenses defying all English equivalent, Kikuyu was also a language surpassing all others in simplicity. There were only three words denoting color: light, dark, and red-brown. If one wished to say that something was blue, it was the "color of the sky." And the number system was so governed by magic and superstition that it was no wonder James's cattle boys could not count their cows. Since it was taboo for a Kikuyu to work longer than six days in a row, to work on the seventh, the traditional day of rest, would mean bringing a *thahu* upon himself. And since the seventh month of pregnancy was the one they believed most likely for miscarriage, the number seven was greatly feared by the Kikuyu. One never planted only seven seeds but six or eight, and one never stopped after the seventh step but went one farther. Even the word *seven* was never to be uttered. It was as James had told her: A good way to understand the psychology of the Kikuyu was to learn their language.

James again.

Grace closed the book and stood. Before leaving the cottage, she took a moment to inspect herself in the mirror.

Her culotte skirt had caused comment in the protectorate. A woman wearing pants! But some had seen the practicality of the divided skirts and had ordered them for themselves. Grace looked at her face. She had even features and protected her complexion from the sun, and her hair was thick and nice. What, she wondered, did James think when he looked at her?

Finally Grace pinned to her collar a turquoise brooch that had been a gift from an American doctor named Samantha Hargrave.

Famous for her fight in America against patent medicines, Dr. Hargrave had been visiting war victims in a London military hospital when she had met Grace Treverton, who was still recovering from her ordeal at sea. The two had talked for a long time, the experienced practitioner fifty-seven years old and the brand-new physician only three years out of medical school. Before leaving, Dr. Hargrave had removed a pendant she was wearing, a turquoise stone the size of a lemon slice, and had given it to Grace. It was for luck, she had said. The stone was very blue; when the luck was used, the color would fade and the stone would have to be passed on to someone else.

It had a curious veining down the center that resembled two snakes twining up a tree, the universal symbol of medicine, or a woman with her arms outstretched. The instant the stone had touched her palm Grace had seen a vision flash before her eyes; it had been as if she were looking through the eyes of another woman and she had seen the bow of a ship and a city of marble domes and columns in the distance. Grace wondered if she had somehow been touched briefly by the spirit of that long-ago woman.

She stepped out onto the veranda and drank in the bracing dawn. Each morning she felt as if she woke up close to the sun. Closer to God, some would say. On this sharp October morning the air was clear and damp with the promise of rain. Directly ahead, through the camphor trees and tall cedars, Grace could see Mount Kenya, where the ancient god of the Kikuyu dwelt. Once again he was being miserly with the rain, hugging the black clouds to him. Every so often a cloud would break away, move across the sky; it would look as if it were about to rain, and then the cloud would dissolve, vanish. Each time hopes would rise; Africans and Europeans would turn expectant faces to the sky, united in one desperate thought: rain.

The long rains, supposed to have begun last March, never appeared. Now the short rains, scheduled for next month, were being prayed for. Grace gazed at the craggy mountain as if it were indeed an irascible old man who was peevishly withholding his blessing. *There* stood her enemy. Mount Kenya. Symbol of all the disease and ignorance in the protectorate. The mountain held its people in superstitious thrall, and Grace knew that in order to save them, she was going to have to fight that mountain.

While waiting for Mario to join her, Grace caressed her small shamba with loving eyes. Overhead weaverbirds chattered in the trees, perched on branches like fat lemons, and starlings the color of deep blue mother-of-pearl played with little waxbills that were mousy gray except for scarlet faces and bills. There was the sweet smell of wild jasmine in the air and smoke from African cook fires. Up on the hill above her, work on the big house was still in progress. She could hear hammers and chisels ringing in the silence.

As Grace drew her cardigan close to her chest, her eye was caught by something amiss. The four chairs on the veranda—their cushions were missing, again! No doubt the work of Sheba's friends. In the night young cheetahs came and played mischievously, pulling clothes off the line, carrying away the veranda cushions. Her welcome mat had disappeared weeks ago and was later found up a tree.

Life at Birdsong Cottage meant constant vigilance to keep one's standards. It would be so easy, Grace realized, to give in and relax the rules of civilization, to allow the animals to have the run of the house, to relinquish the thatch roof to white ants, to allow one's clothes to run to rags, to let one's hair go uncombed, to forgo the evening bath; and some isolated settlers had done just that. The Stone Age, Grace knew, could be just a broom or a fork away.

Mario came out of the house. He carried a warm cooking pot, a bag of grain, and a string of onions flung over one shoulder. He was a bright young Kikuyu who had been educated by the Italian fathers at the Catholic mission; there he had been converted to Christianity and had been given the name, following widespread practice, of the priest who had baptized him. When he had come of age and had gone through the circumcision ceremony of manhood, he had gone in search of employment with the white man, as so many African males were doing now that there was no warrior class for them to enter. The cattle ranches were always their first choice, for cattle herding was an ancient and honorable occupation for men; James never lacked for cowhands. They shirked farm work like planting and picking because that was woman's work and therefore demeaning. Mario had not been able to join Valentine's house-building gang because he was from another clan and therefore an outsider, so Grace had hired him. She couldn't pay much, only two rupees a month, but he ate well and slept in a rondavel behind the house.

He spoke English with an Italian accent, this young Kikuyu with the name of a Roman priest, and he wore khaki shorts and shirt, just like the native levies of the King's African Rifles. "Ready, Memsaab Daktari," he said, and showed her the pot.

It had simmered all night, a stew of stunted vegetables mixed with maize meal. There was no meat because the Kikuyu would not eat wild game and Grace could not spare one of her own goats, nor was there any chicken because the men would not touch it, chicken being eaten only by women. But what Grace *had* dropped into it the night before was a rusty horseshoe, a traditional preventative against anemia.

She had begun feeding the villagers a month ago when the last of their own grain had run out and their vegetable plots failed. They were now starving because the Kikuyu did not believe in preparing for the future. They grew only enough to eat and to use as barter, believing that tomorrow would somehow take care of itself. For that same reason it would never have occurred to them to dam the river, as Valentine had done, to ensure a water supply in times of drought, and even now, with the reservoir available, they did not try to think of an efficient means of delivering that water to their dying shambas. Every morning the Kikuyu women and little girls trudged to the man-made pond, filled their calabashes, and carried the water back up to the village, their bodies bent double. To dig a furrow to eliminate this daily toil would have meant change, and change was taboo.

Grace and the boy left the veranda and struck off down the path that led away from Grace's house. To their right lay the trickling river; to their left rose the grassy overlook, which was now totally depleted of forest. From this path, looking up, Grace could just see the roof of Bella Two.

It had been eight months since Grace and Rose's arrival in Africa, and Valentine was obsessed with having the house done by Christmas. He drove his Africans day and night, striding about the construction area with his whip, shouting, giving the boot to anyone he found sitting down. It had become the focus of his entire life: to have Bella Two finished in time for the gala celebration that was going to mark the official opening of the house. And it was expected to be quite the event. They all were to continue to live in the camp right up until the big night, when more than two hundred guests would arrive from all over the protectorate and sit down to a fabulous feast. There would be music and dancing, and afterward, when the guests all were comfortably housed in makeshift huts and tents around the grounds, Valentine would escort his wife for the first time upstairs to their new bedroom.

Abutting the southern boundary of Grace's thirty acres was the clearing where Mathenge and his family had lived and which Valentine was now converting into a polo field. The chief had ordered his wives back across the river to live with the main clan, but two women had disobeyed: elder Wachera, his wife's revered grandmother, and young Wachera who was apprenticing with the old medicine woman. Of the seven original huts, only two still stood.

A few weeks ago Grace had observed a strange confrontation between Mathenge and his wife's grandmother. Elder Wachera had politely informed the young chief that someone was tearing down the huts, and he had respectfully explained why, telling her to join the others across the river. The grandmother had quietly, almost shyly reminded him of the holiness of that ground because of the ancient fig tree, and the young warrior, in a diffident manner, had courteously asked her to obey his wishes.

It had been a bizarre exchange. Clearly two revered ranks were at odds. Elderly Kikuyu were so honored in the tribe that it was taboo to utter their names, especially that of a medicine woman who spoke for the ancestors. But young warriors, particularly one who was now a chief and very nearly had the status of a *mzungu*, were also to be obeyed. As a result, neither had backed down. Wachera returned to her hut, there to remain forever, she declared, while Mathenge had stood proudly, his face a mask.

Valentine, however, had vowed that his plans were going forward, and he would have the old woman bodily removed if necessary.

When Grace and Mario pushed through a stand of whispering bamboo to reach the path to the village across the river, they were halted by the sudden appearance of Mathenge. He did not see them but walked with a purposeful step toward the plantation.

Grace held her breath. There went her adversary, the man she must win over, who had the power to grant her success or failure in Africa. A man she was afraid of.

And he was the most beautiful human being she had ever seen.

Mathenge was very tall with broad, rounded shoulders and a surprisingly narrow waist and hips. He wore a *shuka* made of americani knotted over one shoulder so that when he walked, his lean flanks and shapely buttocks were exposed. His hair was done in Masai fashion, in two sets of braids, front and back, plastered down with red ocher. Such a hairstyle took hours to arrange and bespoke the man's vanity. His face, too, told of utter conceit. Mathenge's Masai ancestry was evident in the high cheekbones and narrow nose, the boldly swung jaw. His manner was aloof, his expression not so much disdainful as that of a man who doesn't bother himself with life's trivialities.

Grace watched him pass, his stride fluid, long arms swinging with supple grace; she realized she was holding her breath.

The Kikuyu did not like straight paths but felt safer meandering. Their minds worked similarly: They never stated a fact directly but hinted at it and skirted around it, leaving one to draw one's own conclusions. In the same way that they feared a blunt statement as if it were a poisoned arrow, so did they avoid a straight road; that was why Grace and Mario now followed a twisting, indirect track to the village.

It ran parallel with an ancient animal path where the recent spoor of giant forest hogs and elands indicated that animals were venturing down to Valentine's reservoir to drink. Because of the drought, much game was coming boldly out of the forest; now, too, new birds appeared among the reeds and bamboo: crested cranes, storks, and Egyptian geese. Mario declared he had even heard a rhino crashing through the bush during the night.

As Grace walked among the juniper and mimosa trees, catching sight of a parrot flashing red and yellow overhead, she felt as if she walked over land that had a soul. There was a pulse here that she had never felt in Suffolk. Here the landscape breathed, the earth gave off a living heat, the plants seemed to whisper, to bend toward her. The air was filled with a sense of expectancy, of waiting. . . .

The village entrance was concealed among trees and vines in order to trick evil spirits and thus to keep them out. Beyond the natural archway lay a clearing with perhaps thirty huts, all round, made of cow dung, and thatched. Blue smoke spiraled up from the pointed roofs to indicate habitation; cook fires must burn day and night, and if a fire went out, it was bad luck and the hut must be destroyed. It was a plain, homely little village because the Kikuyu had no art or architecture, did not carve designs or sculpt. Despite the lack of a harvest and the Spanish flu that had weakened the clan, the village was an anthill of industry. Everyone was working. From the very littlest girls tending goats to the married women pounding meager handfuls of millet to the grandmothers who sat with legs stretched in the sunshine weaving baskets, the scene proved the maxim that one never saw a Kikuyu woman idle.

In their leather aprons stiff with dirt and grease, arms jangling with beads and copper, they tanned goatskins, stirred their paltry stews, and worked at their primitive pottery, using no wheel and baking the pots in the sunlight. With the exception of a few young women each wearing a woolly patch of hair on her head to indicate she was unmarried, all the heads were smooth-shaven and gleamed like brown billiard balls.

There were no men in the village. Either they were working for Valentine on the opposite ridge or they were enjoying a beer drink under the shade of a tree. As Sir James had once said to Grace, "The women are the toilers; the men, the loiterers."

When some children saw Grace, they dropped what they were doing and came hesitantly toward her. It was supposed to be a mark of status to have flies about oneself because that indicated the ownership of goats. The more flies meant the more goats and therefore more wealth and status in the tribe, and to brush the flies away was a terrible breach of etiquette. But Grace didn't care about etiquette when these little ones came forward and she saw their faces plastered black with flies. She shooed the flies away with her hand.

Protocol had to be followed before the food could be distributed. All the women smiled shyly at Grace and waited while elder Wachera came forward. Her venerable old body was nearly hidden beneath ropes of cowry shells and bands of beads. She walked with dignity and smiled, revealing gaps where her incisors had been extracted in girlhood as a sign of beauty. She extended a calabash to Grace. It contained a greenish mixture of sour milk and spinach, which Grace drank, knowing how little the family could spare it but knowing also that to refuse would give offense. Wachera said, *"Mwaiga,"* a long, drawn-out Kikuyu word that means "All is well, come or go in peace," the hail and farewell of all Kikuyu conversation. The medicine woman spoke demurely but with stateliness, being the senior and most honored woman in the village. She did not look directly at Grace because that would have been impolite.

The dialogue then twisted and turned like the village path, hinting at the drought, suggesting the famine, with Grace struggling through and occasionally helped by Mario. She could not go directly to the point of the food she had brought as that would have been bad manners. Grace tried to curb her impatience. The children were *starving.* Their little arms and legs like sticks and their blown-up bellies were inclined in the direction of the cooking pot like blossoms following the sun.

Finally Wachera insinuated that the lid might be lifted and that if some of the stew left the pot, she would not mind. Even then the children did not rush forward. Mothers came up, giggling behind their hands because they were unused to the presence of a white person, and made sure the handout was polite and orderly. None of the adults helped herself until the children were fed. Then Grace told Mario to hand the sack of grain to Wachera. As she received the sixty-pound bag and swung it easily onto her back, the old Kikuyu woman flashed Mario a look of disdain for having carried the sack into the village himself.

Grace was now officially welcome in the village and was free to move about. She went first to the huts of women she had been seeing as patients. There was little she could do for them; they were down with the Spanish flu, for which there was no cure. All she could do was talk to them, check their vital signs, and make sure they were being cared for. The huts were smoky and dark, the stuffy air stung with the smell of goat urine because the goats were always brought into the huts at night, and the flies were overwhelming. Grace knelt by each woman, carried out what examination she could, and murmured words of encouragement. Her eyes watered in the foul air and from the frustration of helplessness. If only these women would come to her clinic! She would put them into clean beds, sponge down their fevers, and see that they ate nourishing food.

One woman lay outside her hut; it meant she was close to death.

Grace knelt by her and felt the dry forehead. Release was only an hour or two away. How had they known, these women of the village? The Kikuyu possessed an uncanny prescience about death. They always seemed to know when it was going to come and were able to move the dying person outside. It was taboo to have someone die in a hut; it was also *thahu* for anyone to touch a corpse, and so the dying were moved while still alive. Once outside, they were left alone, waiting for the hyenas to come and finish them because the Kikuyu did not bury their dead.

Grace knew better than to try to help the woman. Once before she had tried to interfere and had caused such an outcry among the clan that she had been barred from the village for days. "Let us at least move her into the shade," she said. But Mario was held back by tribal taboo.

"Mario!" she whispered. "Take her legs; I shall take her arms. We'll lay her under that tree."

He did not move.

"Damn it, Mario. Remember the Lord Jesus and the story of the good Samaritan."

His black face worked in indecision. Finally, reminding himself that these were lowly Kikuyu, having not yet become Christians and therefore to be scorned, he made a show of his fearlessness of them, of the old medicine woman in particular, by picking up the woman all by himself and carrying her to the shade.

In front of another hut Grace found a young mother sucking on the top of her baby's head. Because the infant was not getting enough fluids, its brain had shrunk, and so the "soft spot," the fontanel, had fallen in. The young mother knew enough to recognize this as a bad sign, but her efforts to correct it were all wrong.

"Tell her the baby needs water," Grace said to Mario. "Tell her to give the baby more milk, more *fluids.*"

He translated, and the young wife smiled and nodded as if she understood, then returned her mouth to the infant's head.

Grace straightened and looked around the village. Her cook pot was empty; everyone was back to work. The grain she had brought was being fed to the goats. In these animals the Kikuyu measured wealth and privilege. A woman with thirty goats could sneer upon a woman with only five. Elder Wachera, it was rumored, owned more than two hundred goats, which practically conferred a queenly status upon her. But the grain had been brought for the people, not for the goats!

"Like an Englishman," Grace murmured, "who will save his gold before his own life."

"Memsaab?"

"Let's see Gachiku now. She must be near her time."

But before Grace could move to the next hut, a voice called out her name.

She turned around. It was Sir James.

10

James Donald had to remove his double terai hat and stoop to clear the arbor that formed the entrance to the village. "Hello," he called to Grace, and waved a fistful of envelopes.

Her heart leaped. The dream came back. The camp beneath the stars, his hard body against hers, his mouth—

"Post is in," he said with a grin. "Thought I'd bring you yours."

He was dressed in khaki drill shorts, sturdy boots with socks up to his knees, and a bush shirt that was partially open to reveal the sunburned V on his chest. "I knew where to find you, of course," he said.

Grace felt her cheeks flush and hoped they were shaded by the brim of her wide pith helmet so that he didn't see. Behind him came Lucille, wearing a dusty slouch hat with a zebraskin band and a canvas bag over one shoulder. Grace thought, but was not sure, that Lucille was frowning. A grimace of displeasure? Or possibly disapproval? But then Lucille's features softened into a smile, and she said, "Hello, Grace. I've brought something for you."

As he handed Grace her mail, James watched. It was always the same: the hurried sorting through the envelopes, hands snapping eagerly, her eyes full of hope, and then the look of disappointment, the mail clasped, forgotten, in her fingers. It was as if, he thought, she was looking for something. A letter perhaps. From whom?

"How is it going, Grace?" he asked quietly.

She looked around the village. All work had ceased; the women were staring. It was because a man had entered their midst. "I don't know what to do, James," she said. "I don't feel as though I'm getting anywhere with them. They let me come and examine them if I bring food, but they won't take any of my medicine or let me treat them. Their idea of a cure is the horrid poisons Wachera boils up."

James squinted across the compound at the formidable old woman, who was regarding him with a closed expression. "She's a powerful old thing," he said. "You'll never win her over. Mathenge's the one you should convince."

Grace didn't tell James she was praying she would never have to meet the young chief face-to-face. Instead, she said, "Missions are guaranteed a sum of three hundred pounds a year from the government if they promise to work with the natives. So far the District Medical Officer has determined that I don't deserve it because my clinic stands empty. He accompanied me to this village once; but there was some sort of ceremony going on, and they wouldn't let me in. He wasn't impressed. He said I shall have to demonstrate more involvement than that to receive the three hundred pounds. And, James, I need that money!"

Grace was worried. Her inheritance was dwindling. Soon she would be relying solely on funds from the Mission Society back in Suffolk.

"I wish I could help," James said. "As it is, we're getting by on bank overdraft, like everyone else!"

She smiled. "I shall work it out. Now then, did you come eight miles just to deliver my mail?"

"I returned your microscope. It's back at your house."

"Was it a help?"

His face darkened, and it made him more handsome than ever. "In a way, yes. It confirmed my worst fears. We've got east coast fever. I've isolated the sick ones and am dipping the rest of the herd. On top of that, another bloody borehole has gone dry." He looked up at the sky. "If we don't get rain this time 'round, we all might as well cash it in."

They listened for a moment to the tinkling of goats' bells. Then Lucille said, "I've brought you a present, Grace."

"Oh, you shouldn't have," Grace said, but her voice died when the book was placed in her hands.

"It's a Kikuyu translation of the Bible. Isn't that clever?"

Grace stared down at the black leather cover, the gold-stamped title. "Thank you," she said uncertainly. "But I don't know that it will help me much."

"Preach the Word of the Lord, Grace. That's how you'll win these people."

"Mathenge doesn't want anything to do with Christianity. He won't allow preachers in the village."

Suddenly the morning peace was shattered by a scream. Grace spun around. It had come from Gachiku's hut. She ran, followed by James and Lucille, but Mario hung back because that was a birthing hut and taboo to men.

Grace went in to the young woman's side and, once her eyes were adjusted to the hut's darkness, saw the large abdomen ripple with contractions. "It's all right," Grace said soothingly in Kikuyu. "Your baby is coming."

She stepped out of the hut and asked for the *muciarithia,* the midwife, who in this instance was old Wachera. But the medicine woman did not move.

"Gachiku is about to give birth," Grace called out. "She needs your help. Mario, explain to her."

But before he could speak, Wachera held up a silencing hand. Her contempt for this young man who was no warrior and who had forsaken the Lord of Brightness for the Christian God forbade her to exchange words with him. To Sir James, who she knew spoke her tongue and whom she respected, Wachera said, "There is trouble with Gachiku's child. It will not come out. For three days she has been in labor, but the baby does not come. It is *thahu.* The ancestors have decreed that the child must not be born."

When James translated, Grace said, "You can't mean that! Surely you aren't going to just let Gachiku die?"

Wachera spoke, and James said, "She says it is the will of God."

"But that's monstrous! We must do something."

"Yes, of course. But it *is* tricky. Once the spirits of the ancestors have decided someone must die, it's the worst of taboos to defy them. They believe Gachiku has a curse on her, and nothing can break a Kikuyu curse."

"I'm not afraid of any curse. Mario, run back to the house and fetch my sterile obstetrics kit."

He hesitated.

"Go on!"

The youth looked at Sir James, who said, "Do as she says, lad."

"Yes, bwana."

"And ether," she called after him. "And the spare sheets from my bed!"

Grace went back into the hut. Her examinations of the villagers had so far been cursory: a feel of the forehead; a counting of the pulse. Kikuyu women were modest and shied away from strangers' eyes. But since Gachiku was in no position to protest, Grace was able to lay her hands on the swollen belly and feel for the position of the baby. It was a transverse presentation, which meant that the baby lay across the birth canal. In order to deliver it, and quickly, Grace would have to reach up and turn it by hand. She lifted up Gachiku's leather aprons.

Grace stared in shock.

She fell back on her heels and felt the hut tilt around her. Then she jumped up and ran outside.

"Dear God," she whispered when James took her arm to steady her.

"What is it?"

"I've never seen anything like it! Gachiku is . . . *deformed.*"

To her surprise, James said, "Yes, but it's not a congenital defect."

"What do you mean?"

"You're not aware of it? The initiation?"

"Initiation—"

"It's what the young people go through when they come of age. The boys are circumcised, and the girls—"

She regarded him in horror. "That was *done* to her?"

"All women undergo the operation in their teens. It marks their entry into the tribe. It is also a test of courage and resistance to pain. Any girl who flinches or cries out is cast out of the clan, cursed."

Grace pressed her hand to her forehead. Then she felt James's strong grip on her arm, and she was able to steady herself. "No wonder she is unable to give birth. She cannot possibly, not with that . . ."

"A lot of Kikuyu women die in childbirth because of the mutilation. The missionaries are trying to abolish the practice, but the Africans have been doing it for hundreds of years."

"I'm going to have to do something to help her, James. And I don't have much time. Will you and Lucille help me?"

"What can you possibly do?"

"A Caesarean section. I will operate and remove the baby abdomi-nally."

His hand fell away from her arm.

"You said you would help me!"

"There are limits to our interference, Grace. You'll have the whole clan up in arms if you attempt something as drastic as that."

"I'm going to try it."

Lucille said, "I'll help you, Grace," and swung the canvas bag off her shoulder.

"You're making a grave mistake," said James.

"Have someone find me the woman's husband. I'll get his permis-sion. Then the clan can't crucify me."

James stepped close to her, angry. "Don't meddle, Grace!"

"I'm not going to stand by and let her die, damn it!"

"All right, supposing you get the husband's permission. If you at-tempt the operation and Gachiku dies, he'll *kill* you, Grace. And I assure you there will be nothing the authorities can do to save you."

"But if I do nothing, then she will surely die!"

"And no one will blame you. Leave her alone, and the clan will let you go in peace. Otherwise, you will never gain their confidence and your clinic will always stand empty."

She glared at him. "Please ask them who the husband is. I'll talk to him. I'll convince him. James, ask them who owns Gachiku."

He asked Wachera, and when the reply came, Grace did not need a translation. Gachiku was the second wife of the clan's chief.

Mathenge.

GRACE HAD WANTED to move Gachiku to her clinic, where there was a proper operating table and good light, but since Wachera would not allow the woman to be moved, and time was growing short, Grace decided to attempt the procedure in the hut. Her wartime reflexes came to her aid; she had performed surgery on a ship that was being bombed, with lights flickering and her only assistant a seasick news correspondent.

James stood outside the hut while Grace and Lucille worked inside. Through the mysterious bush telegraph, women from the neighboring villages heard of what was happening and began to appear in great numbers. So, too, had Mathenge heard, and he now strode through the entrance arch.

The gathering of women and children parted like a sea before the young chief and fell back to close behind him. There was nothing hurried in his step; his face was set in an indifferent expression. But James braced himself. Mathenge was not like the peaceful Kikuyu who attended mission schools.

They greeted each other in the usual complex ritual, mentioning ancestors and crops as if they were two old friends idling the time away. From within the hut came the periodic moans and cries of Gachiku, but Mathenge gave no indication of noticing.

Finally he squatted in the dust and invited James to do the same. The women looked on as their chief and the white bwana gradually moved in on the issue at hand.

"You sit before the hut of a lady mine," Mathenge said.

"It is so," James replied in Kikuyu. Sweat trickled down between his shoulder blades.

"There is someone inside the hut with the woman I own."

Blast you, thought James. *You know damn well what's going on inside that hut.*

"The mother's mother of first wife has said the ancestors have put *thahu* on second wife. Perhaps Memsaab Daktari does not know this."

James scooped up some dirt and let it sift through his fingers. A show of nonchalance was vital. Mathenge was offering Grace a way out that would save face for both of them, but James knew she would refuse it.

They continued to sit in silence with not even the jingle of goats' bells disturbing the air. The sun grew hot. The eyes of the many women remained fast on the two men. Mathenge sat as still as a statue, while James listened to his own pulse thunder in his ears.

Lucille was in that hut. . . .

"She is my favorite wife," Mathenge said.

Startled, James looked up, and for an instant the bold warrior's gaze met his. Then Mathenge averted his eyes, as if embarrassed at being caught in an emotion, and he said quietly, "It troubles me that there is *thahu* on Gachiku."

James felt a flutter of hope. "Could Wachera be wrong about the ancestors?" he ventured. "Perhaps there is no *thahu.*"

But Mathenge shook his head. Despite the love in his heart for second wife, his fear of the medicine woman was stronger. "Memsaab Daktari must stop."

Christ, thought James. *And he wants me to do it!* "I haven't the authority to stop her."

The chief tossed him a look of disdain. "The bwana cannot control his women?"

"I do not own the memsaab. She belongs to Bwana Lordy."

Mathenge thought about this. Then he turned, barked an order into the crowd, and bare feet were heard running out of the compound.

To James he said, "Second wife must not be touched. She is under *thahu.*"

"Kikuyu *thahu* cannot harm Memsaab Daktari."

"Thahu harms everyone, bwana. You know that. Kikuyu *thahu* will destroy the memsaab."

James swallowed. The order that Mathenge had given was to fetch the warriors who were working on Lord Treverton's house. The tension in the air mounted until he thought he could feel it crackle, and James wondered if Grace was about to trigger an "incident."

Suddenly Mathenge stood. The women fell back. James also rose and, being as tall as the chief, met him eye to eye. "I swear by Ngai, Mathenge, that the memsaab is only trying to save the lives of your wife and baby. If you order her out, Gachiku will die."

"The ancestors have said she must die. But if she dies under the hand of the memsaab, then it will not have been an honorable death, and I will seek revenge."

"And if Gachiku lives?"

"She will not live."

"The memsaab's medicine is very strong. Perhaps it is stronger than Wachera's."

Mathenge's eyes narrowed. He strode past James and entered the hut. Everyone looked on with held breath; even the hut stood in a strange silence. James frowned. He didn't hear Grace or Lucille. Nor, for that matter, did Gachiku make a sound. What had happened?

Finally the chief came out of the hut and said to the crowd, "The woman I own is dead."

"What!" James turned and went inside. What he saw made him stop short.

Lucille was at Gachiku's head, holding an ether cone over her sleeping face, while Grace knelt at the young woman's side. She had already made the incision; the sheets were soaked with blood.

"You're in the light," Grace said, and James stepped to one side.

He had seen blood before, had watched army surgeons perform during the war, had even witnessed childbirth, but nothing had prepared him for this.

Grace's hands flew. Her rubber gloves snapped as she picked up instruments, used them, dropped them, snatched up towels, sponges, cut, and sewed. The air in the hut was hot and close and heady with ether fumes. Lucille calmly regulated the anesthetic drip on Gachiku's face while Grace worked with such concentration that her blouse was soaked through with perspiration.

It seemed hours to him, yet it was a quick operation. It had to be. Once the baby was out and in Lucille's hands, the blood had to be stopped and Gachiku kept alive. James watched in fascination as the two women worked rapidly, as if they had done this together a hundred times, their heads bowed over the young woman, hands fluttering, caring, restoring to whole. When the last abdominal suture was in and Lucille was patting Gachiku's face to waken her, James found that he was pressed against the mud wall and his back hurt.

Grace finally turned and looked up at him. There were tears in her eyes, caused by what he didn't know. "James," she whispered, and he reached down to help her up.

"Will she live?"

Grace nodded and leaned against him. She trembled in his arms; her skin smelled of iodine and Lysol. Then she took hold of herself and walked out into the sunshine. The lookers-on murmured in horror; taboo of taboos, she had the blood of another person on her clothes.

"You have a daughter," Grace said to Mathenge, "and your wife is alive."

He turned away.

"Listen to me!" she cried.

He spun around. "You lie!"

"Go inside and see for yourself."

His eyes flickered to the hut and then came back to her face. There was no politeness in him now, no show of manners. He had to demonstrate his superiority over this interfering *mzunga*, who clearly needed a husband to beat her. He stared down at Grace, who came as high as his shoulders and threatened her with his strength. In the days of the great raids his father had carried off many Masai women, subjugating them in the way Mathenge would like to break this memsaab.

To his fury, she met his gaze equally.

Inside the hut Lucille finished washing the baby and wrapped her in a small blanket. When she started for the door, James stopped her.

"Why not show the baby to the father? When Mathenge sees—"

"He'll kill it. We have to wait for him to come into the hut on his own. It's the Kikuyu way."

Lucille took the baby to sleeping Gachiku and placed it at her breast.

When James and Lucille came out of the hut, it was in time to see a line of men file into the compound, many still carrying hammers and saws.

James felt the back of his neck prickle. "Jesus," he whispered, "we've got to get word somehow to the District Police."

There was a stirring in the crowd, and those closest stepped aside to allow Wachera into the circle. She came slowly forward, her venomous gaze fixed on Grace. "The hut is cursed!" she cried. "It has been defiled, and it must be burned."

"What?" said Grace. "Surely you're not going to—"

"There is *thahu* here! Bring fire!" To her granddaughter's husband the old woman said, "You must burn the hut with the bodies of your dead wife and child inside. Then you must slay these two memsaabs who caused this sacrilege."

"Wait a minute!" shouted James, stepping forward. "The woman and child are not dead! Go and see for yourself, Lady Wachera. You will see that I do not lie."

"How can they be alive? The baby could not come out. This I felt with my own hands."

"I brought the baby out," said Grace.

"No one has the power to do that."

"The white man's medicine does. Listen!"

They all turned toward the hut. A mewling sound came from within. The cries of a newborn.

"But Gachiku was dead!" said Mathenge. "I saw with my own eyes. Her belly was cut open!"

"She was not dead, merely asleep. Go and see. She will waken. Your favorite woman, Mathenge!"

He was caught in indecision. "You haven't the power to bring the dead back to life."

But Grace said, "I have and I did."

"Not even Ngai has that power," he said, but his tone was cautious.

Lucille spoke up then, her voice ringing. *"Our* God has that power! Our Lord died and came back!"

Mathenge considered this, his look suspicious. Then he turned to Mario. "You worship the white God, toad. Is what they say true? Does He make the dead live again?"

"The mission fathers taught me so."

Mathenge turned to Grace. "Prove it."

"Go inside the hut and see with your own eyes."

But the young chief would not be tricked. He knew that to enter the hut would mean an admission that he thought the white man's medicine was stronger than his own. "We will kill someone," he said, "and you will bring him back to life."

In front of the excited onlookers Mathenge gestured for Mario to step up, and when the young man didn't move, two men seized him and threw him to the ground.

"Kill him," said Mathenge.

One of the men raised a hammer, and Grace shouted, "Stop! *I* will do it."

"You?"

"It is *my* medicine that you question. It was I who put Gachiku into the sleep like death and I who gave her life again. You wanted proof of *my* power, Mathenge."

Their eyes locked for an instant. Then he nodded once, and Grace went into the hut for the cone and bottle of ether.

Mario shook terribly, and his eyes rolled in fear. "Don't be afraid," she said in English, smiling to comfort him. "You will sleep only; then I will waken you."

"I am afraid, Memsaab Daktari."

Lucille said, "Trust in the Lord, Mario. He will not forsake you." As added solace she pressed the Kikuyu Bible into his hands; he clutched it as he lay down.

A strange stillness descended upon the village. Grace knelt at Mario's head, uncorked the bottle, placed the cone over his nose and mouth, and slowly poured. When the pungent fumes rose up, everyone retreated in fear.

They all watched as Mario's eyes closed and his body relaxed, the book falling from his hands. Finally Grace sat back and said, "He sleeps. Just as Gachiku slept."

Mathenge studied the recumbent body. Then he gave an order and a glowing ember was brought. Before Grace could stop him, Mathenge stamped the hot coal onto Mario's neck and held it there until the flesh was seared. The young man did not stir.

A murmur went through the crowd. Mathenge then called for a knife.

"No," said Grace. "Do no more. You have your proof. He feels no pain. He sleeps deeper than the sleep of night."

"Now waken him," said the chief.

Grace chewed her lip. Her shaking hand had not controlled the ether dosage with the exactness it required. A few extra drops had fallen.

. . .

"Why does he not wake up?"

"He will," she said.

A few minutes passed; Mario did not move.

"I do not see him coming to life."

"He will." Grace leaned forward and placed an ear to Mario's chest. There was a heartbeat, slow and weak. Had she given him too much? Did Africans, for some reason, require smaller doses?

Mathenge called for a torch, and Wachera smiled in triumph.

"Wait," said James. "It takes time. He must travel through the spirit world before he comes back to this one."

Mathenge gave that some thought. When the torch was brought, burning high and bright, he took it in his right hand and held it in readiness.

Still, Mario did not move.

James knelt next to Grace. "Is he going to be all right?" he asked softly in English.

"I don't know. Perhaps these people are highly sensitive to anesthesia—"

"Wake him now!" came Mathenge's sharp voice.

Grace patted the boy's cheek and called his name.

"Behold the white man's medicine!" cried Wachera, and she received a rumble of approval from the onlookers.

A baby's cry came from within the hut, and when Mathenge turned in its direction, the medicine woman said, "A trick! That is the cry of an evil spirit to lure you into *thahu*. Your child is dead, my son!"

"His child is alive!"

"And what about the boy at your feet?"

Grace looked down at Mario's face. *Please wake up*, she thought. *Open your eyes. Show them the power we have.*

"Mario!" she said out loud. "Wake up!"

James took the boy by the shoulders and shook him. The eyes remained closed.

"Dear God," whispered Grace, "what have I done?"

"Come along, Mario," said James, slapping him smartly on the cheek. "Wake up now! Naptime's over!"

In disgust Mathenge turned away and strode to the hut with the torch held high.

Grace shot to her feet. "No!" she screamed. "Your wife lives! Go and see for yourself!"

"You have lied. Your medicine is powerless. The ancestors have put *thahu* on us."

Grace reacted before she could think. Her hand shot out and sent the torch flying away from the hut. Stunned, Mathenge stared at her. For a woman to strike a man, a *chief* . . .

"Memsaab Daktari," came a weak voice.

All eyes switched to Mario. His head was rolling from side to side.

"That's the spirit, lad," said James, continuing to shake him gently. "Wake up now. Show the people we don't lie."

Mario's eyes fluttered open. He focused them on Mathenge. Then he suddenly rolled over and retched into the dirt.

"You see?" cried Grace. "I did not lie! My medicine is stronger than yours."

The young chief looked from Grace to the medicine woman, back to Grace. For the first time his handsome features were molded in uncertainty.

When he finally started walking toward the doorway of the hut, Wachera flung herself forward and blocked the way. "Don't listen to the *wazungu,* my son. It will mean *thahu!*"

"If their god can do this thing, then my new daughter lives and there is no *thahu.*"

Wachera slowly straightened her aged body, drew herself up with dignity, and stepped out of his way. Mathenge entered the hut.

Everyone watched and waited.

Finally the young chief came out and in his hands lay the naked body of his newborn daughter. "She lives!" he shouted as he held her high. "And lady mine lives also! She came back from the dead!"

Hurrahs erupted from the crowd.

Mathenge approached Grace, his face proudly set once again. He handed the baby to her, then bent and picked the dusty Bible off the ground. Hefting it, he said, "You will teach me about your God."

And elder Wachera, the medicine woman, retreated into the shadows of a hut.

11

The house was ready.

As Rose put in her last stitches for the morning, she could not contain her excitement. Today was a *beautiful* day because tomorrow she was moving into the house!

She hummed as she folded the tapestry frame and handed it to the African girl, who carried it. Mrs. Pembroke, the nanny, settled ten-month-old Mona into her carriage and tucked the blankets in around her. The only other members of the group were two little African boys, one to carry the food hamper and the memsaab's parasol, the other to take care of the monkey and two parrots. Rose carried her bag of yarn and led the way back to camp.

There was music in the glade: the rustling of the dry, brittle eucalyptus branches; the wind whispering through tall bushes; and birds, high in the foliage, flitting about in flashes of bright colors, calling, singing, chattering away. Normally Rose was reluctant to leave her special glade, which was hidden and protected by the forest and where Valentine had built for her a pretty little white gazebo, but today she did not mind. She was anxious to begin final preparations for the move.

Valentine had such a love of ceremony! The house had been ready for a week, the furniture in place, curtains up, carpets laid, the smell of new paint freshening the December air. But he insisted upon a formal opening. The servants had been rehearsing all week; smiling Africans in long white kanzus and scarlet jackets had practiced lining up along both sides of the steps leading to the front door. A red carpet was to be rolled down! First Rose would enter, carrying a bouquet of flowers, with Valentine at her side, then Grace and the Donalds, with all the guests gathered on the circular drive to watch and applaud.

Rose shivered in anticipation. Her gown had arrived two weeks before from Doeullet of Paris, the *very* latest style, worn by the Queen herself. The eyes of their two hundred guests, Rose had no doubt, were going to pop when they saw her arrive in the decorated pony cart and climb the steps.

She had not seen the inside of the house yet and was delirious at the prospect of entering for the first time. That was what had made her fall in love with Valentine when he had courted her; he had such a dramatic flair, such a marvelous sense of *surprise,* and was so clever at organizing such things.

Rose looked over her shoulder and said to the nanny, "Do come along, Mrs. Pembroke. You are such a slow coach!"

"I'm sorry, Your Ladyship," the elderly woman replied as she tried to maneuver the baby carriage over the dirt path.

Despite the bouncing and jostling ride, Mona sat up without complaining, her big eyes taking in the surrounding forest. She was a quiet little thing and never fussed, much to Mrs. Pembroke's relief, and pretty, too, in her frilly dress with matching bonnet. And intelligent, the nanny thought. Mona was already putting words together and starting to walk without help. At ten months! Not that her parents paid much notice. Whenever Lady Rose did pay attention to her daughter, it was in a childish way, playing with Mona as if she were a doll. And His Lordship—well, if there were a child in the family, one wouldn't know it by him!

There was so much yet to be done. Although Rose's biggest trunks had already gone up to the house, there were still her personal effects to be packed: toiletries; cosmetics; night things. The roses had yet to be planted, of course. And her hair to be done. Grace had offered to do it for her, copying from a picture out of an American magazine. They were going to do the shocking new marcel style.

"Do hurry, Mrs. Pembroke," she said again. Rose wore a pale pink gauze dress with a scooped neckline and large flounce collar that seemed to float about her. The moonlight-colored hair, soon to be cut short and crimped, was piled on top of her head, escaping in wisps and filaments. As Rose passed through shafts of sunlight, she looked like a forest sprite, translucent and ephemeral.

When the curious little group emerged from the woods and onto the cleared ridge above the dry river, they could see Birdsong Cottage below, the primitive clinic to which a beaten path now led, and farther along, the clearing with its lone hut and ancient fig tree.

Rose called out and waved to her sister-in-law, but Grace did not hear. There was a crowd under the thatch of her four-poster clinic: pregnant women and ailing babies and men with toothaches. Ever since that remarkable operation in the village two months ago, Grace's reputation had spread through Kikuyuland like a brush fire. Each morning now she woke to find Africans waiting to see her. And Lucille Donald came down three times a week to teach Bible to the children.

Everything was going so wonderfully! Rose felt as if her feet weren't touching the ground. Gone was the shock of last March, when she had arrived to a dismal scene. Even though the rains never came and even though everyone complained of the desperate situation the economy was in, Rose saw no reason to be unhappy.

As she made her way along the ridge, Rose slowed her step. She couldn't believe her eyes. They were at it again, the old woman and her granddaughter. They were building their hut one more time! Which was this? The fourth? Valentine had had the other huts all torn down, and Mathenge's family had gone across the river. Only the medicine woman and her young apprentice stubbornly remained, rebuilding their hut each time the tractor pushed it down. It was a mystery to Rose.

She recalled the last time the two women had come into the camp. The grandmother had led the way, walking with head held high like a dowager empress, bedecked in all her beads and copper and shells; behind her, the younger one, carrying the little boy on her hip. So polite the two had been! Bowing, smiling shyly, speaking in such soft voices that they could barely be heard. Grace's boy Mario had translated: They wished no offense but wanted only to alert the bwana that for some reason their hut kept falling down and that they would like the hut to stay up as that was where they lived and where they must remain because it was their sacred duty to serve the ancestors who dwelt in the fig tree.

And that had been their fourth visit! The patience and stamina of the two Kikuyu women had impressed Rose. All four times they had come humbly, bringing gifts of goats and beads, assuring Valentine that they accused no one and desired no trouble, wanting only to remind the spirits in the wind that the hut stood on holy ground and that it should not be allowed to fall down.

What curiosities the two Kikuyu women were to Rose. Look-alikes nearly, except that the grandmother was smaller and darker, as old Kikuyu women eventually became. There had been a quiet dignity about them; even the boy on his mother's hip had been respectfully silent, as if sensing the gravity of the situation. Valentine had reminded them that the land was his, since he had bought it legally from Chief Mathenge, and had sent them away with sacks of grain and a precious bag of sugar.

But there they were now, toiling again, as Rose looked down, the old medicine woman and her granddaughter, putting up the hut by themselves, patiently, silently. She wondered if they knew that Valentine had ordered the fig tree to be uprooted tomorrow, to open up the new polo field.

Farther along the river, beyond the tented camp, stood a symbol of Valentine's unshakable optimism. It was a brand-new pulper just out from the West Indies. He wouldn't be using it until the first coffee crop came in, in two or three years, but the pulper was ready, waiting for the moment when it would strip the soft red shell off the first berries and release the coffee beans within.

While Mrs. Pembroke put Mona down for her nap in the nursery tent, Rose went to the makeshift greenhouse to collect the cuttings she had brought out from England.

Not only had they survived, but they now flourished with new blossoms. All the way from Suffolk into the heart of an African drought. She put them into a wheelbarrow now and led the Kikuyu gardener up the path toward the house.

Where the formal drive met the dirt road there was a large, imposing gate with a stone arch that was inscribed with the Treverton coat of arms and the name of the estate.

It brought a smile to Rose's lips to recall the look on Valentine's face when that stone had been delivered last month. The Swahili stonecutter in Mombasa had worked lovingly and painstakingly on the carving, making the letters perfectly matched, putting extra flourishes at the corners. It was an artistic accomplishment, everyone agreed, and certainly worth more than Valentine had paid for it. There was only one thing wrong with it: The name was misspelled.

"Bella Two," Valentine had ordered, in memory of Bella Hill, his ancestral home back in England. He had added, "Not T-O-O, mind you, as in *also*, but Bella Two, meaning the 'second house.' Do you understand?"

The man had insisted that he understood perfectly and then had sat down to a four-month job of doing it wrong.

The look on Valentine's face . . . And then everyone had burst out laughing. Sir James had quickly made the best of a bad situation by saying, "Very clever, Val. Whatever made you think of it?"

Carved permanently in stone was BELLATU. And it meant in Swahili, Sir James had hastened to explain, "totally and completely Bella."

Valentine had had the long drive planted with giant poinsettia trees so that the approach to the house was very dramatic. The dwindling supply of precious water had been tapped for these bushes to ensure their blossoming for the gala celebration. Petals like tongues of flame exploded from every branch and littered the barren ground like a scarlet carpet. This was the way the guests would come tomorrow, after they were first shown to their quarters among the many tents and temporary huts Valentine had had put up in a nearby field. There stood a village, a clean little shantytown that would vanish after the guests were gone but that, for a few days, would be alive with parties, laughter, fox hunts, and endless champagne. It was the way things were done in the protectorate when guests had to travel long distances to an event, arriving with servants and animals.

Rose fought the impulse to sneak a look inside the house. Ever the showman, Valentine had even had all the draperies closed so that Bellatu remained a sealed secret. He hadn't even allowed her to see the color of the paint for the interior.

It was a magnificent house on the outside and so different from the stodgy mansions of England.

Bellatu was two-storied, gabled, built of fieldstone with a deep veranda all the way around, and had an air of tropical luxury, of gracious living. It was a new and innovative style, created especially for East Africa, and it spoke of new beginnings. The dining room at the rear had tall French doors which opened onto a multilevel flagstone terrace.

Flower beds were freshly stocked with blooming plants; Rose knew they must have cost Valentine a fortune in this drought. But she was not going to plant her roses here; they were going to go in front of the house.

Last June there had been a ceremony in Nairobi at which Lady Rose had officially presented some of her rosebushes to the town. There had been a band playing, and a banquet afterward, and a rowdy celebration. A plaque had been erected among the roses:

ROSA GALLICA OFFICINALIS

These roses, which came from the
gardens of Bella Hill in Suffolk, England,
are believed to have been first planted there
after the War of Roses, when Henry Tudor, in
1485, gave lands to a faithful soldier in reward
for fighting for the Lancastrian cause. To honor
his king, the new earl of Trever's Town planted
on his estate red roses, symbol of the
House of Lancaster.
Lady Rose, countess of Treverton, brought
these cuttings to British East Africa in
February 1919.

It was on such occasions that Rose, like her flowers, bloomed: when there was pageantry and ceremony, when the right food was served, the correct protocol followed, and the proper people were in attendance. Then she opened up and glowed. She felt herself come to life, in love and loved.

Valentine had invited only the best of British East Africa society to the celebration of their new home. Some were coming from as far away as Uganda, the Sudan, the coast, even Tanganyika, which was British now that it had been won from the Germans. There would be officers of the king in smart regimental uniforms, with ladies on their arms; titled personages; people with wealth and position in the protectorate; and those without but who were no less glamorous: the white hunter surrounded by legend, the brothers who had explored the Congo, a famous writer, and two screen actresses. It was going to be the Event of the Year, perhaps of the decade, and Rose, finding her place at last in this strange country, was going to reign over it all.

She hurried now. She dug the earth with her bare fingers. The house! she thought. A proper house at last! No more tents, no more insects and lizards. A *real* bed in a *real* bedroom. One for Rose, one for Valentine. In these past months he had come to respect her wishes; that unpleasant business was forgotten. He hadn't approached her bed and most likely would not in the future.

She planted the first rosebush.

THE TRACTOR HEADED for the fig tree.

"Cut the bloody thing down," the bwana had said, "and then we'll be rid of those pestering women."

Two strong Africans had sawed through the tree's ancient trunk; the tractor would push it over and then pull up the stump. Bwana Lordy wanted the job finished by this afternoon. The *wazungu* were already arriving in their wagons and motorcars and on horseback; he wanted the polo field to be ready.

THE SPIRIT OF the river was angry. That was why young Wachera and her grandmother had traveled far for their water, rising before dawn and striking into the heart of an unfamiliar forest, walking many spear throws to reach the mountain slopes where a few creeks still trickled. Now they were in the land of wild animals. The two Kikuyu women were guests and had no wish to offend the animal spirits or the spirits in the rocks and trees of this place so far from their home, so they sang as they walked and left offerings of maize meal and beer along the way.

The river spirit was angry because of the wall the bwana had built across its throat, choking it, causing the waters to back up and swell and grow out into a pond where never before had there been a pond. It was to take care of the people during the drought, the bwana had said. While the other clans died of thirst, Chief Mathenge's family had water. But this was wrong, the medicine woman had told her apprentice. The Children of Mumbi must not offend the spirits of nature to satisfy their own selfish needs. The river was being strangled, and that was why there was *thahu* in Kikuyuland.

They carried large calabash gourds and sat patiently while each gourd slowly filled. Young Wachera grew sad as she thought of her husband.

After the birth of Gachiku's daughter Mathenge had followed the road to the white man's mission, and there he had listened to tales of a miraculous god named Jesu who had died and come back to life and who promised the same returning to life for any who worshiped Him. At the mission Mathenge had been bewitched. He had seen the thing called a "bicycle," and he desired one of his own. He had ridden in a "motocah" and had fallen under its spell. He had been given charms called "coins" and had seen how they were more valuable than goats. He had been shown how to "speak" symbols that were drawn on paper and had been told that in this skill lay all the power in the world. In the white man's village Mathenge's head had turned; he had witnessed the might of the *mzungu,* in his guns, his boots, his tins of food. And Mathenge had returned to his family by the river a changed man.

"The white man has the better way, lady mine," he had said to young Wachera the night he left her forever. Mathenge had come to the hut wearing white man's clothes because the mission fathers had told him that nakedness was an abomination to the god Jesu. "This is the new age. The world is changing. Ngai on his mountain is dead; there is a new god. Shall the Children of Mumbi perish for not worshiping the new god and learning his ways? Remember the proverb that says the pretty girl walks past the house of a poor man. Will you have the other tribes of the world walk past the Kikuyu door?"

Wachera had listened in respectful silence, her tears to be shed later so as not to shame herself before her husband. Little Kabiru, their son, toddled about, unaware of the great farewell being spoken.

"I was made chief, lady mine, and it is my duty to take care of our people. Remember the proverb that says cattle that have a limping leader never reach the good grazing grass. I will learn the reading of the white man, and I will sacrifice to the god Jesu. The mission fathers showed me an image of the bad god whom they call Satan, and his skin is the color of the Kikuyu. They have shown me that black is evil, and I do not wish to be evil. They washed my forehead and called me Solomon, which is my new name. I am like the white man now, I am his equal. And my son here, who is called Kabiru for his grandfather, will go to the mission and will also be washed and will receive a new name and thus be the white man's equal."

Mathenge went away for six passings of the sun and returned with the child, saying, "Now his name is David, and he is a Christian. The white man will treat him as a brother."

Then Mathenge had said, "God Jesu says that I commit a sin by owning more than one wife. You defied me, lady mine, by not moving to the other side of the river when I commanded. Therefore, you are no longer my wife. I shall live now as a Christian man with Gachiku, and with Njeri, my daughter whom Jesu restored to life. And when my time comes to die, I will be restored to life, as Jesu promises."

Afterward Wachera had clasped Kabiru to her breast and lamented as if Mathenge had died. It was the worst calamity for a Kikuyu woman to be cast out by her husband, for then she was cast out by the clan and no longer had a family. Wachera wept not only for the loss of her beloved mate but for the emptiness of her womb in the years to come. She clung to Kabiru and wailed, she washed him with her tears as if to wash away the white man's baptism, but in the end, because it was the wish of the man she desperately loved, she called her son David. And when her hut was torn down a fifth time, she did not rebuild it but moved into the hut of her grandmother, where the three lived in love and mutual solace.

The gourds were full; it was time to return. Because young Wachera had the additional burden of David, who rode on her hip, the grandmother carried more gourds, and so her load was heavier, what the white man would measure at ninety pounds. Bent in half and facing the ground with leather straps digging into their foreheads to hold the heavy calabashes in place, the two trudged in silence through the unfamiliar forest back to their hut beside Valentine's reservoir.

THE LATE-AFTERNOON air was filled with smoke as the men burned what was left of the gigantic fig tree stump; the river quiet was jarred by the grinding of chains and tractor motor.

Wachera and her grandmother came through the trees in time to see the ancient roots, like the gnarled fingers of a protesting hand, rise up out of the ground in a shower of dirt. The two women stopped and stared. A team of ten men was hauling away the stump and filling in the cavity left behind. All that remained of the massive trunk and great spreading branches of the sacred tree were bundles of freshly chopped logs.

Elder Wachera slowly removed the calabashes from her back. "Daughter," she said, "take me into the forest now. It is time for me to die."

Young Wachera stared at her. "Are you ill, Grandmother?"

The medicine woman spoke calmly but with an echo of fatigue and age in her voice that the granddaughter had never heard before. "The home of the ancestors has been destroyed. The sacred ground is defiled. There is great *thahu* here. My time in this world is over. Take me now, Granddaughter."

The arm she held out was steady. Wachera put her calabashes on the ground, shifted David to her other hip, and took her grandmother's hand. They turned their backs on the Kikuyu men in white man's clothes who were chopping and burning the sacred tree and returned to the forest.

They walked in silence; only little David, fourteen months old and unaware of the catastrophe that had struck, gurgled and cooed. Although she did not want to accept it, young Wachera knew that her grandmother was indeed about to die. It was the Kikuyu way not to bury the dead but to leave the body to be devoured by hyenas. A person must not be allowed to die in a hut, for then the hut was made unclean and must be burned; a corpse could not be touched, for that was taboo. And so the sickly and dying, while yet alive, were either taken or went on their own to die alone and thus not bring *thahu* upon the homestead.

They reached a place that was uninhabited by people. The grandmother sat on the dusty ground littered with twigs and dry leaves, and for the first time her movements were those of an old woman. Young Wachera marveled at how suddenly her grandmother had aged. The tired joints creaked; arms and legs moved stiffly when only a short while before, while carrying the calabashes, the medicine woman had been as spry and nimble as the granddaughter fifty years her junior.

Elder Wachera sat on the earth and stretched her legs out before her. "Soon I will be taken by the Lord of Brightness," she said softly. "And I will return to live with our First Parents, Kikuyu and Mumbi."

Placing David on the ground, young Wachera sat opposite her

grandmother and waited. Something terrible had happened, something the young woman could conceive only vaguely, something beyond her grasp but which one day she believed she would understand.

"There is sorrow in Kikuyuland," elder Wachera said at last, her breathing becoming labored. "The time has come for the old ways to pass. I know now that I was born to see the sunset of the Kikuyu. The Children of Mumbi will turn their backs on Ngai, on their ancestors, on the tribal laws. They will strive to become like the white man. The old ways will die and be forgotten.

"Mathenge will never come back to you, Daughter. The white man has cast a spell on him. But the man who once owned you will not be happy in his new life, for there is the proverb that says the knife once sharpened cuts its owner. But he is not to blame, for there is another proverb that says a man's heart feeds on what it likes."

She fell silent. The sun began to creep out of the forest, leaving behind long shadows like snakes reaching out for the two Kikuyu women.

"You know, Daughter, that we live in our descendants. A man must own many wives and have many children so that our ancestors live eternally. But the white man is teaching us that this is wrong. Already Kikuyu men are forsaking their wives. There will not be enough children to receive the souls of departed grandparents, and so the spirits of our ancestors will wander the earth homeless. Soon there will be no more fig trees, and there will be no one left to communicate with our fathers and mothers of the past. They will be lost."

With shaking hands the medicine woman removed a bracelet from her wrist—it was made of elephant eyelashes and therefore contained strong magic—and handed it to her granddaughter. When she spoke again, her voice was thinner, her breathing more irregular. It was as if her life were seeping out of her old bones, just as life was departing the roots of the dying fig tree. "You will eat an oath now, Granddaughter. And then you will leave me."

The forest was growing dark and menacing. No Kikuyu ever went abroad at night because of the many dangers from animals and evil spirits. But the young woman wanted to remain with her grandmother until death had claimed her. "I will not let them take you while you live," she said in a tight voice, referring to the hyenas, which even now had come out and were prowling nearby.

Elder Wachera shook her head. "It matters not to me that they feast on my flesh while I live. The hyenas are to be honored and respected, Daughter. I will not cry out. You must go, but first the oath."

Wachera was terrified. Oath eating was the most powerful form of Kikuyu magic; it bound one's soul to one's word. To break such an oath meant instant and terrible death.

"You will promise me now, Granddaughter, by the earth that is our Great Mother, that you will protect the old ways and keep them forever and ever." The old woman scooped some soil into her hand and held it out. Making mystical signs over the dirt, she closed her eyes and said, "Someday the Children of Mumbi will turn against the white man and cast him out of Kikuyuland. When that time comes, they will want to return to the ways of their fathers. But who will be here to teach them?"

"I will," whispered young Wachera.

The medicine woman placed the dirt in her granddaughter's hands. "Swear by the earth our Great Mother that you will keep the tribal ways and that you will communicate always with the ancestors."

Wachera lifted her hands to her mouth and pressed her tongue to the dirt. Swallowing, she said, "I swear."

"Swear also, Wachera, that you will be medicine woman to our people and will practice the rites and magic of our mothers."

Again Wachera ate the soil and swore the oath.

"And promise me, my soul daughter . . ." The old woman labored for breath. Her body seemed to grow small and shrink before her granddaughter's eyes. "Promise me that you will take revenge upon the white man on the hill."

Wachera ate the oath, promised revenge against the *mzungu,* and watched her grandmother die.

12

She had walked through the night forest with no fear, for she knew the spirit of her grandmother walked at her side. Wachera marched with a purposeful step, eyes blind to the shadowy shapes of heads and flanks around her, ears deaf to the sounds of hyenas feasting on human flesh. She pushed through tree and bush with David embraced to her strong young body, courage and determination filling her with every step as if the power of her grandmother were swelling in her veins. With each tree passed, Wachera's shyness and humility vanished; with each rock stepped over and each twig cracked, her youthful fears and uncertainties were broken and cast aside. Wachera grew as she walked, in spirit and in stature. She had memorized every word elder Wachera had spoken; she would remember them until the day she died.

At last she came out of the forest to the clearing where the sacred tree had once stood and where there was now a lone hut in the moonlight. Holding her baby, the only one she knew she would ever have, young Wachera, now the medicine woman of the clan, turned her eyes to the big stone house on the hill.

"I SAY, RATHER like a coronation, isn't it?"

This was said by His Excellency the Governor, who, because of his exalted rank in the protectorate, stood closest to the front steps of the house. The excitement was palpable in the night air. Torches blazed along the curved drive down to the dirt road where latecomers were still arriving. The assembled guests murmured in anticipation, thrilled with the spectacle Treverton had orchestrated. Wineglasses sparkled in the moonlight; pink gins sloshed around in tall tumblers. Everyone eagerly awaited the arrival of the earl and his countess, after which they'd all get a good look inside the magnificent new house and then be fed a proper feast.

"They tell me it's all lit with light bulbs. Treverton's installed some sort of generator, the first electricity in the province."

"I understand there's to be polo tomorrow," someone else said. This was Hardy Acres, the manager of Nairobi's biggest bank, to whom almost everyone present was in debt.

"If the weather holds," added the man next to him. Faces turned to the night sky, where moon and stars shone. Still, a few wondered, didn't the air feel unusually damp tonight? And wasn't there the barest hint of a breeze? All it would take was one good wind and the clouds would tumble down off Mount Kenya and bring . . . *rain.*

"I say," came another voice. "Here they are!"

Valentine Treverton understood that in British East Africa one could substitute showiness for taste and get away with it because that was part of the magic of living in the protectorate. Like others, Treverton was affected by the equatorial sun; style became ostentation, and his sense of pomp verged on parody. Everyone accepted it and loved it. So when the wagon came down the drive, drawn by ponies decked in Arab tassels and bells, the cart festooned with ribbons and flowers, the driver an African in full Treverton livery down to the crest on his jacket and green velvet top hat, the guests had to applaud. East Africa settlers loved a good show.

It was understood that the rules were different here and were often made up on the spot. Weekends of hunts and drinking and target shooting helped one forget that the crops were withering in the fields, that the Africans were dying of starvation and disease, and that a very real threat lingered near that one might have to pack off to England, a failure.

Bless Valentine Treverton, everyone thought. He was as good as his word and was certainly delivering tonight. His guests adored him for it.

Lady Rose looked stunning as she stepped down from the cart, holding, of all things, a bouquet of madonna lilies. Where had Treverton managed to get *those,* in this drought? And the countess's hair!

Already the women were making a note to cut off their own old-fashioned Gibson style for the free, new-woman marcel wave that was scandalous in Europe but that Lady Rose had suddenly made acceptable. Her long, beaded gown trailed behind her. She smiled and nodded as she mounted the steps, her hair gleaming like polished platinum in the torchlight. Valentine, proud and dignified, walked at her side; he was decidedly the most handsome man at the affair. Dr. Grace Treverton followed, more conservatively dressed than her sister-in-law; Mrs. Pembroke was with her, carrying ten-month-old Mona; and last came Sir James and Lady Donald, the Trevertons' best friends and most honored guests.

The doors were opened by two smiling servants, and Valentine led his wife into her new home for the first time.

It was every bit as fabulous as she had imagined it would be—even more! Valentine had planted little surprises everywhere: an antique highboy displaying her Spode china, which had nested in a crate for nearly a year, the wonderful grandfather clock in the parlor that swung with time, and a portrait of her parents which he had secretly sent for and which now hung in the formal dining room. And the biggest, best surprise of all: a Christmas tree in the center of the living room, cut down from the Aberdare forest and laden with lighted candles, tinsel, gingerbread ornaments. At its base lay drifts of artificial snow.

Rose was overcome. She turned to him, said, "Valentine, dearest," and went into his arms. When they kissed, everyone cheered, except for the Kikuyu servants, who, being members of a tribe that did not kiss, wondered why the memsaab and bwana would put their mouths together.

Miranda West, having arrived from Nairobi the day before and at work in the kitchen since before dawn, saw to the orderly serving of her masterpieces. Because two hundred guests could not all sit down together, the banquet was served buffet style, the guests being attended upon by Africans wearing scarlet Zanzibar waistcoats embroidered in gold over long white kanzus and white gloves. Miranda's fried potato cakes accompanied roast gazelle, rainbow trout from Valentine's dwindling reservoir, spur fowl baked in honey, and ham from the Rift Valley. Drop scones were eaten with butter and jam; Miranda's potted salmon was spread onto cottage loaf; and even the punches were her own creations; from cut glass bowls with dippers and matching glasses were offered the famous badminton and claret cups. The food brought sighs of ecstasy and melancholy from the homesick crowd as everyone tasted England and suddenly remembered what they had forsaken for this uncertain new life. There were even musicians with violins and an accordion who played Christmas carols. Bellatu glowed in the night, on its lonely hilltop, like a kingdom that came to life once every hundred years. For miles around, natives in their dark, smoky huts huddled together with their children and goats, afraid of the dark, listening to the baffling sounds of laughter and music of the *wazungu*. A solitary elephant trumpeted on a nearby mountain slope, as if to remind the revelers of where they really were.

The guests spilled out onto the veranda, on the lawns, and a few had even found their way secretly up to peek at the bedrooms. Valentine never left Rose's side. They were a charmed couple, sprinkling magic and blessings on everyone they touched. Treverton's luck in the protectorate had become legend in this past year; while everyone else's crops perished from lack of water, his seedlings were strong and green. He even had a mystifying way with the Africans who were loyal to him and seemed never to run away or sit down on their jobs. People crowded around the earl and his beautiful wife, hoping that some of the enchantment would rub off.

Grace escaped to the terrace, where she stood at a clipped hedge and looked down at the Chania River.

"I think your brother's outdone himself," Sir James said as he joined her. "This night will be the topic of gossip for years to come."

She laughed and sipped her champagne.

"How on earth can Valentine afford all this?" James asked.

Grace did not reply. She knew her brother was drawing heavily upon the income from his Bella Hill rents, and she prayed his good judgment would tell him when to stop. The Suffolk estate was not a bottomless money well.

Three men walked by, their white dinner jackets ghostly in the moonlight. "When I'm on safari," one of them said, "I prefer sleeping in the open. The sky makes a good roof, provided it doesn't leak!"

James lifted his brandy glass and smiled at Grace. She was caught in that smile, in the creases around his eyes.

One of the trio, as they vanished around the hedge, said with slightly slurred words, "I hear there's a monstrous big tusker out Lake Rudolf way." And the conversation, fading, swung around to elephant hunting.

James grew thoughtful. An absent look stole across his face; the glass remained at his lips, untouched.

"Is there something wrong?" Grace asked.

"I was just remembering . . ." He set the glass on the edge of a marble birdbath. "My father hunted for ivory. When I was old enough, he took me on safaris with him. I recall that I had just turned sixteen when we went to Lake Rudolf."

James didn't look at her as he spoke; his voice grew distant. "That was back in 1904. We were tracking an old bull that my father had wounded with his first shot. I was in camp while he went on ahead, and he found it. The elephant charged my father, and before he could get off a second shot, his gun jammed. He turned and ran, with the gigantic tusker thundering after him. According to the gun bearer who fetched me, my father flung himself to one side just as the elephant was upon him. It spun around, came back, and tried to gore him with its tusks. By the time I got there, my father had managed to crawl behind the elephant's chin so the tusks couldn't reach him, but the beast was pounding him with its knees. I shot off several rounds and dropped the animal, but by then my father was dead. It was a long trek back, several hundred miles with just me and the native porters. The whole time I was beside myself with worry about how I was to break the news to my mother. But when I reached Mombasa, I learned she had died of blackwater fever."

He looked at Grace, his expression gentle. "That was when I went to England to live with relatives. When I returned to British East Africa, I was twenty-two and married. I bought the land at Kilima Simba and imported Ayrshire cows to crossbreed with the native Boran bulls. Since then I have had no stomach for hunting."

He studied her for a moment, then said, "You're truly happy here, aren't you, Grace?"

"Yes."

"I'm glad. People who don't love East Africa have no right to be here. This is the only world I know. I was born here, and I shall die here. These others"—he gestured toward the noisy house—"who come here to make a quick fortune, who exploit the land and the natives— they are criminals. Those with no love for this land should go home."

"*This* is my home now," she said in a quiet voice.

James smiled and quoted softly, " 'Here in a large and sunlit land, Where no wrong bites to the bone, I will lay my hand in my neighbor's hand, And together we will atone.' "

He paused and seemed about to say something further when a voice came between them. "There you are!"

They turned to see James's wife come through the French doors.

Once again, as she had several times in the past ten months, Grace thought she caught a look of displeasure, or pain, cross Lucille's face. But each time it was quickly replaced by a smile, as it was now. "I'm afraid the noise has gotten a bit much in there," she said. "Someone is dancing a Highland fling!"

James laughed. "Can you picture these merrymakers getting up in the morning for polo?"

"My brother will see that they do! He's been exercising his ponies for a month. We should see quite a match. Have you any bets on, James?"

"I'm afraid," said Lucille, "that we won't be here for the matches. We'll be leaving first thing in the morning."

"Leaving?"

"Lucille wants to go to the Methodist mission in Karatina for Christmas service."

"But Father Mario is coming from the Catholic mission! We shall have a lovely mass on the front lawn."

Lucille's smile hardened. "I don't wish to attend a Roman service. It's bad enough that I get to Karatina only four times a year. You know, Grace, you would be wise to write to your Mission Society for a minister instead of for the nursing sisters you've been requesting."

"But I need nurses, Lucille. Desperately. I can't seem to train the Kikuyu to touch sick people."

"You're going about it the wrong way. A minister would turn these heathens from their abominable practices and make Christians of them. Then you would have all the help you require."

Grace stared at her.

James said, "Listen! They're playing 'Silent Night.'"

As the partyers quieted and the laughter subsided, the strings of the violins rose to fill the night. Soon the house and grounds rested in silence as the Christmas hymn was lifted up to the cold equatorial stars so far from home. A few smoky clouds, as if drawn by curiosity, detached themselves from Mount Kenya's grasp and drifted across the sky.

Grace stood between James and Lucille; they gazed into the brightly lit rooms of Bellatu and upon the large, very diverse family that was united in a single, familiar song. Voices began to join in. Some contributed harmony. The African servants stood by with fixed expressions as the *wazungu*, rowdy one moment and reverent the next, grew sad-eyed and nostalgic.

Miranda West came out of the kitchen. Across the living room, standing by the Christmas tree, she saw Lord Treverton, his baritone leading the chorus. Miranda was thinking of the new year, 1920, and of the promise it held. There was only one way to make the earl hers, and that was to give him the one thing he wanted most: a son.

Valentine, by coincidence, was thinking the same thing but on different terms. Holding Rose's hand as they sang "Silent Night," he thought of the failure of Dr. Hare's bromide to solve the problem and of the new tack he intended to take tonight. The powder in Rose's nightly chocolate had only put her to sleep, and he didn't want her that way. He wanted her to respond, to make love to him. It had been living in tents, he concluded, that had spoiled everything. And Rose's sense of delicacy and decency . . . But tonight for the first time he would take her up to their bedroom, where they would begin their proper married life together, beneath the canopy of the Treverton ancestral four-poster bed.

Lucille, standing next to her husband on the terrace and feeling the damp night air close in on her, tried with all her heart to sing the bitterness and anger out of her soul. Lady Donald, ten-year resident of the protectorate, rancher's wife, and devoted mother, harbored a terrible secret: She detested British East Africa and cursed the day she had left England.

"Memsaab!" came an urgent whisper through the hedge. "Memsaab!"

Grace turned around to see Mario, his eyes wide and frightened in the darkness.

"Come quick, memsaab! Something bad has happened!"

"Where? What is it?"

"It is Chief Mathenge. You come now!"

Grace and James exchanged a look. Then James said to Lucille, "You stay here, darling. I'll go with Grace."

They followed Mario down a serpentine path, off the house grounds, around the edge of the woods, and along the river embankment. He was leading them to Birdsong Cottage.

"What is it, Mario?" Grace said as they rounded her house. "Where is Chief Mathenge?"

"He is in back, memsaab."

When Grace and James came around the corner and through the gate of her little vegetable plot, they stopped short. In the dark they could make out a shape sprawled among the maize and bean plants. "Bring me my torch, Mario," Grace said as she ran to Mathenge's side.

The young chief was lying on his back, looking as if he slept, but when Grace felt for a pulse, she found none. And his skin was cold. James, kneeling opposite, looked at Grace. "What is it? What happened to him?"

"I don't know. . . ." Her eyes searched his body. She saw no wounds, no blood. But it was too dark really to see. Black clouds now covered the moon.

When Mario returned with the flashlight, Grace turned it on Mathenge's face. Her hand froze.

"My God," said Sir James.

Mario cried out and jumped back.

Grace stared at the beautiful sleeping face, half hidden by the ether cone. She moved the flashlight along his body and found the empty ether bottle in his right hand.

"My God," murmured James again. "How did this happen? Who did this?"

Grace felt herself go cold and numb as she looked down at Mathenge's eyes, closed in eternal sleep. There were no signs of violence about him; his clothes were unrumpled; his hair, still fixed in the Masai warrior style, lay neatly braided on his forehead. He looked, in fact, as if he had come into the garden to lie down for a peaceful nap.

"I don't think anyone did this to him," Grace said slowly. "He did it himself."

"That's not possible. Kikuyu don't commit suicide."

She regarded James with damp eyes. "He didn't intend it to be a suicide. He hadn't planned on dying. He expected to wake up as Mario had—"

"Good God," James murmured, his look incredulous, "he wanted to know the secret of the white man's power!"

"It's Christmas," she said with a sob, "the birthday of his new god. He *believed*—" She started to cry.

James came around, drew Grace to her feet, and took her into his arms. As she wept on his shoulder, more clouds rolled down from Mount Kenya and began to fill the sky, obliterating the stars, making the night deeper and darker.

"It's my fault! It's all my fault!"

James held her tightly. "It's not your fault, Grace. You're not responsible for Africa's innocence."

She cried awhile longer, then drew back, wiping the tears off her cheeks. At her feet lay the body of the beautiful, once proud chief whose spear the white man had taken away. As she shivered in the shelter of James's arms, Grace stared down at the dark, pathetic shape among the vegetables and realized that something profoundly significant had just taken place. With Mathenge's childlike death went the last of Africa's true warriors. And something else . . .

"Will there be trouble, do you suppose?" she asked as they went back to the house.

James didn't think so. There was no foul play involved, no causes for revenge against another clan. Mathenge would be quietly buried, and a new chief would be appointed in his place.

They arrived to find Hardy Acres, the well-fed banker, dressed as Father Christmas and distributing gifts from a huge sack. Grace skirted the crowd and went to her brother, who sat like a king presiding over the dispersing of his largess. Each gift was wrapped and tagged with a name: perfume or lace handkerchiefs or silver combs for the ladies; hunting knives or silk cravats or crocodileskin billfolds for the gentlemen.

She approached him from behind and whispered in his ear.

"Not now, old girl," he said merrily.

"Valentine, you didn't hear me. I said there's been an accident."

"You're the doctor, you take care of it."

A few comic gifts scattered among the crowd caused occasional eruptions of laughter. Then a rumble, too loud for laughter, brought everyone to fall silent and look up. Thunder crashed overhead.

"I say," began Mr. Acres, "you don't suppose . . ."

"Val," said Grace, taking advantage of the lull, "you have to come with me. It's Chief Mathenge—"

"Where *is* the chap? He was invited to this, you know."

"Good Lord," said Sir James, "did you invite his wife as well?"

Grace looked up, just as everyone else turned toward the front door. A shocked silence filled the room; two hundred pairs of eyes stared in disbelief.

Wachera stood like a statue beneath the crystal chandelier of the entry, looking as if she had materialized on the spot. She gazed at the sea of white faces, an exotic figure against the mahogany hat-rack, the brass umbrella stand. Wachera was dressed for a special occasion.

A leather dress and aprons covered her strong, slender body. Row upon row of beaded necklaces lay across her breast and shoulders, rising up along her neck, appearing to support her head. Great circles of beads stood out from her ears, which were pierced on the tops and sides as well as at the lobes. Her arms up to her elbows and her ankles up to her knees were glorious with beads and copper bangles and leather bands stitched with cowry shells. Strings of beads crisscrossed her forehead; copper headbands encircled her black, shaved skull; a single thong strung with three beads came down between her eyes and rested on the bridge of her nose. Her eyes, wide and slanting above prominent cheekbones, looked upon the stunned crowd with a hooded expression.

Recovering from his shock at seeing her, Valentine rose and said, "What the devil is *she* doing here?"

Wachera took a step forward, and the crowd parted. It was then that Grace saw the little boy David, Mathenge's son, naked except for a necklace, clutching his mother's hand.

Valentine motioned to the servants to remove her, but they did not move. For all their Christian names and fluency in English, for all the white man's gloves they wore, the servants were Kikuyu nonetheless and afraid of a medicine woman.

"What do you want?" Valentine finally demanded.

Wachera walked toward him, and when she was a few feet from Valentine, she stopped and regarded him.

Their eyes locked, and then Lord Valentine slowly sat back down.

Surely, he thought, this was not the same shy and self-effacing girl who had come into the camp in humility, bowing and offering him gifts! Valentine narrowed his eyes and looked around. Where was the grandmother?

And it was not a humble murmur that now filled the room when Wachera spoke, but the voice of a proud and defiant spirit. Wachera spoke in Kikuyu, which few present understood but which Sir James translated.

"You have defiled sacred ground," the medicine woman said. "You have destroyed the home of the ancestors. You have committed uncleanliness against the Lord of Brightness. You will be punished."

Valentine was stupefied. "What the devil is she talking about?"

Wachera continued: "I call down the Spirits of the Wind." She lifted the sacred divination gourd from her belt; it contained magic charms collected by a nameless ancestress centuries ago. When she shook it, the rattling filled the house. "The ancestors place *thahu* upon this sinful place!" She turned and shook the rattle toward each corner, saying, "Evil spirits dwell there. And there. And there." She raised the gourd over her head. "And under your roof. Until this land is returned to the Children of Mumbi, you will know sickness and misery and poverty all the days of your life. Until this land is returned to the Children of Mumbi, the chameleon will visit this unclean house."

"The chameleon!" said Valentine, shifting impatiently in his chair. If the servants wouldn't remove her, then by God *he* was going to.

James said, "The chameleon is a symbol of the worst bad luck to the Kikuyu. By inviting a chameleon into your house, she is wishing you—"

"Until this land is returned to the Children of Mumbi," she said in a deadly tone, "your children will drink of the dew."

"Now what the bloody hell does *that* mean?"

"It's a Kikuyu proverb. To drink of the dew means to vanish."

"All right," said Valentine, standing. "This has gone on long enough. Get out of my house."

"Thahu!" cried Wachera. "A curse upon you and your descendants until this land is returned to the Children of Mumbi!"

"I said get out!" He looked around. "Where the devil is Mathenge? I thought these people kept their women in line! You there!" He pointed to two terrified Africans. "Show this woman the way out." But they were frozen with fear. By tomorrow morning they planned to be far away from this house with *thahu* upon it.

"Very well then!" shouted Valentine. He strode toward Wachera and reached out to seize her arm. At that exact moment a great clap of thunder shook the house. And then came the soft whisper of rain.

"Hey!" cried one of the guests. "It's raining!"

The crowd broke up as everyone ran to the windows and doors. They dashed outside into the downpour, faces and hands lifted to the glorious wet, hugging one another, laughing and delirious with joy.

The rain pounded the roof, drove against the windows, while thunder filled the thirsty valley.

"Well!" said Valentine in a triumphant tone. He faced Wachera squarely, feet apart and hands on his hips. "If this is your idea of a curse, then I welcome it!" He threw back his head and laughed. Then he turned on his heel, took hold of Rose's hand, and led her across the room to join the rain-soaked crowd on the veranda.

Only Sir James and Grace remained behind, and little Mona in her high chair. Wachera paused to give the three a long, considering look, then she turned to walk away, her hand holding fast to David.

"Wait," said Grace. "I have something to tell you. It's about Mathenge."

Wachera stopped and leveled a poisonous gaze upon Grace. "My husband is dead," she said in Kikuyu, and although she did not add, *And you killed him,* it was in her eyes.

THERE WOULD BE no polo match or fox hunting tomorrow; the field where the guest tents stood would be a knee-deep mud morass by morning; travel back to distant homes and farms would be nearly impossible and wretchedly uncomfortable. But no one minded. The long-prayed-for rain had come at last, and it was coming down so torrentially and steadily, with no end to the rolling black clouds, that everyone knew crops and investments were going to be saved.

Grace had returned to Birdsong Cottage to find that wild animals had already dragged Mathenge's body away, and she decided sadly that this was probably how he would have wanted it. Now she was asleep in bed with Sheba, the great, snoring cheetah, pressed against her back. Sir James and Lucille were comfortably situated in one of the guest rooms in the big house, as were the governor, and Lord and Lady Delamere, while the two hundred other guests were inconveniently but happily making do with leaky tents and damp cots. Only one person was not at peace with the outcome of the evening. Lady Rose, as she sat at her vanity table brushing her newly cut hair, was puzzled.

After a decorous frolic in the rain she and Valentine had bidden good night to their guests and retired to the second floor, where hot baths awaited them. She had been pleasantly surprised to see how nicely Valentine had furnished and decorated the upper half of the house: the tubs with hot and cold taps; indoor plumbing with ceramic toilets; Turkey carpets on the cedar floors; paintings and photographs on the walls. There was a homey warmth to it all, especially with the storm raging outside. And yet . . .

Rose felt strangely unsettled. Valentine was in the bath, singing above the steam. He had shown her into this bedroom and told her he would join her soon. Here Rose had found her trunks unpacked, with everything hung up and put away, her toiletries and cosmetics laid out on the vanity. Clearly this was her bedroom. Then which was Valentine's?

He came out of the bathroom in silk monogrammed pajamas and dressing gown, his black hair moist and curling over his forehead. "Merry Christmas, darling," he said as he came to stand behind her. "Did you have a good time?"

She looked at his reflection in the mirror. She felt the warmth of his body through her satin peignoir. How handsome he was, how perfect. *Let him hold me tonight before I go to sleep.* "It was wonderful, Valentine. It was better even than I dreamed. But, oh, this rain will spoil the rest of the fun. I had so looked forward to luncheon on the front lawn tomorrow. Mrs. West was going to serve a proper high tea."

He placed his hands lightly on her shoulders. "The rain is badly needed, darling. Now James's cattle won't die and our coffee won't fail and Mr. Acres won't have to foreclose on just about every mortgage in the protectorate."

Valentine came around and knelt at her side. "I have a present for you," he said.

Her eyes twinkled. The champagne, the altitude . . .

He handed her a small box wrapped in Christmas paper. Rose tore it open and exclaimed at the jade and emerald necklace it contained. "Four continents went into making that," he said. "Do you like it?"

She threw her arms about his neck. "Valentine, dearest! It's exquisite! But I haven't wrapped *your* present yet. I was going to give it to you in the morning."

"It can wait." His arms went about her waist. "Happy?"

She buried her face in his neck. "I've never been happier. The house is perfect, Valentine. Thank you."

He felt like shouting with joy. It was turning out exactly as he had planned. All the months of hard labor, of driving the natives with his whip, of making those wretched long trips down to Nairobi, of aching for his wife, wanting her . . .

His mouth sought hers.

Valentine kissed her gently and chastely while Rose rested content in his arms. But when the kiss grew passionate and his mouth moved on hers, she drew back and laughed. "It's been *such* a day, darling! And I am so very tired."

"Then we shall go to bed."

He drew back the covers on the four-poster, folded the comforter at the foot, and bent to remove Rose's slippers for her. She sat on the edge of the bed and sighed languidly. How was it possible, she wondered, that she had found and married the very man she had dreamed about since girlhood? He was so gallant, such a gentleman, like a knight in armor—

He removed his dressing gown and draped it over a chair. "What are you doing, darling?" she asked.

"I know it's been my habit to sit up late after a long day," he said, coming around the bed and drawing back the covers on the other side, "but tonight I will make an exception."

She was sitting up with the sheets drawn to her chin. Rose had no idea about a habit of sitting up late; she and Valentine had barely seen each other in the evenings of the past ten months. What she had meant was, Why was he getting into her bed?

"I really am tired," she said cautiously. "Wouldn't you prefer to go to your own bedroom?"

He laughed. "Darling, this *is* my bedroom."

She stared at him.

Valentine stood by the bed and looked down at her. "When we were in the tents, it was reasonable to have separate quarters. But we're in our own house now, darling. And we *are* married."

"Oh," she said.

"It'll be all right," he said gently. "You'll see. We just have to get used to one another again. Like we were back at Bella Hill."

Bella Hill! Rose shrank into her pillows. At Bella Hill he had abused and humiliated her, and she had hated him for it. But these ten months in East Africa had made things better. Surely he didn't mean to— Surely Grace had explained to him—

"What's wrong?" he asked. Valentine reached out to touch her, and Rose recoiled. Thunder rolled down from the mountain and exploded overhead.

"I thought you were going to have your own room."

Now he saw the fear on her face, the stiffening of her body. Thunder clapped again and the house shook. *Christ,* thought Valentine, *not again! Not still!*

"Rose, you're going to have to accept the fact that I'm your husband, not a fond cousin or brother. I have a right to sleep with you."

She started to tremble. Her eyes grew big and frightened, like a gazelle's, as if he were about to shoot her. He had seen the look on many a hunting safari; he didn't deserve it in his own bed.

"Damn it, Rose," he said, grabbing her arm.

"No!" she cried.

"Rose, what on earth—"

"No! Please . . ." Tears filled her eyes.

"Oh, for God's sake."

"Leave me alone!"

Lightning flashed and illuminated the room. Rose was ghost-pale; her skin went cold beneath his fingers. Then came the thunder again, closer now. The air was charged; it was electrified, as if the storm had somehow invaded the bedroom. Valentine felt his anger grow, and his passion.

"I will not put up with this any longer!" he shouted. "It's been ten months since the baby was born. There is nothing wrong with you."

She yanked free and tried to run, but Valentine pulled her back onto the bed. With one hand he pinned down her wrists; with the other he tore furiously at her peignoir. The satin came away from her white skin, and she screamed again.

"Go on," he growled. "Let our bloody friends know. Do you think I care?" She struggled beneath him, tried to escape; one hand came free, and she clawed his neck. "I want what's mine," he said. "And if you won't give it to me, I'll take it any way I can."

Lightning tore across the sky around Mount Kenya, casting a brief, harsh light on the craggy summit of Ngai's lofty home. The walls and foundation of Bellatu trembled; the trees in the forest, the tall eucalyptuses of Rose's little glade all were whipped in a frenzy. The storm came down upon the Treverton Estate like a punishment, washing away soil, drowning tender coffee seedlings, driving the new river into a raging flood that broke its dam and swept up over its banks.

Wachera, the Kikuyu medicine woman, sat inside the hut that was going to be her home for the next seven decades and stared up at the windows of the white man's house on the hill. In one of them, on the second floor, the lights winked out.

PART
TWO
1920

13

Well!" said Audrey Fox as she tested the soap in the cooking pot to see if it was cool and dry. "We're legitimate now! Not a protectorate anymore, but a colony! Still, I don't much care for calling it *kee-nia*. That means 'ostrich' in the local tribal language, doesn't it? Wasn't that why they named the mountain *kee-nia*, because it resembles a male ostrich? I rather liked the sound of British East Africa. And besides, it sounded *British*, which is what we are. Kenya is an *African* name."

Mary Jane Simpson, who was holding her wriggly son while Grace examined his ear, echoed her friend's sentiment and then shouted, "Lawrence! I'm telling you for the last time, leave that cat alone!"

They were in Lucille Donald's kitchen at Kilima Simba, five women and a host of noisy children. While Mrs. Fox sat down to roll into balls the soap she had been making all morning from mutton fat and banana-leaf ashes, Cissy Price checked the diapers of the two toddlers in the playpen. Mona was dry, but Gretchen was wet. After clearing a spot on the crowded kitchen table, Cissy laid Gretchen down and proceeded to change her. Despite the cold June day, the kitchen was hot and the faces of the five women glowed.

"This'll do it," Grace said as she dipped some cotton into simsim oil and packed it into the boy's ear. "Mind where he sticks his head from now on, Mary Jane. This country is a menace to ears."

As she reached for the next child, Grace could not help a quick glance out the kitchen window. Sir James had not yet come out of the barn.

This morning he had said he had a surprise for her, something special he wanted to show her, and had asked if she would wait around a bit before running off home. But then a stockman had come to say that a cow was having difficulty calving, and James had dashed off, leaving Grace to wonder, *What sort of surprise?*

"Being a colony will benefit us greatly," said Lucille. She was kneading bread dough and dividing it up into baking tins. This evening, when her guests departed, each would leave with a fresh-baked loaf. She in turn would receive some of Audrey Fox's homemade soap, as would the others, as well as some wool, which Mary Jane Simpson had brought from her sheep farm to exchange for bread and soap and medical services. Grace had come with her doctor's bag.

Next up was little Roland Fox, who had jiggers in his toes.

"Used to be," said Lucille, testing the Dover stove for temperature, "the kitchen boy was the house doctor. We had to rely on him for all our emergencies. He was an expert on digging out jiggers."

"I'd rather die!" declared young Cissy, who had come to the Nanyuki area only the month before and was already wishing she were back in England. Like the two women who had come to the Donald farm with her today, Cissy's husband had been awarded a land grant through the Soldier Settlement Scheme. Led by visions and dreams, he had brought his family out in a covered wagon, and now they scratched a rugged subsistence on their struggling farm. These get-togethers at the house of one of them, typical of Kenya life, were their sole source of entertainment and companionship and an opportunity to trade what produce or goods they had in excess for items badly needed.

Cissy finished changing Gretchen's diaper and returned her to the playpen, where the two little girls, sixteen months and thirteen months old, played quietly. "What do you do if you have a *real* emergency?" asked Cissy.

"You pray," said Lucille, and she slid her bread pans into the oven.

Grace worked on Roland's foot, only barely paying attention to the conversation. The women, it seemed to her, all were talking at once, and a pack of kids yelled and shouted and made gunshot noises all through the house. It was bedlam, and Grace desperately needed to think.

Problems crowded her mind this morning.

This past June week had been full of ceremonies and festivities commemorating Kenya's new status as crown colony. Like royalty, Valentine and Rose had been in Nairobi, presiding over events which had culminated in the unveiling of the bronze statue of King George V, donated to the colony by Valentine. It was a week of races, fox hunts, parties, and speeches.

In Nairobi Valentine and his wife stayed at the Norfolk Hotel, the only place where anyone who was anyone stayed.

But they had separate rooms. They managed to explain it with a lie: that Rose suffered from night asthma attacks and did not wish to disturb her husband's sleep. Everyone accepted the story with a wink and a nod. Bush telegraph made secrets impossible in East Africa. When Rose learned she was pregnant after the gala Christmas party at Bellatu, the news was all the way to Tanganyika within a week. And when she miscarried three months later, that, too, was common knowledge, including the fact that the baby had been a boy. Since then a rumor circulated that the earl and countess slept apart for whispered reasons.

"Tell him, Grace," Rose, while still bedridden from the miscarriage, had said to her. "Tell Valentine he must never touch me again." It was much the same plea Grace had heard from her before, but this time Rose had been surprisingly frank and open about it. "I find the whole obligation revolting. Now I know why they call it the *master* bedroom. Just be thankful you're not married, Grace."

And what could Grace have replied? That her own feelings were exactly the opposite? That she ached for that intimate contact between lovers? That she fantasized about sleeping with Sir James? Rose would never have understood.

As she bandaged Roland's toe, Grace stole another glance out the window.

"How is the clinic doing, Grace?" Audrey Fox asked.

Sending Roland off to play with the others, with an admonishment that he was to wear shoes at all times from now on, Grace set about straightening up her supplies. This visit had not been as demanding as some: just a bottle of aspirin for Cissy's monthly cramps; a quick look at twelve-year-old Henry's throat, which was sore, she determined, not from illness but from too much yelling; a lotion for Lucille's chapped hands; a routine check of Mary Jane's pregnancy; and the few minor complaints of the kids. Now she was finished. She should pack up and go home. But James had asked her to wait. A surprise for her, he had said.

"The clinic is doing fine, thank you," she said as she put her instruments to soak.

Grace sometimes wondered if the other women ever noticed what a private person she was, that she never participated in the usual exchange of feminine intimacies. They sat in the kitchen and talked of menstruation and babies, of bedroom problems and conjugal secrets, of strange dreams lately, of premonitions and intuitions; they shared tea and listened to the weather and compared measles and whooping cough and the relative development of one another's babies. But Grace rarely said anything at such times other than in the capacity of doctor. She never talked of her personal life or feelings. Perhaps they did not expect her to; perhaps they regarded her more as physician and counselor than as a fellow woman. Or maybe it was just as simple as the fact that she had neither husband nor babies.

But I could tell you things, she thought as she dried her instruments and returned them to her bag. *I could tell you about the soldiers on the warship and the confessions they made, the propositions I received, the very correct officers knocking on my cabin door late at night. I could tell you of my dreams and needs and loneliness. And of this love growing within me like an unwanted child—love for a man I can never have.*

But *was* it love she felt for James Donald? It was a riddle Grace tried to unravel morning and night. This longing for his touch, the continual thinking of him no matter what she was doing, the way her heart jumped whenever he appeared unexpectedly—was it love? Or was it merely a product of her loneliness, of her natural urges which remained unsatisfied? But if that were the case, if she were merely another frustrated spinster, then surely she would welcome the attentions of the men who demonstrated an interest in her. Some were charmers; some she might even fall in love with. And yet all she could think of was James.

She considered the ring on her left hand. The women all had noticed it, but Grace had never felt compelled to explain it. *Let them wonder,* she thought. *At least this ring is proof that at one time I was wanted by a man.*

Grace stared at her hand. She was stunned. Where had *that* notion come from, that she wore the ring as a flag, as something to flaunt before people who pitied her? *Is that why I still wear it?*

"How is the earl's plantation doing, Grace?" asked Mary Jane Simpson, whose husband owned a bacon factory.

Or do I wear this ring—Grace covered her left hand with her right and closed her eyes. She was coming close to being afraid of her own thoughts. *Do I wear this ring as armor, as protection against the fact that James will never look upon me as anything but a friend?*

"Grace?"

She looked up. Mary Jane's face was puffy from pregnancy, her maternity smock faded from having been worn for six previous babies. And for an instant, inexplicably, Grace did not like her.

"The plantation is doing fine," she said.

"The Christmas rain destroyed most of his crop, I heard."

"Yes, but Valentine purchased a new lot of seedlings and planted at once. The estate is doing better than expected, in fact."

"I'm surprised at that," said Lucille as she fed wood into her stove, "considering the curse that medicine woman put on Bellatu."

"Oh, Lucille!" said Cissy. "You don't believe in that, do you?"

But Lucille's mouth was set as she said, "That woman is an agent of Satan. You mark my words."

Grace pictured the round mud hut that stood just at the southern end of the polo field. In the nine months since Valentine had first ordered the huts torn down and Mathenge's family moved across the river, the young medicine woman had put up an astonishing fight. When she had rebuilt her hut yet again, after the Christmas opening of Bellatu, Valentine had asked the authorities to do something about her. Officer Briggs and two askaris had escorted Wachera across the river and had burned down her hut. The next morning she was back, rebuilding it. Exasperated, Valentine had then installed a tall chain link fence around the entire polo field, so that Mathenge's widow was cut off. He ultimately chose to ignore her, deciding that it was beneath him to engage in games playing with an African medicine woman.

Grace, on the other hand, could not ignore Wachera Mathenge. Despite the growing popularity of Grace's little clinic, Wachera continued to ply a healthy business in magic and, to Grace's thinking,

witchcraft. Although, because of Chief Mathenge's acceptance of the
white doctor, some of the people came to Grace with their ailments,
the majority stubbornly sought out the medicine woman. Grace feared
that as long as Wachera was allowed to practice what Grace regarded
as mumbo jumbo, the Africans would remain in ignorance and darkness. She had begun talking with the authorities about getting tribal
medicine officially outlawed.

The back door crashed open, depositing two wild-haired boys into
the kitchen. "It's a new heifer, Ma!" they shouted, dirty hands seizing
jam tarts off a cooling tray.

"Mind your manners," said Lucille. "Look who's here."

"Hullo, Auntie Grace," said eight-year-old Geoffrey and five-year-old
Ralph as they crammed tarts into their mouths. They shuffled self-
consciously among the women and diapers, then let out whoops and
tore off through the house.

"Those boys are wild," Lucille said. "I'll be glad when we can send
them to the European school in Nairobi. They worry me sometimes.
I can't see to them properly. I can't be doing all things at once."

"They're just boys," Cissy said.

Lucille sank into a chair and brushed hair from her face with a hand
covered with flour. "James is gone before sunup and gets in when the
boys are asleep. I've got Gretchen and nappies all day and all the
household chores as well. I can't grow vegetables here, the well has too
much soda in it, and the groundwater is good only for cattle, not crops.
So I have to take the wagon to the nearest native market, where they
cheat me blind."

They all sat in silence, the other three farm wives hearing their own
stories in her words. Then Lucille said quietly, "Do you know what I
did back in England?"

They leaned forward. People rarely spoke of their past lives, of what
they had done before coming to East Africa, as if life had not existed
before Kenya. "I owned a little shop in Warrington." Her voice grew
soft, her expression wistful. "I sold ribbons and thread. It made me no
great fortune, but it was a comfortable and respectable living. I had a
place upstairs, where I lived with my mother. And I was walking out
with a boy who was a clerk at the ironworks. We had a secure and
reliable life, with church every Sunday and the vicar to tea and Tom
placing the odd guinea on the pools."

Grace had heard it before, how Lucille's life had changed when James Donald had walked into her shop. She had fallen head over heels for him and had packed it all in to come to Africa with him. Whenever Lucille spoke of it, Grace always heard an element of regret in her voice.

Grace wondered if James was aware of it. She also wondered now, as she studied Lucille's sagging shoulders and limp wrists, if he was aware of how tired his wife was looking lately.

"Still," said Lucille, pushing herself up from the chair and returning to the hot stove, "farming life is an honest and Christian life. And the good Lord has blessed us."

These last words reminded Grace of another of her latest worries: the letter in her pocket.

It had come last week. A notice from the Mission Society back in Suffolk informing her that until a proper inspection could be made of her mission, all monetary support to her clinic would be suspended.

The back door opened again, and this time Sir James entered. He removed his broad-brimmed bushwhacker's hat, stamped mud off his boots, and said, "Hello, ladies." When his eye caught Grace, his smile broadened. "You're still here. I was hoping you hadn't left yet. There's something I want to show you."

The cold wind was refreshing as she stepped outside and took a deep breath. Beyond the few trees protecting the homestead, a vast savanna, green now after the long rains, stretched to the distant blue mountains. Cattle grazed on enormous tracts of new grass; farmhands worked among fodder crops, singing as they went. The sky was a stunning blue with shreds of white clouds about Mount Kenya's craggy summit. Grace felt her spirit soar up to the pale sun.

As she walked at James's side, wishing she could do this every day of her life, Grace said, "The boys announced the birth of a new calf."

"One of our dairy cows. They usually require close management during calving. This was a case of hind legs first; but I got it turned around, and we delivered successfully. Thank God I've got the best stockman in the protectorate."

"Haven't you heard? We're a colony now."

He laughed. "Yes, I forgot. It will take me forever to catch up. I still think Edward is king!"

As they crossed the busy compound from the house to the dairy, stock boys and cattle boys called out greetings to Grace. They all knew her; she was a familiar face around Kilima Simba. She had treated the injuries of some of these men when she came to visit Lucille or when she brought the microscope for James to borrow. The Donald farm was noisy and busy: to her left, beef cattle were being prodded through a footbath; to her right, cows were lining up to enter the milking bails. Calves romped in small paddocks; hay was being laid out in a feeding field; a skittish Guernsey bull was being handled by three Africans. Kilima Simba was one of the biggest cattle ranches in Kenya; it supplied much of the beef and dairy products of East Africa. And yet, like so many other farmers, James Donald continued to operate on a bank overdraft.

"Mind where you step," he said, taking her elbow.

"What is it you want to show me?"

"You'll see!"

"You're being very mysterious."

"It's a surprise. Something I've been working on for quite a time. Didn't want to tell you about it until it was all done. I think you'll be pleased."

They came around the corner of the dairy where James's Chevrolet truck was being loaded with milk cans destined for the Nyeri and Karatina markets. "It's in here," he said, opening a door into the dairy. "Slippery. Be careful."

It was cool inside the small stone building, and dark. James led her across to the other side to another door.

This one opened onto a shed that had been built onto the dairy; it was made of log walls and corrugated tin roof. Two windows admitted sunlight and fresh air; an old carpet covered the dirt floor. Grace stood in the middle of the six-foot by six-foot space, speechless.

"Have I surprised you?" asked James.

"Yes . . ."

Shelves from floor to ceiling covered two walls; a workbench took up the third. Every bit of surface was littered with tins and boxes and bottles and books. The bench looked like a chemist's, with racks of test tubes, culture dishes, jars of chemicals, and, in the center, a shiny new microscope.

"What do you think?" said James. The room was so small, not much bigger than a closet, that he stood almost touching her.

Grace looked away. "How nice for you."

"It took me awhile," he said as he ran his hand along the smooth surface of the workbench, touching the few pieces of laboratory equipment as if they were holy relics. "I had the devil of a time getting all these shipped. Believe it or not, a good deal of it came from Uganda. They're quite advanced there in scientific research."

"It's marvelous," she said quietly, thinking about all those occasions in the past fourteen months when the message would arrive from James asking to borrow the microscope, and Grace would drop everything and get on her horse and ride out to Kilima Simba, where he would be waiting with a big smile and effusive thanks. They would spend an hour together bent over some slides; then they would diagnose the latest scourge infesting his cattle; and finally another hour, the best hour, with brandy in front of a roaring fire. Grace lived for those visits.

"The world is becoming modern, Grace," he went on. "The days of old-fashioned cattle ranching are over. Today's herds have to be managed with microscope and hypodermic syringe. And I couldn't just go on borrowing yours."

"I haven't minded."

"I know. You've been wonderful about it. But now that I have my own laboratory I shan't be bothering you again."

Grace was silent. She stood with her back to him, watching through the window some cattle boys notching the ears of newly inoculated cows. James was so close to her that she could feel the warmth of his body.

"Grace," came his quiet voice, "is there something wrong?"

"No," she said too quickly. Then: "Well, yes."

"What is it?"

"It's nothing I can't work out."

He put his hands on her shoulders and turned her to face him. Except for the brief moment when she had cried in his arms, with poor Mathenge's body at her feet, and in Gachiku's birthing hut after the Caesarean section, Grace had never been this close to James. "You're a very private person, aren't you?" he said with a gentle smile. "You never tell your troubles to anyone. Do you think that's good for you?"

"I tell it all to my journal. Someday, after I'm gone, a stranger is going to read it and be quite puzzled."

"Tell me what's bothering you, Grace."

"You have enough worries."

"So you don't need friends then?"

His hands were still on her shoulders; she wanted to keep them there forever. "Very well," she said, reaching into her skirt pocket. "You know that I've been writing to the Society back home to send trained medical help. This is the organization that sends me a small check every month, made up of contributions from various parishes around Bella Hill. That, plus the three hundred pounds I receive yearly from the government and my own income from my inheritance, is what has been keeping my clinic going. However, because of rather involved economics and some bad investments on my father's part, my income from his estate has been cut. I was just worrying about how to make it up when this letter came."

James read it with a frown. "They won't send you any more money until they've come out and made an inspection of your clinic? What the devil for? Do they think you're cheating them?"

Grace turned away, pulled a stool out from under the workbench, and sat on it. "There are certain missionaries in this district who have been complaining that I'm not running my place properly. I don't have a minister, and I don't hold services. I'm not converting the natives. I think one of them has written a letter to the Society about it, and now a team is coming out to see if I deserve its charity. James, if the Society cuts off its support, then the government here will take it to mean that I am not running a legitimate mission and will withhold the three hundred, and I shall lose everything!"

"It won't happen."

"How do you know? Oh, the arguments I've had with those sanctimonious prigs! They count their success in how many souls they've saved! They tell me it's not enough that I heal the Africans or teach them hygiene and health, I must preach the Gospel at the same time! They were positively stupefied when I told them I refused to denounce the Kikuyu god and that I thought Ngai was merely another spelling for God Almighty!"

James gazed down at her. Grace's eyes were bright; her cheeks, crimson. Her light brown hair, lately cut and crimped in the new "bob," stood out under her pith helmet. He had to smile. "Did you really stupefy them, Grace?"

She looked up into his smile and shook her head. "Yes, damn it," she said with a laugh she couldn't help. "And I enjoyed it!"

Then they laughed together, and Grace marveled at how much better she suddenly felt. "I'm glad you've got your own laboratory, James," she said at last, meaning it. "You'll work wonders in here. You'll probably get a new bacterium named for you."

"I'd rather not!" He held out his hand, and she took it. "Besides," he added more quietly, "I'm expecting you to come and show me how to use all this."

"If I'm still around."

As they left the shed and entered the cool darkness of the dairy, James said, "You'll still be here, Grace. And you'll do all right. You have many friends in Kenya."

"I hate to go begging."

"Can you ask Val for help?"

"Never. He's the last person in the world I would admit helplessness to. I would never hear the end of it."

"You're very independent, aren't you, Grace? You prefer to do everything on your own. And you don't need anybody. At least that's what you want people to think. Watch it here, there's water—"

Grace's foot suddenly slid on the wet concrete, and she lost her balance. James caught her. They held each other for an instant; his arm was tight about her. Then he released her, and they laughed again.

But later, when Lucille's friends were loading their wagons with barter and kids, James stood for a long time at the end of the drive and watched Grace ride away on her horse, down the lonely dirt track toward Nyeri, her medical bag tied to her saddle, her pith helmet reflecting the westering sun.

He thought about the other thing he had planned to show her and was glad now he had changed his mind. It was from an old issue of the *Times.* Old by date, but new here in Kenya, where overseas newspapers were seldom seen and then came weeks late. This paper had already passed through many homesick hands and would go from Kilima Simba to other ranches in the Nanyuki area and eventually over the Aberdares to settlers in the Rift. James took out of his back pocket the one page he had kept for himself. It was sacrilege to clip the paper, to disfigure it in any way; an unspoken rule kept the *Times* intact until it disintegrated with the last reading. But this page, a listing of personal advertisements, James had felt duty and honor bound to hide from other eyes.

It was because of one small item in the middle of the last column. A tiny box with a message that said:

> *Jeremy Manning,*
> *You can find me in the Nyeri*
> *District of Kenya, East Africa.*
> Grace Treverton

James stood at the gate still watching until long after Grace had vanished and the sky was growing dark.

14

V alentine laughed and flung down his cards. Then he gathered up the winnings, strode to the steps of the hotel veranda, and threw the money to the ricksha boys lined up on the street. Going back into the bar of the Norfolk Hotel, where he was clapped on the back and congratulated, Treverton ordered drinks for everyone, including champagne for the guests in the dining room. It was his last night in Nairobi after a week of celebrating the new colony; tomorrow he and Rose would make the silent journey back to Bellatu.

She was asleep now, in her own hotel room. "Her Ladyship's asthma" was the excuse. The broad smile on Valentine's face buried the pain that none of his friends could see—the pain of being despised by the wife he loved, a hurt which no amount of alcohol could numb.

But he tried. The gins kept coming, and the tab ran up. Lord Treverton's credit was good all over East Africa. There was no end to his wealth. Besides, spending made him feel good. Giving money to others made him feel less impotent.

Valentine carried liquor well. He never staggered or fell down, never got sick or out of control. He merely got merrier with each glass, and more generous. That was why, as he was walking down the street half an hour later, in the direction of Miranda West's establishment, Valentine greeted everyone he passed, handed rupees to black children, and tried to think of something nice he could do for Miranda.

She had been a true friend these past months. Miranda was the first one he had told about Rose's miscarriage. She always listened to him, never making judgments or giving advice or saying anything much at all. The only person, he was certain, in all of East Africa with that blessed gift! There were other things about Miranda that he liked. For one thing, she never asked him for anything, the way everyone else seemed to. He offered her money to get new lobby furniture, and she said she didn't need it; he said he would put in a word at the Land Office in her favor for the purchase of a certain plot abutting her hotel land, and she had said no, thank you. She was a woman who could stand on her own two feet and didn't go running to others for help. Miranda was a lot like Grace in that respect. Another thing he liked about her was that she didn't flirt with him, or act coy, or play any of the usual female games. Miranda was honest and forthright and had no time for the light sexual fencing Valentine seemed to encounter at every gathering. She wasn't interested in getting into his bed, he knew that; she never expected a compliment or any of the attentions women usually wanted from him. Miranda West was a comfortable woman to be with, plain and simple, and he wanted to express his thanks tonight before he left Nairobi.

The lobby was barely lit and deserted; the dining room, closed and dark. He found an African sweeping the stairs who said, "I fetch the memsaab for you, bwana."

"No, don't bother. I'll surprise her."

Miranda wasn't in the least surprised. She had been watching him from the window of her private apartment. Only an eye like her own, familiar with the earl, could see the slight variation in his gait that meant liquor. So . . . Valentine was coming to her drunk.

"Lord Treverton!" she said when she opened the door. "What a pleasant surprise!"

"I trust I am not disturbing you."

"Not at all. Do come in. Can I offer you a drink?"

"It's been such a week, Miranda!" he said, sinking familiarly into an easy chair even though he rarely visited her in her private rooms. He took the whiskey and downed it in one gulp, saying, "Wish the railway went all the way to Nyeri. I detest the long trip home." Because it would take eight days, with a camp every night to outspan the oxen and Rose's accusing silence to drive him mad.

"It will one day, Lord Treverton," she said, refilling his glass.

Valentine propped his feet up on a stool, long legs stretched before him, and stared into his glass. He was having the devil of a time pushing that rail line through. The economy of the colony was picking up now, prosperity was peeking around the corner, but despite his influence with the Legislative Council and his communications with the Secretary of State for the Colonies, the railhead remained stubbornly at Thika. And Valentine *needed* that train to come to his property!

In the short interval between the two rains, back in January, Valentine had had the drowned seedlings pulled up and replaced with new ones, at great cost. Then the March rains had come, and within fifteen days the plants had sprouted blooms, beautiful white flowers with a scent very much like orange blossom. It wouldn't be another three or four years before the coffee harvest was in, but it could take that long to build the railway. That train would guarantee the best prices and distribution for his beans; without it Valentine would have to rely on wagons and thus be the last to the Nairobi market when all the competitive buying was done.

"I was hoping you would come by tonight," Miranda said, walking to a mahogany sideboard littered with doilies, bric-a-brac, and pictures of the royal family. "I set this aside special." She came back with a fancy round cake tin. "Rum gingerbread for Lady Treverton."

Valentine looked at the fake Wedgwood tin, thinking of all the care that had gone into the cake inside, wondering how on earth Miranda managed to find the time for such offerings in her demanding schedule, and was suddenly overcome with sentiment. The widow West was a good woman. Her husband had to be dead; no man would purposely stay away from her.

She sat in the chair opposite and folded her hands in her lap.

"You've done your hair different," he said.

"Three months ago! It's the new look."

His face darkened. All the women in Kenya were chopping their hair off now because Rose had done it. Dresses were straightening out natural curves, and hemlines were rising. White women had the vote in the colony finally, and more and more were taking up cigarette smoking. The "new woman"! Was that what the war with Germany had been fought for?

Valentine felt his spirits start to slide. As a man who rarely let his natural optimism flag, who never allowed himself the indulgence of self-pity, and who had really only once in all his time in East Africa felt true despair—on the night of his unforgivable attack on Rose—the earl of Treverton now let melancholy engulf him. Swallowing his whiskey, he said, "What's the world coming to, Miranda?"

She formed a sympathetic smile. Miranda heard familiar signals in his tone, saw a look creep into his eyes that she had seen in the faces of many lonely men. She refilled his glass.

"What do women want, Miranda? Can you tell me that?"

"I only know what I want, Lord Treverton. Not all women want the same thing."

"I want a son," he said quietly. "It's all I've ever really wanted. I've got that great monster of a house and five thousand acres and no one to pass it on to. I need an heir. But my wife . . . the doctors have said she can't have any more children. . . ."

Miranda knew that was a lie. According to the bush telegraph, it wasn't that Lady Rose *couldn't* but rather that she *wouldn't* have children.

Suddenly Valentine looked at her and said, "You need a man, Miranda. You shouldn't be alone."

"I've the hotel to keep me busy. There's the staff and guests. I'm never alone."

"I mean at night, Miranda. After the hotel duties are done and your guests are all tucked in their beds. Don't you miss a man then?"

She looked down at her hands. "Sometimes."

"You're the subject of much speculation, Miranda."

"Am I?"

"There isn't a man in East Africa who can claim to have known you intimately."

"And I aim to keep it that way."

"Why? Because you're married?"

"Oh, no, Jack's dead. I'm certain of that."

"Why then? God knows you can have your pick of men."

"I've got my reputation to protect. You know that a woman on her own can't afford to sleep around."

"I didn't mean to sleep *around*," he said quietly. "I meant . . . just one man."

"Who would I choose? I own this hotel, and it earns a nice income. How would I find a man who isn't after my money?"

"There are men in Kenya who don't need your money."

"True. But I have no affection for any of them. Before I give myself to a man, I should have to have some fondness for him."

His black eyes contemplated her. She was just like Rose, he thought. Not in looks or in any tangible way, but she guarded her virtue in the same way Rose did.

This realization suddenly made Valentine feel lusty. And the whiskey was finally getting to him. Thoughts began to run together; the room grew hot. And the pain he had been carrying around for six months was beginning to dissolve.

"There *is* someone who interests you, isn't there?" he asked softly.

She hesitated.

"Who is it?"

Miranda returned his gaze with equal intensity. She was so close now, so close. . . .

"*Is* there someone, Miranda?"

She nodded.

"Who?"

"I'm sure you already know," she whispered.

He rose and swayed over her. "I want to hear it, Miranda. I want you to say the name of the one man you would go to bed with."

She felt dizzy. Her face burned. She whispered, "You know very well who it is. It's yourself—"

Valentine reached down, pulled her to her feet, and covered her mouth with his. "Don't say no to me, Miranda," he said in a tight voice. He kissed her lips, her neck. He unbuttoned her blouse and kissed her throat. When his hand slipped down to her breast, he whispered, "Don't refuse me, Miranda!"

And Miranda, surrendering in his embrace, murmured, "I shan't, Valentine. I shan't."

15

I feel like a squirrel in a wheel [Grace wrote in her journal]. I keep treating the same ailments over and over, often with the same people. They come to me with fevers and colds and flu, with intestinal parasites, with tetanus, with malaria, ringworm, and sores that never heal. They consider my simple remedies with Epsom salts and quinine miracles, but I am not happy with this. What I must do is teach them to change their ways of living. Those terrible huts with no ventilation, sleeping with goats, drinking the water that they also wash in and wade their animals through! And the poor little children who are burned by the unguarded cook fires! They come to me and I give them medicine and they return to their filthy homes and continue their unhygienic practices so that I see them again next week, the same people with the same ailments. Or perhaps a few of them have died at last from their unabated afflictions. And I cannot seem to make them understand that it is not enough to come for treatment when the ailment arises, but that they must do something about their living conditions and eradicate the causes of their sickness in the first place!

Grace put down her pen and massaged the back of her neck. She sat at her dining table writing by the light of a hissing petrol lamp. Outside a tender African night hugged the river. The smell of wild jasmine filled the air; a solitary owl hooted mournfully.

She was alone in her cottage. Mario was in the village attending a ceremonial dance, and Sheba was out for a nocturnal prowl. As Grace gazed into the shadows that inhabited every corner, she thought of the pile of mending that must be done, of the bandages that needed to be rolled, the letters to be written to friends in England, long overdue. But it was ten o'clock. She had been up since dawn and would be getting up again in a few hours to begin another long day.

She picked up her pen and wrote:

I desperately need help. I need teachers. I cannot cure the Africans' malnutrition or parasitic diseases if they do not change their lives. By myself I am almost helpless; it is impossible for me to reach all of them. I must stay here and see to the people who come to the clinic.

If only the medicine woman weren't nearby! Wachera is my bane. She is the major obstacle in my progress. Wachera advocates maintaining the old customs and ways. The people fear and respect her; they do whatever she says. When Wachera's medicine fails to help them, then they come to me. But it is always she they go to first. A path is beaten to her hut. They go to her for love potions, for charms against sickness. She conducts the old religious rites among the Kikuyu. They believe she is their direct link to God and the ancestors. As long as Wachera is allowed to practice her superstitious nonsense, I shall make little headway among the local people.

How I wish Valentine had been successful in moving her back across the river. And how I wish he had persisted! But she continually returns to that place by the river, and Val has given up, not considering it worth his bother. He has become quite used to the sight of that hut near the southern goalposts of the polo field, but for me that hut is a mockery and a constant reminder of my helplessness!

I have asked Lucille Donald to come back. She stopped the Bible teaching in January because, she said, the rains had ruined the track and travel to and from Kilima Simba was daunting. But when the road dried, she still didn't return. She declares that she has too much to do on her own farm to make the long ride down here and try to teach the Bible to the few children who bother to attend. Besides, the Bible is not what they need. I told Lucille that—that the children needed to learn something more useful, such as reading and writing, health and safety—and we had that argument back in April. Lucille has not come back since, and so now I see that she must have been more deeply chagrined than I had thought at the time, when I had told her that Christianity was going to come second at my mission!

But perhaps that will have to change. The Society delegation arrives next week from England, and I must be prepared for them. I will not lose everything I have worked for. I cannot let them force me to give up my dream. But I have come up with a plan that I believe will work. However, it calls for Lucille's cooperation. . . .

Grace closed her journal, returned it to the drawer she kept it in, and went to the front door. Before opening it, she wrapped a shawl around her shoulders. Cold darkness stood a few feet beyond her veranda. Hawk moths and emperor butterflies flitted around the single paraffin lantern that hung from a beam. To her right the forest delivered up the rhythms of African drums; on her left, high above her, piano chords drifted out of Bellatu—Rose playing again, trying to fill the silence within those walls.

Grace started.

Something was moving along the path toward her house.

Reaching out for the rifle that hung in readiness on the porch, Grace tried to delve into the darkness to see what it was.

Presently a human figure came into view. A man who limped. James!

"Hello," he called. "I see you're still up."

Grace clutched the shawl over her breast. He had never visited her at night before.

"I won't keep you," he said as he climbed the steps. "I know it's late, but I'm on my way home from a visit with the DO in Nyeri and thought I'd drop in at the house and have a talk with Valentine. But he's on safari again, so I looked over the ridge on the chance you might still be up, and I saw your light on. Here," He held out a brace of partridge. "These are for you."

"Thank you! Do come in."

When James, so tall and travel-dusty, filled her tiny living room, Grace was suddenly struck by how small and feminine her cottage seemed.

"Would you like a cup of tea?" she asked.

He hesitated, and when Grace lit more lamps, she saw that his manner was rather awkward. She put the kettle on to boil and measured three teaspoons into her china pot. "It's Brooke Bond's new Countess Treverton blend. Very expensive, but Rose gives me packets of it. Please sit down."

"Are you sure I'm not keeping you up?"

She sat in the second chair and folded her arms and saw that not only did James seem uncomfortable, but it appeared that something was troubling him.

"I wasn't ready for bed yet," she said. "I still have a million things to do. Was your visit with the DO an official one?"

"Yes. I got wind that some chaps from the Northern Frontier were sneaking cattle down this way from a quarantined area. They'll spread rinderpest like wildfire if they aren't caught. And there will go my entire herd! Anyway, patrols are out. I imagine they'll be caught. Oh, before I forget." He held out a leather saddlebag. "From the DO's wife. In appreciation for the tooth extraction, she said."

Grace went through the bag like a child at Christmas. "Bless her!" she cried as she brought out a tin of mixed biscuits, a plum pudding, and jars of preserved ginger, jam, and honey.

When she set the things aside and handed the bag back to him, Grace saw disturbed lines etched in his face. "James, is there something wrong?"

He looked into the cold, dark fireplace and thought for a moment. Then he said, "Some of my chaps have come down with dysentery, and I'm all out of cod-liver oil. I was wondering . . ."

She rose and went to her medical cupboard. She came back with a bottle and placed it on the table between the two Morris chairs. "You're welcome to anything I have, James."

"Thank you," he said, and then fell silent.

They listened to the night for a few minutes, Grace wondering about the real reason for his visit. Then James finally said, "How is the clinic going?"

"We're managing. But it's the *teaching* that's a problem. I've written so many letters requesting nurses and teachers to come and work in the villages. Instead, I'm getting an inspection team. But you know, James," she said, leaning toward him, "I've come up with a plan. I was wondering if Lucille would help me out while the Society members are here. Perhaps be teaching a class when they come through. Bible stories, that sort of thing. It would certainly help. What do you think? Shall I ask her?"

He looked at her squarely, and Grace knew the answer before he said, "Lucille won't help you."

"Why not?"

"Because she was the one who sent the letter of complaint to the Mission Society."

Grace stared at him.

James looked away. "I found out this morning. She told me."

The night seemed to creep in closer, as if trying to peer through the windows of the cottage. The oleander bushes near the veranda rustled; then came the nervous twitter of hyenas on the scavenge. Finally the kettle whistled, and Grace went to it. She poured half the hot water into the teapot, then stopped, put the kettle down, and came back into the living room.

"Why, James?" she whispered. "Why did she do it?"

"I'm afraid I really don't know. I was as shocked as you are. I can't really explain what's happened to Lucille." He regarded Grace with an unhappy expression. "When we were first married and I brought her to East Africa ten years ago, she seemed so enthusiastic about living here. But you see, she and her mother had been very close. Lucille's father died when she was a child, and she has no brothers and sisters. When I met her, she and her mother were living above a small shop, quite devoted to one another. There was bad feeling when we left. Lucille and her mother parted badly. Mrs. Rogers didn't want her daughter to be a settler's wife."

James reached into his shirt pocket for a pipe. He made a ritual of filling and lighting it, then continued. "So we decided the best thing would be to bring Lucille's mother out here when we were settled. East Africa is a good place to spend one's retirement, provided one has a proper house and comfortable living. We started saving and planning. Mrs. Rogers was going to live with us at Kilima Simba. I believe that dream was what made the shock of her new life bearable to Lucille. And it *was* a shock at first. She cried for days when she saw the ranch. But then she began exchanging letters with her mother and sending brochures about the protectorate, and her mother warmed to the idea. It was to be this year that she was going to join us."

"What happened?"

"She died, quite suddenly and unexpectedly. She was only fifty years old. Lucille was beside herself. It was just two years ago now, and as the war was still on, there was no way Lucille could go back home for the funeral. I believe that was when she began to change."

"Change? How?"

"In small ways, so small that I only see them now in retrospect. She brought out the old family Bible and began reading it in the evenings. Then she got involved with the Methodists down in Karatina. When she heard that Valentine's sister was coming here to set up a mission, she was ecstatic."

"I see," said Grace as she got up and went back to the kitchen. After pouring the tea and handing him a cup, she said quietly, "Did she tell you what she wrote in her letter to the Society?"

"No." James stirred his tea thoughtfully, watching the spoon go 'round and 'round. "I think now I made a mistake bringing Lucille to East Africa. She was only nineteen, and I was twenty-two. And Lucille had rather a romantic streak in her. When we finally arrived at Kilima Simba, she was speechless with disappointment."

"A lot of wives, and husbands, too, are shocked when they see their new land for the first time."

"I should have known better. I was born here, grew up here. I should have seen how different this life was from the one she'd been brought up in." James set aside his cup and went to stand by the fireplace. His normally calm demeanor was marred by abrupt gestures and a barely constrained tension in his body. "Grace, if you only knew how terrible I feel about all this."

"And I thought Lucille liked me," she said softly.

"But she does like you." Then he added more quietly, "We both do."

Grace could not bring herself to look at him, would not allow herself to succumb to his tone, to his masculine presence filling her house. She was suddenly angry and sad at the same time and confused by the betrayal of a friend. "Whatever shall I do when the delegation comes?"

"I would like to help."

She shook her head. "I'm afraid there's nothing you can do. I was wrong to think of deceiving them. The people in Suffolk are contributing to what they think is a Christian ministry. They have a right to know where their money is going." She stood and squared her shoulders. "I shall simply have to think of a way to appease them, or convince them of the value of what I'm trying to do here, or maybe even come up with a way to do without them. I don't know."

James stepped close to her; his eyes caught hers and held them. "Grace, tell me this won't hurt our friendship."

Her throat tightened. "Nothing in the world could do that, James."

"You will still visit us at the ranch, won't you?"

But she hesitated.

He spun around and drove a fist into his palm. "How did things get so mucked up? I thought she was happy. She *seemed* happy." His body taut, he paced as far as the tiny room would allow. "She's been so good with the farm and with the children. In ten years she's never complained." He stopped suddenly and faced Grace with a pained expression. "Lucille's a good woman, and I don't know what I'd do without her. But . . . I was beside myself this morning, when she told me about the letter. I shouted. I said some unkind things. I didn't mean them, but all I could think of was—" He lowered his voice. "Grace, you're one of the best things to happen to this country and to me. I could only think that if Lucille had somehow ruined our friendship. . . ."

White ants rustled in the thatch overhead; lizards scuttled along walls and timbers. The house was alive, as were the garden and forest beyond. The two in the cottage listened to the chorus of life all around them, lost for a moment in each other's eyes, caught in the nearness of their bodies and the intimacy of the moment. Then James said, "The hour's late. You should go to bed, Grace."

"Surely you're not going home now! It's not safe."

"Rose has offered me a shakedown up at the house."

Grace wanted to say, *Stay here with me,* but instead, she took a lantern from a hook and handed it to him, saying softly, "The path from here up to the house is dangerous at night, James. Please take care."

She opened the door, and he walked onto the veranda. Replacing his wide-brimmed hat on his head, James turned and looked down at her with eyes cast in shadow. "I promise you one thing, Grace. I will do everything in my power to help you."

16

Peony sat with her face buried in her hands, her thin shoulders hunched over, shaking with sobs. "I don't know what I'm gonna do!" she wailed. "I shall kill myself!"

"Oh, hush," said Miranda as she held a glass of brandy to the girl. "Here. Drink this and stop crying. You won't solve anything that way."

The maid lifted her swollen face. "Solved! How can this be *solved?*"

"There's ways."

Her eyes widened. "Oh, no, mum," she breathed. "I could never do *that.*"

Miranda sat at her desk and drummed a fingertip on the green blotter. What a day it had been! First there was the stealing discovered in the kitchen and the mess of having to find out which of the boys was doing it. Then one of the guests had come down with fever and panicked all the others. Now *this.*

Peony, Miranda's English maid, was a pale young girl who had come out on the last boat with her fiancé, who had died of blackwater in Mombasa. Miranda had hired her and put her to work. Peony had performed cheerfully and diligently these past eight months and was saving her money to go back to England.

"How far along are you?" Miranda asked.

"'Bout two months."

"And the father? Does he know about it?"

Peony looked miserable. "He don't know, mum. He's long gone from here. I—I don't even know his name."

Miranda shook her head in disgust. These girls! Like rabbits, some of them, coming to Kenya, showing no discretion, going mad at the

sight of so many men. One settler wife in the Limuru district made a lucrative business in performing abortions.

Miranda stood up and went to the window. It seemed to her that each time she looked out Nairobi got busier. Was it her imagination, or did five new motorcars appear each time her back was turned, a hundred new men looking for adventure, twenty new women looking for rich husbands? She was beginning to hate Kenya.

Valentine had not come by to see her since their one night together.

Across the way a wagonful of Dutch farmers pulled up. They would spend the day buying, trading, collecting mail, and then return to their hardscrabble acres at the back of beyond. Good God, thought Miranda. Why did they look so proud? What was so honorable about plowing dirt where nothing grew except malaria and sleeping sickness?

She hadn't gotten even so much as a note from Valentine. Early that next morning he had crept from her bed and returned with his wife to his plantation in the north. In all the time since he hadn't stopped by. And he'd been in Nairobi. Miranda had seen him.

When Peony started to cry again, Miranda's bitterness grew. The perverse way life sometimes worked! There was that girl, hysterical because she was pregnant after a one-night fling with a nameless boy, and here was Miranda, desperate to get pregnant but unable to.

She stared down at the street. One of the Boer wives was pregnant and flaunting it in public. Times were changing. Confinement and hiding pregnancy were a thing of the past. The war had done away with the old conventions and clothing fashion. There were maternity frocks now, and women paraded their bellies with pride.

Except for me, Miranda thought, resenting the young Boer wife. *I should be walking down the street like that.* Word would get around that it was the earl's baby she carried; he would set her up in some nice place, perhaps a house in Parklands, where she could live like an empress while someone managed the hotel for her and deposited the profits into her account. But she needed a baby to make that come true, and for that she needed Valentine in her bed again.

Miranda's shoulders slumped. It was no use. Valentine wasn't coming back. Any fool could see that. He'd been drunk, and when he had sobered and realized what he had done, he had regretted it.

"I don't wanna have one o' them operations," Peony wailed. "I was raised Catholic!"

Miranda turned around, her look contemptuous. "You should have thought of that before you gave in to your weakness. If you don't want to get rid of it, then do you want to keep it?"

Peony's eyes went as round as coins. "No, no, mum! What would I do with a little un? It's not as though I loved the boy I slept with. He don't mean nothing to me. I don't want the baby. But I couldn't . . . kill it."

"Then what choice have you?"

Peony twisted the hem of her apron. "I thought perhaps someone would adopt it."

Miranda stared at her.

Peony looked small and pathetic in the big easy chair, the outlines of her bony shoulders showing through the fabric of her cheap dress. But she was healthy, Miranda knew that. And the baby would be, too.

Miranda narrowed her eyes, an idea dawning. "You say the boy doesn't know?"

"Oh, no, mum! And I'll never see him again to tell him."

"Does *anyone* know?"

Peony dumbly shook her head.

Miranda smiled. "Then I'm going to help you."

"Oh, thank you—"

"But you'll have to promise me you'll keep it a secret. Now, here is what we are going to do. . . ."

ROSE HAD WRITTEN him a note: "Mrs. West's macaroons, one doz. And Bristol cake, please."

It was the only way they communicated anymore, either through Mrs. Pembroke, the nanny, or by written notes. He had found this one in his dressing room when he had been getting ready for his trip to Nairobi. Rose was already out of the house, of course, in her eucalyptus glade.

Valentine was tempted to pretend he hadn't seen the note or that Mrs. West was no longer in the baking business, but he knew that lies would not save him. He wasn't being honorable. Unpleasant as it might be, he could not go on avoiding Miranda forever; he had to face her and lay the thing to rest.

Miranda glided out of the kitchen with her hands held out and, to his surprise, greeted him warmly.

"You've been busy, Lord Treverton," she said, motioning to one of the boys who was setting up tables for tea. "Two beers," she said in Swahili, then turned to Valentine. "You must have a terrific lot of work on your hands, what with weeding and mulching and pruning five thousand acres of coffee. It's all I hear about from the other growers."

Valentine looked around, thinking the dining room a rather public place. But it was deserted at this hour between lunch and tea. And the staff was working quietly on the other side of the room. "I'm sorry I haven't been by, Miranda. I just really didn't know what to say to you."

"It's all right," she said softly. "It really is."

"I'm not normally like that. I feel such the cad. I hadn't meant for it to happen. Too much gin at the Norfolk, you see."

"Of course. I understand."

"Well, then." He placed his hands flat on the table, feeling immeasurable relief. "I must say, Miranda, you're a good sport!"

She laughed. "What did you think I was going to do? I'm not a green girl fresh off the boat, after all. And I do trust your discretion. After all, there is my reputation to think of."

"You have my word of honor."

"And *your* reputation to protect, too."

"Well, yes."

"Especially now."

"Now?"

The beers arrived. Miranda poured them into glass mugs and waited until the boy had gone back into the kitchen before she said, "It's quite the coincidence you should stop by today, Lord Treverton. I was just about to go out and look for you."

He gave her a cautious look. "You were?"

She sipped her beer. "Oh, I'm afraid the boy brought cold ones. I've started keeping some on ice for the Americans. They drink their beer cold, did you know that?"

"Miranda, why were you going to go looking for me? Surely you know that what happened that night cannot be repeated."

"I hadn't expected it would be. The reason I'm glad you stopped by is that I have something to tell you."

"And what is that?"

"I'm pregnant."

"What!"

A waiter appeared through the kitchen doorway. Miranda waved him back, and he disappeared. "Please, Lord Treverton, we must be discreet."

"You're pregnant," he said.

"Yes."

"Are you sure?"

She sighed. "Yes."

"Why are you telling me?"

"Because it's your child."

"Mine!"

"It certainly isn't anyone else's."

He stared at her. Then he said, "Good Lord," and stood up. Valentine took a few steps, then turned around. "What are you going to do about it?"

"Do? Why, I'm going to keep it, of course."

"There's a woman in Limuru. A Mrs. Bates—"

Miranda shook her head. "I could never do that. And could you? Knowing it was your own child? And there's a very good chance that it's a boy. My family's known for having boys."

She paused, to let that sink in; then she said, "I'm not asking anything from you. I'm not that kind of woman. I'll take care of him, raise him as my own. No one will know you're the father. I just thought you should know, is all."

Valentine looked down at her, his expression dark and thoughtful. She returned his look with a forthright, honest gaze.

Then he thought of his father, the old earl. There had been talk of a woman in London and a little boy. Valentine's father had set them up in a flat on Bedford Square.

A boy. A *son* . . .

He came back to the table and sat down. "I'm sorry, Miranda," he said, earnest and serious. "I hadn't intended for this to happen."

"Neither had I, but there you are. I've spent years protecting my reputation. And now it's gone down the drain because of a moment of weakness."

"It was my fault."

"It takes two."

"I'll help you, of course."

"I'm not asking for it."

"Nonetheless . . ." Valentine's thoughts began to race. He pictured the members of his club, the knowing glances that were exchanged when he entered a room, the conversations that stopped abruptly. Valentine knew that the whole colony talked about him and Rose, speculated on their marital problems. *The earl of Treverton can't manage to father an heir.*

"When is the baby due?" he asked.

"In March."

"Very well then," he said as he reached into his pocket for his billfold. "This will be a start."

17

It was the worst possible time of the year to come to Kenya—just before the rains, when the grass was dry, the fields empty of crops, the whole land looking withered and forsaken by God.

As I shall be, Grace thought, *if I am not careful today.*

The delegation had arrived the day before. They were staying at the White Rhino Hotel in Nyeri and would soon be at Birdsong Cottage to begin their inspection. Feeling responsible for the situation, James had offered to come help, but Grace had declined, believing she must face the delegation on her own.

The morning was young and fresh as she walked the path toward the little compound that comprised her clinic. Night mist still curled along the ground; dew sparkled on leaves like glass flowers. Grace saw the flash of a paradise flycatcher up in the trees, its long scarlet tail catching the early sun. A cinnamon bee-eater flew across her path. The air was full of song and chatter. On the other side of the river blue smoke from the Kikuyu cook fires hung low in the trees.

Grace's mission consisted of three structures: the outpatient clinic, which was a thatch roof on four posts; the school, which was no more than logs laid out like benches facing an olive tree to which the blackboard was nailed; and a mud hut for seriously ill or injured patients. A quiet and orderly crowd was already waiting for her: women with babies on their backs; old men squatting in the dirt playing an interminable game with pebbles.

When the delegation, three men and two women, finally arrived, coming down the path from the plantation above, Grace was well into her routine.

As she had not yet met them, introductions went around. The Reverend Sanky headed the group and was accompanied by his wife, Ida. There were no questions at first; they merely watched Grace minister to the Africans as the patients came up one by one, with Mario assisting her. There were the usual burned children, whom she treated with permanganate and clean bandages, sending them away with reminders to their mothers of the hazards of the open fires in the huts. There was a man with a goiter whom Grace could not help; a severe case of elephantiasis, which she referred to the Catholic hospital in Nyeri; a man who three days ago had cut his hand, which, because it had gone unattended, was now badly infected. Many of her patients presented ailments they had already come to her for in the past, some of them several times. These problems arose from unsanitary living conditions, and although Grace repeated the same cautions over and over, about keeping the hut clean, penning the goats outside, washing one's body regularly, wearing sandals, keeping flies away from the face, the advice was never taken.

Mr. Sanky and his companions watched in silence, writing down notes in little books. They strolled around, inspected the equipment on the table—laryngoscope, reflex hammer, hypodermic syringes, tongue depressors, forceps, and scalpels—read labels on bottles, glanced at her charts, and listened.

An old man with sores all over his body kicked up a fuss when Grace reached for a hypodermic syringe. Mario translated: "He says he already have shot, memsaab. Yesterday, at the Catholic mission."

"I see," she said, filling the syringe from a bottle labeled "Neosalvarsan." "He had this particular shot?"

"He says yes, memsaab."

"Ask him if he also had a shot for cloud infection."

There was a brief exchange, then: "He had that one, too, memsaab."

"Very well then. Hold him please, Mario."

While the old man protested, she jabbed him in the arm.

"I say," said Mr. Sanky when the elder, complaining loudly, had gone away, "what was that all about?"

She spoke while she looked inside a woman's mouth. "The man had yaws. He needed a shot of Neosalvarsan."

"But he told you he'd already had one."

"These people are deathly afraid of injections, Mr. Sanky," Grace said as she reached for a pair of pliers. "They always lie and insist they've already had the shot."

"But how could you be sure he *was* lying?" Mrs. Sanky asked as she watched Grace pull a bad tooth from the Kikuyu woman's mouth.

"Because he insisted he had also had a shot for cloud infection, and there is no such thing."

"You made it up?"

"Mario, please tell the woman to rinse with this and spit it out." Grace washed her hands in a basin of soapy water and said, "It's a way of finding out if they're telling the truth. If he had told me he had *not* had a shot for cloud infection, then I might assume he was telling the truth about the Neosalvarsan shot. I've had some of these people vigorously assure me they have had a *chocolate* shot."

The clergyman and his wife exchanged a look.

Another member of the delegation said, "Just now you gave that woman her extracted tooth. Why?"

"I had to; otherwise she would think I might use it against her in black magic."

"Dr. Treverton," said the other woman in the group, "why is your morphine red? Morphine is not red. In fact"—she pointed to the medicinal vials on the table—"all these should be colorless solutions, and yet they are different colors. Why?"

Grace took a baby from its mother and proceeded to treat a burn on its leg. "I discovered that these people think all colorless liquids are water and that therefore, they won't work. Once I added dyes, they were convinced of the power in them. It is also the same if a medicine is bitter-tasting; they trust it more. In that respect the African is no different from the Englishman who goes to a Harley Street doctor."

"Dr. Treverton, are you able to take care of *all* the ailments that are presented to you?"

"Many of them. I rely rather heavily on 'Vaseline on the outside, quinine on the inside.' It gets me through most cases. The rest I send to the Catholic hospital."

At this all five exchanged a look. Mr. Sanky said, "Could you spare some time for us now, Dr. Treverton?"

"Certainly." She gave the bandaged baby back to its mother, warning her to watch him around the cook fire and knowing the warning would go unheeded; then she washed her hands and told Mario to keep an eye on those still waiting and guard against theft.

"These people steal from you, Dr. Treverton?" Mrs. Sanky asked as they walked down the path to the river. The group had requested a visit to the nearby village.

"Yes, they do."

"They seem to have no morals."

"On the contrary, the Kikuyu are a highly moral people with their own rigid set of laws and punishments. They just don't happen to think it's wrong to steal from the white man."

Mr. Sanky, walking beside Grace, said, "So far, in your treatment of these people, we've observed lies, trickery, and superstition—on *your* part, Doctor."

"It's the only way to communicate with them. They wouldn't understand otherwise."

"Who lives there?" asked Ida Sanky. She was pointing to the lone hut at the edge of Valentine's polo field.

"It belongs to a local healer named Wachera."

"I thought witch doctors had finally been outlawed."

"They have been. Wachera would be fined or imprisoned if she were caught practicing tribal medicine. The people go to her in secret."

"If you're aware of such secret practices, Dr. Treverton, I trust you have told the authorities."

Grace stopped at the riverbank where the wooden footbridge, built by Valentine, led across to the village. "I have, Mr. Sanky. Believe me. I have been trying to put a stop to what that woman is doing. She is my biggest obstacle in my fight to educate the Africans."

"Can't you talk to her? Reason with her?"

"Wachera will have nothing to do with me."

"Surely the woman sees that our ways are better!"

"On the contrary. Wachera is waiting for the British to pack up and clear out of Kenya."

"I have been doing some reading," said a young man in the group. "Is it true that the wives sleep with their husbands' friends?"

"It's a very old tribal custom that is deeply rooted in their complex age-group systems. And it is done openly, at the wife's discretion and with the husband's approval."

"Fornication, in other words."

Grace turned to the clergyman. "No, not fornication. The sexual mores of the Kikuyu are different from ours. For instance, they have no word in their language for rape. Their sexual attitudes might seem promiscuous to us, but they do have very strict taboos—"

"Dr. Treverton," said Mr. Sanky, "your fondness for these people is obvious to us, and we are not insensitive to what you are trying to accomplish here. However, our feeling is that you are going about it the wrong way."

"How so?"

"Back there, when you treated those patients, you never once spoke of the Lord, you never explained that your power came from Him, you didn't try to bring any of those people to Jesus, although you had ample opportunity."

"I'm not a preacher, Mr. Sanky."

"Precisely, and that is your main problem. You have neglected their spiritual needs, and so the Africans continue their evil practices. There is the operation, for example, wherein young girls are surgically mutilated. What have you done, Dr. Treverton, toward the missions' efforts here in Kenya to get that practice abolished?"

"In order to treat the illnesses of these people, Mr. Sanky, I must have their trust and friendship. If I start preaching to them and condemning their tribal traditions, they will stay away from my clinic. The Catholic mission has lost a lot of its African members because the priests cut down sacred fig trees."

"Surely you don't condone the worship of trees."

"I don't, but—"

"You see, Dr. Treverton," said an elderly member of the group, "the primary purpose for a medical mission here is an evangelistic one. We wanted a clinic here not to heal their bodies but to bring these people to Jesus."

"I've told you that I'm not a preacher."

"Then you need one."

"By all means send me a preacher," she said. "But send me also nurses and dressers!"

"You seem to be doing well enough on your own, Doctor," said Mrs. Sanky. "Why do you need so many assistants?"

"To teach the Africans self-help."

"Self-help?" said the clergyman.

Grace spoke quickly and earnestly. "My real goal is to train the Africans to take care of themselves. If I could just have a team in the village, someone to show the Kikuyu healthier ways to live, then my patient roll would drop dramatically. And if I could teach other Kikuyu the way I have taught Mario in basic first aid and treatment—"

"You're speaking of autonomy for these people."

"Yes, I am."

"Then how would they be brought to Jesus? If the Africans were able to get on for themselves, they would see no reason to come to Christian doctors, and therefore, evangelizing would be impossible."

Grace stared at the five, who looked out of place in their tightly buttoned jackets and neckties, the two women in corsets. They looked as if they were ready for an afternoon at Wimbledon instead of a trek through the African bush. Jeremy came suddenly to her mind. Grace now recalled a conversation she had had with him one night as they were walking on the deck. "The first thing we shall build, darling, is a house for inpatients," he had said. "Outpatients are difficult to hold on to, but patients in bed are a captive audience and so much more receptive to spiritual teaching."

It was strange. She had never really thought about it before, Jeremy's emphasis on the proselytizing aspect of their mission. And the more she considered it now, the more she could see Jeremy standing in this group.

She thought of the money this delegation represented, the monthly contribution from the Mission Society in Suffolk. They were her last resort, these five who were clearly not pleased with her methods. She would not go to Valentine for help, not with Miranda West walking around Nairobi in maternity clothes and all East Africa whispering about whose baby it was. Grace had no intention of being supported by her brother the same way he supported his mistress.

"I will gladly accept a preacher, Mr. Sanky," she said quietly. "His help would be most welcome."

The clergyman smiled. "We are sympathetic with what you have been going through here, Doctor. It certainly cannot have been easy for you. And since you have been so cut off for the past year and a half, it is not surprising that the course of your work went astray. I have a man in mind; he's doing work right now in Uganda. The Reverend Thomas Masters. He'll do the ticket. Get your people to build him a house right away, as I shall send him out on the next train."

"Will he bring medical personnel with him?"

"Mr. Masters will want to assess the medical need first."

"Shouldn't *I* be the one to make that assessment?"

"Mr. Masters will be in charge of your mission from now on, Doctor. All decisions will rest with him."

Grace looked at Mr. Sanky. "In charge! But . . . this is *my* mission."

"Built with *our* money, Doctor. It is time we took a hand in its supervision." Mr. Sanky looked around at the wild river, the untamed forest, the tops of thatched huts through the trees, and saw a land ripe for the likes of the Reverend Thomas Masters—a stern and forbidding man of unshakable righteousness who had put Satan on the run in four African countries.

18

The rains had stopped three days before, and Nairobi seemed to have sprouted colors overnight. As Miranda West walked down the street toward the King Edward Hotel, she passed walls matted with scarlet, orange, and pink bougainvillaea, private gardens crowded with newly blossomed geraniums, carnations, and fuchsias. The trees that lined Nairobi's muddy streets were arrayed in red Nandi blossoms, lavender jacaranda buds, white bottlebrushes. It was Christmas, and the world, fed by the short November rains, was shouting life and new growth. Miranda West's ample body, as she walked along, waving cheerily to people, was also a celebration of birth. She was six months pregnant and showing every day of it.

Once at the hotel, she stopped in the kitchen to pick up a tray of soup and sandwiches, then went up to her apartment, where she removed the pillow from under her smock and laid it aside. After putting on a dressing gown and making sure she was not seen, she climbed a private stairway to the attic.

Peony was sitting on the bed, reading a magazine.

"How are we today?" Miranda asked as she set the tray down.

The room had been done in flowered wallpaper, carpet, curtains, and such furnishings and extras—books, gramophone, rocking chair—as Peony had requested. It was as comfortable as Miranda could make it; but there was no disguising the fact that it was a jail, and Peony was beginning to chafe at it.

"Christmas in two days," she said, "and here's me missing out on everything."

"You won't miss out. I shall bring you some goose and Christmas pudding. And I've got a present for you."

Peony looked over the tray of sandwiches and said, "What? Ham paste again?"

"My customers pay a lot of money for my ham paste."

"I'd sooner have a jam buttie."

Miranda curbed her irritation. She knew it wasn't easy for the girl to stay cooped up for twenty-four hours, seeing no one but Miranda. But it would be worth it, as she reminded Peony now. "Only three more months, my girl, and you'll be on your way back to England with money in your pocket."

Peony looked fretful. "You sure those people are going to go through with it? The ones who are going to adopt the baby?"

"I promise."

"How come they ain't never come to see me? I should think they'd want to look the mother over."

"I told you, they wish their identity to remain a secret."

"Well, as long as they keep to their end of the bargain."

Miranda sat on the edge of the bed and patted the girl's hand. "You've nothing to worry about. As soon as I take the baby to them, you'll get your boat ticket back to England."

"*And* the five hundred pounds?"

"In cash. Now then, shall we see how we're doing tonight?"

As Peony slid down in the bed so that she was lying flat, she said, "Why do you always say 'we'?"

"It's what nurses say, isn't it? And aren't I your nurse?"

Peony gave her a suspicious look. "You *are* going to get a proper doctor to deliver it, aren't you?"

"I've already told you that. The couple have got one in mind. I'll send for him the minute your labor starts. Now, tell me how you feel."

It was the same every day: Miranda would come in, measure Peony's abdomen, feel all around it, and ask questions such as "Have you a good appetite? Do you have any aches or pains? What does the baby *feel* like?" Out came the tape measure now, and Miranda saw that she was going to have to let out her pillow again.

"No more morning sickness?"

"Not for five days. I guess that's passed."

Peony had been wretchedly ill the first few months, bent over a basin, unable to keep anything down. So Miranda had refused breakfast and lunch for those weeks and had complained to anyone who would listen that she was having morning sickness.

"But my back aches now," Peony said.

"Where?"

"Here. And I'm forever running to the toilet!"

Miranda smiled. She would remember that. "Are you sleeping all right?"

"Well enough. Can you get hold of any fish? I'm sure craving fish."

"What kind?"

Peony shrugged. "Just fish. Expecting a baby sure makes you crave funny things—I *hate* fish!"

Miranda rose from the bed and said, "You shall have the best fish money can buy. Is there anything else?"

"I'd like a magazine that's not six months old!"

"Now you're asking for a miracle. But I'll see what I can do."

"I don't like this, you know. I don't like it one bit. I'll go crazy if I don't get out."

Miranda stood at the door with her hand on the knob. "You know that isn't possible."

"Just for a walk! Ain't expectant mothers supposed to get exercise?"

"The couple doesn't want you to be seen."

"Who would know? *Please*, mum. Just let me get out for a bit. I won't do nothing, I promise."

"Peony, we settled all that back in August. You agreed to abide by every condition they set down. If you take one step outside this room, the deal is off, and you're on your own, pregnant and penniless. Is that understood?"

Peony toyed with a strand of her hair.

Miranda smiled and said gently, "It'll all be worth it once it's over. You'll see. Just as long as you sit tight."

Reaching at last for a sandwich and biting into it, the girl said, "Aw right, I won't go nowhere."

When she left, Miranda turned the key in the lock.

"MY MORNING SICKNESS has stopped, but I've got the most unexpected craving for fish!" Miranda wrote in the letter to her sister in London.

"My back aches, and I make frequent trips to the toilet; but it's only three more months, and then I shall be set up quite comfortably. Lord Treverton is building me the most beautiful house in Parklands. I'll move into it as soon as the baby is born. You will come and live with us. We shall have such a good life!"

Miranda put her pen down, folded the sheet, and slid it into the envelope along with a photograph of herself in her maternity smock. The hour was late; as she started to wonder whether or not to work on enlarging her pillow tonight, she heard a sound beyond her door.

Miranda froze. Her apartment was above the kitchen at the top of a private stairway; it was cut off from the rest of the hotel and guests. She looked at her clock. It was midnight.

She listened. There was someone outside her door.

Peony! Sneaking out after somehow picking the lock!

Miranda jumped up and ran to the door, which she flung open to surprise the girl and grab her before she was seen. But Miranda received a shock.

"Hello, darlin'," said Jack West.

She drew back.

"You look as if you've seen a ghost. Don't you recognize your own husband?"

"Jack!" she whispered. "I thought you were dead."

"Yeah, well, I wanted it that way. Ain't ya gonna invite me in?"

A stocky red-haired man in sweat-stained khaki and beard down his chest, he walked past her. He looked around the apartment. "You've done all right for y'self, Miranda. All right indeed."

She quickly closed the door. "What are you doing here?"

He turned and raised bushy orange eyebrows. "What am I *doing* here! Why, I'm yer husband, darlin'. Ain't I got a right to be here?"

"No! Not after you abandoned me."

"Abandoned! I told you I was going to Lake Victoria to look for hippo."

"That was seven years ago. I never heard from you."

"Well, yer hearing from me now. Ain't ya gonna offer me a drink?"

Miranda tried to think. Her mind raced: the girl hidden upstairs; the pillow with the ties on it; Lord Treverton. She poured Jack a whiskey and said, "Where've you been all this time?"

He sat in the very chair the earl had sat in six months ago and put his dirty boots on the footstool. "Here and there. The hippos didn't pan out, but I managed to make a bit of a profit on the war, scouting for the Germans and spying on the British. After that I did a little ivory poaching in the Sudan."

"Why did you come back to Nairobi?"

"Because I heard of a gold find in the Nyanza, and I aim to cash in on it."

Miranda spoke with caution. "Then you're not here to stay?"

"Not while there's gold to be found out there!" He tossed the whiskey down in one gulp and held his glass out for more. "Quartz reefs backing onto limestone have been spotted near Lake Victoria. They say they're just like the gold-bearing formations in Rhodesia. D'you know what gold fetches these days? Four pounds an ounce!"

"Then why are you here and not *there?*"

The second glassful went down and he took a third. "I need a kit. I figure five salted mules and a couple of trusty wogs'll do it. Plus the equipment. That's what I'm in Nairobi for." When he'd drunk the third whiskey and a flush had come to his cheeks, Jack West thoughtfully fingered his beard. "But you see, I don't have the money for all that. And when I heard that my own wife had a prosperous hotel in town, well . . ."

Miranda turned abruptly and went to the small safe that stood beside her bed. "How much do you need?" she asked.

"Now, now," he said, coming to his feet, "what's your hurry? Can't get fitted out at this hour, can I? The business part of our little visit can wait till morning."

Miranda went cold. She turned and said, "Jack, we're not married anymore."

"Of course we are!" He started toward her. "And by God, you've gotten to be a handsome woman in my absence."

She backed away from him. She tried to think. Her plans, so fragile, so chancy . . . Jack could spoil it all. "When do you leave for the Nyanza?" she asked.

"Tomorrow. As soon as I get my kit together. But right now I've got another sort of mining on my mind!"

Miranda stood still and let him come nearer. Gold prospecting in

Kenya, she knew, could take years. Once he was out of town, she would file for a proper divorce, as she should have done long ago. No one need know that he had come back or that she had seen him or that he was still alive. She would placate him, send him on his way. . . .

He was close enough for her to smell the whiskey on his breath, and when he reached for her, she didn't resist. She let him touch her. She thought of everything that was at stake. She closed her eyes.

19

Grace was desperate.

In her six days of searching Nairobi for sources of financial aid, she had come up with very little. Although the East African Women's League had pledged support, and contributions were promised from the governor and other concerned people, the majority was of the shared opinion that as the sister of one of the wealthiest men in East Africa Grace didn't need their help. One had only to look at the ostentatious stone house Valentine had built for his mistress and bastard child to know that he could well afford to support his sister in similar style. If they'd only known. Grace had already gone to Valentine, and he had refused.

It had not been easy for her to turn to him. She was already angry with him over the Miranda business. Poor Rose, as isolated as she was, had still heard the rumors and had come to Birdsong Cottage one night in a state of hysterics, saying that it was all her fault, that she wasn't a proper wife to Valentine, that she could produce only girl children or miscarriages. Grace had given her sister-in-law a sedative and taken her back up to the house, where Valentine was not in residence because he had been in Nairobi visiting *that* woman.

Grace looked up at the lowering sky. It was March now; the long rains were due to break. She knew she must be getting back up north before the roads became bogs and lakes, but first she had to find a way to make the mission hers again.

The Reverend Thomas Masters from Uganda had turned out to be an abominable man.

He had begun at once saving souls, pouring on the baptismal water and listening to the witnesses of illiterate Africans. He gave them *wazungu* names and promised them eternal life just for saying a few words in a language that they didn't understand. The Africans came to him because they wanted the magic and power of the white man's name, and as a consequence, the village was starting to be populated with Thomases, Johns, and Rachels. They mimicked his prayer words and thought they were becoming like the white man.

The clergyman had also taken over control of the money sent by the Mission Society, requiring Grace to make written requests before buying supplies; she had to account to him for every inch of bandage, for every stitch of suture. And if he thought she was being wasteful, he forced her to make do with less.

Through his prince-nez glasses and down his long, thin nose, the Reverend Thomas Masters found endless criticism of Grace Treverton. Especially on the issue of Wachera. He declared that he couldn't understand why Grace hadn't taken care of that problem long ago. "Don't just ignore her," he had said. "Bring her to Jesus. Once she walks in righteousness, the medicine woman will denounce her witchcraft, and the rest of her people will follow."

Still, for the sake of receiving the financial support of the Mission Society Grace had tolerated everything until the night Mr. Masters had questioned her relationship with James Donald—a married man.

James had come to visit her, arriving late one afternoon with a brace of spur fowl and some butter and cheese from his dairy, and he had sat and talked with Grace until well past sunset. The clergyman had come to the door to speak with Grace and had stood stock-still when he had seen Sir James in her living room. Afterward had come the lecture on appearances and the responsibility of living like a Christian woman, of setting an example for the Africans, and Grace had told the clergyman to mind his own business. The exchange, she knew, had been reported to the Mission Society.

That was when she had decided to seek Valentine's aid.

She had found him in the northern acreage of the estate, atop Excalibur with whip in hand, overseeing the mulching and weeding of the seedlings. The long rains were due, and he was racing against time. While Grace talked to him, Valentine kept his eyes on the field hands, every so often shouting an order, interrupting her, his manner maddeningly fragmented. Sleepless nights were etched on his face; the obsession to create the wealthiest plantation in Kenya burned in his gaze. "Get on with it, Grace," he had said impatiently. "The rains will break any day now. You are taking up precious time."

After she had stated her purpose, he had said, "I gave you two years, Grace. And here it is, you've been in Kenya for two years. And you've failed."

"I haven't failed. I just need some help."

"You swore up and down you didn't need me. You promised me you'd never bother me with that project of yours. Wahiro!" he called out. "Bring some more fertilizer down here. And tell them to spread it properly this time!"

"Valentine—"

"Healing them is one thing, Grace. I don't mind that. But teaching them, *educating* them, is another. Where would I be if these chaps suddenly decided to run things for themselves? Give them enough education, and they'll want to take over. And then we can all pack up and go back to England. Is that what you want?"

Grace had burned with fury. She had wanted to lash out at him about Miranda and the baby, to remind him of poor Rose and little Mona, two years old and unloved, to point out what a mess he was making of his own life; but she had known that it would only create an ugly scene and that it would alienate her brother from her further. So she had decided to risk the trip down to Nairobi, aware of the impending rains and that the roads would soon be not only unusable but downright dangerous; more than one wagon or automobile had disappeared into a sudden muddy swamp with driver and passengers never found. Her friends in Nairobi were her last hope. She had to get rid of the Reverend Thomas Masters.

But now even her friends had not been able to offer sufficient aid. A bank loan was her last resort, although she had no idea how she was going to pay it back.

She watched a dusty Model T rattle by, then crossed the dirt street to Hardy Acres's bank.

MIRANDA LEANED OVER the ceramic bowl and vomited.

She clutched the edges of the table while her body shuddered; then she sank down into the chair, exhausted. Her eyes gazed dully at the window, where a light rain had begun to wash the panes. She felt no emotion—neither joy that the rains had come, ensuring another year of prosperity for Kenya, nor distress at the thought of what a mess the mud was going to make of her hotel. She was thinking of nothing at all. Her worst fears had been confirmed.

She was pregnant.

The first suspicion had entered her mind back in February, when she realized she had missed a period. She had held out on a false hope, which had grown fainter and fainter with each morning of sickness, until now there was no doubt and no hope. All those weeks of interrogating Peony had taught Miranda enough to diagnose her own condition.

Her dispirited gaze moved from the window and settled first upon a crumpled letter on her desk—the message that had arrived the day before from Jack's gold prospecting partner informing Miranda of her husband's death in an incident with a wounded rhino. Then her eye went to the ludicrous cushion on her bed, the pillowcase that was stuffed with rags to approximate a nine-month belly. And finally Miranda looked up at the ceiling because Peony was up there, in the attic, waiting out her last hours. . . .

There was no choice for Miranda but to go to Mrs. Bates in Limuru. Her dirty business was an open secret in Kenya; Miranda could name three women who had been relieved of their mistakes in Mrs. Bates's kitchen. But there was the problem of when to do it. The Limuru woman would not terminate a pregnancy that had gone past four months, and Miranda was past three. She would have to go soon. But when?

Peony was due any day. Miranda could not leave her. She had lied to the girl about a doctor's being on call; Miranda planned to deliver the baby herself. Secrecy was paramount. She would take the baby, throw away her pillow, and put Peony on the first train bound for the coast.

But now there was this new complication.

Miranda checked her watch. It was getting on to teatime, and she had not looked in on Peony since morning.

Her mind stumbled about for answers. When to go to Mrs. Bates? What if Peony was mistaken about her dates and the baby didn't come for another two or three weeks? Miranda would have Lord Treverton's baby and still be pregnant!

She looked at the tray that was to go up to Peony. On it lay a magazine that was full of romance stories and gossip about American film stars. On the back page were classified advertisements for "hard to come by" items. The advertisers had post office box addresses, required cash in advance, and promised quick and discreet delivery of "female regulators," guaranteed to work.

Miranda rose wearily and picked up the tray.

She knew nothing about delivering babies but decided it could not be too complex, its being a rather straightforward, natural process. She had found a book, *Home Childbirth*, which had turned out to be useless because it had been published twenty years ago at the turn of the century and was so discreet that it got no more technical than "First, place a modesty screen around the mother." So Miranda followed her instincts. In Peony's nightstand there was a pile of freshly laundered sheets and towels, soap and a bottle of sterile water, a basin for washing, and tea towels with safety pins for afterward. All going well, Miranda reminded herself now as she opened the attic door, she should have her baby in a day or two, Peony safely on the train, and herself making the quick trip to Mrs. Bates's farm.

When she entered the attic room, she cried out and dropped the tray.

Hastily locking the door behind herself, Miranda ran to the bed and felt Peony's wrist. At first she couldn't find a pulse. Then it was there, but weak.

"Peony?" she said. *"Peony?"*

There was no movement on the shockingly white face. Miranda looked at the blood soaking into the mattress, covering Peony's dress and legs, and tried to stay calm. The girl was still alive. Working quickly, Miranda drew Peony's clothes off, spread a new sheet under her, and tried to stop the blood flow.

What had happened?

Miranda began to tremble. She had no idea what to do. She felt the girl's abdomen. The baby was alive, moving. Then she saw a contraction and the emergence of more blood.

Miranda jumped up, left the attic, ran down the stairs and into the kitchen, where a boy turned to her with startled eyes. *"Daktari,"* she said, pulling him aside. The others in the kitchen stopped work and stared. "Quickly!"

"Daktari Hare?"

"Any doctor! Hurry! Tell him it's life and death!"

MR. ACRES'S OFFICE was simply a mesh cage at the back of the tiny bank, which itself consisted of nothing more than a bit of floor space, a counter with a grille, and one teller's window, where a young Hindu was counting out money.

"Dr. Treverton!" said Mr. Acres, rising and straightening his waist-coat. "I certainly hadn't meant for you to come out in this weather. It could have waited until after the rains."

"I beg your pardon?"

"You're here because of my message, are you not?"

"What message?"

"Well, this *is* a coincidence." He pulled out a chair for her and sat behind his desk. "I sent a note up to the DO in Nyeri town, asking him to pass it along to you. It's about your bank account."

She gave him a puzzled look. "What bank account?"

He went through some papers on his desk, cleared his throat, and brought forth a ledger. "An account has been opened in your name, Dr. Treverton." He leaned forward and opened the book. "Here it is. See? That is the sum that was deposited, five hundred pounds. You may draw upon it as often as you wish, provided you do not exceed that amount within a twelve-month period."

Grace blinked down at the neat columns, at the line with her name printed on it. "I don't understand."

"Yes, well, I rather thought it would come as a surprise to you. You see, this account has been opened by a person who will make yearly deposits of five hundred pounds, to be used by you as you see fit."

She stared at him. "I don't understand. *What* person?"

"I am not at liberty to divulge that information, Doctor. The identity of your benefactor must remain unknown to you."

Grace looked at him. Rain pattered on the corrugated iron roof of the small bank, creating a noise inside. A leak appeared, and the young

Asian was immediately on the spot, setting a bucket under it on the floor.

"Mr. Acres, I don't know what to say."

"I quite imagine. Five hundred pounds is a lot of money."

"And you can't tell me who did this?"

"Anonymity is part of the conditions. Were such information to be somehow disclosed, the benefactor will terminate the account. I cannot even tell you if these funds originate here in Kenya or elsewhere."

Grace continued to stare at the ledger page with her name and the remarkable numbers after it. *Kenya or elsewhere.* Who on earth?

And then a voice echoed in her mind: *I shall make it up to you somehow, Grace.* Sir James had said that to her the night he had told her about Lucille's writing the letter to the Society. *I promise you I will make it up to you.*

"But he can't afford it."

Mr. Acres looked over the rim of his spectacles. "Did you say something, Doctor?"

She shook her head. Of course, he would want the account to be anonymous, and of course, she was going to respect that. And the first thing she was going to do after sending Mr. Masters packing on the very next train to Mombasa was ride out to Kilima Simba and tell James about her good news.

"Memsaab Daktari! Memsaab Daktari!" shouted the rain-soaked kitchen boy as he ran into the bank.

Hardy Acres shot to his feet. "What is this!"

The Asian teller tried to grab the muddy boy but missed. "Daktari!" he said as he came up breathlessly to Grace. "The memsaab needs you at once. She says it is life and death. *Haraka haraka!*"

"What has happened?"

"You come! Something bad!"

"Who sent you?"

"Memsaab Westi!"

Grace exchanged a look with the banker. Then she said, "Tell Mrs. West that I must stop first for my medical bag. I'm staying down Government Road with the Millfords."

* * *

WHEN GRACE FINALLY hurried into the attic, shedding her raincoat and dropping her umbrella, she found a frantic Miranda pacing beside a bed that, at first glance, appeared to contain a corpse. In the instant it took for her to close the door and cross the room, Grace's trained eye took in two important details: that the girl on the bed was in the middle of childbirth and that the widow West was suddenly no longer pregnant.

Grace sat on the edge of the bed, snapped open her bag, and withdrew the stethoscope. "What happened?" she said as she listened first to Peony's chest, then to the abdomen.

"She started labor this morning—"

"It's evening now. Why didn't you call in a doctor before this?"

Miranda stood in petrified silence.

Shooting the woman an angry look, Grace proceeded to examine Peony.

She found the worst possible situation: The placenta was breaking up, and the poor girl was bleeding to death. It was too late now for hospitals or surgery; Grace was going to be lucky if she could save the baby. And for that she was going to have to fight.

"We are too late to save the girl," she said as she made hurried preparations to bring the baby out. "But I might still be able to save the child." She looked up at Miranda. "That was what you wanted, isn't it? This child?"

Miranda swallowed and nodded.

Valentine! Grace thought as she hastily unwrapped her sterile instruments. *You fool!*

The night grew long and dark; the shadows of the two women loomed on the walls and wavered in the glow of a hurricane lamp. Rain fell continually against the windows as Nairobi withdrew into sepulchral silence. Grace worked quickly, using her instruments, the sheets, and towels. There was the umbilical cord to deal with, wrapped around the baby's neck, and the blood flow, as ceaseless as the rain. Miranda assisted her; they sat with their heads together, doing all the work because Peony was beyond helping them.

The girl died just before the baby gave its first cry. Grace said, "It's a boy," and Miranda fell away from the bed in a dead faint.

20

District Officer Briggs was clearly uncomfortable. "It is, ah, most extraordinary, Your Lordship," he said as he pointedly avoided looking Valentine in the eye. "Quite a baffling case."

They were sitting on the veranda of Bellatu, drinking morning tea in the brief sunshine break in the rain. Already clouds were gathering to shed another blessed deluge upon Treverton's five thousand acres of coffee.

"Apparently it, ah, happened four nights ago," Briggs said. "One of the kitchen boys said Mrs. West sent him out for a doctor. The girl was named Peony Jones, came out from England about fifteen months ago and worked as a maid at Mrs. West's hotel. Your sister has confirmed what happened that night. She filed a report the next morning with the police."

Valentine sat with a stony expression, teacup forgotten in his hand.

The officer shifted in his chair, wishing this messy business hadn't fallen to him. "So, ah, as I was saying, Mrs. West's car was found on the Limuru Road, not far from the Bates farm. Dr. Treverton said she had no knowledge of that. In her report she states that she left immediately after delivering the Jones girl's baby. Apparently Mrs. West drove out to Limuru the same night the maid died. We don't know the purpose of the trip."

Briggs glanced at Valentine's fixed stare and went on. "There was a baby with her, most likely the one your sister delivered in the attic. It was still in Mrs. West's arms when she was found; they had both drowned in the mud. It appears the car got stuck, and Mrs. West tried to go the rest of the way on foot in the rain and didn't make it."

Valentine looked out over the rows of green coffee bushes speckled with white flowers. Beyond them Mount Kenya stood cloaked in mystery and majesty.

"But the, ah, really baffling thing of it all," Briggs continued, "is that, ah . . . the baby she had with her was half black. The Medical Officer concluded that the maid had had sexual relations with an African."

Valentine didn't blink. He looked like a man hypnotized.

"There is just one more thing, Your Lordship. The Medical Officer has also reported that Mrs. West was pregnant at the time of her death . . . about three months along."

Finally Valentine looked at the District Officer. "Why are you telling me all this? Mrs. West is of no concern to me."

Briggs stared at him for a moment, then looked away, a bright flush rising up his neck. Fumbling for his hat and swagger stick, the officer got to his feet, began to say something, then hurried down the steps and away.

THEY HAD HAD only one week of rain, and already the Cape chestnuts were bursting all over in a froth of pink flowers and aloes were blossoming in bright red clumps among the rocks. The spur fowl was singing its musical scales, and the rainbird answered in its flutelike song.

Rose hummed along with nature as she sat in the protection of her gazebo, stitching the tapestry and looking, in her pale pink cardigan, tan woolen skirt, and green scarf as if the rain had produced her as well. She was not alone in the glade. Mrs. Pembroke sat with Mona, looking at a picture book; an African girl squatted by the picnic hamper, ready to serve hot pies and chocolate; and three invisible Kikuyu men stood on guard among the eucalyptus trees. Rose's pets were with her also. A black-faced vervet monkey was curled up in her lap, and tethered to a post was Daphne, an orphaned bushbuck that Rose had rescued when it was no bigger than a cat.

On a sturdy frame was stretched the white linen that had become Rose's entire life. She had so far stitched in outlines and possibilities, a sketch in thread. On one side Mount Kenya was starting to materialize, its craggy peak with a bit of cloud done in perle cotton; the slopes would be covered in Persian yarns and Florentine stitchery; and the vast rain forest with its ropy vines and dense brush was slowly going to come to life with embroidery floss and French knots. Rose could see it in her mind—complete, breathing, *alive*. There remained only one space that eluded her: slightly off center, between two gnarly trees. The rest of the scene was all in balance; every spot had its subject and every subject had a place. Except for that one mysterious vacancy. No matter how she studied it or tried to place things into it, nothing worked. It was the one spot in Rose's tapestry that could not be filled.

When Mrs. Pembroke discreetly cleared her throat, Rose looked up and, to her immense surprise, saw Valentine coming through the damp trees.

He walked up the steps of the gazebo, knocking moisture from his shoulders, and said, "I would like to be alone with my wife, if you please."

No one moved. Rose looked up at him, bewildered, trying to sense his mood. Then she nodded to the nanny, who took Mona and the African girl with her.

When they were alone, Valentine went down on one knee next to Rose. "Am I disturbing you?" he asked softly.

"You've never been here before, Valentine."

He looked at the linen. The dotted outlines in various colors of yarn made no sense to him. He praised it nonetheless. Then he asked, "Are you happy here, Rose?"

His face was level with hers; she saw how gentle his eyes were. "Yes," she whispered. "I'm very happy here, Valentine."

"You know that's all I ever want, don't you? For you to be happy?"

"I think so."

"The night of the Christmas party, Rose. What I did to you—"

She placed her fingertips on his mouth. "We mustn't speak of that. Not ever again."

"Rose, I need to talk to you."

She nodded. "I heard about Mrs. West, Valentine. And I was sorry to hear it."

Pain replaced the gentleness in his eyes. He reached up and clutched the back of her chair. "I love you, Rose," he said in a tight voice. "Do you believe me?"

"Yes, Valentine."

"I suppose it's too late to expect you to love me in return, but—"

"I do love you, Valentine."

He gazed into her pale blue eyes and saw that she meant it. "I must have a son," he said quietly. "You have to understand that. I need a son to inherit what I am building."

"Won't Mona do?"

"Of course not, darling. You know that."

"You want me to give you a son," she said.

"Yes."

"It frightens me, Valentine."

"I won't hurt you, Rose. I won't let any harm come to you. And I have nowhere else to turn." He bowed his head. "If you do this for me, I shall make you a promise. Give me a son, Rose, and I will never come near you again."

She laid a cool, slender hand along his cheek. Tears filled her eyes. Valentine had come back to her; he was hers to love again. "Then I will do it," she said.

ON AUGUST 12, 1922, Arthur Currie Treverton was born. Rose had kept her part of the bargain. And Valentine kept his.

PART
THREE
1929

21

Mona had already decided she was going to run away. All she had to do was choose the right moment.

Her solemn eyes took in the crowded streets of Paris as the limousine made its way toward the train station; she saw pedestrians on the sidewalks turn to watch the stately procession of shiny Pierce-Arrows. Mona rode with her mother in the first car; in the next one came Sati, Mona's Indian ayah, with Lady Rose's personal secretary and a little African girl named Njeri. Two more cars followed with Rose's many trunks and the purchases collected during her shopping trip and her two lady's maids. Gleaming black with curtains closed to hide the passengers inside, the Pierce-Arrows created a spectacle as they inched their way through the Place de la Concorde.

Mona felt her heart grow heavy. In their eight weeks in Paris, spent mostly in the George V Hotel because the noise and crowds of the city distressed Rose, Mona had not been able to dissuade her mother from going on to Suffolk. Now they were headed for the station where they were to board the boat train that would carry them to England, where Mona was going to be abandoned.

What a monstrous city this was, with its grotesque buildings and naked statues and gawdy bridges spanning a cold, flat river. Mona's first glimpse of Paris had terrified her. She had never seen so many people, heard such a din. And the sky barely showed between the rooftops. It led her to think of the beehives made by the Wakamba tribesmen. Everyone in Paris was in a hurry. People rushed along the sidewalks with their collars turned up, their faces pinched and red. They went from cement walkways to asphalt roads to stone walls. There was no wilderness here; it all was planned and orderly. Jazz poured from windows and doorways, and wild-looking American girls called flappers sat at sidewalk cafés, showing off their cigarettes and smoky silk stockings. Mona wanted to go home, back to Bellatu and Aunt Grace's mission. She wanted to run free again, to cast off these horrible clothes her mother had bought for her at a place called a salon. She longed to be with her friends again—Gretchen Donald, and Ralph, who was fourteen and terribly handsome and on whom Mona had an enormous crush.

Why, *why* did she have to leave Kenya?

"Mummy," she began tentatively.

Rose didn't look up from the novel by F. Scott Fitzgerald she was reading. "Yes, dear?"

"Couldn't we maybe just put it off for a bit? Just until I'm older?"

Rose laughed softly. "You'll enjoy boarding school, darling. *I* did."

"But why must I go to school in England? Why can't I go to the boarding school in Nairobi?"

"I've already explained, darling. You want something better than the Nairobi school. You're the daughter of an earl; you must be educated correctly, as befits your station."

"But Gretchen and Ralph go there!"

Rose laid aside her book and smiled at her daughter. The poor child! At ten years of age she could hardly be expected to understand. "You are going to grow up to be a lady, Mona. Gretchen Donald is going to be a farmer's wife. There *is* a difference."

"But I don't want to be a lady! I want to live at Bellatu and grow coffee!" Mona wanted to cry. She knew the real reason she was being taken to England. It was because her parents didn't love her. "I promise I shall be good from now on, Mummy! I shall always do what I am told, and I shall pay attention to my lessons, and I shan't make you and Daddy angry with me anymore!"

Rose looked at her in surprise. "Why, Mona, darling, whatever put such silly notions into your head? Boarding school isn't a punishment. You should be looking forward to it."

She lifted her hand, and for an instant Mona thought her mother was going to touch her. But the gesture had only been to adjust the veil covering Rose's eyes. The book came up again, and her mother withdrew from her once more.

Mona sniffed. She couldn't remember having ever been caressed or held by either of her parents. As far back as she could remember, she had always been in the care of a succession of nannies, all of whom either went back to England or found a husband in Kenya; then had come the governesses, a constant turnover of young women who soon got bored with the isolation of Bellatu. That was why Rose had finally given in and hired Sati, Mona's first ayah. Indian or African nursemaids and companions were becoming the accepted thing in Kenya as English help was becoming harder to keep. The Trevertons were among the last to resist; now Mona's constant company was a young woman from Bombay who wore brightly colored saris and heady spice perfume and who was the only one who ever showed Mona any physical affection.

When they arrived at the train station, people stopped and stared at the elegant and mysterious woman emerging from the limousine. These eight weeks in Paris had been Rose's first contact with the world of fashion in more than ten years; she had adopted the latest styles at once. The black felt hat pulled tightly over her head, covering her forehead and eyebrows and revealing eyes blackened with too much mascara, gave Rose a provocative mystique. She wore a black wraparound Chanel coat with an upstanding fox collar that hid the lower part of her face so that she bore a striking resemblance to Pola Negri, the popular screen vamp.

Mona knew that everyone thought her mother must be a film star; in shops around Paris people had approached Lady Rose for her autograph. Mona felt painfully conspicuous as she stood close to her mother and watched the trunks and packages go onto the baggage cart. When Sati and Njeri came out of the second limousine, a murmur rippled through the French crowd.

Despite her fashionable drop-waisted dress and strapped shoes, nine-year-old Njeri caused a sensation with her shaved head and loops of Kikuyu beads strung through holes in her ears. Rose's maids, both Africans in black uniforms, and her private secretary, Miss Sheridan, also in tight cloche hat and upstanding collar hiding her face, closed in around their mistress to form a protective knot. Together they all hurried after the baggage cart, anxious to be on the train.

There was a moment of confusion before boarding. A mob congested the platform, kissing and embracing, waving farewell. Mona was overwhelmed by the press of fur coats and rapid French speech; she hung close to her mother while Miss Sheridan went in search of a conductor to assist them.

When Mona saw how Njeri, also intimidated by the railway crowd, stayed close to Lady Rose, her resentment of the little African girl swelled.

Njeri had first caught Rose's notice one day last year, when she had come tentatively into the eucalyptus glade to stand as still and timid as a gazelle and watch the memsaab sitting in the gazebo. Mona had watched in child's jealousy as her mother, taken with the shy little girl dressed in rags in the same way she was touched by stray animals, had coaxed Njeri into the gazebo with a macaroon. The next day the little girl had returned—with her brother! And Mona's jealousy had turned to anger to see her mother give them both sweets.

David, the eleven-year-old son of Wachera, the medicine woman, had not come back after that; but Njeri had returned every day, and Rose, enchanted by the little girl, who seemed starved for attention and who was clearly in awe of the memsaab, allowed her to stay.

When plans for the European trip were made, Rose had asked Mona's Aunt Grace to obtain permission from Gachiku to take Njeri along—"As a companion for Mona," Rose had said. But Mona knew the truth: Karen von Blixen had caused a sensation by traveling about Europe with a little African boy in her entourage; Lady Rose wanted to do the same.

Mona, receiving little enough attention from her mother, desperately resented Njeri's intrusion. In fact, she resented all the African children who received attention from her aunt Grace in the mission school and who, because of their poverty, were the frequent recipients of Lady Rose's charitably donated castoff clothes. But more than anyone, Mona disliked Njeri's brother, David, whom she thought an arrogant boy and who had one day, down by the river, impudently declared to Mona that his mother had told him this land was *his* and that one day all the white people were going to leave Kenya.

That was why Mona could not go to the academy in England. She had to return to Kenya, to show David Mathenge that the land was *hers*.

And so, when the first good opportunity arose, she was going to run away.

THE CARS CREPT along the gravel drive toward the stately mansion, where a line of servants stood out front: footmen in livery, maids in uniform; old Fitzpatrick, the butler who had fled Kenya back in 1919 three months after his arrival there. The March wind made skirts snap like pennants, and the staff of twenty ogled the newcomers in silence. They had never seen Africans before, and there was a dusky beauty in lemon yellow silk who looked as if she had just stepped out of the *Arabian Nights*. Sati, the ayah, was unimpressed—she had seen British mansions before—but the two Kikuyu maids, shaven-headed and awkward in their shoes and uniforms, stared openmouthed at the three-story house with its towers and turrets and thousand windows.

"My dear Rose!" said Harold as he came down the steps. He took her gloved hands and stared into the furtive eyes barely seen between veil and fox collar. "It *is* Rose, isn't it?"

Harold had grown fat. He bore little resemblance to his older brother Valentine, who, at forty-one, was still athletically trim and showing only touches of silver at the temples. "Surely you didn't have to bring all of Africa with you!" he said in a forced joking manner. Then he said, "Come along. Edith is anxious to see you."

The elegant George V Hotel in Paris had awed Mona with its grand lobby and chandeliers. But *this* house. It was like a palace! It took her breath away as she entered the dark hall lined with standing suits of medieval armor, ancient tapestries on the walls, darkly brooding portraits of people long dead. It made Bellatu seem a mere cottage, and it would have been her home, she knew, if her father had not fallen in love with East Africa eleven years ago.

Edith Treverton was in the drawing room with another woman and two young girls. Edith greeted her sister-in-law with exaggerated enthusiasm, introducing the visitor as Lady Ester and one of the girls as her daughter, the Honorable Melanie Van Allen. The other girl was Edith's daughter, Charlotte, Mona's cousin.

"Rose, how good it is to see you again after all these years!" Edith declared, kissing the air next to Rose's cheek. "We all truly believed you and Valentine would be on the first boat back to England! How *do* you stand living in the jungle?"

Mona sat self-consciously on a brocaded chair, surreptitiously watching the two girls, both of whom were slightly older than her and very stylishly dressed in the latest drop-waist fashion. Her aunt Edith did not make much of an impression, nor did Uncle Harold, who did not look at all like her father or Aunt Grace.

While the adults talked, the young ones sat in polite silence, Charlotte and Melanie handling their cups and plates with extraordinary finesse. Their training, Mona soon learned, had been obtained at Farnsworth's Academy, the very school in which she would be enrolling the next day. "Charlotte will show you around," Edith said. "She's thirteen and will have a different set of friends, of course. But you *are* cousins."

Charlotte and her friend exchanged a secretive, amused look, and Mona wanted to vanish into the upholstery.

"You know, Rose," said Harold, frowning at the African girl who hovered near the doorway, "I hadn't expected you to bring a pickaninny with you. What shall we do with her?"

"She sleeps outside Mona's door."

Edith looked at her husband. "Perhaps it would be best if we put her in the servants' quarters. Your letter was so vague, Rose, we had no idea what to expect."

The conversation became adult and boring, about who had died, moved away, married, and had babies. All the news of Suffolk was wrapped up in speech beyond Mona's understanding or interest, and while Charlotte and Melanie resorted to whispering and giggling, Mona stared out the window and wondered if the long rains had come to Kenya.

Dinner, she discovered to her dismay, was to be taken separately— her mother with Uncle Harold and Aunt Edith and Lady Ester; she with the two thirteen-year-olds. "But, Mummy," Mona protested as she was getting settled in a bedroom that was big and cold and damp, "you and I *always* eat together. Why do I have to eat in the nursery?"

Rose laid out Mona's things, her manner distracted. "Because it is the way it is done here, Mona. It's the *proper* way of doing things."

"But I thought we were proper at Bellatu."

Rose sighed, and a troubled expression briefly crossed her face. "I'm afraid we've let things slide a bit over the years. I just hadn't noticed. Africa does that to one. We shall have to correct that. Which is why, Mona, you are going to attend Farnsworth's Academy. By the time you come out, you will be a polished young lady."

Mona was engulfed with despair. "When will that be?"

"When you are eighteen."

"But that is *such* a long time! I shall perish from being away from Kenya!"

"Nonsense. You'll come home for holidays. And you'll soon make friends among the lovely girls at the school."

Mona started to cry. Rose came and sat next to her on the bed and said, "Now, now, Mona. What a bother over nothing!" She laid her arm lightly about her daughter's shoulders; it felt to Mona like a mist. Her mother's perfume enveloped her, and she ached to be held by warm flesh. "Listen, poppet," Rose said quietly, "when I get home, I shall start on the tapestry again. Why don't you tell me what to put in the blank spot? In ten years I haven't been able to think of what should go there. I'll leave that to you. Would you like that?"

Mona sniffed back her tears and drew away from her mother. It was no use. There was simply no way to make her parents understand the pain in her heart, her anguish at being sent away, the certain knowledge that she wasn't loved and that they were, in fact, glad to be rid of her. *If only I were pretty or smart,* she thought, *then they would love me.*

And if I were suddenly to disappear, then they would realize how much they missed me.

"WHAT IS IT like, living among naked savages?" asked Melanie Van Allen, a pert girl with bangs and shingled hair and an eye that looked as if she sought out trouble.

"They're not naked," Mona said as she moved the food around her plate.

The three were sitting at a table in what was called the nursery and were being waited on by footmen. Njeri was in the corner at a smaller table, eating in glum silence.

"I once read," said Charlotte, "that they are cannibals and don't believe in God."

"They believe in God," said Mona.

"Yes, now that they've been made Christian."

"Do you actually play with her?" Melanie asked, pointing to the African girl at the other table.

"No. She was brought along as my companion."

"Don't you have any *white* friends?"

"There's Gretchen Donald. And Geoffrey and Ralph, her brothers. They live on a cattle ranch called Kilima Simba."

Charlotte whispered something to Melanie, and they both giggled.

"Ralph is very handsome!" Mona said, thrusting out her chin.

Melanie leaned across the table, her eyes flashing. "Do you shoot lions and tigers?"

"My father does. But there are no tigers in Africa."

"Of course there are! You don't know very much about your own country, do you?"

Mona closed her ears and eyes and took refuge in a vision of Bellatu. She saw the golden sunshine and the flowers; she saw Arthur, her little brother, with his perpetually scraped knees, and against the blue sky, the silhouette of her father astride his stallion. She heard the cheers of the rowdy polo matches that took place on the field down by the river and smelled the aroma of the bull roasted every New Year's and divided among the Africans who worked the estate. Mona felt the sun on her bare arms, the red dust beneath her feet, the highland wind play with her hair. She tasted Solomon's millet cakes and Mama Gachiku's sugar-cane beer. Her thoughts swirled in a kaleidoscope of English, Swahili, and Kikuyu. She yearned to be sitting not at this odious dining table but in Aunt Grace's cottage, rolling bandages and sharpening needles. She thought of Ralph Donald, Gretchen's brave and dashing brother, who ran wild like an antelope and who enthralled her with stories of the bush.

"I must say your manners are appalling."

Mona looked at Charlotte.

"I was talking to you. Are you deaf?" Charlotte turned to Melanie and said in a suffering tone, "She's my cousin, and so *I* am expected to show her off to the school! What will they think of her? Of *me?*"

Melanie laughed. "Trudy Greystone bet with me that your cousin would wear a grass skirt and have a bone through her nose."

Mona's chin trembled. "Kenya's not like that."

"What's it like then? Do you live in a hut?"

"We have a *grand* house."

"Bellatu," said Charlotte. "Whatever is *that* name supposed to mean?"

"It means—" Mona frowned. The name had something to do with *this* house, Bella Hill; she knew they were somehow tied together. It had to do with the fact that this glorious mansion was more her house than Charlotte's, that her aunt and uncle and cousin were only guests here, *caretakers,* Rose had once said. But it was all too complex for Mona.

"Oh, well," said Charlotte with a martyr's sigh, "you'll learn manners at the academy. They'll see to that!"

MONA FOUND NJERI sleeping on a cot outside her door, and she woke her, whispering, "Get up! We're running away!"

Njeri rubbed her eyes. "What is wrong, Memsaab Mdogo?" she said sleepily, calling her by the name Rose insisted she use, which means "little mistress."

"Get up! We're running away."

Mona was wearing her riding habit, red velvet jacket and white breeches. It seemed more suited to running away than a dress did. And she carried a bundle of things tied in a pillowcase: her hairbrush and comb, facecloth, a half-eaten bag of sweets, and a few articles of clothing.

"Where will we go, Memsaab Mdogo?" Njeri asked, getting up from the cot and shivering.

"Just away. They must not find us for a long time. They must think I am dead. And when they do find me, they will never think of sending me away from Kenya ever again."

"But I don't want to run away."

"You'll do what I say. You heard what my uncle called you. A pickaninny! You know what that means, don't you?"

Njeri shook her head.

"It means *stupid.* You're not going to be stupid, are you?"

"But I don't want to run away!"

"Be quiet and come along. We'll stop first in the kitchen and get some bully beef and maize flour. We shall be gone a long time, and we'll need food."

Unhappily Njeri followed her down the dark hall, terrified of its shadows and peculiar flat people on the walls. Mona carried a flashlight, which spread a dim beam on the carpet before them. Their steps were muffled on the thick weave; the house slept on in night silence.

At the end of the hall the flashlight swept briefly over something that caught Mona's attention. She stopped and stared up at the portrait, holding the light on a familiar face.

"Why," she breathed, "it's Aunt Grace! Looking ever so pretty!"

Njeri looked up, mystified. She recognized Memsaab Daktari.

"But hasn't she got funny clothes on?" Mona said. Then she realized that it wasn't her aunt at all, but a woman who looked very much like her.

Mona moved the light away from the portrait and resumed walking down the hall without having realized two things: that the face she had just seen was that of the grandmother she had never known—Grace and Valentine and Harold's mother, Mildred—and that its features bore a striking resemblance to her own.

When they rounded a corner, Mona stopped short, and Njeri bumped into her. "Someone's coming!" Mona hissed. They scrambled back around and ducked into an alcove.

The two children watched with wide eyes, their teeth chattering with fear and cold, as a portly figure in a dressing gown went up to a closed door. It was Uncle Harold. He knocked and entered, closing the door behind himself.

When she heard voices inside the room, Mona crept forward and pressed her ear to the wood. She recognized her uncle's voice and then her mother's.

"I'm sorry to disturb you at this hour, Rose," Harold was saying, "but what I have to tell you is very important and can't wait until morning. I'll come right to the point. Rose, you've got to tell Valentine to stop his spendthrift ways."

"Whatever are you talking about?"

"He hasn't answered any of my letters. The next shall come from the family solicitor, you can tell him that for me. Rose? Will you please put down that yarn and look at me?"

There was a murmur, and then Harold boomed, "At the rate Valentine is going, there will be nothing left of Bella Hill! He's selling land right and left. It's barely half the size it was ten years ago."

"But he *owns* Bella Hill, Harold," said Rose's gentle voice. "He can do what he likes with it. After all, it's not as if this were *your* house."

"Rose, I appreciate the fact that my brother allows us to live here. But I cannot stand by while he ruins the family inheritance and home. You must tell him to curtail his spending."

"Oh, Harold, you're imagining things."

"Rose, the coffee farm is running at a loss. It has been ever since he started it."

Mona heard her mother laugh. "What nonsense! We have parties every weekend, houseguests. We are hardly impoverished, Harold!"

He made an exasperated sound. "And another thing," he said. "Here. Read this. It's a letter from Grace. She wants you to come home at once. It's something to do with your son."

"Poor little Arthur. He can't help being a clumsy boy. You know, he's forever falling down, banging his head, cutting his elbows. It infuriates Valentine."

"Rose, this is serious. Read the letter."

"Harold, I'm frightfully tired right now."

"There's one more thing, Rose. You can't enroll Mona in Farnsworth's tomorrow."

"Why ever not?"

"Because it's an expense Valentine cannot afford. I won't have him selling off more Bella Hill land just to send his daughter to an expensive school."

"Of *course* we can afford to send Mona to Farnsworth's!"

"Rose, you are living in a fool's paradise. Hasn't Valentine told you anything about your financial affairs? That farm is being run on a bank overdraft and proceeds from Bella Hill sales! It's only a matter of time before the whole thing collapses!"

"Mona is going to the academy, and that's all there is to it."

"I'm afraid not, Rose. In order for her to attend that school, she must have a sponsor here in England who will be responsible for her. That is one of the rules. I am taking back my offer to be that guardian. You must take Mona back with you to Kenya, on the first available boat. As far as I'm concerned, the matter is closed."

"Then I shall find someone else to sponsor her."

"Who? You have no family left, Rose. Do be reasonable. Keep the child in Kenya, where you can be near her. I know for a fact that Lady Ashbury's niece attends the European school in Nairobi and that it is very highly regarded. You'll see, Rose. It's the best thing."

On the other side of the door the two children looked at each other. Then Mona slumped against the wall and smiled.

She was going home.

22

"Daktari! Daktari!"

Grace looked up to see Mario running into the compound. He thundered up the steps of her new thatch clinic, past the crowd of patients waiting on the veranda, and burst in. "Memsaab Daktari!" he cried breathlessly. "Come quick!"

In their years together Grace had rarely seen Mario so excited. "What is it?" she said as she handed the child she had been examining to the nurse.

"My sister! She is *dying!*"

Grabbing her medical bag and pith helmet, Grace followed Mario down the veranda steps and through the compound that was formed by six thatch buildings. They ran between clotheslines where mattresses and sheets from the inpatient ward were airing, past the goat and sheep paddock, through the cluster of huts where her ten employees were housed, out through the fence that enclosed Grace Treverton Mission, across Valentine's polo field, past Wachera's hut, across the wooden bridge, and up the opposite slope, where women harvesting ripe beans in the fields paused to watch the memsaab fly by, her white skirt billowing, the familiar black bag in her hand.

Mario led his mistress along narrow paths between acres of maize that was in cob and taller than them, across patches of sweet potatoes and pumpkins growing over the ground in tangled mats, past one village, then another, until Grace was out of breath and clutching her side.

At last they came to Mario's village, nestled in the hills overlooking the Chania River, a collection of round mud huts with cone-shaped papyrus roofs giving off spirals of blue smoke. When they entered the village, Grace saw that no one was working; people were standing about, and a strange silence hung in the air. She pushed through and saw to her surprise one of the priests from the Catholic mission, a young man named Father Guido, fetching something from the pack on his bicycle.

"What has happened, Father?" she asked as she drew close.

His face looked darkly angry beneath the broad rim of his sun hat. His black cassock was dusty and sweat-stained; he, too, had come in a hurry. "There has been another secret initiation, Doctor," he said. And then Grace saw what he was retrieving from his pack: items used in performing the last rites.

"Dear God," she whispered, and followed him.

Several elders barred the way to the hut; mothers and aunts raised their hands and cried for the *wazungu* not to interfere.

"Who is in there with her?" Grace asked Father Guido.

"Wachera Mathenge, the medicine woman."

"How did you hear about this?"

"From Mario. This village is nearly all Catholic. The girl is named Teresa; she attends our school. *Kwenda!*" the priest said to the grim-faced elders. "You must let me enter! Teresa belongs to the Lord!"

Grace studied the fixed expressions of the men and women, law-abiding Kikuyu who normally deferred to the authority of a priest. But this was no ordinary situation.

The missionaries had been trying for a long time to abolish the practice of circumcision on girls, which involved the surgical removal of the clitoris. It was officially outlawed in Kenya and called for a fine or imprisonment for anyone caught engaging in the ritual. On the surface the initiations appeared to have stopped. But in fact, they had only gone underground. Grace knew that such savage rites were now being conducted in secret places where the local police could not find out about them.

"Please let me see her," Grace said in Kikuyu. "Perhaps I can help."

"*Thahu!*" cried an old woman who must have been Teresa's grand-mother.

Grace felt Father Guido shift nervously at her side. The entire population of the village stood around them in a tight circle; tension and hostility were in the air. "When did the initiation take place?" she asked the priest quietly.

"I do not know, Dr. Treverton. I only know that twelve girls were involved and that Teresa is dying from an infection to the wound."

Grace appealed to the elders. "You *must* let us enter!"

But it was useless. For all their education and Christianizing these people were still strongly tied to the old ways. They went to church every Sunday at Father Guido's mission and then went into the forest to practice the ancient barbaric rituals.

"Shall I call the District Officer?" Grace said. "You will all be put in jail! He will take away all your goats and burn your huts to the ground! Is that what you want?"

The elders remained impassive. They blocked the doorway of the hut with arms folded.

"It is wrong what you have done!" cried Father Guido. "You have committed an abomination in the sight of God!"

Finally one of the elders spoke. "Does not the Bible tell us that Lord Jesu was circumcised?"

"Indeed, it does. But nowhere does it say His blessed mother *Mary* was!"

Several pairs of eyes blinked. One elderly aunt glanced over her shoulder.

"Have we not taught you that the old ways are bad? Did you not embrace the love of Jesus Christ and promise to keep His laws?" Father Guido pointed a shaking finger toward the sky. His voice rang over their heads. "You will be cast out of heaven for what you have done! You will burn in the hellfire of black Satan for your evil sins."

Grace saw the stony faces start to break. Then Mario stepped forward and pleaded in rapid Kikuyu with his relatives to let the holy man and the memsaab into Teresa's hut.

There was a moment of silence, in which seven Kikuyu elders matched the stares of the two white people; then the old grandmother stepped to one side.

Father Guido and Grace entered the hut and found Teresa lying on a bed of fresh leaves; the darkness was filled with the drone of flies and the pungent scent of ceremonial herbs. Kneeling at her side was Wachera.

While Father Guido knelt opposite, opening his small bag and removing the silk stole and holy water, implements for the administering of the final sacrament, Grace bent to examine the girl.

The wound had been treated in what Grace knew to be the ritualistic way, a strict formula handed down through the generations. Special leaves had been dipped in antiseptic oil and bound between Teresa's legs. They had been changed recently, no doubt by the specially appointed "nurse," who would bury the old leaves in a secret, taboo place where no man might accidentally walk. Teresa would also have been fed special food of a religious nature, Grace knew, and she would have eaten it off a banana leaf.

The whole process of initiation into womanhood was a sacred and holy thing, something few whites had ever witnessed, and it was as sacred and meaningful to the Kikuyu as the mass conducted at the altar was to Catholics. But it was a cruel and inhumane practice which caused a great deal of pain and suffering and blood loss and a deformity that created problems for the woman in later life, such as difficulty in childbirth. Grace had joined the missionaries in the fight for its abolition.

Mario's sister was very pretty, Grace could see in what little light came into the hut. About sixteen years of age, she guessed, with delicate features and a touching innocence about her. Teresa's eyes were open. Grace gently closed them—because the girl was dead.

While Father Guido solemnly murmured the prayers of the last rites, Grace bowed her head and felt the sting of tears.

She was not praying; she was clenching her teeth in frustration and anger. Teresa was the fourth girl Grace had seen die as a result of blood poisoning after an initiation, brought on by the knife of the medicine woman who had performed the operation. She had also heard of other girls dying from infections that might have been cured if a European doctor had been called in time.

Grace looked up and met Wachera's eyes.

For an instant the air inside the hut was charged; the energies of the two rivals—Wachera and Grace—seemed to clash within the mud walls.

Then Grace said in Kikuyu, "I am going to see that your evil practices are brought to an end. I know the black magic you practice. I have heard from my patients. I have tolerated you long enough. Because of you and others like you, this child is dead."

While Grace trembled with anger, the medicine woman gazed back with a masked expression. Wachera was still beautiful, tall, and slender, with her head shaved, rows of beads and copper covering her long arms, her supple body dressed in soft hides. She was an anachronism among Christianized Kikuyu; Wachera existed like a ghost from their ancestral past. She gazed at Grace Treverton in arrogance and pride. Then she rose and left the hut.

GRACE RETURNED TO her mission to find Valentine pacing back and forth in front of the clinic building. When she saw what he had in his hand and the little boy who crouched in terror by the veranda steps, she knew why her brother had come.

"Look at this!" Valentine shouted, flinging the object at her. It hit Grace in the chest and fell to the ground. She picked it up and saw that it was one of Mona's dolls. "I caught him playing with it again!"

"Oh, Valentine." She sighed. "He's only seven years old." Grace walked past her brother and squatted beside Arthur, who, she saw at once, had received another parental thrashing.

"I will not have you mollycoddling him! You and Rose are turning my son into a Percy boy!"

Grace put her arms about Arthur, and he burst into tears. "Poor little thing," she murmured, stroking his hair.

"Damn it, Grace! Listen to me!"

She glared up at him. "No, you listen to me, Valentine Treverton! I have just seen a child who was *truly* ruined, and I will not listen to your shouting over something ridiculous. Another girl has died because of an initiation, and I was unable to save her. What are you doing about these initiations, Valentine? They're *your* people. You should care!"

"What's it to me what a bunch of blacks do? My only concern is for my son. I will not have him playing with dolls!"

"No," she said slowly. "You don't care what the Africans do. And you care more about yourself than about your son."

A deep flush raced up his neck as Valentine glowered at his sister, then turned and walked away.

Inside the cool thatch building that was her clinic, Grace comforted Arthur. He had bruises about his neck and shoulders.

"Hello," said a soft voice as a silhouette filled the open doorway.

Grace looked up. Her heart leaped. "James. You're home."

"I got in last night and came straight to see you— Hello, what's happened here?"

"Valentine again."

James stepped inside and said, "Hello, Arthur."

"Hello, Uncle James."

"My brother thinks he can terrorize his son into manhood," Grace said quietly, trying to keep the anger out of her voice so as not to frighten the boy. "I'm going to stop these beatings if I have to . . . You'll be all right, Arthur. You're not hurt badly."

"Have you written to Rose about it?"

"She should be arriving any minute now, in fact. Her letter wasn't very precise—you know Rose."

"Then Mona is in school in England?"

"Yes. At the academy Rose went to as a girl."

"You'll miss Mona, won't you?"

"Yes, terribly."

Grace gave her nephew a kiss on the head, then set him down on the floor, a boy who was too small for his age and who had inherited his mother's dreamy temperament. "Go on now, love," Grace said gently. "Go and play."

"Where shall I go?" he asked, bewilderment in his large blue eyes.

"Where would you *like* to go, Arthur?"

He pretended to think a moment. Then he said, "May I go and see the babies?"

She smiled and patted him on his way. Valentine had forbidden Arthur to set foot in Grace's maternity hut, but she had decided not to heed her brother's orders.

"James!" she said as they walked out of the clinic. "What a wonderful surprise to see you!"

They stepped outside, and when Grace looked at the way the sunshine brought out the auburn highlights in James's dark brown hair, she felt the familiar rush of love and the ache that never left her. Each time he went away she felt a part of herself go with him. When he came back, she was whole again.

"I missed you," she said.

They followed the path toward her house, passing the thatch buildings she had added. One of them was the small maternity clinic where Arthur spent most of his time looking at the newborn babies.

As James and Grace walked up onto the veranda of her cottage, she said, "What is the news from Uganda?"

"The same as always. Sleeping sickness, malaria, blackwater. Nothing new, I'm afraid. And you, Grace? How has the mission been these past four months?"

She went into the house and returned with two glasses of lemonade. Handing one to James, she said, "You've been gone *five* months. We have a new henhouse and a new blackboard for the classroom."

He laughed. "Here's to chickens and education," he said, and they drank.

James studied Grace over the rim of his glass. She looked as neat and crisp as usual. Despite the demands of running her mission school and clinic, Grace was always dressed in a clean white blouse and skirt, her short hair always in place. And she was even more beautiful, he thought, than when he had last seen her.

"Is something troubling you, Grace?"

"There's been another initiation. Mario's sister died." She sat in a wicker chair. "I have to be firmer with these people, James. I've got to put my foot down and make them realize that the old ways are bad for them. This is the twentieth century. Modern medicine is reaching a peak that is unknown in all of history. We work miracles these days. But *still*, when they're frightened, they run to a tribal healer."

"Traditional healing isn't all bad, Grace."

"Yes, it is. It's witchcraft, plain and simple. Who knows what that woman puts into her concoctions!" Grace waved a hand toward Valentine's polo field and the hut at its end.

Wachera's homestead was now, after so many years, such a familiar part of the scene that it no longer aroused comment. Indeed, many European farms were now peppered with "squatter" homesteads—the small plots of Africans who had come out of the Reserves and who chose to work for the white man and live as a tenant on his land—so that Wachera's presence at the end of the polo field was no longer the oddity it had once been. The young medicine woman, Grace knew, lived a strange, secret life, going silently about her ancient business like a shadow at the periphery of one's vision. But Grace knew what she did. Her patients told her.

Mathenge's widow led the people on spirit hunts whenever an epidemic struck, she supervised planting ceremonies before the rains, she made magical charms to keep children safe, she delivered babies, she brewed love potions, she talked to the spirits of the dead, and she read the future. She also, Grace suspected, wielded the knife during the initiations of girls.

"I think," Grace said quietly, "that the District Commissioner is going about it the wrong way. Simply making something illegal doesn't make it disappear. What we have to do is outlaw the perpetrators of such barbarism. Wachera and people like her must be removed, and then the old practices will die naturally."

"How do you propose to get rid of her? Valentine tried without success."

"I don't know. I shall go down to Nairobi and organize the missions into a more unified effort. The Africans must be made to see that traditional healing is bad and that the white doctor is the person they must go to."

James took out his pipe and lit it. "I'm afraid I disagree with you, Grace. I still maintain there is a lot of good in traditional healing. Remember when I had that outbreak of dysentery among my chaps and I was all out of Epsom salts and castor oil? It was the old Kikuyu rhubarb remedy that saved them."

She shook her head. "We never took smears, James. We never did a microscopic analysis. You don't know for sure it was dysentery or even amoebic."

"Not everything has to be diagnosed through modern medicine, Grace. You know, there is such a thing as being too one-sided."

"You wouldn't be saying that if you had seen that poor girl this afternoon."

Suddenly a group of boys came running around the corner of the classroom hut, laughing and looking back over their shoulders. When they saw Grace on the veranda, they immediately drew up to attention and presented serious faces. "Jambo, Memsaab Daktari," they said, and marched by like little black soldiers.

"Merciful heaven," she murmured, rising from her chair, "what *are* they up to now?"

At the rear of the long structure that was the school, she found a little girl lying on the ground, covered in mud. "Wanjiru," Grace said, going to her.

Helping the nine-year-old to her feet and brushing the dirt off her dress, Grace said, "There, there, Wanjiru. You're not hurt, are you?"

Close to tears but holding them back, the little girl shook her head no.

"Would you like to go home?"

She shook her head more fiercely.

"Very well then. Go and find Memsaab Pammi and tell her I said you could have a sweet."

The child mumbled a shy *asante sana,* then turned and ran to the entrance of the schoolhouse, where Miss Pamela was having a tea break between lessons.

"Is she one of your pupils?" James asked as they walked back to Birdsong Cottage. "I didn't know you had female students."

"She is my first girl, and I'm afraid she's having a terrible time of it. You know what a struggle I've had trying to get girls to come to my school. Three months ago a woman from one of the villages upriver brought her daughter to the school and enrolled her."

"That took courage."

"Indeed! The woman is a widow with nine children. She has a very hard life, and she told me that she wants something better for Wanjiru. She's the first African woman I've heard express that sentiment. I'm thrilled to have the girl, of course, but the boys tease her mercilessly. They taunt her and tell her she'll never marry and she'll be *thahu* because she was doing a man's thing. Yet she comes every day, more determined than ever. And she's a good learner, which I think the boys also resent."

When they reached the veranda, Grace said, "Something must be done about the plight of African women, James. You know, we had a locust invasion two months ago and the men blamed the *women* for it! They said it was because the women were wearing short skirts and God sent the locusts as a punishment."

She turned to him. "James, I have measured some of the loads these women carry. One woman was carrying as much as a hundred and eighty pounds! And the birthrate is so high. You see many women with eight or ten children, working their farm plots all alone because their men have gone to work for the white man. Now that young African men are becoming educated, they don't want to stay on the farms anymore. They want to work in the cities. They come home for visits, get their wives pregnant, and disappear again. And they are very much against education for their wives and daughters."

James looked at her, at the face that had gotten brown in ten years, with creases around the eyes and a chin just as determined as ever. It was a face which he pictured often and which visited him in dreams. "Can we walk, Grace?"

The Africans who worked at Grace's mission no longer wore goat-skins and *shukas* but trousers and shirts and European-style dresses. Heads were no longer shaved but covered with closely cropped hair. A few still sported wooden cylinders in their earlobes and copper beaded bracelets, but for the most part the only adornment was a small cross on a chain.

Grace paused at the back of a wooden shed to inspect the rows of waterpot filters that were being readied for distribution among the villagers. Each filter consisted of two round clay pots, the smaller one seated in the mouth of the larger. She demonstrated to James how they worked. "The top pot contains a layer of clean sand, a layer of clean gravel, and finally a layer of broken brick. The water is poured in through the top, and as it drips through these layers into the pot below, it is cleansed of impurities, especially the guinea worm. I'm trying to install one in each village hut, with a lesson in the vital importance of water purity."

"This would be something valuable to include in your book," James said.

Grace laughed. James had begun pressing her to write a health manual for nonmedical rural workers. "When would I have time to write a book?"

They walked past a clothesline where mattresses were airing. These were made of americani stuffed with dried corn sheaves and, like the filters, were Grace's invention.

They climbed the path up to the ridge and emerged onto a view that might have been a painting. Rows of lush green coffee bushes, heavy with ripe berries, covered five thousand acres. The landscape was not flat but rose and fell in waves and hillocks like a gently undulating sea, the dense green interrupted by stripes of red dirt and tall breaks of jacaranda trees bursting in purple flowers. It was May now, and the long rains had ended; women and children moved along the rows, picking the berries and filling their sacks. Trucks awaited them at the edges of the fields, and men transported the berries to the dryers and tumblers down by the river. Mount Kenya guarded the distant border of the immense vista, sharp and dark against a clear sky, its snow-streaked peaks shining in the sun. Directly facing the mountain across the valley was Bellatu, lifted skyward on perfect green lawns and terraced gardens.

Several shiny automobiles were parked in the drive. Grace recognized one as belonging to Brigadier Norich-Hastings. The others, except for the two Oldsmobiles which belonged to Valentine, were owned by her brother's current houseguests.

Bellatu was never quiet. Now that cars were commonplace in Kenya, and a road, although still dirt and impassable during the rains, came all the way to the estate—and now that the train reached Nyeri town— it was but a day's journey from Nairobi. Valentine's house had become the social center of Kenya; there was always a party, a fox hunt, a polo match going on which drew East Africa's rich and fast set to the coffee plantation. A legend had grown up around Bellatu. To those who only ever glimpsed the fabulous house from a distance, it seemed that the people inside must be eternally young and beautiful, they did the smart things and drank champagne, and only the wealthy and aristocratic were visitors. The twenties had been a boom decade for the Kenya gentleman settler; Treverton coffee was now shipped all over the world and in great demand. Grace's brother reigned like a king—and he was never alone.

Grace stared at the house, hearing, when the wind shifted, music and laughter.

She resented Valentine for what he was doing to Arthur, trying to bully him into being a man. The boy had received more than one severe beating for being caught with his sister's dolls, and his awkwardness and spells of falling were not, as Valentine argued, staged for attention but were possibly the result of a neural problem. Grace had begged her brother to send Arthur to specialists, but Valentine had told her to mind her own business. No son of his was weak or handicapped, and any sign of weakness or effeminacy was going to be knocked out of him.

When had Valentine changed? she wondered. It had been a gradual process. Ever since that terrible business with Miranda West, it seemed to Grace, and then with the birth of Arthur. Everyone in Kenya knew that Valentine kept an African mistress in Nairobi, in the very house he had built for Miranda. She was a beautiful Meru woman who wore expensive clothes and drove her own car.

James walked past Grace, his boots crunching the red earth, and squinted in the sunlight. She watched his hard, lean body as he reached for a strip of eucalyptus bark and began to shred it, deep in thought. His frequent visits to Uganda of late, which were for Lucille, who had developed a passion for the inland African country, were more wearing on Grace than her long days filled with hard work. She missed him sharply. When he was so many miles away, in such dangerous territory, she lost her appetite and tossed and turned at night. But when he was at home on Kilima Simba, she was comforted, knowing he was there, just a few miles away. There was the constant anticipation of his unexpected visits. They were what had kept her going these past ten years, what gave her energy to get through days of frustration and setbacks. Grace would come out of the clinic and James would be standing there, dusty and sweaty from the long drive, usually with a gift—something from the dairy, a kill for the pot. He would stay awhile; they would sit on her veranda and talk quietly like the two old friends they were, sharing troubles, offering help and advice, laughing, or even just sitting in silence, close together but not touching, as the African day winked into night.

Then he would leave, and Grace would lie in her bed so badly in want of him that sleep sometimes never came.

"Grace," he said now, "I have something to tell you."

She looked at him.

"Lucille and I have decided to move to Uganda and live there. Permanently."

23

G race stared at him. Then abruptly she looked away.
"I'm sorry," he said. "We only decided it on this last visit."
"When will you go?"
"As soon as I can arrange shipment of our things. Lucille stayed
behind this time. She's in Entebbe, getting our new house in order."
Grace walked a few steps from him and reached out to a eucalyptus
tree to steady herself. Its shade seemed to swallow her; the day felt
suddenly dark, as if clouds covered the sun.
"What about the ranch and the children?" she finally said.
"I'm leaving the operating of the ranch to Sven Thorsen. He's been
with me for two years and is quite capable of managing it on his own.
Geoffrey will stay on at Kilima Simba. He's seventeen now and keen
on ranching. But Ralph and Gretchen will go with us."
"What will you do in Uganda?"
"Lucille has joined the Scottish mission there. She wants to dedicate
herself to its work."
"And you?"
"I've been offered an administrative post in Entebbe."
She turned and looked at him. The sun shone down on a man whose
arms were sunburned and whose body was lean from years of rugged
outdoor living. "You'll work in an *office?*" she said.
"I'm forty-one, Grace, and not getting younger. Lucille thought I
should slow down. And I'm, not needed around the ranch the way I
used to be. It's practically running itself, and it's doing well. Sven will
oversee things."
Grace knew the Donalds were doing well financially, that their days

of overdraft and making do were over. It had come as no surprise to
her when, last year, Hardy Acres had informed her of an increase in
the yearly deposit into her account.

"I will miss you," she said.

"And I, you." He came up to her, standing close and looking down
with intense eyes. "It was not an easy decision to make, Grace. But you
know how unhappy Lucille has been."

"Yes."

"She's a different woman in Uganda. She's genuinely happy there.
I can't refuse her."

"No."

Her senses were assailed: the smell of his body, the coarse look of his
safari jacket, the sound of a voice at once commanding and humorous
and tender; his overwhelming *nearness.* James had always been there
for her, if not as a lover, then as someone to love; he was the secret
passion that was better than no passion. Dreams of him had made her
nights less lonely, her bed less empty; his quiet, reliable strength had
helped her through days of frustration and failure; he had shared her
triumphs, too. The physical loving that she ached for could never be,
she had always known that, but there was the occasional touch, the
fingers on her arm—and an embrace under the trees out of the rain,
at a homecoming, through ten New Year's Eves. . . .

A long time ago Grace had removed Jeremy Manning's engagement
ring; she had taken James Donald into her heart and kept him there,
her secret soul mate. But now a terrible door was opening, and he was
walking through it. For the first time Grace was aware of her age.
Suddenly years seemed significant. *I shall be forty next year.*

"I will miss you," she said again.

"I'll come tomorrow and say good-bye."

Tomorrow? she thought. The beginning of the true meaning of
loneliness came to her. She saw the nights stretch before her, like a
string of desolate little train stations where there was no light, no life.
She saw herself in the future, sitting on her veranda, prim and chaste,
gazing through the darkness past the mission she had built, across the
polo field, where, she realized, there was a little hut where another lone
woman—Wachera—sat at her cook pot, stirring, stirring.

Grace drew back. "Say good-bye to me now, James. I don't know what I shall say to you tomorrow."

He put his hands on her arms. Their grip was tight. He bent his head to kiss her.

"Auntie Grace! Auntie Grace!"

They turned. A spidery little figure was flying down the drive from the gate where one of the Treverton cars stood with a door open. It was an imp with an impossible haircut and outlandish imitation-adult clothes, and it sprang through the air to clamp arms about Grace's waist. "Oh, Auntie!" Mona squealed. "How I've missed you!"

It came too quickly, joy upon grief. Grace dropped to her knees and pulled her niece into a desperate embrace. The girl started instantly to talk of ships and trains, of France and horrible cousins, then said, "Don't cry, Auntie Grace. I'm back now, and I shall never leave Kenya ever again!"

"Mona," Grace said in a tight voice, "what are you doing here? What happened to the academy?"

"Uncle Harold said I couldn't go! Auntie Grace, are you all right? Why are you crying?"

"I'm just so happy to see you, darling. Look at you. A proper young lady now."

"I was nine when I left; now I'm ten and a third. England was horrid, Auntie Grace. I'm ever so glad I came back."

Seeing Rose coming now toward her, Grace stood up and went to her sister-in-law. "Welcome home, Rose," she said.

"It's wonderful to be back," Rose said as she linked an arm through Grace's. They walked to the ridge and looked down at the churning river. The banks were thickly green and bursting with wildflowers of every color. "How I missed this place! And I'm so anxious to get back to my tapestry!"

Grace, numb, moving like an overrehearsed actor, watched little Njeri come shyly out of the car. The girl stayed close by Rose, as if afraid. Grace looked at the child with sharp affection; Njeri was the baby she had lifted from Gachiku's womb. "Njeri," she said, bending down, "don't you want to go home and see your mama?"

The nine-year-old hung back and shook her head.

"She's become quite attached to me, I'm afraid," Rose said with a laugh, patting the girl on the head. "Aren't you, Njeri? You should have seen the attention she got in Europe. And she's such a help to me. She loves to spend hours brushing my hair. Njeri can go home later. She wants to stay and help me sort my new yarn."

Mona was watching. She swallowed back her jealousy and pain and reached for her aunt's hand.

Grace stared at Rose. This was all too unreal. Here was Rose after an eight-month absence, acting as if she had just arrived for tea! Why wasn't she asking about Arthur? About Valentine? And why had Mona come back with her instead of staying behind at the academy?

Grace's head swam. She wasn't ready for all this—the homecoming and the leave-taking with James.

"Auntie Grace," said Mona, tugging her hand, "are you crying because of me?"

She looked down at her niece and said, "I'm happy because you're home and also sad because Uncle James is going away. He and Aunt Lucille are going to live in Uganda."

Mona looked up at James, her eyes round. "Are Gretchen and Ralph going, too?"

"I'm afraid so," he said.

Then Mona, too, looked sad, and tears formed in her eyes.

Grace knelt and took the girl's face in her hands. "Don't worry, Mona," she said softly. "You and I still have each other." She thought: *You may have to come and live with me. It's all too strange. Your mother seems less present, less real than ever. I will mother you, Mona; you will be the daughter my body will never have. There is a love emptiness in you, dear child, as there now is in me. We need each other.*

"Where is Valentine?" Rose suddenly asked.

"I'M TELLING YOU, Treverton, London has got to be made to listen!" Brigadier Norich-Hastings put down his glass and strode to the lead-paned window that gave onto a spectacular view of Mount Kenya. "We need to have one of us go and present our case in person to His Majesty's government."

"Hugh is right," said Hardy Acres from the deep comfort of a wing chair.

Valentine was sitting behind his desk, chair rocked back and feet propped up. He swirled his glass and watched the whiskey go 'round and 'round.

A fourth man in Valentine's study, Malcolm Jennings, was a rancher from the Rift Valley who owned more than a hundred thousand choice acres in the Central Province and who therefore had a personal interest in the colony's politics. He hadn't spoken yet, but he did now. "South Africa's got the right idea. We should follow its example and form a white union. Say, Uganda, Kenya, and Tanganyika. Maybe even Northern Rhodesia. We need to reinforce the policy of white domination in East Africa, remind the wogs who really rule here."

"I'm bloody sorry *this* was printed," said Acres, flinging a Kenya newspaper to the floor. His friends knew what he was referring to: the white paper published recently in London by Lord Passfield, the new colonial secretary. In it he withdrew his support of the white settler demands in Kenya and stated that "the British objective in the Colony was a ministry representing an electorate in which *every* section of the population finds an effective and adequate vote," adding that this was very nearly impossible to achieve in a country where less than one percent of the population had the vote!

"If the wogs read *this*," said Acres, "it'll start trouble."

"Trouble's already started," said the brigadier grimly. "Passfield's forbidden the governor to restrict meetings of the Kikuyu Central Association. He's bloody well *inviting* them to start a revolution! Now they're asking for land grants in the Highlands. Before you know it, the wogs will get permission to grow coffee!"

The three men looked expectantly at their host. Valentine appeared not even to be listening to them. His dark eyes were staring moodily at a photograph in a silver frame on his desk.

He was thinking of Arthur. He shouldn't have hit him so hard, but the boy did infuriate him at times. Where had the child gotten such peculiar notions? Here it was May, and Arthur hadn't even touched the Christmas presents his father had given him: the set of toy soldiers with miniature cannon; the rifle; the hunting knife.

He picked up the photograph and looked hard at it. His heart broke at the sight of Arthur's innocent, cherubic face, the sweet little smile, the khaki shorts he never seemed to keep buttoned. *My son,* cried

Valentine's tormented mind. *You are what I live for, what I built this house for. I never want to hurt you. I just want you to grow up to be a man.*

"Treverton?" said Hardy Acres.

I'll make it up to you, my son. I'm sorry I hit you. I promise you I won't do it again. . . .

"Valentine?" said Malcolm Jennings. "Are you with us?"

He looked up. "I beg your pardon?" He put the picture down and got up to go to the whiskey cart. "I'm not worried about an uprising. All my chaps ever want to do is sit under a tree and drink beer."

"Then you're blind, Treverton," said Jennings.

Valentine ignored the effrontery. His thoughts were still upon Arthur, wondering if maybe it was time to take the boy on his first hunting safari.

"We came here for your opinion in this matter," said Brigadier Norich-Hastings. "Talk to us, Valentine."

"My chaps have never had it so good," he said distractedly. "I give them all the americani and bicycles they want. They're as docile as sheep. And they'll stay that way as long as I continue to treat them right."

The three men exchanged a look. The brigadier said, "Valentine, open your eyes! Some of these wogs are starting to grouse that the Highlands are rightfully theirs and that they never voluntarily gave them up!"

Valentine refilled his glass, stared at it thoughtfully, then took a drink and turned to his companions. "Who were you thinking of sending to London?"

"We thought you would be good, Valentine."

"Me!"

"After all, you hold a seat in the House of Lords. Your name isn't without certain influence. And you're a good speaker. They'll listen to you."

Valentine rubbed his chin. The thought of returning to England did not appeal in the least. The last time he had been there was at an exhibition in 1924, when he had represented Nairobi coffee, now called Kenya coffee. And in Rose's one letter from Suffolk she had described England as being just as cold and damp and unwelcoming as ever.

"Well? What do you say?"

"Perhaps . . ." He could take Arthur with him. Get the boy away from Rose's and Grace's feminizing influence.

"We haven't much time. The situation is getting more and more serious every day. If we're going to hang on to our land, we'll need the support of His Majesty's government."

"I say," said Hardy Acres, coming to his feet, "isn't that your car? The one you sent to the train station?"

Valentine went to the window and looked out. The Cadillac was pulling up the drive, empty but for the African chauffeur.

He walked out onto the veranda and shielded his eyes from the sun. A stiff breeze swept across the five thousand acres of lush coffee bushes and stirred his hair. This was the very spot he had stood upon ten years before, describing his dream to Rose and Grace. The scene which stretched away before him now was the very vision he had had in his mind on that long-ago day. "Where is the memsaab?" he asked the driver.

"She has gone with Memsaab Daktari, bwana," the man said, pointing to the ridge.

"HELLO THERE! WELCOME home!" he called, taking off his hat and waving it at Rose and Grace.

Rose waved back, then said to her sister-in-law, "That silly Harold. The notions he gets into his head!"

"What do you mean?"

"Look at Bellatu! Of *course,* we have money!"

Puzzled, Grace watched Rose pick her way delicately down the path to where Valentine greeted her with a kiss on the cheek. "I missed you," they said together.

Then a miniature person came running, down below them, from the doorway of the maternity hut. "Mama!" called Arthur, his chubby little legs pumping.

Valentine looked down. "What are you doing in there!" he shouted, his voice ringing across the river. "I've told you not to go in there anymore!"

Arthur stopped short and stared as his father flew down the hill.

"You deliberately defied me!" Valentine said when he reached him. He took Arthur by the collar and shook him.

Up on the ridge Grace and James watched. When she saw Arthur suddenly collapse to the ground, kicking and writhing, Grace gave out a cry and ran down the path.

By the time James and Rose joined them, Grace had managed to wedge a stick between Arthur's clenched teeth. He was twisting and turning in the dirt, eyes rolled back in his head, strange sounds coming from his throat. The adults stared down in horror; Mona came up silently.

It ended as quickly as it had begun. Grace started to lift the unconscious boy into her arms, but Valentine stepped in. Cradling him against his chest, he followed his sister into the clinic hut, where Grace did a thorough examination of Arthur.

Finally she said, "Epilepsy," and Valentine shouted, "No!"

"I've told you before to get the boy to a specialist," said Grace. "Now you'll *have* to do something!"

"There is nothing wrong with my son!"

"Damn it, Valentine, there is! And if you don't take him, then *I* will!"

He glared at his sister, matched her stubborn will heartbeat for heartbeat; then his shoulders slumped slightly.

"There are specialists in Europe," Grace said more gently, "men who are doing research on this condition."

"On insanity, you mean."

"Epilepsy has nothing to do with insanity. It has nothing to do with mental faculties at all. And epilepsy is nothing to be ashamed of. Julius Caesar had it. So did Alexander the Great."

Valentine turned a malevolent look upon Rose. "This comes from your side of the family," he said in a tone that shocked them all. Then he gathered the limp body of his son into his arms and drew it tightly to him. He pressed his mouth to the mop of grapefruit-colored hair that was damp with perspiration. Arthur seemed so small, so fragile. *My son. The only son I will ever have.* When Rose reached out to the boy, Valentine stepped back and said, "Don't touch him."

To Grace he said, "I will take him to England. I'll take him to every specialist in London. I'll go to the Continent if I have to. I'll spend every penny—" His voice broke.

They watched him go down the veranda steps and up the path toward the house, Arthur's doll-like arms and legs flopping. Rose took a different path, the one that led through the forest to her eucalyptus glade; she went so quickly that she looked like a woman in flight. Little Njeri trotted behind like a puppy, while Mona hovered in the shadow of the veranda, uncertain of what to do. Then she, too, headed off in the direction her mother had taken.

Out in the sunlight again, pushing hair from her face and taking in a deep breath, Grace looked around the little cluster of thatch buildings that was her mission. James came to stand at her side. "Are you going to be all right?" he asked.

"Yes."

He took her hand and held it tightly between his. "I'll stay awhile, Grace. Until Valentine leaves for England with the boy."

But she turned to him and said, "No, James. You don't belong here anymore. Your life lies far to the west, where Lucille and your children are waiting for you. They need you more than we do."

"I want you always to remember, Grace," he said quietly, "that if you ever do need me, all you have to do is send word and I will come. Will you promise me that?"

She faced the setting sun and nodded. "Let's say good-bye now, James. You must get started on your journey. It's a long way to Uganda."

24

A ll this land, my son, that you see around you and even beyond, belongs to the Children of Mumbi and to no one else."

David sat and listened to his mother as she talked while preparing their supper. Two plump sweet potatoes wrapped in banana leaves were growing soft over steam; millet grains burst in boiling water and thickened into porridge. Although many of the women in the village across the river were adopting the European custom of eating three meals a day, Wachera still practiced the old tradition of sitting down to one huge dinner in the late afternoon.

"The Children of Mumbi were tricked by the *wazungu*," she said, "into giving up their land. The white man didn't understand our ways. He saw forest where there were no huts, and so he took it because he said there was no one living there. He did not know that the ancestors lived there or that the forest would one day be cleared for the huts of our children's children. The white man does not think of the past or of the future; he sees only what is today."

David gazed worshipfully at his mother. She was the most beautiful woman he had ever seen. Now that he was approaching the threshold of manhood and would soon undergo the circumcision initiation, he was becoming aware of the way men looked at her; and women, too. The former was a hungry look; David knew that his mother was desired by men and often received offers of marriage. The latter was a look of envy—from women who secretly admired Wachera's life of freedom, with no man as her master. And everyone regarded the medicine woman with awe and respect.

Although she had no husband and only one child—under other

circumstances, reasons to pity her—Wachera was a revered woman among the clan because she was the keeper of the old ways. David had seen important people come to this hut over the years; his childhood was one long chronicle of chiefs and elders visiting and taking counsel with his mother, of women bringing their secrets and paying for charms and potions, of men offering their manhood. The little hut Wachera and David shared had heard the woes and joys of the Children of Mumbi, spoken through many mouths under many full moons. David was proud of his mother; he would die for her.

But there was so much he did not yet understand. He was eleven years old and anxious for manhood and the wisdom it seemed to bring. He wanted her to speak faster, to tell more, to shine light on the dark mysteries that plagued his young soul.

David sat on a troubled brink. Much of him was still child, so little yet man. But the child part longed for manhood and feared it might never come. There was another part of him, too, the Kikuyu part that looked enviously and longingly upon the white man's riches—his bicycles; his telegraph; his gun. David Kabiru Mathenge yearned to own such things, to possess such power, to be accepted into that elite corps. Long ago his father had had him baptized. Now David belonged to Lord Jesu, or so the *wazungu* said. Yet he was not the true brother they had promised he would be; he was not their equal. And so he resented them.

"Do not love the *wazungu*," his mother often told him. "Do not give them respect. Do not recognize their laws. But also, my son, do not take them lightly, but always remember the proverb that says a wise man faces a buffalo with caution."

"We will eat now," Wachera said at last, scooping millet stew onto banana leaves. "You will recite for me the list of ancestors back to the First Parents. Then we will go into the forest, where a secret meeting is to take place. A great man is coming to speak to the Children of Mumbi. You will listen, David Kabiru, and memorize his words, as you have memorized the list of ancestors."

WANJIRU HAD STAYED late at the school hut to help Memsaab Pammi, the teacher. This was not done out of love for the memsaab or out of a sense of duty to the school; the nine-year-old girl always looked for excuses to avoid the boys who walked the same path to her village and who teased her mercilessly along the way.

It was not that she was afraid of them; Wanjiru was afraid of nothing except the chameleon, which all Kikuyu feared. It was that her mother worked so hard to be respectable, and Wanjiru's dresses, torn or muddied at the hands of the boys, caused great grief.

Her chores done, Wanjiru said *kwa heri*, good-bye, to the memsaab and left the thatch classroom. The sun was setting. She would have to hurry if she was going to be home before dark. When she passed through the gate where a sign read GRACE TREVERTON MISSION, Wanjiru hesitated. Before her spread a flat bed of lush grass that was perplexing in its uselessness. No animals grazed there; no crops were grown. Yet it was tended by gardeners and inspected by the bwana who carried a whip. Once Wanjiru had seen horses galloping up and down the field with white men on their backs swinging great sticks, while at the sides, under the shade of camphor and olive trees, memsaabs in white hats and frocks called out as if their men were warriors.

But it was not the polo field which Wanjiru now contemplated; it was the hut at the end where two people she could just see in the waning light were finishing their supper.

She knew who they were. Wanjiru's mother often went to the medicine woman when the children were sick. And once the widow of the legendary Chief Mathenge had come to Wanjiru's village to speak to the people of the ancestors, and the family had celebrated with a great beer drink. Wachera fascinated the little girl. Even though the *wazungu* had forbidden the medicine woman to practice her ancient arts, she defied them; her defiance made all the people of the clan in awe of her. The boy, who Wanjiru knew was named David Kabiru, had only recently begun attending Memsaab Daktari's school. His mother had sent him to learn the ways of the white man, he had boasted, in preparation for the day when the Children of Mumbi would claim Kikuyuland as theirs again.

Wanjiru found the mother and son preparing to go into the forest. She heard Wachera speak to David in a grave voice. The little girl sensed something important in what they were about to do; as her curiosity mounted, she decided to follow them.

The way was long and fraught with evil spirits and golden eyes blinking in the bush. Wanjiru followed close behind, undetected, her young mind knowing how worried her mother was going to be but unable to resist the lure of the mysterious mother and son.

Eventually the medicine woman brought the boy into a glade where, to Wanjiru's surprise, many men were sitting in silence. She recognized a few from her own village. Most were dressed in *shukas* and blankets and carried staffs in place of spears, but a few were in European clothes because they worked at one of the missions. The little girl watched them as she crouched in the bushes.

There were no women at the gathering, but none of the men seemed to mind the medicine woman's presence. Indeed, a place was cleared, and a gourd of beer was handed to her. As if she were a man! Wanjiru thought, her eyes growing big.

More men arrived, coming silently and materializing suddenly out of the night. No fire had been lit; the glade was washed in the light of the full moon, a time when important business was conducted. The men sat on the dirt, on boulders, on fallen logs; they shared sugarcane beer, a few chewed *miraa* leaf stems to keep alert, and some passed around a bottle of *colobah*. Wanjiru knew what this last drink was; it was highly prized among Kikuyu men because it was the white man's liquor and illegal for Africans to possess, and thus it was called "color bar."

Wanjiru watched as the men sat in typical African patience. No one carried a watch; none cared about the movement of time. What Wanjiru did not know was that they had come here out of curiosity; word that a man named Johnstone was coming here tonight had passed from mouth to mouth. He was going to speak about the Kikuyu Central Association. Because of this, there were men hidden in the trees as guards. And every man at this meeting had taken a sacred oath of secrecy in order to weed out possible government informers. What they all were gathered here for tonight was illegal.

Presently a strange sound disturbed the forest silence. It was like the rumble of an elephant's belly, distant at first and growing louder until a few men jumped to their feet, prepared to flee. But it was the man Johnstone, arriving on his English motorbike.

The few who had heard him speak before commanded the group to silence and introduced him as Johnstone Kamau. A tall, powerfully built Kikuyu with a strong voice and piercing gaze, who wore, everyone saw, a tribal ornamental belt called *mucibi wa kinyata,* he strode into the center of the circle.

The men sat spellbound as he spoke of the destiny of the African, of the need to unite, of the need to become educated. Wachera and her son listened; little Wanjiru listened.

"In the old order of African society," Johnstone Kamau said, "with all the evils that are supposed to be connected with it, a man was a man, and as such he had the rights of a man and liberty to exercise his will and thought in a direction which suited his purposes as well as those of his fellowmen; but today an African, no matter what his station in life, is like a horse which moves only in the direction that the rider pulls the rein. . . . The African can only advance to a 'higher level' if he is free to express himself, to organize economically, politically, and socially, and to take part in the government of his own country."

When he was finished, silence rushed in behind his words. He looked around at the faces of his audience, pausing briefly to study the beautiful young medicine woman in ancestral dress. Then he said, "We are free to speak here."

A man named Murigo from Wanjiru's village said, "What are you telling us? That we should drive the white man out of Kikuyuland?"

"I speak not of revolution but of equality, my brother. Which of us here feels he is the equal of his white lord and master?"

Another man, Timothy Minjire, said, "The *wazungu* have given us so much! Before they came, we lived in sin and darkness. Now we have Jesu. We are modern in the eyes of the world."

Several men nodded in agreement.

"But what have you traded for those things?" said Johnstone. "We gave them our land, and they gave us God. Was that a fair trade?"

"The bwana is good to us," said Murigo. "Our children are healthier now; my sons are learning to read and write; my wives cook with plenty of oil and sugar. Before the coming of the bwana we had none of these things."

"But we were *men.* Can you say that of yourselves now?"

Looks were exchanged around the circle. One elder rose to his feet, glared imperiously at young Kamau, and strode away into the darkness;

several others jumped up and followed. Those who remained continued to regard the upstart with suspicion.

"We are millions while they are only thousands," boomed Johnstone. "Yet they rule over us!"

"Does not a handful of elders govern all the Kikuyu?" argued one man.

Johnstone gave him a piercing look. "Do a thousand hyenas rule over a million lions?" He pulled a newspaper from his hip pocket and waved it like a club. "Read!" he cried. "Read the white man's own words. He *admits* that one percent of the population of our country decides all the laws, and *that* percent came here as strangers whose ancestors dwell in other lands."

The audience murmured.

"They took away our spears and our war bells!" he shouted. "They have made women of our men. And now they seek to abolish the sacred initiation of girls, teaching them to read and write instead so that our women are made men. The *wazungu* are turning the Kikuyu upside down! They are slowly destroying the Children of Mumbi! And you go like sheep, kissing the hand that plunges the dagger! Wake up, sons of Mumbi! Act now before it is too late! Remember the proverb that says the family of 'I'll do it' was overtaken by the family of 'have done it.' "

He stroke across the circle and came to stand before an elder seated on the dirt. The old man wore a blanket and carried a staff; around his neck hung a small metal container. *"Mzee,"* said Johnstone in a quieter, more respectful tone, "what is that necklace you are wearing?"

The man regarded him with caution. "You know what it is. You carry one yourself."

"Yes!" cried Johnstone. "It is the *kipande*, the identification the *wazungu* force us to carry. But because most of you do not wear clothes with pockets, as I am able to do, you must wear your identification around your neck, *like a dogtag!"*

The audience froze. A chill descended over the group as the eyes of the *mzee* met those of the firebrand. After a moment the dignified elder came to his feet, and he said in a soft, deadly voice, "The white man came and brought us out of the darkness. He showed us the greater world, of which we knew nothing. He brought us medicine and God, roads and books. He brought us a better way. This *kipande* which

I wear tells other men who I am. I am not ashamed of it. And I do not have to listen to you."

He made a stately turn and departed from the clearing as if leaving his own throne room. The rest of the elders also rose and left with him. But the younger men remained, and these Johnstone now addressed. "It is seven years since the massacre in Nairobi of our own people over the detainment of Harry Thuku. Thuku is still in jail for his activities in *uhuru*, independence. A hundred and fifty of our men and women, who were unarmed themselves, were gunned down in the street like animals. Will we continue to allow this?"

He met the gaze of each man in the circle, caught the look in each one, and held it with his own magnetism, until they had to look away. "I tell you this," said Johnstone Kamau with quiet force, "if one of you here works for a white man, then he is no African. Do you hear me?"

"Eyh," said a few of the men. *Yes.*

"Is not our manhood worth more than sugar and oil?"

"Eyh," they said a little louder.

"Shall we continue to ride in third-class train cars while the white man rides first? Shall we put up with the indignity of requiring a pass to travel from one village to another? Shall we suffer their rules that forbid us to smoke in the presence of a white man, that force us to lift our caps when he passes, that make us stand up when he walks by? Or will we live like men?"

"Eyh!" they cried.

Wanjiru felt her young heart begin to race. This charismatic man, Johnstone Kamau, spoke with magic in his voice. She understood little of what he said, but the power in his delivery heated her blood. Her wide, unblinking eyes watched as a few more men in the group, disagreeing with the radical and afraid of the police, got up and marched away. She saw nervous, excited glances go around the circle; men shifted uncertainly on their buttocks. Some murmured in support of him, others remained silent. She thought of him as a stick stirring embers. The old dead coals fell to the wayside, warm ones sat glowing weakly on the edges; but the hot new ones, red and burning, poured their heat into the center of the cook fire. These were the young men, Wanjiru saw, youths in khaki shorts who had been taught to read and write but didn't have a shilling in their pockets. They were discontented young men flaring into flames from the hot breath of Johnstone Kamau.

To her surprise Wanjiru saw the medicine woman slowly rise and approach the young man. The group fell silent. She went up to him, and they exchanged words of respect. Then Wachera, widow of the legendary Mathenge, said, "I have a vision, son of Mumbi. The ancestors have shown me your future. You will lead the people back to the old ways. You will free us from the yoke of the *wazungu*. I have looked into your tomorrows, and I have seen what you will one day be: You will be Kenya's lamp, you will be *Kenya taa.*"

Johnstone's eyes flickered; a look passed briefly over his face. Then he smiled and nodded and watched her walk away.

When Wachera came back to her son, she reached for his hand and said, "You will remember this night and this man, David."

Wanjiru overheard. She would remember, too.

$$25$$

Thunder cracked. The interior of Birdsong Cottage was briefly bathed in the white glow of lightning. Grace picked up Rose's letter. It began:

My dear Grace,

The weather is frightfully awful here, and I am going mad with being bound up in the house. Bella Hill is such a gloomy place! When Valentine is home (he spends so much time in London speaking in Parliament on behalf of the whites in Kenya), he and Harold argue so fiercely that it's all I can do to keep sane.

But I have been doing some wonderful stitching! I found the most beautiful shade of red in one of the village shops. I shall use it for the petals of my hibiscus flowers. Did I tell you that I had decided to put hibiscus in my tapestry? I don't know if they grow on the slopes of Mount Kenya, but they seem appropriate somehow. What do you think of a variation on the Hungarian stitch for the sky? Is it too much? I am still at a loss over the blank spot. I cannot fill it in for the life of me. The mountain is coming in nicely; some of the trees have received their final bark detailing. Now I shall turn my attention to the leopard lurking behind the ferns. It will no doubt take a year or two out of my life! But what on earth do I put in the blank space?

In answer to your last two letters, there is nothing yet to report on Arthur's condition. You needn't scold me, Grace. Just because I don't mention him doesn't mean I don't care. One Harley Street specialist had the audacity to tell Valentine to take Arthur to a Freudian! What a row that caused!

Why are Novembers always so dreary in England? Have the rains come to Kenya? I do pray so. My roses and delphiniums will be needing it. I received a letter in the post this morning from Lucille Donald in Uganda. She talks of nothing but her good works.

It appears we shan't be home for Christmas after all. Even after we leave England, the boat takes six weeks. My heart rests in Kenya, with you all.
                                        Love,
                                        Rose.

Grace sighed and put the letter down. It had been written on delicate stationery of rose pink and teal blue, the Treverton colors, with the lion and griffin crest at the top. Rose's florid handwriting had filled the entire page without saying anything, as usual, Grace thought.

She looked up at the underside of her thatch roof as more thunder growled down from Mount Kenya. Wind rattled the dry papyrus, joining the crackle of her fire. Grace was alone except for Mario asleep in his rondavel and Mona in her bed in the recently added room. With Valentine and Rose in England, the big house was closed up.

Grace tried not to think of empty Bellatu. It only reminded her of her own emptiness.

She poured a second cup of tea and listened to the wind. She had Mona. It if weren't for that, Grace knew the loneliness would overwhelm her.

Bringing her mind out of the shadows that closed in on her, she tried to concentrate on the latest problems demanding solutions. There was the trouble with the smallpox lymph, which arrived inactive from England because it did not travel well; inoculation had been a ritual in futility. There was the "nappy project" she was having difficulty launching: sending nurses into the bush to demonstrate to African women the making and *need* of diapers for babies. There was still the trouble with children burned from falling into cook fires and dehydrated infants who were not receiving fluid therapy in time; the need to check the water filter pots in all the huts to see if they were being used. Dysentery was breaking out again; parasites were becoming more of a problem, instead of abating; malnutrition was on the rise as the population continued its boom growth; newborn babies were dying of tetanus because of unsanitary delivery conditions—the list seemed endless.

Grace battled two immutable obstacles: lack of education among the Africans and the persistent local preference for tribal doctors. The first she knew she could vanquish with schools, books, and teachers; the second was trickier. Despite increased pressure from the missions upon the Africans to turn away from the local medicine people, traditional healing was only being driven farther underground. Many was the night when Grace, unable to sleep, had stepped onto her veranda for some air and had seen, in the moonlight, furtive shapes enter Wachera's hut.

There was her enemy. Wachera had to be stopped.

Setting Rose's letter aside and reaching for the one she had received from James, Grace listened to the thunder growing closer. She knew it was only a matter of time before the storm hit. She wondered if Mona would sleep through it. James had written:

We have the same problems here in Uganda as you do. The villages are too far apart and too deep in the jungle for medical missionaries to see to everyone. These people are dying from the simplest things! Diarrhea, dehydration, malnutrition, infections—all of which can be prevented or cured if only there were some way to educate the Africans in basic health. So many times, Grace, I have gone into a village and seen the needless suffering and thought: If only there were some sort of guidebook that nonmedical personnel such as Lucille and I, or indeed that the natives themselves could refer to! You are the person to write that book, Grace. We pray that you will someday.

Her eyes misted; she put the letter down. A book. To take the place of a doctor. With simple explanations and drawings. That was what James envisioned. Grace stared into the fire for a long time, contemplating his dream and listening to the storm draw near.

"YOU'RE NOT AFRAID of a bit of lightning, are you?" Mona asked.

David wore a stoic face. He wished he could run back to the hut where his mother slept. But that would have looked like cowardice, and he had to show the bwana's daughter that he was unafraid.

She had dared him to do this.

They had encountered each other down by the river that afternoon, Mona boldly announcing her *permanent* return to Kenya, David retorting that she would not be here long. They had argued then over whose land this was, David's authority being his mother, Mona's, her father.

Out of that quarrel a dare had emerged: to meet at midnight on taboo
ground. The one who was the braver was the rightful owner of the land.

And so David was here, at this late hour, crouched against the thatch
wall of the surgery hut—to prove his bravery to Mona. A cold wind cut
through his thin shirt; lightning tore across the sky, illuminating the
heavy black clouds that were bringing the rain. He didn't like storms;
no Kikuyu did. This was not normal rain, he knew. Angry storms such
as the one that was coming were rare; it made the Children of Mumbi
wonder if God was angry with them—not the *mzungu* God Jesu, to
whom they sang songs on Sunday and whom they praised in good
times, but Ngai, the ancient god of the Kikuyu, to whom they reverted
when their primeval fears surfaced.

The wind whipped Mona's short black hair. Her Magyar-cut khaki
overalls, covering a long-sleeved blouse, ballooned out around her. She
had gone to bed fully dressed, and her aunt Grace hadn't known
because when she had come in to kiss her niece good night, Mona had
had the covers drawn up to her chin.

"Let's see how brave a warrior you are," she said. "I dare you to go
in there!" She pointed to the doorway of the surgery hut.

It was a small structure, not much bigger than the hut David's
mother lived in. There was no veranda, just an opening with a wooden
door, which David now pushed with the flat of his hands. The door
creaked away from him, and lightning cast a brief light on the wooden
floor, cabinets, electric lights suspended from the beams, and a crude
operating table.

This was Grace's cleanest hut; it was as free from insects and rodents
as any thatch structure could be. Here she performed surgery that she
did not send down to the big hospital in Nairobi: minor operations and
emergencies. David had never seen the inside of this place, which the
mission workers regarded with great awe because Memsaab Daktari
worked very powerful magic in here. Surely it was taboo for him to
enter!

"Go on!" whispered Mona close behind him. "I dare you!"

David swallowed. His mouth was dry; his pulse raced. Each clap of
thunder seemed to shake the ground. Lightning flashes lit up the
mission compound in quick, eerie scenes. The trees at the perimeter

were whipped into a frenzy; a great rushing noise whistled down from Mount Kenya, as if Ngai were breathing fury.

David stood frozen with fear.

"Go on!" shouted Mona, the wind snatching the words from her mouth and carrying them away. "Or are you a coward?"

With fists curled at his sides, his thin body shaking from fear and cold, David closed his eyes and took a step forward.

"Go on—go all the way in!"

The hut shook as thunder and wind clapped and swirled around them. Thatch flew from the roof. Dust came up in funnel clouds, stinging the children's eyes. Fingers of fire streaked across the black sky. In the forest nearby a tree was struck and began to burn.

Mona gave David a shove. He fell forward onto his hands and knees. She pushed him again; the wind came up behind her and slammed her into the hut. The door crashed shut.

Both children cried out.

The walls of the hut shuddered as the wind shot through cane and papyrus. David and Mona looked up.

The roof was burning.

They ran to the door and tried to push it open, but it was wedged tightly closed.

They were trapped.

SMELLING SMOKE, GRACE set aside her journal and went to the window.

Three huts were on fire.

"Dear God," she whispered. "Mario! *Mario!*" She flew out the front door, down the steps, and around to the houseboy's rondavel, where he was already coming out, pulling up his shorts.

Mission workers started to appear, blinking sleepily, running to the burning huts. When Mario headed for the surgery hut, Grace cried, "No! Leave the equipment. Save the patients!"

They went straight to the long hut that was the inpatient ward and saw that the two night nurses were already leading people outside. Two walls were on fire; the roof was ablaze.

The wind carried sparks from hut to hut until every structure was on fire. Flames reached up to the sky as workers struggled with stretchers, wrestled with wheelchairs and furniture. Grace tried to supervise the chaos, shouting over the roar of the wind and fire. But panic seized the crowd. Men dashed into burning huts and got themselves trapped trying to rescue tables and chairs. Oxygen tanks exploded; glass was heard shattering above the noise of the inferno. People ran to and fro, waving their arms, screaming, while Grace caught them, gave orders, tried to direct the safe evacuation of the patients.

"Memsaab!" shouted Mario, tugging at her nightgown. "Look!"

She turned. Her house was on fire.

Mona!

"Mario, where's Mona? Have you seen her?"

He ran toward the cottage but was thrown back when flames exploded from a hut. Grace picked him up and dragged him to safety. She ran toward her house, calling Mona's name. As she passed the surgery hut, which was half ablaze, she thought she heard voices calling out.

She ran to the door and pressed her ear to it. Smoke billowed out through cracks. The roof was a cone of fire. Grace listened. She heard the children's voices, calling feebly.

"Mona!" Grace tried to open the door.

Men came running with banana leaves. They pounded the flames that were licking down the walls. Someone threw handfuls of dirt. Grace pushed at the door with all her might; then one of the Africans pulled her away and shoved with his own body.

The hut started to cave in. The cries of the children could no longer be heard.

Soon the entire compound was a blazing hell, and the Africans began to retreat in fear.

Grace screamed and pounded on the door. Cinders and sparks showered down on her. Heat seared her face and lungs. "Mona!" she cried.

Finally the door gave way and smoke poured out. Covering her face, Grace fell to her hands and knees and reached inside. The ceiling was starting to come down. She felt a limb and seized it and pulled with all her strength. David's body came out just as a chunk of flaming papyrus fell. It struck Grace on the head. She tugged at David until he was out of danger. Then, fighting heat and smoke, she ran back for Mona.

And then the rain broke.

It burst from bulging clouds and washed down on the inferno. The flames shrank; a great hiss began to fill the air. The thunder and lightning moved on; the rain came down hard until it was falling like a river.

Grace slogged in the mud, tripping on her nightgown. Thatch once flaming now grew sodden and heavy. She plunged through steam and smoldering papyrus, slipping and sliding, searching for Mona.

The Africans withdrew, then vanished into the deluge.

Grace found Mona, trapped beneath the instrument cabinet which had fallen over. Before she could get hold of the child, the roof collapsed beneath the force of the storm and buried the girl. Grace dug frantically, tearing at the soaked thatch until her hands bled. Mona lay motionless, one pale arm flung out at an unnatural angle.

The rain came down on Grace with punishing force, plastering her hair to her face. She tried to lift the cabinet but could not. She called out for help, the wind driving rain into her mouth. Grace could not see more than a foot or two in front of her. The rain was like a solid wall. And it was quickly turning the charred floor of the hut into a lake. Mona had only moments before been in danger of burning to death; now she would drown if Grace did not get her out in time.

"Help!" she cried. "Someone! Mario!"

She looked around in desperation. The compound was deserted; black remains of huts and hospital furniture hissed in the downpour. "*Help!*" she screamed. "Where *is* everyone?"

Then she saw a shape emerge through the driving rain. It came slowly toward her.

"Please help me," Grace sobbed. "My little girl is trapped. She might still be alive."

Wachera stared down with a stony expression.

"Damn it!" cried Grace. "Don't just stand there! Help me lift this cabinet!"

The medicine woman said just one word: "*Thahu.*"

"This is no bloody *thahu!*" shouted Grace, tugging at the cabinet, ripping her nails. "It's a storm, nothing more! Help me!"

Wachera didn't move. She stood in the downpour, her leather dress drenched, rain running off her shaved head.

Grace shot to her feet. "Damn it!" she shouted. "Help me save this girl!"

The eyes of the medicine woman flickered to the pathetic arm stretched out from under the cabinet. The water level was rising around Mona's lifeless body.

"I saved your son!" Grace screamed.

Wachera turned her head. When she saw David, stirring to consciousness in the mud, her expression changed. She looked from the boy to the white woman, then down at the cabinet. Without a word she bent and took hold of one end. Grace seized the other, and together, panting and struggling, the two women managed to drag the heavy piece of furniture off the girl's body.

Grace dropped to her knees and gently turned Mona over. Wiping hair and mud from the shockingly white face, she said, "Mona? Mona, darling? Can you hear me?"

Grace felt the side of the girl's neck and found a pulse. She put her cheek to the gray lips and detected a faint breath. Alive. But only barely.

She tried to think. She sat up with her niece in her arms and looked around the compound. Where was everyone?

As if reading her mind, Wachera said, "They all have left you. They fear *thahu.* They fear the punishment of Ngai."

Grace ignored her. Cradling the lifeless girl against her, she looked frantically around for shelter. All the huts were destroyed; her own house was gutted, the wind sending rain into what was left. Her mind struggled; she couldn't think clearly. She sat in the mud, trying to keep the rain off Mona's face.

My instruments, my medicines, my dressings . . .

All gone.

Then she thought of Bellatu. Its bedrooms and dry beds. There would be some sort of medicines in one of the bathrooms; dressings could be made out of sheets.

Grace tried to stand. The blow to her head had made her dizzy. Blood trickled into her right eye. *Get to the house.* But the road—it would be impassable!

Through the rain she saw her own Ford truck sunk up to its running board in the mud. The road to Nyeri would also be one long bog. No one, she knew, would be able to get through.

Holding Mona tight against her, Grace tried again to stand. She slipped and fell. Then she saw the ugly gash in the girl's leg. She tried to find Mona's pulse.

I'm losing her!

The third time Grace managed to stay on her feet. She began to stumble through the rain, toward the path that climbed up the ridge. Mona was a dead weight in her arms; the stormy world around her tilted; the ground seemed to move beneath her.

Grace started to sob. She plodded through knee-deep mud, her feet catching on the hem of her nightgown, the rain pushing her back, Mona growing heavier and heavier. She had to get to the house, or they both would drown out here, alone, in the mud. . . .

And then two arms, shiny black with rain, reached out, and suddenly Grace's burden was lifted. Wachera took up Mona with ease and turned away. Grace stared after her.

She saw the boy follow his mother; they were heading for the polo field. "Wait," Grace whispered. Her head swam. She put a hand to her forehead, and it came away bloody.

Cold and wet and numb, Grace staggered over the ruins behind the African medicine woman, who walked in the direction of her hut.

26

G race opened her eyes.

There was little to see, just the smoky interior of an African hut. She tried to move. Every joint and muscle in her body hurt. Her mind was a fog; she couldn't remember where she was, what had happened.

She lay still and listened to the rain patter on the thatch, recognizing the smells in the hut. They were at the same time familiar and alien. Someone was talking. Singing? She tried to move again. The hut swung around her. She felt sick.

I'm hurt. I must go slowly.

Bit by bit the fog lifted from her brain, and her thoughts began to coalesce into a sharper focus. The rain. There had been a storm. And a fire . . . Mona!

Grace sat up abruptly. The hut tilted. In the darkness she saw the glow of hot stones over a cook fire and the silhouettes of three people— one sitting, two recumbent. As her eyes grew accustomed to the dark, Grace recognized Wachera's face, her coppery features set in deep concentration. Then there was David, asleep on a bed of banana leaves, his body covered by a goatskin. Across the small hut lay Mona, white as death.

Grace opened her mouth. Her lips and tongue were dry; she had difficulty speaking. "Mona . . ."

But the medicine woman held up a hand and said, "You are not well. Your head received a bad wound. Lie down."

"I must see to Mona."

"I have taken care of her. She lives. Now she sleeps."

"But . . . she was bleeding."

Wachera got up from her place at the cook fire and went to the girl. Lifting the goatskin blanket, she pointed to the wounded leg.

Grace stared. Mona's thigh was clean, and a dressing of grass and leaves had been tied in place by a leather thong.

"It needed suturing . . ." Grace said, her head swimming.

Wachera reached up to the circular wall, where, Grace saw now, many gourds and leather pouches hung. Taking one of these, Wachera spilled something into her hand and held it out for Grace to see. In the brown palm lay iron needles of different sizes, strips of sheep tendon, and bark string. "The wound is closed," Wachera said. Then she returned the things to the pouch and the pouch to its hook.

Grace watched her with eyes that refused to stay focused. The image of the young medicine woman blurred; she seemed to retreat down a long tunnel. Grace heard the singing voice again and realized it was herself. Why was she singing? No, not singing . . . groaning.

She sank back onto the bed of banana leaves. There seemed to be not an ounce of strength in her body. *My patients,* she thought. Where was everyone? Mario. Her head throbbed. She put a hand to her temple and felt something leafy there.

Grace closed her eyes and lost consciousness.

WACHERA SQUATTED NEXT to the little girl and murmured magic spells as she removed the leaves and inspected the wound. There was a lot of angry redness and swelling, which meant evil spirits had invaded the flesh, so she took some leaves from a pouch on her belt, put them in her mouth, chewed for a moment, then applied them to the wound that had been stitched with bark string. When new dry leaves were tied in place, Wachera examined the burn on the little girl's back. There was enough aloe juice in the gourd for one more treatment; then she would have to send David out for more. But where was he?

She looked at the doorway. It was still raining. The downpour had not stopped since its onset; the whole world was gray and watery.

Wachera covered the little girl again with the warm goatskins and turned to the memsaab, who was still unconscious. Wachera studied her. She had never been this close to a white woman, had never touched one. She stared at the curiously colorless skin, at the brown hair flimsy as cornsilk; she lifted the hands and marveled at their lack of calluses. This *mzunga* was like a newborn lamb, all white and soft. It amazed Wachera that such women survived in Kikuyuland. Yet they did, and more were arriving every day with their helmets that were wider than their shoulders and their clothes that protected every inch of their vulnerable skin.

What made them come? Why were they here?

The medicine woman sat next to the sleeping memsaab and laid a hand on the cool, dry forehead. The throb of life at the memsaab's throat, which was the energy of her ancestral spirit, was strong. She was healthy. She would live. But she would be half blind. There was nothing Wachera could have done about the memsaab's loss of sight.

David came in, shook the rain off himself, and squatted by the fire. He stole a glance at the white girl sleeping in his bed. He wished she would die.

Dropping some bark and roots into a pot boiling on the cook stones, Wachera instructed her son to go to the river and collect three lilies the "color of a goat's tongue." But he must not try to cross the river to the other villages, she warned, because the water was rising and its spirit would grab him and pull him under. She embraced David, thanking Ngai for sparing him, then watched him go back into the rain.

When she returned to the preparation of the infusion, Wachera found the memsaab awake and looking at her.

"How is Mona?" Grace asked.

Wachera nodded to indicate that all was well.

Grace tried to sit up. She was surprised to find her nightgown dry and herself clean. Then she realized the medicine woman must have bathed her.

The hut was smoky and dark. The daylight coming through the doorway was pale; a curtain of rain fell steadily. Grace tried to orient herself, blinking in confusion. It was then that she realized there was something wrong with her sight.

Reading the memsaab's face, Wachera said, "You were struck on the head. Here," she added, pointing to her own temple.

Grace felt the leaf dressing on the right side of her forehead. She didn't remember being struck by the burning thatch. Then she moved her hand in front of her right eye and couldn't see it.

"I could not save your sight," Wachera said.

Grace looked at her in surprise. "How did you know I could not see out of this eye?"

"It is the old knowledge. When a head is struck here, the sight is lost." She reached for an empty gourd, filled it with the infusion, and handed it to Grace.

"What is it?"

"It will strengthen you. Drink it."

Grace looked down at the hot liquid. Its steamy aroma was not unpleasant, but she didn't trust the medicine woman. "What is it?" she said again.

Wachera didn't answer. She turned away from the memsaab and went to the little girl, who had begun to stir. Cradling Mona in the crook of her arm, she brought a gourd to the dry lips. Mona drank, her eyes closed, her body limp. Grace started to protest. She wanted to push the medicine woman away from her niece and take care of Mona herself. But Grace felt sick again. She lay back down, setting the gourd on the earth floor.

She thought about her eye. She knew that a blow to the temple could detach the retina; the same wound had blinded Admiral Nelson. And there was no cure for it. But how had this African woman known that?

Grace tried to fathom her strange weakness, her inability to get up off this primitive bed. *I must get help. I must get word out. . . .* She thought of the mission workers, of her patients, of Mario. They had to be brought back to the mission, to rebuild the clinic. She pictured Birdsong Cottage as she had last seen it, charred and gutted with the rain pouring in. Everything ruined.

She listened to the rain. It lulled her. She watched the medicine woman patiently feed tea to a half-conscious Mona. The pungent scent of the infusion filled the hut. It seemed to invigorate, even in vapor form. What was in the tea? Grace reached for the gourd; her trembling hand knocked it over, and black tea spilled out, seeping into the floor.

Wachera worked silently and slowly. She turned Mona onto her side, checked the dressings again, then tucked the goatskins in all around. Returning to the cook fire, she picked up the gourd Grace had knocked over, refilled it, and came to sit at the memsaab's side. This time, when Grace struggled to sit up, Wachera put a strong arm around her shoulders and supported her. The medicine woman brought the tea to Grace's lips, and she drank.

"Do you have pain?" Wachera asked.

"Yes. In my head. Terrible pain . . ."

David came in then. He set the three lilies down and retreated to the wall, where he sat cross-legged and watched. Wachera left the memsaab to work on the flowers. Separating roots and leaves, she dropped the petals into a measure of hot water, stirring it as it boiled. Grace lay helpless as she observed the simple process of making a decoction. Her head throbbed. She began to feel ill again.

When the new brew was cooled, Wachera returned to Grace's side, helped her sit up, and brought the gourd to her lips. But Grace drew her head back. "Water lilies?" she said weakly. "I can't drink this."

"It is for head pain."

"But . . . it might be poison."

"It is not poison."

Grace looked up into the dark face inches from her own. Wachera's eyes were like the brown pebbles found in the river bed. They seemed depthless. Grace looked at the pinkish tea. Then she drank.

"How do you feel?" Wachera asked a short while later, as she began to prepare millet stew on the cook fire.

"I'm feeling better," Grace said, meaning it. The pain in her head was subsiding, and strength seemed to be returning to her body.

She was able to concentrate now, to organize her thoughts. She looked at the boy sitting sullenly against the wall, wondered what he and Mona had been doing in the surgery hut, then asked Wachera if it was possible to get word to others where she was.

Wachera stirred the millet, the beaded bracelets on her arms making a clacking sound. "The rain is very bad. My boy cannot go. I cannot go. When the rain stops, we will try."

Grace imagined the world beyond the mud wall; she had seen storms like this before. The river would be swollen and churning; all paths and roads would be ribbons of mud; wherever people were they would be stranded there; and of those unlucky to be caught abroad in the rain, some would drown.

When she was given a gourd of millet stew, Grace found she had appetite and ate with relish. Wachera first fed Mona, who seemed to hover in a half-awake limbo; then she took some stew herself. David gobbled his down and curled up on his side to sleep, his back to the others in the hut.

GRACE WAS THE first awake. She stared up at the underside of the thatch, listened to the continuing rain, then slowly sat up.

Wachera was still asleep on her side next to David, her body curved spoonlike against his, her arm covering him. Grace fought a spell of vertigo, then was able to shift from the leafy bed. She went to Mona and immediately checked the girl's vital signs.

Grace sat back in alarm. Mona was burning with fever.

She undid the leaf dressing on Mona's thigh and gazed in astonishment at the track of neat stitches. There was redness but no drainage. Then she inspected the burn on the girl's back. It would leave a scar, but because of Wachera's quick action, there was no sign of infection.

So Mona burned from some other cause. And it could be anything; the cold rain; the medicine woman's mysterious brews; something brought on by the bite of an insect, which lived in disconcerting profusion in this hut.

Mona needed something to reduce her fever, and quickly. Without a proper thermometer Grace could not determine the exact degree of the temperature, but she knew the child was dangerously hot. Grace got up and went to the doorway. There would be aspirin up at the big house, in Rose's bathroom. But the rain stood like a solid wall between Wachera's hut and the ridge; the path to Bellatu, Grace knew, would be gone.

Hearing a sound, Grace turned and found the young African woman awake and reaching for a leather pouch. Wachera seemed unaware that the memsaab was out of bed and standing at the doorway; in single-minded concentration she proceeded to draw roots out of the bag and begin to pound them between two stones. She then stirred the pulp into a gourd filled with cold rainwater and took it to Mona. When she lifted the gourd to the girl's lips, Grace said, "Stop!"

Wachera ignored her.

Mona's eyelids fluttered, her mouth opened, and a bit of the juice went in.

Grace flew to Wachera and grabbed the gourd. "What are you giving to her?"

"Acacia," said the medicine woman, using the Kikuyu name for the tree. "This will draw the fire out of her body."

"How do I know it won't kill her? How do I know it isn't your medicines that are making her sick?"

Wachera turned a cold, flat stare upon Grace. Then she reached out and took a firm hold of the gourd. "My medicines do not make the child sick. She has the evil spirits of sickness in her body."

"Nonsense. There are no such things as evil spirits."

"They exist."

"Show them to me."

"They cannot be seen."

"And I tell you there are no such things. Mona is ill because she took some germs into her body. Tiny things which we call 'microbes' are making her sick."

"Show me these microbes."

"They're too small to be seen—" Grace blinked. She let Wachera take the gourd and watched Mona sip the medicine in her half sleep.

When the gourd was empty, Wachera pounded more acacia roots, stirred them into cold rainwater, and drew the goatskin off Mona. Using a soft chamois, she sponged the girl's feverish body from head to foot.

THEY SAT FACING each other with the cook fire between them, Grace wrapped in goatskins against the cold drafts, Wachera stirring another millet stew. Every so often Grace looked through the door where she could see her brother's polo field turning into a lake. She looked at the sleeping form of Wachera's son, at Mona, who tossed and turned in fever, and finally at the medicine woman.

Grace had never been this near to Wachera, had never gotten a really good look at her. But now that she did, she saw what she had missed before: that the Kikuyu woman was, in fact, beautiful, her body not yet ravaged by time and hard living, and there was dignity in her eyes. There was also, to Grace's surprise, compassion.

Grace watched the nimble brown hands add bits of vegetable to the stew. Copper bracelets glinted in the fire's glow; earlobes stretched with rings of beads brushed dark brown shoulders. Wachera had lived alone in this hut for nine years, shunning the company and security of the village to hold on to a patch of seemingly insignificant ground, her only companion a little boy. How could she stand it? Grace wondered. Wachera was still young, and certainly she must be desirable to the men of her tribe. How could she give up so much for a fight that was futile and in which she was totally alone?

"You're on your own, Grace." Valentine's voice suddenly echoed in her memory. "I won't help you with your mission. You've made your choice to come to Africa and take care of a bunch of natives that ultimately will never appreciate you. I don't agree with what you're doing. You won't receive any help from me."

Then Grace pictured her own little cottage and the shadows in it that were her only companions.

Wachera looked up. Their eyes met. Grace shivered and drew the goatskins more tightly about her. There were unspoken questions in the medicine woman's gaze; Grace saw the studied curiosity, the wanting to know, and realized the look must mirror her own.

Finally Wachera said quietly, "Why did you come?"

"Come?"

"To Kikuyuland. Was it because your husband came?"

"I have no husband."

Wachera frowned. "The one they call Bwana Lordy—"

"He is my brother."

"Then who owns you?"

"No one owns me."

Wachera stared. This was a concept alien to her. They were speaking in Kikuyu, and there was no word in that language meaning "spinster." Only very young girls were unmarried. In the Kikuyu tribe all women were married.

"No one owns you," Grace said.

"That is true." Wachera was an oddity in her tribe. And were it not for the fact that she was the medicine woman and the widow of the great Mathenge, she would be an outcast. She looked over at Mona and said, "Is she your daughter?"

"She is the daughter of my brother's wife."

Wachera's eyes widened. "You have no babies of your own?"

Grace shook her head.

The millet stew bubbled; drafts rattled the bamboo frame of the hut. The young African woman retreated into baffled thought.

"I knew your husband," Grace said softly. "I respected him."

"You killed him."

"I did not."

"Not by your own hand," Wachera said, her tone hard. "You poisoned his mind first."

"I did not turn Mathenge from the Kikuyu way. We are not all alike, we *wazungu*, just as not all Kikuyu are alike. I was opposed to the destruction of the sacred fig tree. I told my brother to leave it alone."

Wachera considered this. Then she looked again at Mona, who was starting to waken, and went to her. The two women examined the burn and thigh wound, and when Wachera began to bathe both in juice from a gourd, Grace said, "What is that?"

"It is the blood of the sisal plant."

Grace watched the long ebony fingers work quickly and expertly. In her own clinic, if she did not protect a wound with iodine or permanganate, a serious infection would result. The medicine woman had neither, yet Mona's wounds were healing cleanly.

Grace looked around the hut, at the gourds and leather pouches hanging from the circular wall, at the magic charms, the strings of herbs and roots, at the belts studded with cowry shells and beaded necklaces that looked as if they were hundreds of years old, and she tried to find the witchcraft she had thought was practiced here.

"Lady Wachera," Grace said, using the Kikuyu form of polite address, "you cursed my brother and his descendants. Why now do you take care of his daughter?"

Wachera took Mona into her arm and raised a gourd of cold herbal tea for her to drink. "What I do here will make no difference to the *thahu*. The future of this child is a very bad one. I have seen it."

Grace looked at Mona's white face, at the fluttering eyelids, at the pale lips drinking reflexively. What indeed *was* the girl's future? Grace found herself wondering. Mona's parents were no parents at all; there was little love in the big stone house for her. And the Treverton inheritance was going to go to Arthur. What did lie in Mona's years to come? Grace tried to picture the teenager, the young woman, the wife and mother, but saw only a blank. Where would Mona go to school, whom would she marry, where would she live, how would she make her way in the world? Grace had never thought of it before, but now that she did, it troubled her.

A feeling of deep possessiveness swept over her. She wanted to take the child away from the dark medicine woman and cradle her back to life. *I gave birth to you,* Grace thought as Mona was laid back to peaceful sleep once again. *On the train from Mombasa, when I nearly lost both of you. Your mother didn't have the strength to bring you into the world; it was my will that gave you life. You belong to me.*

"I save the daughter of your brother's wife," Wachera said quietly, "because you saved my son."

Grace looked at David standing in the doorway, contemplating the rain. He was a lanky, pensive boy who she suspected would one day be as handsome as his father.

"We should not be enemies, you and I," Grace said at last to Wachera, surprised herself with the revelation.

"We can be nothing else."

"But we are alike!"

Wachera gave her a suspicious look.

"We are the same," Grace said with passion. "Is there not a proverb that says the crocodile and the bird are both hatched from an egg?"

The medicine woman looked at the memsaab long and consideringly; then she reached up and untied the leather thong that held a leaf dressing to Grace's forehead. Feeling the light touch of Wachera's fingertips, and knowing without having to look at it that her head wound was healing well, Grace tried to think of the words that would express what had come so suddenly and unexpectedly into her heart.

"We both serve the Children of Mumbi," she said softly as Wachera dabbed the wound with sisal juice, taking care that none ran into Grace's injured eye. "We both serve life."

"This is not your land. Your ancestors do not dwell here."

"No, but my heart does."

They shared a gourd of sugarcane beer, passing it back and forth in silence, both listening to the rain and staring at the thickening stew. Presently other sounds joined the steady patter of rain: donkeys braying; men shouting; a car motor grinding. Grace then recognized the voice of Mario drawing close to the hut.

When she started to rise, Wachera stayed her with a hand. "Twenty harvests ago," she said, "you brought Njeri from Gachiku's belly. Gachiku was my husband's favorite wife. Njeri was the joy of his eye."

Grace waited.

"The *thahu* that we feared never came. Njeri, who is my son's sister, is a girl now, and she will bring honor to our family."

"Memsaab!" came Mario's voice outside the hut. Feet made sucking sounds in the mud. "Are you in there, memsaab?"

"Lady Wachera," Grace said softly, "I shall never be able to thank you enough for what you have done. You saved my little girl's life. I am in your debt for always."

Their eyes met one last time.

"Good-bye, Memsaab Daktari," Wachera said.

27

The Chevrolet truck raced down the dirt road, kicking up gravel and stones and leaving a long red-dust cloud in its wake. James Donald gripped the steering wheel with white knuckles; he watched the road for potholes and boulders as he maneuvered the vehicle at top speed. When it flew down the ridge in a great noise of gears grinding and chassis squeaking, women in the fields straightened up from their work, and the men constructing the new stone buildings of Grace Treverton Mission shielded their eyes and commented among themselves that the *wazungu* always seemed to be in a hurry.

Finally the truck jolted to a stop amid a shower of sand and debris; before the motor died, James was out of the cab and running. A few Africans who recognized him waved and called out, but he was oblivious of them. His long legs carried him through the busy compound and up the veranda steps of the recently repaired Birdsong Cottage. A startled Mario was asked a breathless "Where is the memsaab?" And before he finished replying, "She is at the village, bwana," Sir James was running back down the steps and off toward the river.

His boots thundered across the wooden bridge; he sweated in the hot sun. When he arrived at the village entrance, he didn't slow his pace. People turned and stared when they saw the white man come flying suddenly into their midst, asking urgently for Memsaab Daktari.

He found her in the center of a circle of women, demonstrating first-aid splinting of sprains and fractures. She looked up when he pushed through. "James!"

"Grace, thank God I've found you!" He reached for her hand. "What—"

"You have to come with me! It's an emergency!" He pulled her through the circle and ran with her, his hand holding tight to hers.

Grace's pith helmet flew off; she said, "James, wait."

He kept running, pulling her along.

"My medical bag is back there," she said, out of breath.

He didn't reply. They ran under the natural arch and down the forest path.

"James, what's happened! When did you get back to Kenya?"

He turned off the path suddenly and plunged into the woods, his grip still firm on her hand. They pushed through bush and over tangled undergrowth; birds flew up out of their way; monkeys complained overhead. "James!" she cried. "Tell me—"

He stopped suddenly, swung around, pulled her into his arms, and put his mouth over hers.

"Grace," he murmured, kissing her face, her hair, her neck, "I thought I'd lost you. They said you were dead. They said you'd been killed in the fire. I came at once."

They kissed hungrily, Grace with her arms about his neck, holding tight to him.

"I drove all the way from Entebbe," he said. "When I got to Nairobi, they said you were alive."

"Wachera—"

"Dear God, I thought I'd lost you." He buried his face in her hair; his strong arms held her so tightly to him that she could hardly breathe.

They sank to the ground in the privacy of wildflowers and bamboo and cedar trees. He covered her with his hard body; she saw the blue African sky through branches. The forest swirled around them as James murmured, "I never should have left you," and then no more words were spoken.

THEY LAY IN her bed, awake and talking softly. It was nearly dawn; soon the mission would be alive with the sound of hammers and chisels, of children singing in their outdoor classroom. This time James and Grace had made love slowly, stretching the night hours to savor each and every minute.

"I was out in the bush when word came," James said. Grace lay in the crook of his arm; he stroked her hair as he spoke. "Every mile of the long drive here I thought I was coming to your funeral."

"I was in Wachera's hut for the first few days after the fire. The storm isolated us."

"I'll never leave you again, Grace."

She smiled sadly and laid her hand on his bare chest. If she never had anything else again, she had last night. "No, James. You must go back. Your life is with Lucille and your children. We don't have the right."

"We have the right by our love for each other."

"And how would we live?"

"I'll go back to Kilima Simba." But even as he said it, James heard the hollowness of his words. The pain of it made him draw her tighter to him. "I have loved you for ten years, Grace. There were times when it was torture just to be near you. I thought going to Uganda would make it easier. But I have thought about you every day since we left."

"And I have thought about you. I will never stop loving you, James. My life and my soul belong to you."

He raised up on one elbow and looked down at her. He memorized every detail of her face, of her hair on the pillow, the curve of her collarbone. The image would go back with him into the Uganda jungle.

"I'm going to write that book," she said, "the medical handbook for rural workers. I shall dedicate it to you, James." She reached up and touched his cheek. The lines in his face were more deeply etched; his skin was more sunburned. She knew he would never be more handsome than he was at this moment.

James kissed her, and they began again, for the last time.

PART FOUR

1937

28

D avid Mathenge stretched in the early dawn. He looked over at his mother's hut, where she still lay sleeping, and thought of the *ugali* left over from their supper the night before.

He was hungry. It seemed to him he was always hungry these days, starved, in fact, not just for food but for other things, for the freedom to change his way of life, for the chance to make the fiery and untouchable Wanjiru his. At nineteen David Kabiru Mathenge was a youth who was all appetite. His tall, wiry body was fired by an energy and restlessness he could barely control. With each dawn that he rose and stepped out of the bachelor hut he had built for himself, it seemed to him that the world had shrunk a little more during the night. Even now he squinted in the morning opalescence and was sure the river had gotten smaller, the bank narrower. He felt as if he were being squeezed in from all sides. David wanted to break out of this suffocating, tiny world and escape into the bigger one where he could breathe, where he could be a man.

Wanjiru.

He had hardly slept for thinking of her, *burning* for her. What sort of magic spell had been cast on him that he was so consumed with sexual desire? But David knew it was not witchcraft that made him hunger for Wanjiru; it was the girl herself.

Perhaps physically Wanjiru could not be considered a beauty. Her face was round and a bit ordinary, but her body was desirable; she was tall with large, jutting breasts and firm, strong legs. However, it was Wanjiru's spirit that inflamed David, the cold fire in her eyes, the heat in her voice, her refusal to be docile and humble even in the presence of men. *Especially* in the presence of men! Wanjiru had disrupted more than one peaceful political meeting under a fig tree by speaking up, boldly and loudly, trying to incite the men into rash action instead of, as she put it, just saying words, words, words. They resented this, of course. The men didn't like Wanjiru; they avoided her because she had gone to school and could read and write and, though they wouldn't admit it, knew more about colonial policy than some of them. She was an outcast among the clan for her defiance of the British and for her intractable stand on elevating the status of African women. Wanjiru embarrassed the young men who were David's friends; she made them uncomfortable. They would laugh nervously when she passed by and make lewd remarks. But there was lust in the eyes of not a few of them, David had seen, when Wanjiru appeared.

She was both a gladness to his heart and a curse. Thoughts of her made his spirit soar, but thoughts of her burdened him also. He found himself thinking more and more of the old custom of *ngweko*, which was still practiced in the villages but which was dying out because of pressure from the missionaries.

Ngweko means "fondling" in Kikuyu, and it was a form of ritualistic intimate contact between young people before marriage. Boys and girls would congregate for dances and parties; partners would be chosen, and the couples would pair off into huts. Once alone, the young man would take off all his clothes, the girl her upper garment, retaining her leather apron and tying it back between her legs for modesty. Then the pair would lie down on the bed facing each other, intertwine their legs, and engage in affectionate fondling of breasts and torsos while carrying on a conversation of lovemaking until they fell asleep. *Ngweko* did not culminate in sexual intercourse, for that was taboo, nor might the girl touch the boy's member, nor he draw aside her apron, and should a boy impregnate a girl, he would have to pay a fine of nine goats to her father and the girl must provide a feast for all the men in her age-group.

Lately David had spent his nights lying in bed thinking about Wanjiru. In his fantasy she would come unexpectedly to his *thingira*, his bachelor hut, with food and sugarcane beer. They would lie down face to face as custom demanded and caress each other. In his dream they had been doing this already for a period of time so that it was now permissible for him to put his penis between her thighs and there experience relief, provided he did not fully penetrate her. But that was not necessary to his fantasy. David would be satisfied with just *orugane wa nyondo,* "the warmth of her breast," which was the Kikuyu way of love.

If Wanjiru were like any other Kikuyu girl, he would approach her father, offer a price, and buy her. Then he would bring her back here, build her a hut next to his mother's, and visit her bed whenever he wished. But Wanjiru was not like any other girl. The first problem was with her education. She was the only educated girl David knew, although he was aware there were others in Kenya and that their numbers were growing. Wanjiru was therefore taboo, unfit to be a wife, and buying her would make David an outcast among his friends. The second problem lay with his mother; Wachera did not approve of Wanjiru because she had sat in a schoolroom with boys and wore European dresses and spoke up in the company of men. But David's biggest problem with Wanjiru was quite simply that she didn't know he existed.

His mother came out of her hut now, greeting him and going down to the river with her waterpot. He watched her, his heart filled with pride.

Wachera had withstood the forces of change and "Europeanization," and because she had defied the white man's law against the practice of tribal medicine and lived by herself without a husband, her mystique and revered status had grown over the years so that now she was a living legend among the Kikuyu.

Unbidden, Njeri came to David's mind.

How different his half sister was from the other two women in his life! She wore dresses such as Wanjiru wore, castoffs from Bwana Lordy's wife, but she had none of Wanjiru's fight and spirit. Also seventeen years old, like Wanjiru, Njeri was docile and uncomplaining in the old way, but she hated the old ways and exhibited a demeaning adoration of the *wazungu.*

Njeri desperately wanted to be white, David knew. She despised her blackness and believed the white man's lies about the inferiority of her own race. She clung to Memsaab Mkubwa as if her life required it, spending all her days in the eucalyptus glade at the memsaab's feet. Everywhere the memsaab went, Njeri followed—ever since the journey to England eight years ago. Thoughts of his sister shamed David. She pierced his heart in a way Wanjiru never could. He had come upon Njeri one day down at the river scraping her body all over with a pumice stone until she bled. She had been trying to scrape off her blackness.

As the morning came to life with birds and monkeys filling the trees with their news, David forced his thoughts away from the three women in his life and reminded himself of the important appointment he must soon keep.

When he had received an unexpected reply to the letter he had written to the *Times* in England, David had called for a meeting of the Young Kikuyu Alliance, the political organization he and his friends had formed two years ago. The meeting today was to serve two purposes: to circulate the petition he had drawn up demanding that the government provide a university for Africans in Kenya and to show his brothers the letter he had received from Jomo Kenyatta.

That name was becoming famous throughout Kenya, with an aura of power about it. Jomo lived in England as a student, and he regularly wrote articles for the *Times,* which made its way into the hands of the hot-blooded Kikuyu youth in the Central Province. In his writings for the English people Jomo Kenyatta explained his tribal ways, clarified African mysteries, and strove to speak to the British public on behalf of black independence. In England he was being labeled "agitator." Among the Kenya youth he was becoming a symbol of their fight.

Everyone knew that the man's name had once been Johnstone Kamau, but the reason for the change and what it meant were unknown and much speculated upon. The prevailing theory was that Kenyatta had named himself for the ornamental belt he wore, the *kinyata,* but David knew the real story. He never forgot the night his mother had taken him into the forest, where a young Johnstone Kamau had addressed a secret group. She had told that young man of her prophecy, that he would one day be "Kenya's lamp," *Kenya taa.*

Recalling that meeting now, David saw that it paled in comparison with the ones now taking place all over Kenya. Nationalism was emerging; African self-awareness was starting to spread. The sparks that Kenyatta had struck that night of eight years ago had ignited a brush fire that the British were helpless to stamp out. The length and width of the colony, among all the tribes from the Luo people on Lake

Victoria to the Swahili on the coast, political consciousness was on the rise.

David had formed the Young Kikuyu Alliance because he and his friends found the Kikuyu Loyal Patriots too moderate and the Kikuyu Central Association admitted only elders. The youth needed an outlet, and they needed a spokesman. David Kabiru was their elected leader for three reasons: He carried the Mathenge name, which spelled power to every Kikuyu; he was an excellent speaker and unafraid to voice his opinions; and above all, he was recognized as being the most intelligent and educated of his peers.

Four years ago he had gone from Grace Treverton's primary school into the Secondary School for Boys in Nyeri, a high school established by the Local Native Council when families, determined to resist the missionary fight against female circumcision and the new rule that said no African who had undergone tribal initiation could attend a mission school, had pulled their children from those schools and had united to build their own. David had left Grace's small school the star pupil. Memsaab Daktari, having seen early the boy's brightness and quickness to learn, had taken it upon herself to give him extra tutoring and gifts of books on special occasions. David had read those books avidly and retained everything.

When he entered the high school, he was already far ahead of the other boys, and so the headmaster had written a special curriculum for David Mathenge, which the boy had followed with stunning success, astounding his white teachers. And when he sat for his final exams, David's results were better than many achieved at the Prince of Wales School, the Europeans' leading school. He now held the O level of the Cambridge School Certificate and had applied to the prestigious Makerere University in Uganda, from which he was now anxiously awaiting word.

In Uganda David was going to study agriculture. His mother had promised him that the Treverton land was going to be his one day, and he wanted to be prepared.

But it was not an easy wait. David was in a hurry to be doing something, to be climbing to higher achievements. When he had left the high school with his precious certificate and a mind that was sharp and full of ideas and thirsty for knowledge, David had found no post waiting for him. The few Africans who held positions in offices or wore the white man's badge had gotten them through "favors" and servility. David Mathenge was simply another educated "boy." Memsaab Grace had gotten him the job that he now worked at for twelve shillings a month, slaving for her brother as a clerk in a wooden shack next to the coffee processing sheds upriver. David sat at a table for twelve hours a day, making marks in a ledger. He recorded coffee production and kept African labor cards. He was allowed no breaks but brought his lunch wrapped in a banana leaf and ate it while he worked; he never handled money, and whenever a white man came into the shed, David had to stand respectfully.

He had not wanted the job, but his mother had encouraged him to take it, reminding him of the Kikuyu proverb that said, "It is the well-fed lion that studies the herd."

David could now hear the grinding of truck motors up on the ridge. The southern acres were being harvested, and the berries were being taken down to the shed, where he was deafened all day long by the roar of processing machinery. Up on that ridge, with bent backs and fingers raw from picking, Kikuyu women and children plucked the red berries from the three-quarter-million trees and filled their sacks.

He lifted his face to the pale blue sky and thought, *That is my land....*

But David wanted more than land. He wanted his manhood back, and the manhood of his people.

"We are not the white man's equals!" he had cried at the last political rally, his handsome black face, the image of his warrior father's, cast in the glow of torchlight. "In Nairobi we are restricted where we may walk. The white man has the run of the city; *we* are not allowed to cross River Road. If we pass a white man and do not lift our hat, he has the right to give us his boot in our backside. There are signs on shops and eating places that say, 'No dogs and Africans allowed.' We are not permitted to wear shoes or long trousers but must do with bare feet and shorts like little boys because they tell us we must not aspire to things we cannot afford to buy. The white men take our women as mistresses and prostitutes, but if an African shakes the hand of a white woman, even if in friendship and with her consent, it means a prison term for him! Not even in the afterlife are we equal, for are we not buried in *separate graveyards?*"

And then, just when the young crowd was at its hottest and David had stirred their blood, he had made his one fatal mistake. "The time has come," he had shouted, "for leadership to be removed from the ineffectual and useless chiefs and handed over to us educated young men!"

That was when Chief John Muchina, the only man in all Kenya whom David feared, had stepped in and broken up the rally.

David hated John Muchina. The man had grown fat on collaboration with the imperialist overlords. He played both sides, placating his simpleminded people with a few roads, a school here and there, pleasing the whites with his bootlicking ways, and in the middle growing rich off both. John Muchina was a Kikuyu elder from the Karatina area; he owned nineteen wives, five hundred head of cattle, a stone house, and a motorcar. He was what the white men called "a good nigger," and as Chief of the Nyeri District, one of the most powerful men in the colony, Muchina had the authority to put David Mathenge in prison—to be at the mercy of interrogation/torture.

But David was no fool. When he had called for today's meeting of the YKA he had made certain first that Chief John Muchina was going to be down in Nairobi deeply involved with the Chief Native Commissioner.

As he strode across the dusty ground to fetch a gourd of goat's milk from his mother's hut, David was stopped by the sight of two horses that suddenly appeared on Bwana Lordy's polo field. When they galloped nearer, David recognized the riders. And he was surprised. Bwana Geoffrey was no stranger to the Treverton Estate, but Memsaab Mona had been away at school in Nairobi. David had not seen her for three years; he now stared at her, the girl who had dared him to go into the surgery hut.

"GIVE OVER, MONA!" Geoffrey whooped, swinging his polo mallet high in the air. "Make way for a champion!"

She galloped ahead of him and reined in her horse at the last minute, causing his pony to shy. She swung her mallet and sent the ball flying. Mona then raced down the field toward the goalposts at the north end with Geoffrey close behind. They made a lot of noise and kicked up a lot of grass sods in their scramble for the ball. This was the end of the field that abutted Grace Treverton's land. On the other side of the fence lay the new road that ran between the towering gates of the mission. Beyond those gates, the cinder-block buildings with their iron roofs could be seen among trees. Inside one of those stone bungalows, working in two modern operating theaters and tending patients in a hundred beds, Grace's well-trained medical staff could hear the calls of the two on the nearby polo field and the crack of a hit ball.

Now Geoffrey pushed his mount back down the field toward his own goal; Mona flew after him, mallet ready to swing. They laughed breathlessly and shouted good-natured insults, each recognizing the other's ability and skill. Geoffrey Donald, twenty-five years old, had a rating of four and was a Number Three, his team's best player. Mona's position was Number One and rated a minus one, but she was only eighteen and had been playing the game for just a year. She was rapidly making progress and a reputation for herself in female polo and was spending these weeks after graduation in practice for the big tournament that was going to be held during Nairobi Race Week.

They reached the south end of the field, where David Mathenge watched them through the fence. Mona nearly had a clear shot when Geoffrey's horse wheeled about unexpectedly to the left, surprising her Arabian and causing it to rear. Startled, Mona was thrown from her saddle, and she landed on the ground flat on her back.

Geoffrey was immediately at her side. "Mona!" He gathered her into his arms. "Mona?"

Her eyelids fluttered. She had difficulty focusing. Then she drew in a breath and laughed.

"Are you all right?"

"I . . . think so. Just got the wind knocked out of me. No harm done."

He helped her to her feet. She leaned against him, feeling a bit dizzy. "You're sure?" he said. And when she raised her face to say yes, he kissed her.

It caught her off guard. Mona had never been kissed before, and she had never dreamed Geoffrey Donald would be the first to do it. So she let him. And it was a long one, with his arms going around her and pulling her against him. But when his tongue touched her closed lips, she drew abruptly back. "Geoffrey!" she said with a laugh.

"I'm in love with you, Mona. Marry me."

"Geoff—"

"You know it's what they've been expecting. It's been understood between our two families for years that you and I would get married."

Suddenly annoyed, Mona pulled away from his arms and brushed grass off her riding pants. Yes, she knew about the "understanding" between the two families, and she had never given it the least thought. Mona knew that her parents wouldn't let her marry just "anyone." She was the daughter of a lord; her full title was Lady Mona Treverton. Geoffrey Donald only just qualified because he was very rich and because his father had been knighted for bravery in the war. But what about marrying for love? What about asking Mona what *she* wanted?

But even if they did ask her, Mona would not know what to say.

For six years she had been attending a girls' boarding school in Nairobi. Whenever she came home for holidays, her only contact with boys was at large gatherings when Bellatu was packed with people. She hadn't had an opportunity to develop a special friendship with a boy or to curry a schoolgirl crush. In those six years she had occasionally encountered Geoffrey Donald, a roughly cut, unpolished hunter/ rancher who worked Kilima Simba when he felt like it, then disap- peared for months on safari. Those times they had met he had been politely indifferent to her, having seen no doubt just another awkward girl who was all eyes and knees and who sat with her cake plate on her lap like an unwanted guest. And then, last year, things changed. Geoff- rey came to her seventeenth birthday party, given not to please Mona but as another excuse for her parents to have a hundred guests to Bellatu, and he had looked at her as if they had never met. To Mona's surprise, two letters had come to her at the school after that, one from the Sudan, where Geoffrey was doing herd control, the other from Tanganyika, where he was hunting lion on the Serengeti. Finally, when she had come home from school once and for all a few weeks ago, Geoffrey had appeared, looking a little more combed and pressed than usual, and now he was almost a permanent fixture around the estate.

Mona was flattered. She had never received so much attention in her life. Geoffrey was good-looking—not as much so as his father, Sir James, but still terribly attractive. He led a romantic, adventurous life, owned a very prosperous cattle ranch, and was generally admired by everyone. But Mona wasn't in love with him.

"I say," said Geoffrey, "who's that?"

Mona looked through the goalposts at David Mathenge, who stood between the two huts that abutted the polo field fence. "Nobody. Just one of my father's boys."

"I must say, he's a sullen-looking chap. I don't think I care for the way he's watching us."

"Come on, Geoffrey. Let's get back up to the house."

But Geoffrey remained where he was. "I'll bet we shocked him with our kiss! They don't kiss, you know. And they don't know what they're missing!"

Mona felt suddenly uncomfortable. David stood in the smoky light of early morning, his naked chest and long limbs resembling those of the Masai warriors she had seen in Nairobi. Strangely, his khaki shorts struck Mona as a mockery—but to whom, to him or to herself, she didn't know.

"Let's shock him again, shall we?" Geoffrey said.

Mona said, "No," too quickly. Then: "Yes," and she impulsively put her arms around Geoffrey's neck.

They don't know what they're missing, Geoffrey had said. Unexpectedly Mona remembered an afternoon of a few weeks ago in her aunt's cottage. Grace had befriended two penniless archaeologists, and she was trying to raise money to fund their digs in Kenya, so she had put on an Indian bun-and-treacle tea for the Leakeys, and during the course of the little party Louis Leakey had spoken knowledgeably and frankly of the Africans.

"It is considered a disgrace," Dr. Leakey had said, "for an African husband not to give his wife complete sexual satisfaction. Prior to marriage the young man is instructed in exactly what to do and what not to do, while his bride is taught by her mother all the best positions and whatever is necessary for an exciting and gratifying sex life."

I doubt David Mathenge is shocked by our kiss, Mona thought. And then added on a deeper, more secret level of her mind: *Our cool, unexciting kiss.*

Geoffrey drew back but continued to hold her by the arms, close to him. He looked into her eyes and said, "You will marry me, won't you, Mona?"

She felt her annoyance rise again. Was this his idea of romance? The rather accidental meeting of lips on a polo field? Then she thought: *But what* do *I want anyway?* Mona had never experienced sexual excitement, had never mooned over a film star the way the girls at school had, never reveled in delicious fantasies or felt the electricity of "his touch." All Mona ever felt inside was a sort of detachment, perhaps even a bit of impatience with the whole thing, and it was starting to worry her.

In fact, it was starting to frighten her. She was turning out to be just like her mother. . . .

"What do you say, darling?"

"I . . . don't know what to say, Geoffrey." His nearness felt strange. In a way it made her giddy; in another way it was unpleasant. The giddiness was not due to the fact that he was a man but simply that he was another human being. Mona wasn't used to physical contact with others. Her father had never hugged her, her mother only rarely; that left Aunt Grace and her brother, Arthur, the only two people whose bodies she had ever felt. Now she was feeling Geoffrey's. And she didn't know if she liked it or not.

"I need time," she said, acutely aware of the grooms leading the horses away, of the chaps stamping the sods back onto the field, of the day growing bright, of David Mathenge watching her.

Suddenly she resented him, the boy who had argued with her years ago over whose land this really was, who had glared miserably at her as she lay in his bed in his mother's hut, recovering from her wounds gotten in the fire. All of a sudden David Mathenge represented all of Mona's problems; he symbolized the source of all her misery. He hadn't *had* to show up that night at the surgery hut so that as a consequence, Mona got badly hurt in the fire and now bore ugly scars that kept her out of swimsuits and made her fear that any lover she had would be repulsed by them. *He* was the root of her unhappiness—David Mathenge, who was always looking so proud when surely he had nothing in the world to be proud of.

She pulled abruptly away from Geoffrey, put her hands on her hips, and called out, "What are you staring at?"

Geoffrey turned around. "Is he still there? I'll send him off."

"No. I'll do it. He's one of ours." Mona walked up to the fence and said, "Did you wish to speak with us?"

"No," David said quietly.

"No, *what?*" said Geoffrey, coming up. "Show some respect, boy."

"No, Memsaab Mdogo."

Mona tipped her chin. "Then shouldn't you be getting back to work?"

His eyes held hers for a moment; something cold and threatening passed between them. Then he said, "Yes, Memsaab Mdogo," and started to back away.

"Damn insolent chap, I must say," muttered Geoffrey. "Got the look of a troublemaker about him if you ask me. I'll have a word with your father. That boy shouldn't be kept on."

As they walked away from the fence, Mona glanced over her shoulder and saw David standing still again, staring at them. She felt a chill rush through her. There was something in his eyes. . . .

She reached for Geoffrey's hand and held it tightly.

DAVID WATCHED THEM go. He was thinking of the ground their white feet trampled. It was the spot his mother had shown him many times; long ago a sacred fig tree had stood there. David made a vow from his heart to his ancestors: One day a new fig tree was going to be planted where the *wazungu* now walked.

29

Wanjiru didn't own a mirror. If she did, she would have been able to inspect her earlobes to see if they were healing properly.

A few young women her age were starting to turn their backs on the ancient custom of ear piercing, because of pressure from the missionaries, who preached against any sort of bodily mutilation. But Wanjiru was proud of her new wounds. They were the legacy of her ancestresses and showed the world that she could withstand pain.

Ear piercing was a terrible ordeal. In childhood the first two holes, the *ndugira*, were made through the sensitive cartilage in the tops of the ears; then, as a girl approached adulthood, the larger, bottom hole was created. She would lie flat on the ground, and a medicine man or woman would jab sharpened sticks through her ears. She had to keep these in for three weeks, stoically bearing the pain, getting little sleep because it was difficult to lie down. Wanjiru's sticks had recently been removed, and Wachera Mathenge, the medicine woman down by the river, had smeared a healing salve on the scabs. Wanjiru's ears still hurt and were not ready for the rings of copper and beads.

But this was a triviality compared with the greater test that was yet to come.

A secret initiation was going to take place. It was the first in a long time, and girls between twelve and eighteen were going to be brought from all over the district to be circumcised into the tribe. Although they could no longer engage in weeks of ceremonial preparations that strengthened the girls and gave them courage to face the knife without flinching—such rituals had been banned, and their sudden appearance would alert the authorities to the approaching initiation—Wanjiru was nonetheless undergoing a personal preparation of her own.

Most of the girls, she knew, were terrified of what was coming; many were going to be forced into it by parents and brothers. But Wanjiru looked forward to the ancient initiation; she welcomed the test of pain and blood.

But there was a more immediate issue on her mind now as she got ready to leave the hut she shared with her two unmarried sisters. A meeting of the Young Kikuyu Alliance had been called at the last minute by David Mathenge, and Wanjiru didn't want to miss it.

Not that the men wanted her there. Women were never admitted to political gatherings, and such women and girls as did attend were there to carry food for their men, to sit and listen in respectful silence, to be invisible at the edge of the important business. Wanjiru, on the other hand, intended to take an active part.

David Mathenge irritated her. Just the thought of him made her pull her one dress angrily over her head and do the buttons up wrong.

He was an oaf, a dolt, a ditherer. It was beyond hot-blooded Wanjiru how such a smart and educated boy could be so slow, so blind, so . . . *weak*. If she were he and had his influential name and an O level certificate and earned twelve shillings a month—if she were a *man* even—Wanjiru knew she could move mountains. Why, she wondered in exasperation as she said good-bye to her mother tilling their small shamba, didn't men use the power they had? If women had that power, what a different world this would be!

This was the same path Wanjiru had walked eight years ago to and from Grace Treverton's mission. In those days the boys had been cruel to her, trying to frighten her into quitting school. She knew now it had been because her presence in the classroom had set them to doubting their superiority over girls. Men were secure in their ascendancy, Wanjiru believed, as long as women were kept pregnant and illiterate, but an educated, independent woman frightened them, made them shift like a herd picking up lion scent. Wanjiru knew she rocked their male security. She did it on purpose, to goad them into action.

That was exactly what annoyed her about David Mathenge. He was a talker, not a doer. And did he think he was fooling anyone by calling this meeting when it was known Chief John Muchina was in Nairobi? Of course, David wanted to avoid being arrested; everyone was familiar with the horror stories of what happened to African agitators in prison.

But Wanjiru had no respect for a boy who stood up and made fine speeches when it was safe and then retreated in silence when authority arrived.

She passed some boys on the dirt road now, young Kikuyu of her own age wearing blankets and grazing their goats. They stared at her—Wanjiru, the freak.

She tossed her head back and walked proudly with breasts forward, buttocks sashaying, bare feet slapping the dirt, and long, strong arms swinging in confidence.

Seventeen-year-old Wanjiru was secure in the knowledge of who she was and where she was going in life. And nearly all this she owed to her mother, who, abandoned by her husband with nine children and a dying shamba, had had the vision and courage to try to change the future. She had chosen one daughter, Wanjiru, and had taught her that she must never be owned by men. After Grace's primary school Wanjiru's mother had seen to it that her daughter was one of the first enrolled in the new Native Girls School in Nyeri, one of a few which were starting to appear the length of the province, places of higher learning called *kiriri,* named for the part of the hut where Kikuyu girls sleep. Wanjiru had just graduated from that high school, and she was going to enter the Native Civil Hospital in Nairobi as one of the first students in a brand-new program to train African women as nurses.

The crowd at the meeting was large. David had chosen a significant site—the spot where a sacred fig tree had once stood on the edge of Nyeri town. To capture further the hearts and passions of his audience, David now climbed onto the giant stump left behind by the Catholic fathers when they had the tree cut down. There was not a Kikuyu present who did not recognize and appreciate the implication behind young Mathenge's gesture.

When Wanjiru arrived, David was already speaking. She pushed through the lines of parked bicycles, the Africans' most prized possessions, and listened.

"When the white men first came here," David was saying, "we thought they were temporary. They seemed to our fathers, and to many of you present here today, as a wandering people in search of a homeland. Out of pity we allowed them to stay and welcomed them to share in the bounty of Kikuyuland. But the white men got greedy, and now we know they are here to stay.

"First, they instituted a hut tax on us, which was alien to our way of life. And the only payment they would accept was coins, which we did not have, and the only way to obtain these mysterious coins was to work for the white man. *On our own land.* Next, they installed the humiliating *kipande* system and made us wear identifications around our necks, the same tags they hang about the necks of their dogs! Finally, they are trying to break up our tribal unity by making illegal our precious ancestral customs such as native healing and the circumcision of girls.

"When we complain, the white man tells us that he is doing this for *our own good,* as if we were children! He tells us that he is teaching us the value of disciplinary work, that he is teaching us the benefit of modern European ways. Instead, he has taught us to behave selfishly and to turn our backs on our family and ancestors!"

The crowd stirred, saying, *"Eyh, eyh."* Wanjiru saw that while there were mostly young men listening to David's impassioned speech, many elders stood on the sidelines, leaning on their tall staffs, their skinny bodies draped in blankets. In spite of herself, Wanjiru began to become infected by David's persuasive oratory.

"The white men brought God and churches to Kikuyuland and preached equality from the pulpit. But I do not see African and European working side by side. White men are dedicated not to us but to furthering colonialism in Africa. They employ us at starvation wages, and we are not permitted in their presence when they eat except as servants. I tell you, brothers, that any form of multiracialism in Kenya would be like a union of a rider and his horse. They part company as soon as the horse has carried his rider to a win in the race!"

The crowd murmured; heads nodded vigorously.

"My brothers," David went on, "we hear the British continuously protesting the treatment of Jews in Germany today. But I ask you, are the Jews in Germany treated any worse than the Africans in all the colonies of this continent?"

"No!" they cried.

"Wait!" shouted an elder from the periphery of the mob. "You are wrong to say what you are saying, David Mathenge! The white man brought us the love of Lord Jesu, and for that we must be eternally grateful!"

"And Karl Marx has told us that religion is the opiate of the masses," David cried back. "You have had the spirit and manhood dulled out of you, mzee, by this Lord Jesu!"

The crowd gasped in shock.

He continued, his voice rolling out over the stunned heads of his audience. "Today the white men dig up gold from where it is buried near Lake Victoria, take it to Europe, and bury it again! They use it to adorn their wives. We wish to adorn *our* wives—and that land where the gold lies belongs to us!"

"But what would you have us do?" cried David's friends. "How can we change what already is? We have no power against the British."

"We must be like the mosquito that lets its presence be known. We must set forth our demands for better schools and a university for Africans here in Kenya. We must go slowly and become educated and prove ourselves in the eyes of our colonial masters. We must remember the proverb that says the string bag is started weaving from the bottom—"

"Proverbs!" came a voice from the rear of the crowd. All heads turned because it had been a woman's voice. "You are good at describing our problems, Mathenge," Wanjiru called out. "But you give us no solutions to them except to utter worthless *proverbs!*"

David frowned. Wanjiru had the exasperating habit of never showing up when she was wanted and showing up when she wasn't! The girl needed a husband, he decided, to keep her in line. He ignored her.

"I have drawn up a petition," he said to the crowd, holding up a sheet of paper, "demanding that the government provide for us a university in Nairobi. I will pass it around, and you will all put your names to it and then—"

"And then the British will wipe their backsides with it!"

Everyone turned to Wanjiru again. This time she elbowed her way through to the front; astonished men stepped aside to let her pass. "I ask you a second time, Mathenge. What solutions do you offer besides useless proverbs and paper?"

He glared down at her. "We will win through unity and word of mouth."

"Unity and *force!*" she cried.

David felt his blood start to burn. His anger and lust rose at the same time. He could think of only one way to deal with this girl, but now was not the proper moment, nor in front of a thousand eyes. "We will launch a peaceful fight for freedom," he said.

"You cannot say 'peaceful fight,' Mathenge. The two words oppose and cancel each other out."

"Through peaceful resistance we will show superiority to the white man, as Gandhi in India is doing."

Wanjiru spat in the dirt. "Does the lion show its superiority to the jackal through peaceful resistance?" She turned to the crowd and raised her arms. "The British do not understand peaceful negotiations because they themselves stole our land by *force.* Violence is the only language they understand!"

The audience shifted like a tide. Half wanted to act immediately, with clubs and spears; the other half looked nervously around for informers and police. Ironically, it was the old men who constituted the former; the young men, the latter.

Wanjiru climbed up onto the giant stump, drew up next to David, and seized his arm. Close to his ear she hissed, "I was there the night you first heard Jomo Kenyatta in the forest! Have you forgotten his message? *I have not!*"

David's eyes flew open. He stared at her, stunned. Her fingers dug deep into his biceps, painfully. Her eyes, inches from his, shot a look through his brain that seemed to sear the back of his skull. *Now. He wanted to take her now.*

"This meeting is over" came a deep, authoritative voice. "Go home now, all of you."

Wanjiru and David looked down and saw Chief John Muchina forcing the mob apart with his silver-tipped walking stick; askaris, soldiers, escorted him.

"Come down from there, David Kabiru," Muchina ordered. "Go home and forget all this nonsense."

David stared down at the formidable chief. On the edge of his vision he saw the crowd starting to disperse, was aware of his friends looking to him for guidance, felt Wanjiru's firm breast pressing against his bare back.

He said, "I am breaking no laws, mzee."

"I told you before, son, not to give such speeches. You are deliberately defying me. Go home now, peacefully, and I will let the matter drop."

"We are gathered here for important business, mzee."

The chief clucked and shook his head. "You are young and restless, David Kabiru, the same as your own father was years ago. Heed the proverb that says, 'Great hurry in digging will break the yam tuber, leaving the best part in the ground, but go slowly and you will reap the whole of it.' "

David jumped down and faced the chief squarely. They formed an odd tableau, the handsome, sinewy youth wearing only khaki shorts and the fat gray-haired chief in his long white kanzu and leopardskin over one shoulder.

"Proverbs," said David. "Is that all you offer us?"

The crowd froze. Wanjiru on the stump caught her breath.

Muchina's eyes narrowed. "I said to go home now, boy, before you are in real trouble."

David thought of the girl standing behind him, her arrogant black eyes watching him. He steeled himself and said, "We are all in trouble, mzee, with chiefs like you."

It seemed that all Africa fell silent then, that an entire continent turned a shocked face toward the mere boy who was challenging the authority of a chief and, behind that chief, the British Empire. What none of the startled eyes saw that August morning on the edge of Nyeri town was the fear in David Mathenge. He knew the risk he was taking; he had heard of the "accidents" that happened in prison to men who opposed Muchina. But there was Wanjiru, watching, listening, doubting David's manhood and bravery. He had to save face in front of the girl; he had to stand fast against Muchina as if he were a warrior of old stalking his first lion. None of the onlookers was aware of the gripping in David's bowels, of the terror constricting his throat. They saw only the sudden and unexpected birth of a new and necessary hero.

John Muchina boiled with rage. As the seconds ticked by, he weighed the situation. These political upstarts were becoming more and more of a nuisance, like that agitator overseas Jomo Kenyatta; they threatened his comfortable arrangement with the British. Old John

Muchina hated this new educated generation. They were intelligent and bright and could make fine speeches, while he could not even read or write and had never gone to school.

"Do you have something to say to me, boy?" he asked in a low, cautioning tone.

A thousand ears hung upon David's reply. Wanjiru, towering over them like a black Liberty, wanted to speak, but even she knew to be silent in the presence of a chief.

A fine sweat broke out over David's body. "This is what I have to say," he said above the pounding of his heart. "I say that the British who appointed chiefs among the Kikuyu did so arbitrarily and with no thought to a man's competence or desire to help his people. I say that the chiefs appointed by white men do not provide adequate tribal representation in the government, that they do not represent tribal tradition, that they exist in a capacity that is foreign to the Kikuyu way of life, and that the chiefs' only interest is in preserving the status quo."

Muchina clenched his jaw. "You speak, then, of your own father, Chief Mathenge."

"I do. It was through his stupidity and the stupidity of our fathers that we now have no land. They had no right to sell our inheritance to the white man."

If David had physically struck the chief, he could have not caused a greater insult, for John Muchina was older than a hundred harvests and therefore was of David's father's generation, and so he, too, had sold his land to the white man in exchange for the badge of office he wore today.

"You are being led toward the prison by your impudent tongue, boy." Muchina lowered his voice so that only David could hear. "If I put you behind bars, you will never see daylight again."

David suppressed a shudder. He turned to the crowd and said in a strong voice, "Look at your chief who tries to run with the impala and hunt with the lion!"

Muchina gestured to the askaris. They started to come forward.

Inflamed, meeting Wanjiru's fiery eyes, David shouted, "Our chiefs are like dogs! They bark when other dogs bark, but they do tricks when they want their British masters to feed them!"

When two soldiers seized David by his arms, his voice rose. "Chief Muchina is a Judas Iscariot!"

"Arrest him."

David struggled against the men who held him. "Listen to me!" he cried to the crowd, which was growing nervous and agitated. A few men had picked up stones; the elders were suddenly hefting their walking staffs and realizing how much they felt like the spears of the old days. "Why do we want to become like Europeans?" David cried. "How many Europeans have you seen who wish to become like the Kikuyu?"

"Eyh!" cried the mob.

Muchina raised his silver-tipped cane to silence them, and when order prevailed, he opened his mouth to speak. Instead, the crowd heard David say, "Remember, brothers, that the man who does not love his country does not love his mother and father and the people of his country. And a man who does not love his mother or father or his own people cannot love God!"

The silver-tipped stick came slamming down on David's head. It made a great obscene cracking noise in the morning stillness. David's head snapped back, but he recovered and turned a venomous eye on the chief. They glared at each other for one cold instant; then Muchina gestured for David to be taken away.

But the crowd was suddenly disrupted. From the rear a commotion began, and it rippled to the front until the chief had to call for order again. This time, when the crowd obeyed, they parted in two halves, forming a path down the center, and at its end stood the reason for the commotion.

It was David's mother, Wachera.

When the chief saw her, a few in the crowd caught the brief tremor in his stolid demeanor. It was no secret that John Muchina went often to the medicine woman's hut in the middle of the night to confer on grave tribal taboos. If everyone in the district was afraid of Chief Muchina, Chief Muchina was afraid of Wachera.

David focused his blurred eyes on her, tried to see her through the blood trickling into his eyes from the wound in his scalp. She appeared to him as almost unreal, as if she were an ancestress who had been conjured up from the mists. She stood in her soft leather dress and aprons, her heavy layers of bead necklaces and bracelets and anklets, her ceremonial belts with their magic charms sewn on. Wachera's smoothly shaved skull was held high as her eyes looked across the space between her and her son. She spoke to him with that look; she said things to him no one else could read.

And he knew in that instant that his mother was not going to rescue him from prison and certain torture.

"White injustice will be the forge that hammers you into manhood, my son," she had said once, and her eyes said it again now. "Suffer first; then you will have the strength and courage to reclaim our land."

When Chief Muchina realized that Wachera was not going to interfere, he barked an order at the askaris and hurried away with his prisoner, leaving behind a confused mob, a mother filled with love and pride and pain, and, on the giant stump of the fig tree, forgotten, a transformed seventeen-year-old Wanjiru, who clutched her hands to her breast and, watching David Mathenge being marched away, saw the new purpose in her life.

30

Arthur Treverton prayed he wouldn't have a seizure.

Today's parade was going to be the biggest ever held in Kenya, and he was going to be the most important person in it. The eyes of the colony, it seemed to the anxious fifteen-year-old, would be upon him as he officially launched the week of celebrations. It was going to be the first chance in his life to prove himself finally.

A red ribbon had been strung across Nairobi's main street, and at an appointed moment Arthur, riding ahead of the parade, was to gallop down the dirt street with his saber held high, swoop upon the ribbon, and cut it before hundreds of spectators, thus marking the official renaming of Central Road to Lord Treverton Avenue.

Arthur was nervous and excited. The grandstands that had been erected on either side of the road, between the Stanley Hotel and the Post Office, were filled with officials and visiting dignitaries. His mother, Lady Rose, was already under her special canopy, smiling serenely and queenlike. Next to her, his father, the earl, was seated beneath a portrait of the King. The boy knew that his father would watch him with the critical, dispassionate gaze Arthur had grown up fearing and adoring.

But even more vital to Arthur than pleasing his father was his performance today in front of Alice Hopkins, who, by virtue of owning the second-largest ranch in Kenya, had also been given a seat in the coveted grandstands.

Alice Hopkins was twenty-two years old, remarkable neither for beauty nor for charm, but something of a legend in East Africa because of her single-handed taking over of a ninety-thousand-acre ranch upon the sudden death of her parents six years ago, when she was only sixteen. Everyone had said at the time that she could never manage the enormous holding alone, and speculation had run high upon who would be the lucky purchaser of the land. Valentine Treverton had been among the prospective buyers and one of the many who had been impressed by young Alice's fight to keep her land and work it with no more help than a few loyal Africans and her brother, Tim, younger by five years. Against immeasurable odds she had saved the sheep and the sisal, had stayed out of debt, had not played into the hands of the fortune hunters who came around, and had emerged solidly successful and independent at age twenty-two.

And she had paid only one price: her femininity.

It was the hard and dour Alice Hopkins, whose mouth had forgotten how to smile, sitting in her khaki trousers and homespun shirt, her sunburned face hidden beneath the wide brim of a man's bush-whacker's hat, whom Arthur Treverton hoped to impress and win over on this August afternoon, because Alice stood between him and her seventeen-year-old brother, Tim Hopkins, with whom Arthur was desperately in love.

The staging area for the parade was the grounds of the Norfolk Hotel. Tables loaded with champagne and food stood beneath trees, and music came from a gramophone. It was mostly young people who had constructed the floats and who would ride on them, and they rushed about now making last-minute adjustments to costumes and checking the engines of the cars pulling the floats, their laughter and excitement filling the cool August morning.

"Do I look all right, Mona?" Arthur asked his sister as he ran his hands down the immaculate jodphurs of the borrowed hunting clothes.

"You look smashing!" Mona said, giving him a hug.

It had been marvelous, she thought, of Hardy Acres, Jr., the banker's son, to lend Arthur his complete hunting outfit. The minute Arthur had put it on, he had seemed to grow two feet. Mona prayed that her brother would perform successfully today. Opening up this parade meant so much to him.

Arthur had no idea that his sister was responsible for his having the honor of cutting the ribbon. When she had heard that that distinction was being awarded to the governor's nephew, and when she had seen how her brother's face had glowed with envy at the news, she had launched a secret campaign to persuade her father that the privilege of opening up Lord Treverton Avenue should, after all, fall to a Treverton. Valentine had finally conceded, not so much, Mona knew, because he agreed with his daughter or because he cared what she thought as because she could be such an annoyance when she took up a cause. Mona knew how to handle her father. She didn't use his love for her as a means of getting her way, as other daughters might, because she knew there wasn't any love there. What Mona did was persist until he gave in, to be left in peace.

And in the end her father had confessed that while the thought of the spectacle of his son galloping down Central Road waving a saber did not appeal to him, he had to admit that at least Arthur would be doing something manly for a change.

Arthur knew none of this. Mona sheltered him from life's bruising realities and from much of his father's disappointment in him. All Arthur knew was that for some reason the governor had reconsidered using his nephew and had invited Treverton's heir to open the celebrations instead. That had been four weeks ago, and Arthur had been a changed boy ever since.

"I *will* be all right," he said to his sister as she straightened his collar, "won't I?"

"You'll be wonderful."

"What if I have a seizure?"

"You won't! You haven't had one for a year, have you? Oh, Arthur, you'll be marvelous! I'm so proud of you!"

He beamed. He couldn't recall when anyone had been proud of him last. It was probably never. He adored his sister; she always managed to give him confidence. He was glad she was out of school for good now and living at home. His secret hope was that she wouldn't marry Geoffrey Donald because then she would move to Kilima Simba and he would be all alone at Bellatu again.

"Would you do me a favor?" he asked quietly, looking around at the crowd getting ready to line up for the parade.

"You know I will." Mona would do anything for her younger brother. After all, with their mother living her own life in the eucalyptus glade and their father rarely at home, all they really had in the world was each other. Mona was also glad she was home from school for good, and by coincidence, she, too, was thinking that she didn't want to marry Geoffrey Donald. "What's the favor, Arthur?"

He pulled an envelope from out of his sleeve and pressed it into her hands. "Give this to Tim, will you?"

She slipped it into the bodice of her harem costume. Mona was their go-between. She was glad Arthur finally had a friend, despite what everyone whispered about their relationship.

"A kiss for luck," she said, and pecked her brother on the cheek. Then, pausing to look at him, at the tender boy's face beneath the hunting cap, and thinking how she was going to take care of Arthur from now on, Mona gave her brother one final hug and went off in search of Tim Hopkins.

The theme of the pageant was the opening up of Africa by the white man. Although the British had been present on the coast of Kenya for more than a hundred years, the year 1887, fifty years before, had been chosen as the "founding date" because that was when the first real settlement of missionaries was established in Mombasa. Geoffrey Donald, who was to ride on the Vasco da Gama float with Mona, enjoyed a unique reputation in that his grandmother had been among those first missionaries, while his father, Sir James, having been born in 1888 to the missionary woman and her explorer husband, enjoyed the singular honor of being one of the first white men born in Kenya.

Dressed in Elizabethan doublet and padded jacket for his portrayal of the Portuguese explorer Vasco da Gama, Geoffrey circled the float and inspected the papier-mâché replica of the town of Malindi and its braces of coconut palms, wishing his father were on hand for today's celebrations. The parade was just the beginning of a week of festivities, and it was only proper that Sir James Donald be here to enjoy the prestige and recognition that were rightfully his. But there had been another outbreak of blackwater fever in Uganda, and Geoffrey's parents were in the jungle, helping the stricken tribes.

He finished his inspection of the float, satisfied that it was the best of them all and that it was going to represent a perfect reenactment of the historic meeting in 1498 between da Gama and the sultan of Malindi, and having made certain that the truck hitched to the massive wagon was capable of pulling it down Government Road, Geoffrey searched the crowd once more for Mona.

He spotted her across the lawn, laughing with Tim Hopkins. Geoffrey pursed his lips. Why was she wasting her time on Tim Hopkins when it was no secret that Tim had eyes only for her brother?

Geoffrey's annoyance dissolved when he took in her costume.

Beneath her head-to-foot wrap of bright pink silk he could make out the harem skirt of such transparent material that one could almost see Mona's legs. He could also see the tight bodice that was like those which Asian women in Nairobi wore—edged in gold and cut high to leave the midriff bare. While it was true that Mona's face was modestly veiled and the pink silk wrap covered her head and that nearly nothing else of her showed, except for hands and feet, Geoffrey realized in mild shock that it was an extremely daring and provocative costume.

Tim Hopkins, dressed in an old-fashioned safari outfit and Victorian pith helmet, was to portray the famous explorer Sir Henry Morton Stanley. On a float decorated with trees and jungle vines, he was going to strike a historic pose with Hardy Acres, Jr.—Dr. Livingstone—commemorating the day in 1871 when the explorer found the "lost" doctor.

As Geoffrey walked up to fetch Mona back to their float, he tried to avoid getting into an exchange with the handsome young Tim, who made him decidedly uncomfortable. But it was unavoidable. As soon as Geoffrey came near, Tim turned his bright smile to him and said, "We've just been talking about the Fort Jesus crowd, Geoff!"

"Oh? Come on, Mona. The parade's about to begin."

"Look at them, Geoff!" she said, pointing to the wagon that supported a balsa replica of the coastal fort. The scenario was supposed to depict the year the Portuguese came down with the plague, and those climbing on board in their costumes looked as if they were playing the part rather realistically.

"Got a bit too heavy-handed with the champagne last night," Tim said. "They've all got hangovers!"

Geoffrey took Mona's arm. "Your brother's getting ready to ride off. We'd better get aboard our float."

"He's not even on his horse yet," Mona said, drawing away, smiling to hide her irritation. Geoffrey's possessiveness was becoming tiresome. "I must find Aunt Grace. She has a pair of earrings to finish off my costume. Remember, I'm the sultan's chief wife!" Turning quickly so that Geoffrey wouldn't see, Mona tucked a folded piece of paper into her bodice—something from Tim which she would give to her brother after the parade. "See you at the float, Geoff!"

Grace was on the hotel veranda, looking, with a troubled expression, across the road at the King's Way Police Station.

Something seemed to be going on. There was an unusual amount of activity around the grounds. Too many policemen . . .

There were quite a few people with her on the veranda—those who hadn't been accorded seats in the grandstands and who didn't feel like standing along the roadside to watch the parade. They preferred to sit in comfort with their gins and watch the parade depart. While she kept an eye on the police station, Grace overheard pieces of conversation.

"I say that the Italian invasion of Ethiopia is the best thing that's happened to us," came the voice of a cattle rancher whom Grace knew. "I'm making money right and left, supplying the Italian Army with beef. You ask Geoffrey Donald. His ranch hasn't done this well in years!"

"It's done us all some good," said his companion. "Provided the Eyeties don't decide to push on down and invade Kenya."

"No fear of that, Charlie."

"There's war brewing in Europe. You mark my words."

Startled, Grace looked at the two men. *War brewing . . .*

"If there's anything I can't stand," said another voice from the far end of the veranda, "it's an educated wog that comes up from Nairobi in a suit and loud tie, talking court English and thinking he knows everything about everything."

Grace returned to staring at the tin-roofed building of the police station. David Mathenge was in there, behind bars. She had been upset to hear of his arrest last week because she knew how much Chief Muchina hated the boy and how certain "special" prisoners were treated in jail. Grace was fond of Wachera's son; she had watched him grow into a fine, educated young man. He had never allowed friendship with Grace, but there was a sort of wary respect between them. Whenever Grace saw him, she could not help recalling the night of the first Christmas party at Bellatu, nearly eighteen years ago, and Chief Mathenge's tragic death.

He is very like his father, she thought now.

A truck pulled up in front of the station, and uniformed men with guns climbed into the back. As it sped off down the road, Grace felt her anxiety rise.

Was trouble anticipated?

An officer emerged through the front door of the police station, adjusting his cap and giving orders to someone inside. As he struck off down the street, Grace called out to him.

"Good morning, Dr. Treverton," he said, coming up to her.

"Can you tell me what's going on, Lieutenant?"

"Going on?"

"Your men seem particularly active this morning. Surely it isn't for the parade!"

He smiled. "Oh, it's nothing to worry about, Doctor. Just a bit of native business upcountry. Something we're looking into."

"What sort of business?"

"We got word that there's a gathering of Kikuyu outside Nairobi. Coming from all over, I'm told. Some from as far north as Nyeri and Nanyuki. We're just going out there to keep an eye on them."

Grace felt herself go cold. Kikuyu coming from as far away as Nyeri. "What do you suppose it means?"

"Who knows? But I assure you it's nothing to worry about, Doctor. We'll see they don't interfere with the parade. Good day to you."

As she watched him go, Grace could not shake the feeling that beneath his smile and relaxed manner, there was a very worried policeman.

"There you are!" called a voice behind her.

Grace turned to see her niece sweep onto the veranda in a cloud of pink silk, her eyes smiling over the veil that hid her face. Grace also saw men's heads turn.

"You should be getting 'round to the Stanley, Aunt Grace. The parade's about to begin."

Grace looked at her watch. She had come to the Norfolk with Mona and Arthur to help with costumes and floats. A seat was reserved for her in the grandstands, and it was time she was driving her car around the back streets to be on hand to watch Arthur cut the ribbon across Lord Treverton Avenue.

"What's the matter, Aunt Grace? You look gloomy. If you're worried about Arthur, don't be! He's such a dear. You should see him on his horse. And that outfit has done wonders for his confidence! I can't wait to see the look on his face tonight when he sees the surprise I have for him."

"And what is that?" Grace asked, distracted.

"You remember. The elephant gun!"

"Oh. Yes. But I wasn't thinking about Arthur just now." Grace was thinking of the unusual police activity, of the gathering of Kikuyu outside the city, and realizing that it could be no coincidence that such a gathering was taking place on the day of the big parade. The Africans were planning something. . . . "I was thinking of David Mathenge," she said, "in that horrible jail."

Mona's smile vanished for an instant. She looked across at the police station, her expression briefly dark and intense; then she was smiling again. "What do you think of my costume?" she asked, twirling around.

Grace forced a smile. She thought Mona's outfit too risqué. But then, Grace reminded herself, this *was* 1937, and young people today were so different from when she was young. Besides, Mona had had little choice in what part to play in the parade. The women riding on the floats had been at a loss to find historical characters from Kenya's past to portray—unless, like Sukie Cameron, one dressed as a man. There were more than enough men in African history, from sultans to explorers, traders to hunters, but women were sadly absent from the centuries, as if they hadn't existed. And so Mona and her friends had had to settle for such pale roles as harem women and the wives of famous men.

There were no Africans taking part in the parade, and no historical African figures were going to be represented.

"Come along then," said Grace abruptly, turning her back on the police station and her mounting worry. "Let's get you into the harem before Vasco da Gama has a fit!"

ARTHUR, AT THAT same moment, as he prepared to mount his horse, was worrying about exactly the same thing—fits.

He hadn't had one in more than a year; Aunt Grace's simple bromides and sedatives were a marvelous stopgap for his incurable illness. Still, the threat of a seizure hung day and night over Arthur Treverton like an ax suspended on a thread. He never knew when one was going to strike, what would bring it on, where he would be when he fell, and in front of whose eyes he would disgrace himself. It was for those reasons that Arthur had never attended school, could not travel anywhere alone, was not allowed to handle a gun, and would never be accepted for military duty, all of which he dreamed of doing one day.

It was not so much the private tutors he minded as he did the missing out on boyhood camaraderie, of belonging to clubs and joining rugby teams. Nor did he so much mind having nursemaids watching over him on hunting safaris as he did his father's refusal to allow him a gun. And as far as the army went, there was no question about Arthur's ineligibility. What sort of earl's son was he, the boy wondered, that he had no school colors or trophies, that he had no buffalo horns or elephant tusks he had bagged himself, and that there was no chance of his ever receiving medals for war service? Someday Arthur was going to be Lord Treverton, and he knew he would feel like an impostor.

As he did now, in this borrowed outfit. He would never own one like it, he would never see military action—even though everyone was saying that Europe would soon be at war again—and he would never be given the chance to show the world that a man lurked within the epileptic boy.

It was for all this that Arthur detested his physical weakness and had been unhappy for all of his life. Until the day he met Tim Hopkins.

It had been during last year's Race Week. Arthur had come to Nairobi with his father and Geoffrey Donald, who had horses entered in all races, and he had encountered Tim at the refreshment tent. The acquaintance had begun uncertainly and tentatively between the four-teen- and sixteen-year-olds, both being painfully shy and unused to casual conversation with strangers. But then, over scones and tea, they had gradually discovered the most amazing thing: that they shared a great deal in common.

Upon the suspected murder of his parents at the hands, it was rumored, of drunk Wakamba tribesmen, eleven-year-old Tim had been taken out of school and put to work by his headstrong sister, Alice, to try to save the farm. In the ensuing five years Tim had received a sporadic education from transient tutors, had been unavailable to join clubs and ball teams, had never gone out on hunting safaris merely for trophies, and now, because of a lung weakness caused by the years of strenuous childhood labor, was exempt from military obligation.

Arthur and Tim had immediately recognized something familiar and comfortable in each other; they had become fast friends at once.

But there had been obstacles over the past year to impede the development of their relationship. Tim's sister, Alice, was fiercely protective of her brother and jealous of anyone who sought his love and attention, and Arthur's father, Valentine, thought Tim Hopkins too rough and lowborn for his son. So the boys stole moments when they could: during the King's birthday celebrations, at every Race Week in Nairobi, New Year's Eve at the Norfolk, and only last month, when everyone in Kenya had turned out at Lake Naivasha to witness the landing of the first Imperial Airways "flying boat" from England.

They even exchanged letters. And it was because of one letter in particular that Arthur's father had thrashed him with his belt and had forbidden him to have anything to do with Tim Hopkins ever again.

Arthur thought of this now as he sat high on his horse, handsome and dashing in someone else's clothes, waiting for the chiming of the hour by the church bells, so he could make his historic ride down Government Road.

What if I have a seizure? What if I fall in front of Tim? Will he be shocked? Repulsed? I should have told him. . . .

Arthur loved Tim beyond words. That was what the thrashing had been for. Arthur's father had found the letter to Tim and had been enraged by the word *love*. It had triggered the beating which Arthur had taken without raising an arm in defense, because he hadn't understood what his father was shouting about, accusing his son of something unnatural and using words which Arthur had never heard before. He had taken the beating without protest and had cried late into the night, the red welts burning his back. He had tried to understand what had happened, and he tried to fathom it now. But all he could come back to was Tim and Arthur's love for each other—the admiration, the sharing bond, the strength they drew from each other, and the solace they exchanged in a hostile, confusing world. It was the one thing in his lonely and bewildered life that finally brought Arthur Treverton happiness.

In the final seconds before he was to start his dramatic ride to the red ribbon, Arthur decided that nothing meant as much to him, with the exception of Tim's friendship, as his father's approval. He wanted a chance to show the earl that he was a man, not a "pansy," as his father declared. Arthur wished desperately to be allowed a chance to do something more heroic than cutting a ribbon.

Hearing murmurs from the floats behind him, Arthur turned in his saddle and saw people stepping down to the ground. He looked at his watch and realized the hour was late. He had been daydreaming while waiting for the church chimes and had not realized that the scheduled moment had come and gone and the chimes had not sounded.

"What's going on?" he called to Geoffrey Donald.

"I don't know. Seems to be something up. I'll go take a look."

Arthur saw his sister climb to the top of a minaret on her float, pink silks fluttering in the breeze, and shade her eyes as she peered out over the crowd. "What is it?" he called to her.

"I can't make it out. There appears to be something going on down the road. The police—"

Angry shouts in the distance silenced the merrymakers. People looked at one another; men jumped down from floats and climbed out of trucks. Then a man burst onto the scene. Everyone recognized him as the church caretaker, who was supposed to have rung the chimes. "I saw 'em!" he cried. "From the bell tower! The wogs are marching on Nairobi! *Thousands* of them!"

Chaos erupted. Arthur fought to control his horse as people began to run from the hotel grounds.

"Mona!" he called. "Can you see?"

"Not yet. It's difficult—" Her hand fell away from her forehead. "Oh, my God."

"What is it?"

"They're coming down King's Way! They seem to be headed for the police station."

"What's it about?"

"I can't tell. But they're carrying signs. Arthur, get me down from here, will you?"

He galloped up to the Malindi float, which was deserted now except for the young harem wife, whose veil fell away from her face as she hastily climbed down from the spire of the sultan's palace. When she was pillion behind her brother, they rode out to the street in front of the Norfolk Hotel, where they found a line of policemen with rifles barring the way.

Arthur and Mona stayed at the back of the crowd and watched from horseback the slow and steady advance of a great mob of people coming down the road. As the Africans drew closer, the Europeans saw that the bell ringer had spoken the truth; there were thousands of them.

Mona tightened her grip around her brother's waist.

Despite their numbers, the Kikuyu were quiet and orderly, marching with determination toward the police station, a few bearing signs that read FREE DAVID MATHENGE and A UNIVERSITY FOR AFRICANS. Mona was stunned by their apparent organization and silent cohesiveness; she had not thought Africans capable of them. Then she saw the likely reason, marching at their head: a young woman whom Mona recognized as having once attended Aunt Grace's primary school.

The great mass of Africans who followed Wanjiru were formidable in their silence. Unified in this way, as the white man had never seen them, they presented a fearsome, collective threat that chilled the blood of every policeman in the line. Although there were women and children in the crowd, and none of the Africans carried a weapon, and none made sounds or threatening gestures, yet they terrified the Europeans who faced them at the end of the street.

Mona sat spellbound. How had they managed it? What mysterious communication network had reached them all over the province and gathered them under one purpose? What united them now and controlled them? She stared at the young woman at the front of the advancing crowd. She walked proudly; there was rebellion and courage in her stride, in the swing of her long arms. And when she raised a hand to stop the mob and she called out three words, "Free David Mathenge!" there was something in her voice the Europeans had never heard from an African before.

A standoff hung in the air. The police stood at the ready, fingers on triggers; the Europeans watched; the Africans waited.

Then a noise was heard in the distance: a car motor that rapidly drew close as it sped along the streets. It came up behind the Europeans. Arthur reined his horse aside; a path was made for the governor and Valentine Treverton. Mona looked down at her father as he passed. The way he strode headlong into a crisis, so fearless and brave!

The governor climbed the steps of the police station and frowned down at the sea of Africans with the look of a father admonishing his children. "Now, now," he said, "what's this all about?"

Wanjiru stepped forward. "Give us David Mathenge!" she cried.

The governor was shocked. A *girl* led this mob? "Now see here. You know you can't do this. Go home, all of you."

"Free David Mathenge!" she repeated.

Valentine stepped up beside the governor and glared at the crowd. "Is this how you think things get done? By a show of force?"

Wanjiru walked to the bottom of the steps, put her hands on her hips, and said, "We are speaking to you in the only language you know! Force is all you understand!" She spoke compellingly, in the crisp, melodious British accent of the educated African. "This is how the Kikuyu vote. We do not put bits of paper in a secret box, as you do, afraid to voice your opinions. We do it openly. We vote by showing ourselves. And what we have voted is that David Mathenge be set free."

"He was arrested legally and within the law," the governor said.

"He was not!" Wanjiru brought a piece of paper out of her pocket and waved it at the two white men. "This is what David Mathenge was doing when Muchina arrested him. It is a petition to obtain a university for Africans in Kenya! David Mathenge was acting peacefully and within the law when Muchina had him taken away in chains! You have no right to hold him!"

Mona felt her pulse race as she listened to Wanjiru's voice. She saw the passion in the girl's stance and thought: *She is in love with David.*

Looking out over the black faces that filled the street all the way to its end and wound back out of sight, Mona felt threatened and excited at the same time. She was filled with a sense of witnessing something profoundly significant.

"Give us our university!" cried a Kikuyu in the crowd.

He was backed up by nods, a low, grumbling murmur, and a sudden nervous shifting of the mob.

"Good Lord," Arthur said quietly to his sister, "I doubt that girl can hold them for long. It wouldn't take much to spark this mob, and once they get out of hand, there'll be blood shed."

The governor signaled to an officer on the porch and whispered something to him. The man saluted and hurried away.

"I tell you again and for the last time," the governor said to the crowd, "send me a deputation. Elect three or four men from among you, and I will listen to your grievances. I will not stand up here and be threatened!"

"It is you who threaten us!" cried Wanjiru. "With your police and your laws and your taxes! You have no right to prohibit our tribal practices. You have no right to forbid worship at the sacred fig trees or the practice of female circumcision! You threaten to erase our way of life altogether! You threaten to wipe us out as a race! If you do not give us what we want, we will call a general strike. Every African in Kenya will sit down and fold his arms. *You!*" She flung an accusing finger at Valentine. "You will get up tomorrow morning and say, 'Boy! Bring me my tea!' And there will be no tea!"

The governor threw down his hands.

"The white men will come to their business offices"—Wanjiru's voice continued to ring out—"but there will be no clerks to do their work for them. The memsaabs will call for their African house girls, but there will be no house girls."

"I'm giving you all one minute to clear the street!"

"Mona," said Arthur very quietly, "look up there."

She looked up and saw soldiers taking places along the police station roof and behind the walls of the compound. A truck rolled silently up; a machine gun stood on its flatbed.

"Dear God," she whispered.

"We'd better get out of here."

"Arthur, look! Something's going on 'round back."

He turned and saw what none of the Europeans or the policemen had noticed: suspicious, furtive activity going on behind the jail.

"What do you suppose it means?" Mona asked.

"My guess is they're going to try to break David Mathenge out of jail." Then Arthur saw something else: Tim Hopkins, in his Stanley costume and carrying a rifle, inching his way unobserved toward the rear of the jail.

Now Mona was genuinely scared. "Shouldn't we warn the police?"

"No. It might trigger an all-out massacre. Tim's got the right idea." Arthur tugged on the rein and guided his horse back to the Norfolk Hotel, where he deposited his sister on the veranda.

"What are you going to do?" she whispered.

"You go inside, Mona. If there's shooting, *don't come out.* Do you hear me?"

"Arthur! Stay here, *please.* Stay out of it."

"I'm going to help Tim, Mona. We can stop them quietly and avoid an incident."

She stared up at him. "Arthur. Please don't go!"

He turned and rode away.

She watched him kick his horse into a light canter so as not to draw attention to himself. Suddenly her brother seemed terribly young and terribly old at the same time. His face was so smooth and sweet, not yet a man's, but the look in his eye and the tone in his adolescent voice that cracked told her that Arthur had just, within minutes, grown up.

She watched him circle the crowd of Europeans and make his way surreptitiously to the rear of the jail; at the same time she listened to the heated exchange between Wanjiru and the governor. Mona suddenly understood. This was the girl's objective: to divert the attention of the authorities while a few of her people set David free.

Frightened, and worried for her brother, Mona pulled her pink silk wrap tightly about herself, looked around to make sure she wasn't being observed, then struck off along the route her brother had taken— toward the rear of the jail.

WHILE SEVENTEEN-YEAR-OLD Wanjiru continued to amaze her own people and the Europeans alike with her oratory, David Mathenge was making his first bid for freedom.

Since most of the police effort was directed toward the street, it had been easy for David's friends to overwhelm the few guards, gain access to David's cell, and get him out. Seeing that he got clear of the compound without getting caught, however, turned out to be another matter. Because David couldn't walk.

He had been tortured.

Not here, in the white man's jail, but back up north in Karatina, in a hut on Chief Muchina's land. Wounds on his feet, which the police doctor had bandaged without asking questions, made it nearly impossible for him to walk. Two comrades got him by the arms and ran, half dragging David, to the gate where four policemen, Africans in the service of King George, lay unconscious. A group of young Kikuyu, wielding clubs and tribal knives, milled nervously on the other side of the gate, watching the end of the alley, where the crowd of Africans was clustered around Wanjiru.

The air seemed to crackle with tension. Wanjiru's words were firing their blood. The youths kept an eye on the cellblock, waiting for David and their friends; they also glanced frequently at the soldiers on the rooftops, who were training their rifles on the mob in the street.

They heard the governor again shouting an order for dispersal, followed this time by a threat to shoot if the crowd didn't clear away.

The small group at the rear gate shifted uneasily. They felt the weapons in their hands, the heat in their veins. Their orders had been to get David Mathenge away quickly and unseen, to a prearranged hideout in the mountains. But the hot-blooded young men were starting to hear not the orders of a mere girl but the thunder of manhood in their ears. These were young Africans who had never known warfare, who had been born too late to experience the pride and excitement of being warriors, who now suddenly resented these white men who had taken away their fathers' spears.

And that was why, when they saw a lone European youth creep into the alley, a rifle in his arm, they lost control.

Several things happened at once. The gang of youths descended upon Tim Hopkins with clubs and knives just as David Mathenge was being brought through the gate. In the same moment Arthur Treverton appeared at the end of the alley, on foot, his ribbon-cutting saber unsheathed.

There was a moment of confusion, which later none of the participants would be able to unravel for the authorities, in which Arthur, seeing Tim fall beneath the blows and kicks, plunged like a madman into the knot of Africans.

David Mathenge shouted, "No! Stop!" and saw the second white boy fall.

Pulling free from the two who supported him, David stumbled toward the fight and grabbed for his crazed friends, shouting at them to stop. He saw a dagger go up and then plunge; he reached for it but missed, falling to his knees next to Arthur's body. Shocked, David saw the dagger go into the white boy's back. He reached for it, pulled it out.

A cry from the end of the alley made the youths stop and turn, startled.

A white girl, dressed like an Asian memsaab, stood at the entrance of the alley, her eyes wide, her hands over her mouth.

The group broke and ran. Two flew over a wall; the rest dashed past Mona and disappeared into the street crowd. She stared at the two white boys lying on the ground and at David Mathenge, who was kneeling by her brother, a bloody dagger in his hand.

Their eyes met.

For an instant time stood still as David Mathenge and Mona Treverton stared at each other. Then, suddenly remembering themselves, David's two companions ran forward and dragged him to his feet.

He held back, to look at Mona with pain-filled eyes. He opened his mouth but was unable to speak. Then his friends pulled him away, and just as shouts from the street were calling for police and the alarm was sounded, David ran, leaving Mona with the body of her brother.

31

Grace put the scalpel down and held her hand out for a hemostat. She looked at her scrub nurse. "Rebecca! A clamp, please!"

The woman looked up from her instrument tray, startled. With a mumbled apology she placed the clamp into Grace's outstretched hand and looked quickly away, embarrassed.

Grace frowned. It was unlike Rebecca to be distracted during surgery. She was one of the hospital's best scrub nurses, vigilant and dedicated, proud to be the only African woman in the province skilled in surgical assistance. But this morning, as they worked in the light of the October sun, Rebecca seemed uncharacteristically inattentive.

"Another clamp, please. I shouldn't have to ask for them."

"I'm sorry, Memsaab Daktari."

"Is there something wrong, Rebecca? Do you wish to be relieved?"

"No, Memsaab Daktari."

Grace tried to read the nurse's eyes. Much of her face was hidden by the white surgical mask, but her eyes, which avoided meeting Grace's, revealed a highly emotional state.

Another of the reasons Grace had singled out this Kikuyu woman for surgery work was her even temperament and ability to remain calm in a crisis. This morning, however, Rebecca seemed to be agitated, and Grace was suddenly concerned.

"Silk tie, please, Rebecca," she said, holding her hand out for something she should not have to ask for. This was a routine hysterectomy. Grace and Rebecca had performed so many together, that they often went through an entire procedure without Grace's needing to say a word.

But now, to Grace's further surprise and rising concern, Rebecca confessed that she had forgotten to put silk on her instrument tray.

"Perhaps you should scrub out," Grace said, signaling to the other African nurse in the operating room. She was the circulator, the member of the surgical team who did not stand at the sterile table. "Bring some silk ties quickly," Grace said to her. "And then see if anyone is available to relieve Rebecca."

As Grace returned her attention to the wound, clamping bleeders that needed silk ties, she did not see the two nurses exchange a secret, worried look.

"REBECCA," GRACE SAID as she removed her white surgical gown and gloves, "I want to talk to you."

The nurse was cleaning up the operating room, her gestures abrupt, her work sloppy. A replacement had not been found; Rebecca had had to stay through the entire hysterectomy, making too many mistakes.

"Rebecca?" Grace repeated.

"Yes, Memsaab Daktari," the woman said, not turning around.

"Is there trouble at home? Are you having difficulties with your children?"

Rebecca had four boys and three girls, ranging from fourteen years old down to one year; her husband had abandoned her during her last pregnancy to live in Nairobi. In all her years of working at Grace's mission, from the day she graduated from the new Secondary School for Girls, through her training with Grace and her years of working in the operating room, Rebecca had been able to keep her personal life from interfering with her work. But now Grace suspected that the responsibilities of being a single mother were wearing her down.

And yet Rebecca now turned, faced Grace fully, and said, "No, Memsaab Daktari. There is no trouble at home."

Grace tried to think. It occurred to her that this morning was not the first time Rebecca had acted strangely. In fact, Grace realized all of a sudden, Rebecca had started to change sometime around the day of the great protest in Nairobi two months ago. Now that she thought about it, Grace was certain that that was when Rebecca had started to act oddly, just days after that terrible afternoon which saw the murder of Arthur Treverton and the miraculous jailbreak of David Mathenge. Was that what troubled Rebecca now? Was her conscience troubled by the reckless actions of a handful of her people?

Rebecca Mbugu was a devout Christian who attended church in Nyeri every Sunday and was involved in many charitable works. Her children all had been baptized and attended mission schools. Many Kikuyu like Rebecca had been shocked by and ashamed over Arthur Treverton's brutal killing and the cowardly escape of David Mathenge. After that day all unity within the tribe appeared to have broken down; Wanjiru lost some of her influence; the Africans had returned quietly to their farms.

That day seemed to have had a specially hard impact on Rebecca, Grace decided now; perhaps she had been in that protesting mob on King's Way.

Grace came up, put a hand on the nurse's shoulder, and said, "If you ever need to talk, Rebecca, or if you need help in any way, you know that my door is always open."

When she left the operating room, Grace again missed the look exchanged between the two African nurses.

Grace Treverton Mission covered nearly twenty acres and consisted of stone buildings, which were the primary and secondary schools, the hospital, dispensary, nurses' dormitory, and vehicle maintenance shed. In the center of this collection that resembled a small town, Grace's imposing house stood. It occupied the spot where Birdsong Cottage had once been, but it was much larger and had been built, after the fire eight years ago, with an eye to permanence.

As Grace crossed the spacious lawn that separated the buildings, she waved to people who called out to her, and she heard children singing in one of the classrooms: *"Old MacDonald ana shamba . . ."*

She had a great deal on her mind. There was the news of a yellow fever vaccine that had just been developed in the United States; her experiments with chloral in treating tetanus; the need to hire a full-time laboratory technician; her plans to travel into French Equatorial Africa at Christmastime. James Donald, on a trip into the Gabon territory last year, had met Dr. Albert Schweitzer and had given him a copy of Grace's rural health manual, *When You Must Be the Doctor*. Dr. Schweitzer had written a letter of high praise to Grace, inviting her to come and visit him at his clinic in Lambaréné, and it was because of this and other things occupying her mind that Grace was unaware of anything amiss on this bright October morning.

For one thing: that the mission compound was unusually quiet.

She climbed the steps of the veranda, where imported California fuchsias were just coming into leaf, and looked around in puzzlement. It was her habit to have midmorning tea out here while she went through the day's mail, and Mario never failed to have the table set, the teapot in its cozy. But the table was bare, with not even a white cloth over it, and the morning mail had not been laid out.

"Mario?" she called.

There was no reply.

She entered the solid tranquillity of her spacious and stately living room. "Mario?" she called again. The house was silent.

She went into the kitchen and found that the kettle hadn't even been put on the stove. She filled it and placed it over the heat, then went back into the living room, where, on a large, ornate desk that overlooked her rear garden, the morning's mail lay.

Wondering where Mario, who was as reliable as the sunrise, could be, Grace went through the envelopes.

In the past eight years James Donald had gotten into the habit of writing to Grace at least once a month, but his latest letter was long overdue. And there wasn't one in this morning's delivery.

Grace was pleasantly surprised, however, to find a royalty check from her publisher in London with a letter suggesting that considering the medical and scientific progress these days, Grace think about writing a revised edition of her manual.

The morning's mail revealed another piece of good news: A letter from the bank informed her that the yearly anonymous deposit into her account, which had not been increased in several years, had just been doubled. The Donald farm, under Geoffrey's keen administration, she decided, must be doing well.

Setting the rest down on the desk next to her journal, Grace called out a third time. But Mario wasn't in the house.

Returning to the kitchen to make tea, Grace saw on the table a newspaper, the latest edition of the *East African Standard,* which had been delivered only this morning and which she had not yet read.

When she saw the headline on the front page, she put the teapot down and picked up the paper.

"Oh, my God," she murmured. Then, thinking of Mona, Grace folded the paper and hurried out.

SHE ENTERED THE big house by the back door and was surprised to find the kitchen deserted, the stove cold. In the imposing dining room the old grandfather clock ticked faithfully in the oppressive quiet. The living room stood in dark, somber tones; the heads of impalas and buffalo looked down on sofas and chairs that had not seen occupants in weeks. Polished surfaces and gleaming silver were the only evidence that the presence of a human, with broom and cloth, ever passed through here.

Grace paused to listen. Bellatu was as silent and unwelcoming as a mausoleum. She knew that Valentine, overwhelmed with grief over the death of his son, was in Tanganyika hunting lion and that Rose was dealing with her bereavement in the only way she knew how—in the cloister of her eucalyptus glade. But where was Mona?

She heard a sound. Turning, Grace found that the living room was not deserted after all. Geoffrey Donald rose from the leather sofa and said, "Hello, Aunt Grace. I hope I didn't startle you."

"Where are the servants?"

He shrugged. "I have no idea. No one answered the door when I knocked. I let myself in."

"Where's Mona?"

"Upstairs. I saw her at the window. She won't come down and talk to me."

"Have you seen this?" Grace handed him the newspaper.

Geoffrey's eyebrows arched. "I say! That's good news, isn't it?"

"I'm hoping Mona will find it so. Perhaps it will bring her some peace of mind. I'll go up and see her, Geoff. Why don't you put the kettle on and I'll bring her down for tea?"

WHEN THE DEAD *are forgotten, they have died twice.*

Where had she read that? Mona couldn't remember. It didn't matter, though; it was true all the same. And that was why she was never going to forget her brother.

Mona was sitting in the window seat of Arthur's bedroom, looking out over the vast acres of coffee toward distant Mount Kenya. In her lap lay the poem written by Tim Hopkins which he had given to her on the morning of the parade and which she had never had a chance to pass on to her brother. She had read it so many times that she had memorized it.

"Mona?" said Grace in the doorway. She came all the way in, shivering and wondering how her niece could stand the chill in the room. As she drew near, Grace studied Mona in concern. The girl had inherited her father's dark good looks, but she had grown pale these past weeks. The Kenya tan common to British settlers had faded to a disturbing whiteness that heightened the blackness of her eyes and hair. She had lost weight; her dress hung on her.

"Mona?" Grace said, sitting opposite her niece in the large window seat. "Geoffrey's downstairs. Why won't you see him?"

But Mona didn't reply.

Grace sighed. She knew that Mona's grief lay enmeshed in a complex web of guilts and punishments. Mona blamed herself for her brother's death because, as she had said, if she had not insisted he be the one to cut the ribbon, he would have been safely seated in the grandstand at the time of the incident. She also blamed Geoffrey Donald, who, Mona had hotly declared, was "doing nothing" while her brother was being murdered. Valentine was also guilty for not having handled the African protest better and for allowing David Mathenge to escape; even Lady Rose, in Mona's convoluted thinking, was culpable insofar as she had never been a good mother to Arthur.

Finally, Mona blamed David Mathenge for her brother's death.

Grace showed her the newspaper.

"He's innocent after all," Grace said while Mona read. "This other boy, Matthew Munoro, has turned himself into the police and has confessed to stabbing Arthur. It wasn't David after all."

Mona took a long time reading it; then Grace realized that she wasn't reading at all but was simply staring down at the page.

"Apparently," Grace explained quietly, "there has been a lot of pressure within the tribe for the real killer to come forward and exonerate David. They want Wachera's son to be allowed to come out of hiding, but he won't as long as he is wanted by the police for murder. They say that Chief Muchina has fallen under a *thahu* and is terribly ill. I would imagine that this boy Matthew decided he would rather face the white man's justice than risk Wachera's *thahu.*"

Mona looked away, her eyes settling on the sea of green coffee trees reaching to the foothills. "David Mathenge is still guilty," she said softly.

"But you yourself told the police you hadn't witnessed the actual stabbing. And the only other person at the scene was Tim, who was unconscious and admitted he didn't witness anything. Mona, this boy has confessed."

"David Mathenge"—Mona's voice continued softly—"is guilty of my brother's death because it was *his* jailbreak that got Arthur killed. Maybe he didn't plunge the dagger into my brother's back, but he's guilty of his murder all the same. And someday David Mathenge is going to pay."

Grace sat back. The whole nightmarish affair had torn the Treverton family apart. Here was Mona, plunged into a morass of grief and self-blame; Valentine had run away to vent his anger and helpless rage on the Serengeti Plains; and Rose had made herself just a little more invisible among her precious trees, her only companion, ironically, Njeri, David's half sister.

"Mona, please come downstairs and talk to Geoffrey."

"I don't wish to see him."

"What will you do then? Never see anyone again as long as you live? This grief will pass. I promise you. You're only eighteen. You have your whole future ahead of you—marriage, children."

"I don't want marriage or children."

"You can't say that now, Mona, dear. There is so much time ahead of you. Things change. If you don't marry, what sort of life would you have?"

"You never married."

Grace stared at her niece.

Then Mona said, with tears rising in her eyes, "Have you ever been in love, Aunt Grace?"

"I was once . . . a long time ago."

"Why didn't you marry him?"

"We . . . couldn't. We weren't free."

"I'll tell you why I asked, Aunt Grace. It's because I know now that I am incapable of love. I have spent many hours sitting here and thinking. And I've come to realize that Arthur and I were different from other people. I can see now that I'm just like my mother, that I was born incapable of feeling love. She never had any love for Arthur, I know that now. She has never loved either of us. When I try to picture my mother, I can't *see* her, Aunt Grace." Mona's tears fell. "She's just a shadow. She's an incomplete woman. Just like her, I'll never be able to love anyone, and now that Arthur's dead, I'll be all alone in life."

When Mona started to cry, memories came rushing into Grace's mind: the terrifying February night eighteen years ago when she delivered an unbreathing baby in a train car; Mona's first laughter, her first steps; the monkeylike creature that had come flying out of the Cadillac, crying, "Auntie Grace! We're home, and I never have to go to England again!" Grace suddenly felt every single day of her forty-seven years.

"Mona, listen to me," she said, taking the girl's hands into hers. "The dagger that fell that day is still falling. It is stabbing all the life and love out of you. Don't let it kill you, too, Mona. Get out of this room. Close it up and say farewell to the ghost that lives here. You belong to the land of the living. Arthur would want it that way. And there *will* be someone in your life whom you can love, I promise you that."

Mona dried her eyes with the back of her hand. Her dark, slate eyes became bleak; her voice was full of loneliness. "I know what lies ahead of me, Aunt Grace. Now that my brother is dead, I am the heir to Bellatu. All this will be mine someday, and I am going to make this plantation my life. I am going to learn how to run it, how to grow coffee, and how to be independent. The only master I shall ever have will be Bellatu. It will be the only thing I will ever love."

There was a light in Mona's eyes that suddenly reminded Grace of another memory, also from eighteen years ago. She and Valentine were standing on this very spot, on a barren hill where the house would someday go, and she was listening to him talk about the plans he had for this wilderness. Grace had heard the conviction in his voice when he had talked about possessing this land; she had seen a strange illumination in his dark eyes as he had described his vision of the future. And Grace suddenly realized that she was witnessing it all over again—in his daughter.

"It will be a lonely existence, Mona," she said sadly. "Just you, all alone in this big house."

"I will not be lonely, Aunt Grace, because I will be very busy."

"With nothing to live for except coffee trees?"

"I shall have something to live for."

"And what is that?"

"To see that David Mathenge pays for his crime."

"Mona," Grace whispered, "let it be. Lay your grief to rest. Revenge never succored anyone!"

"He'll come back here someday. He'll come out of hiding, from wherever he is, and he'll come back here. And when he does, I will see to it that David Mathenge pays for my brother's murder."

A door slammed downstairs. Footsteps thumped through the house. Finally, Mario's voice rang down the hallway. "Memsaab Daktari!"

"Good gracious," said Grace, getting to her feet. "I'm in here, Mario."

He burst in. "Memsaab! In the forest! You must come."

"What is it?"

"An initiation, memsaab! A big one! Very secret!"

"Where? Initiation for whom?"

"In the mountains. Over there. For *girls,* memsaab."

Grace suddenly understood the odd behavior of her nurses, the absence of the Bellatu staff, the mission compound strangely quiet. They had been amassing for a huge secret initiation, the first in years. It was the forbidden ceremony of female circumcision—the clitoridectomy—the operation that had killed Mario's sister.

"Memsaab," he said, "the girl Njeri Mathenge—"

Grace flew past him and down the hall.

Mona remained in the window seat, listening to their footsteps fade. She looked out and saw Grace and her houseboy hurry across the lawn to the path that led down to the mission.

A moment later a car—an official car—pulled up from the opposite direction. When Mona saw a district officer get out, she left her window seat and went downstairs.

Geoffrey stood up when she came into the living room. "What's going on?" he said.

"A policeman's just arrived. It must have to do with the initiation."

But the officer wasn't there for that reason at all. He had brought a telegram, which he now handed to Mona. "It's for Dr. Treverton, but no one down at the mission seemed to know where she was. I was wondering if you would give it to her."

Mona frowned down at the yellow envelope. When she saw that the telegram had been sent from Uganda, she quickly opened it.

It was from Ralph, Geoffrey's brother, and it said: AUNT GRACE. SERIOUS OUTBREAK OF MALARIA. MOTHER IS DEAD. FATHER DYING AND ASKING FOR YOU. COME AT ONCE. BRING GEOFFREY.

"Oh, my God!" she cried.

Geoffrey took the telegram, and before he could react, Mona was running down the veranda steps in the direction of the river.

When she reached the ridge, where she could see the mission compound, the polo field, and Wachera's hut, Mona could not see her aunt anywhere.

32

The ceremonial surgery was called *irua*, and it consisted of three steps: the removal of the clitoris, the trimming of the labia, and the suturing shut of the vulva.

Its purpose was to discourage lust in girls, to curb sexual promiscuity, and to make masturbation impossible. With the sensitive part of the genitals cut away and the vaginal opening reduced to the width of a little finger, it was believed that girls would be deterred from experimentation before marriage. Later each girl, upon being purchased by a husband, would undergo an examination to assure him of her virginity, and an incision would then be made to allow for intercourse.

Irua was one of the oldest, most revered rituals of the Kikuyu; it marked a girl's official entry into the tribe and celebrated her passage into womanhood. Those who underwent *irua* were honored and respected among the clan; those who did not were outcast and taboo.

Wachera had been preparing her instruments and medicines for days.

It had been many harvests since she had last performed the sacred *irua*—her people's fear of the white man's reprisals had stopped the practice of many important Kikuyu rituals—and so she felt proud and honored to be performing it today. The ancestors were pleased; they had told her so. Just as they had told her of her son's hiding place—in the land where the sun slept.

However, they hadn't told her when he would come home.

But Wachera was patient. She had faith that her son would someday return to Kikuyuland and take his place as a leader of his people. On that day, Wachera was certain, David would reclaim his land stolen by the white man and drive him out of Kikuyuland.

For was not her *thahu* working?

The terrible curse Wachera had spoken many harvests ago in the bwana's big stone house had finally claimed the life of the bwana's only son. The rest of the *thahu* would work in time, the medicine woman believed, wiping out the seed of the man who had torn down the sacred fig tree. The day would come when the bwana and his family would no longer exist, and it would seem as if they had never been.

Still, the fruits of revenge were small succor for the pain Wachera carried night and day in her breast, the pain of missing her only son, of yearning for him, of worrying about his safety and happiness. She received some consolation, however, from the knowledge that David was undergoing a special trial of manhood, just as the warriors of old had done. Whatever he had suffered at the hands of Chief Muchina and in the white man's jail, whatever hardships he now endured in the lands to the west, Wachera knew that her son would return a warrior, a true Mathenge.

She paused in her final preparations to listen for the girls' singing, which would indicate they were coming from the river, ready to be operated upon.

No one helped the medicine woman in her secret work. *Irua,* because of its sacred nature, required special ritualistically clean and spiritually pure attention. Not just anyone could wield the surgical razor, in the same way that not just anyone could observe the procedure. Only those women who were themselves circumcised and in good standing with the tribe could watch. And men were so taboo as to incur punishment should they try to spy on the ritual.

Wachera knew that what she was going to do today was denounced by the white man. It wasn't against his law; no matter how hard the missionaries had tried to stamp out the ancient ritual, they had not succeeded in making it officially illegal. Yet they strove in other ways to turn the Children of Mumbi away from the traditional practices, and in such ways the missionaries were being largely successful, as in the instance of barring any circumcised child from their schools. The missionary schools were the best, and since most parents wanted their children to grow up with the white man's advantages and education, they entered into a sad bargain with the missionaries, giving up the ancestral ways in order to receive the crumbs that fell from their white overlords' table.

Such had been the feeling in Kikuyuland until the day of David Mathenge's arrest.

But from that time on, through the persuasive speeches of the girl Wanjiru and others like her, the Children of Mumbi were starting to see what an empty covenant they had entered into with their white oppressors. On the day of the big protest in Nairobi, when David had escaped and the soldiers had fired shots into the defenseless crowd, the Kikuyu had had their eyes opened. One by one they had come to Wachera, asking her what they must do. And she had said, "Return to the ways of the ancestors, who are unhappy."

Even though many Kikuyu did not agree and refused to take part in today's *irua,* believing the missionaries, who called it monstrous and barbaric, true Children of Mumbi were bringing their sisters and daughters into the forest to be circumcised.

She listened again for the singing.

While Wachera worked in the privacy of the initiation hut, girls from all over the district, ranging in age from nine to seventeen, were bathing up to their breasts in the icy waters of the river. While female elders of the tribe stood guard on the bank to be sure that no man or non-Kikuyu spied on them, the initiates shivered and froze in water meant to numb them, for there would be no anesthetics used in the surgery. They sang the ceremonial songs and dropped leaves into the river as a symbol of drowning their childhood spirits. They would stay in the freezing water until they had little feeling below the waist; then they would follow a path to a specially built homestead in the forest.

Wachera had bathed at the river before dawn and shaved her head. Now she painted her body with sacred paint—white chalk from Mount Kenya and black ocher. She chanted as she painted herself, holy words which made the chalk and ocher strong medicine against evil spirits. When this was done, she checked again her healing leaves, the "banishers" that made spirits of infection flee, and the mixture of milk and soothing herbs that would be sprinkled on the fresh wounds. Sweet-smelling leaves were set aside for the last part of the operation, when they would be bound between each girl's legs before she was carried to the healing hut. Lastly, Wachera inspected her iron razor. It was sharp and clean, as her grandmother the elder Wachera had taught her.

Few of *her* girls ever felt pain at the time of cutting or died from blood poisoning.

Singing in the distance brought Wachera to the door of the newly built initiation hut. She saw aunts and mothers merrily constructing the ceremonial arch of banana plants, sugarcanes, and sacred flowers at the entrance of the temporary homestead. This arch was a medium of communication with the ancestral spirits; no one but the initiates might pass under it. Other women were laying out fresh cowhides on the ground; the girls would sit on these during the operation. And still others were preparing the feast of roast sheep and sugarcane beer which would follow the ordeal.

Irua was one of the most solemn yet joyous celebrations among the Kikuyu. Wachera's heart swelled to see her people united again in the old ways. Surely the God of Brightness was pleased! Surely this returning to the ways of the ancestors was a sign that the white man was soon to leave Kikuyuland! It meant that her son David was soon to come home.

Wachera Mathenge, for the first time in many years, was suddenly very happy.

GRACE DIDN'T HAVE to ask Mario where the girls were. She could hear them singing down at the river.

Before she reached them, her way was barred by men—the fathers and brothers of the initiates, Mario explained—who were passing around calabashes of sugarcane beer. They were polite to Memsaab Daktari, but they would not let her pass. Already there was a district officer, Assistant Superintendent Shannon, who had left his car on the road and trudged through the bush with two African askaris. And arriving at the same time as Grace were two missionaries from the Methodist church in Nyeri and a very disturbed group of priests from the Catholic mission.

"Hello, Dr. Treverton," Assistant Superintendent Shannon said as he came up to her. He was a tall, stiff military man who ran a tidy district and who knew when to keep out of "native" affairs. "I'm afraid this is as far as they'll let us go," he said, nodding in the direction of the happily drunk fathers and brothers. "The girls are in the river. But they'll come along this path. It'll be your only chance to see them."

"Where is the ceremony to take place?"

"Up there, through those trees. They've been weeks at clearing a homestead."

"I hadn't expected to see you here. Are you going to try to stop it?"

"I'm not here to interfere, Doctor. I'm here to keep the peace and see that no nasty business comes out of this." He was referring to the missionaries, who were looking stormy and in a mood to obstruct. "Believe me," the officer said quietly, "I don't condone what the natives are doing, any more than you do. But I haven't the authority to break it up, and I wouldn't want to try if I had it. Those Africans outnumber my small force, and they're quite drunk. They've been stirred up by some political agitators. These people are getting harder and harder to control."

"I hadn't even heard a *word* about this!"

"None of us had. They kept this one a real secret. It's all wrapped up in the David Mathenge business."

"Do you have any idea where he is?"

"Only rumors. Some say he's in Tanganyika; others, in the Sudan. The governor hasn't the manpower to search all East Africa for him, and now that this other boy has confessed to killing your nephew, well, quite frankly, Doctor, I don't think anyone gives a hang where David Mathenge is."

"*Mi scusi, signor,*" said a white-haired priest, coming up to the police officer with a distressed look. "You must stop this abomination!"

"They're not breaking any laws, Father. And I advise you not to interfere. If you try to, I'm afraid I shall have to detain you."

"But this is outrageous! *We* are not the ones performing the ungodly ritual! For the sake of those poor girls, you must stop them!"

"Father Vittorio," Shannon said in practiced patience, "You know as well as I that these people will not listen to me. And if I try to stop them, there will be bloodshed. Wait until Sunday, Father, and then lecture them from your pulpit."

The elderly priest glowered at the policeman, then turned to Grace. "Signora dottoressa," he said, "surely *you* want this stopped?"

Yes. Grace wanted it stopped. She felt so strongly against *irua* that six years ago she had gone to Geneva, where, under the auspices of the

Save the Children Fund, a conference on African children had been held. Grace, along with several other European delegates, had spoken out against the barbarous custom, declaring that it was the duty of all governments under which the custom was practiced to make it a criminal offense. Clitoridectomy was practiced not only in Kenya but throughout all Africa and the Middle East; hundreds of tribes from the Bedouin in Syria down to the Zulu of South Africa forced little girls to suffer a painful and traumatizing ritual that posed complications in later life, especially in childbirth. Grace had told the members of the conference about Gachiku and the Caesarean delivery of Njeri.

However, the conference members could not wholeheartedly agree to total abolition of a people's sacred and deeply ingrained social custom and opted instead for education of those people to help them turn away from such practices by their own wish.

As far as Grace knew, there had not been an *irua* in this province for years. If what Officer Shannon said was true, that this mass ritual was tied up somehow with David Mathenge's arrest, then today's *irua* implied something far more significant than a simple tribal get-to-gether.

It was meant to be a slap in the white man's face.

"Here they come," said one of the Methodists.

It was the only time during the whole ritual when others might look upon the initiates. As the girls, naked except for a single necklace each, followed the path from the river to the homestead, they sang ancestral songs of a mournful nature, in slow and gentle voices. The girls walked in pairs, with their elbows bent and pressed to their ribs, hands raised and curled into fists with thumbs inserted between first and second fingers, to indicate a readiness to withstand the coming pain.

Grace was shocked into immobility. Nor did the priests or missionaries react because they had not been prepared for the sight that now passed before their eyes.

The girls were grave and stately, singing in perfect beautiful harmony, their heads newly shaved, their nude bodies gleaming with river water. They didn't look to either side of the path or behind themselves, for that would have been bad luck; they didn't acknowledge the Kikuyu men, who now stood soberly at a respectful distance, or the Europeans, who stared speechless. The initiates walked as if in a trance; they mesmerized themselves with their melodious chant; their slender bodies swayed as they walked.

Their ages, Grace guessed, ranged from seventeen down to eight or nine. Such a broad span would not have been known in former times, but since there had been no *irua* in recent years, the older ones joined the younger. And she knew most of them. There was Wanjiru, the articulate fighter who had orchestrated David Mathenge's escape from jail; there were the nurse Rebecca's three daughters; there was Njeri, David's half sister and Rose's companion.

Grace could neither move nor speak.

When had they organized this? How had they managed to keep it a secret? There were a hundred girls, at least, in the monstrous procession! Why hadn't a single white person gotten word of it?

Grace suddenly felt cold. For the first time in her eighteen years in East Africa she felt a strange, dark fear. There was something awesome about these innocent naked girls, something raw and primeval. Grace had the sensation of looking back into time. It was as if she were watching girls who had lived a hundred years ago, on their way to the ancient test of strength and courage and endurance.

And it frightened her.

When the girls were out of sight, the Kikuyu men closed in behind them and warily watched the Europeans.

"Why don't you all go home?" Assistant Superintendent Shannon said quietly to the missionaries. "There's nothing you can do here."

Recovering from his shock, Father Vittorio turned on the District Officer. "Are you going to stand there, knowing what those poor girls are about to go through?"

Shannon glanced at the Africans, then presented a smile to the priest. "Take care now, Father. They're watching us. And they're the male relatives of the girls. If you make a wrong move now, I shall be powerless to save you from them."

The priest looked at the Africans. He knew many of them. One was the groundskeeper of his church; another took care of his priestly vestments. These were men who came regularly to mass, who knelt at the altar rail to take holy communion, who brought their children for baptism and Christian names, but who were now, the priest saw, strangers.

Father Vittorio blinked. He experienced a sudden revelation that for some reason struck fear in him: that savage Africa still beat in these Catholic hearts.

While the Europeans continued to argue over what to do, while keeping an eye on the Africans who blocked the path to the homestead, Grace discreetly left the group and went into the bush. No white person, as far as she knew, had ever witnessed an actual *irua*. She herself had seen only the aftermath: Mario's dead sister and Gachiku trying to give birth.

She followed the direction of the path and eventually saw, through the trees, the sacred arch decorated with flowers. A few Kikuyu men stood guard. Grace continued through the forest, circling the clearing that was the homestead. Finally she came upon a boulder surrounded by Cape chestnut trees. Climbing up, she saw that it gave her an unobstructed view of the homestead below while she herself remained concealed.

She watched with held breath.

Assistant Superintendent Shannon was right. It was one thing to interfere with childbirth, as she had done with Gachiku, but another to intrude upon a most sacred and solemn ritual. In this Grace knew she was powerless to stop them, as was the officer with his askaris. And the Kikuyu also knew this. The *irua* about to be performed was a blatant nose thumbing to the white authorities. Since the debacle of Pageant Week, when a thousands-strong mass of Africans had been humbled in the eyes of their white masters, they had sought, and found, a way of lashing back.

This was active rebellion, and everyone knew it.

The girls filed into the compound, where mothers were waiting. Grace knew a little of the rules of the ritual. Traditionally a girl had a sponsor, another woman of the tribe who became a kind of second mother. But these girls, she saw, went to their real mothers. Perhaps not enough women had been available. After all, Grace realized, large though this group was, it did not represent the entire Kikuyu population in the province. The majority was staying safely, and wisely, away.

The girls went to their mothers, who were waiting on the cowhides, and sat down. They were taken in groups of ten, while the rest formed a protective circle around them. From her vantage point Grace could see over the heads of the women. Each girl sat down with her legs open, while her mother sat behind her and interlocked her own legs with those of her daughter, to keep them open and steady. The girl reclined in the arms of her mother, her head back so that she looked up at the sky. When the girls were thus positioned, an elderly woman passed among them, sprinkling a liquid—ice water, Grace suspected—on each girl's genitals. This was supposed to numb the area further and retard bleeding, but Grace knew it would have little effect.

Held thus by her mother, each girl was expected to keep her eyes skyward and was not to move, to cry out, or even to blink while the operation was being performed. To flinch in any way was to bring disgrace upon herself and her family.

Grace was not surprised to see Wachera, painted in black and white, appear from inside the hut.

Wanjiru was the first candidate. She lay back in her mother's arms and, as far as Grace could see, not only showed no signs of fear but looked as if she were proud, as if she welcomed this terrible test. And when Wachera's razor did its work, Wanjiru remained serene.

Grace closed her eyes.

When she looked again, Wanjiru was being carried, bandaged with leaves, to the healing hut.

Grace watched as the next girls were attended to. The littlest ones cried. A few screamed. Not many were like the radical Wanjiru.

Grace felt time stand still. The women sang in their haunting, primitive harmony, rejoicing upon each mutilation, as their mothers had done for them, and their grandmothers, and so on back into history in an unchanging, unbroken ancestral legacy. With the cutting of each girl, Grace felt the grip of European civilization slip away. She listened to women with Christian names singing songs of praise to Ngai, the god of Mount Kenya. And she felt herself go numb.

But when the next group of girls came to the cowhides and she saw a terrified Njeri lie back between Gachiku's legs, Grace came suddenly alive.

Wachera performed her quick, skillful surgery upon four girls before she reached Njeri, and when Grace saw the fear in the seventeen-year-old's eyes, saw how she struggled against her mother's hold, and when she remembered the day she had brought the baby out of Gachiku's abdomen, Grace cried, "Stop!" and climbed down the boulder.

The singing ceased. The women turned.

It was the worse sacrilege—a non-Kikuyu and, from what they understood of white ways, uncircumcised, coming into their presence. Grace's intrusion brought *thahu* upon the sacred *irua*. But the women were too shocked to react. They drew back as she made her way to the inner circle.

"Wait," Grace said breathlessly as she drew up behind the kneeling medicine woman. "Please stop!"

Wachera rested back on her heels, razor in hand, paused a moment, then rose to her feet and faced Grace. She did not appear surprised to find the memsaab in her midst; in fact, Grace realized, Wachera seemed to welcome the interruption. *As though this were a chance at last for us to fight,* Grace thought.

"Please do not do this, Wachera," Grace said in Kikuyu. "Please let the girl go. Look how frightened she is."

"She will not disgrace her family."

Grace appealed to the girl's mother. "Gachiku, isn't this your favorite child? Isn't this the daughter of your beloved Mathenge? How can you do this to her?"

"I do it because I love her," Gachiku said in a tight voice, not meeting Grace's eyes. "And to honor my dead husband."

"Would you have your daughter suffer in childbirth as you did?"

Gachiku didn't reply.

"Give the girl to me," Grace said to Wachera. "She belongs to me! I gave her life when everyone else would have let her die. Your grandmother, the elder Wachera, would have let her perish. And Chief Mathenge, too. I saved Njeri! But not for this!"

"She belongs to Kikuyu. She will be made a true daughter of Mumbi."

"Please, Wachera! I'm begging you!"

"Begging? As my grandmother once begged the bwana your brother not to cut down the sacred fig tree?"

"I am sorry for that, Wachera, truly I am. But I am not responsible for my brother's actions."

"Where is my husband?" cried Wachera. "Where is my son, David? Where are my unborn children? If your brother had not come to Kikuyuland, I would have all my family at my side today. Instead, I am alone. Go away. You do not belong in Kikuyuland. Go back to where your ancestors dwell."

Before Grace could respond, Wachera dropped to her knees and worked her hasty skill upon Njeri.

The girl's scream tore the air, sending birds into flight from the surrounding trees.

Wachera poured the herb milk on Njeri and then applied the healing leaves. She said, "Now this girl is a true daughter of Mumbi."

Grace looked down. She began to tremble as Njeri's weeping filled her eyes. For as long as she lived, Grace knew, she would never forget the girl's scream.

As Gachiku helped her daughter to the healing hut, Grace turned to the next woman on the cowhide. "Rebecca," she said in an even voice, "I have taught you surgery. I have taught you about cleanliness and infection. You know that what you are doing here today is harmful. You know that you place your daughters at great risk. Let them go. Because if you don't, then you will never work at my side again."

The Kikuyu woman with the small gold cross around her neck gazed impassively at the white woman.

"And I say to all of you," Grace called out, looking at each woman in turn, "if you do not stop this evil practice now, you are never welcome in my mission again. If you are ill, do not come to my clinic. You will not be welcome there."

They stared back at her.

"They will not listen to you," Wachera said, "because I have told them that your clinic will not be there much longer. The day when the white man leaves Kikuyuland is near at hand. We are returning to the old ways, and you will be forgotten."

Grace regarded the face hidden behind black and white paint, the face of a woman whom she had thought she knew but who she realized now was a stranger. And Grace sensed a premonition, cold and gray, pass over her like a cloud briefly obscuring the sun. She thought of the few thousand whites ruling over millions of Africans, she heard Officer Shannon say, "They're getting harder and harder to control," she looked down at the bloodstained cowhides, and suddenly she knew beyond a doubt that some terrible, irrevocable threshold had been crossed here today.

With great dignity, her bearing a cover for the anger in her heart, the trouble in her soul, Grace turned her back on the medicine woman and walked from the compound. When she reached the sacred arch of the ancestors, she heard behind her the resumed soft, harmonious chant of the African women.

33

M ona reached over and took her aunt's hand not because she was afraid of the airplane flight, but because Grace looked as pale as death.

This was not a pleasure trip; they were going to a funeral.

Mona studied her aunt's tight profile. Grace seemed oblivious of her niece in the seat next to her. Mona told herself that it was because she sat on her aunt's "blind," side, the side of the injured eye. Unaware she could not see them, anyone not knowing Grace Treverton might stand or sit on her left. Giving her aunt's unresponsive hand a squeeze, Mona returned to staring out the window.

The Avro monoplane was flying low over dense forest and jungle. From the air Mona thought Africa looked far wilder and more intimidating than it ever did on the ground, but it was also more breathtakingly beautiful and compelling. This dark continent was her home, its rivers ran in her blood, its trees were rooted in her flesh; she believed that because she had been born here, she loved Africa with a passion that surpassed anyone else's, especially people like her father, interlopers in a land they barely understood. Mona wanted to remove the glass from the window and stretch her arms out to embrace it all, to shout down to the herds grazing on the plains below, to call to the herdsmen leaning on their tall staffs. Mona believed that because of her unique love for Africa, she would never become disillusioned with it or embittered.

She glanced at her aunt again.

Grace had said little since receiving the telegram from Ralph Donald three days ago. Something had happened at the *irua* ceremony, Mona suspected, but Grace wouldn't talk about it. All she had said was "I wasted my time while James lay dying."

And now she was afraid she was too late.

Grace had insisted they wear black. Not even for Arthur had Mona worn black; she simply didn't own anything that was darker than brown. Light colors were the most practical in an equatorial climate. But they had found an Indian *duka* in Nairobi that had been able to supply them with mourning dresses and little black hats with black veils.

Mona felt the airplane shudder, watched its canvas-covered wings dip and sway in the East African winds. Only last week a twin-motor Hanno carrying mail into Uganda had crashed upon landing.

She thought about death. She thought about Arthur in his solitary grave in the burial plot behind Bellatu, the first grave on a patch of ground waiting for future Trevertons. He had been dead only two months; it seemed two years. And now perhaps Uncle James, whom Mona barely remembered.

Geoffrey Donald was sitting in the rear of the plane, down where the cabin narrowed and where he shared a window with two Catholic nuns traveling to a mission at Entebbe. Geoffrey's loss of his mother had made Mona suddenly sympathetic toward him, had made her feel an unexpected tenderness for him, so that now, as the plane banked and came into its final leg of the flight, she thought about Geoffrey Donald.

BECAUSE GRACE HAD sent a wire to Ralph concerning their flight, he was at the landing strip outside Entebbe, waiting for them. He wore a black band on the sleeve of his khaki outfit.

The brothers embraced solemnly; then Ralph turned to Grace, who said, "I'm sorry for your loss, Ralph." Finally he turned to Mona and took her into his arms. "I'm glad you came," he murmured, and she looked at him, this tired-looking man, who was so colorless compared with his brother. She wondered what she had ever seen in him.

"Your father—" Grace began as she stood by the open door of Ralph's Chevrolet.

"He's on thirty grains of quinine a day, but he's stabilized."

Grace bowed her head and whispered, "Thank God."

"It's been a nightmare," Ralph continued, "what with absolutely everyone coming down with the malaria." His voice broke.

Geoffrey laid an arm around his brother's shoulders.

Ralph wiped his eyes. "It was madness. Some sort of unusual strain, the experts at the Makerere medical department tell us. Mother went swiftly, thank God. She was hardly ill. And then Gretchen put up a big fight. She's all right now, but I'm afraid you won't recognize her."

"Ralph," Grace said softly, a catch in her throat, "please take us to your father now."

SIR JAMES WAS sitting up in bed, insisting to his daughter than he couldn't possibly swallow another cup of tea. When the four came into the bedroom, he cut himself off in mid-sentence and stared like a man who couldn't believe his eyes.

Geoffrey went to him, sat on the edge of the bed, and embraced his father.

"Thank you for coming," Gretchen said to Mona and Grace.

Mona was shocked. Ralph had warned her that she wouldn't recognize her old friend. Gretchen looked years older than eighteen. "We came as quickly as we could," Mona said. "We decided that flying would be faster than the train."

"You're very brave. I could never get on an airplane."

"I'm sorry about your mother, Gretchen."

Her friend's eyes filled. "Well, at least it was quick. She didn't suffer."

Then Geoffrey rose from the bed, and Mona looked at her aunt. But Grace seemed unable to move. So Mona went and shyly said, "Hello, Uncle James. I'm glad you're feeling better."

"Well, *getting* better," he said in a weak voice but smiling. "It's good to see you, Mona. You've grown into a lovely young lady."

An awkward moment followed. James gazed across the room at Grace. Finally, he held out an arm, and she went to him.

Mona watched as her aunt went smoothly and naturally into his arms, burying her face in his neck, crying softly. And how James's hands stroked her back, her hair, how *he* comforted *her*. And suddenly Mona knew: This was the long-ago love her aunt had spoken of, the man she could never marry.

Grace drew back and studied James's haggard face. The years and harsh living in Uganda and this final illness had etched their work in his features. The cheekbones were sharper; the mouth was thinner.

"We were afraid we were going to lose you," she said.

"When Ralph told me you and Mona and Geoffrey were coming, it was the perfect medicine. I decided right then that I wasn't going anywhere."

"I'm sorry about Lucille."

"She was happy here, Grace. She did a lot of good work and has left her mark. Many people will remember her with love. When she was dying, she said she didn't mind. She had done her work and she was going to the Lord. If there is a heaven, she's there now."

He sighed and rested his head back on the pillow and said, "But I'm through with Uganda, Grace. I want to go back to Kenya. I want to go home."

ENTEBBE WAS A small port town on the north shore of Lake Victoria, and it was the administrative center of Uganda. A young African lurked among the official buildings, as he did every day, in the hope of catching news from home. When he saw four white people emerge from the Provincial Commissioner's bungalow, and he recognized the two women as Grace and Mona Treverton, David Mathenge retreated into the shadow of the building and watched them cross the dirt road.

He could almost taste the sweetness of revenge.

Because of them and others like them, he had had to flee his homeland, live in exile, and be hunted down for a crime he didn't commit—a shamed man. But his mother had promised him that the land would someday return to the Children of Mumbi and that her *thahu* upon the Trevertons would someday be fulfilled. The white people were currently the masters of East Africa, but David Mathenge vowed that they would not be so forever. He would return to Kenya someday, when he was prepared, when he had learned what he had to learn, and he would see to it that he had his revenge.

34

The radio was playing a Glenn Miller song, and Rose hummed along with it as she went through her wardrobe, trying to decide what to wear.

She looked through the bedroom window to let the weather be her guide. Since it was a gloriously sunny day splashed with the colors of newly blossomed flowers, and since she was going to overstitch the wild gardenias on her tapestry today, she settled upon a primrose yellow dress of moss crepe.

It was impossible to get new dresses these days. The war in Europe had brought the fashion industry to a standstill. Styles hadn't changed in five years; dresses still had padded shoulders and below-the-knee full skirts. Worse, clothing in England was rationed, and the only "new look" to come along in years was called the "utility suit." Rose found it all baffling. Wartime had made uniforms and working clothes the guideline of high fashion!

She sat at her vanity to let Njeri comb out her hair. After Rose had had her hair cut for the night of the gala opening of Bellatu, twenty-five years ago, she had let it grow out again, so that it now tumbled down her back to her waist. It was still the color of a harvest moon, still youthful and shiny, and had not a single gray hair, despite the fact that Lady Rose Treverton had just celebrated her forty-fifth birthday.

The radio broadcast crackled, faded, then died out. Rose gave the radio a mournful look. It seemed one couldn't depend on anything anymore.

She found matters not much better downstairs in the kitchen, where, a few minutes later, she came upon one of the African house girls buttering the bread *before* toasting it. "And the tea supply is getting lower," she murmured when she looked into the caddy. Supplies from Nairobi were infrequent and rarely complete. So much had to go to the war effort—to the feeding of Kenya's troops and the thousands of Italian prisoners coming into the colony—that little was left, it seemed to Lady Rose, for the civilians to pick over.

If Valentine were here, she was certain, such would not be the case.

But Lord Treverton had signed on to the King's African Rifles four years ago, when Italian forces had invaded northern Kenya. He had been there ever since, first fighting the campaign in Ethiopia that had signaled the collapse of the Italian Army in East Africa and now an officer in the intelligence section of the Occupied Enemy Territory Administration, policing the border between Kenya and Somaliland. He had been home only once in all that time.

And now, by great irony, Rose thought as she rationed out Countess Treverton tea into her teapot, after so many Kenya boys had fought and died in that bitter battle with the Italians, her own husband nearly dying from a septic wound, eighty thousand Italian POWs were being held in camps all over Kenya, requiring to be fed and clothed.

She resented it and wondered why the British government didn't just pack them all off back to Italy.

"Good morning, Mother!" Mona said as she came through the kitchen door, a rifle in her hand. "Finally got the leopard that's been at the pigs! I've told the chaps to give you the skin when they're done with it."

Rose gave her daughter a disapproving look—for several reasons. The first was Mona's inappropriate behavior. The Honorable Mona Treverton should not go stamping about the bush with a man's rifle, shooting leopards. The second was the way Mona spent her time these days. In her father's absence Mona had gradually taken over the running of the plantation, to the point of working in the midst of their Africans and even fixing machinery with her own hands! But lastly and most important, Lady Rose did not approve of her daughter's unladylike appearance.

Mona wore trousers and boots, with a khaki blouse tucked inside her belt. She wore her black, shoulder-length hair in a pageboy caught up in a common scarf knotted on top of her head. And from where Rose sat at the table monitoring the toast, she could see her daughter's hands as she washed at the sink; they were rough and brown from farm work.

"Where's Tim?" Rose asked, referring to the young man who had once been Arthur's friend and whose life Arthur had saved in the alley seven years ago. He had become a familiar figure around the Treverton plantation.

"He's gone up to Kilima Simba to join Uncle James in the search for the Italians."

"Italians?"

"I told you about it yesterday, Mother." Mona tested the tea, poured two cups, and joined Rose at the table. "Three prisoners escaped from the camp near Nanyuki. There's a large manhunt out for them."

"But why? There are Italians practically running loose all over. James has several working on his ranch, and your aunt Grace has two of them in her hospital kitchen. They're free to come and go, it seems to me."

Mona picked up the bundle of mail that lay untouched on the table; her mother wouldn't get to it for days, she knew.

Mona was aware of Rose's feelings toward the Italians. They were responsible for Valentine's being absent from Bellatu, and they were an expensive burden on Kenya—eighty thousand of them, requiring a pound of meat per day each. That was why there was such a steady slaughter of wildlife going on in the forests, with trucks driving past Bellatu every day loaded with zebra and eland carcasses. Rose was enraged over the mass, reckless hunting, and she blamed the Italians for it.

"These three were special prisoners," Mona explained as she looked through the envelopes. "Officers. One is even a general, I'm told. They had been kept under strict guard. Apparently, when they escaped, one of the guards was killed, so things are in an uproar."

Rose lightly buttered the toast, cut off the crusts, and handed a plate to Mona. "I hope Tim and James are careful."

"Yes, and I wish you wouldn't go into the glade today, Mother. Or at least if you do, please take a couple of chaps with you."

Rose shook her head. "The escaped prisoners can hardly have gotten down this far. I should imagine they would have headed north, toward Somaliland. Perhaps your father will capture them. In any case, I don't care for this subject—"

"Mother, I do wish you would be realistic! These men are desperate and dangerous! The guard they killed—they butchered him. He was *mutilated*. Please stay in the house until—"

Rose stood abruptly. "You've upset me, Mona. You really have, with your talk. I shall go without breakfast."

"Mother—"

"Come along, Njeri."

Njeri Mathenge, who had been at the counter putting together a lunch of strawberries and cream, cold meat pies, and soft cheeses, said, "Yes, memsaab," took up the picnic basket and Rose's parasol, and followed her mistress through the back door.

As soon as Rose was in the garden, in the fresh air and sunshine, she felt better. And the farther along the path she walked, with Bellatu receding until it disappeared behind the trees, and the deeper she went into the last, untouched reserve of forest where no one, except for herself and Njeri, ever went, the more she felt the troubles in her heart lift and vanish.

The glade was nearly the same as it had been the day she had found it twenty-five years ago. The gazebo was weathered, its paint peeling, but the trees were lush and green, the flowers a mass of color, with birds and insects filling the frangipani-scented air with song and drone. This was a world apart from the greater, ugly world where men killed and where innocent wildlife was slaughtered. Rose disliked that world; she put it from her mind.

The tapestry was secured to a large, folding frame that scrolled from left to right. As she worked, Rose turned one of the rods so that the fabric was taken up and thus kept clean. It was almost finished. Huge, as large as a tablecloth, the tapestry was covered entirely in bright flosses and yarns and fancy stitches. All that remained was the blank spot in the midst of jungle ferns and vines—the few inches which had eluded her all these years. Rose decided she would put an elephant into it, perhaps, or an African hut.

And after that, what? The tapestry had taken her twenty-five years to do. If she began another one now, Rose estimated that it would take her to the end of her life. When she died, two tapestries would show that she had lived.

A small greenhouse stood at the edge of the clearing, embraced between two mighty chestnut trees. It had been built years ago when Rose, finding she sometimes tired of stitchery, had decided to develop an interest in floriculture. The walls of the greenhouse were made of stone, but the roof was a glass skylight. There was a window; its panes had grown opaque over the years so that looking in, one could make out only indistinct shadows and smudges of color. Here was where Rose planted and nurtured her precious flowers. She sent away for catalog seeds and bulbs; she experimented in hybridization; she pruned and made cuttings and talked to her plants as if they were children. Rose won ribbons every year at the Nairobi Flower Show; it was said that she grew the most stunning orchids in East Africa.

Also in the greenhouse, among the tables of delphiniums and budding irises, stored between two lilies of the Nile whose majestic blue crowns were just beginning to blossom, were folding chairs which Rose brought out on those occasions when she felt like working in the sun, like today. While Njeri erected the tapestry frame out on the grass, Rose went down to the greenhouse to fetch a chair.

As she followed the narrow footpath, she did not see, on the ground, spots of fresh blood leading to the door.

MONA WATCHED HER mother leave the kitchen garden and wondered if she should call up a couple of chaps and send them down to guard the glade. Then she decided her mother was probably right. There was no reason why the escaped POWs would head in this direction; they would more likely head west over the Aberdares or north toward Ethiopia. In fact, James Donald and Tim Hopkins were concentrating their search north of Nanyuki, and Mona prayed they would be careful. Hunting for men, she knew, was not the same as hunting for animals.

Tim had come to replace the lost brother in Mona's life. After the day of Arthur's murder, seven years ago, she and Tim had sought each other out for solace and comfort, talking about Arthur, keeping his memory and their love for him alive. Over time Tim had come to see Arthur in Mona, and Mona had seen her brother in Tim. There had evolved a gentle friendship, of which even Alice, Tim's possessive sister, once she was assured their relationship was platonic, approved.

Poor Tim had tried desperately to enlist when war broke out, but because of his lungs, he had not passed the physical exam. The recruit-ing officer had assured the despondent Tim that he would be a great help to Kenya's cause by staying on his Rift Valley ranch and providing the colony's troops with food and supplies. As a result, Tim and Alice Hopkins—like James Donald on Kilima Simba and Mona Treverton at Bellatu—were growing rich off the war.

Returning to the stack of mail on the table and thinking of all the things that must be seen to today—the problem with puff adders near the stock corral; what to do about the porcupines that were getting into the potato patch; the continued resistance of her father's Africans to taking orders from her—Mona picked up the latest copy of the *East African Standard* and looked at the picture on the front page.

Grace had gone down to Nairobi to represent the Trevertons at the swearing-in ceremony of Eliud Mathu, the first African member elected to the Legislative Council, Kenya's governing body. It was a momentous occasion, one which most people had insisted would never happen—an *African* in government?—and there sat Mona's aunt be-tween the governor and Mr. Mathu. The caption beneath the picture read: ". . . also in attendance was Dr. Grace Treverton, known fondly among her people as 'Nyathaa.' "

That was the Africans' name for Grace, Nyathaa, which means "Mother of all goodness and love."

As Mona sipped her tea, she thought about her aunt. Grace Trever-ton's name had become legend in Kenya and was spreading the world over. The seventh edition of her health manual, *When You Must Be the Doctor,* with its simple and touching dedication "For James," was being used by soldiers in the battlefield. Grace's energy seemed limit-less to Mona. At fifty-four she was showing no sign of slowing down. Indeed, Grace seemed to be picking up speed, like a whirlwind, travel-ing all over East and Central Africa, distributing the new yellow fever vaccine donated by the Rockefeller Foundation, visiting clinics and bush hospitals, treating wounded troops in Nairobi, and, lately, giving speeches on her newest cause: the preservation of Kenya's wildlife.

It was no wonder, Mona understood now, that Grace did not marry James after all. They had discussed it endlessly, upon their return seven years ago from Uganda. But in the end both Grace and James had had to admit that marriage for them wasn't logical. They had their separate lives and projects; Grace couldn't move to Kilima Simba, or James to the mission; she traveled here, he traveled there. They would hardly see each other, they realized, and as there could be no children for them, marriage seemed almost redundant.

And so they were good friends, taking days at a time together when they could, spending brief holidays at the coast, Grace getting into her old Ford and driving to Kilima Simba for a day or two. It was an arrangement both had come to enjoy and be happy with.

There were three letters from overseas. The first was from Mona's Aunt Edith at Bella Hill.

Since Uncle Harold had been killed at the beginning of the war when a German bomb had struck his London men's club, and since Mona's cousin, Charlotte, having trained as a nurse, was now in the South Pacific, fighting the Japanese, Aunt Edith was all alone at Bella Hill—except for seventy-eight children, who had been evacuated from London during the blitz. Edith had written:

> They fill these gloomy old walls with their laughter. I love them all as if they were my own. We had only Charlotte. I had always wanted more. I have no doubt that many are orphaned; some have not heard from their parents since the start of the bombing. Whatever will be done with them after the war? This enormous old house will seem so empty then.
>
> Now that Charlotte's married her American flier, I shall be completely alone here, and I don't look forward to that. Too many memories and ghosts. Holding on to Bella Hill was always Harold's idea. He and Valentine fought for twenty-one years, as you know, over Valentine's reckless selling off of Bella Hill land to pay for Bellatu's losses. Now I say he is welcome to it. Bella Hill is, after all, your and his house, Rose. Perhaps you would like to come back here and live? Whatever you decide to do, I have made up my mind that, after this war is over and the children are restored to their families, I shall move down to Brighton and live with my cousin Naomi. I would appreciate a yearly allowance from Valentine. . . .

The second letter was from Mona's father. She hesitated before opening it. It was not addressed to her; it was meant for his Kikuyu headman.

She knew that this letter contained orders for the running of the farm. And Mona resented it. Since his departure in 1941 Valentine had sent letters regularly to Bellatu, instructing his various African headmen on how to run the plantation. When Mona had written back to him, suggesting she be allowed to oversee the work, he had replied with an emphatic no. Mona's dream, born seven years ago, to learn the operation of the vast coffee estate, had never materialized. No amount of arguing or trying to reason with her father—"What about after you're dead? Who'll run the farm then?"—had moved him to decide to teach her to follow in his footsteps. That was to have been Arthur's right.

Mona had shown the headmen the first few written orders sent down from Ethiopia, where her father had been fighting—orders regarding pruning, mulching, boreholes, and irrigation. But then circumstances had started to change. Kenya's troops demanded to be fed. And there were the thousands of Italian POWs whom her father was sending down to the camps, also needing food. The government had requested that farmers utilize their land to the best practical advantage, and that had meant to Mona less coffee growing and more mixed farming.

Again she had written to her father and had explained; again he would not heed her, insisting they continue with coffee only. So Mona had embarked upon a plan of her own. In her father's study was a large collection of books on agriculture, gathered over the years. Mona had read and studied them, had listened to the advice of other farmers, had gone into Nairobi to see what was needed, and then had returned and commenced to forge a new set of "orders" from her father. The first crop to go into the newly cleared acres had been maize, and she had been very successful at it.

Mona received help from Sir James and from Tim, who walked the furrows with her and pointed out this, that, and guided her along. Too, her headmen were good farmers. They could feel when the rain was coming, when the soil was too poor, when locusts threatened, how to defend against army worms. As a result, Mona's deception was a small victory over her father.

She dreaded his return after the war. There would be a terrible row, she knew, over what she had done, and then he would take charge again, forbidding any further interference on her part. That she knew she would not be able to bear. In these four years Mona had come, for the first time in her life, to feel as though Bellatu were really *home*. She had never before felt so belonging, so a part of these five thousand acres of green trees. She had come home on school holidays like a guest, sleeping in a room that could have belonged to anyone, eating with parents who were practically strangers. But *now*—

Bellatu was hers. And she was going to keep it.

The third letter was from Geoffrey.

Mona poured herself a second cup of tea before opening it, putting off the moment to savor it. She looked forward to his letters; lately she lived for them.

Geoffrey Donald was in Palestine, doing "police work." He couldn't say much about what he was doing, but Mona had pieced together from news accounts the dangerous situation he was in: With so many European Jews fleeing the Nazis and finding refuge in Palestine, the indigenous Arabs were feeling pushed and therefore were fighting back. In retaliation, certain secret Jewish groups were launching counterattacks to remind the British of their commitment to Zionism. It was not the safest corner of the world to be in, but Mona was glad Geoffrey was there instead of somewhere like Burma, where Kenyan troops were suffering heavy losses. He wrote now:

The war can't last forever, and when it's over, we'll see a new world come from it. You mark my words, Mona. Things will be different. It will be a Modern Age, and I intend to be part of it. I've got it in mind to do something drastically new when I get home. Tourism, Mona. This war has opened up the world. It's made people move around and see other places. It's sparked interest in travel. In the past tourism was a sport for the rich, but I believe that the ordinary man, once he's gone back to his ordinary life after fighting in exotic places, is going to want to see more. And I aim to put Kenya on the sight-seeing map. Let me know what your thoughts are on this; you know how I value your opinion.

I picked up a marvelous trinket for you the other day. An old Arab brought it round to the garrison, wanted too much money for it, but I got him down. He claims it's a genuine antiquity. It's a bit of old scroll, no doubt manufactured in his backyard, but it looks like the real thing. Might make a nice decoration over the fireplace at Bellatu. Hope you're in good health, Mona. Thank you for the chocolates. You're a darling.

She carefully folded the letter and slipped it in her pocket. She would read it several more times during the day, as she drove around the estate overseeing the field hands, and then that night, she would lie in bed and think about Geoffrey.

It had come to her at last—love. Mona had heard that wartime did that, that the threat of danger and death made people turn to one another. Wasn't there an old family story about Aunt Grace and a shipboard romance during the first war? Mona marveled now, as she left the kitchen to start her day's rounds, at how easily love had come to her. Seven years ago, as she had stood in Sir James's sickroom in Uganda, she had looked at Geoffrey and had wondered if perhaps she could someday love him the way her aunt loved his father. And so she had decided to wait and see. "I'm not refusing you," she had said to Geoffrey on their return to Kenya when he again asked her to marry him. "But I'm only just out of school. Let me get used to the idea." He had agreed, and they had spent the next two years as a "couple," making the rounds of parties together, being part of the young smart set. They had even kissed; but Mona had not been able to allow further intimacy, and Geoffrey, respecting her wish, had not pressed.

And then war had broken out, and everything had changed. Suddenly the world was upside down. All the young men of Kenya got into uniform and began leaving for mysterious parts of the world—Geoffrey to garrison duty in Palestine, where he commanded a "colored" regiment. The letters had started coming from him after that, and Mona had begun to miss him more and more until she felt stirrings of desire—her first—and she realized with great relief that she was not, after all, like her mother: incapable of love.

When Geoffrey came home for good, Mona decided, she was going to say yes to him.

ROSE PAUSED BEFORE the door of the greenhouse. She saw that the padlock had been wrenched off and was lying in the dirt.

Another break-in! she thought in alarm. *The fourth this year!*

It had never happened before the war, when Valentine was always around. But since the bwana had been gone for so long, some of the local people were starting to disregard the laws. Usually they stole only the tools—things they could sell—but one time they had taken some valuable plants. Worried, Rose rushed inside.

A hand shot out from behind the door and seized her. She was pulled back, her arm was twisted up behind her, and a man's voice said close to her ear, "Do not move, signora."

Rose stared at her rows of silent flowers as she felt the sharp edge of a knife blade touch her throat.

35

R ose stood frozen, with the knife at her throat and the man against her back, holding her in a painful grip. She looked at the half-opened door and thought of Njeri a few yards away, setting up the tapestry frame. Rose opened her mouth; the knife bit into her neck.

"No sound!" he whispered.

She closed her eyes.

"Do not move, signora. Listen to me."

She listened; she waited. He was having difficulty breathing. She felt his body shudder. The hand that clutched her bare arm was hot and damp.

"*Per favore . . . mi aiuti . . .*" The grip started to slip. "Please," he whispered, "help me. . . ."

Suddenly the knife fell away, and Rose was free. She jumped back as the stranger sank to his knees. The knife clattered to the stone floor.

"Please," he said again, clutching his chest, his head bowed, "I need—"

Rose stared down at him. There was blood on her arm—*his* blood.

She watched him crumple to the floor, where he lay on his side. His eyes were closed; his face was distorted in pain.

"*Ascolti,*" he breathed. "*Chiami un prete.* Bring me—"

Rose fell back against the wall.

"Please," he groaned. "I beg of you, bring me *un prete.*"

She started to shake. She saw the blood on his shirt and the grass stains and grime of his having fled through the bush. He was barefoot; his feet were cut and bleeding. And his face was streaked with dirt and sweat.

"A priest," he said. "I am dying. Please, signora. Bring me a priest."

Rose moved away, terrified. She stumbled over a clay pot; she groped for the door. Mona's voice echoed in her mind: *They butchered a guard.*

And then she saw something that made her stop.

Red stripes of blood were soaking through the back of his shirt.

She stared down. She was confused; she tried to think.

"Who—" she began. "Who are you?"

He didn't answer.

"I'm going for a policeman," she said. Rose shook so badly that she was afraid her legs were going to give way.

But he didn't respond, didn't move.

She continued to stare at the bloody stripes on his shirt. Then, cautiously, as if approaching a dangerous, injured animal, Rose took a step toward him. She paused, watching him. Then she took another step, and another, until she stood over him.

The stranger lay curled on his side, his eyes closed, gasping for breath.

"You're one of the escaped prisoners, aren't you?" she said in a shaky voice.

He lay moaning.

Rose wrung her hands. "Why did you come *here?* I can't help you!" Her eyes were fixed on the stripes on his back; blood continued to seep through the fabric of his shirt.

She was filled with terror.

"You're the enemy," she said. "How dare you ask me for help? I'll send word to the men who are searching for you. They'll know what to do with you."

He whispered one word: "Priest . . ."

"You're mad to think I'll help you!" she cried. "Dear God—" Rose could see that he was in terrible pain. And she thought: *He's dying.*

When she realized that he couldn't hurt her now and that he had probably never intended to, she slowly knelt and looked at the stripes on his shirt. She was overcome. "They whipped you . . ." she murmured.

His eyes opened briefly. They were dark and damp; they reminded her of the eyes of a wounded antelope. His body shook. He moaned.

"Help me," he whispered. "In the name of God . . ." His eyes closed. His body grew still.

Rose chewed her lip.

And then suddenly she was on her feet. "Njeri!" she called, going through the door of the greenhouse.

The African girl looked up, startled.

"Go back to the house," Rose said breathlessly. "And fetch me some soap and water and towels. Bring them back here."

Njeri looked puzzled.

"Hurry!"

"Yes, memsaab."

"And blankets," Rose called as she hurried down the path that led from the glade.

As she ran down the steps that led to the mission area below the forest, Rose tried to think of where her sister-in-law would be at this hour. Grace would know what to do for the man; she would take care of him.

But when Rose turned onto the gravel drive that led to Grace's house, she remembered in dismay that Grace was in Nairobi!

Rose stopped at the intersection of three dirt roads and looked around. She twisted her hands. Seeing the smear of blood on her arm, she thought of the infirmary, a small cinder-block building where minor injuries were treated.

She approached it uncertainly, afraid to be seen and having no idea what she was going to do when she got inside. But when Rose went up the steps and walked through the door, an idea came to her.

There was a new "miracle" drug Grace had spoken of recently, something that stopped infection and saved lives in even the most extreme cases and that was going to revolutionize medicine. But what was it called?

Rose couldn't remember.

The infirmary was unattended. Its one room sat in sunlight, clean and shining and waiting for patients. Rose looked around. The attendant would no doubt be arriving any minute, coming from his breakfast. Rose would have to hurry.

The name of the miracle drug, it seemed to her, began with *P.* She went to the medicine cabinet and peered through the glass doors. She tried to read the labels. Some were familiar to her; most were not. And none began with *P*. When she saw the morphine bottle, she decided to take it.

As she was about to hurry out, she saw it: a small carton of newly delivered medicine. The name was on the box: penicillin. Grace's miracle drug.

Seizing a few other items but having no real idea what she needed or in what quantity or even how to use them, Rose bundled everything into a linen towel and quickly left the infirmary.

When she arrived at the glade, she found Njeri sitting in the gazebo with a bucket of water, a bottle of floor soap, one towel, and no blanket.

"Hand soap, Njeri!" she said. "For washing hands. And a blanket and pillow. Run! And don't talk to anyone."

Rose pushed open the door of the greenhouse and looked in. The stranger hadn't moved. He lay in the diffuse light coming through the skylight, his battered body an obscenity among the colorful blossoms and potted fruit trees.

She felt a strong emotion rush through her, an emotion that was at once familiar and yet alien. Rose had experienced this compulsion many times in the past—to rescue injured or orphaned animals and to protect and nurture them. But never before had she felt it toward a human being. It baffled her. This man was an enemy; her husband was in the north fighting Italians. And yet Rose did not see an enemy in the poor, abused body lying among her flowers. She was observing the prisoner not with her eyes but with her heart, and her heart saw only a living creature in need of help.

She knelt at his side. He was still alive but, she feared, only barely. "Can you hear me?" she said. "I'm going to try to help you. I've brought medicines."

He lay on his side, unresponsive.

Rose reached out, hesitated, then touched his forehead. It was hot.

She looked around the greenhouse. There was a clear space on the other side of her workbench, wide enough for a man to lie down. Setting aside her infirmary bundle, Rose walked around and slipped her hands under his arms.

But she couldn't move him.

"Please," she said, "you must help me to move you."

He groaned.

She started to panic. He lay exposed near the open door. Hardly anyone ever came to the eucalyptus glade, but if someone did, the stranger could be seen.

And then Rose realized she had to hide him. It wasn't an action she questioned. Deeper, more complex currents were compelling her now: the instinct to protect any injured creature from its predators.

She looked around again. There were her new rosebushes, lined up along the nearest wall and taking in the gentle sunlight, awaiting transplantation. Hurrying, Rose dragged the heavy pots over the stone floor until she decided there was enough room for the man. Then she came back to him and, by pulling and pushing, managed to move him out of the way of the door.

Having first covered the floor with a blanket, she then laid the stranger down among her roses.

THERE WAS NOTHING Njeri Mathenge would not do for her mistress.

Even though it was Memsaab Grace who had given birth to Njeri when she had lifted her from Gachiku's womb twenty-five years ago, and even though it had also been Memsaab Grace who had tried to save her from the terrible *irua* ceremony seven years ago, it was Memsaab Rose to whom David Mathenge's half sister was steadfastly devoted.

Njeri could not remember a time when she had not longed to live in the big stone house and be near the beautiful lady who looked like a sunshine spirit. From her earliest years, when she had run away repeatedly from her mother's shamba to spy on the lady in the glade, Njeri had always sensed a special magic in her memsaab. A sweet sadness engulfed the bwana's wife; she walked with an aura of melancholy that no one else seemed to sense but that the gentle Njeri, in her unique perception, felt sharply.

They were always together, Njeri and Lady Rose. In the early days Njeri had crept from her mother's hut to sit with the lady in the glade, who never questioned the little girl's sudden appearance one day but who accepted her with a smile and fed her from the ever-present wicker basket. In those days Memsaab Mona, the lady's daughter who was the same age as Njeri, had also been in the gazebo with them, taking lessons from governesses. But then Mona had gone away to school in Nairobi, and Njeri had had the lady all to herself. After that Memsaab Rose had taken Njeri into the household as her personal maid, paying the girl three shillings a month, which Njeri turned over to her mother. Njeri now lived the perfect life: She wore the memsaab's castoff dresses; she slept outside her bedroom door in the big house; she brought up Lady Rose's morning tea and then spent an hour combing out the waterfall of hair.

Njeri could not understand why her brother, David, or the girl Wanjiru didn't like the *wazungu*. Njeri worshiped them and their whiteness and wonderful ways, and she thought how dark and unwelcoming Kikuyuland must have been before they arrived.

She chuffed along the path with her blanket, pillow, and bar of the memsaab's special Yardley Lavender soap, and she did it unquestioningly. Njeri never questioned her mistress's orders or actions, and never would.

But when she walked through the door of the greenhouse, Njeri cried out and dropped her things.

"Hush!" said Rose. "Come here and help me!"

Njeri couldn't move. Old Kikuyu taboos rooted her to the stone floor.

"Njeri!"

The girl gaped at the man lying facedown on the blanket, his shirt removed, his back exposed. The memsaab was touching him—his wounds, his blood.

Rose jumped to her feet, snatched up the dropped soap, and took Njeri by the arm. "Stop gawking and come and help me! The man is hurt."

Njeri went woodenly and knelt opposite the memsaab, but she couldn't bring herself to touch him. She watched as Rose gently washed the half-healed stripes on his back, watched those slender white hands, which never touched anything unclean or unbeautiful, bathe away the old blood and dirt, carefully dry the wounds, and then apply a healing salve.

Finally Rose sat back and said, "That might help. I don't know what else to do. I think he has a dangerously high fever. He might die from it. Some of these wounds are infected, and they're causing the fever."

Njeri's eyes moved over the stranger's back. Then she saw what her mistress must have also seen: old scars among the new. "He has been punished many times, memsaab."

Rose studied the bottle of penicillin. She had no idea how much to give him. Too little, certainly, would be useless. But could too much kill him? What on earth *was* penicillin anyway?

Her hands trembled as she filled the hypodermic syringe, doing it the way she had seen Grace do it, with two fingers through the metal rings, her thumb guiding the plunger. It was a heavy, cumbersome instrument, the needle seeming somehow much too long.

When the drug was drawn up, Rose then looked down at the unconscious stranger and murmured, "Where do I inject?"

Deciding that vaccinations ordinarily went into the arm, she cleaned a small patch on the hard muscle just at the shoulder and sank the needle in.

He didn't react.

Dear God, Rose prayed as she slowly depressed the plunger, *let this be the right amount.*

When she was done, she sat back and studied him. The stranger slept deeply—too deeply, she thought. And then she noticed what a clean, handsome profile he had.

She felt the pulse at his neck. It didn't feel right. It was as though his heart were struggling; each beat felt like a desperate plea for help.

Reaching out, Rose stroked the black hair matted to his forehead. "Poor man," she said softly, "whatever did you do to deserve such inhuman treatment?"

She withdrew into silence, her blue eyes settling upon the dark head. Time came to a halt; the air grew moist and heavy with the smell of rich earth and exotic blossoms. Something skittered along the skylight. The sun moved behind a tall eucalyptus, softening the hues and shadows in the greenhouse. The two women, white and African, sat while the injured stranger slept between them.

DURING HER LONG vigil at the sleeping man's side Rose was overwhelmed with a sense of helplessness and utter uselessness. With the body of this poor man stretched before her, his life beating slowly away, she loathed her weakness and inability to do anything.

Near sunset Njeri reminded her mistress of the coming dark. Rose was terrified of the night and always took care to be home before daylight faded. But now she was reluctant to go.

She laid a hand on the burning cheek and thought: *You will probably die in here sometime during the night, alone, in pain, and with no one to comfort you.*

But the dark did frighten her, and so at last Rose was compelled to leave the greenhouse. After making sure he was as warm and comfortable as possible, she paused at the door to look back at the pathetic form sleeping in the gloom.

She thought of her tapestry. It was all she had to show for her life. And thinking of it, for the first time Rose despised herself.

SHE COULDN'T SLEEP.

After slipping into the house unseen, to avoid running into Mona, Rose had gone straight to her bedroom, where she now sat in the light of a hurricane lamp, gazing out the window at the dark forest.

Unable to bear the silence, she turned on her radio, hoping for some music, but instead she heard the voice of a late-night news broadcaster. She quickly turned the volume down and listened to the faint report: "Two of the Italian prisoners who escaped from the Nanyuki camp have been found. The third is still at large. He has been identified as General Carlo Nobili, the duca d'Alessandro."

So he had a name now.

Rose thought of him lying in the cold greenhouse, slowly dying. Would he waken, she wondered, and be terrified in his last moments of life? She thought of the wounds on his back—the old ones and the new—that spoke volumes of his cruel treatment in the camp. *No wonder he escaped. Perhaps the murdered guard deserved to die.*

Then she thought: *I should have done more for him. But what? What could I have done?*

Rose started to cry.

She buried her face in her hands and wept. The bedroom door opened, and a ribbon of hallway light fell across the carpet as Njeri, who had never seen her mistress cry, looked in, baffled and afraid.

Rose turned and looked at her maid. "Why am I so useless?" she cried. "Why am I such a useless, *ridiculous* woman? Anyone else might have saved that poor man! If Grace had been here instead of in Nairobi! *She* would have known what to—" Rose stared at her maid. "Grace!" she cried. "Of course!"

Jumping up from the window seat, Rose said, "Why didn't I think of it before?" and ran from the bedroom.

Njeri followed her mistress downstairs and found her in the library— a musty, rarely used room that was all leather and brass and lined from floor to ceiling with books.

"It must be in here!" Rose said as she frantically searched the shelves. "Help me, Njeri! It's this big and this thick," she said, outlining an invisible book with her hands. "The cover is made of paper, not leather. And it's—it's—" She moved along the shelves, rapidly scanning the spines. "It's a green book, Njeri. Hurry!"

Bewildered, the African girl, who had never learned to read, went to one wall and slowly searched the leather and gold books for one made of green paper. Behind her she heard her mistress exclaim, "Oh, we *must* have a copy! Surely Grace gave one to us!"

Rose flew along the bookcases, rising onto her toes, then dropping to search the lower shelves. There were so many books, so very many. . . .

"Memsaab?" Njeri said.

Rose turned. When she saw the manual in the brown hands, she cried, "Yes, that's it! Grace's book! Bring it over here, into the light."

It was the fourth edition of *When You Must Be the Doctor,* published back in 1936, still crisp from having never been looked through, and yellowed and dusty from neglect. Rose ran her finger down the table of contents. "Here," she said, tapping the page. " 'Wound Infections.' 'Fevers.' 'How To Take Care of a Seriously Ill Person.' "

She pulled a pad of paper and a pen from the drawer and began writing.

NJERI TREMBLED WITH fear as a short while later she and her mistress stood on the threshold of the kitchen door, facing the darkness. Like most Kikuyu, the girl had an instinctive fear of the night.

This time their arms were loaded with carefully packed bundles, made up from a list gotten from the manual. Rose had found a thermometer and aspirin in her bathroom cabinet, and sugar, baking soda, and salt in the kitchen, to which she had added Vaseline, cotton balls, a watch with a second hand, three thermoses of boiled water, and two flashlights—all recommended in Grace's manual.

Looking across the garden at the black wall of forest, where the kitchen light ended, Rose was overcome with dread. Then she thought of General Nobili lying on the cold stone floor of the greenhouse, and her resolve came back.

"Let's go," she whispered, and started down the steps.

She looked back. Njeri stood frozen.

"I said come along!"

The girl stayed close behind her mistress as they hurried down the path. "Pray that he is still alive, Njeri," Rose whispered as they plunged into the trees. "Pray that we are not too late."

They ran through the forest, with unseen ghosts and imagined animals snapping at their heels, and arrived at the greenhouse shaking with fear and cold. Rose went straight to the general and found that he was still alive.

While Njeri held the flashlight, which trembled in her hands so that its beam quivered over the unconscious man, Rose opened the manual to the page headed "How to Examine a Sick Person" and went through a methodical check of his vital signs.

Because his pulse was weak and thready, and his skin damp, indicating that he was in shock, Rose turned him onto his side and elevated his feet with bricks. His respirations were a reassuring sixteen per minute, and when she lifted his eyelids and shone a light in them, she found his pupils equal in size and reactive to the light—good indications, according to Grace's book. But his temperature was too high.

So Rose, following the instructions in the book, turned to the page headed "Very High Fevers" and read: "Brain damage can result if a high fever is not brought down immediately."

She pulled the blanket off him, as the book instructed, so that the night air could cool his body; then she poured a cup of water and dissolved two aspirin tablets in it. Lifting the general's head in the crook of her arm, she put the cup to his lips. He didn't drink. She tried again. The aspirin was necessary to bring the fever down.

She turned to the book for help and read in bold print: "NEVER GIVE ANYTHING BY MOUTH TO AN UNCONSCIOUS PERSON."

Rose set the cup aside and settled the general's head back on the pillow. She continued to read. Under the heading "Danger Signals" she found "A day without drinking liquids—see page 89." She turned to that page and read, in the unsteady beam of Njeri's flashlight, about the dangers of dehydration.

Rose looked at her watch. She estimated that he had been unconscious for twelve hours. "He must have fluids soon," she murmured, "or he will die of dehydration. But what can I do? I can't get him to drink. He needs the water, and he needs the aspirin to bring the fever down. It's a vicious circle!"

She gazed down at the face bathed in the glow of the flashlight. She wondered how old he was, where he came from, if he had a family who was worrying about him.

Njeri's teeth began to chatter.

"Go back to the house," Rose said. "I'll stay with him."

But Njeri crossed her legs and sat down on the floor, the flashlight cradled in her skirt.

"If I send for medical help," Rose said softly, "then he will be returned to the camp. But if I try to take care of him by myself, he might die. What shall I do?"

She felt his forehead again. It seemed cooler and drier than before. She searched for his pulse and thought that it had slowed a little, felt stronger. His breathing, too, appeared to be easier now.

"Njeri, give me that basket." Rose mixed a rehydration drink according to the recipe in Grace's manual: sugar, salt, and baking soda into clean water. She tasted it to make sure it was "no saltier than tears," as Grace had written, then set it next to the cup with the dissolved aspirin, in readiness. If he regained consciousness, she would give him both to drink.

But if the general did not regain consciousness by dawn, Rose decided, then she would go for help.

SUNRISE BROKE OVER the top of the stone walls of the greenhouse, sending pinpoints of light through the overhanging eucalyptus branches. Rose stirred in her blanket, aching from having slept on the floor. She raised up and searched for Njeri in the milky light. It appeared that her maid, now that it was day, had left.

Rose looked at the stranger. His eyes were open. He was staring at her.

They watched each other for a long moment, Rose wrapped in her blanket, the general lying on his side facing her, his head on the pillow.

Remembering the feel of the knife at her throat, the painful way he had twisted her arm, Rose was suddenly wary again.

He opened his mouth. He tried to speak. But all he could do was make a dry, throaty sound.

Rose picked up the rehydration drink and held the cup to his lips. He sipped at first. Then he drank it all down and let his head fall back to the pillow.

"Are you in pain?" she asked gently.

He nodded.

She brought the second cup to his lips, the one containing aspirin, which must have been bitter, for he grimaced. But he drank all that, too, and when he rested back on the pillow, he seemed to breathe more easily. "Who—" he began.

"I am Lady Rose Treverton. And I know that you are General Nobili."

His dark eyes were fixed on her questioningly. Then he said, "Did I hurt you?"

She shook her head. Her hair, having come down from its pins while she slept, tumbled over her shoulders.

General Carlo Nobili stared at it almost in wonder. "I know who you are," he whispered. "You are one of God's angels."

Rose smiled and laid her hand on his forehead. "Rest now. I'll bring you something to eat."

"But where—?"

"You're safe here. And you can trust me. I am going to take care of you and see that no harm comes to you ever again."

The general closed his eyes, and his body relaxed.

36

The explosion occurred exactly at noon, during the Muslim call to prayer. Extensive damage was done to the police fortress on the outskirts of Jerusalem, and five British soldiers were killed.

"It's that bloody Menachem Begin," David Mathenge overheard his commanding officer, Geoffrey Donald, say.

And thus began the intensive manhunt for the underground terrorist that brought David out of his cot in the middle of the night to muster with his regiment and wait in the cold and damp September night for orders from Captain Donald.

It was coincidental that David was in Geoffrey Donald's African regiment in Palestine. When he had volunteered to join the British Army at the outbreak of war, he had not expected to be assigned to mere garrison duty but had hoped to be able to fight Hitler's racist Nazis. Nor had David expected to find himself under the command of a man he had despised for seven years.

Ever since the day of his escape from the Nairobi jail and subsequent exile in Uganda, David Mathenge had carried a special hatred for the Trevertons and, because of his friendship with that family, also for Geoffrey Donald, a man whom David was now forced to salute.

David had been in Palestine for four years and was by now familiar with its various fighting camps—Arab, Jewish, British. The terrorist bomb that went off in the British police fortress had to be the work of Menachem Begin's Irgun; it couldn't have been the work of the Haganah, the Zionists' secret army, David knew, because it always gave advance warnings so that people could escape. The fight was over whose homeland this mandated territory was. It seemed to David

Mathenge, who, like all Kikuyu, was deeply tied to the land and understood territorial possession, that this was a *tribal* issue.

There were the Arabs, who had lived here for centuries, being pushed off their ancestral lands by European refugees, Jews fleeing Hitler. The Jews claimed this land as their own by right of ancestral legacy. And in the middle sat the British, catering to both parties, making and breaking promises with both. It was no wonder, as far as David was concerned, that Menachem Begin, fed up with Churchill and his empty words, had turned his terrorist tactics not upon the Arabs, his natural enemy, but upon the British. That was why the police fortress outside Jerusalem had been targeted.

David was utterly miserable.

What had happened? Where had his life gone wrong? Four years ago, when the colonial government had launched a massive recruitment drive for the King's African Rifles, David Mathenge and thousands of other young Africans like him had eagerly joined up, believing that Hitler was going to invade Kenya and cart them away in chains. The young Africans, newly out of school, unemployed and anxious for action, had been convinced that they were marching off to fight a monstrous evil and that they were going to have the glorious opportunity to defend their country, freedom and democracy, and their way of life. Outfitted in a smart new uniform and a hat with the side brim turned up and fixed with a plume, David had paraded proudly before the eyes of his white officers, feeling like a warrior going into battle, and had left his homeland to discover that the world was a far, far bigger place than he had ever dreamed. At the time he believed that joining the British Army was the smartest thing he had ever done.

Now he realized that it wasn't. David decided that the smartest thing he had ever done was to stay on in Uganda after Chief Muchina, ill and dying—from a *thahu,* people whispered, placed on him by Wachera—had dropped all charges against David and had declared the arrest a false one. David had been free to go back into Kenya, but he had opted to stay in Uganda and attend Makerere University, from which he had graduated three years later with a degree in agriculture.

He had learned farming and farm management. Now he was ready to take back his land from the Trevertons.

But when will that be? he asked himself as he left the barracks, rifle slung over his shoulder. For years his mother had been promising the reinstatement of his lands. Had she not placed a *thahu* on the Trevertons? And didn't Wachera's curses always work? But not quickly enough for David. "The Treverton coffee estate is doing well," Wanjiru had written in her last letter. "The white girl Mona is running it herself." This was not what David had joined the King's African Rifles for—to waste his time in a dry, godforsaken country where the people were determined to annihilate one another, with him in the middle, the target of both sides because he was a British soldier, while the Trevertons grew fat on his land!

David was overcome with misery.

What was there to love in this arid Palestine? In the summer the heat was killing, and hot winds seared one's lungs; in the winter there were gray, relentless rains and a biting cold he had never felt back in Kenya. David's heart was heavy for his homeland. He yearned for the forests, for the clean mists of Mount Kenya, for the songs of his people, for his mother's cooking, and for Wanjiru's love.

Wanjiru . . .

She was more to him now than just the woman he loved and hoped to marry; Wanjiru had come to personify all the things he was homesick for. Wanjiru was Kenya. He longed for the comfort of her embrace.

When David saw the large transport trucks starting to line up, their headlights filling the compound with unnatural brightness, he realized that a massive search was being organized. Where would it be this morning? he wondered as he walked over to one of the trucks and struck up a conversation with the driver.

"Petah Tiqva," the man said, referring to a small town not far from Tel Aviv.

David nodded and leaned against the fender. The mandatory authorities were fond of saying that "bloody Petah Tiqva is a nest of terrorists." And they weren't wrong. British intelligence was well aware that the groves and woods surrounding Petah Tiqva concealed armories and were the secret training grounds of rebel forces. It was a dangerous area to search; British soldiers didn't like going into Petah Tiqva.

It seemed to David that this was all his duty ever consisted of these days: searching for the elusive Menachem Begin. If David wasn't manning roadblocks and inspecting every car coming into and going out of Tel Aviv, then he was searching through hotels or interrogating pedestrians in the street or knocking on doors at midnight and getting people out of bed. The search for Begin was escalating; the British were frantic to find the man who was sabotaging their communications and civil offices. And now that David Ben-Gurion, leader of the Jewish Agency and Begin's archrival, had as much as declared war on Begin, cooperating fully with the British in their search, all Palestine was being turned upside down.

There was even a reward posted: fifteen thousand dollars to the man who delivered Menachem Begin to the authorities.

He must be a fierce warrior, David Mathenge thought, to have thoroughly confounded British intelligence for four years, to have pulled off so many successful acts of sabotage, to maintain such strong leadership over his underground army, the Irgun, and all without having once been caught. To be constantly on the move, always one step ahead of his searchers, was, in David's opinion, the work of a clever and brave man. In fact, the British had only a vague idea of what Begin looked like. When they conducted house-to-house searches, David and his men were told to look for a "Polish Jew, in his thirties, who wears glasses and who has a wife and small son."

"I hope they find the bastard this time," the truck driver said as he lit a cigarette. "That bloody Begin thinks all we're good for is target practice. And I don't like going into Petah Tiqva. One of these days it's going to be booby-trapped. You mark my words. Begin's going to start a bloody civil war. The Arabs will sit back and laugh while the Jews kill one another off, doing Hitler's work for him."

David looked at the driver, a ruddy-faced man who spoke with a Scots accent. It was only on such occasions as this, when mustering for duty or manning a post, that white soldiers talked to the men of David's regiment. Otherwise, there seemed to be an invisible barrier or some strange, unuttered law against racial mingling.

It had surprised the Africans, when they had arrived in the mandate, to discover they had separate quarters and a separate mess from the rest of the battalion. Back in Kenya it was accepted that the Africans didn't mingle with the white settlers—that was simply the way it was and always had been—but they had expected the army to be democratic. After all, they all wore the same uniforms and served the same cause, didn't they? Only last week David had learned that African soldiers received less pay than their white counterparts.

This had come as a shock. A few of his comrades had complained about the discrepancy, declaring that a private was a private, black or white, and should receive the same pay. But the officers, all white, had reminded the African grumblers that they were better off than their countrymen back home and should be thankful that the army took them instead of leaving them behind to toil like women on the farms.

David watched the trucks line up, the armored cars and tanks, the machine guns, and road-blocking equipment. He knew that they were going to surround Petah Tiqva entirely, penning in the unsuspecting inhabitants, and that his regiment would be sent in to conduct a search for Begin.

He recalled now an incident in Haifa in which three soldiers had encountered a booby trap. He himself had been just a few steps behind them and had narrowly escaped being killed.

Was Begin waiting for them right now in Petah Tiqva? David wondered. Was this an Irgun ruse? Would today bring his Palestinian tour of duty to an abrupt, bloody end?

David didn't want to die. He wanted to go home. To Kenya. To Wanjiru.

Sitting down on the bumper, he pulled her letter out of his pocket and read it in the beam of the headlight. She had written:

We are praying for the rains. Last week I had leave from the hospital. I went up to visit your mother. We went into the forest and found an old fig tree, where we prayed together for rain.

Your mother is well, David. I read your letters to her, over and over. But I do not read the newspaper to her, the accounts of the war in Palestine. We read of the bombings, David, of the land mines, of the torture and murder of British soldiers. What is this fight all about? Why are you there? If Masai and Wakamba were fighting, would Kikuyu step in between? No. Let Arab and Jew work out their differences. This is not your fight, David. I do not understand why you are there.

David looked up from the letter and gazed at the horizon, which was streaked with the orange promise of dawn. Was the sun rising over

Kenya right now? he wondered. Was his mother fetching water from the river? And Wanjiru—was she stirring in her bed, thinking of him?

What am *I fighting for?*

Another incident came back to him now, one that had also taken place in Haifa and had haunted him ever since.

It was six months ago, and David was on patrol. During a routine search of a hotel he had come upon a man who had so stunned him that both he and his partner, a Luo named Ochieng, had stopped and stared.

The man was wearing an American uniform and had the rank of captain. But he was *black.*

"Excuse me, sir," David had said to the American. "Just a routine check."

They began talking. Because of David's accent, the captain had thought he was from England. "From Kenya, sir," David had explained. Finally, he had gotten up the nerve to say, "I beg your pardon, sir. But how is it that you are a captain? In the British Army there are no black commissioned officers."

The American had smiled and said, "Well, Private, it's because I have a college degree."

"So have I," David had said, and it was the American's turn to stare.

The look on that captain's face had followed David in the subsequent months; he saw it everywhere: in his sleep; in the desert; in the faces of the Jews he interrogated. It would not leave him for even a moment. The American had not said another word, but his eyes had said, *Shame.* . . .

But for whom—for the young private or for himself—David could not guess.

There was suddenly a lot of activity. The men were falling into rank, orders were being shouted. David saw a Jeep pull up; Captain Donald stood to address the troops. He gave a familiar speech but this time peppered it with strong words. The thrust of it: to find Begin at all costs before any more British lives were lost.

As David climbed into the transport truck, he translated the commanding officer's speech for his partner, Ochieng, who spoke only his native Luo and Swahili. As David explained their orders, that they were to conduct a house-to-house search in the Hassidoff quarter of Petah Tiqva, he considered the unfairness of the situation.

Here was Ochieng, illiterate, a peasant from the Lake Victoria region who barely understood anything he was told to do but who placidly followed orders, who liked to look at himself in his uniform, and who would, after the war, like the eighty thousand other African troops, return to Kenya to his former primitive and unquestioning life. And there was David Mathenge, one of the very few educated Africans in the regiment, the only one with a college degree, a man full of ambition, who would receive not one iota of recognition as being different from Ochieng. It brought back to David's mind the look in the American captain's eyes. The utter *shame* of it.

But if, David started thinking as the trucks pulled out, he was indistinguishable to his white officers because of his color, then he must make himself different in another way. There was a hefty price on Begin's head and a medal for the soldier who found the terrorist and brought him in.

David Mathenge was going to find Menachem Begin.

HASSIDOFF WAS A workers' district surrounded by orange groves. The tanks and armored cars of the occupation army, working with the Palestine police, circled the area, while soldiers went up and down the streets, calling through loudspeakers, "Curfew! Stay in your houses! Anybody who leaves risks his life!" The men jumped down from the trucks, wished one another "good hunting," and the search began. As David and Ochieng headed down the road toward the first house, an Arab shepherd boy with his flock waved to them.

Within minutes prisoners were being rounded up and pushed into the trucks; many still blinked from sleep, for dawn had only just broken. These were suspects who were to be taken to police headquarters for questioning. It was a surprisingly quiet and cooperative operation. People watched from their windows; they answered their doors and showed their papers. Although the soldiers were outnumbered by the inhabitants—several of whom, it would be later learned, were indeed members of Begin's Irgun—the soldiers had the weapons and the people were unarmed.

David did the questioning while Ochieng stood guard with his rifle.

It was not easy to search for a man whom they only suspected was here and whom no one had ever actually seen. But David was determined. The wanted poster on the wall of the barracks displayed an old photograph of Begin. It showed him in a Polish Army uniform, standing next to a pretty young woman, his wife. David had memorized every detail of that blurry picture: Begin's hairline; the shape of his eyes; the thrust of his mouth. And the woman's too, Aliza Begin.

David encountered nervous young Jews, whom he sent to the waiting trucks, and men whose papers were not in order and a few who protested. Most of them, he knew, would be released by the day's end, with little or no information gotten from them.

David knocked at each door while Ochieng stood with rifle raised. Each door, they knew, could be a trap, could open with gunfire.

The morning wore on. David's anxiety mounted. Captain Geoffrey Donald toured the streets in his Jeep, questioning his men, directing them. Ochieng became jumpy. He expected any moment to hear the crack of bullets, the thunder of a bomb.

David knocked on the door of a modest little house, and it was opened by a short, smiling man.

"Hands up," David said. He searched the man. Finding no weapons, he said, "Your papers," and the man complied.

He was Israel Halperin, the identity papers said in English and Hebrew, a refugee from Poland.

"What is your profession?" David asked.

The man smiled, spread his hands, and said something in a language David didn't understand. When David stood back and said, "You'll have to go to police headquarters," another man suddenly appeared, as if he had been standing behind the door, listening.

He was taller than Mr. Halperin, wore a beard and a long black coat. He said his name was Epstein, a rabbi. "My friend does not speak English. Perhaps I can translate for you?"

David studied the rabbi. He bore no resemblance to the photo on the wanted poster. After Ochieng searched the rabbi for a weapon, David asked him, "What does this man do?"

"He is a lawyer. He is preparing for his examinations here in Palestine."

David looked the smaller man up and down. He had a shy manner and a congenial smile. "How long have you been here in Palestine?" David asked him.

Mr. Halperin replied, and the rabbi translated: "Four years."

"David!" said Ochieng. He spoke in Swahili. "I saw a movement over by that door."

David motioned for his friend to investigate. Ochieng led with his rifle and inched around the second doorway while the two Jews watched, seemingly unconcerned. A moment later a woman emerged, holding a small boy in her arms. Ochieng stood behind, his rifle trained on her, his stance edgy.

"Who is she?" David asked.

Mr. Halperin spoke, and the rabbi said, "She is his wife."

David stared at the woman. She was familiar. His heart began to race. He looked again at Mr. Halperin, looked into eyes that met his calmly and with assurance. Could this unassuming little man be the fearsome Menachem Begin? David suddenly saw a resemblance to the picture in the wanted poster. The eyebrows, the set of the mouth . . .

Shouts echoed in the street, and the roar of truck motors. A few citizens protested, calling insults to the soldiers.

David and Mr. Halperin looked at each other for a long time. Then David said, "You will come with me."

"My friend," said the rabbi gently, "what has Mr. Halperin done?"

David peered into the house. He looked for signs of others lurking there, for evidence of terrorist activity, but all he saw were stacks of books. "He is to be questioned by the police."

Then Mr. Halperin spoke; it sounded like a question.

Rabbi Epstein said, "Mr. Halperin wants to know, if you are a soldier, what are you fighting for?"

David was slightly taken aback. "Into the truck, all of you! The woman and child as well!"

But Mr. Halperin, calm and unperturbed, spoke again. While he spoke, the rabbi translated: "You are African, my friend, a member of an oppressed race. Why are you fighting for the British? Why do you fight for men who subjugate you?"

David hesitated, and the diminutive man went on, in a quiet, compelling voice. "Do you know what is going on in the world? I will tell you. In my hometown in Poland we Jews numbered thirty thousand. Today there are but ten left. It was our home, yet we were driven from it. What is happening in *your* home, my young African?"

Mr. Halperin's dark eyes were steady on David's face; they had a penetrating look, a persuasive power. "What have you been promised in return for fighting for the British, my friend? India has been promised independence in return for fighting in the war. Have you Africans been promised as much?"

David blinked. He looked past Mr. Halperin at Ochieng, who, not understanding English, stood impatiently with his rifle aimed at the woman and child. David was drawn back to Mr. Halperin's penetrating eyes. "If you have been promised nothing," Mr. Halperin, through the rabbi, continued, "then you fight for nothing. You were colonized years ago because you had no weapons, no education to match the British. But now you have knowledge of weapons, you have education. *What are you waiting for?*"

David stared down at the man who barely came to his shoulders. Mr. Halperin was pale, his hair receding, his voice soft. But there was a strange power about him from which David could not break away.

"There are things more precious than life, my oppressed friend," the Polish Jew said. "And more horrible than death. If you love freedom, you must hate slavery. If you love your people, you cannot but hate those who oppress them. I ask you, if you love your mother, would you not hate the man who sought to kill her? And would you not fight him at the cost of your own life?"

A memory flashed in David's mind. He was seventeen again, standing on the stump of a fig tree and crying out to Chief John Muchina, "The man who does not love his country does not love his mother. . . . And a man who does not love his mother . . . cannot love God!"

David was shaken. It was for those very words that he had been arrested and tortured and driven into exile in Uganda.

How could he have forgotten?

Suddenly he was acutely aware of the uniform he stood in, of the British tommy gun slung over his shoulder, and of the identity papers of "Mr. Israel Halperin" in his hand.

"Go!" whispered the soft-spoken Jew. "Go back to your homeland in peace and let us do here what we must do!"

"What have you got there, Private?" came a voice from behind.

David turned. His commanding officer was standing up in the Jeep, his eyes hidden behind sunglasses. He carried a swagger stick; the buttons of his uniform were polished and gleamed in the sun. He was Geoffrey Donald, friend of the Trevertons.

"Nothing, sir," David said abruptly, returning Mr. Halperin's papers to him. "Everything is in order here." He signaled to Ochieng, who came running out of the house. As the door closed behind him, David heard a quietly spoken *"Shalom."*

37

E veryone in the district knew that the greenhouse was haunted.
      Around their cook fires at night the Kikuyu spoke in hushed tones
of the spirit that lived there; children in school talked of the ghost;
women at the market murmured. It was not long before word of mouth
had reached every African in the area so that soon no one, not even
would-be thieves, ventured near the taboo greenhouse in the glade.

Njeri had done her job well.

Rose sang as she left the house on this beautiful December morning.
Like every morning now, she had taken great pains with her hair, with
her clothing. She tried different perfumes; she chose just the right
jewelry. She was desperate to please Carlo, to win his smile. But that
was exactly what General Carlo Nobili had done every day for three
months—smile at Rose.

Back in October the remains of a white man had been found in the
forest near Meru. It was surmised that he was the third of the escaped
Italian POWs and that he had met his fate in the jaws of wild animals.
The remains were sent to his ducal estate in Italy; the manhunt was
dropped; the case was closed. No one—not Grace or Sir James, nor
Mona and Tim Hopkins—knew of the mysterious occupant of the
greenhouse or that Rose had ceased to work on her tapestry weeks ago
and that she now went every day to the glade for a much different
purpose.

She paused at the edge of the drive and shielded her eyes from the
sun.

Mona was driving a truck loaded with sacks of coffee beans. Rose
marveled at her daughter's obsession with the estate. It was like a

madness. Mona was as fiercely possessive of Bellatu and its five thousand acres as Valentine was, and so Rose decided that Mona was
definitely her father's daughter. But what about when the war was
finally over, Rose wondered, and Valentine returned to resume control
of the plantation?

Rose felt a chill in her soul.

Valentine.

She hoped he would never return.

The general was in the greenhouse, cutting delphinium seedlings
with a knife. He had planted them in seed boxes two months ago, one
of his first tasks after convalescence. Rose paused in the doorway to
watch him. He stood in the refracted sunshine that came through the
skylight; a soft, gauzy aura seemed to envelop him. Nothing was in
sharp focus. The dark blue and lavender blossoms surrounding him
appeared to blur; leaves of light green blended into those of emerald.
The man himself was transformed: Rose thought he resembled a myth-
ical figure—so tall and slender, his dark head bent—like an olive-
complected god walking in some Olympian garden.

He looked up. She hadn't made a sound, but he had sensed her
standing there. "Rosa," he said softly.

She came in and set down the basket that contained their breakfast.
"Isn't it too soon to divide the seedlings?" she asked, coming to stand
next to him and looking down at the box.

"Not in Kenya! This country is fantastic, Rosa! Such a mild climate
you have here, with no winters, no spring or fall. Nothing lies dormant;
flowers bloom all year round!" He turned his radiant smile upon her.
"It is a gardener's paradise."

Carlo Nobili, Rose had discovered, was an expert on flowers. Back
on his ducal estate in northern Italy, he had spent years cultivating and
experimenting, crossbreeding, producing new hybrids, and creating a
vast flower garden that was the envy, he boasted, of the Vatican itself.
When, during his rocky convalescence on the bed she and Njeri had
made out of straw and blankets, the general had remarked upon the
excellence of Rose's plants, speaking knowledgeably, they had discovered an interest in common. In the weeks since, as their chaste and
gentle friendship had evolved, they had spent their hours sharing this
interest, learning from each other, telling of experiences, of successes

and failures. He had taught Rose how to cut back begonias so that they would have a longer flowering life; she had shown him how to cultivate the stunning opalescent blue delphinium that was native to Kenya and that she had found in the forest and transplanted in her glade.

He looked at her now, at the way the diffuse sunlight haloed her pale hair, softened the colors of her dress. This greenhouse hidden in the heart of a wood seemed, to the duca d'Alessandro, to be enchanted. He knew he lived a bewitched existence beneath its glass roof and among its rich soil, its heady floral perfumes, its great, nodding leaves, visited daily by this beautiful, pure woman, whom he had yet to touch and who, he was certain, must have stepped down from a Botticelli canvas.

"Did you sleep well, Rosa?" he asked, standing close to her.

Her breath caught. "Yes. And you, signor?"

"You have made a palace for me here." He swept his arm toward the corner, where a crude straw mattress, a rug, a folding chair, and a washstand with pitcher and basin made up his hideaway. "And you must call me Carlo."

Rose blushed and reached for the basket.

Her inability to call him by his first name was something she couldn't explain. Certainly, the duke believed, the intimacy of her having nursed him in his illness, of bathing his wounds, of feeding him like a child, and then of helping him take his first steps—surely, the duke thought, after days of this she could call him Carlo. And yet, incredibly, she could not!

He had watched her change during his recovery, from the gentle but firm nurse who had taken over his life and had done everything for him to a shy, timid creature that seemed now on the verge of running from him. It was almost as if, he thought, the more he had regained his strength, the more she had lost hers. The more his power grew, the more hers diminished. Now she could hardly meet his eyes.

She unpacked the basket, spreading out a fresh tablecloth, and set out the hot scones, butter, jar of honey, and pot of Countess Treverton tea. While they ate, Carlo spoke quietly about his home, the estate where he lived alone, his wife having died five years ago in childbirth. He and Rose discussed gardening, paintings, music, and books, but neither brought up the subject of the war or of his terrible experiences in the POW camp. They never touched upon the very thing that had brought him to this place and that kept him here now.

Every day Carlo saw the unspoken question in her eyes: *Why do you stay?* As if she feared that he would one day vanish. And every day he asked himself the same question, finding only no answers, just the sense that the longer he stayed, the more he had to stay.

For now he lived for this stolen spell, a charmed piece of time cut from the nightmarish fabric of war, as if past and future did not exist. All too soon, he knew, he would somehow have to find his way back to his army, back to the ignominy of defeat.

The morning was spent in fertilizing Rose's prize orchids, in soaking them and rotating them from sunlight to shade. Carlo asked questions as they worked. "Why do you keep them in such small pots, Rosa? I would think larger would be better for them."

The first time he had asked her a question, weeks ago, Rose had not known what to say. She was so out of practice in answering questions— not even her African house staff came to her for orders—that she had first been at a loss. But in time, as she had gotten used to Carlo's queries and had realized that he *listened* when she spoke, she grew comfortable explaining things. "These are South African orchids—disa orchids. They like small pots because they like to crowd against the sides."

They washed their hands in the afternoon when Njeri brought them tea, setting it out and then leaving. As Carlo and Rose ate the little sandwiches, they became aware of the darkening day. Clouds were rolling across the sky.

When the first drops spattered on the skylight, Rose said, "I must go now."

But Carlo suddenly took her hand and said, "No. Do not go. For once, Rosa, stay with me."

She felt her heart tumble. She looked down at the dark hand that held her wrist—his first real touch. And it excited, frightened her.

"Are you afraid of me, Rosa?" he asked softly.

Carlo stood. He came close to her. "Stay," he whispered. "Stay with me tonight."

"No . . ."

"Why not?" With his other hand he touched her hair. "Do you want to go, Rosa?"

She closed her eyes. "No."

"Then stay."

His nearness made her dizzy. The scents of a hundred flowers, in the warm, moist greenhouse, pressed in on her. She felt his fingers on her hair and holding her wrist. Although their relationship was platonic, thoughts of Carlo Nobili filled her every waking moment and her dreams as well. By day she approached him demurely chaste, but by night she fantasized. . . .

When she felt his lips on hers, her eyes flew open and she drew back. But he held her and said, "Tell me you do not love me, Rosa. *Tell me.*"

"Signor, please let me go."

"My name is Carlo. I want to hear you say it." His grip tightened on her wrist. "Do you love me? If not, say so and I will let you go."

She looked into his dark eyes and was lost. "Yes," she whispered. "I do love you."

He released her. He smiled and tenderly took her face between his hands. Rose braced herself, but she barely felt his kiss. "Tell me what you are afraid of, my dear one," he murmured. "We are alone in here. No one can see us. Let me make love to you. I have wanted to do so since I first opened my eyes and saw one of God's angels."

"No . . ."

"Why not?"

You'll hate me, she thought. *I'll disappoint you, and then you won't love me anymore. Like Valentine . . .*

She bowed her head. "Because . . . I don't like it."

"Then I must see to it that you do." He put his arm around her and led her to the bed. She stiffened and prepared to resist him, but to her surprise, instead of making her lie down, he invited her to sit.

The rain came down heavily on the glass roof. Carlo lit a hurricane lamp and sat next to Rose on the bed. He put his arm around her shoulders and drew her back so that they both rested against the wall. For a long time they sat and listened to the rain.

Rose was confused. Part of her wanted him; part rejected him. She felt something close to desire for him, but it went no further than simple things—a touch, a kiss. Beyond that a wall of fear stood before her.

He started to stroke her hair. He kissed her forehead. He murmured in Italian. She felt the warmth of his body through the silk shirt he wore; she felt his firm muscles, the harnessed masculine strength. Carlo had the power, she knew, to force her, as Valentine had once done. If he did that, then the spell would be broken forever.

But there was nothing demanding about Carlo's actions. Rose sensed none of the urgency she had felt with Valentine. Ensconced in the warmth and glow of the greenhouse, surrounded by a jungle of ferns and vines and tropical flowers, with the rain pelting overhead, she began to grow languid. She leaned into Carlo's embrace. She tucked her legs beneath her and rested her head on his shoulder. It was becoming dreamlike—his soft voice, his touch, his comforting nearness.

Then his hand went down to her thigh.

"No," she said.

"Please," he whispered. "Let me take care of you, my dear one."

She tried to relax, tried to admit him into her body, but as his hand drew higher, she began to panic.

"Rosa," he said when he felt her go rigid, "look at me."

"I—"

"Look at me."

She drew her head back. His eyes were inches from hers. They seized her and held her while his hand continued its gentle exploration.

"Open your legs," he whispered. "Just a little."

"No."

"Open yourself to me, Rosa."

His hand moved inward.

She gasped and stiffened.

"Shhh," he said. "Do not fight me. Relax, my dear one."

"What are you—" she began. She was breathless.

"Keep looking at me, Rosa. I love you. I am telling you how I love you."

Something strange was happening to her. Rose was startled. Carlo's hand moved slowly; his eyes looked into hers.

She said, "Oh!"

"Come to me, Rosa," he said. "Come to me."

She was captured by his gaze. She couldn't move. But something was happening. "Wait," she whispered. "I'm going to—"

"What? What are you going to?"

His hand continued its rhythmic caress.

"Yes," she whispered. "Oh, yes."

Then he touched her. Rose cried out as the wave swept over her. Then she seemed to collapse in his arms.

Carlo took hold of her chin, lifted her head, and pressed his mouth to hers.

"Carlo!" she breathed. "Oh, Carlo!"

"Tell me what your dream is, my dear one. Tell me your dreams."

Tears came to her eyes. She had had a dream once, years ago, when she had first come to Kenya. She had dreamed of becoming a real woman. She had thought East Africa would make her complete. Instead, the highland winds had carried her spirit away.

But tonight, beneath the driving rain, in Carlo's arms, Rose began to dream again.

She jumped up suddenly, and went to the door. "Njeri," she called through the pouring rain. The girl was sitting in the gazebo, waiting for her mistress.

"Njeri, go back to the house. I shall be staying here. If anyone telephones or comes to visit me, tell them I am in bed with a headache and don't wish to be disturbed. Do you understand?"

Njeri looked uncertainly at her mistress standing in the doorway. Then she said, "Yes, memsaab."

Closing the door behind herself, Rose turned and looked at Carlo.

He gazed at her with great tenderness. "And now, my dear one," he said, "will you dream with me?"

"Yes."

"And will you no longer be afraid?"

"Yes," she said. "I will no longer be afraid."

SHE FOUND HIM standing in the glade, gazing up at the moon and stars. His hair was blowing in the light breeze, his face set in concentration. He looked so tall and beautiful, Rose thought, without a shirt, so that the moonlight played its nacreous glow over his sinewy arms and chest. He was so magnificent that he seemed to Rose to have just been created, like Adam in Eden, new and magical and alone.

But when she drew near, she saw the scars on his back, and her heart ached for him. There had been nights, in these two months of living together in love, when Carlo had cried out in his sleep. Rose had comforted him, and he had wept, finally telling her about the camp, of the atrocities inflicted upon his men. Guilt lay heavily upon the soul of Carlo Nobili. He was a troubled, deeply anguished man. He believed that he had abandoned his men and that he should have perished with them.

She came up to him and touched his arm.

"The war is ending," he said into the wind.

"I know."

He turned and looked down at her. "The end of our time here together has come. We can no longer go on like this."

She nodded.

"Will you stay with him?" Carlo asked.

It was a subject both had carefully avoided in the past eight weeks. But the question came as no surprise to Rose; she knew it would have to be asked one day. "No," she said. "I will not stay with Valentine. I won't live with him anymore. I don't want to be here when he comes home."

"What about your daughter? Your home?"

"Mona doesn't need me. And Bellatu has always just been a house to me, never a home. You are my home, Carlo."

"Then you will go away with me?"

"Yes."

"Wherever I say? Wherever I go?"

"Yes."

"I do not know what I will do, where I will go. My family believes me to be dead. I do not know what awaits me in Italy. Perhaps I will not return to my home but start somewhere new, in a new place. Does that frighten you, Rosa, that I am a man without a home?"

"I am not afraid, Carlo."

He drew her into his arms and pressed his face against her pale gold hair. "What did I do in my life to deserve you, my dear one? When I think of my years of sorrow, after my wife died . . . and the long, lonely years in the house of my ancestors, thinking that I would never love again. I was only half alive, Rosa, before I met you."

He kissed her, very gently, then said, "I cannot promise you anything more than this, my dear one. This, and my eternal love and devotion to you."

"It's all I ask. It's all I've ever wanted. I'll leave all this behind, right now, if it's what you wish."

He nodded. "Then we will leave at once."

AT THAT SAME moment Valentine was standing on the platform of the Nairobi train station and wondering again if he should telephone ahead and let Rose know of his unexpected leave or put it off just a little longer and make his homecoming a surprise.

He wanted to make a show of it, a grand spectacle just like the old days, when everyone in the colony had said that Valentine Treverton was a master showman.

Six blessed weeks lay ahead of him, of being in his own home, in his own bed, and eating real food. After three years in the wretched desert fighting the Italians, Valentine had but one thought in his head: to set foot inside Bellatu again.

He was even looking forward to seeing Rose. Perhaps, he hoped, four years of loneliness would make her receptive to him.

And so, finding a boy to carry his bags, Valentine headed away from where the telephones were and looked for a taxi. He had decided to make his homecoming a surprise.

38

Wanjiru had danced in the rain. Now she lay back on her new bed of goatskins, her naked body wet and shining, ready for David to come to her.

She had waited for a long time for this night. There hadn't been an opportunity, five years back, when David had finally returned to Kenya from his Uganda exile, for them to enjoy each other. He had signed on for the army and had gone away, almost at once, to that terrible Palestine, where he had almost died.

That was why David was home now, before the war was over, because of wounds received when his Jeep had hit a land mine. After twelve weeks in a hospital in Jerusalem, and four more in Nairobi, David was home at last, and he was *hers.*

There had been two marriage ceremonies: the civil one, which the British authorities required, and the Kikuyu one, which the tribe required. It was the second one they were celebrating on this drizzly April night. All the family had come from the village across the river to share Wachera's happiness. David had paid thirty goats to Wanjiru's mother—a handsome price! He and his friends had then erected the walls of a new mud hut, after which, following ancient custom, Wanjiru and the women had spent the morning putting on the roof. Two weeks ago David's mother had made the ceremonial cut upon Wanjiru that would allow sexual intercourse, undoing the work she herself had done on Wanjiru at the *irua,* eight years ago. The wound had healed; Wanjiru now lay ready for her man.

* * *

IT SEEMED TO David as if the celebrating would go on all night.

He was morose. He wished he could be as joyous as his kin all were, dancing and passing around calabashes of surgarcane beer. But they were blissfully ignorant people; they were able to be happy, whereas David, too educated and too worldly for his own good, sat in the glum shadow of reality.

For his wounds and service to the Crown, the British had given David a medal and an early honorable discharge. But nothing more. He had returned home to find there was no employment for him, that there was no place in Kenya for, as one person had put it, an "educated nigger." Although there were African teachers in "native" schools, and African clerks in some government offices, and a growing number of Africans in private business, no one seemed to need a bright young man of twenty-seven with a college degree in farming and an ambitious look in his eye.

A calabash of beer was put into his hands, and he drank.

He knew Wanjiru had gone into her new hut, which he and his friends had built next to his mother's. But he couldn't face his bride just yet. He was too full of anger, too bitter to go to her in love. So he drank down all the beer and reached for more. Across the fire, around which the young people danced, David saw his mother watching him.

David estimated that his mother was fifty-five years old. If she had stopped shaving her head, she would no doubt show gray hairs. But her face was still smooth and beautiful; her long neck was graced with row upon row of beaded necklaces. She still wore the old-fashioned dress made of soft hides, and great loops of beads stood out on either side of her head.

Wachera symbolized for her people the vanishing ways, a vanishing Africa. David saw his mother as a sort of sacred icon that represented the old order being erased from this land. She made his heart ache. All these lonely years! Without a husband, with no other children, living alone in a hut that had been torn down repeatedly and that she had rebuilt until the white man finally left her alone. David's mother, Wachera Mathenge, was now a legend all over Kenya because of her stand against the Europeans.

Since his return David had spent many hours talking to his mother, while she had listened in silence. He had told her of his struggle in Uganda, as a student on his own, to graduate at the top of his class and of his painful, homesick years in Palestine, when his only comfort had been thoughts of coming home. And now, of how emasculating that homecoming really was, returning to discover that he was, after all, only a second-class citizen.

"They praise us in the newspapers," he had said to her over the cook fires in her hut. "And on the radio. The government praises its 'colored' troops; Parliament cheers its 'native' heroes. They instill in us pride and self-esteem; they teach us to read and write and to fight for a unified cause—Luo and Kikuyu side by side. But when we return to Kenya, we are told there is no place for us, no jobs, and that we must go back to our homes on the native reserves!

"Mother! All over the British Empire colonies are gaining their independence. I ask you: *Why not Kenya?*"

David knew that he was not alone in his cry. Although the outbreak of war had brought an abrupt halt to a budding political awareness among Africans, which he had taken part in back in 1937, it was being rekindled. Even now, as he emptied another calabash of beer, David knew that convening in Nairobi was a secret meeting, a session of the Kenya Africa Union, in which certain key leaders—young, educated, and energetic men—were outlining their plan for Kenya's independence. It was also rumored that Jomo Kenyatta, the famous "agitator," was planning to return to Kenya, after a seventeen-year absence. With such forces in motion, and with the imminent return of seventy thousand African troops once the war was over, David was certain that the face of Kenya was going to be altered forever.

It meant that his land would be returned to him.

He rose on unsteady legs and turned to look up at the ridge that rose above the river. Just over the tops of the trees he could see the lights of Bellatu, that monstrous stone house which had been built with Kikuyu blood and sweat. Thinking of the white people inside that house—the Trevertons—David thought: *Soon* . . .

His mother came up to him and said, "Go to your wife now, David Kabiru. She is waiting."

He went into the hut and stood just inside the doorway. A smoldering cook fire filled the air with smoke; it was warm and close within the mud walls; the smell of rain and beer filled his head. When he saw Wanjiru, stretched out, voluptuous and naked, a lump gathered in his throat.

He felt like an impostor.

A woman had the right to have a *man* for a husband. By Kikuyu law, if she was not sexually satisfied, if he did not give her children, if he could not perform like a man, then she had the right to cast him off and return to her family. David wanted desperately to show her how much he loved and desired her, to take her as a warrior should and give her pleasure. But he felt useless. He felt impotent.

Wanjiru raised her arms and he went to her. Sinking down, David pressed his face between her large breasts and tried to tell her what was in his heart. But he had drunk too much beer. His tongue would not obey. Nor would any other part of his body.

Wanjiru was patient at first, understanding more about men than most new brides did because she was a trained nurse. She caressed and soothed him. She murmured Kikuyu endearments. She moved her body in enticing ways. But when her efforts failed to coax a satisfactory response from him, when he remained limp in her hand, she felt her old anger flare up.

Eight years ago she had had to goad David Mathenge into manhood, when he had stood on a tree stump spouting proverbs. Now she must do it again—on their wedding night!

She sat up. "David, what's wrong?"

He was devastated. The beer, his feelings of humiliation, his sense that the manhood had been cut out of him . . .

"The *thahu* is not on them!" he cried, flinging out an arm and pointing up in the direction of Bellatu. "It is upon *me!*"

Wanjiru was shocked. And when she saw tears gather in his eyes and heard the tone of self-pity in his cry, she was revolted. Nothing made her more contemptuous of a man than his acting like a woman.

"Leave me," she said, "and come back to my bed when you are a man."

David stumbled from the hut. He glanced over at his cousins and uncles celebrating around the fire, then turned away from them and disappeared into the night.

* * *

"I SAY," SAID Tim Hopkins when Sir James came to join him on the terrace, "there appears to be something going on down at the old medicine woman's hut. What do you suppose it is?"

James looked up at the dark sky and wondered how long the rain would hold off. Chancing going back to Kilima Simba in the middle of a storm might be risky. He decided to take Valentine up on his offer of a shakedown for the night. "Val says Wachera's son got married. They put up a new hut for the wife."

"That will make three huts down there then at the end of the polo field."

"Yes, and Val is furious. He's declared that he's going to tear the whole lot down in the morning, the old woman's hut included this time."

Good, Tim thought. *I hope the bastard does it. The Kikuyu won't stand for it, and they'll want revenge. Maybe this time they'll feed Lord Treverton to their goats!*

Grace appeared at the French doors. She hesitated, looking at young Tim talking quietly with James in the misty night. Grace wore glasses now, but because of her blind right eye, one lens was made of plain glass.

"James," she said, coming to join them.

He saw that she was troubled. "What is it, Grace?"

"Rose has just told me the most remarkable thing!" She glanced back through the French doors into the dining room, where servants were setting the table for dinner. "I'm still in shock over it. She called me up to her room just now and told me the most extraordinary story! Mona is up there now, no doubt hearing the same thing. James, Rose is planning on leaving."

"What do you mean, leaving?"

"She's going away, out of Kenya. Rose is leaving Valentine!"

He said, "What?" so loudly that Grace had to caution him to be quiet.

"Valentine doesn't know yet. Rose is going to tell him at dinner."

"This is absurd. Is she drunk perhaps?"

"She's quite sober, James. You see . . . there's another man."

James and Tim stared at Grace.

"Rose has a lover," she whispered.

"Nonsense," James said. "She's telling you stories."

"I don't think so. If you recall, I told you sometime ago that my sister-in-law had somehow changed over the past few months. She suddenly became animated, assertive. She began giving orders to the house staff. She actually *fired* two house girls. And she even challenged *me* on one occasion, telling me to mind my own business! Mona and I discussed it at the time, and considering that Rose is forty-six, I decided that it was due to that time of life. But now Rose tells me that she has had a lover all these months and that the two of them are running away in the morning."

James frowned. "I don't believe it. If Rose has had a lover all this time, word would surely have gotten around. You know how like a gossipy small town Kenya is!"

"Apparently they were able to keep it a secret. The man himself is unknown to any of us, and she kept him hidden."

"What on earth are you talking about?"

"Rose said it's one of the escaped Italian prisoners, the ones you and Tim searched for back in September."

"But that was seven months ago! Surely if the man had gotten down as far as Nyeri and was trying to hide, we would have found him."

"Not where Rose kept him."

"Where?"

"In her eucalyptus glade. In the *greenhouse.*"

James and Tim looked at each other. "She *kept* him there?" the younger man asked.

"At first he was injured, she said. She nursed him back to health. Afterward they met in secret in the greenhouse."

James shook his head. "It's preposterous. This is not at all like Rose." He thought for a moment, then added, "And is that where he's supposed to be right now, this Carlo?"

"In the greenhouse. Waiting for her, she says. They're going to leave at first light."

James stared at Grace for a moment, then turned away and paced the glistening stones of the terrace. It was starting to rain again. "Do you believe her, Grace?"

"At first I didn't. But she's so calm about it, she's acting so incredibly levelheaded. And the *details*. Well, yes, as a matter of fact, I do believe her."

"Should we try to stop her?"

"I don't see how we can. She's very determined. And then again, do we have the right to interfere?"

"Valentine is going to be furious."

Grace pulled her cardigan tightly about herself. "I know," she said, and hurried back inside out of the rain.

Inside the house, where the aroma of roasting lamb mingled with the smoky fragrance of a roaring fire, Valentine stumbled back from the open window through which he had overheard every word of the conversation. He leaned against the wall, staring.

MONA TOUCHED LITTLE of her dinner and wondered how her mother, considering what she was planning to do at dawn, could eat. And yet there was Rose, cutting her lamb, taking a second helping of sweet potatoes, all the while smiling, charming, engaged in small talk with Tim Hopkins.

Grace and Sir James ate in silence, frequently glancing across the table at each other, while Valentine talked.

"I'll tell you what the coming thing is," he said to James as he refilled his wineglass. "Groundnuts. I'm going to clear about three thousand acres and plant groundnuts."

Mona looked at her father. "They won't work," she said.

"Why not?"

"The elevation here is too high for groundnuts."

"And how do you know that?"

"I tried it two years ago, and they perished."

"Then you did something wrong."

As her father resumed talking to Sir James, Mona felt the color rise in her cheeks. This airy dismissal of anything she had to say infuriated her. Mona had expected a terrible row when her father returned from the north, and she had been ready for it. Instead, to her great surprise and disappointment, he had driven over the estate, had seen what she had done, and had said vaguely, "You were lucky. But of course, all this will have to go."

No anger, no shouting. Just a simple, humiliating disregard of her labors and accomplishments. It was worse, Mona decided, than the expected tirade.

"You'll stay out of my affairs from now on," he had said after that. "*I'll* see to the running of this farm."

Mona had replied, "And what am *I* supposed to do?"

And Valentine had said, "Hang it all, girl! You're twenty-seven years old! Get married!"

That was a week ago, and Mona still smoldered over it. *Get married,* he had said, meaning, *Get out of my hair and be another man's burden.* Her father had even gotten her age wrong.

Mona thought about her mother. What a shock it had been to hear of the love affair and the plan to run away. At first Mona had been upset, and then she worried for her mother's mental state. Soon, however, Mona had begun to envy her mother's new life, her discovery of love and passion and utter dedication to one man. She recalled the look on her mother's face when she had spoken of her dear Carlo; Mona had felt a pain in her heart, and then she had felt happiness for her mother. *Yes,* she had finally said to Rose. *Do it. Follow the man you love. Get away from Father. I wish I could do as much.*

As she pushed her food around her plate and listened to *him* go on about plans for *his* farm, Mona thought of Geoffrey Donald, who was due to come home from Palestine soon. Marrying him was going to fit in perfectly with her own plan. Geoffrey didn't want to work Kilima Simba anymore; he wanted to start a tourist business. And he could do that, Mona decided, as easily from Bellatu as from anywhere else. Instead of her moving out when she got married, as her father was no doubt anticipating, Mona was going to bring her husband *here* to live. Because Mona Treverton was never going to relinquish possession of the plantation. Not to her father, not to anyone.

"Did you know, James," Valentine said as he poured himself more wine, "that there's talk of a *new* soldier settlement scheme? It's a plan to bolster the economy after the war. Bring in more white settlers at low land prices."

"I've heard the rumors, and it seems to me that there isn't enough land now as it is."

"The plan is to move the squatters back onto the native reserves. All the Kikuyu in this district will have to return to the original land the government set aside for them."

"They won't do it willingly, not the way they did in the old days." James exchanged a glance with Grace. There was a palpable tension at the table. Valentine's amiable mood seemed forced, and he was drinking too much.

While Valentine was in the middle of saying something further to James, Rose pushed her chair back and stood. "I'm going to say good night to you all now. But before I go up, I have something to say."

Her guests, expectant, apprehensive, turned to her. The man at the other end of the table, they all knew, was possessed of a powerful and destructive temper.

Rose looked beautiful. For the occasion she had put on one of her best dinner gowns; it was long and sleek and black, with rhinestones around the low neckline. She wore her hair piled on top of her head, fixed in place with an orchid.

"Valentine," she said, "I have something to say to you."

They all waited.

"I'm leaving you, Valentine. I'm going away in the morning, and I'm never coming back."

She paused. The other four at the table wanted to look at him, but no one dared to move.

Rose was serene and in control of herself. "I have found someone who loves me just for me, Valentine, not for what he can produce out of my body. A man who cherishes me, who listens to me, who treats me as his equal. My life with you is over. I shall start anew, far away from Kenya. I lay no claims on your money or on Bellatu. And I give you back your title. I was never a good countess."

She stopped. She gazed down the length of the table at him. Those near to Rose could see the thumping of her heart beneath her breast.

"No, Rose," Valentine said with a sigh. "You're not going anywhere."

Grace looked at her brother. She saw the fire in his eyes, the throb at his temple.

"Yes, Valentine. I am leaving you, and you cannot stop me."

"I will not allow it."

"You can't bully me anymore, Valentine. I am no longer afraid of you. Carlo taught me that. He also taught me how to love. It was something I have always thought myself incapable of, because you killed it in me years ago. I could have loved you the way you wanted, Valentine, but your impatience and disregard of my feelings drove me away from you. Even my own daughter, whom I could have loved if you had but made one gesture when I arrived here with her. If you had acknowledged my baby, uttered one word of appreciation or affection, then I would have let myself love her. Instead, you made me feel guilty for having produced her. And so I punished myself, and her, for it.

"And your son, Arthur, whose only desire in all his short life was to please you—you drove him away also. He was killed because he was trying to be brave, to make you proud of him. I have found love again, and I am not going to let this chance pass me by. I do not hate you, Valentine. I simply do not love you. And I don't want to live with you anymore."

She looked at the others, said, "Good-bye," and walked from the dining room.

The five at the table sat motionless, listening to the whisper of rain. Grace waited for the explosion from Valentine, braced herself for the fury.

But all he said was "It's late. And it's raining, so you'd best all stay here tonight. No use getting wet!"

They watched him stand up from the table and walk to the whiskey cart. One by one they slowly rose. Mona and Tim left first, to their separate rooms; then Grace murmured to James that she was going up to Rose.

When the two men were alone, James tried to say something.

But Valentine turned a gallant smile to him. "She won't go, you know. She doesn't really mean it. Rose doesn't have what it takes."

"I think she means it, Val."

He tossed back the whiskey and poured another. "Well, she might think she means it now, James, but you'll see. Come morning, Rose will still be here. I guarantee that."

James stepped up to him. "Valentine," he said, "why not just let her go?"

Valentine laughed, softly and without rancor. "You just don't understand, James," he said, dropping a heavy hand on his friend's shoulder.

"I built this house for *her.* All this—for my lovely Rose. You surely don't think she's going to leave it, do you? Now go to bed, my friend. Tomorrow my coffee trees will start blooming with white blossoms. Think of it! Thousands of acres of them!"

He smiled. "Sleep well, James. And don't worry about Rose and me."

GRACE WOKE UP suddenly.

She blinked in the darkness, trying to think what had wakened her.

Then she realized it was the sound of a car motor.

She tried to read the dial of her bedside clock. It was either five past four, or one-twenty, she couldn't tell. Had she only dreamed of hearing a motor? Or had someone actually driven away from Bellatu in the middle of the night? Tim, perhaps, worrying about his sister alone on their farm.

Grace looked at the head sleeping on the next pillow. The sound hadn't wakened James.

She listened to the silence of the big house and thought: *The rain has stopped.*

As Grace drifted off to sleep again, she thought the floorboards in the hallway creaked, as if someone were tiptoeing by.

39

Early in the morning, just before dawn, on April 16, 1945, a European midwife from Grace Treverton Mission was driving her car down the deserted road from the town of Kiganjo, where she had labored all night delivering a baby. In the darkness ahead she saw a car parked on the right side of the road, facing away from her, its motor running, and its taillights casting two red beams on the muddy road. As she slowed down and drew near, she saw that someone sat inside the car, in front on the right side, the driver's seat. She pulled up alongside and found a man asleep. Recognizing him as the earl of Treverton, the nurse called to him and asked if he required assistance. When he didn't wake up, she got out and looked through the passenger window.

The earl was slumped against the driver's door with a bullet hole in his left temple, a gun in his hand.

She drove immediately to the Nyeri police post, where she roused Third-Grade Constable Kamau, who then woke the corporal on duty. Together with two askaris they followed the memsaab back to the Kiganjo Road, where, a mile beyond the turnoff from the main Nyeri road, they found Lord Treverton's car.

In the feeble light of dawn the policemen circled the car and argued among themselves over what should be done. The nurse noticed, in the meantime, fresh bicycle tire tracks in the mud, leading up to the passenger side of the parked car and then doubling back toward the direction they appeared to have come from—Nyeri. But by the time the corporal acted and returned to the post to put in a call to Inspector Mitchell, who lived in Nyeri, and by the time the inspector was on the scene, all evidence of the bicycle tracks had been trampled away.

"Good God," Mitchell said when he looked into the car, "the earl's shot himself!"

Having to report such a thing to the family was unpleasant duty. And what a sensation this was going to cause! Why, the earl was even in his uniform! It must have been depression over the war that had driven him to it, the inspector decided as he followed the winding drive up to Bellatu. Not a few fighting men had come home to commit suicide. But Lord Treverton?

It was nine o'clock in the morning when Inspector Mitchell of the Nyeri police knocked on the front door of Bellatu and told the African houseboy he wished to speak to Lady Rose.

Dr. Grace Treverton came into the living room instead. "My sister-in-law isn't home, Inspector," she said. "Lady Rose left for a trip early this morning. Perhaps I can help you?"

"Well, Doctor," he said as he turned his homburg around and around in his hands; Inspector Mitchell hated this part of his job, "it's about His Lordship the earl."

"I'm afraid my brother hasn't come down to breakfast yet. So far Sir James Donald and I are the only ones up."

The inspector nodded. He was well acquainted with Sir James. "Well, Doctor, since you're the earl's sister, then I can tell you, and you can inform Lady Rose when she returns."

"Tell me what, Inspector?"

The house was ominously still. A clock ticked somewhere; animal heads with magnificent horns stared down from the walls. Inspector Mitchell wished the earl hadn't chosen this district in which to kill himself.

"I'm afraid your brother won't be coming down for breakfast, Dr. Treverton, because he isn't here."

"Not here? Of course he's here."

"He was found in his car early this morning on the Kiganjo Road. One of your midwives, a Nurse Billings, found him."

"What do you mean, found him?"

"I'm sorry to say that His Lordship drove out in his car sometime during the night and committed suicide with a pistol."

Grace sat motionless. She gazed at the police inspector through gold-rimmed glasses. Then she said, "Are you saying that my brother is *dead?*"

"I'm very sorry, Doctor."

"Are you sure it's Lord Treverton?"

"Quite sure."

Grace stood up. "Pardon me, please," she said, and left the living room.

When she returned a moment later, Sir James was with her. "Tell me what happened, Inspector," he said as he sat on the sofa next to a visibly shaken and upset Grace.

The policeman repeated everything and added, "The motor was still running when the nurse found him. We don't think he had been dead long. The body will be taken to the police post. You can, ah, see him there."

Grace said, "Oh, my God," and Sir James took her into his arms.

"Thank you for coming by, Inspector," he said in a tight voice when the policeman rose. "I'll come to the station later and verify identity."

"That would be most appreciated, Sir James."

The inspector turned to go but stopped when he saw Rose Treverton standing in the doorway of the dining room.

He stared at her. A large bruise covered her left cheek.

"What has happened?" she said.

James and Grace looked up. "Rose!" said Grace. "You're still here!" When she saw the bruise, she got up and went to her sister-in-law. Grace whispered, "What on earth has happened to your face?"

But when she reached out to touch the black-and-blue cheek, Rose drew back. "Why is this policeman here?" she asked.

"Rose," Grace said in a tight voice, "please come and sit down. I'm afraid there's some bad news."

But she remained in the doorway. "What is it?"

The inspector shifted self-consciously. He had glimpsed Countess Treverton on occasion—in her box at the Nairobi Racecourse or riding by in her chauffeured car. She was always beautiful and every bit the aristocrat. Her appearance now shocked him: the disheveled hair, half pinned up, half falling down; the rumpled dressing gown; the circles under her eyes; and that monstrous bruise.

Grace said, "Rose, there's been an—" She stopped. She had been about to say "accident."

"Is someone hurt?"

Grace, unable to speak, turned to Sir James, who said, "Valentine is dead, Rose."

Rose flinched, as if she had been struck.

"Apparently he shot himself—" James's voice caught.

Rose looked confused. "Valentine is dead?" she whispered. "He *killed* himself? But where?"

"In his car, Your Ladyship," the inspector said. "On the Kiganjo Road. Sometime during the night. I offer my deepest condolences."

She turned woodenly and moved to one of the dining room chairs. She put her hand on it as if to pull it out but simply stood, her eyes searching the polished surface of the table. "Valentine," she murmured. "Dead . . ."

Then she buried her face in her hands and cried, "I hadn't meant for that to happen! Oh, Carlo!"

After the inspector had gone, James and Grace helped Rose into the living room. "Rose," said Grace in a numb voice, "what happened last night? How did you hurt your face? And why haven't you gone away with Carlo?"

Rose stared into her lap. "Valentine hit me. He came upstairs and said he was going to stop me from leaving him. We had a row. He struck me across the face."

Grace waited. "And then what happened?"

"I don't know. He knocked me unconscious. I only just woke up a few minutes ago. I didn't hear him leave the house—" Rose started to sob. "You must believe me! I hadn't meant for him to *die!*"

"WELL," INSPECTOR MITCHELL said as he walked into the small, plain police station, "this'll be one for the gossips!"

An African constable looked up from his Corona typewriter and grinned.

Mitchell shook his head and hung his hat on a peg. "Nothing like a high society suicide to get the tongues wagging!"

As he was about to sit down at his desk to his morning tea and toast, another constable came running in. "Bwana! Come quick!"

With a sigh, and asking himself why he had ever left his peaceful Cheshire to emigrate to Kenya, Inspector Mitchell followed the constable outside and around back into the police yard. Lord Treverton's car was there, its door and trunk open, undergoing an inspection by two constables.

When Mitchell came around to the rear, he stopped cold and looked into the trunk. "Good Lord! Who is it?"

Third-Grade Constable Kamau said, "We don't know yet, sir. There appear to be no identity papers on him. But we haven't searched him thoroughly. I wanted you to see him like this before we moved him."

"Dead, I suppose?"

"And for a long time, I think."

"Get the photographer out here."

Mitchell gazed down at the body in the trunk and felt all appetite for breakfast evaporate. The victim, wearing only trousers and a white silk shirt, was barefoot and bound with rope at the ankles and wrists. He had been shot through the head.

"EXECUTION STYLE?" SAID Superintendent Lewis of the Criminal Investigations Division in Nairobi. He had just arrived in Nyeri, after receiving a call from Inspector Mitchell, and was accompanying the inspector out to the police yard.

"It looks that way," Mitchell said. "Trussed up like a sacrificial goat. Shot once, cleanly, through the head."

"Any idea who he is?"

"None at all. We've asked around. Appears to be a foreigner. No one knows him, and no one's been reported missing."

They came to the car and looked into the empty trunk. Blood was spattered near the wheel well.

"I reckon he was made to climb in," Mitchell said. "His hands and feet were tied, and then he was shot. The earl saved himself the trouble of trying to get a body into the trunk."

Superintendent Lewis, a short, plump man with bifocals and a walrus mustache, stroked his chin in thought. He'd been called in on the Treverton case because it now involved a murder. "Are the pictures ready yet?"

"Not yet, Superintendent. But I've told the man to hurry with the developing."

Lewis walked around to the left side of the car and looked in. Directly across, on the driver's door, he saw a small bloodstain, just about on level, he estimated, with where the earl's head would have been as he sat behind the wheel.

"The motor was running, you say?"

"Yes, Superintendent. The way I see it, Lord Treverton put the man in the trunk, shot him, then drove off with the intention of dumping the body where animals could get at it or of burying it. But somewhere along the way, on the Kiganjo Road, he was overcome with guilt and remorse, pulled over, and put the gun to his own head."

"Has the pathologist arrived yet?"

"He's on his way up from Nairobi."

Superintendent Lewis looked all over the inside of the car, noted the few things scattered about—a pair of men's gloves, an old magazine, a blanket neatly folded—then settled his small, intelligent eyes on the passenger seat. There were flecks of dried mud on it. Stepping back, he looked down at the running board and saw two big smudges of mud, which might or might not be taken for footprints.

"Does the family know about this development yet?" he asked Inspector Mitchell.

"Not yet. I informed them of the earl's death this morning. I thought I'd wait until you took a look at the situation before I followed up."

The superintendent looked at Mitchell over the rim of his bifocals and said, "If you don't mind, Inspector, I'd like to be the one to break this news to them."

Inside the police office the two men sat over the newly developed photographs. Superintendent Lewis lingered a long time over the shots of Treverton, his head, in profile, leaning against the window, a small round hole with powder burns in his left temple. There was also a photograph of the gun in his hand, resting on the seat at his side. In the picture bits of mud on the passenger seat could be seen. And the mud appeared to be fresh.

* * *

THEY WERE SITTING at the breakfast table with cold cups of tea before them when Rose came in and said, "He's not there!"

James got up and helped her into a chair, while Mona poured from a fresh teapot and pressed the steaming cup into her mother's hands. But Rose didn't drink. "Carlo isn't in the greenhouse!" she said. "Where could he be?"

Tim Hopkins got up and went to the window. He looked out at the deserted coffee fields, listened to the silence from the river, where the processing machinery stood idle, and heard, far away, the song of mourning in the Kikuyu village. The earl, he knew, would be greatly missed.

But not by him.

"Where would Carlo have gone to?" Mona asked, sitting next to her mother and laying a hand on her arm.

Rose shook her head as tears gathered in her eyes.

"Perhaps he got worried because you hadn't shown up as planned," James said. "Maybe he's at the train station."

Tim said, "Someone's coming. Oh, it's that police inspector again. Got another bloke with him this time."

"Grace," said Rose, seizing her sister-in-law's wrist, "I don't want to talk to them! Please keep them away from me!"

"Don't worry, Rose," Grace said bleakly. Her face was white and drawn; she hadn't touched her tea. "James and I will see to everything."

But Superintendent Lewis wanted in particular to ask Lady Rose a few questions. His first was how she had come by the bruise on her face.

She twisted her hands in her lap and didn't meet his eyes as she said, "I fell."

"You fell?"

"Last night. I tripped on the edge of the carpet and hit my jaw on the edge of the dressing table."

"Do you know what time your husband left the house last night?"

"No. I was—sleeping."

"Do you know *why* he left the house in the middle of the night?"

"Superintendent," said James, "is this really necessary? Lady Rose has suffered a terrible shock. Surely I can answer your questions. I was in the house last night, too."

His bushy eyebrows rose. "You were? Well then, perhaps you can help." He pulled a small notepad out of his breast pocket, flipped it open, and said to James, "You were close friends with the earl, were you not?"

"We've known each other for years."

"Was Lord Treverton right-handed or left-handed?"

"He was right-handed. I say, what is this all about? And why has CID been called into this?"

"Because, Sir James, there has been a serious development in the case since the earl was found this morning."

"What sort of development?"

He reached into his breast pocket and withdrew a photograph. "It seems a murder was committed as well."

Lewis watched their faces as he told of the body in the trunk and of his theory that Valentine shot the man and was on his way to disposing of the body when he, too, was killed.

"We are trying to identify the victim. Perhaps you know him?"

They bent their heads over the grisly photograph. Mona turned away, her hand pressed to her mouth. Tim said, "Jesus Christ," while James and Grace looked at it, stunned.

But when Rose leaned over and saw the body of Carlo in the trunk, bound hand and foot with a bullet wound in his head, she suddenly screamed, "Valentine, you monster!" and collapsed to the floor in a faint.

"RATHER AN INTERESTING reaction," Superintendent Lewis said back at the police station. "Wouldn't you say?"

Mitchell sipped his tea, his eyes focused on the bare block wall of his office. "I'd say that Lady Rose knew the chap."

"That was my impression. The others reacted predictably enough. I didn't see any sign of recognition on their faces. They were simply looking at the shocking photo of a dead body. But Her Ladyship . . . now there was a reaction."

"Superintendent?" Dr. Forsythe, the young pathologist sent up from Nairobi, came in. "I've just started the autopsy you ordered on the earl, but I had to stop because there's something you must see."

"What is it?"

"You won't believe it. You had better come see for yourself."

The police "mortuary" was actually an all-purpose room adjoining the one barred cell. The body of Carlo Nobili lay under a canvas on top of some packing crates; Valentine Treverton was lying stretched out on a table, naked.

The pathologist didn't have to point out to the superintendent what had caught his attention. The detective had seen stab wounds before.

It was very neat, just to the left of the breastbone, and practically bloodless.

"This is what killed him," Dr. Forsythe said, "not the bullet in the head. I'd stake my reputation on it."

Mitchell whistled. It looked so harmless, just a slit in the skin, about an inch and a half long, with a trickle of dark blood.

But Lewis knew how deadly that insignificant-looking mark could be. Stab wounds, especially those that entered body cavities, such as the belly or chest, rarely produced a lot of blood. The damage was done internally. He had no doubt that the knife had cut a major vessel, possibly even the heart itself, and that when the earl's chest was opened, they would find it filled with blood.

"You definitely say this is the cause of death?" he asked the doctor.

"I'll be more positive when I look inside, but judging from its location, I'd say yes. And when I look closely at the head wound, it appears to me to have been inflicted *after* death."

"To make a murder look like suicide!" Mitchell said.

The man from the CID turned on his heel and strode back into the office, where he retrieved the police photographs from Mitchell's desk. He studied in particular the ones of the passenger seat, showing mud. When the inspector joined him, Lewis said, "The car was at the side of the road, as if the earl had pulled over for a reason, and he left the motor running as if he hadn't intended on staying parked for long. Do you know what I think? I think someone caught up with him and got him to pull over. Someone who was carrying a knife."

"You know," Mitchell said as he picked up the case file and thumbed through it, "now that I think of it, the woman who discovered the car, Nurse Billings, said something in her statement about bicycle tire tracks around the car. Where is it? Here."

Lewis read the nurse's report of the tracks leading up to the passenger side of the car and then doubling back toward Nyeri. He put the paper down and said, "I've got another scenario for you, Inspector. Tell me what you think of this. The earl shot the bloke in the trunk. We'll figure motive when we've got the victim's identity, and we can go to Lady Rose for that. Ballistics in Nairobi will tell us if the same gun fired both bullets. No doubt the earl did do the trunk murder and was, as you say, on his way to getting rid of the body. But then, let's say . . ." He began pacing the small floor; he stopped and turned to Inspector Mitchell. "Let us say that someone followed the earl and caught up with him on the Kiganjo Road. He flagged him over, and the earl stopped probably because he *knew the person on the bicycle.* That person then walked to the car, climbed into the passenger seat, tracking mud because it had just been raining, and stabbed the earl once, through the chest. Then the person panicked and, seeing the gun His Lordship had used on the man in the trunk, decided to make it look like suicide."

"Surely he'd know the stab wound would be detected."

"Not necessarily. There was no blood on the earl's clothing. And if no autopsy was going to be performed, it could very easily have been missed. And it damn near was missed, because *I* ordered the autopsy only after you discovered the bloke in the trunk."

"Which means," Mitchell said slowly, "that chances are the person with the knife didn't know about the man in the trunk."

Lewis's eyebrows arched. "Maybe"—he stroked his chin—"maybe that person thought he was *preventing* the earl from committing the murder, not knowing he was too late."

The two policemen stared at each other. The enormity of the case, which had taken place in Mitchell's normally peaceful and uneventful district, started to settle upon the inspector's shoulders. He developed a pronounced stoop within minutes.

"I want every possible witness rounded up," Lewis said abruptly, pulling out his notepad and starting to write. "I want every lead, no matter how insignificant, to be traced. I want that bicycle found. I want the knife found. But I'll tell you one thing, Mitchell. Things aren't quite right in that big fancy house on the hill."

* * *

GRACE PAUSED ON the veranda of Bellatu to pull the black veil of her hat down over her eyes. Today was the second time she had worn black since her service in the navy, twenty-six years before.

She watched as everyone got into the line of cars waiting to go to the Treverton family plot, where Valentine was going to be laid to rest next to Arthur, his only son. Grace was shaken. She desperately needed James's arm to lean on.

Morgan Acres, the banker's eldest son, was the Treverton family lawyer, and he had just told Grace the most astounding thing.

Valentine's will had been read that morning, revealing no surprises: Rose was left a rich widow, heiress to the Bellatu coffee estate plus the ancestral estate, Bella Hill, back in England. But after the others had left, Mr. Acres had taken Grace aside and told her that regrettably, because of His Lordship's death, the annual contribution to her mission bank account, which had been started years ago, would now end.

Grace had been so stunned that she had had to sit down. "Valentine?" she had said. "My *brother* was the anonymous benefactor? I had always thought it was James. . . ."

After all this time, Val, she thought sadly. *And I never got a chance to thank you.*

James finally came out onto the veranda and took Grace's arm. They climbed into a limousine, which they shared with Rose and Mona, and the procession moved out. Tim Hopkins rode at the end in his own truck, thinking of the grave he was about to visit, which he had not been to in eight years—Arthur's grave.

The line of cars moved slowly down the dirt road that skirted the vast estate toward the lonely spot where a section of ground had been fenced off. Africans stood along the road, waving a sad good-bye to their bwana. David Mathenge was there, with his mother, watching silently as the grieving white people went to put another of their kind into the ground.

SUPERINTENDENT LEWIS WAS studying the photos pinned to the bulletin board—pictures of Lord Treverton's car and of the earl's body—and the map of the murder scene, with a dotted line showing the route Nurse Billings claimed the bicycle had taken, when Inspector Mitchell came breathlessly in.

"We've got it!" he said, and held out a large envelope to the detective.

Lewis took it and hefted it thoughtfully. He was tired. The two policemen had been five days at the investigation, using every available man on the small Nyeri force and borrowing forensic specialists from Nairobi. They had had little sleep, too much coffee, and both men had red eyes. The contents of this envelope were the culmination of their five-day search.

Yesterday they had found the bicycle.

It had been abandoned in the bush approximately halfway between the earl's car and the town of Nyeri, tossed on its side with a punctured rear tire. The detectives surmised that when the tire had blown, the murderer had dragged the bike into the bush and then made the rest of the way home on foot. The bicycle had been identified as belonging to the Treverton plantation.

Their interrogations had been thorough and intense. Both had gone out with a pair of askaris, talking to anyone, no matter how remotely connected with the earl, who might give a shred of evidence, the tiniest clue. They had even questioned the Africans who worked and lived on Treverton's land, including the medicine woman, Wachera, who just kept saying something about a *thahu*. But the most telling interviews had been with the family members themselves.

Lady Rose wouldn't talk. She had said not one word since her collapse five days earlier, when she saw the photo of the dead man. She had sat still and silent through the questioning, her face abnormally pale so that the bruise stood out all the more. It was Dr. Treverton who had answered the detective's questions.

The man in the trunk, she had explained, was an escaped Italian POW named Nobili.

"No one else in the district knows him," Superintendent Lewis had said. "How is it that you do?"

"Rose spoke of him to me."

"Where did he live?" Lewis asked, holding his pencil ready to write down the address.

But when she paused too long and then finally told him about the greenhouse and Rose's intention to leave Kenya with Nobili, Lewis had seen the greater and clearer picture.

And now, here was final proof, according to Inspector Mitchell.

Three men had been put on the estate grounds to watch the comings and goings of the family, to question the staff, and to search for any possible clues. This morning one of the askaris had reported that rubbish was being burned in a pit not far from the house. It was routine work; the estate workers burned the trash on a regular basis, usually once a week. Lewis sent someone from Forensics to give a look through. This envelope contained the findings.

He opened it, and when he saw what was inside, he nodded in satisfaction. As far as Superintendent Lewis from the Criminal Investigations Division was concerned, the case was closed.

THEY STOOD BENEATH a dark gray sky, a handful of people with bowed heads around a hole in the ground. Reverend Michaelis, the minister from Grace's mission, read the eulogy as the coffin was lowered. There was sadness and bewilderment and shock in the hearts of the mourners. But one was full of bitterness and hatred; another, of grim satisfaction that the earl was dead.

James said a mental, heartfelt prayer and farewell to his friend, who, twenty-eight years before, had saved his life near the Tanganyika border and who, out of pride, had sworn James to secrecy. James knew that Grace thought it was he who had saved Valentine's life, but Valentine had made James promise never to tell of his extraordinary act of valor in which he had almost lost his life saving James.

Mona said good-bye to a stranger. The plantation was hers now.

Tim Hopkins, standing apart from the others, gazed down at the headstone of the only person he had ever loved. He prayed that Arthur, in heaven, could now look down upon his father in hell.

A short distance away, on the other side of the wrought-iron fence, stood a few Africans: the house staff, sincerely sad to see their bwana go; Njeri, who was mourning not for the man in the grave but for her poor sorrowing mistress; and David Mathenge, who thought with a cold heart: *Adhabu ua kaburi ajua maiti,* a Swahili proverb which meant, "Only the dead know the horrors of the grave."

As she threw a handful of dirt onto her brother's coffin, Grace was filled with a sense of his death's marking the end of an era. Change was in the air; she could feel it. An old familiar and beloved Kenya, she feared, was slipping away, and something new and frightening was coming to take its place.

Superintendent Lewis and Inspector Mitchell waited until the funeral was over and the mourners were returning to their cars. They approached Lady Rose, who walked between her sister-in-law and Sir James.

The detective from the CID apologized for the intrusion and held out something for her to see. "Can you identify this, Your Ladyship?"

Rose didn't look down. She stared at his face with unfocused eyes, like a woman walking in her sleep.

But Grace and James looked at what was in his hand: a piece of linen, scorched and bloody.

"Is this your monogram, Lady Rose?" the detective asked.

She stared past him.

"This handkerchief was found in your rubbish pit this morning, wrapped around a bloody dagger. Now, Lady Rose, do you have anything to tell me about the night of your husband's death?"

She gazed past him, out over the acres and acres of flowering coffee trees.

Lewis reached out and took from Lady Rose's hand the handkerchief she had been carrying. He held it next to the charred one, and the policemen compared them. The monograms were identical.

"Lady Rose Treverton," Superintendent Lewis said quietly; "I am arresting you in the name of the Crown for the murder of your husband, Valentine, the earl of Treverton."

40

The sensational trial of the countess of Treverton began on August 12, 1945, four months after her arrest. It took the prosecution that long to prepare its case against her. In the meantime, she was incarcerated in a special cell in the Nairobi jail, where, after appealing to the judge and prison authorities on her behalf, Rose's attorney obtained permission for her to be allowed to work on her tapestry.

It was the second of only two requests Rose made.

The first had come immediately upon her entering the prison. Rose had not uttered a word since seeing the photograph of Carlo's body; now she asked that Morgan Acres, the family lawyer, be summoned. The two spent three hours alone together in her cell, during which time Rose gave Mr. Acres explicit instructions on what to do with General Nobili's body. Mr. Acres was not at liberty to discuss the plans with the rest of the family, at Lady Rose's request, but when, a week later, Grace and Mona saw a work force from Nairobi arrive at the eucalyptus glade with trucks and tractors and building materials, they knew it was Rose's doing. The body of her beloved Carlo, in the meantime, was kept in a Nairobi mortuary.

The second request, for her tapestry, had come a week after that, and she had made the request of Grace.

"It isn't finished," Rose said as she sat on the iron bed with her hands folded in her lap, gazing through the bars of her window at the distant Athi Plains.

"Rose," Grace said, sitting in the one chair of the plain cell, "listen to me. This whole thing is trumped up. That detective from CID doesn't care if he's got the right person or not; he just wants to close his file! He's basing his case against you on purely circumstantial evidence. Why won't you speak up? Tell them Valentine knocked you out and that you were *incapable* of riding a bicycle in the middle of the night on a muddy road! Rose, your silence looks like an admission of guilt. For goodness' sake, defend yourself!"

Rose kept her blue eyes on the African vista far beyond the stone prison and said softly, "I stopped working on the tapestry the day I met Carlo. Now I must finish it."

"Listen to me, Rose! While you're letting them crucify you, you're letting Valentine's murderer go free! That handkerchief was stolen from your bedroom, and you know it!"

But Rose would speak no more. So Grace and Rose's defense attorney, Mr. Barrows, King's Counsel, brought up specially from South Africa, had presented Lady Rose's request to the chief warder, pointing out the extraordinary circumstances of her situation—that there were thirteen hundred prisoners in the Nairobi jail, only eight of whom were Europeans, and Rose was the only white woman. Exceptions were made, granting the countess the right to her tapestry, food brought in from the Norfolk Hotel, where it was prepared personally by the head chef, chocolates, and bedding, a rug on the cold stone floor, and, as prisoners were required to keep their own cells clean, the daily visit of Njeri, Lady Rose's personal maid, who took care of her mistress during the entire ordeal.

"YOUR SISTER-IN-LAW IS making my job very difficult, Dr. Treverton," said Mr. Barrows, the barrister from South Africa. "She won't talk to me. She won't even look at me. Her silence is quite damning for her, you know."

"If they find her guilty, then what?"

"As a colony Kenya has the English system of jury trial. And the same punishments. If Lady Rose is found guilty of murder, she will hang." The barrister rose from the couch and strode to the edge of the veranda, where he lapsed into deep thought.

For the duration of the trial Grace and James, Mona, and Tim Hopkins all had come down to Nairobi and taken rooms at the club, which was not far from the courthouse. They now sat on the eve of the trial opening in a private members' room, which was all leather and rattan, zebraskins and animal heads.

"You know, Doctor," Barrows said softly, "the Crown has a strong case against your sister-in-law. First, there is the motive. These love triangles are always such a messy business. Lady Rose admitted to four people—yourselves—in front of house servants, that she was going to leave her husband for another man. Jury sympathy is going to go to Valentine, Doctor, *not* to your sister-in-law. Secondly, there is the knife, which the pathologist has determined beyond a doubt is the same as that which killed the earl. It is a knife that your sister-in-law used for years in her greenhouse, to prune her plants, and it was found in one of her own handkerchiefs."

Mona said, "Anyone could have taken that knife from the green-house and stolen a handkerchief from my mother's room."

"I quite agree, Lady Mona. But unfortunately your mother will not testify to such. She doesn't deny wrapping the knife in the handker-chief and trying to dispose of it in the weekly rubbish fire. In fact, Lady Mona, your mother has not once, so far, denied committing the mur-der! Now then, thirdly, there is the fact that she cannot account for her whereabouts at the time of the murder, nor has she any witnesses who can. You all were fast asleep, you say."

Mr. Barrows came back to the sofa and settled his lanky frame into it. "I'm afraid cases of this sort are decided upon emotions rather than upon cold facts. The Crown is going to try to make Lady Rose look like a hard, cruel, and callous woman. They'll drag out the whole sordid love affair in the greenhouse and paint Valentine as the ultimate cuckolded husband. Bear in mind, Miss Treverton, that the jury will be all male. And they will hang Lady Rose for her adultery, I can assure you of that."

"But we can't let that happen!" said James.

"No, we can't. And I'm going to try my damnedest to get the jury to sympathize with *us.*"

"In the meantime," said Tim quietly, "the real murderer goes free."

"That is not our concern right now, Mr. Hopkins. We must concen-trate on bringing in a verdict of not guilty for Lady Rose."

Mr. Barrows peered at his companions from under reddish brows. Hard little green eyes that betrayed the genius of the South African barrister, who was known for winning difficult and sensational cases, fixed upon each of them. And then he said, "Before I walk into that courtroom tomorrow, I want to be certain that I have *all* the facts of this case. I want no surprises. If any of you now, has something he or she is not telling me, or if any one of you has thoughts heretofore unexpressed regarding this case, any suspicions, *anything at all,* then tell me now."

IT WAS IN an almost festive atmosphere that the trial opened the next morning. Nairobi's Central Court had become the focus of the war-weary colonists, who, anxious for a good show, crammed into the Edwardian sobriety of the courtroom, lined the walls three people deep, and packed themselves into the public galleries. The glass dome overhead shed diffuse light upon settlers who had come from as far away as Moyale, upon ranchers and farmers, upon men in uniform, upon women in their best dress normally reserved for Race Week. The roar was deafening as everyone eagerly awaited the commencement of what promised to be a spectacle. All the ordinary, hardworking Kenya folk, who had entertained themselves these past four months with rumor and gossip and speculation, latching upon newspaper reports of the "greenhouse love nest," and exhausted from six years of war and sacrifice, had come in hopes of glimpsing the sordid, intimate lives of their aristocracy.

Shortly before the prisoner was brought in, the entrance of one more spectator caused at first a stir and then a shocked silence as she made her way through the crowded African gallery, where the people stepped aside for her. By the time Wachera, the medicine woman, reached the railing and looked down over the courtroom, the Europeans in the surrounding galleries and those down below all looked at her in astonishment.

There wasn't a person in the courtroom who had not heard of the legendary Kikuyu woman who continued to defy European authority and who was a spiritual force behind the largest tribe in Kenya. She stood at the railing like an empress surveying her subjects. At any other time the white men and women might have found her costume quaint and amusing, or tasteless and out of place here, but there was something, this morning, about the tall, strong body dressed in hides and covered head to toe in beads and shells, her head smoothly shaved and crisscrossed with beaded bands, that struck a wrong note in the minds of the Europeans. Wachera reminded them of something they preferred not to think about: that this had once been *her* land, and they were the latecomers.

Stories of an old *thahu*, pronounced at a Christmas party long ago, had also made their way into the gossip columns. The Europeans thought of it now, as they stared at the medicine woman, and wondered if she had come to see the fruits of that curse.

Two Trevertons dead, they thought. *Three to go . . .*

The Lord Chief Justice, Sir Hugh Roper, in black robes and white wig, entered the court and took his place on the bench. And then Lady Rose was brought in from the cells. She walked to the dock like a woman in a trance and seemed not to hear a court official read the indictment. She stood like a statue, her eyes glazed and barely blinking. The courtroom was silent as everyone stared at the pale, slight figure. Many were mildly disappointed; she didn't look like an adulteress or murderess at all.

As the counsel for the Crown stood to make his opening address, Rose suddenly turned in her seat and looked up, over her shoulder, at the African gallery.

Wachera's eyes met hers.

Rose was taken back twenty-six years; she was standing again on the ridge, holding baby Mona in her arms and looking down upon an African girl with a baby on her back.

Wachera was also remembering, as she now looked down upon the *mzunga,* that day of fifty-two harvests ago when she had looked up at the ridge and had seen the vision in white, wondering what it could mean.

And then the trial began.

It was eventually to run for ten weeks, in which time witness after witness was called, from the most obscure worker on the Treverton Estate who had never even laid eyes on his employer, to members of the family themselves. Specialists were brought in. They included Dr. Forsythe, the pathologist, who demonstrated by matching a flaw in the knife blade to a groove in Lord Treverton's rib, that this was indeed the murder weapon, and who had determined upon autopsy that the earl was already dead from massive internal bleeding when the bullet was put through his skull.

Servants were questioned. "Are you an askari on the Treverton Estate?"

"Yes, bwana."

"Do you know during which hours you were patrolling the grounds on the night of April the fifteenth?"

"Yes, bwana."

"Can you tell time?"

"Yes, bwana."

"Please look at the courtroom clock on that wall over there and tell us what time it is."

The askari squinted at the clock and said, "It is lunchtime, bwana."

So much of the questioning, on both sides, seemed tedious and irrelevant.

"You are Lady Rose's dressmaker?"

"I am."

"Was Lady Rose in the habit of coming to Nairobi for fittings or did you go up to the house?"

"We worked it both ways, depending on the rains."

On days when gardeners were questioned, or when the most insignificant of evidence, such as the earl's letters to his wife from his post on the northern border, was studied to the point of madness, the spectators thinned out, and there were even empty seats. But as the barristers slowly worked their way to the crux of the trial—the love affair and the murder itself—the audience grew in size again.

Njeri Mathenge, the countess's personal maid, was called to testify. While she was being questioned, her eyes moved nervously from Lady Rose to Wachera up in the gallery back to Lady Rose.

"Were you with your mistress when she found the escaped prisoner in the greenhouse?"

"Yes."

"Speak up, please."

"Yes."

"How often did the memsaab visit the man in the greenhouse?"

"Every day."

"At night as well?"

"Yes."

"Did you ever observe them while they were in the greenhouse?"

Njeri looked at Lady Rose.

"Please answer the question."

"I looked through the window."

"And what did you see?"

Njeri's eyes shifted to her mother's co-wife, Wachera, in the gallery. Then she looked at David. And back to Rose.

"What did you see, Miss Mathenge?"

"They were sleeping."

"Together?"

"Yes."

"In the same bed?"

"Yes."

"Were they wearing clothes?"

Njeri started to cry.

"Please answer the question, Miss Mathenge. Were Lady Rose and Carlo Nobili naked in bed together?"

"Yes."

"Did you ever observe them to do anything other than sleep?"

"They ate supper together."

"Did you ever observe acts of a sexual nature between them?"

Njeri bowed her head, and tears fell onto her hands.

"Miss Mathenge, did you ever see Lady Rose and Carlo Nobili engage in sexual intercourse?"

"Yes."

"How many times?"

"Many . . ."

Through it all, Rose sat pale and silent in the dock, as though far removed from the courtroom. She never spoke, never looked at the witnesses, seemed not even to be aware of what was going on. If she was innocent, people started to ask themselves, then why didn't she speak up?

"SHE WON'T TALK to me," Mona said when she joined the others in the small, private members' room at the club. A plate of sandwiches sat untouched in the middle of the table, but the whiskey and gin were being paid earnest attention to.

The strain of the trial was starting to show on the young woman. Her dark eyes stood out on her pale face. "I said to her, 'Mother, you have to speak up and defend yourself.' But she just kept stitching that blasted tapestry."

"Is it possible," James said, "that she did it?"

Grace shook her head. "I don't think Rose is capable of murder. Especially in that way—a knife so expertly used."

"There was a time when we wouldn't have thought my mother capable of harboring an escaped prisoner of war and having a secret love affair with him!"

Grace looked at her niece. "Don't be so hard on your mother, Mona. Think how she must be suffering."

"She certainly didn't think how *we* might suffer because of her selfishness! All those horrid people in the courtroom, their ears wagging as that wretched prosecutor parades our family business in public! And *you!*" She turned to Barrows, her mother's lawyer. "Why did you bring up that awful Miranda West business?"

"I had to, Miss Treverton," he said quietly in his South African drawl. "The Crown is trying to build its case on your mother's moral turpitude. He's convincing the jury that your father was a saint, that he had practically done the world a favor by killing the Italian, and that his own death was the greatest loss Kenya has ever known. By bringing up his affair with Mrs. West, I reminded the jury that Valentine Treverton was a man with weaknesses and flaws and pointed out that long before your mother embarked upon her one adulterous affair, your father had already engaged in several."

Tears rose in Mona's eyes. She wished with all her heart that Geoffrey were home. He was due to arrive any day.

"What do you suppose they're building in the glade?" Tim Hopkins asked, to change the subject and ease the tension around the table. "It looks like some sort of pagan temple."

Because she could not be away from her mission for long, Grace made frequent trips back up north and, while there, checked on the progress of the mysterious concrete structure Rose had commissioned to be built among her eucalyptus trees. It was quite large—a good deal

GREEN CITY IN THE SUN 417

of the forest had had to be cleared for it—and decidedly churchlike. The teams worked night and day, as if racing against time. Grace had ventured a look inside and had found it curiously empty. Marble columns supported a vaulted ceiling; the walls and floor were bare. But last week something had been installed inside, and the building was no longer a mystery.

The workers had placed an alabaster sarcophagus in it.

And now stonecutters were etching words into the lintel over the doorway: SACRARIO DE DUCA D'ALESSANDRO.

"It is Carlo Nobili's final resting place," she said quietly.

"A *crypt?*" said Mona. "She's burying him in her glade behind my house? That's monstrous!"

"Mona—"

"I'm going out for some air, Aunt Grace. And then I think I'll have supper alone in my room."

Grace tried to stop her, but Mona was already crossing the spacious lobby of the club, causing heads to turn and whispers to follow her.

Out on the street in front of the club Mona stopped and leaned against a sycamore tree, her hands in the pockets of her slacks. People in passing cars stared at her; a group of women on the veranda murmured while casting glances her way. An old newspaper fluttered in the street. It was not a Kenya paper but a piece of the *New York Times,* with its front-page story of the continuing trial of the scandalous Treverton murder. Mona fought back her tears and anger, her feeling of humiliation and of having been betrayed.

Across the street, gathered in the brief, smoky twilight, a group of Africans in military uniforms talked quietly while passing around a single cigarette. When a white couple came along, the soldiers stepped off the sidewalk and tipped their hats as required, and Mona realized that one of them was David Mathenge.

He had sat in the gallery every single day since the beginning of the trial. He and his mother watched the proceedings like vultures, Mona thought, like two big blackbirds waiting for their prey to breathe its last. She hated them, just as she hated the white people who came to listen and to gloat and to watch the ignoble downfall of the family they had once worshiped.

David happened to look her way. Their eyes met.

"Mona!" called a voice from behind.

She turned. Grace was at the entrance of the club, waving to her niece to come inside.

"What is it?" Mona said as she came up the steps.

"I've a surprise for you! Come along!"

Puzzled, Mona followed her aunt into the lobby and found a knot of people standing beside the enormous flagstone fireplace. When she saw who was at the center of the group, Mona cried, "Geoffrey!" and ran to him.

He caught her in his arms and hugged the breath out of her.

"Geoffrey!" she cried again. "How wonderful to see you!"

"Mona, you're as beautiful as ever. I had hoped to get home sooner, but you know military red tape!" He drew back and gazed solemnly at her. "I'm so sorry about Uncle Val and Aunt Rose."

She looked up at Geoffrey and thought he had gotten taller and more handsome in his five years in Palestine. He looked so much older, too, as though the hot wind and sands of the Middle East had weathered him. Although only thirty-three, Geoffrey Donald was graying at the temples; his mustache, too, was silvering. Mona saw the lines of war and hardship etched around his eyes and recalled how close he had come, on more than one occasion, to being killed by a terrorist bomb.

They hadn't spoken of marriage since just before the war, when she told him she needed time. He hadn't brought it up in his letters, no doubt waiting for her to make the next move, as she definitely was going to do, now that he was home. *I shall be able to see my way through this nightmare,* she thought, *now that you're here. . . .*

"And this is Ilse," he said, stepping aside and holding his hand out to a young blond woman.

"Ilse?" said Mona.

"My wife. Ilse, this is Mona, the dear old friend I've told you so much about."

Mrs. Donald extended her hand, but Mona could only stare at the blond hair, the blue eyes, and shy smile.

"I'm afraid Ilse doesn't speak much English."

Mona looked at Geoffrey. "Your wife? I didn't know you had gotten married."

"None of us did," said James, resting a hand on his son's shoulder. "Apparently Geoff has arrived before his letters!"

"I'm so happy for you," Grace said. "And welcome to Kenya, Ilse."

"Thank you," the bride said in a soft voice.

"Ilse's a German refugee," Geoffrey explained, unaware of the profound effect his news was having upon Mona. She had to back away, had to lean against the sofa for support. "Her family were all taken to Hitler's camps," Geoffrey went on. "She was gotten out by sympathizers and smuggled into Palestine. We had the devil of a time getting papers for her. And they damn near wouldn't let us marry."

"How dreadful," murmured Grace. The one Nairobi movie house was showing the news films that were now arriving in Kenya—American films of places called Dachau, Auschwitz. . . . "We shall certainly do our best to make Ilse welcome here, Geoffrey. How unfortunate that you should come home to this terrible trial."

"It's been written up in the Jerusalem papers for months. I couldn't believe it! I shall go and visit Aunt Rose if I may. And if there's anything I can do to help—"

"Mr. Barrows is an excellent attorney."

"I've heard of him."

"You'll meet him at supper."

"I should think," James said, "considering Geoff's return and the new bride, that champagne isn't out of place. I'll reserve the table nearest the aviary; the service is always best there."

"Pardon me," said a discreet voice. "Might I have a word with you for a moment, Captain Donald?"

Everyone turned to see Angus McCloud, one of the club's officers, standing a few feet away.

"Yes?" said Geoffrey. "What is it?"

The man looked nervous. "Could we, ah, speak in private, Captain?"

Geoffrey bristled, as though he already knew what McCloud wanted to discuss.

"What's the problem?" said James. "There *is* a table available for dinner, isn't there?"

The Scot reddened. "If we could just step over here—"

"Say it right here, Mr. McCloud," Geoffrey said, "in front of my wife and friends."

Grace turned a puzzled look to James. "What is going on?"

"I'm afraid it's club policy, Captain Donald," Angus McCloud said. "I didn't make up the rules; I am simply enforcing them. If it were up to me, you understand . . ." He spread out his hands. "But there's the matter of all the *other* members."

"Good God," said James suddenly, "you're not saying what I think you're saying!"

McCloud's embarrassment deepened.

"Geoffrey," said Grace, "tell me what this is about."

His jaw was tight as he said, "It's about Ilse. She's a Jew."

"And?"

"And there's a club rule barring Jews from the dining room."

Grace looked at Angus. He avoided her eyes.

James said, "To the devil with the rules. We shall be dining here tonight and at the aviary table."

"I'm afraid I cannot permit it, Sir James, if Mrs. Donald is among you."

"You can't possibly mean that you would—"

"Never mind, Father," Geoffrey said as he reached for Ilse, who looked at him questioningly. "I don't care to eat in this bloody club. I don't care to be a member, thank you. My wife and I will go where we are welcome. And if we are welcome nowhere in Kenya, then we shall go somewhere in the world where we are!"

"Geoffrey!" James called after him as he strode out.

Mona, shaken and still sitting on the back of the sofa, stared after the couple, at the dashing figure in uniform and the pretty woman with him. Then she turned abruptly and ran from the lobby, down the garden path to her bungalow, where she locked the door behind her.

ROSE WAS QUIETLY stitching when Grace came in. Outside a smoky night stretched from the barred window out to a horizon that met crystalline stars.

Grace paused to look around the humble cell that had become Rose's home. Then she sat and said, "Rose, will you talk to me tonight?"

"Is Carlo's resting place nearly finished?"

"Yes, it is, Rose."

Sighing, she anchored her needle, pushed the tapestry away from her, and, for the first time in months, looked her sister-in-law straight in the eye. "When it is complete, please give the mortician instructions to place Carlo there. And then ask Father Vittorio to say a mass for him."

"I will."

"You know, Grace," Rose said quietly, "Valentine was not an evil man. He was simply incapable of love. Carlo was a sweet and gentle man who wished no one harm. He had been tortured in the prison camp. I saw the scars on his poor body. Valentine had no right to kill him the way he did, like an animal, tied up and helpless. I hope Valentine burns in hell forever."

41

The trial went steadily from bad to worse for Rose, until even Barrows was starting to give up hope. All testimony, it seemed, pointed accusingly right at the countess.

Superintendent Lewis, of the Criminal Investigations Division, was put on the stand. "Superintendent," said the counsel for the Crown, a rotund man who filled out his black robe and whose white wig sat atop a bald head, "did you ask Lady Rose how she came by the bruise on her face?"

"I did."

"And what was her reply?"

"She said she fell and hit the edge of the dresser."

"And yet she told her family that her husband had struck her! In other words, Lady Rose told two different stories, one of which is therefore a lie. Or maybe even *both* are lies. Would you agree, Superintendent, that it is possible Lady Rose could have sustained that bruise while riding a bicycle, the tire of which blew, sending her down to the ground?"

Inspector Mitchell, of the Nyeri police, was put on the stand several times.

"You said, Inspector, that Dr. Treverton had been under the impression that Lady Rose had left for a trip that morning?"

"Yes. But there was Her Ladyship in a dressing gown. It hardly looked to me like she was planning on going anywhere."

"What was Dr. Treverton's and Sir James's reaction when they saw Lady Rose in the doorway?"

"They were quite surprised. They were under the impression she'd already left."

"Left for where?"

"Well, she had planned to run off her with Italian boyfriend."

And later: "Inspector Mitchell, will you tell us please what Lady Rose's reaction was to the news of her husband's death?"

"She said, 'I hadn't meant for that to happen.' "

"And what did she mean by 'that'?"

Counsel for the defense rose to his feet. "My Lord, this is an improper question."

"Yes, Mr. Barrows."

"Did Lady Rose say anything else?"

"Yes, she said one word."

"What was that word?"

"Well, it was a name actually. She said, 'Carlo.' "

Grace watched her sister-in-law throughout the proceedings, studied the masked expression, the face that seemed to be growing paler and thinner. What on earth, Grace wondered, was going on behind those staring blue eyes?

Finally the counsel for the crown called Dr. Treverton to the stand. She looked out over the ogling white faces, the packed courtroom, the greedy eyes up in the galleries.

"Dr. Treverton, did you examine the bruise on Lady Rose's face?"

"I did."

"And in your professional opinion, would such a blow have rendered her incapable of riding a bicycle on the night of April the fifteenth?"

"She told me she was knocked unconscious."

"Please answer the question, Doctor. Does such a blow to the face *always* render a person unconscious?"

"Not always, but—"

"Have you any medical way of proving whether or not Lady Rose was, in fact, knocked unconscious?"

"No."

"Dr. Treverton, please tell us what your sister-in-law said to you after Inspector Mitchell had delivered the news of His Lordship's death."

"Rose said that she hadn't meant for him to die."

An easel with a floor plan of Bellatu pinned to it was brought out. "Dr. Treverton, is this a plan of the upper story of Bellatu?"

"Yes."

"Please point out the room where you were sleeping. The one

marked with the red *X?* Thank you, Doctor. Now then, we can see by this floor plan that your room was second to the last in that wing. Can you tell us, please, whose bedroom that last one was?"

"Lady Rose's."

"You mean Lady Rose *and* Lord Valentine's."

"No. My brother's bedroom was across from mine."

"I take it, then, that the earl and the countess did not sleep together?"

Grace glared at the pompous barrister. "They had separate bedrooms. I don't know whether or not they slept together."

"Very well then. The last bedroom belonged to Lady Rose. And she shared it with no one else?"

"That's correct."

"Therefore, when you heard footsteps going past your door in the middle of the night, they can have come only from Lady Rose's bedroom?"

"Or going *to* it—"

"Now then, Doctor, you've told us that you looked at your clock. What time did you hear the car motor?"

"As I told the police, it was either five past four or one-twenty. I didn't have my glasses on."

"Since the time of the earl's death has been established as being approximately three in the morning, then we must assume you heard the car motor at one-twenty and that the footsteps you heard were coming from Lady Rose's room and going out of the house."

"It could have been anyone out there in the hall! There is a bathroom—"

"Dr. Treverton, were you alone in your bedroom that night?"

She stared at him. "I beg your pardon?"

"Where you alone in your bedroom that night, Doctor?"

"I don't see that that has any bearing on this case."

"But it does. We are endeavoring to establish the whereabouts of everyone on the night of the earl's murder. Please answer the question. Were you alone?"

Grace looked over to where James was sitting with Geoffrey and Mona. He smiled.

"No, I was not alone."

"Who else was there with you?"

"Sir James was with me."

"I see. And was he sleeping on the floor or perhaps on a chaise?"

"No."

"Then tell us, please, where Sir James was."

"He was in bed, with me."

A rumble went through the crowd, and Sir Hugh had to call the court to order.

Barrows's assistant scribbled a note on a pad and slid it along the table. It read, "They're out to hang the whole bloody family."

Finally the counsel for the Crown began his closing remarks. "Gentlemen of the jury." His voice boomed over the congested courtroom. "We have shown you what happened on the morning of April sixteenth of this year, on the Kiganjo Road, a mile beyond the Nyeri turnoff. You have heard expert testimony proving beyond a doubt that the weapon found in Lady Rose's handkerchief and burning in her rubbish pit was the one that killed the earl of Treverton and that the knife belonged to Lady Rose. You have seen the results of laboratory analysis that has linked conclusively the mud on the passenger seat and on the running board of the earl's car to that of the mud found along that particular stretch of the Kiganjo Road. You have heard witnesses testify to a car leaving Bellatu in the middle of the night and footsteps coming down the hall from the direction of Lady Rose's bedroom soon after. And we have found the bicycle that was abandoned in flight, a bicycle traced to the Treverton Estate.

"Now then, gentlemen of the jury," the barrister said, "taking all of this and adding to it the motives which compelled Lady Rose to commit the act, we can reconstruct what happened that night."

He described it all for them again, in such vivid prose and compelling oratory that not a single person in the courtroom did not see the lonely road, the earl pulling over, the bicycle rider getting in, the knife plunging, the gunshot to the head, and the panicked flight of the murderer.

"It is inconceivable," the counselor went on, "that carrying a body in the trunk of his car, Lord Treverton would stop on a dark and deserted road for a stranger. Therefore, we can conclude that the person who followed him on the bicycle *was well known to the earl* and that he admitted that person freely into his car!

"I put it to you, gentlemen, that that person was Lady Rose, the earl's adulterous wife, who, fearing for her lover's life and having been struck across the face by a deservedly angry husband, followed him out of fear and revenge in the hope of stopping him from bringing harm to Carlo Nobili, an enemy of the Crown!

"I warn you, gentlemen, not to be deceived by looks. That woman sitting in the dock is not as helpless as she would have us believe. She is a woman who knowingly harbored an enemy soldier, who kept his whereabouts a secret when she knew of the widespread manhunt for him, and who then engaged in a sordid and illicit sexual affair with him. Such a woman, I say to you, is not beyond committing cold-blooded murder!"

While the prosecutor spoke, a bailiff made his way from a side door to the table where Mr. Barrows sat and handed him a note.

Barrows read it, then stood at once. Sir Hugh Roper, the Lord Chief Justice, recognizing an interruption, turned to Barrows, who requested permission to make a submission in the absence of the jury. The courtroom erupted in surprise and speculation when the Lord Chief Justice declared an adjournment and called the two barristers into his chambers for a private conference. To bring a halt to the proceedings at such a late time—in the middle of the Crown's closing remarks!

No one strayed far from the building while the legal conference was going on. In fact, word got around so that more spectators pushed their way inside when the court was reconvened, and everyone watched in excited wonder as a new, surprise witness was called by Mr. Barrows.

"Will you please tell the court your name?"

"Hans Kloppman."

"Where do you live, Mr. Kloppman?"

"I have a farm out near Eldoret."

"Would you please tell us what brought you to Nairobi Central Court today?"

"Well, y'see, my farm is isolated. . . ."

While he spoke, nearly every person in the courtroom, especially the members of the jury, saw a man who, although not personally known to them, was nonetheless very familiar to them: the Kenya farmer. They all saw the tanned face, the dusty work clothes, the honest, coarse hands. Either he was very much like themselves or he resembled a good friend, a close neighbor. Everyone listened to what Hans Kloppman had to say, and no one doubted his word.

"My farm is isolated. I don't get much news. I been out of touch these past months, and it was only when I went into Eldoret for supplies that I heard about this trial. And that's when I knew I had to come and speak my piece."

"Why, Mr. Kloppman?"

"Because you've got it all wrong. That lady didn't commit no murder."

"How do you know that?"

"Because I was on the Kiganjo Road that night, and I saw the person on the bicycle."

The courtroom erupted; the judge called for silence.

When all was orderly again, Mr. Barrows asked the Boer farmer to tell the court exactly what took place on the Kiganjo Road, on the night of April 15.

"I been into Nyeri town on business and visiting friends. I was driving in my van down Kiganjo Road when I seen this car parked ahead, on the right-hand side. The headlights were on. As I got near, I seen someone climb onto a bicycle, turn it around, and ride it down the road as fast as he could."

"*He*, Mr. Kloppman?"

"Oh, it was a man all right. And he pedaled that bike like it was on fire! Went right past me, didn't even seem to notice me. Pedaling and swerving on that mud like the devil himself was after him."

"And then what, Mr. Kloppman?"

"So I drive up to the parked car and I seen the motor is still running. I look inside and seen a man asleep, and I think, *Well, I've had to stop and sleep one off myself*, so I left him in peace."

"You say, Mr. Kloppman, that the bike rider was a man. Are you sure?"

"Oh, I'm sure all right. I didn't see his face; he had a hat pulled down over it. But he was a broad-shouldered man, and very tall. The bicycle looked too small for him. And he had to be strong, to pedal through that fresh mud."

"Mr. Kloppman, will you please look at the defendant, Lady Rose, sitting in the dock? And will you tell us please if there is any possibility that woman could have been your bicycle rider?"

The farmer looked at Lady Rose. His face registered surprise. "That little thing? Oh, no, sir!" he said without hesitation. "It wasn't her, all right. I'm telling you, it was a *man.*"

The court was thrown into chaos.

"MOTHER?" MONA CALLED as she knocked on the bedroom door. "Are you awake?"

Balancing the breakfast tray in one arm, she opened the door and looked in. The bedroom was empty; the bed had not been slept in.

Mona set the tray down and hurried downstairs. She had a good idea where her mother was.

It had been three weeks since the end of the trial. Mr. Kloppman had been subjected to intensive questioning and scrutiny by the prosecution but in the end the jury had reached a verdict of "not guilty" on the grounds that they could no longer be convinced of Lady Rose's guilt "beyond reasonable doubt." Since her release Rose had spent every daylight moment in the glade, seemingly unconcerned about recent events. She had cleaned and blocked and framed the completed tapestry. Last night Rose and Njeri had taken the enormous stitched work and hung it in Carlo Nobili's mausoleum.

Mona followed the path through the woods that stood behind Bellatu. Before she got there, she could see the marble roof of the *sacrario,* like an ancient Greek temple hidden in a sylvan paradise. Rose had spent a great deal of money on her lover's final resting place; she had also set up a perpetual fund for its future care and upkeep.

The gazebo and greenhouse were still in the glade, but the forest on the north side had been cleared. The mausoleum shone brightly in the morning sun. It was an incredible monument considering the short time in which it had been built. Mona estimated that it was about the size of the small Presbyterian church in Nyeri and that it would hold, if there were pews inside, perhaps fifty people. But the mausoleum was a hollow shell, its only contents a plain alabaster sarcophagus.

Mona stopped short and stared at the gazebo.

Then she cried, "Oh, God!" and ran to it.

The African girl had used a stepladder. She had tied one of Lady Rose's silk scarves around her neck, thrown the other end over the central beam supporting the gazebo roof, kicked the ladder out from under, and hanged herself.

Mona knew without close examination that Njeri was dead.

"Mother?" she called. Mona looked around the tranquil glade. Birds and monkeys chattered in the trees. Shafts of sunlight played upon the forest floor. The greenhouse stood like a jewel in the sun, the blossoms within shimmering in multicolored facets through the skylight. *"Mother!"*

She ran to the mausoleum. The double doors were unlocked. Pushing on them, Mona saw the cold darkness of death yawn before her.

The single flame at the head of General Nobili's sarcophagus, meant to burn perpetually, gave off an eerie glow. Mona stood silhouetted in the doorway, staring at the duke's stone coffin, at the figure that rested gracefully, tragically upon it.

Lady Rose appeared to sleep. Her eyes were closed; her face was as white as the alabaster lid upon which she lay. Thin red ribbons of blood led from her wrists and pooled on the stone floor.

Later the coroner would report that she had died before dawn but that she would have had to inflict the wounds shortly before midnight. It appeared, therefore, that Lady Rose had died slowly in the dark and cold, alone with her beloved Carlo.

42

David Mathenge stood at the roadside, watching the trucks roll by. He knew who drove them, what they meant; it was white immigrants arriving in Kenya to start farms offered by Britain under a new soldier settlement scheme.

Such a plan had been used once before—back in 1919, when the Crown had wondered what to do with soldiers returning to Britain after the first war who had no jobs and nowhere to go. The solution, it seemed to David, had been to pack them off to the colonies. Now again, in these early weeks of 1946, returning soldiers, finding a financially ruined Britain and no employment for themselves, were receiving grants for farmland in Kenya's "white highlands." Of course, in order to make room for the newcomers, African "squatters" were being moved off the choicest land and being forced back onto the native reserves.

It was madness.

What shortsighted men, David wondered, were governing the empire that they thought Africans would tolerate such an outrage a second time?

Already the seeds of rebellion were being sown. Young Kikuyu were asking one another, "If there is plenty of room on the richest land for white settlers, why can no room be found for *us?*" The answer, that a major economic depression would strike if something weren't done soon and that only Europeans, not Africans, had the capital and international contacts to make profits in a hurry, did not satisfy the restless young Kikuyu. "Give us a chance," they had said to their deaf colonial masters. And thus were the "Nairobi wild boys" born.

Nearly a hundred thousand African troops, returning to East Africa after having fought in some of Britain's bloodiest campaigns, had come home to find big new houses in Nairobi, cars, hotels, and shops full of luxuries. These were men who had been trained in many useful skills, who sought honest occupations. Fifteen thousand of them had been trained to drive trucks; they had come back to a country in which there were only two thousand trucks. There were simply no jobs to absorb this sudden influx of educated and skilled young men who believed they deserved compensation and recognition for their service in the war. Those who did find employment discovered that their wages were far lower than what they had received in the army. Bitter and resentful, and unable to channel their grievances into normal legal means, these homeless, landless young men—the Nairobi wild boys—were starting to collect in secret meetings throughout the province. And this time, David knew, they would succeed where their predecessors, who had been stopped back in 1939 because of the war, had not.

And there was a difference between today's hotheaded youths and those of David's early political days: The Nairobi wild boys had been taught how to fight—by their white officers.

But it was not something David could dwell upon right now. Because of his own immediate problems, he could not afford the luxury of worrying about his countrymen. For one thing, he, too, was unemployed; for another, Wanjiru was pregnant at last.

Turning his back on the road, David Mathenge, twenty-eight years old and troubled about his future, strode back toward the river where, on the bank below, three huts stood around a cultivated shamba. His mother and wife were down there now, tilling the plots, tending the goats, carrying water, mending the roofs, making beer, and cooking his supper while he, their son and husband, their protector, their *warrior*, was as useless as a calabash gourd with a hole in it.

Frustration filled his mouth with a bitter taste.

There should at least have been some consolation in the knowledge that the Treverton Estate was in trouble. But even that brought no pleasure to David. In fact, when he had heard of Memsaab Mona's difficulties with the field hands, he had found himself not gloating, as he once would have, but thinking what unfortunate news it was. After all, that land was *his* and would be returned to him one day, according to his mother's promise and prophecy. And so he hated to see the land go neglected simply because the headmen, who had once loyally served the earl, now refused to take orders from his daughter, a mere memsaab.

David paused on the red-earth road that turned away from the ridge and went into the estate, and he thought of the two women he lived with: the indomitable medicine woman, who watched her son in a kind of wordless chastisement, and his dissatisfied wife, who complained about the slowness with which men got things done. Wanjiru had tried to goad David into joining the Kenya African Union, the new militant political organization that was coalescing all over the country. But David had had enough of fighting in Palestine. He also knew that unarmed Kikuyu, no matter how numerous, would be no match for the tanks and airplanes of Britain.

If change was going to come to Kenya, he believed, it must be achieved through rational thought and careful process. But what power had he and others like him, educated but jobless, to start the wheels moving toward that necessary change?

It was all that had occupied David's mind this past year, ever since his return from the Middle East. In order to be listened to, in order to convince those in power, and the rest of the world, what a righteous cause Kenyan independence was, then he himself must be a responsible, thinking man. The British, he knew, did not pay attention to the Nairobi wild boys or to the KAU hotheads. They did, however, sit down and talk with African teachers, businessmen, and men of some influence.

As a landowner of considerable acreage, in the heart of the choicest land in the choicest province, then David Mathenge would be listened to. He would be a leader.

Land . . .

He hungered for it—as a root does for water, he thought, as a bird does for the sky. He had been born to the land, he was tied body and soul to it, and all this would have been his if his father had not been duped nearly thirty years ago into turning it over to the white man. Wachera's words rang again in David's ears as he gazed out over the

Treverton farm: "When someone steals your goat, my son, it is roasted and eaten and you forget it. When someone steals your corn, it is ground into meal and eaten and you forget it. But when someone steals your land, it is always there and you can never forget it."

David would never forget that these rich acres had been stolen from his ignorant father, that they were David's legacy, and that they should rightfully be returned to him. But force and impulsiveness, he knew, such as were the mainstays of the Nairobi wild boys, would never get him his land back. Careful planning and caution, he told himself, to move like a lion, to study the prey, to follow it and be on constant alert for its one moment of weakness—these were going to be David Mathenge's weapons.

He was going to get his land back, legally and honorably and in a state of prosperity.

He looked out over the five thousand acres of coffee trees and made his decision.

DAVID FOUND MONA Treverton in the southeastern sector of the estate, not far, in fact, from the fateful turnoff on the Kiganjo Road. She was standing on the flatbed of her truck, shielding her eyes and turning a complete circle.

"Damn!" she murmured, and was about to climb down when she saw David.

He looked up at her, suddenly remembering things: how she had sat so stoically through her mother's trial; the way she rode a horse on the polo field; the night of the fire when they both had been caught in the surgery hut.

Mona stared down at him, feeling suddenly cold in the warm sun. Several times, during the trial, she had glanced up to find David Mathenge watching her. He watched her in the same way now, his face a mask.

"What are you looking for, memsaab?" he asked in English.

"My field hands. They've run off again. It's the fourth time this month." She climbed down from the truck and pushed a few strands of black hair from her face. "These berries are ready to be picked."

"Where are the women and children?"

"I sent them to the northern section, to do the weeding. I need those men!"

David studied her. The memsaab was angry and frustrated, he saw, a woman now alone in the world, in that big house on these five thousand acres, with no husband, no man.

She thrust her hands into her pockets and walked a few steps away. Mona turned her face to the rolling hills of green coffee trees, the scarf on her head fluttering. She took in a deep breath to steady herself. "How can I get them to work for me?" she said quietly.

"I know where the men are," David said.

She turned. "You do?"

"They have gone to a beer drink at Mweiga. They will be gone for days."

"But the coffee must be picked! I don't have *days!* In a week my entire crop will be lost!"

He thought, *My crop,* then said, "I can bring the men back for you."

Mona gave him a wary look. "Why would you do that?"

"Because, memsaab, you need a manager and I need a job."

Her eyes widened. "You want to work for me?"

David nodded.

She stared at him.

"Do you think you could do it? I mean, all this—" She held out her arms.

He told her of his studies in Uganda, the diploma he had received.

Mona thought about it. She was uncertain. Could she trust him? "I've been trying to find a manager, in fact," she said slowly. "But everyone wants to start his own farm. No one wants to work for someone else. I would pay you a good salary, and you can build a house for yourself on the estate."

"I will need to have complete authority over the workers. I will need to have unlimited freedom. It is the only way."

Mona considered that. Then she thought of the red figures in her ledgers, of the debts mounting up because the farm had gone neglected during the trial and the months following, and she said, "Very well then. We have a deal."

When she held her hand out, he looked down at it, taken aback.

GREEN CITY IN THE SUN

She continued to hold her hand out.

Uncertain, David Mathenge brought his right hand up and took hold of hers.

"You can start at once," she said quietly.

He looked down at the two hands, brown and white, clasped.

PART
SIX
1952

43

When Wanjiru's labor pains began, she knew there was something wrong.

Placing a hand on her lower back and her other on her abdomen, she straightened and took a few deep breaths. Mama Wachera had cautioned her to be careful with this pregnancy, but Wanjiru, stubborn and unable to be idle for even a moment, had ignored the advice of her mother-in-law and had come into the forest to collect lantana leaves.

It was David's fault, Wanjiru decided as she waited for the contraction to subside. His mother was entering that stage of life when she should have the help of her son's several wives on the shamba, instead of having to make do with just one. But David had married only Wanjiru and, in the seven years since, had not even spoken of buying another wife. That was why Wanjiru, because Mama Wachera required the healing leaves for her medicines, had had to cross the river today and go in search of lantana.

Wanjiru was more resentful of David's selfishness than was Mama Wachera, who was too forgiving of her irresponsible son. Wachera claimed that there was still plenty of time yet for David to buy more wives and that he was too busy now with running the Treverton Estate to see to his duty to more than one woman. As it was, the old woman declared, Wanjiru didn't see her husband as much as she would like. How much worse, then, if she had to share him? Wanjiru disagreed. Even just one more co-wife would ease the work on the shamba and give David's mother and her daughter-in-law time to rest in the sun.

Another pain came on, and Wanjiru placed both hands on her abdomen. *She must not lose this child.*

In her seven years of being David's wife, Wanjiru Mathenge had had six pregnancies. Of those, one had resulted in miscarriage, one in stillbirth, and three had not lived beyond infancy. Only the last, Hannah, a robust little girl who was back at the shamba with her grandmother, had survived. Wanjiru was desperate for another healthy child. And she prayed that this one would be a boy so that the spirit of her father could live again.

On the matter of the child's name David and Wanjiru had argued. She wanted to call him, if a boy, Kamau, after her father, as Kikuyu law dictated. But David wanted his children to have *mzungu* names because, he had said, "We will one day be a free and independent modern nation. We must fall in step with the rest of the world." Sarah, if a girl, he had said, and Christopher if a boy. As headstrong as she was, Wanjiru was nonetheless subservient to her husband and had to obey him. In her heart, however, the boy would be Christopher *Kamau* Mathenge.

When another sharp and painful contraction came on, Wanjiru looked at the sky to read the hour of the day. Sometime back the European authorities had imposed a curfew on the Nyeri District. It was because of "certain illegal activities," they had said. There were "gangsters" working in the area, and proscribed meetings were taking place at night. They were referring, Wanjiru knew, to an elusive, nebulous organization that, for reasons no one seemed to know, called itself Mau Mau. Its members hid in the forest, struck suddenly and unexpectedly at random white farms, then disappeared into the mists of Mount Kenya. It was a radical fringe element, the authorities declared, small in number and without leadership—not to be bothered about at all, really, except that a few white settlers had complained of cattle being stolen. And so the curfew had been established. Between sunset and sunrise no African could be out of his or her hut.

Wanjiru saw by the descending sun, a watery circle in the rainclouded sky, that she had time yet before she must head back to the shamba. She looked for a place to sit, to ease the burden of her body, and to discern if the pains were possibly a false alarm.

She had had premature pains like these with Hannah, a month before she was due. Wanjiru had merely rested for a few days, the pains had subsided, and Hannah had stayed within her mother until the Lord of Brightness had called her forth. So it would be with this one, Wanjiru consoled herself as she settled down upon a log.

However, as she sat and waited for relief, as the air grew damp and cool and the sky grew grayer and darker, Wanjiru began to realize in alarm that not only were the contractions not subsiding, but they were coming closer together and intensifying.

Deciding that she had better start back, Wanjiru stood and turned in the direction of the river.

She froze.

Moving through the trees was a large, dark shape. It was accompanied by sounds familiar and frightening to her: rumbles and grunts, the noise of bark being stripped from trees.

An elephant!

She watched and listened. How many were there? Was it a lone rogue, or was it a herd? Were they females with babies, or were they young bachelors? Suddenly scared, Wanjiru saw the tops of trees sway and shiver as the giant beast grazed its way through the forest. It was their habit, Wanjiru knew, to migrate down from the bamboo forests at the beginning of the rains, to feed in the less dense woods and where the ridges were not so steep. But she had never seen elephants this far down the mountain before.

Wanjiru tried to sense the direction of the wind. If there were babies in the herd, or if it was an angry old bull, then her scent would cause alarm and trigger a charge.

Wanjiru looked right and left. She heard the slow, heavy tread of feet on each side of her, the "belly rumble" that was elephant talk, the snap of twigs and bark. They were on three sides of her—a large herd!

Wanjiru looked over her shoulder at the thickening forest and the beginning of the mountain slope. The trees behind her did not move; there were no sounds among them. She decided she would make her way slowly backward, away from the herd and then circle them, toward home.

She went a short distance into the woods and was stopped by a severe contraction. Wanjiru bent over and clutched herself, stifling a groan. She looked back; the elephants were drawing nearer; she saw the flash of white tusk between trees.

Her fear mounting, Wanjiru hastened her retreat up into the denser forest, moving as quickly and silently as her bulk would allow, pausing only when pain gripped her, and glancing back frequently to measure the distance between herself and the elephants.

If the matriarch of the herd caught a whiff of human scent . . .

Wanjiru moved as swiftly as she could through the descending gloom. Although daylight was now rapidly dying, she dared not try to circle back toward home, not until she was certain she was giving the elephants a wide margin.

A ropy vine lay across her path; her foot caught on it, and she fell. She cried out.

Wanjiru lay where she was and strained to listen. The low growl of the elephants, as they communicated with one another in the forest, was all around her. She lay perfectly still in the lowering darkness on the hard, damp ground.

The herd was moving, she thought in rising panic, at the pace of a snail. They just seemed to stand in a spot and strip the trees, their ears making swishing sounds, their massive feet crushing everything underfoot. The forest grew dark; sounds changed from daylight melodies to sinister, nocturnal calls. Wanjiru was terrified of the night, and now she was about to be caught in it.

Only one thing worse could happen to her, she decided as she waited in agony for the elephants to move on, and that would be for the rain to break.

And it did, just as she was picking herself up to head back home.

The rain was just a gentle drizzle, but Wanjiru could see only a few feet in front of her—the dreary shapes of trees and giant bush. She stumbled for cover under a chestnut tree and was struck by a violent contraction. She cried out again and fell to her knees.

It lasted longer than the previous pains, and she felt the ominous shifting of her pelvic bones.

The baby was coming.

No! she thought in panic. *Not here, where the wild beasts of the forest will steal him from me!*

Wanjiru struggled to get to her feet. She pulled herself up along the tree trunk, scraping her palms until they bled, and then, once she was standing, tried to conquer the pain so that she could walk.

Forgetting the elephants, the lantana leaves in her abandoned basket, and the white man's curfew, Wanjiru managed to push away from the tree and take a few halting steps out in the light rain. She was able to walk. She clutched her abdomen and moved blindly into the drizzle, unaware, in her physical agony and in the confusion of the rain, that she was heading in the wrong direction.

WANJIRU HAD NO idea how long she had been walking. Night seemed to have come to the forest long ago; the rain had been falling steadily for hours. Her kanga, a piece of brightly colored cloth which she wore around her head in a turban, was soaked and plastered to her shaved scalp. Her skirt clung to her legs, making walking nearly impossible. But she pressed on through the rain and the darkness, scrambling over boulders and fallen logs, feeling her way among trees that were growing closer and closer together, trying desperately to find the direction home.

She knew where she was. Wanjiru was stumbling up the slope of the mountains the white man called the Aberdares. To them the range was a national park, but to Wanjiru it was Nyandarua, "Drying Hide," the forest of her ancestors. She also knew that helpless, alone, and about to give birth, she was now in the territory of the deadly buffalo and black leopard.

Once the pain was so severe that she collapsed and lay for a long time in the mud, the freezing rain washing over her, rocks and dead branches cutting into her.

Wanjiru's hands and feet were numb; she felt none of the lacerations or the warm blood seeping from her wounds. She was barely even aware of the wet, the sharp cold, her hunger pangs. Wanjiru was centered in her belly, where her child was demanding to be released. But she held him in her; she carried her pain and torture inside her body, through the black forest and into the terrifying night.

Dear God, she prayed in desperation as she stumbled, fell, then pulled herself up from the mud and plunged into the arctic void. *Lord of Brightness, help me!*

She pressed on. Sobs wracked her body as wet branches slapped her face and stung her arms. Her bare feet slipped over the muddy forest floor. The rain continued to come down, heavy and hard, seeming to invade even her skin and soak her to the bones. Wanjiru thought of her warm, dry hut, the bed of goatskins, the *ugali* stew bubbling on the cook fire, and the comforting presence of David's mother, patiently brewing medicinal tea. But the last thing this nightmarish forest contained, Wanjiru knew in despair, was warmth and dryness.

Thunder clapped, and the ground shook. Wanjiru heard the trumpeting of startled elephants. She wondered where they were, if it was the same herd, if she was heading away from them or toward them. An icy wind cut through her sodden clothing, making the labor pains sharper.

She plunged on, into the night.

THE RAIN FINALLY stopped, and eerie mists swirled up from the ground. Wanjiru had to push through branches laden with water, the cold wind blowing over her wet body. She felt as if the world were turning to ice and that she was going to be swallowed up in the freezing lakes and fogs of the forbidding mountain.

Something warm trickled down between her legs. The birth pain was one continuous ribbon of fire. She ran out of breath. She fell against a tree. Wanjiru knew now that she was far from home, that she had been lost and wandering for hours, and that the baby was going to be born in this cold, dark hell. All around she heard the scuttlings of wild animals; she sensed hyena eyes fastened greedily upon her, waiting for her to fall one last time. Wanjiru had heard the women in the marketplace tell of a woman who had been caught in the fields in childbirth and how hyenas had dragged the newborn baby off.

I'll kill my son first, she thought as she clutched the tree, gasping, straining to keep the baby inside her just a while longer. *And then I will kill myself. . . .*

Wanjiru felt as if her body were being torn apart. She cried out. Then she screamed.

She slid to the ground, tearing her cheek on the rough bark, tasting blood, *seeing* blood, and hearing, in the dense mist, the clicks and grunts of evil, scavenging animals.

"Go away!" she screamed.

Wanjiru felt around the wet ground for a weapon. Her hand curled around a rock. She tried to throw it, but she was too weak. Life was draining out of her; a sturdy, new life was pushing its way from her body. Her pain rose up and out of her skin and flew away to the low-hanging clouds and misty bamboo forests. Wanjiru was at the top of the mountain, and she knew she would never get down again.

But her baby would not be food for the beasts. She would not let the wild animals of this terrible forest feast upon the grandson of the warrior chief Mathenge.

Dazed and weak, the child nearly born, Wanjiru began to dig feebly into the mud. A grave, just big enough . . .

IT SEEMED TO her that she slept and that she was warm and dry. Half of her told her that it was an illusion, that she was still out in the cold, digging a grave for her baby. But another part of her told her that this was very real.

She was back at the Native Hospital in Nairobi, where she had worked for five years as a nurse before leaving to live in the Nyeri District as David Mathenge's wife.

She was having an argument with someone. "Why are our uniforms different from yours? Why are our wages so much lower than yours? Why are you called 'sister,' while we must answer to 'maid'?"

The face of her white supervisor materialized before Wanjiru. It was the self-righteous countenance of a woman who told Wanjiru that African nurses simply didn't qualify for the same status as white ones.

And then Wanjiru, in her strange dream, remembered that this was why she had left the nursing profession. "We are discriminated against," she had complained to David. "African women receive the same training and do the same work, but we are not considered the equals of the white sisters. Why should I trouble myself?"

At that point Wanjiru opened her eyes and realized, after some minutes, that she was staring up at the ceiling of a cave.

She lay thinking, trying to discover if this was real or another dream. The bed of dry leaves underneath her seemed real enough, as did the pain in her hands and feet. The air in this mysterious cave was warm and dry but gently illuminated by a fire in the center of its rocky floor.

Silhouettes of people hunched together and eating squatted around that fire.

Wanjiru stared at them. Then she explored herself; she felt inside her body and realized that the baby was gone.

She tried to speak; it came out as a groan. One of those by the fire got up and came to her. It was a woman holding a newborn baby.

"Your son," she said quietly.

Bewildered, Wanjiru reached up and brought her son, Christopher, to her breast, where he began feeding at once. She studied the woman who knelt at her side. By her features, Wanjiru guessed that she was a member of the Meru tribe.

"Where am I?" Wanjiru was finally able to say.

"You are safe with us. Don't worry, sister."

Wanjiru looked around the large cave, craning her neck. She saw more people, many more, along the walls, sleeping in corners and on stony shelves. She saw furniture made of bamboo, large crates with English words printed on them, rifles stacked in the shadows. A strange silence filled the cave, considering the number of people it housed; but the aromas were familiar and comforting, and the woman at Wanjiru's side smiled reassuringly.

"Who are you?" Wanjiru asked.

"We found you in the forest and brought you here. You are among friends." The woman paused, then said, "The soil is ours." She looked down at Wanjiru, as if expecting a particular response.

But all Wanjiru, in her exhaustion and confusion, could say was "I—I don't understand. *Who are you?*"

The woman's smile faded, and she said solemnly, almost sadly, "We are *uhuru*, sister. We are Mau Mau."

44

M ona thought the train would never come.
And then there it was at last: the whistle; the rumbling track; the smoke puffing up to the blue sky. People swarmed all over the platform—those, like Mona, meeting arrivals and others ready to clamber aboard and fight for a good seat for the ride up to Nanyuki. She stayed back by her Land-Rover as she anxiously watched the train slow down and come to a stop. She paid no attention to the first- and second-class cars, in which whites and Asians rode, but fastened her eye upon the third-class car. Finally—it seemed to take forever—she saw him step down.

"David!" she called, waving.

He looked up, smiled, and waved back.

Mona pushed through the mob and met him halfway, saying, "I was beginning to think you'd never come! I've missed you, David! How was Uganda?"

They put his bags into the back of the Rover, then pulled away from the noisy depot, with Mona driving.

"I was unable to bring back any mealybug parasites," he said as the car took the paved road. "But I did stop at Jacaranda Research Station and observed the research going on there. A few of the parasites have emerged."

"Any success with stopping the mealybug?"

"So far, no."

"There have been two outbreaks of coffee berry disease in the Upper Kiambu District."

"Yes, I heard. But only a small amount of the crop was lost, and the outbreak has been contained."

They followed the narrow road that was one of the many paved by Italian POWs during the war; it wound through the hills between Kiganjo and the Treverton Estate, a rich, verdant farming region where small, round Kikuyu huts stood among plots of maize, banana, and sugarcane. African children at the roadside stopped and called out to the passing car. Women trudging along the parallel path, bent over, hauling water and wood by straps across their foreheads, raised their hands in greeting. Mona waved back, feeling suddenly happy and elated after two months of running the farm without David.

"What else did you learn at Jacaranda?" she asked, glancing at the man at her side. Mona had heard her Aunt Grace say only a few days ago that David Mathenge was the image of his handsome warrior father.

"They still consider banding grease the most reliable control of mealybug. The Coffee Board recommends Synthorbite and Ostico. Jacaranda Station is experimenting with dieldrin, a new insecticide supplied by Shell chemicals." David shifted in his seat, rested his arm out the window, and looked at Mona. "How is the farm?"

"I was able to sell this last crop at four hundred twenty-five a ton."

"That's up considerably from last year."

She laughed. "And costs for running the farm are up, too! David, I'm so glad you're back."

He regarded her for a moment, then looked away. Green hills and red-dirt tracks sped by; thick stands of banana plants were etched against the blue sky. Spirals of smoke rose up from countless cone-shaped thatched roofs. It was a peaceful, familiar scene, and David had sorely missed it. He had also missed Mona.

"Will you stop and have tea with me?" she asked as she steered the Rover around to the side of Bellatu. She parked it between a battered Ford truck and a dusty Cadillac limousine, the former being in use every day, the latter having not moved since Lady Rose's funeral seven years before. "Or do you want to rest?"

He climbed down and knocked the dust from his trousers. "I slept on the train. I would love some tea."

Mona said, "Good!" and preceded him up the steps to the kitchen door.

As they entered, Mona said, "I've had to have another talk with

Solomon. I caught him warming the toast in front of the fire this morning."

"What is wrong with that?"

"He was holding the toast between his toes!"

David laughed. Mona, also laughing, was about to say something more when she was startled by the sudden appearance of someone standing in the doorway of the dining room.

"Geoff!" she said. "I didn't see your car."

"Father dropped me off. He's gone down to the mission to see Aunt Grace."

"Is Ilse with you? We were about to have tea."

Geoffrey cast a quick, disapproving look at David, then said, "I'm afraid this isn't a social call. We need to talk in private, Mona. I've some rather upsetting news to tell you."

"What is it?"

He looked again, significantly, at David, who quickly said, "I will have that tea later, Mona. I must go down and see my mother and Wanjiru."

"David"—she reached out and touched his arm—"please do come back and have lunch with me."

"Yes," he said. "We'll need to go over the books."

"Really, Mona," Geoffrey said when David had gone, "I don't understand why you let that boy of yours call you by your first name."

"Don't be such a toffee nose, Geoffrey," she said, marveling once again to think that she had once considered marrying this stuffy man! "As I've told you before, David Mathenge is not a 'boy'; he is my manager. And he is my friend. Now, what's the upsetting news?"

"Have you turned on the wireless this morning?"

"Geoffrey, I was up before dawn and spent the entire morning down at the processing sheds. Then I had to go and collect David at the train station. No, I haven't listened to the wireless. What *is* it?"

Geoffrey would have liked to say something about that, that Mona could easily have sent someone else to fetch David, that it would, in fact, have been more proper for her to do so, but Geoffrey, knowing it was useless to argue with her, turned to the reason for his unexpected visit. "The governor has declared a state of emergency in Kenya."

"*What?*"

"Late last night, in an effort to put an end to Mau Mau, Kenyatta and several of his cronies were arrested."

"But there's no proof that Kenyatta is behind Mau Mau! Only two months ago he publicly denounced these acts of terrorism!"

"Well, they've got to be stopped somehow, and I'll wager everything I have that with old Jomo behind bars and unable to get messages out, the violence will cease."

Mona turned away, her hand pressed to her forehead. "What does it mean, a state of emergency?"

"It means that until the gangsters come out of the forest and give themselves up, we'll be living under special police conditions."

She walked to the tile counter where a yellow plastic radio stood between an electric coffeepot and an electric orange squeezer. Since 1919, when it was built, the kitchen of Bellatu had undergone several renovations, the latest having been two years ago, when a modern gas stove had finally replaced the old Dover wood burner.

Mona turned the radio on, and "Your Cheatin' Heart" filled the air. Turning the dial, she briefly picked up a broadcast from faraway Cairo. Then she found the Nairobi station.

"There is no doubt that Kenya is facing trouble," said the voice of the Governor, Sir Evelyn Baring, "but I appeal to all citizens to keep calm and be careful not to create alarm by passing on rumors. I signed a proclamation of a State of Emergency throughout the Colony, a grave step that was taken most unwillingly and with great reluctance by the Government of Kenya. But there was no alternative in face of the mounting lawlessness, violence, and disorder in a part of the Colony. This state of affairs has developed as a result of the activities of the Mau Mau movement. In order to restore law and order and to allow peaceful and loyal people of all races to go about their business in safety, the government has made emergency regulations to enable it to take into custody certain persons who in its opinion constitute danger to public order."

Mona looked at Geoffrey. "What does he mean, certain persons?"

"For this purpose," Sir Evelyn went on, "there has been a redistribution of police and military forces, and in addition, a British battalion is being brought in by air to Nairobi, the first troops having arrived last night. HMS *Kenya* will also arrive at Mombasa in the course of today."

"Troops!" she said, turning off the radio. "Is all that really necessary? I had no idea things were so bad!"

"They weren't at first. Mau Mau, whatever the hell *that* is supposed to mean, began, as you know, with a few fringe lunatics, Nairobi wild boys, unemployed and broke, who took to hiding in the forest and making occasional, arbitrary strikes, mostly for food and money. An African policeman or two came up missing; cattle were stolen; someone's hut was burned down. But it seems that more and more dissatisfied young natives are joining them, and it's escalating. I'm afraid it's caught us all a bit off guard."

Mona felt suddenly cold. She went to the stove and set the kettle on to boil. *Mau Mau* was a term she had first heard about two years ago, when few people outside the Secret Service paid much attention to it. And then incidents began occurring: police headquarters burglarized and ammunition stolen; someone's plot of maize set ablaze; threatening notices appearing mysteriously all over Nairobi. Last month a gang of Africans had raided the Catholic mission, locked the missionaries in a room, and made off with cash and a shotgun. A week later the body of a strangled dog was found hanging in Majengo market as a warning from Mau Mau to all white settlers. Finally, just two weeks ago, a senior tribal chief, a man much respected by both Africans and whites, had been assassinated in broad daylight.

Geoffrey came all the way into the kitchen, folded his arms, and leaned against the sink. "The final straw," he said quietly, "occurred early this morning. You know Abel Kamau, the dairyman up at Mweiga?"

Mona nodded. Abel Kamau was one of those African soldiers who had returned from the war with European wives. The Kamaus had settled just a few miles north of Bellatu, to live a quiet, peaceful existence. They were one of the very few interracial couples in Kenya and were so ostracized by everyone, shunned by Africans and whites, cast out from both his family and hers, that they had few friends and led a lonely existence. Mona had met them and had found them to be congenial, likable people. They had a four-year-old son.

"They were attacked in their beds during the night," Geoffrey said. "Massacred. Abel and his wife were barely recognizable, the police said, because of the numerous panga slashes."

Mona reached for a chair. "My God. And the boy?"

"He's alive, but they don't think he'll live. The thugs gouged his eyes out."

"Dear God, *why?*"

"They use eyes in their oathing ceremonies." Geoffrey took the chair opposite Mona and sat at the table. "They were a Mau Mau target because they had broken racial taboos. As you know, it's as offensive to an African as it is to whites to intermarry. Abel Kamau's big crime was that he was married to a white woman and also that he was a loyalist. The ones Mau Mau seem to be targeting, besides a few isolated whites, are Africans who support the colonial government."

The kettle was whistling. Mona looked at it but didn't move. "What on earth was that poor little boy's crime?" she murmured.

"His father had slept with a white woman."

Mona finally got up from the table and went through the motions of making tea. Her joy of that morning, the result of David's return, had died. "Do the police have any idea who did it?"

"They know exactly who did it. Kamau's houseboy, Chege."

Mona spun around. "That's not possible! Chege is a sweet and kindly old man who wouldn't hurt a fly! Why, he was Abel's father's best friend!"

"Yes, that's the monstrous part of it all. Mau Mau are starting to work through people who are close to their targets."

"But how can they? Chege was *devoted* to Abel and his wife!"

"Love and devotion, Mona, are nothing compared with the power of a Mau Mau oath."

She knew about the oaths, had heard about them all her life. Oathing was what bound a Kikuyu to his word; it was an integral part of tribal social structure and was so steeped in ancestral superstition and taboos that few Kikuyu could go against an oath once taken. "But how could they make someone take an oath against his will and then make him commit a hideous crime?"

"They're forcing people through the oath. They terrorize them into taking it. Chege was most likely abducted, carted off into the forest, forced through an obscene ritual, and then released."

"But how could they be sure he would carry out their orders?"

"Mau Mau can be certain of anyone they've forced to take an oath,

Mona. If the oath itself doesn't terrify the poor bastard into carrying out their demands, then the threat of execution by them does."

Mona put the teapot, cups, sugar, and milk on a tray and carried it out of the kitchen. She found Ilse, Geoffrey's wife, sitting in the living room, looking at a Sears catalog advertisement for "handbags for the pigtail and Coke crowd." Ilse had gotten quite fat in her seven years of marriage to Geoffrey and was even heavier now because of pregnancy.

"Dear me," she said, putting the catalog aside, "such badness! And to think that it so near to us has happened!"

When Mona saw how pale and shaken Ilse was, she remembered that the Kamau homestead was less than a mile from Kilima Simba.

Deep in thought, Mona stirred her tea. Although she had never heard Kenyatta speak, she had read excerpts of his speeches in the newspaper. He was the leader of the Kenya African Union, the powerful and growing political organization which, Kenyatta had declared, was dedicated to ending the color bar in Kenya and to obtaining more land, more education, more leadership for Africans, with the ultimate goal being self-government. "We are looking for one thing," the charismatic Jomo had said, "and that is peace."

Despite Kenyatta's repeated denunciations of Mau Mau, the government had nonetheless decided that he and the KAU were behind the terrorism and therefore had had him arrested. A dangerous move, Mona thought, and possibly a very foolish one.

"There's nothing to worry about, Mona," Geoffrey said. "This Mau Mau business will fall apart without their leaders. Baring's promised that Kenyatta will never again be a free man. And to show the terrorists that we mean business, we've got the equivalent of six battalions currently positioned throughout the province, in addition to the three Kenya battalions of the King's African Rifles, a Ugandan battalion operating in the Rift, and two companies of Tanganyika battalions. Last night the Lancashire Fusiliers were flown down from the canal. They landed at the Royal Air Force station at Eastleigh and have been set up in Nairobi as a command reserve. We're also creating a home guard, making use of African ex-soldiers who fought in the war and who are loyal. I tell you, Mona, I for one am glad to see that we're finally showing them a firm hand. We're demonstrating to the wogs and to the world that we can defend this colony on a moment's notice, by the air and by sea."

"I wonder . . ." Mona said. She was staring out the large living room window, which admitted a glorious day that shed equatorial sunlight on Bellatu's somber, elegant old furniture. Bright pink and orange bougainvillaea framed the deep veranda, rows of green coffee trees undulated over a gently hilly landscape, and in the distance, purple and snowcapped, Mount Kenya stood in cloudless majesty. "I wonder, Geoffrey, if the governor's move isn't, in fact, an error. By bringing in such military force, he is as much as admitting to the world, and to Mau Mau, that the white settler government of Kenya is incapable of defending the colony alone."

"Good God, Mona, you talk as if you wanted the wogs to run the country!"

"I don't think their desire for self-rule is unreasonable."

"Well, I'll agree with you in part. I've been screaming for self-rule for years, you know that. There's no bloody sense in our having to answer to Whitehall any longer. But I mean *white* self-rule."

"Geoffrey, there are forty thousand of us in this country and *six million* Africans! It must be evident to you and everyone by now that the Rhodesian apartheid model will never work here in Kenya. We don't have that right."

"You're wrong, Mona. We do have the right. Don't forget what miracles our tiny minority has performed in East Africa. The British taxpayer, Mona, the hardest hit after the war, has poured great sums of money into this colony, money which has helped the Africans! When one considers everything we've done for them, actually brought them out of the Stone Age, and how we've taken care of them all these years, it's appalling that the current situation has been allowed to develop. If you ask me, Mona, we were fools not to accept Montgomery's plan when we had the chance."

"What plan was that?"

"Back in 'forty-eight Field Marshal Montgomery introduced a plan to establish military bases here in Kenya because he had foreseen exactly the dissension we have today. Because we didn't listen to him, the Africans have played right into Communist hands, and that is exactly what we are facing now. The whole of Mau Mau, I tell you, is based on Communist lines."

"Oh, Geoffrey," Mona said impatiently, "I still say it is their country as much as it is ours, and we shouldn't discount the needs and feelings of six million people."

Geoffrey gave Mona a wry smile. "Do you really think they are capable of self-rule?" He laughed. "I can hear the wogs now! 'Give us the job and we'll finish the tools!' "

"You're being unfair."

"And I say they're being bloody ungrateful! But what can you expect? The Kikuyu language doesn't even have a word for 'thank you.' We had to teach it to them."

Geoffrey stood abruptly. He hated these arguments with Mona. She infuriated him. Everything about her annoyed him: her political views; the way she lived—especially the way she lived.

Mona was a good-looking woman, he thought, could be quite stunning, in fact, if she didn't insist on parading about like an ordinary farm woman. She had inherited a rather fetching combination, in his opinion, of her mother's beauty and her father's dark good looks, and she should be capitalizing on it with better clothes and a trip now and then to the hairdresser. But Mona insisted on drawing her long black hair into a plain ponytail and wearing men's shirts. She hadn't an ounce of style, he thought, spending her days in the coffee fields, working alongside her Africans. Mona seemed to have inherited none of her parents' gentility. The days of champagne and polo parties were, sadly, long gone; they seemed to have died with Valentine. The upstairs guest rooms, Geoffrey knew, had been closed up long ago. Limousines no longer pulled up the drive; gay celebrations had ceased to fill these somber rooms. The only visitors Mona entertained were men from the Coffee Board, growers like herself, with whom she smoked cigarettes and drank brandy and discussed world market prices. What Mona needed was a man to remind her of the woman she was. And Geoffrey decided he was that man.

A pang of conscience made him look at his wife, who sat in a cotton maternity smock, fat and complacent, her sole interest in life their children. Ilse had let herself go. After four babies and now pregnant again with the fifth, she had lost all sexual desirability. She was a good mother, Geoffrey admitted. But as a bed partner she had lost her appeal long ago. What had he been thinking to marry her because she had been persecuted and he had felt sorry for her? Instead, he should have come home to Mona!

It was getting more and more difficult for him to curb his desire for Mona. It amazed him that she could lead such a celibate life. It was unnatural. Surely she, too, longed for intimacy with a man. Yet, amazingly, there were no men in her life other than strictly business contacts. Geoffrey was certain that there must be a yearning in her somewhere, that at night, alone in her bed, she must be reminded of her sterile life. Mona must be ripe, Geoffrey decided, for the right man to come along. One of these days, Geoffrey promised himself, or one of these nights he was going to give in to his lust and come to Bellatu and find her alone. And she would be just as ready for him as he was for her.

"Anyway," he said as he strode to the window, his body, still lean at forty, silhouetted against the October sunshine. "I mean to show the Mau Mau gangsters that I am not intimidated by them. With me it will be business as usual, despite what the bad press has done for it. Once this Mau Mau nonsense has died down, and it will, I promise you that, then I shall have my customers again."

Geoffrey was referring to his embryonic tour agency, which he had started after being released from the army. His prophecy that the war would spark a new age in tourism had come true. All over the world soldiers returning home had regaled their families with stories of the exotic places they had seen: Paris; Rome; Egypt; Hawaii; the South Pacific. These discoveries, along with the recent introduction of commercial jet travel, which drastically reduced traveling time, had triggered a sudden worldwide fad for sight-seeing. The Donald Tour Agency, which operated out of Geoffrey Donald's living room at Kilima Simba, was still in its early, struggling stage, Kenya not yet implanted in the minds of would-be holiday travelers. So far Geoffrey only took out hunting safaris, but his intention was to establish something altogether new: *photographic* safaris.

"I'm working on a new advertising campaign," he said as he returned to his tea and changed the subject with, in Mona's opinion, maddening agility. "I'm having a brochure drafted, with photos of lions and giraffes and natives and a reassurance that the Manchester laborer can enjoy two weeks of African adventure in guaranteed safety and comfort. Now that we've got these wildlife preserves, thanks to the diligent work of Aunt Grace, we might as well cash in on them."

"But even with our wildlife," Mona said, "I don't see what else Kenya has to offer to the average holidaymaker. One can get tired of just taking snapshots of animals every day."

One of Mona's problems, Geoffrey decided, was that she lacked imagination. "That's going to be part of my new program. The brochure will have pictures of the Nairobi hotels. I'll emphasize the luxury, the cuisine, the nightlife. Now that Nairobi has finally achieved city status, I mean to put it on the world map."

Mona laughed. "All you need now is a jingle or a slogan. How about "Welcome to Nairobi, City in the Sun?"

As she collected the empty teacups, she didn't see Geoffrey pull a small notebook out of the pocket of his khaki jacket and write something down.

"Now, you're not to worry," Geoffrey said a few minutes later as he and Ilse prepared to say good-bye in the kitchen. His hand was on Mona's arm, holding tightly. "I can guarantee that with Kenyatta cut off from his forest thugs, they'll come slinking out with their tails between their legs and this whole business will blow over."

He stepped closer to her. Mona could see the sunburned creases around his eyes. "But if you do get frightened," he said quietly, "if you should wake up and think there's someone in the house, give me a ring on the telephone, and I'll be over here in an instant. Will you promise to do that?"

Mona stepped away from him and handed a basket to Ilse. "Some honey for the children," she said.

Outside Geoffrey paused on the steps and said, "I say, is your boy being questioned?"

Mona looked out. Three askaris of the Kenya Police Reserve, in navy blue pullovers and tall red fezzes, were standing a short distance down the drive and appeared to be examining David's identity papers.

Geoffrey turned to Mona. "I want you to be careful with that chap."

Geoffrey's intense dislike of David Mathenge was no secret. His constant criticism of Mona's relationship with her African manager was a source of contention between them. "I trust David," she said.

"Nevertheless, in these next few weeks, until the emergency has passed, I want you to be very careful around him."

Mona parted with Geoffrey and his wife as they took the stairway that led down the ridge to the mission, while she continued along the drive to where David stood with the askaris.

"What's the problem?" she asked.

The three soldiers were polite and spoke in the clipped, melodious British accent of the educated African. "Pardon the intrusion, memsaab, but a farm was burned this morning, and we are questioning everyone."

"Farm? Which one?"

"Muhori Gatheru's farm. His house was destroyed, and all his cattle have been killed. It was the work of Mau Mau."

"How do you know that?"

"They left a message. It said, 'The soil is ours.' "

"What does that mean?"

"It is the Mau Mau oath."

"I can vouch for Mr. Mathenge. He was on the train from Nairobi this morning."

"Pardon, memsaab, but the train was delayed at Karatina for some time this morning, and Muhori Gatheru's farm is at Karatina."

"Still, I vouch for him. Good day."

On their way to the house, where she and David would spend the afternoon going over the ledgers, bills, and correspondence and discussing David's visit to Uganda, where he had hoped to find a solution to their problems with mealybug infestation, Mona said, "I can't believe this horrible Mau Mau business is happening! You've heard of the state of emergency?"

"Yes."

Entering the kitchen, she said, "I'll have Solomon make us some sandwiches. Oh, where *is* that lazy old rascal?"

"Don't worry for my sake, Mona. I'm not hungry. I ate on the train."

"What delayed the train at Karatina? Do you know?"

He paused, then said, "No."

Mona had long ago converted her father's study to her own, packing away all his trophies, awards, and photographs. Chintz curtains now replaced the heavy drapes, and the stolid furniture, brought out from

England thirty-three years ago and starting to show wear, had been covered in bright floral fabric.

Mona took her place at the large oak desk while David drew up a chair and sat alongside.

"How is the baby?" she asked as she pulled the ledgers out of their drawer.

"My son is fine."

"And Wanjiru?"

"We argued again." David sighed. "I have been gone for two months, and my wife greets me with complaints."

Mona knew about the arguments. Wanjiru wanted co-wives, to keep her company and to help with the work on the shamba; she wanted David to get himself elected to the leadership of the local KAU chapter; she wanted him to move out of the manager's cottage he had built six years ago and live with her and his mother down by the river.

Wanjiru did not cease in repeating these demands, and David, Mona knew, never budged an inch. And she was glad. On the KAU work Mona had no opinion, but it pleased her that he had not sought second and third wives and that he preferred to live alone in the small house down by the road. The reason this pleased her, Mona told herself, was that it left David free to concentrate on working the estate.

But what Mona did not know and what David was not going to tell her was that today his argument with Wanjiru had been on a new issue. It had been about Mau Mau.

"Christopher is a fine little boy," Mona said as she handed David the stack of bills that had piled up. "Only seven months old and already starting to crawl!"

David looked at Mona and smiled. "You should have children," he said quietly.

She looked away. "I'm past that! At thirty-three I can hardly think of starting a family!"

"All women should have babies."

"I have the farm. I'm satisfied." Mona hated it when David brought up the subject of her single status. His male presumption that a childless woman was an unhappy woman annoyed her. There was more to marriage and babies, she had once tried to explain to him, than a man simply buying a wife for a few goats. There was the matter of love.

"I used to be afraid I was turning out to be like my mother," she had told him one rainy night back in April, when they had been warming themselves by the fire after a vigorous day on the estate, "because I had mistakenly thought she was incapable of love. And then I discovered that my mother was a woman who can love only one man in her life and then love him so completely and totally that she absolutely cannot survive without him."

Mona had stopped herself then, suddenly realizing how close she was coming to things too private to confess. No one, not even her Aunt Grace, who was Mona's closest friend and confidante, knew of Mona's decision to wait out her life entirely if necessary, alone and childless, for the right man to come along. Settling for just anyone, merely to be married, seemed to Mona to bring only unhappiness and regret.

David's shirtsleeves were rolled up. As he separated the bills into different piles, his bare arms moved in and out of the sunlight that spilled across the desk. Mona found herself watching the movement of muscles beneath the dark brown skin.

She picked up the letter from Bella Hill. "My dear Lady Mona," the agent had written, "I do hate to bother you with these matters, but the unavoidable fact is that something *must* be done or else we shall lose the last of our renters."

Mona put the letter aside. She was in no mood to read about Bella Hill's seemingly interminable problems. When her aunt Edith had moved out to live in Brighton with her cousin, Mona had had the Suffolk mansion converted into apartments, with cheap postwar rents. Returning soldiers had snapped them up and moved their new brides into them. But as prosperity returned to England, as life-styles improved, as the wives began to produce children, and as wear and tear began to take their toll on old Bella Hill, the ancestral estate that had once been a source of revenue when Bellatu was in need had become a financial drain. Renters, complaining of bad plumbing and insufficient heating and wanting modern improvements, were moving out faster than the agent could replace them. Mona knew she was going to have to do something about the poor old white elephant, and soon.

Bella Hill . . .

She glanced at David. He was running up figures on the adding machine, his head bent, his handsome face molded in concentration.

She was remembering three incidents. The first, twenty-four years ago, had taken place in a gloomy hallway of Bella Hill, when an unhappy little Mona had tried to force David's sister, Njeri, to run away with her. The second incident had come close on the heels of the first: Mona and David trapped in the burning surgery hut. But the third episode she recalled now, as she watched him work, had happened seven years ago, shortly after he had taken the job of estate manager.

"I want to apologize to you, David," Mona had said to him. "I was cruel to you when we were children, and I am sorry about that. I nearly got us both killed."

A look, one which Mona had not been able to read, had crossed his face, and then he had said, "It happened a long time ago. It is forgotten."

As if sensing her eyes upon him now, David looked up from the adding machine and smiled. "I almost forgot," he said, pushing away from the desk. "I have brought you something from Uganda."

She watched him reach into his pants pocket and bring out something large wrapped in a handkerchief. He held it out to her.

Puzzled, Mona took it. David had never given her a present before. And when she took away the handkerchief and saw what it was, her puzzlement turned to shock.

"Good heavens," she whispered. "It's beautiful!"

"This is the necklace the people of Toro make. Do you see these green beads? They are malachite from the Belgian Congo. And this is carved ebony."

Mona stared at the necklace that lay in the sunlight. It was a stunning creation of polished copper, chunks of amber, ivory rosettes, and iron links—African and primitive, yet strangely modern, almost timeless. A work of art, it seemed to Mona, that had no business hanging about someone's neck.

"Here," David said, "let me put it on you."

He went to stand behind her. She felt his hands sweep aside her hair. She saw the necklace come down before her eyes, felt it settle heavily and comfortably on her breast. David's fingers brushed her neck as he fastened the clasp.

"Go to the mirror, Mona. Look at yourself."

She couldn't believe her eyes. Mona thought she looked different, no longer ordinary but transformed in some way. The necklace lay against her cotton blouse in a kind of glory that made everything else—the room, the furniture, the sunshine outside—seem prosaic.

"It's magnificent, David," she said.

"The women of Toro wear these."

"The women of Toro are beautiful. It looks wrong on me."

"As soon as I saw it, I thought of you, Mona."

She pictured the Ugandan women of Toro, with their dark, slender necks and proud heads. "I don't do it justice," she said. "I have the wrong skin for it."

David said, very quietly, "There is nothing wrong with your skin, Mona."

She looked at his reflection in the mirror. He was standing close behind her. Their eyes met in the glass.

When Mona turned around to thank him, the stillness was shattered by the sudden blare of a radio voice.

It was the Kikuyu-language noon broadcast. Solomon, in the kitchen, had turned it on. The newscaster was reporting the Mau Mau slaying of Abel Kamau and his European wife. Their four-year-old son, he went on to say, having sustained severe eye wounds, had just died in King George Hospital.

45

Wanjiru and her mother-in-law sang together as they worked. It was a simple song, with the same words repeated over and over, and they sang it in pleasing harmony, changing it, making it up as they went. It was a hymn to Ngai, the god who lived on Mount Kenya; it was a prayer for *uhuru*, freedom.

Mama Wachera's heart was heavy with sadness on this cool, crisp day before the beginning of the rains. As she dug sweet potatoes and trimmed off the leaves to feed to her goats, the elderly medicine woman thought about her daughter-in-law's imminent departure. She did not want her son's wife to go, but Mama Wachera would not try to stop her. There was a call in the younger woman's heart, David's mother knew, a summons that only Wanjiru could hear and that she was compelled to answer. Mama Wachera had borne loneliness before; she would bear it again.

What a strange pass the world had come to! Not even her Bag of Questions could have foretold for Mama Wachera the internecine war that was tearing Kikuyuland asunder today. Nor even the most prophetic of her dreams could have shown her Kikuyu brother fighting Kikuyu brother, while the other tribes of Kenya looked on. How the ancestors must be lamenting, Mama Wachera thought, to see the forest fighters come down from the mountain and slay their African brothers and to see the comrades of those murdered men retaliate by hunting down and torturing any whom they suspected of being in league with the forest men. How had such madness come about?

Mama Wachera straightened and gazed up at the grassy ridge overlooking the river.

It had begun with the coming of the white man, she decided. *They* were the cause of this terrible war that was destroying her tribe. They had come many harvests ago, with their covered wagons and milk-skinned wives, and had started to spread their poison. When would it end? the old medicine woman wondered. When would Kikuyu stop killing Kikuyu and unite to drive the white man out of Kenya? When would they see the foolishness and shame of this fruitless war and combine their fighting strength against their one true enemy?

Mama Wachera thought about her son and wondered where David's loyalties lay.

Like many Kikuyu men, he chose to work for the white man and to live in a stone house near his job, leaving his wife to work the shamba. Wanjiru was luckier than most women, for David did not live far from her hut. The wives to be pitied were those whose husbands left them for jobs in Nairobi, where they lived in flats and drank European beer and slept with prostitutes. Those poor wives seldom saw their men, sometimes not for years, while Wanjiru was visited by David once a week, when he would stay the night in his *thingira* hut and eat food prepared by his wife and mother. On those visits David Mathenge honored his women with gifts of americani, sugar, and oil. In many ways, David's mother admitted, her son acted in true Kikuyu fashion.

But how, she wondered when she saw a truck pass along one of the dirt tracks among the Treverton coffee trees, could he work for the very woman whose father had stolen his land? It was a mystery Mama Wachera could not fathom. But being a respectful mother and mindful of her son's privacy, she would never think to ask him.

Mama Wachera went to the other side of the shamba, where Wanjiru was harvesting pumpkin leaves, and checked her banana plants.

She knew that her daughter-in-law had taken a Mau Mau oath. Many years ago, on the night of a terrifying storm, as her grandmother lay dying and waiting for the hyenas to devour her flesh, a young Wachera had eaten a similar oath. Oathing was part of the Kikuyu way of life; it was as old as the mists on Mount Kenya. Without oaths the Children of Mumbi would cease to be. But the oath Wanjiru had eaten had been disturbingly altered. For reasons unfathomable to Mama Wachera, her daughter-in-law had sworn her oath while holding the *mzungu* Bible; she had eaten the soil and pledged her word upon Jehovah.

What did that mean? Why such a subversion of sacred tribal ritual?

Mama Wachera feared that this evil Mau Mau was going to destroy the old ways forever. Those men in the forest, she decided, were not true, honorable Sons of Mumbi, but exactly what the white men called them, "thugs." Tribal discipline was breaking down, Kikuyu society was disintegrating, and misguided young men were jeering at their elders.

They do not fight for the soil, Mama Wachera thought as she filled her basket. *They fight to be wicked and to defy the ancestors.*

The hymn came to an end as the two women walked back to their huts, where twin spirals of smoke rose up from cook fires. Wanjiru knew that her mother-in-law did not approve of her decision to go. She knew that they would never agree on this issue, because Mama Wachera was an old woman, over a hundred and twenty harvests old by her own reckoning, which was sixty years in Wanjiru's estimation, and living in the past. When they talked about the Children of Mumbi's taking back the land that was rightfully theirs, all Mama Wachera could speak of was *thahu.* "They have been cursed," she repeatedly told Wanjiru. "I told them that they shall know only misfortune and misery until the land is returned to the African. And see? They have known misery. All dead, save for two, and no sons to inherit the land."

Such antiquated thinking and such stubbornness annoyed Wanjiru, but having been brought up to be modest and respectful in the presence of her elders, she had not argued. *Fighting*—that was what Wanjiru believed in. Only war was going to restore the stolen land to the African. "The tree of liberty is watered by blood," she had told her mother-in-law.

But Wanjiru was fighting for reasons other than simply to take back the land. Like many women who were joining Mau Mau, Wanjiru was fighting for her daughter's rights. She envisioned a future in which Hannah would have the freedom to go to school without being taunted by cruel boys, as had been Wanjiru's unfortunate girlhood experience; the freedom to work outside the home alongside men; the freedom to choose and pursue an honorable career; the freedom to walk at her husband's side as his equal, not behind as his beast of burden. Kikuyu mothers, Wanjiru believed, owed this fight to their daughters.

"Take the bark of the thorn tree," Mama Wachera instructed her son's wife now as Wanjiru prepared to depart. "From the youngest branches. Roll it in salt, and suck on it. This will cure stomach ailments and diarrhea."

Wanjiru listened while her mother-in-law spoke. They were packing a basket with medicines and healing charms. On top of these went boiled arrowroots and cold sweet potatoes, a few bananas, and some maize meal. When the basket was full, Wanjiru wrapped it in the blanket she was going to use for a sling, wedged a large calabash of water next to it, and down the sides she tucked the bullets and three pistols which had been smuggled to her that morning. Lastly she included hastily written notes and messages from wives to their freedom fighter husbands in the forest.

When all was ready, Wanjiru put two dresses on over the one she already wore, wrapped a bright red *kanga* around her shaved head, and swung, with her mother-in-law's help, the heavy blanket sling onto her back. A strap across her forehead held the sling in place so that her hands were free to carry Christopher, who was tied across her breast in a kanga, and Hannah, whom she held on her hip.

Outside the hut Mama Wachera paused to place a blessing upon this daughter, whom she suspected she might never see again. "I will take care of David for you," she said.

"David is my husband no longer," Wanjiru said, and then added the words which, by Kikuyu tradition, a woman could dissolve her marriage, "*I divorce him.* Do not fear for me, for I was born only once and I shall die only once."

Mama Wachera watched sadly as, bent beneath the weight of her burden, with a baby at her breast and a child on her hip, young and strong Wanjiru set out across the river and ultimately out of view.

SHE WALKED IN the afternoon sunshine, following a path that bisected newly planted fields waiting for the rains. Wanjiru walked in the warmth and laziness of the day, with flies droning in the hot sun, dust rising up from beneath her bare feet. Christopher, nearly a year old and very heavy, slept against his mother's comforting bosom, while three-year-old Hannah's head nodded upon her mother's shoulder.

It was not long before Wanjiru was joined on the path by a woman younger than she, who was wearing four dresses, a yellow *kanga* on her

head, and a sling full of food and water on her back. She emerged from
the bush and fell wordlessly into step at Wanjiru's side. Later they met
up with old Mama Gachiku, the mother of Njeri, who had been lifted
out of her belly by one memsaab and who had hanged herself in the
gazebo of another. Mama Gachiku, like Mama Wachera, was the
widow of the legendary Chief Mathenge, and she carried the Kikuyu
machete, called a panga, with her.

Presently they came upon a stream. After helping each other off with
their burdens, the women knelt and drank. They cooled their clean-
shaved heads in the rushing water, then rewrapped their *kangas* into
turbans. Mama Gachiku and the younger woman shared a cold sweet
potato while Wanjiru fed both her children from her breasts.

They took up their burdens again and continued up the gentle slope
of the mountain, not speaking, concentrating on their destination.
More women appeared on the path until by the time they plunged into
deep woods, they numbered twelve.

They followed Wanjiru, who had passed this way many times on her
secret missions, smuggling food and guns to the freedom fighters hiding
in the forest. When the women came upon a waterfall, Mama Gachiku
cut an arrowroot leaf, folded it, filled it with water, and passed it among
her companions.

They pressed on, silent and determined, each led by a vision that
impelled her. Mama Gachiku saw the body of her poor daughter,
hanging from a rafter in the eucalyptus glade—Njeri, bewitched by the
white man's ways and driven to a shameful and dishonorable death.
Nduta saw the face of her husband, beaten senseless by members of
the Kenya Police Reserve. Njambi and Muthoni were fueled by the
memory of their father's murder at the hands of white Kenya boys. And
Nyakio, the youngest of them, was driven by the memory of her brutal
rape by four drunken British soldiers. The twelve women had been
given the oath by Wanjiru; they all had sworn to turn their backs on
their old lives in order to fight for freedom. They had all made the
honor-bound decision to fight until the last white man was cast out of
Kenya and, if necessary, to die trying. Each knew that the oath, once
taken, bound them body and spirit to their word. If any one of them
should betray that trust, if any should pass information to the authorities about the secret camp in the forest, if any should disobey a com-

mand given by the field marshal, then she would die a terrible death.

As the day grew cool and dark, as the forest became all shadow and shape, the women moved closer together and followed Wanjiru's red turban as if it were a beacon.

Finally, before the light went from the forest altogether, Wanjiru brought her group to a halt at the base of a massive, ancient fig tree. Saying nothing, she relieved herself of her load and her children, helped the others do the same, then went to kneel at the foot of the tree.

The others joined her. The women knelt in a circle, with their foreheads pressed against the tree trunk, and they chanted a prayer to Ngai, the god of their ancestors. Then Wanjiru sat back, scooped up a handful of rich black soil, gazed down at it, and said, "The soil is ours."

Her companions did the same until all twelve were chanting softly, "The soil is ours. The soil is ours." Lastly, just before the final curtain of night descended over the woods, Wanjiru took some dirt into her mouth and chewed solemnly. Her sisters in war did likewise. They ate the earth, renewing their oath, and swore once again that the soil was theirs.

46

When the sign was unveiled, Mona was not surprised to see that it read WELCOME TO NAIROBI, CITY IN THE SUN.

The three hundred people present at the ceremony at this quiet roadside at the edge of Nairobi Wildlife Park, standing in the shade or sitting on folding chairs, clapped and praised Geoffrey Donald for his ingenuity. The slogan certainly gave their city an improved international image, they all declared, which was especially needed with Mau Mau being reported so heavily in the foreign press. This was bound to improve trade with overseas tour operators.

Mona stole a glance at her watch. She disliked these staged rituals, but she knew they served a very necessary purpose in the troubled colony. For one thing, to engage in familiar ceremony during a time of turmoil created a sense of unity and stability among the white settlers. For another, these events were meant to demonstrate that race relations were, in fact, good in Kenya, despite Mau Mau, and that the majority of Africans were obedient, law-abiding people. Nearly half the crowd today was "native," sitting on the ground or leaning on walking staffs, listening to Geoffrey Donald's speech. There were several prominent chiefs in the crowd, proud Kikuyu elders in their characteristic mix of Western and African dress. One such man was stately old Irungu, the powerful and influential chief who had convinced his people to attend this event and thereby show proof of good feelings toward the whites. Irungu wore khaki shorts, a checkered tablecloth around his shoulders, and, on his feet, sandals made from car tires. He wore traditional plugs in his earlobes; a gourd of tobacco was hung about his neck, and a thong which held his snuff container. He had wristwatches on both arms and was seated next to the deputy governor, who wore a somber navy blue suit and Eton tie. Mau Mau appeared to be the farthest thing on the minds of these dignified leaders.

Mona checked the time again, paying no attention to Geoffrey's speech, and scanned the edge of the crowd for David. But all she saw were "Tommies," British soldiers standing with their Sten guns in a large, protective circle around the audience. Any gatherings of Europeans with African loyalists were feared to be prime targets for Mau Mau, even though, as yet, in the five months since the emergency was declared, no such anticipated trouble had materialized.

It was noon. Mona wondered where David was.

She wished she weren't expected to attend these functions, but because she was a Treverton, and Kenya whites were locked into their precious traditions, she had no choice. Years ago her parents had fulfilled the settlers' craving for aristocracy. Now it was up to Mona and Grace to play the part. She hated to be called Lady Mona, but it pleased farm wives to do so. Even more, on this dreadfully hot day with dry, blasting winds, did Mona hate the royal blue gabardine suit she had to wear, with its fashionably tight-fitting jacket, tight-fitting sleeves, cinched waist, and wide, flaring skirt. To add to her discomfort, she wore white gloves and carried a white plastic purse, and her feet were squeezed into impractical white pumps. She couldn't wait to get home and into comfortable pedal pushers and sloppy, man-tailored shirt.

She felt those in the audience around her start to fidget. A cough here, a shooed fly there, and many makeshift fans attempting to cool hot faces. The November rains had never come; then the February rains had failed to arrive. It was now March with no sign or smell of impending rain. This was no time, Mona decided as she thought about her coffee trees wilting in the hot sun, for Geoffrey to demonstrate his talent for long-winded speeches. Revenue from tourist shillings and dollars was the thrust of his uninspired talk, and apparently he was going to achieve such a feat single-handedly by carting middle-class holidaymakers around on African adventure safaris.

Mona closed out Geoffrey's drone, which seemed to her to get more nasal and la-di-da with each passing year, and thought about David.

He had driven down to Nairobi with her that morning, a trip which now took on the average of only three hours because of the new paved road from Nyeri. They had had to stop only twice for tire punctures and once for radiator boilover. Then she had let him take the Mercedes while she had come out to the unveiling ceremony with Geoffrey and Ilse.

David was using the Mercedes to search for his wife. Because it was unusual to see an African driving such a fine car and he was bound to be stopped and questioned, Mona had given him a letter of permission. But he was supposed to have been back by now; she hoped he hadn't run into trouble. Some of the Home Guard, African ex-soldiers who had volunteered to fight Mau Mau and who abused their temporary police privileges with arrogance and Gestapo-like methods, were known to beat up someone first and ask questions later. Mona tried to reassure herself that David could take care of himself.

Still, she worried. In fact, Mona was starting to worry more and more about David. Mau Mau incidents were on the increase. Instead of "blowing over," as Geoffrey had predicted back in October, the campaign of terrorism had escalated, and the majority of targets were loyalists—Africans who worked for or were friends of Europeans.

David had gone into Nairobi to search for Wanjiru, who had disappeared mysteriously a few days ago with the two children.

Since the declaration of the state of emergency Kenya's roads were seeing an unusual and inexplicable mass movement of women and children. Mona had watched them trudge along the dusty paths that bordered her estate, silent, marching women with loads on their backs and children clinging to their skirts. Where were they going? everyone asked. What had triggered this bizarre exodus? "Something is brewing" was the speculation. Whatever it was, thousands of women were streaming into Nairobi, the majority of them frightened by Mau Mau and hoping to join their husbands in the city. David had gone there on the thin hope that Wanjiru had joined that exodus and that he would find her there.

When the crowd laughed at one of Geoffrey's jokes, Mona was brought out of herself. She suddenly realized she had spent the morning thinking of David. Again.

She couldn't pinpoint when David Mathenge had begun to insinuate himself into her thoughts, appearing unbidden, in the form of an image of his beautiful smile or the memory of something he had said. Mona would be reading a book or arranging flowers, and she would find herself thinking about him. It seemed, in fact, once she really considered it, to have begun a long time ago.

When Mona searched her memory, she found David there all the way back to her childhood. As a girl she had resented him because of her mother's attention to his sister; as a teenager Mona had watched him grow into an arrogant political agitator; then she had blamed him for her brother's death; and lastly she had heard about David's heroic actions in Palestine and his receiving a medal. He had attended her mother's trial every day and had then taken the job as her plantation manager, which he had been working at these past seven years. It had come as something of a shock to Mona to realize how much a part of her life Wachera's son had been; in fact, Mona had discovered to her mild surprise that there never really had been a time in her life when she had not given some thought to David Mathenge.

But now she was beginning to find, in rising dismay, that those thoughts were turning into feelings. And they, too, she discovered upon examination, had been with her for a long time.

A pair of giraffes, grazing on a nearby flat-topped thorn tree, paused to look at the crowd of people. Mona watched them as they stood still, their tall, gawky bodies backdropped by yellow plains that stretched away to lavender hills; then they turned and moved on. They seemed unconcerned with the human presence. Perhaps these two had not learned to fear humans, Mona decided, because they lived on a protected reserve. Hunting and poaching were outlawed in this area, thanks to Grace Treverton and her unrelenting campaign for the preservation of Kenya's wildlife. It was through such areas that Geoffrey Donald drove his handfuls of vacationers, guaranteeing them good photographic opportunities of the lion, giraffe, elephant, and zebra.

Mona returned her attention to the road and felt her worry mount. David was late.

HE DROVE SLOWLY, anticipating the next roadblock, the next interrogation at the hands of half-educated, swaggering home guards who liked to push men like him around.

David clutched the steering wheel until his fingers dug into his palms. He had spent hours searching, and he had not found Wanjiru.

But what he had found had appalled him.

Thousands of homeless and husbandless women were living in the African estates of Kariorkor, Bahati, and Shauri Moyo Locations, crowded into dismal one-room apartments that had no plumbing or cooking facilities, making do with water from community taps in the streets, living in filthy, squalid conditions because they had left their farms, where they felt vulnerable to Mau Mau attacks, for the imagined safety of the city. In his search David had learned how the majority of these helpless women managed to survive—by attaching themselves to men in return for sexual favors. A passbook system had been established on the declaration of the emergency: It was designed to help the authorities monitor people's movements and to aid in identifying and capturing rebels. Each Nairobi resident was required to obtain a passbook, and the requirements needed to qualify for one were proof of employment for a man, support for a woman. Any woman who could not produce a husband or any male responsible for her, like a brother or father, was labeled a prostitute, arrested, and deported to her village, where she no longer had a home. Since none wanted to be returned to the shambas, the women either hid and lived in fear of being found out or managed one way or another to obtain "husbands."

Outraged at the filth, the smell, the wretched existence of these unprotected and abandoned women, David had gone through the tenements, and he had prayed with each fearful or sullen expression he encountered that he would not find his wife and children here.

In the end he had not, and now he was on the road going out of the city to meet Mona at Geoffrey Donald's new sign.

Was this the time, David asked himself as he channeled his anger and frustration toward the man he hated, to be writing slogans and attracting tourist trade? With Jomo Kenyatta, an innocent and peaceful man to David's thinking, undergoing an unfair trial and cruel detention, with twenty thousand African children out of school because the British had closed the Kikuyu Independent Schools, with people being murdered in their huts, with women being terrorized and raped by undisciplined Home Guards and giving themselves to strange men in exchange for protection, with Kikuyu killing Kikuyu and the whole of Kenya falling apart and disgracing itself in the eyes of the world—was *this* a time to be making speeches and unveiling signs? *My God*, David thought, *the man must be as stupid as his face.*

But David knew that Geoffrey Donald was not a stupid man; on the contrary, he was very smart and therefore to be watched with great caution. That was one of the reasons David hated Geoffrey. Another was Geoffrey's close friendship with Mona. The man tried to run her life, David had observed, forever giving her unnecessary advice or criticizing the way she did things. Mona, for reasons beyond David's understanding, tolerated it. He also didn't like the fact that Geoffrey was always over at Bellatu and that he seemed to spend more time with Mona than with his own wife. But what David disliked most of all about Geoffrey Donald was the way he sometimes looked at Mona.

David recalled now how Geoffrey and Mona had once ridden horses on the polo field. He remembered the day she'd fallen off her horse and Geoffrey had lifted her up and kissed her.

David's grip tightened on the steering wheel.

Quite a few African soldiers, stationed overseas during the war, had had intimate relations with white women—prostitutes mainly, but also European women who were curious about African men and hadn't grown up with the racial prejudice most Kenya white women had. Those soldiers had done a lot of boasting. European women, they had declared to their comrades in the segregated barracks, were more responsive and more easily satisfied than African women were because they had not undergone the *irua* operation. More than that, the soldiers had bragged, European women appreciated the amorous skills of the African warrior.

It had disgusted David, whose heart and body had burned for Wanjiru. And after the war he had disapproved of those men who had brought back European wives. It was an insult, he had said, to their African sisters.

When he finally sighted the crowd at the roadside, David slowed the car and let it roll to a stop. He looked for Mona among the audience, which, he noted in resentment, was cleanly divided between African and white, the former sitting out in the hot sun on the ground, the latter on chairs under the shade. He had been told that later there would be refreshments at the Norfolk Hotel, with the whites inside the coolness of the elegant dining room, the "natives" out on the lawn. So much, he decided bitterly, for racial integration.

He saw Mona sitting near the dais.

As he stared at her, David recalled again that morning of sixteen years ago when he had seen Mona and Geoffrey riding on the polo field. He pictured them now—the way they had stood with their arms around one another, their mouths pressed together. Kikuyu men who had discovered kissing, in their exposure to European women, had declared it the greatest gift civilization had brought to Africa.

David watched Mona as she discreetly searched the edge of the crowd. When her eyes met his, her mouth lifted in a brief smile. He thought he saw a look of relief pass over her face, as if she had been worrying about him.

He cursed his feelings for her; they felt like a betrayal of his people.

As David listened to the applause for Geoffrey Donald's vapid speech, he tried once again, as he had so many times, to analyze and understand, and therefore to figure out, how to rid himself of his growing desire for Mona Treverton.

As a thinking, educated man David Mathenge believed that any difficulty could be overcome and solved through rational, conscientious process. He spoke about it at KAU meetings, urging his comrades not to take the terrorist way out, explaining that, as he had seen with his own eyes in Palestine, such action only provoked a like counteraction, with the result being a never-ending war. "We must have the respect of all the nations of the world," he said repeatedly. "If we are to stand on our own and govern ourselves as other countries do, then it must be as honorable men. Mau Mau is dishonorable. I do not want an *uhuru* gotten by such means. Mau Mau must not win." It was the only way, he believed, to rid Kenya of an unwanted evil. Therefore, in the same way David hoped to rid himself of his unwanted feelings for Mona.

When had the desire begun? He didn't know. Possibly the birth of this second, unwanted hunger had happened at the time of the death of his love for Wanjiru, six years ago, when she had driven his love for her out of his heart with her sharp voice, her cutting words, her open scorn for his belief in a peaceful revolution. Perhaps, when his heart was suddenly emptied of desire and affection for his wife and left cold and wanting, he had been vulnerable. But why Mona Treverton? he wondered. A woman who was, in fact, his enemy. Why hadn't he turned his affections to any one of the many husbandless women in the village, all of whom would have been anxious to please him and not a few of whom were young and pretty? Why this white woman, who was too pale and skinny by African standards, whom he had once hated, and who lived a life alien to his own and had no real knowledge or comprehension of the Kikuyu way of life?

I could teach her, his traitorous heart whispered.

It was not, however, as simple as that. There were insurmountable obstacles to the outrageous fantasy David entertained.

Kikuyu men who married white women were cast out of the tribe and disinherited because it was taboo for a Kikuyu man to lie down with an uncircumcised woman. He brought shame to himself and to his family; he dishonored his father's name and his ancestors. His mother, David knew, would be devastated if she suspected his feelings for the white woman—a hundred times more so because this particular white woman was among those she had cursed on Christmas Eve nearly thirty-four years ago.

David pounded the steering wheel.

It was all so convoluted! David respected and feared and believed in his mother's *thahu.* He believed that Mona was truly doomed, as her brother and parents had been. He wanted to save Mona from his mother's curse. But to defy Wachera would be to dishonor himself and revile his ancestors. He would be no better than Mau Mau and therefore not a man worthy to live.

But there was an even greater obstacle to his madness. There was the question of Mona's feelings toward him.

On the day she had hired him as her estate manager, Mona had apologized to him for her cruelty to him when they were children. Her voice had been so sincere, her smile so warm, and she had held out her hand to him—a gesture that would put an African in jail were it to be witnessed—that David's resentment of her and his plans for revenge had been shaken. In the seven years since, she had treated him as a friend and equal. Those occasions in which he was aware of their racial separation were few and far between. But surely, he told himself as he watched the audience break up now that Geoffrey's speech was over, surely that was all David was to Mona: a friend!

Lastly, there was the color bar.

This was what made a mockery of his insane desire for her and what convinced him that Mona would only ever look upon him as a friend, the fact that, quite simply, Kenyan Africans and Kenyan whites never crossed that crucial line.

David started the car and drove closer. He parked, got out, and waited for Mona to finish talking with Geoffrey. There was a great deal of handshaking and congratulating among the whites, while the Africans slowly dispersed and began the long, hot walk to the Norfolk for their free refreshments.

Geoffrey escorted Mona to her car, his hand on her arm, both of them laughing. When he saw David, Geoffrey said in a not too discreet voice, "Really, Mona, don't you think it rather irregular that you let that boy of yours drive your car?"

She stopped and pulled her arm away. "I wish you hadn't said that, Geoff. And I'll thank you not to say anything like that in my presence again."

He watched her go, a cold, smoldering look on his face.

"I'm sorry, David," Mona said quietly. "I'm sorry you heard that."

"He is entitled to his opinion, as long as I am entitled to mine."

She smiled. Then, remembering the reason for his needing the car, she asked what success he had had in Nairobi.

He gazed past her and out across the plains. Mona was wearing the lavender scent again. "None. I found no trace of Wanjiru or anyone who could give me information. I fear now that she is not in Nairobi after all." It was not that David wanted his wife back—she had divorced him; she was free to go—but the children were his, and it was for them, Christopher and Hannah, that he searched.

He was about to say something further when a great roar suddenly filled the sky. Everyone looked up to see four New Zealand jet fighters streak across the blue. They were heading for the Aberdare forest in the north.

"That'll show 'em we mean business!" someone said. "That'll put the fear of God into the Mau Mau bastards!"

A police car appeared on the road, driving at a furious rate, not slowing down for people in the way but only when it drew near to the deputy governor. Before the car had stopped, a white policeman in khaki uniform jumped out and came running with a piece of paper in his hand. Everyone watched as the deputy governor read the dispatch. When he said, "Oh, my God," Geoffrey took the paper and read it.

"What is it?" Mona asked.

"There's been a massacre in the village at Lari! Mau Mau locked the huts and set fire to the roofs! A hundred and seventy-two people were either burned alive or slashed to death with pangas when they tried to escape!"

"When?"

"This morning. No one knows the identities of the attackers. . . ."

Geoffrey looked at David.

47

On June 14, 1953, four African women walked into the dining room of the very posh and elegant Queen Victoria Hotel on Lord Treverton Avenue and sat down at a table spread with Irish linen, china, and silver.

The white patrons in the dining room fell into a stunned silence as the four calmly gave food orders to the shocked African waiter. The women, who wore cotton print dresses and *kanga* turbans on their heads, requested *irio* and *posho*, traditional Kenya dishes, which, of course, the Queen Victoria did not serve.

Recovering from their shock and realizing what this was about, the indignant white customers got up and left. A few minutes later the police arrived. The four women put up a terrific fight, which resulted in the destruction of much china and crystal, flower vases, and the dessert cart. Three were arrested, but one managed to escape, running through the kitchen with her baby bouncing on her back. Before disappearing down the alley and from there into the warrens of Nairobi's crowded African sections, she turned and hurled a rock through one of the Queen Victoria's windows. It had a note tied around it which read, "The soil is ours," and it was signed "Field Marshal Wanjiru Mathenge."

"JAMES, I HAVE already told you, and I mean it! I will *not* carry a gun." Grace put the revolver back into his hands and walked away.

"Damn it, Grace! Listen to me! We have a desperately bad situation here! All the missions are being hit. You heard what happened to the Scottish mission last week."

Grace pressed her mouth into a stubborn line. Yes, she had heard about it; it had made her sick, and she hadn't slept since. What the Mau Mau terrorists had done to those poor, innocent people! It was even worse than the Lari Massacre back in March. And this strike had taken place in broad daylight! Mau Mau were getting bolder, their tactics viler.

The government, in Grace's opinion, had made a big mistake in finding Jomo Kenyatta guilty and sentencing him to seven years' hard labor. He should not have been arrested in the first place, to her thinking; there was no proof that he was the force behind Mau Mau. And now, instead of putting a stop to the "freedom" movement, the unjust treatment of Kenyatta had only served to fan the flames. Thousands—jobless and dissolute young desperadoes who had nothing to live for and who cared only for killing and stealing—were fleeing into the forests every day.

The heaviest Mau Mau activity was in the area around Bellatu and Grace Mission. The Royal Air Force was now steadily and systematically bombing the Aberdare forests nearby; Tommies were seen in great numbers, setting up roadblocks, interrogating everyone; all telephones had been taken over by the government, all conversations were screened, and only English was allowed.

Mau Mau was escalating, not just in the number of freedom fighters in the forest but in general Kikuyu sympathy. African children were being taught to sing hymns substituting the word *God* with *Jomo;* servants, once loyal and trusted, were becoming the willing or unwilling agents of Mau Mau; white settlers were now asked to lock their house staff out of the house at 6:00 P.M. and not to let them back in until morning. All over, no one knew whom to trust, whom to suspect.

And the atrocities were mounting—on both sides. Loyalist headmen were being murdered daily; the missions attacked; settlers' cattle mutilated; home guards torturing suspects by burning their eardrums with cigarettes. The oath-taking ceremony, which had once been described in the newspapers, was becoming increasingly more savage and obscene—children were now used, and animals—so that such descriptions were no longer printable.

The whole world, it seemed, had gone mad.

"I'm asking you for my sake, Grace," James said as he followed her into the living room. "I won't rest until I know you're protected."

"If I carry a gun, James, it means that I intend to kill someone. I will not kill, James."

"Not even in self-defense?"

"I can take care of myself."

In exasperation he holstered the gun and set it on the table. Absolutely every settler in the province had taken to wearing a gun except for this stubborn, obstinate woman. At sixty-four Grace still carried herself with the determination of the old days, that square-shouldered, stiff-upper-lip willfulness that had been one of the reasons he had fallen in love with her. But she was gray-haired now and wore glasses. In the eyes of Mau Mau, a frail, defenseless white woman!

Mario came in, a little stooped and completely gray after all these years with Memsaab Daktari. He brought a tray of tea and sandwiches and was about to set it on the table when he saw the gun.

"These are bad days, bwana," he said sadly. "Very bad days."

"Mario," said James as he picked up the gun so that the tray could be set down, "we suspect there is an oath giver in this area. Do you have any knowledge of that?"

"No, bwana. I do not believe in oaths. I am a good Christian man."

Yes, thought James darkly. And another prime target for Mau Mau. Was this Grace's defense? An aging houseboy whose devotion to his white mistress could mean his death sentence?

"Memsaab," Mario said, "Daktari Nathan says he will need your help in surgery this afternoon. There are twelve more boys needing to be done."

"Thank you, Mario. Tell him I will be there." Grace sat down next to the radio. "Poor Dr. Nathan. He's doing twenty circumcisions a day now. And I understand the Nairobi hospitals are swamped with cases."

It was all because the tribal circumcisers—witch doctors—had been rounded up and jailed as Mau Mau suspects. Kikuyu parents, frantic to maintain tradition, were turning to local hospitals, where surgeons performed the operation under less than traditional conditions. Only the girls continued to be circumcised in the old way, by Mama Wachera.

Grace turned the radio on. When "Doggie in the Window" came through, she murmured, "Everything is American now."

She shifted the dial. The Nairobi news broadcast reported first on international events—in the United States the Rosenbergs, accused spies, had been executed; the USSR had exploded its first hydrogen bomb—and then the voice of General Erskine, the new head of the East African Command, came on.

First he announced the government ban on the KAU and its restriction on the formation of any African political group. Then he said, "From bitter personal experience, you know more about Mau Mau than I do. I only know that this Evil Creed has led to crimes of the greatest savagery and violence and that respect for law and order must be restored without delay. I have been sent by the War Office and shall get on at once with this task. I shall not be satisfied until every loyal citizen of Kenya can go about his work in peace, safety, and security."

"So," James said quietly, "General Erskine is here. I would say that they have sent in the big guns."

AFTER THE BROADCAST James and Grace left her house and followed one of the paved lanes that crisscrossed the thirty acres of Grace Mission. This location had been decided on as being the best for emergency settler meetings. The mission was central to most farms, and one of the schoolrooms could accommodate the large crowd that always attended. When they arrived, they found Tim Hopkins standing on a box in front of the blackboard, calling for attention.

It was uncomfortably hot in the classroom, even with all the windows open. Nearly a hundred angry and frightened settlers, with gun holsters on their hips and rifles in their hands, sweated in heat that had oppressed the colony unabatedly since March. The tension in the air was due to more than just Mau Mau: with the continuing drought there was a prediction of ninety-five percent crop failure.

"Can we have it quiet, *please?*" Tim called, but to no effect.

Everyone, it seemed, was talking at once. Hugo Kempler, a rancher from Nanyuki, was telling Alice Hopkins about his thirty-two cows that had been poisoned by Mau Mau. "Autopsy found arsenic in their maize."

Alice, in turn, told of the disappearance of her entire labor force. "Sixty of them, all gone off in one night. That was last week, and not a one has come back. My sisal and pyrethrum are going unharvested. If I don't find labor soon, my entire farm will go bust."

Finally, because he was unheard over the din, her brother pulled out his gun and fired it into the air. The crowd was instantly silenced.

"Now listen!" he shouted, wiping his perspiring face with a handkerchief. "We've got to do something! There's an oath giver in this area, and we have to find him! And fast!"

A rumble of agreement went through the crowd. Mrs. Langley, who had come out to Kenya with her husband in 1947 upon India's independence, stood up in her prim cotton dress and gun holster and said, "We've tried talking to our chaps, but we get nowhere. We try bribes or threats, but they just won't talk."

Heads nodded; murmurs went around. They all knew it was impossible to get the Kikuyu to talk about Mau Mau. Although many Africans were sympathizers, many were not, but they kept silent out of fear. Only last month a man who had given evidence in Nairobi in a special Mau Mau court was later seen being forced into a car by four men and hadn't been seen since. Even those who testified under police interrogation and signed statements did not then later show up in court and were unlikely ever to be heard from again.

Mr. Langley stood up next to his wife. A small, weathered man, he had left India because, like hundreds of others who had swarmed to Kenya in 1947, he could not abide living under "native" rule. "I lost my best headman two nights ago," he said. "He was locked inside his hut and burned alive with his wife and two children. And then all my dogs were poisoned." He paused. There were tears in his eyes. "We hadn't been hit until then. It was done by our own chaps, I'm sure of it. They'd been loyal until they were forced to take the oath."

Fear stood out on every settler face. The power of the oath, once taken, was their biggest, most insidious threat. Devoted houseboys, treated for years like family, could overnight be made into assassins. Even if the oath was forced upon him, once a Kikuyu had eaten the raw dog flesh and drunk the cup of blood, he could not disobey a command from Mau Mau.

"The trouble is," Tim said, "we have to find a better way to fight these monsters. How can you fight an enemy that never shows itself? We all know how it is for Mau Mau. They live in hidden camps in the forest, they're supplied with food and clothing and medical supplies by women who smuggle them all in, and they're provided with information on the movements of the security forces. They have an incredible network of communication—using hollow trees as letter boxes! Only last week they were successful in staging a boycott of Nairobi buses, and they've stopped Africans from buying European cigarettes and beer. The wogs are far more impressed by fear of Mau Mau than by any desire to restore law and order!"

Everyone started talking again, and Tim had to shoot his pistol once more. "What we've got to do," he shouted, "is find out who the oath givers are! That's our priority. Then we have to find the secret underground. Find out who's smuggling guns and ammunition to Mau Mau. And once that's done, cut the bloody lines to them and starve them out of the bloody forest!"

Mona, who stood at the rear of the classroom with Geoffrey, stared at Tim Hopkins. She had never seen him like this. His face was red; his eyes blazed. He was exploding with anger and bloodlust. In the past few months Tim had become what the people called a "Kenya cowboy," a self-appointed vigilante with a contingent of riders, a sort of farmers' cavalry, whose purpose was to aid isolated farms. Such private forces were manned mostly by the sons of settlers, European boys born in Kenya who were fighting to hold on to land that they believed was as much theirs as the Africans'. Young men like Tim resented the word *native* in reference to the black tribes, arguing that Kenya-born whites were just as "native" and had just as much right to ownership of this country. While some of these cowboys were compelled by noble purpose and acted in a civilized way, many of them were just as sadistic and barbaric as Mau Mau. They were known for arbitrarily stopping Africans and giving them thorough beatings with little or no cause. Tim, Mona prayed, would not turn into one such as they.

"What I do not understand," said the soft-spoken voice of Father Vittorio, "is why the government simply does not give them what they want."

"Why should they do that?" asked Mr. Kempler.

"The Africans are not asking for so much, are they? Better wages, trade unions, the freedom to grow coffee, the elimination of the color bar—"

"We give in to the niggers," shouted another man, "and they'll take everything!"

"But Mau Mau would be finished if the government gave the Africans economic and political equality with us."

"Why don't we just hand over the whole lot and pack up and leave?"

"Gentlemen!" Tim called. "Please! Let's not fight among ourselves. We have to decide on what to do about this oath giving."

Mona grew impatient. Nothing new was being said at this meeting, the heat was deplorable, and the gun holster hung heavily and uncomfortably around her hips. Stepping back a few feet so that she stood by the open doorway, she looked around the mission compound. It seemed unusually quiet today.

She thought about David. At that moment he was working in the hot sun somewhere on the estate, fighting to save her crop. She knew she should be with him.

Mona recalled their conversation of two days ago, when they had paused in their work to sit under a tree with a thermos of cold lemonade. David had spoken softly, his voice barely louder than the drone of bees around them: "Violence does the African cause harm. It is essential that the solutions to our problems be based on truth and nonviolence. I saw what terrorism did to Palestine, and I see what it continues to do now in the new state of Israel. I doubt that in thirty years the fighting between Arab and Jew will have ended. We all should follow the great example of Mahatma Gandhi.

"You know, Mona, Mau Mau would be finished if Britain would only grant economic and political freedom to Kenyans. But instead, they have committed the blunder of banning the KAU. My political party had nothing to do with Mau Mau. We met peacefully and tried to work out our differences through legal channels. But the government has proscribed the KAU, and that was a big mistake."

David always talked to her that way—honestly, directly, and with an aim to make his position clear. Not like Geoffrey, who lectured her and talked down to her as if she were a child. On that sultry afternoon under the tree, when they sat alone and far away from prying eyes, sharing the lemonade, David had said, "A new world has come out of this last war, Mona. Britain is no longer master of the world. She must see that Asia and Africa are rejecting her. Once people break out in violence, it goes on and on, and in the end the government will make concessions—we know that. Why, then, not make the concessions *now?*"

He had turned to face her, his voice earnest. "British policy over the past fifty years has forced the Africans to resort to violence in order to wrest bit by bit a measure of human freedom. Look at the tragic examples of Ireland, Israel, Malaya, and Cyprus. I wonder, Mona, when Britain will learn the folly of the repression and the denial of human dignity!"

A hot breeze came up. Mona stepped outside, hoping for relief. The air was heavy. Flies and bees filled the heat with their hum. The corrugated tin rooftops of the mission's many buildings shimmered in the sun and sent up transparent heat waves. The silence was profound. It seemed to Mona as if the world slept. Grace Mission, normally a center of constant activity, appeared to be sleeping through the oppressive afternoon. In fact, she realized in puzzlement, there wasn't the usual pedestrian traffic about. It seemed that within the past few minutes everyone had disappeared: nurses; patients; doctors in white lab coats; visitors bringing food and flowers.

Inside the classroom James was trying to tell the panicked settlers not to lose their heads when Mona saw a car suddenly appear on one of the paved lanes. It was approaching at a terrific speed, the driver pressing the horn. When she saw David jump out and come running toward her, she went to meet him.

"What is it, David?"

He seized her arm. "You must get away! *Now!*"

"What—"

He started to pull her away.

The others, having heard the horn and the screech of brakes, ran to the door and windows and looked out. "Run!" David shouted to them. "Mau Mau!"

And then it hit.

They appeared from out of nowhere, all at once, surrounding the classroom. Men with pangas and spears and rifles materialized from the bushes and trees, their long hair twisted into the formidable dreadlocks of Mau Mau.

David ran with Mona as shooting erupted all around them. Flaming torches flew through the air, crashed through the classroom windows. From inside came screams.

A flying rock narrowly missed Mona's head. Bullets whistled past her ears as she ran with David, his hand tight on hers. They reached a small storage shed. Mona stumbled and fell. David caught her up and pulled her to him. In the brief shelter behind the shed he held her tight, and she clung to him. They heard the frenzied yelps of the forest men as they besieged the classroom. Gunfire thundered; glass shattered. There was screaming and shouting. In the distance came the wail of the alarm siren.

Mona and David held on to each other for a moment. Then he drew back and said, "Go to my mother's hut! You will be safe there!"

"No."

"Mona, damn it! Do as I say! They are after *us!* Don't you understand?"

"I won't leave you!"

He pulled the gun from her holster. "Run to the car as fast as you can. I'll keep them off with this."

"No!"

A spear clattered on the tin roof of the shed. A bullet exploded in the masonry by Mona's arm. David took her hand again; they dashed from the shed and fell into the shelter of a large hedge. Mona stared in shock at the scene before her.

The classroom was on fire; bodies of Mau Mau and settlers were already strewn on the ground. She saw David raise the gun, aim, and fire. A terrorist, about to throw a fire bomb, froze, then dropped. David fired again. Another Mau Mau fell. At the classroom windows she saw Geoffrey and his father shooting through broken glass at the onrushing Africans. A woman—Mrs. Langly—came running out. A Mau Mau spear went through her stomach.

There seemed to be hundreds of them, feral men waving pangas and spears, dressed in rags, their faces wild and filled with bloodlust. Mona saw one trying to climb through a rear window of the classroom. "David!" she screamed. He fired. The man fell dead.

They kept coming. They dropped as settler bullets found their marks. But Mau Mau, too, were shooting guns, their bullets going through windows and finding targets inside. Flames leaped everywhere. Smoke billowed up to the placid sky. Two more white men came out of the classroom, stumbling and coughing. Both fell beneath the pangas of Mau Mau lying in wait.

Mona saw Mr. Kempler drop to his knees as six Africans slaughtered him with their blades.

Father Vittorio came out waving a white cloth. A fiery torch was thrust at him; his black cassock burst into flame.

Mona heard David's gun click. He said, "I need more bullets," and she stared at him.

"I haven't any!"

A Mau Mau spotted the two behind the hedge. He gave out a yell, and a gang of comrades followed him. David and Mona jumped up and ran. They zigzagged along the garden paths that lay between mission buildings. They jumped over hedges, dashed around corners. The Mau Mau followed, yelping like hunting hounds, hurling rocks and spears, firing pistols.

The entrance to the mission, a broad, arching wrought-iron gate, appeared before them. Beyond it lay the polo field, grown over with weeds and yellow from the drought. At the far end of that, on the other side of a rusting chain link fence, stood the huts of Mama Wachera and the woman who had once been David's wife.

"Go to my mother!" David said again. "She will protect you! I will go this way, and they'll follow me."

"No, David. I won't leave you!"

He looked at her.

Then he said, "This way!"

They found the door of the machine shop standing open. Inside it was cool and dark; cars and trucks stood in various stages of repair. It was, like the rest of the mission, deserted. David took Mona's hand; they darted inside.

They moved quickly and silently between the autos, stepped around oil drums, dodged hanging tires. Then the light from the doorway was blocked by the silhouettes of their pursuers. The terrorists hesitated.

David led Mona into the darkest corner, where they crouched behind a workbench. He searched for a weapon and seized a bicycle chain. Mona held on to him. She could hardly breathe; her mouth had gone dry with fear.

They watched the silhouettes shift in the doorway, heard the men argue quietly among themselves.

Mona felt David's muscles tighten. His body was hard, coiled to spring. She trembled. He put his arm around her and drew her closer to him.

Suddenly a shape loomed up beside them, and a hand shot out of the dark. Mona screamed. She seemed to fly up out of David's hold; her feet left the ground.

David saw the massive hand that had seized her by the hair. He saw the second hand raise up, the bloodied panga poised to come down across her throat.

He flew at the man, driving the chain against the Mau Mau's head.

The hand released Mona. She fell among the tools and car jacks. Dazed, she saw the two men struggle. Then she saw the others come rushing in.

She fumbled frantically in the dark. Her hand fell upon a tire iron.

The first Mau Mau to reach her received a cracking blow across his shins. He cried out and dropped his spear.

Mona stood up and lashed out again. She heard the satisfying snap of bone as the iron came down on his shoulder.

But now the others were upon them. She saw David overwhelmed by them; he fell beneath blows and kicks. She felt hands reaching for her, pulling at her clothing. She tried to fight. She struck out blindly with the iron. But she knew there was no hope.

David. . .

Suddenly the terrorists drew back and began to run from the garage. Mona blinked in bewilderment. Then she heard the police sirens, the roar of airplane engines.

She dropped to her knees and reached for David. He was on his side, moaning. "They're gone. . ." she said. "The soldiers have arrived."

After a moment they were able to help each other up. They stood in the darkness, arms around each other for support, then staggered out into the sunlight.

When they arrived at the classroom, where a bucket brigade was dousing the fire and where soldiers were putting handcuffs on captured Mau Mau, Mona ran to her aunt, who was bandaging Mr. Langly's head.

"Eight of us dead," Grace said. She herself had received no wounds, but her face was smudged with dirt; her silver hair had come out of its bun and trailed over her shoulders. "They killed eight of us. . . ."

Mona looked around. She saw Sir James, Geoffrey, and Tim conferring with the command officer. She saw Mrs. Kempler, weeping over her husband's barely recognizable body, being comforted by a nurse. The captured Mau Mau were being treated roughly; several received knocks on the head with clubs. At the periphery of the brutal scene a few Africans looked on with blank expressions. Mona knew who they were—mission workers. Where had they gone to? she wondered. How had they known about the attack?

And then poor old Mario, trembling and crying, came running from the house and stood over Grace, wringing his hands.

Mona turned to look back over her shoulder. She saw four British soldiers surrounding David. One of them suddenly delivered a fist into David's stomach. He dropped to his knees, doubled over.

"Stop!" Mona cried, running to them. Geoffrey, hearing her, also came running.

"Stop!" she screamed, pushing through the soldiers. She knelt next to David and put her arm around him. "What the hell do you think you're doing?" she screamed at the soldiers.

"He's a suspect, Miss Treverton. We're getting information from him."

"This man is no suspect, you idiot! He's my estate manager!"

"Looks like Mau Mau to me," said another.

"What's this all about?" said Geoffrey as he came up.

"This boy was resisting arrest, sir. We're taking him in for questioning."

"You are not!" said Mona. "And he isn't a *boy!*"

Geoffrey looked down at Mona. She was kneeling in the dirt next to David Mathenge. "They have to take him in, Mona. They have to question everyone."

"Don't you dare touch him. *David saved my life!*"

The soldiers looked at one another.

Geoffrey scowled down at her.

"He came to warn us," Mona said. "You know that, Geoffrey."

"Yes, and he came a bit late to help, don't you think? I wonder how he knew of the attack."

Mona glared up at him, her arm protectively around David.

Geoffrey met her gaze for a moment, saw the challenge in her eyes, the determined set of her mouth—for an instant it was like looking at the face of Valentine Treverton—then slapped his thigh and said to the soldiers, "You heard her. This boy was helping us fight the Mau Mau. He isn't one of them. You can let him go."

When Geoffrey and the soldiers were gone, Mona said, "Are you all right, David?"

He nodded. But there was a nasty cut on his forehead, a bruise on his cheek; a trickle of blood came from the corner of his mouth.

"Come on. Aunt Grace will see to you."

But David said, "No." He moved out from under Mona's arm and stood. "I will go to my mother. She is a medicine woman."

Mona watched him limp away; then she went to where Mrs. Kempler was sobbing uncontrollably with her husband's blood on her hands.

Not a few people at the scene that day, bitter and angry and filled with thoughts of revenge—both African and white—had noticed how Mona Treverton had put her arm around David Mathenge.

48

The rains had come at last.

A gentle drizzle whispered beyond the heavily draped windows of Bellatu, wetting the red and lavender bougainvillaea that grew along the pillars and eaves of the veranda. Inside, a comforting fire crackled in the living room, casting fingers of yellow glow over furniture, zebras-kins, and elephant tusks crisscrossed on the walls.

David closed the ledger book and said, "It is late. I must go."

Mona didn't reply. She quietly restored neatness to her desk, where they had been working all afternoon, trying to find a way to meet the growing debts of the farm since the crop failure. New seedlings were now being watered by the tardy rains, but revenue from that future harvest would not arrive in time. Her only solution to saving the estate, Mona had decided, was to sell Bella Hill.

"I will write to Mr. Treadwell first thing in the morning," she said as she stood with David and turned out the desk lamp. "I'll tell him that I accept his offer. It's a good price, I think. And Bella Hill will make a good boarding school. I don't mind losing it. That house holds only bad memories for me."

For an instant Mona and David looked at each other in the darkness of the study. Then Mona turned abruptly and headed for the light and warmth of the living room.

She was frightened. She had been debating all day showing David the note she had found in her letter box. Ordinarily she would have told him about it at once. But in the two weeks since the Mau Mau attack on Grace Mission their relationship had altered drastically.

Something now lay between them, Mona realized, something dark and shapeless and terrifying. It was like a giant sleeping lion—unthreatening when not aroused, but deadly if disturbed. It was the lethal passion their mutual desire had given birth to, which had brought them to the terrible threshold of racial taboos.

Mona could not stop thinking about the day of the attack. She concentrated on the memory of the feel of David's hand holding hers, the way he had pulled her to him, the firmness of his body, the tight embrace within his arms. She had looked up into his eyes in that moment, as they stood in the brief shelter of the storage shed, and she had seen mirrored in his look her own desperate yearning. For one fleeting instant he had tightened his hold, their bodies had come together, and then they had separated and run.

She relived it over and over, was obsessed with it, not in a loving, cherishing way but fearfully. Mona was afraid of the perilous brink she and David had reached. In former times they would simply have been scorned by society and cast out from among family and friends. But now, because of the nightmare of Mau Mau, because racial hatred had reached monstrous proportions, because the country was ruled by panic and terror and suspicion, Mona knew that their love for each other was suicidal.

She had to fight it. For her life, she had to. And for David's.

That morning, in a village near Meru, a gang of Home Guards, on the pretext of routing out a Mau Mau sympathizer, had burst into the house of an African businessman who was married to a European woman. The gang had tortured the man, raped his white wife, and left them both dead.

"I will help you lock up the house," David said as they entered the living room. "It's time to send the servants home."

It was an ignoble way to live. Throughout the Central Province—at the Donald ranch, in Grace's house at the mission, in Bellatu—white men and women were locking their African servants out of the house at sunset and letting them in again in the morning. "Solomon has been with my family for years," Mona had protested when the District Commissioner insisted she comply with the rule. "He wouldn't hurt me!"

"Begging your pardon, Lady Mona, but if he's been forced to take an oath, then you aren't safe with him. And until we find the oath giver that's working in this area, you can consider all your servants as dangerous."

Geoffrey had then installed a siren on her veranda and two rockets—one by the kitchen door, the other by the front door. Lighted, they shot far into the sky and exploded so that they could be seen by the lookout post on Allsop Hill in Nyeri, a tower built by a Sikh named Vir Singh and manned by Asian Combat.

Although many Europeans were abandoning their farms and moving to the relative safety of Nairobi or even giving up their homes altogether and fleeing to England, some remained on their land, determined not to give it up. With the help of sirens and rockets, and periodic overhead surveillance by airplanes and helicopters, the settlers stood their ground.

Her supper had been laid out on the kitchen table by Solomon. Mona said good night to her maids and houseboys and locked the door behind them. Taking a flashlight, David went upstairs and all over the house, making sure that windows and doors were locked, that balconies and verandas weren't harboring anyone. Then he returned to the kitchen and prepared to leave.

He paused at the door and looked at Mona.

"I'm frightened," she said quietly.

"I know."

"It's dark out. And it's a long way to your cottage. Mau Mau could be out there—"

"I have no choice, Mona. I have to go. It is past curfew. I will go quickly."

"David, wait." She reached into her skirt pocket. "I found this in my letter box this morning."

He read the note. It contained two words: "Nigger lover."

"Who could have done it?" she said, glancing at the closed curtains over the kitchen windows and feeling the dark night that crouched on the other side. For as long as she lived Mona would never forget the sight of Mrs. Langly with the Mau Mau spear through her stomach, Father Vittorio running and screaming, his cassock aflame, and David, in the garage, falling beneath kicks and blows.

"I'm afraid you and I are in a unique position, Mona," he said darkly. "Instead of having just one enemy, both sides hate us. We are caught in the middle of something that is not of our doing and over which we have no control."

Mona held her breath. David was coming dangerously close to rousing the unspoken thing that slept between them. In the past two weeks they had worked hard together around the estate, uprooting the dead coffee trees, planting new seedlings, rarely speaking except on farm matters, and then parting to go to their separate homes before night fell. They had existed in a kind of hermetically sealed world, a sterile place where Mau Mau was unheard of, where hatred and love were locked outside. But this afternoon they had had to address the issue of Bellatu's serious financial losses. And they had worked past the curfew hour.

Now they were trapped. Night had caught them.

Mona had an idea who had written the note. She suspected a hot-headed settler son named Brian who had once been arrested for mistreating one of his African cattle boys. Brian had slung a rope through the man's pierced earlobes and then had galloped off on his horse while holding the other end of the rope so that the poor man had had to run behind.

"Why has it come to this, David?" she whispered. "What have we done to deserve this?"

He looked long at her, his eyes sad, his face troubled. Then he reached for the doorknob.

"Don't go," she said.

"I have to."

"Mau Mau might be out there, waiting for you. Or a vengeful white boy."

"I can't stay here."

"Why not? You would be safe here."

He shook his head. "You know why I cannot stay, Mona." His voice was soft, barely heard above the whispering rain. "It is one thing to be with you in daylight, with other people around, doing farm work, but it would be something altogether different for me to be in this house alone with you at night."

She stared across the room at him. Her heart raced.

"Mona," he said in a tight voice, "you and I can never be. Perhaps in another place, at another time, among people who are tolerant. But we are here in Kenya in the midst of a shameful racial war. We must not take that final, irreversible step because once it is taken, we can never cross back to the side of guiltlessness and safety."

"Is it so wrong, the way we feel?"

"For you and me, yes."

He unlocked the door and was about to turn the knob when a crash came from the direction of the living room.

Mona's eyes widened in fear.

"Give me your gun!" David whispered. Then he said, "Stay here." But she followed him as he walked slowly from the kitchen through the dark dining room. At the doorway to the living room he paused, Mona close behind him, and looked around.

No lamps had been lit. The only light came from the strong fire in the fireplace. The hearth was illuminated, revealing brass coal hods, andirons, intricate brickwork, an elephant's foot holding a poker, and the three leather sofas facing the fire. But there the light dwindled. It was scattered among mahogany tables, flickering on a poorly defined periphery. Things seemed to move with the firelight: magazines; ashtrays; an antelope's foot that was a cigarette lighter. And then beyond inky shadows hugged the walls, hiding bookcases and other doorways. Occasionally a mounted animal head was caught in passing glow; the staring glass eyes of an oryx or gazelle glinted.

David crept forward, close to the wall. When he reached the velvet drapes that covered the large windows facing Mount Kenya, he stopped, raised the gun, and parted the drape. Mona, behind him, peered over his shoulder.

The veranda was dark and rain-swept. A single bulb over the steps cast a misty circle of yellow light upon wicker furniture, potted palms, and red and lavender bougainvillaea petals.

David and Mona saw the shards of broken pottery, the scattered soil, the azalea tree lying on the veranda floor. A few feet away they saw what had knocked it over: a small, clumsy shape rooting curiously among the potted plants.

"A hedgehog!" Mona said.

"No doubt seeking shelter from the rain."

David turned to Mona, laughing. She, too, laughed, nervously, in relief.

Then their smiles faded, and they stared at each other in the intimate half glow at the edge of the firelight.

"I want you to promise me," David said quietly after a moment, "that you will move out of this house tomorrow and go and stay with your aunt Grace. Tim Hopkins is with her; you will be safer there than here. Do you promise me, Mona?"

"Yes."

He fell silent again, his eyes searching her face, following the line of her hair, her neck, shoulders. "It's not safe for you to be alone," he said at last, thinking of the note. "Someone other than Mau Mau has threatened you now."

"And you."

"Yes. . ."

David brought his hand up and gently laid it on her cheek. "I have wondered so many times," he said, "what your skin feels like. So soft . . ."

She closed her eyes. His hand was hard and calloused. Its touch made her feel faint. She felt her breath catch in her throat, the sudden straining of her heart.

"Mona," he breathed.

She reached up and touched his cheek with her fingertip. She traced the lines of his face, from his nose down to the corner of his lips, the furrow between his eyebrows, the creases at the edge of his eyes.

David's hand moved to the back of her head. He drove his fingers into her hair. He bent to kiss her but hesitated. When their lips did meet, it was tentatively, as if taking a first, uncertain step. Then she put her arms around his neck, and she encouraged the kiss, guiding him, showing him how it was done. Their bodies came together in the flickering fire's glow.

After a moment David drew back and undid the buttons of her blouse. He marveled at Mona's small white breasts, which his hands covered completely. She parted his shirt and laid her palms flat on his chest. When David was naked, Mona saw the legacy of his Masai ancestry—in the finely sculpted buttocks and strong, lean thighs.

David picked her up and laid her down in front of the fire. He explored her body. He touched her. Mona responded because she had never known the *irua* knife.

He placed his mouth over hers again, and she arched her body up to receive him. They lay in the dancing light of the fire, black skin against white.

MONA WOKE SUDDENLY, wondering what had wakened her. She turned to the man next to her in bed—David, sleeping soundly. How long had she slept? She stretched. She had never felt so good. She had never been so happy.

They had made love several times, each better than the last. David had been taught the arts and skills of his warrior forefathers; Mona had delighted him with her intense, unexpected responses.

"Mona!" came a voice from downstairs.

She sat up. That was what had wakened her! Someone coming into the house!

It was Geoffrey. He was moving about downstairs and calling her name.

Mona jumped out of bed and pulled on a dressing gown. Glancing back at David to be sure he still slept, she went out into the hall and closed the door.

She met Geoffrey in the living room, where a few red coals still glowed in the fireplace. "What on earth are you doing here, Geoffrey?"

"Christ, Mona! You took ten years off my life! When I found your kitchen door unlocked, I didn't know what to think!"

She put her hand over her mouth. She and David had left the house open!

"What are you doing here?" she asked again, noticing that Geoffrey's mackintosh was drenched, that rain dripped off the brim of his hat. He was carrying a rifle, and hovering in the doorway to the dining room were two soldiers of the Kenya Police Reserve.

"A routine patrol during the night found a dead cat hanging on the gate to Bellatu. You know what that means."

Mona knew what it meant. It was a Mau Mau signal that the inhabitants within were going to be the next victims.

"So we're conducting a general roundup of all wogs in the area. But when I got to David Mathenge's cottage and discovered he wasn't home, in fact, that it looked like he hadn't been home all night, I decided to come up here to ask you if you knew where he was."

Mona clutched the dressing gown over her breasts. The house was abominably cold.

"What time did he leave here last night, Mona?"

Last night? "What time is it, Geoffrey?"

"It's nearly dawn. I've got several patrols out searching for him. I've always suspected that boy of being a Mau Mau sympathizer. He might even be the oath giver we've been looking for."

"Don't be so ridiculous. And would you please send those men outside? I'm not dressed."

Geoffrey gave the askaris an order in Swahili, and when they were gone, he said, "Do you know where David Mathenge is?"

"He had nothing to do with the dead cat."

"How do you know that?"

"I just know it, that's all."

"I don't understand how you can trust him so blindly. What sort of hold does David Mathenge have over you anyway?"

"I know he's innocent."

"Well, I want to take him in for questioning. It's time he was detained. You've stood up for him too long. Now tell me, what time did he leave last night?"

Mona didn't reply.

"Do you know where he went? Do you know where he is right now?"

She chewed her lip.

"If you don't tell me, we'll find him anyway, and it won't go too well for him under questioning, I can guarantee that. He's broken the curfew law."

"That's not David's fault. I'm responsible for that."

"What do you mean?"

Mona tried to think. If David was suspected of having a hand in the dead cat business, then he would be tortured under interrogation. But if she spoke up for him and proved he couldn't have done it because he was with her all night, then she would be confessing to what they had done.

Before Mona could make a decision, Geoffrey said, "What the devil!" and she turned around to see David in the doorway.

He was wearing only trousers and was holding a pistol. "I heard voices, Mona," he said. "I thought you were in trouble."

Geoffrey was too shocked to speak.

Mona went to David and put her hand on his arm. "We left the kitchen door open, David. Geoffrey came to tell me that a cat was hung on my gate during the night. He thought you had done it."

She looked at Geoffrey. "But David couldn't have done it," she said, "because he was here with me all night."

Several looks marched across Geoffrey's face before he was able to speak. "So," he said, walking up to Mona, "I had a suspicion about this. But I couldn't be sure. After all, I told myself that Mona certainly wouldn't sink so low."

"You had better go, Geoffrey. This is none of your concern."

"I'll say it isn't! I want nothing to do with this! My God, Mona!" he cried. "Sleeping with a nigger!"

She slapped him hard across the face.

"Get out," she said in a deadly tone. "Get out or I'll use this gun on you. And never come to my house again."

He opened his mouth to say something. Then he gave David a venomous, threatening look, turned on his heel, and marched out.

When they heard the kitchen door slam, Mona covered her face with her hands and went into David's embrace. "I'm so sorry!" she cried. "He's such a hateful person! It's all my fault, David!"

"No," he said quietly, stroking her hair. He fixed his eyes on the cracks of milky light coming through the drapes. It was dawn. "It is no one's fault, Mona. We are simply the victims of forces beyond our understanding." He stepped back and held her by the arms. "Mona, look at me and listen to what I have to say. This is not a world we can live in; our love would not survive. Someday they will have you looking at me and thinking, *nigger*, or I shall look at you and think, *white bitch*. And our beautiful love will be destroyed."

He spoke passionately. "There must be a future in which we can live together and love each other freely and without fear. We must be able to live as husband and wife, Mona, not creeping about in the cover of night. I love you with all my heart, more than I have ever loved anyone, and yet while that man was insulting you, I was unable to defend you! I cannot be stripped of my manhood, Mona, for then I might as well be dead! I can see now that I have been wrong all this time, that the only way to make the future ours is to fight for it! I can no longer be the white man's 'boy'!"

She looked up at him, mesmerized, terrified.

"I am going to do now what I should have done long ago, Mona. And I do it for us. Just remember that I love you. It may be a long time before you see me again, but you will be with me in my heart. And if you are ever afraid or in danger, and you need to contact me, go to my mother. She will know what to do."

"Where are you going, David?" she whispered.

"I am going into the forest, Mona. I am going to join Mau Mau."

49

This was going to be the biggest Mau Mau strike to date. And Field Marshal Wanjiru Mathenge was going to lead it.

As she counted the last of the dynamite sticks which had been smuggled to her, she felt the heady rush of pulse in her brain, tasted the bite of fear and excitement. It was the same exhilaration she felt whenever she went into the forest, smuggling guns, leaving food and communications in hollow trees for the freedom fighters. She was giddy with anticipation of the big strike she was about to lead: the bombing of the Norfolk Hotel.

There was to be a meeting there this afternoon. The governor and General Erskine had called a general council of white settlers in an effort to plan a new, major offensive against Mau Mau. One of Wanjiru's lieutenants, a beautiful young Meru woman named Sybill, had slept with one of the governor's aides. He had unsuspectingly told her about the secret meeting.

Things were happening so quickly now! Mau Mau had stepped up its fight. The war was expanding to incredible proportions. Wanjiru knew it was because there was a new leader in the forest, a man who had appeared suddenly one day in July. Wanjiru had never seen him—she took her orders from someone under him—and his true identity was known only to Mau Mau high command. To Wanjiru and the rest of the freedom fighters, and to the Europeans as well, he was known as Leopard. Whoever he was, wherever he had come from, Wanjiru admired him. Since his joining up with the forest armies, Mau Mau had launched a massive push against the whites. Leopard had brought to Mau Mau new tactics, new ways of fighting; he had a soldier's experience and cunning and seemed to know the internal workings of the British military. The successful strikes against the settlers in these past few months all were his doing, as was today's attack, which had been in the planning stages for weeks. Once pulled off, the bombing of Nairobi's most important hotel with Kenya's leaders inside was going to be a crippling blow to the whites.

This was Wanjiru's first time in Nairobi since the incident at the Queen Victoria Hotel. After she had thrown the rock through the hotel's window, she had run into the forests and taken part in organizing new camps, making homemade guns out of pipes, supervising the women, and forming secret, underground communications networks. Field Marshal Wanjiru had risen in the Mau Mau ranks and was now considered the most powerful of the women freedom fighters. The British had launched a widespread hunt for her; there was a bounty of five thousand pounds on her head.

She had arrived in Nairobi a week ago, traveling on foot from the Aberdares in disguise. Friends had made for her a Muslim *buibui,* a black veil that covered her entire body, leaving only a slit for the eyes. She had brought Christopher and Hannah with her from the secret forest camp, trudging in the hot sun, begging for food in villages, drinking from streams. As she neared the city and had been stopped at roadblocks, she had pretended to speak not English, Swahili, or Kikuyu but a Somali dialect which none of the soldiers knew. She had looked harmless enough—a refugee from the Northern Frontier District, traveling with two babies—so that the soldiers had passed her through. Once she was in the city, however, things were different. She had to have identity papers. It had been arranged for her to become the "wife" of a Mau Mau sympathizer, a Muslim who worked for the Uganda Railway and who therefore was away from his room most of the time. The man had taken Wanjiru to the Labor Office on Lord Treverton Avenue, where she had been fingerprinted, photographed, and issued a passbook under the name of Fatma Hammad.

Now, on this scorching October noon as the hour for the bombing drew near, Wanjiru padded Sybill's stomach with the last of the dynamite.

She had been at it all morning. At sunrise Wanjiru had gone to the market near to Shauri Moyo, the tenement block where the Muslim sympathizer had a dingy room. At the market Wanjiru had met certain women, as had been arranged, and had passed to them, among ears of corn and in calabash gourds, sticks of dynamite with hurried, whispered instructions to meet at the Norfolk at one o'clock.

Although the attack on the hotel had been Leopard's idea, the means had been Wanjiru's. Men were not free to move about Nairobi. Tommies and Home Guards stopped everyone, conducted searches, made arbitrary arrests. But women, Wanjiru had observed, were less likely to be harassed. Although many were stopped and questioned and taken away in trucks, most were left to go about their interminable shopping, washing, vegetable selling, and childbearing—the never-ending rut of the African woman.

Baskets and gourds could be searched, Wanjiru knew, even the slings that held babies on women's backs. But pregnant bellies were seldom given close scrutiny by soldiers. That was why Wanjiru had instructed her women to pad themselves well and to keep the dynamite close to their bodies, and that was why she now made a last-minute adjustment to the wad of sheets over Sybill's abdomen.

Each woman had been assigned a place. Three days ago Wanjiru had surveyed the hotel grounds, drawn a picture, and penciled in the positions of her saboteurs. While she and Sybill sweated in the ovenlike room of Shauri Moyo, they were gathering there now—eighteen women going unnoticed on the crowded sidewalks, one pausing to pull a splinter from her foot, another to nurse her baby, and so on, until they surrounded the grounds in an inconspicuous and seemingly unrelated circle. Wanjiru was going to be the last one to arrive. At one o'clock she was going to cry, "Mothers of Kenya!," upon which her sisters were to light their sticks and hurl them through the windows of the Norfolk.

A plan of which Leopard had highly approved.

When Sybill was done, she wrapped a bright yellow kanga around her shaved head, hoisted her heavy load of onions onto her back—she was going to spread them out on a cloth in front of the hotel, pretending to sell them—said to Wanjiru, "The soil is ours," and left.

When she was alone, Wanjiru commenced with her own final preparations. As she created a pregnant belly from the remaining pillow, she paused to look at her two babies asleep on the iron bed. Hannah was getting to be a big girl, and Christopher, at eighteen months, was strong and handsome. He looked exactly like his father, David.

With that thought Wanjiru's look darkened. She scorned the man she had divorced and chastised herself for ever having loved him. David Mathenge was a coward, she decided, a man who brought shame to the Children of Mumbi. She hoped he was miserable, working on the white bitch's estate.

As she recalled Mona Treverton, Wanjiru's spirits lifted. Sybill's report on today's secret settler meeting had included a grain of wonderful information: that Dr. Grace Treverton and her niece, Mona, were going to be there.

What will you do then, David? Without your memsaab?

She roused the children. "Come along, my babies. We are going for a walk."

They were languid and moved slowly in the heat. Hannah put on her one dress, which was dirty and torn and too small for her growing body. Christopher wore only a pair of shorts. Both were hungry and barefoot. As she prepared to leave the tenement building, taking up her basket of arrowroots, which she was going to pretend to sell on the sidewalk in front of the Norfolk, Field Marshal Wanjiru Mathenge reaffirmed her resolve. *I do this for my babies, for their future, that they may never have to suffer the degradation their parents did.*

After the July rains the city had turned green. As Wanjiru walked in the sun, with Christopher on her hip, Hannah walking alongside, holding her hand, the arrowroots weighing down upon her back and the explosives tucked against her belly, she recalled how Nairobi had looked when she had come here sixteen years ago as a girl, to be the first nursing student at the Native Hospital. The city had seemed so much smaller and quieter then. Lines had been clearly drawn; rules of race and society had been simple. The Africans stayed on their squalid estates; the whites had all the rest. In those days, it seemed now to Wanjiru, a kind of innocent peace had enveloped Nairobi; people hadn't paid much attention to the speeches of teenagers like herself and David. In those days the African "knew his place."

When she passed the spot where the great, failed protest had occurred, on the day of the parade when the Treverton son had been killed and David had fled to Uganda, she saw how things had changed. There were bigger buildings, paved roads, more cars and people, and it made her feel almost nostalgic for the passing of the old days.

But they were bad days, she reminded herself as she turned down the road toward the Norfolk. *They were wrong days; we fight now for better ones.*

She paused on a street corner and looked around. Nairobi had turned into a military camp. Not since the war had so many uniforms been seen on its treelined streets. British Tommies patrolled up and down, ignoring the sullen looks of Africans. And the Home Guards, Kikuyu like herself and just as villainous, in Wanjiru's mind, as the whites, swaggered with their police badges and baton sticks. She didn't know which she feared more.

As she neared the Norfolk, Wanjiru spotted her sisters among the pedestrians. There was Ruth, idly filling her gourd from the street water tap; Damaris had taken off her sling and was readjusting it on her back; Sybill had spread out her cloth of onions; Muthoni sat on the curb, nursing her daughter; and there was old Mama Josephine, who had written a letter to Queen Elizabeth for Kenyatta's release, appealing to the queen's maternal instinct. They blended in with the crowd on the sidewalks, just a few random African women going about their mundane tasks. The soldiers, having examined their passbooks, had dismissed them as insignificant and unworthy of further concern. Wanjiru knew that also at their stations were the rest, women who appeared to have nothing on their minds but who were, in fact, sharply alert and waiting for a deadly signal.

Parked along the street, Wanjiru saw in satisfaction, were the cars of the white settlers, being guarded by bored soldiers. She recognized the one which belonged to Mona Treverton; it was the same car the earl had been murdered in eight years ago.

So—they were all inside, like sheep in a pen, waiting for the slaughter. Wanjiru looked up at the clock on the church tower. It was ten minutes to one o'clock.

"Hold there, mama!" came a voice behind her.

She turned and smiled at the pair of Home Guards approaching her. Because she could not afford to be hampered today, Wanjiru was not wearing the protective *buibui*.

"Your passbook, mama."

She handed it to him.

While the one askari scrutinized her photograph and data, the other, a young Embu man, looked Wanjiru up and down.

"What are you doing here, mama?" the first asked her as he handed back the passbook.

She turned so they could examine her basket of arrowroot. "I'm going to sell them."

"Why here? Why not at the market?"

"Ha! Too much competition at the market! And I need the money! My lazy no-good husband spends all our money on beer!"

"There are easier ways for a good-looking woman like you to make money," the second one said with a smile.

"Sir, I am a devout Muslim. What you say insults me!"

They gave her a thoughtful look. Wanjiru wanted to glance up at the clock but dared not.

"Where are you from?" asked the first.

"Where it says in my passbook."

"Tell me where."

She tried to keep up her smile, her unconcerned manner. Wanjiru had passed through many such brief detainments; she must keep her head through this one. "Up north," she said. "Near the border."

"Today is Friday, mama," said the second soldier, who no longer smiled. "Why are you not at the mosque?"

Wanjiru's heart leaped. She had forgotten! "My husband goes for both of us. Allah understands the need."

The second askari gave her a long, considering look. He narrowed his eyes at her, and Wanjiru, for a panicked instant, thought he looked familiar. But she could not remember from when or where. Then he whispered something to his companion. Wanjiru felt the sweat trickle down her back, thought of the women surrounding the Norfolk. Would one or two become nervous and start the attack before they heard her signal?

She desperately wanted to move on, to get to her position. Yet she had to appear to be in no hurry and untroubled before the two askaris.

Finally, to her immense relief, they said, "You may go, mama. And stay out of trouble."

"*Inshallah,*" she said with a wave, and turned away.

She looked up at the clock. Four minutes to one. She saw Sybill giving her an edgy look; others, too, were starting to shift uneasily.

Wait, thought Wanjiru. *Do not act yet. . . .*

Surprise attacks were what Leopard had taught his forest fighters. He had shown them what the British Army had trained him to do and what he had seen terrorists in other countries do. Wanjiru knew it was vital that the women light their sticks at the same time and throw them together. It must be done in one quick move before the soldiers could react. Or else all would be in vain.

She was stopped at the curb by traffic congestion. Wanjiru looked across the street at Sybill, who was getting to her feet and reaching into her dress. It was two minutes to one, and the women all were surreptitiously bringing out their matches. When the minute hand stood at one minute to one o'clock, they were to produce their dynamite and listen for her cry.

The traffic came to a halt. Horns honked; exhaust filled her head. Deciding that there was no time, Wanjiru held tightly on to her children and plunged between the autos and trucks, creating more cacophony of horns and brakes. When she reached the other side, jumping up onto the sidewalk just as a military motorcycle whizzed past, her eyes met Sybill's.

Wanjiru put her hand through the pocket of her dress, where she had made a hole. She felt the dynamite.

She looked up at the clock.

The women waited for the signal.

The hand of the clock moved slowly to the twelve. Wanjiru's pulse rushed in her ears. The sound of traffic and people seemed to recede. All that existed were the hands of the clock and the stick of dynamite in her grasp. Just a few more seconds. . . When the hand was straight up on the twelve, she was going to shout, "Mothers of Kenya," and eighteen sticks of dynamite were going to crash into the dining room where the white settlers were gathered.

The last few seconds now. . .

"Mama!" called a voice.

She spun around.

The two Home Guards were running across the street.

Wanjiru froze. Should she call the signal or flee?

"What is—" she started to say. But they had their guns out and fired into the air.

The people on the sidewalk scattered instantly. British soldiers came running down the steps of the Norfolk, their Sten guns pointed at Wanjiru. Behind her she felt Sybill jump up and run. The other women, too, were escaping.

"You are Wanjiru Mathenge!" said the Embu askari. "I thought I knew you from somewhere!"

"You are mistaken!" she cried, and realized with a pounding heart where she had seen him before: He had been an orderly at the Native Hospital years ago.

"We'll see about that," said a British corporal, who roughly took her arm. "You're coming in for questioning."

Hannah started to cry. Wanjiru gathered her up and, with the two children in her arms, followed the soldiers into the military truck.

50

M ona wrote:

My dearest David,

It has been four months since you left. I miss you more than I can say. As you asked me to do, I am now living with Aunt Grace, and Bellatu is locked up. The farm, I am sorry to say, is failing. After your disappearance many of the field hands deserted me. A few loyal ones have stayed on, but I think most of the crop shall perish. I received the money from the sale of Bella Hill. It will help for a while; after that I don't know.

I heard on the wireless yesterday that Wanjiru was arrested in Nairobi. They said she was taken to Kamiti Women's Detention Camp and your two children are with her.

I had hoped I would see you in these past four months, my dearest, and would be able to give you these letters myself. But I realize now that we shall not be reunited until this terrible conflict is over. I shall do as you instructed; I shall take these letters to your mother. You said she would know how to contact you.

Do you still believe, David, my love, that there will be a place for us in the new Kenya? I pray that you are right.

Hearing footsteps on the veranda, Mona looked up to see Grace come in, wearing a crisp white lab coat with a stethoscope around her neck. "I came to see if you've heard anything about the shipment I'm expecting. Any word?"

"Nothing, Aunt Grace."

Grace frowned. She desperately needed the new Salk polio vaccine from America, and she prayed the shipment hadn't been waylaid by Mau Mau.

"I'm for a cuppa," Grace said. "How about you?"

Mona never ceased to marvel at her aunt's seemingly inexhaustible energy. At nearly sixty-five Grace continued to run her enormous mission with the verve and efficiency of a much younger woman.

Mona put her pen down and followed her aunt into the kitchen, where Mario was slicing ham for their cold supper. At sunset he would be locked out of the house.

"Thank goodness the tea plantations are unaffected by Mau Mau," Grace said as she measured Countess Treverton tea into the pot. "Britons would surrender if their tea was threatened!"

The houseboy looked over his shoulder with a grin.

Mona returned his smile and shook her head. Grace's dauntless attitude in the face of so much danger was what had kept her mission going when others had been abandoned. There had been two more Mau Mau attacks, and still, she stood her ground. Despite the troops stationed close by, despite the daily news reports of mutilated African corpses, hamstrung cattle, cats impaled on fence posts, and despite the constant racket of airplanes going over the forest, calling for the terrorists to come out and surrender, Grace managed to maintain her equilibrium and her optimism.

"It's no use turning on the news," Mona said as she set the table. They were going to sit in the warm sunshine, next to a window framed with flowers. "They're still searching for the oath giver in this area. The authorities are concentrating on that right now; they say that once he's found, a lot of the danger will be removed."

Grace stood at the stove waiting for the kettle to boil. She studied her niece who wore her usual Capris and oversize man's shirt. "I don't mean to be rude, Mona," she said, "but I do believe you're putting on weight. Surely it can't be because of Mario's cooking!"

"Yes, I'm putting on weight," Mona said with her back turned to her aunt. "But it has nothing to do with Mario's cooking. I'm pregnant."

Grace looked at her niece through gold wire-rimmed glasses. She blinked and said, "*What?*"

Mario, who had known Mona since she was a little girl, turned around.

Mona continued to set the table, placing paper napkins on the sandwich plates. "I'm going to have a baby, Aunt Grace. David Mathenge's baby."

Mario dropped his knife. It clattered on the linoleum, jarring the afternoon peace.

"Mona!" Grace whispered. "What on earth were you thinking!"

"I was in love, Aunt Grace. I am still in love. David and I care very much for each other."

"But. . .he's *vanished!*"

"Yes. He told me he had to go, and I let him."

"You know where David Mathenge is?"

Mona paused. A lump was gathering in her throat; tears rose in her eyes. She had not been able to bring herself to tell anyone that David had become one of *them.*

Grace stared at her niece for a moment, then gave Mario a significant look. Understanding, he discreetly left the kitchen. Grace and Mona sat down. They faced each other.

"My poor dear," the aunt said, "what are you going to do?"

"Do? I'm going to have David's baby."

"And then what? How will you live?"

"As I have lived the past thirty-four years. As anyone lives, one day at a time. Waiting for David to come back to me."

"Then you do know where he is?"

"Yes."

Grace looked into her niece's eyes and read an answer that she preferred not to know. "And what of the child? What sort of life will it have?"

"It will be loved, Aunt Grace. It was conceived in love; it will be raised in love."

"What if David never comes back?"

"He will—" Mona's voice caught. "Then I shall raise the child on my own, and I will teach it to be proud of its father, of its *two* races."

Grace looked down at her hands. She listened to the song of birds outside her window, the reason why her first house, which had burned down on this spot many years ago, had been called Birdsong Cottage. She was thinking of the night the surgery hut was on fire and of the children's voices she had heard calling from inside.

"Mona," she said slowly, "you must know that if David does come back, he will no longer be the same man. He will have changed."

"I don't believe that."

"If he has joined Mau Mau, then he has taken the oath and he can no longer be trusted."

"Not David."

"You know the power of the oath, Mona! It can turn rational, intelligent men into monsters. It's a kind of psychological sickness. They *believe* in the binding of the oath. David is a Kikuyu, Mona!"

"He's different."

"Is he? Have you heard about the prisoners in the detention camps? Africans who had once been loyal headmen but who had turned on their white friends are being put through rigorous rehabilitation programs. The government has real witch doctors going about the camps giving anti-Mau Mau oaths! Mona, don't you see? David is one of them! And he joined them voluntarily, not against his will. Even when a man protests his loyalty to the government, he cannot be trusted, especially a man who willingly joined Mau Mau."

Mona stood abruptly. "David will never harm me. I know that."

"Mona, listen to—"

"Aunt Grace, I need your help with something. I want to ask a favor of you."

Grace's mouth formed a thin line. "What is it?"

"I've been writing letters to David. I want to get them to him."

"Well, you know where he is."

"I don't know *exactly* where he is, and I don't know how to pass these letters on to him. He told me that if I should need to communicate with him, I should go to his mother. He said that she would know what to do."

"Yes," Grace said sadly, feeling for the first time since the onset of hostilities the true crime of this obscene war. "There's an underground network. Messages are left for them in hollow trees."

"Mama Wachera will know how to get my letters to David."

"And what do you want me to do?"

"She doesn't speak English, and I know only a little Kikuyu. Will you go with me and explain it to her?"

Grace looked up. "To Wachera's hut?"
Mona nodded.
"I haven't spoken to that woman in years. Not since the *irua*
. . . when I tried to save Njeri."
"Please," Mona said.

THE POLO FIELD had not been used since Rose's suicide. Mona always
spoke of opening it up again or of turning it into a large garden, but
she never got around to it. Now it was overgrown with weeds, its fence
rusting. Grace had lately been thinking it would make a nice addition
to her mission, as a playing field for the three hundred African students
in her school.

A beaten path went along the grassy bank. Mona and Grace followed
it after passing under the iron archway of the mission gate. Two British
soldiers offered to accompany the women, but they assured the men
that there was nothing to fear from Mama Wachera. Africans in both
camps respected the legendary medicine woman and left her in peace.

As she neared the cluster of humble huts, Grace was assailed with
memories: of the rainy day she had arrived back in 1919 in the ox
wagons, baby Mona in Rose's arms; of her first handshake with James;
of the day Valentine had had the fig tree cut down, on a spot near the
southern goalposts; of the night of the fire and the subsequent days
recuperating in Wachera's hut. Walking now along the edge of the
medicine woman's shamba, where beans and maize awaited the rains,
Grace felt her modern mission with its electricity and latest medical
equipment slowly slide away behind her as she stepped into another
era—the Kenya of long ago.

Mama Wachera was sitting in the sun, stripping leaves off what
Grace recognized to be a healing plant. The medicine woman chanted
as she made her medicine and then stored the mixture in gourds
marked with magic tokens. Wachera wore the costume for which she
was known: beaded necklaces; copper bracelets; massive earrings that
had stretched her earlobes down to her shoulders. Her shaved head
gleamed in the sun; ceremonial charms and sacred talismans jingled on
her wrists.

She looked up at the silver-haired memsaab in white coat and metal-rubber ornament around her neck. They had not spoken in many harvests.

Mona was apprehensive in the presence of the elderly African woman. She had heard so much about Wachera; this hut had stood here for as long as Mona could recall. And there was an elusive, dreamlike memory: of a fire, and then of rain, and finally a bed of goatskins and gentle hands cooling her fever. Mona knew that Mama Wachera had once saved her life.

Grace addressed David's mother with extreme politeness and respect, speaking in the excellent Kikuyu that she had perfected over the years. In return, Mama Wachera was exceedingly polite and modest but did not, Grace noticed, offer a calabash of beer.

"These letters, Lady Wachera," Grace said, holding out the bundle tied in a string, "are for your son, David. We were wondering if you could get them to him for us?"

Mama Wachera gazed up at Grace.

They waited. Flies buzzed in the heat; an errant cloud covered the sun. But the medicine woman didn't speak.

Mona said, "Please," in English, and then tried to explain in her own rudimentary Kikuyu how much the letters would mean to David.

Wachera's eyes went to Mona's waist, then back up to her face. There was contempt in the look, as if the African woman knew what secret lay beneath Mona's shirt.

"Lady Wachera," Grace said, "your son would be very happy to read these letters. We don't know where he is. We only know that he went into the forest. But when he left, he told my niece that she could contact him through you. He said that you would help."

Mama Wachera looked up at the woman who had long ago built a strange hut comprised of nothing more than four posts and a thatch roof but who now owned many stone buildings with paved roads and automobiles. She said, "I do not know where my son is."

Nonetheless, Grace laid the bundle on the ground next to the medicine woman, said, *"Mwaiga,"* which means, "All is well, go in peace," and turned away.

As they took the path back to the mission, Grace said to Mona, "Don't worry. She knows where David is. And she would want to carry out his wishes. She will get the letters to him."

51

Simon Mwacharo, one of the camp warders, both hated and lusted after Wanjiru Mathenge. He had her brought to his office again and again, at all hours of the day or night, interrupting a meal or rousing her from sleep, to interrogate her, to break her spirit.

"Who is your immediate superior in Mau Mau?" he asked her a hundred times. "What are the lines of communication? How do you receive your orders? Who is Leopard? Where is his camp?"

Mwacharo conducted these random interrogations in his office, a hastily constructed shack of corrugated tin walls and roof, with just a table, chair, and radiophone inside. He always questioned Wanjiru in the presence of a white officer and four askaris, and he kept at it for hours, keeping her standing on the stone floor, whether it was a fiercely hot day and the hut turned into an oven or cold rains filled the office with a biting cold. Wanjiru either shivered or sweated, she was weak and exhausted, but she always remained silent. Since coming to the Kamiti Maximum Security Camp, she had uttered not one word to the authorities.

Eventually, after an hour or two of rapid-fire questions, Simon Mwacharo, having learned nothing, would release her.

But he was a determined man. Wanjiru Mathenge had been given the rank of field marshal by Mau Mau; she had been labeled "hard-core" by the authorities and given a black card, which meant she was among the most dangerous of the detainees. To wrest information from her, Mwacharo knew, would be to earn praise for himself and possibly a promotion from his superiors.

He had been interrogating Wanjiru for five months. He knew that she was bound to break eventually.

* * *

"WATCH NOW, HANNAH!" Wanjiru said to her four-year-old daughter. "Pay careful attention to what I do because someday you are going to be a medicine woman like your grandmother."

Stories about Mama Wachera, her father's mother, were what little Hannah liked best, even better than tales of Mount Kenya. She wished her mother would tell one now, instead of showing her how to remove a nasty old jigger from a toe.

"There," Wanjiru said to the elderly Embu woman who sat on the dirt with her back against the barracks wall. "Wash it well, mama, and be careful where you step."

She cleaned her needle, one of her most precious possessions, pinned it to her collar, and turned her attention to the next woman.

The three thousand female detainees of the Kamiti Detention Camp occupied only a quarter of the eleven-thousand-acre prison; they were segregated from the men's section by a high chain link fence, guard towers, and rolls of barbed wire. The inhabitants of Kamiti were considered dangerous political prisoners, and therefore, it was a maximum security camp; conditions were harsh for both the men inmates and the women and children, the food was deplorable, the cells were overcrowded, and medical help was stretched too thinly to be of any help. That was why Wanjiru, because of her training as a nurse, had become almost the sole health care worker in Compound D.

After examining the next woman's arms, which had festering wounds as a result of torture, Wanjiru said gently, "Be sure to keep them clean, mama. And let the sunlight of Mother Africa heal them."

Wanjiru felt so helpless. With no medicines, no bandages, and no proper food it was impossible for her to do much for these suffering, outcast women. Still, she did her best. She drew upon her formal training received from British nursing sisters, who had taught her modern medicine and hygiene, and upon the traditional healing she had learned from Mama Wachera. Sometimes just having Wanjiru Mathenge look at their ailments or listen to their troubles made the inmates feel better. They were lucky to have her, the women all agreed.

Having seen to the last woman, Wanjiru stood and took hold of her daughter's hand. It was time to collect the water from the communal borehole.

She walked with Christopher strapped to her back. He was two years old and getting heavy. Wanjiru could have left her children in the care of other women in the compound, as most mothers in the camp did, but she had never, since the day each was born, let them out of her sight. She would not be separated from them now.

The sky was gray and lowering as she trudged under the eyes of the white and African guards up in their tower, where the British Union Jack fluttered in the wind. She passed large groups of women, sitting or lying in the dirt or lined up against the barracks walls, out of the cold, many of them inadequately dressed. She wondered again what crimes these poor creatures had committed. Surely, she thought, out of the three thousand women in the camp, there were perhaps only fifty who were Mau Mau like herself. So what had the rest done to deserve such treatment?

They have no husbands, she thought. *They are unwanted. They are considered useless. And that is their great crime.*

The water was brackish and dirty; but it was better than no water at all, so Wanjiru constantly urged the women of her compound to keep themselves and their children clean. Disease was the biggest enemy in the Kamiti camp, and Wanjiru was forever lecturing on the tactics of how to fight it.

She paused with her calabash gourd to look out through the enormous rolls of barbed wire that coiled around the camp. This was a desolate place. She could see far into the distance, where heavy rain fell upon the mountains. In the rising wind she heard again the pronouncement at her trial: *Charge: terrorist activities against the Crown. Sentence: governor's pleasure, maximum security, life.*

Life. . .

Were they truly going to do that to her? Keep her and her children behind wire for the rest of their lives? Wanjiru was only thirty-six years old; *life* was a very long time.

She felt Christopher, warm and heavy on her back, and Hannah's tiny hand in hers, and she was suddenly gripped with panic and fury. What crimes have these little ones committed, except to have been born with the right to freedom?

A female warder came along. She was a tall Wakamba woman leading two vicious dogs, who prodded Wanjiru to go back to her barracks. Wanjiru thought of David. Where was he? What was this war doing to *him?*

"ONCE UPON A time," Wanjiru said quietly above the sound of rain, "a very wise medicine woman lived in a hut on the bank of a river. She lived with her grandmother and her son, and they were very happy there on the bank of that river, which gave them water and fed their crops of maize, millet, and beans. One day a strange man came to the river. The medicine woman had never seen anything like him before. His skin was the color of the pale green frog, and he spoke in a language unknown to the Children of Mumbi. The medicine woman called him Mzungu, because of his strangeness."

The women in Wanjiru's cell, huddled together against the cold, paid close attention to her tale. They had never heard this story before.

"Now Mzungu told the medicine woman that he liked this place by the river and that he would like to live there. She said that he was welcome because there was enough food and water and sunshine for all. So he went away to build his house in another place by the river.

"The medicine woman and her grandmother and son lived in peace by the river. They were very happy and loved one another. And they didn't mind Mzungu for a neighbor. But then one day Mzungu got greedy."

Christopher wriggled in his mother's lap. She had told this story before; he wanted to hear the one about how the wild turkey got his spots. Hannah, curled up against her mother's side, was asleep with three fingers in her mouth.

In this cell, which had been constructed to hold ten people, twenty-six women, some with small children and babies, sat along the cold, damp walls or lay on the floor, listening to Wanjiru's story. It didn't matter that it wasn't a familiar, traditional tale—although those were the best—only that she provided them with distraction so that they could forget for the moment how tired they were from having worked all day in the fields, growing food for the inmates, or carrying murram for new roads, or burying the many dead. They all were hungry, but Wanjiru stopped them for a while from thinking of their supper of badly prepared maize porridge served without salt or sugar.

"Mzungu told the medicine woman that he wanted more land, that what he had wasn't enough. So she said, 'Take what you need; there is plenty for all.' So Mzungu took more land and made his shamba bigger."

The rain drove down on the corrugated tin roof and against the one window of the cell. Although it was still day, the light in the barracks was dim, and there were no lamps or light bulbs. There was nothing for the women to do except sleep and waken in the morning to another day of hardship, of wondering where their husbands were, of wondering when they were going to be released, of not knowing why they were in prison.

It had to do with Mau Mau, they all knew that. But, most wondered, did the government really think *all* these women were freedom fighters? Like toothless old Mama Margaret over there, or lame Mumbi? A "rehabilitation witch doctor" had come through Compound D that afternoon, administering antioaths to the women. For many it had seemed a useless ritual because they had not taken oaths in the first place.

"Mzungu came again to the medicine woman's hut and told her he needed still more land. And she said, 'Take what you need; there is plenty for all.' Mzungu did this day after day, until it was no longer a long walk to his shamba. It was right next to hers! Then he said, 'I need more land,' and she said, 'Take what you need; there is plenty for all.' But Mzungu now wanted the land upon which the sacred fig tree stood, and the medicine woman said politely, 'No, my friend. You cannot have that ground, for as you can see, it belongs to Ngai, the Lord of Brightness.' "

Wanjiru's audience murmured, pleased with the medicine woman's response. But when she told how Mzungu uprooted the tree anyway, they all cried out.

"The medicine woman put a *thahu* upon Mzungu and all his generations to come and said that he would be cursed until the day the sacred land is returned to the Children of Mumbi."

The women clapped and agreed all around that it had been a satisfying story. Then they settled down for the long, hungry sleep, trying to get comfortable in the one blanket each had been provided with, some trying with dry breasts to suckle babies, others weeping in memory of the homes they had been wrenched from. For most, there had been the sudden, surprise roundup in their villages; the women had been carted away in trucks separately from their men, riding away down the road to see soldiers enter their huts and come out with their arms full.

"Mama Wanjiru!" called an urgent voice in the doorless doorway of the cell. "Come quickly! Mama Njoki is very ill!"

Wanjiru went with the woman into the next cell, where Njoki was sitting propped up against the wall. In the watery light that came through the window, Wanjiru saw that the woman's tongue was swollen and bright red. There were also sores on her body, and her skin was curiously loose in places. "How do you feel, mama?" Wanjiru asked gently. "Have you had vomiting?" The woman nodded. "And diarrhea?" Another nod. "Does your throat burn?" Wanjiru saw how the woman's hands opened and closed repeatedly in a grasping reflex which Njoki could not control. She also recognized that delirium was not far off and beyond that, death.

"Are there others?" Wanjiru asked the woman who had summoned her.

Yes, there were others, but none as sick as Mama Njoki.

"I must see Simon Mwacharo," Wanjiru told the female warder who watched over the barracks. "It's urgent!"

The white British officer, Dwyer, was in Mwacharo's office. They had been playing cards beneath the thunderous sound of rain on the corrugated roof. Both were surprised to see Wanjiru, rain-soaked, come in. Mwacharo experienced the brief hope that she had come to give him the information he wanted, but that hope was dashed when she said, "There is an outbreak of pellagra in Compound D."

"How do you know?"

"I have seen the victims. Some are very sick. They will die if we don't have an improvement in our food. We need something more than maize!"

"What are you talking about?" said Officer Dwyer. "That's all you people ever eat."

"We need green beans! Maize alone is deficient in vitamin B."

His eyebrows shot up. "How do *you* know something like that?"

She gave the white officer a contemptuous look. "I was trained as a nursing sister in Nairobi. I understand the connection between nutrition and health. And I tell you the food in this camp is unhealthy!"

Officer Dwyer was momentarily impressed. He had never come across an educated African woman before. "Why *should* we feed you? To build up your strength so you can go back into the forest and fight us some more?"

"So," said Mwacharo, coming up to her, "do you want me to set out a banquet for you every night?"

"Just let us grow beans. Or have the *daktari* dispense vitamin tablets. The pellagra will spread if we don't stop it now."

Mwacharo grinned, and Wanjiru suddenly went cold.

"What will you do in exchange?" he asked.

"Please give us better food," she said softly.

The warder put his hand on her breast and squeezed. Wanjiru closed her eyes.

"When you give me the information I want," he said, "about the secret underground of Mau Mau and about Leopard, then I'll see you get your vitamins."

MAMA NJOKI DIED the next day, as did two other women and three children. Wanjiru was taken off the rock quarry, where she engaged in an endless labor of breaking rocks, and was put on burial detail. In the evening she went through all the cells of Compound D and saw that the pellagra was getting worse.

She began her protest among the women of her own cell, and from there it spread to the entire compound. "Mothers of Kenya!" she cried. "They are killing us with their miserable food! We must unite and resist! We cannot let them murder us in this insidious way! Do not let tribalism keep us from forming a united front! We should not be Kikuyu or Luo or Wakamba; we must remember that we all are Kenyan mothers and are fighting for our children's future!"

As a punishment for her insurrectionist talk Wanjiru, along with Mama Ngina, Kenyatta's wife, was made to carry the prisoners' excrement pails.

But she continued to preach to the inmates, stirring them up, so that finally Wanjiru was locked up in solitary confinement, without her children, for twenty-one days. But even from there Wanjiru continued to organize a food strike. Knowing that the guards were non-Kikuyu, she sang songs at night, her voice ringing out over the compound, and in her Kikuyu songs she told the mothers of Kenya to refuse the gruel that was given to them in the morning, and to lay aside their hoes, and to refuse to carry murram until the food was improved.

When she was released, blinking in the sun, three weeks later, Wanjiru found to her joy that her plan had worked; the women had listened to her songs and had done as she instructed. The food boycott had resulted in a concession of bean plots and a weekly distribution of vitamin tablets.

But it was too late, she learned, for little Hannah.

"We did what we could," the women in Wanjiru's cell told her. "But the help came too late. Now she cannot eat."

Wanjiru sat and rocked the listless child in her arms, singing a Kikuyu lullaby while Christopher watched with big, solemn eyes. In the middle of the night Hannah stirred, said, "Mama," and died.

The next morning Wanjiru herself dug the grave, one of many from the pellagra outbreak, and returned her daughter to the earth of Mother Africa.

THEY HAD BEEN at it for hours; Wanjiru could hardly stand up any longer. Simon Mwacharo never ceased his interminable questions: "Who did you take orders from? Where was your forest camp? Who is Leopard?"

It even proved to be too long a session for Officer Dwyer, who finally got up and left.

"Let me sleep," Wanjiru said. "Please. . ."

"After you tell me what I want to know. Give me the Mau Mau information, and you can have anything you want. I promise."

Wanjiru felt light-headed. She hadn't eaten in more than a day, and Simon Mwacharo had kept her standing for hours.

"Stupid woman," he said, "your stubbornness will be your death sentence, don't you know that? And if you don't care about yourself, then what about your son?"

She thought of Christopher, back in the cell in the care of the other women. *If he must die for* uhuru, *then so be it,* Wanjiru thought. *I will not betray my cause just to save my life or my son's.*

"Tell me what I want to know," Mwacharo said, "or I shall force it from you."

He walked to the door and locked it. When he gave a signal to the four askaris, Wanjiru suddenly came alert.

"You've had this coming for a long time," he said as he started to unbuckle his belt. "With your vitamins and boycotts and superior ways. I'll show you what you really are. I'll show you what you deserve. And cry out all you want; if anyone hears you, he won't interfere."

The guards shoved Wanjiru to the floor. Two pinned her arms down; the others held her legs.

Simon Mwacharo unbuttoned his pants and said, "When I am done with you, these four askaris will take turns on you."

Wanjiru looked up at the ceiling in horror. She concentrated on the hills and valleys of the gray tin, recalling the green hills and valleys of her home in the Nyeri District. She thought of the sweet-smelling pine forests, of the running streams and waterfalls, of the abundance of birds and flowers, of the children singing in the village, of women working joyfully in the sun, of the husband she had once so loved—

Wanjiru threw back her head and screamed, *"David!"*

52

M ona had been sitting by the window, looking out, for nearly two hours when at last her vigil was rewarded. "Uncle James!" she said, jumping up.

She hurried out onto the veranda of Grace's house to meet him, her three-month-old baby in her arms, but as soon as she saw the expression on his face when he got out of the car, she knew that his trip to Nairobi had been in vain.

"I'm sorry, Mona," he said, limping up the stairs. James was sixty-six now, and the old leg wound from World War I was giving him trouble. "I made extensive inquiries, and David Mathenge simply was not among those rounded up."

"Which means he's still in the forest."

"Or he's dead," James said, putting a hand on her shoulder. "You must accept that possibility, Mona. Many were killed."

James Donald was referring to Operation Anvil, which had taken place three months ago, in April—a massive campaign against Mau Mau launched by the British which had resulted in the arrest and detention of thirty-five thousand Africans. Since Mona had not heard from David in the year since his disappearance and had received no reply to any of the letters she continued to give to Mama Wachera, she decided he must be in a detention camp and therefore unable to get word to her.

So James had offered to use his influence and make some inquiries. He and Geoffrey, Grace, and Mario, the houseboy, were the only four who knew that David had joined Mau Mau and that the baby in Mona's arms was his.

The colony buzzed with speculation about Mona Treverton's illegitimate child. Whose could it be? She had seemed such a nice, decent woman, the gossips declared, but then look how her mother turned out. The consensus was that the baby was Geoffrey Donald's. He was always at Bellatu.

Mona didn't concern herself with the rumors. The child had little hair on her head and was creamy-skinned. She looked like any baby. But Mona knew the time would come when her daughter's African ancestry would start to show, and then eyebrows would certainly rise. She hoped that by then Kenya would have solved its differences and that her daughter would not have to suffer a social and racial stigma.

There must be a future for us, David had said to Mona on that June night of a year ago, when they had made love and sworn eternal devotion, *where we can walk side by side in the sun as man and wife.*

Will there be such a future for us? Mona wondered as she went with Sir James into the kitchen, where Mario was preparing lunch. *A future in which David and I can marry without being outcasts, in which we can ride together in the same train car, walk into a hotel dining room together and sit at a table and order a meal?* Late at night, when she lay in bed with her baby cradled in her arm, Mona's yearning love for David made her believe that such a future was not only possible but very near. In the light of day, however, as she strapped the revolver around her waist and heard the news reports of more killings, more atrocities on both sides, she saw that beautiful future fade like a tea rose exposed to too much sun. In Kenya whites had always ridden the train first class, the Africans third, and they never sat at a meal together. Her fantasy was outlandish; she might as well wish for the moon.

"*Jambo, bwana,*" Mario said as he poured James's tea. "*Habari gani?*"

"*Mzuri sana,* Mario. And yourself?"

"These are bad times, bwana. Very bad."

Bad, yes, James agreed, but improving daily. In the three months since Operation Anvil the British had started to see a definite decline in Mau Mau strength. Although not all of the thirty-five thousand who had been rounded up were Mau Mau, by casting such a wide net, the British had coincidentally snared a few big fish. Now, if only they could get the oath giver in this area, and the Mau Mau high command, such as Dedan Kimathi, or the one they called Leopard, then this rebellion, James was certain, would be snuffed like a flame.

And after that, what?

James stirred sugar into his tea, deep in thought. Beyond the window, bees droned among Grace's marigolds and pansies, the usual busy traffic of the mission rattled down paved lanes, British Tommies patrolled the perimeter, guns ready.

There was no doubt in James Donald's mind that Mau Mau had changed Kenya forever. Once this civil war was over, he knew that drastic innovations were going to be seen. Already something which no white settler would have dreamed had happened: The first African minister had been installed in the government.

But if the Africans expect self-rule, James thought, *then whom would they choose to lead them?*

"Have you seen Geoffrey?" he asked.

"He was here earlier," Mona said as she commenced to give Mumbi her bottle. "He and Tim Hopkins have joined the DO in another search for the oath giver. They plan a surprise roundup."

James took a slice of bread and buttered it. He didn't know what had happened between his son and Mona, only that it had been bad enough to have caused an irreparable rift between them. The two had not spoken to each other, it seemed to James, in nearly a year. And whenever Geoffrey came to visit with Ilse and the five children, Mona made excuses to leave the room. It had, he suspected, something to do with David Mathenge.

"Mario," James said, "I seem to have used the last of the jam. Would there happen to be—"

To his surprise, the houseboy was no longer there.

THE MISTS CREPT down from Mount Kenya in tendrils. They curled around tree trunks, swallowed grass and bush, burdened each leaf and petal with heavy drops of moisture. By midnight the forest had been transformed into a smoky, shadowy realm, a kind of netherworld like the one the Kikuyu believed their ancestors inhabited.

Two men walked alone through the fog, their hair bejeweled with mist, their ragged clothes wet. They had come a great distance, from the cloud-covered moorlands on top of the Aberdares, where giant bamboo forests and murderous bogs hid their secret freedom camp. They walked with caution, their senses, after their having lived so long in the forest, honed to animal sharpness. They heard as a leopard hears, they scented as an antelope scents, and they walked as if on paws, silently, lethally. There was danger all around them, they knew, not just from the wild beasts of the forest but from the British soldiers who had begun to infiltrate the mountain woodland in new guerrilla tactics.

These two were Mau Mau. They were desperate men, and they were on a mission.

They stopped suddenly, together, and listened. Not far away was a camp. They could hear the bamboo popping in the cook fire. The leader of the two crept forward, his rifle at the ready. He walked with thumb on the safety catch, finger on the trigger. If the soldiers were suddenly alerted, it would be snap shooting.

But the Tommies, he and his companion saw through the trees, were eating bully beef and trying to get warm under canvas tarpaulins. They looked pale and miserable and out of place in this silent jungle of mists and vines.

The two Mau Mau moved on. Their destination was too important to be sidetracked by the killing of a handful of Tommies.

Their orders had come from the very top, from Dedan Kimathi himself, the supreme Mau Mau commander. Underground intelligence had told of a white infant being kept in the house of Memsaab Daktari, Grace Treverton. Kimathi wanted that baby, and he wanted it alive.

Ever since Operation Anvil, which had crippled Mau Mau to the extent that many freedom fighters were cut off from supply lines, starving, diseased, and in rags, Kimathi had decided to launch the largest recruitment to date. At this moment his men were making raids upon Kikuyu homes, dragging the inhabitants out for forced oathings. It was the only way he could increase the size of his army. But because these were hard-core loyalists, Kikuyu who had resisted Mau Mau for two years, Kimathi knew the oathing would have to be of a particularly potent and virulent kind. There would be no dogs or virgins used in this ceremony, but the child of a white memsaab. Once the taboo flesh had been eaten, none of those forced into the oath would be able to disobey Kimathi's orders.

When at last the two—the leader, named Leopard, and his companion, the oath giver—emerged from the forest, they found a world bathed in moonglow. Tidy little shambas patched the grassy hillsides paralleling the river; fingers of smoke rose up from cone-shaped roofs; the sprawling Grace Mission, looking like a small town, slept behind locked windows and doors. The two Mau Mau could see soldiers making silent rounds. One of the forest men, the oath giver, pointed his companion toward the large house in the center of a garden and trees, where Memsaab Daktari lived. The baby was in there, he said, in the room that faced the giant sycamore. And that window, he assured his comrade, was unlocked.

Before striking off down the path that led to the river, Leopard paused. Spread before him, looking eerie and ghostly in the moonlight, was the forgotten rectangle of the polo field, embraced at the southern end by three little Kikuyu huts. His eye traveled up the opposite ridge, where, illuminated by the light from the full moon, a magnificent two-story house stood on a rise like a jewel on black-green velvet. That house was also dark. He thought of its inhabitant, asleep in the dark; he recalled the bed she slept in. And for a moment he was overcome with grief.

But all this—the peaceful river, the three little huts, the house on the hill—was gone now, forever. . . .

MONA TOSSED AND turned in her sleep. Unpleasant dreams visited her; she awoke more than once, her heart thumping.

When she woke up this time, her eyes snapping open, she stared up at the dark ceiling and listened to the silent house. In the bedroom down the hall Aunt Grace and Uncle James were sleeping. Tim Hopkins had spread a bedroll in the large pantry off the kitchen. In these days of the emergency the settlers who had stayed in Kenya clustered together for safety.

Mona listened to the house. Her heart thumped. *Had* she heard a sound?

But the house was solidly locked; James and Mario had seen to that. And there were soldiers all around.

She lifted her head from the pillow and looked at the silhouette of the crib at the foot of her bed. Her daughter, the joy of Mona's life, dreamed peacefully in baby innocence.

And then, suddenly, the moonglow from the window was blocked by a shadow. Mona gasped and sat up. Reaching for her gun, she jumped out of bed and switched on the light.

She cried out.

Two Mau Mau, their clothes in rags, one with a beard and long hair, the other with a trusted and familiar face, suddenly filled the tiny room. She raised her gun, started to shoot. And then her eyes met those of the bearded one.

"David?" she whispered.

He stared at her. A look of confusion swept over his face.

She looked at the other man: Mario. His face was the same, but his eyes! There was a wildness in them, a savageness that struck terror in her. And then all at once Mona knew: They were after the baby.

"No," she whispered. "David, don't do this! She's our child! *She's your daughter!"*

He looked down into the crib. His face was like that of a man who has been wakened from a deep trance. He seemed disoriented, as if surprised to find himself there.

"David!" she cried. "You never got my letters!"

In a sudden, swift move Mario reached into the crib and seized the baby. "No!" Mona screamed. She fired the gun. It splintered the wall.

Mario raised his panga and started to throw it at Mona. David grabbed his arm, but Mario shoved him back, and David landed hard against the wall, dazed.

The bedroom door burst open. James rushed in, a club in his hand. He swung at Mario. But the panga found him first. Clutching his neck, James dropped to his knees.

Mona dashed forward and tried to pull the baby from Mario's arms. He wrested the gun from her hand and fired, missing her.

Then David was on his feet again and wrestling with Mario. The grip on the child loosened; she tumbled to the floor and landed between the scuffling feet of the two men.

Mona, down on her hands and knees, tried to reach her.

Mario's gun went off. David flew back, his hands on his chest.

Mona ran to him. He fell into her arms.

And then another shot was fired. Grace Treverton was suddenly in the doorway, her pistol held between both hands. She fired a second time, and Mario fell dead to the floor.

DR. NATHAN QUIETLY closed the door to Grace's bedroom and said, "She'll sleep now. I've given her a sedative."

"Yes," said Geoffrey. He was numb with shock. He had driven as fast as he could from Kilima Simba after receiving the phone call, only to arrive minutes after his father died of the panga wound.

Tim Hopkins, who had arrived on the scene after the last fatal bullet was fired, roused himself now from his stupor and looked around the crowded kitchen. It was full of soldiers badgering sleepy-eyed Kikuyu with their questions. The oath giver, it was found out, had been Mario. But what David Mathenge had to do with Mau Mau, no one seemed to know. "I say," said Tim, "where's Mona?"

"I don't know, and I don't give a damn." Geoffrey truly hated her now. This was all her fault. He was glad her black lover was dead, as was their half-breed baby. It was just punishment, in Geoffrey's mind.

"Pardon me, sir," said one of the soldiers. "If you're referring to Miss Treverton, she left the house a little while ago and took that path up there."

Tim looked through the open door. The Tommy was pointing up to Bellatu. "And you let her go? You idiot!"

He ran out of Grace's house and climbed the wooden stairway up the grassy ridge.

At the top he paused and looked around. It was a clear night, with full moon and stars. The wilting, unharvested coffee trees stood in thousands of moonlit rows, sweeping away to a silvery, misty Mount Kenya. He turned toward the house. It was dark. But the back door was open.

He went inside and listened. He heard sounds overhead. Running through the dark dining room and living room, Tim took the stairs two at a time until he was on the second floor. He paused and looked down the length of the gloomy hall. The air smelled old and musty. He saw frail light spilling from one of the rooms.

When he reached it, Tim found Mona in a dusty, cobwebby room that looked as if it hadn't been used in years. Dominating it was an enormous old canopy bed, its spread and ruffles yellowed with time. And there was a vanity table, cluttered with dried-up perfume bottles. Mona was on her knees, frantically going through a dresser drawer.

"Mona?" he said, coming in. "What are you doing?"

She held a shaky flashlight, while with her other hand she madly went through lace and silk and satin.

Squatting next to her, Tim said quietly, "Mona? What are you doing?"

"I can't find it," she said.

"Can't find what?"

"I—I don't know." Negligees flew out of the drawer, dainty rose-pink nightgowns, and lingerie as delicate as spider webs. "But it *must* be here."

He looked around. Mona had gone through all the drawers in the room. Things were strewn on the floor—clothing, papers, photographs. He remembered with a chill that this had been Lady Rose's bedroom, closed up years ago. And then he recalled the night of the earl's murder, the desperate bicycle ride.

"Mona," he said gently, "what is it you're looking for?"

"I don't know. But it must be here. It was here once. . . ." She started to cry.

Tim put his arm around her and tried to comfort her. Mona turned into his embrace and wept against his chest. He brought her up to her feet and held her tightly, while she sobbed and cried out all her grief and anguish.

"I feel such pain! Oh Tim, the pain!"

He didn't know what to say. But he understood what she was feeling because he had felt it once long ago, when he had come to in the alley and had been told that Arthur had died trying to save his life.

"Tim! Tim!" she sobbed into his neck. "Hold me! Please hold me! Don't let me go!"

He tightened his embrace. She clung to him. Tears rose in his eyes, with memories, with sympathy.

"I feel such *pain*," she whispered. "I can't bear it."

Her mouth came up to his. He let her kiss him.

"Don't leave me," she said. "I can't bear it."

He cried with her, feeling the old pain all over again and the empty, loveless years that had followed Arthur's death. When she leaned against him, as if no longer able to stand, he guided her to the dusty bed that had made the long journey from Bella Hill in 1919.

He laid her down and held her, tried to soothe her. She cried in his arms. She clung to him. She kissed his face. She said things he didn't want to hear. And she whispered, "The pain, Tim. Make the pain go away. I can't bear it. . . ."

And so Tim Hopkins, who had never loved a woman, thinking now of Mona's brother, the only person he had ever loved, and knowing from her hands what she wanted from him, comforted her in his own clumsy, anguished way.

PART
SEVEN
1963

53

It fascinated Deborah the way the sunlight dappled the water. Like amber on diamonds, she thought.

She knelt on the riverbank, enveloped in a shaft of golden sunlight, a barefoot little girl whose long black hair had escaped its ponytail and now hung half down her back, half over her shoulder. She was motionless and looked as if she had sprung from the clay, like the bamboo and ferns and river grass that surrounded her. Her white cotton dress caught the morning sun and softened it; the myriad greens of the lush foliage around her cast gentle hues over her nut brown limbs. There was a woodlike aura about her, as though she were a forestland nymph.

Deborah remained so still because she was watching a pair of otters cavort in a pool among the riverine boulders. Their red-brown bodies were sleek in the sun; their little round heads with short ears bobbed in and out of the water, their whiskers twitching. They seemed to be aware of the little girl as they played; Deborah was certain they performed especially for her.

As the warmth of the sun penetrated the fabric of her dress, the eight-year-old was lulled into a drowsy complacency. Her large black eyes contemplated the rippling water, became hypnotized at the yellow, brown, and gray pebbles shining on the river's bottom, like the eggs of lazy birds, she thought, or the castoff jewels from some old king's treasure. She dipped her hand in. The water was icy. That was because it came from the tops of the mountains, Deborah knew, from a place her governess had said was called the Aberdares. This water had traveled all the way down from misty, moorland peaks, through forests so deep no human had ever gone inside, along secret streams, and over waterfalls to splash finally down this ravine that was called the Chania River.

Deborah loved the river. It was the only world she knew.

Overhead chatter startled her out of her dreamy state. Shading her eyes, she looked up to see a family of colobus monkeys making its way among the Cape chestnuts. Deborah laughed. She called out to them. They looked like beautiful adornments on the lichen-covered trees, their long white mantles and bushy tails draping the branches like pale moss. They whistled to one another and regarded the little girl with elders' eyes. They were used to her; she was always here at the river.

Deborah threw herself onto her back and looked up at the sky through the branches. It was a never-ending blue. No sign yet of the rains her mother was hoping for.

Closing her eyes, she inhaled the heady perfumes of the river's edge: the moist earth; the grass and trees and flowers; the crystalline mountain air that swept down from the Aberdares. She felt a pulse beneath her hands; she heard the wind breathe. Africa was *alive*.

Deborah opened her eyes with a start.

There was a boy, standing a few feet away, watching her.

Deborah got to her feet and said, "Hello. Who are you?"

He didn't answer.

She studied him. She had never seen him here before; she wondered where he had come from. "Do you speak English?" she asked.

He stared at her, warily. Deborah thought he looked ready to turn and run. So she asked in Swahili, "Do you speak English?"

He shook his head no.

"Swahili?"

He nodded slowly.

"Good! I speak Swahili, too! What's your name?"

He hesitated, and when he spoke, his voice was soft, shy, "Christopher Mathenge."

"I'm Deborah Treverton, and I live in that big house up there."

She pointed to the top of the grassy ridge. Christopher turned and looked up. The house couldn't be seen from down here by the river— just rows of dead coffee trees. "Where are you from?" Deborah asked.

"Nairobi."

"Oh, Nairobi! I've never been there! It must be very big and wonderful! How I envy you!" She reached into her pocket and then held out her hand. "Would you like a sweetie?"

The boy looked at the candy in her palm. He seemed uncertain. He was so *serious,* Deborah thought.

When Christopher finally took one, she said, "Take two; they're awfully good!"

They ate the candy together, and by the time all the pieces were gone, Christopher was starting to smile.

"That's better!" Deborah said. "You're new here. Where do you live?"

He pointed to the mud huts clustered at the edge of the abandoned polo field. "Oh!" said Deborah, feeling a delicious thrill. "You live with the medicine woman! That must be terribly exciting!"

Christopher didn't look too sure about that. "She's my grandmother."

"I don't have a grandmother. But I do have an aunt. She owns that mission over there. Do you have a father?"

He shook his head.

"Neither do I. My father died before I was born. I live all alone with my mother."

They looked at each other in the diffuse, tree-broken sunlight. It suddenly seemed very significant to Deborah that this boy also had no father, and she sensed something sad about him. He was older than she was—he looked as if he was around eleven or twelve—but they had something important in common.

"Would you like to be my best friend?" she asked.

He frowned, not understanding.

"Or do you already have a best friend?"

Christopher thought of the boys he had only barely known in Nairobi. Because his mother moved so often and they had lived in so many places since their release from the detention camp, Christopher and his little sister, Sarah, had never been able to make permanent friends. "No," he said quietly.

"Don't you have *any* friends?"

He looked down and dug his bare toes into the earth. "No."

"Neither do I! *We* shall be best friends! Would you like that?"

He nodded.

"Very well then! I'm going to show you my special place. Are you afraid of ghosts?"

He gave her a suspicious look.

"My special place is supposed to be haunted. But I don't think it is! Come with me, Christopher."

They followed the river while Deborah kept up constant chatter. "I'm supposed to be doing my lessons, but Mrs. Waddell is taking a nap. She's my governess, and she isn't very good. I *was* going to the white school in Nyeri town, but they closed it because so many white people are leaving Kenya that there weren't enough pupils anymore to keep the school open. Why do you suppose that is? Why are all the white people leaving Kenya?"

Christopher wasn't sure, but he knew it had something to do with a man named Jomo Kenyatta. Christopher's mother had told him all about Jomo, who had spent as much time in jail as she had and who had been released at the same time, two years ago. The whites were afraid of Jomo, Christopher had heard. They thought he was going to take revenge on them for having kept him in prison for so many years.

"Actually I *do* have a friend," Deborah said as they skirted the polo field. She swung her arms as she walked and kicked stones with her bare feet. "His name is Terry Donald, and he used to go to the white boys' school in Nyeri; but that was closed down, too. He has two brothers and two sisters, and they're all in boarding school in Nairobi. But Terry's too young to go there. He's only ten. He has a tutor to give him lessons. He lives in Nyeri town. His father used to own a big cattle ranch called Kilima Simba, but they sold it last year. *Africans* bought it. Can you imagine that? Terry comes and plays with me. He's going to be a hunter when he grows up, and he already has his own gun!"

They paused at the busy entrance to Grace Mission. A paved road passed under the impressive wrought-iron arch and widened into a treelined street that had a stop sign at the end and a policeman's kiosk. Large stone buildings stood among old Cape chestnuts; there were people everywhere. From one of the three school buildings came the voices of children singing.

"It's the biggest Christian mission in Kenya," Deborah said with pride. "And my aunt Grace built it many years ago. She's a doctor, you know. I'm going to be a doctor when I grow up. I'm going to be just like her."

Christopher tried not to stare at this strange, talkative white girl, but he was curious about her. And he envied her. She seemed so sure of herself and of the world around her; she knew what she wanted to be. For Christopher, such confidence was alien. Life in the detention camps had been unsure from one day to the next; he had grown up knowing only insecurity. People he knew and grew to love suddenly were gone the next morning. And there had been another little sister, a long time ago, who had died in his mother's arms. When they had finally been released from detention, when Christopher was nine and Sarah six, they had known only the nomadic, rootless existence of living here and there in Nairobi, of being watched by the police, of his mother's doing menial jobs for the few shillings that fed and clothed them.

But things were going to get better from now on, Christopher's mother had assured him. She had finally gotten a permanent job at a hospital in Nairobi, as an ayah, a "maid," even though she was a registered nurse. That was why he and Sarah had been brought here to live with their father's mother. Christopher's mother shared a flat with two other nurses; she couldn't afford to keep her children with her. But soon, she promised him and his sister, things were going to change. Now that Jomo was prime minister of Kenya, Africans were going to be the equals of whites; Christopher's mother was going to be called "sister" and receive the same pay as white nurses.

The two children went around the perimeter of the mission and came upon a flight of rickety wooden stairs. They climbed the ridge, and Christopher finally saw the big house.

"It's called Bellatu," Deborah said. "It's terribly big and lonely. My mother is almost never home. She works out in the fields. She says she is trying to save the farm."

The young African boy stared at the house, which reminded him of the wonderful places he had seen in Nairobi. This white girl must be terribly rich, he decided, his boy's eye not seeing the peeling paint, the unmended shutters, the dying flower garden, the dried-up fountains. Bellatu was only a ghost of its former glory, fading and sad, but to Christopher Mathenge it looked like a palace.

He followed the strange girl down a narrow forest path that plunged into trees and dense undergrowth. It was an old path, he could see, which had not been walked on in a long time. Presently they came upon a peculiar clearing in the middle of a ring of eucalyptus trees. In the center stood a rotting structure that had no walls; on the far edge was a small stone building with a glass roof. But directly across was a most remarkable sight. It reminded Christopher of the churches in Nairobi.

"There's an old caretaker," Deborah said in a lowered voice, "but he's deaf. Would you like to go inside?"

They slowly approached the stone facade, which had engraved writing neither child could read, and mounted the steps. Christopher had expected to find people inside, so he was surprised to discover that it was empty except for a big stone block in the center. Strangely a flame glowed at one end of it.

"Look here," Deborah whispered. She took Christopher's hand and led him to a wall. There they saw, in the dim light, an enormous tapestry hanging in a wooden frame.

Christopher was awed. He had no idea what it was. It looked like a picture, yet it wasn't. The trees and grass and sky looked so real. The golden eyes of the leopard peering through giant fronds made him quake. And there was Mount Kenya!

Deborah's captivation was with just one spot on the tapestry, off to the side and looking slightly out of place—as if it had been an afterthought.

It was the figure of a man. He stood shrouded in mountain mist, looking as if he was trying to hide behind the ropy vines and sweeping moss. He gazed out from his linen world with dark, solemn eyes. He was very handsome, Deborah thought, with his high forehead and large, straight nose. Like a prince, perhaps, out of a fairy tale. And he was dark-skinned, but not like the Africans. She had no idea who he was or what he was doing trapped in that jungle of yarns and threads.

She looked at the boy at her side. When she saw that he was impressed, that he was not afraid of her "ghosty" place, she was glad. "You're very brave," she whispered. "You must be a warrior!"

Christopher looked at her. Then he stuck out his chest a little and said, "I am."

They left the mausoleum, with its forbidding, silent block of stone and curious, faint rust stains on the floor, and went to the glass-roofed building. It was in shambles, with the glass all broken and nothing inside but dead plants. Deborah and Christopher did not go all the way in, but from the doorway they could see something that looked like a bed, all tattered and overgrown with weeds and vines.

"What would you like to do now?" Deborah asked when they were once again on the sunlit path. "Are you hungry?"

Christopher could not remember a time when he had *not* been hungry. So when Deborah suggested they go up to the big house and see what was in the kitchen, his mouth watered, and he was suddenly very glad he had gone to look at the white girl lying on the bank of the river.

They found treacle buns still warm from the oven and a pitcher of cold milk. They ate with their fingers and wiped their hands on their clothes. Then Deborah said, "Would you like to see my most favorite place of all? It's terribly *secret.* No one knows about it. Not even Terry Donald!"

"Yes," said Christopher, feeling important and full and enjoying his adventure with the white girl. He sensed the big house standing around and over him, and he wondered what it must be like to live in such a grand place, to have a kitchen that provided endless food.

So again Deborah took Christopher Mathenge's hand and led him through the unused dining room, through the living room, and up the stairs to the scary, thrilling locked rooms above.

MONA KNOCKED THE dust off her pants and removed her straw sun hat. As she hung it on the peg inside the kitchen door, she saw that Solomon was not preparing lunch as he was supposed to be. In fact, there was no evidence, other than the tray of warm treacle buns, that the houseboy had attended to his usual morning chores. Mona was not surprised. Ever since the election of Jomo Kenyatta to the office of prime minister, back in June, old Solomon had become less and less faithful to his duties.

But it was not only Solomon, Mona knew. A rare disease had infected all of Kenya's native population; it was the illness of arrogance and greed.

As she looked through the morning post, which consisted of notices from creditors and banks and offers to purchase Bellatu, Mona reflected upon the unfortunate pass the colony had come to.

Although Mau Mau had been defeated back in 1956, and an end came at last to the hostilities, it was really just a Pyrrhic victory for the British. Mau Mau might have lost the battle, but it seemed now to Mona, on this terrifying eve of Kenyan independence, that they had won the war. In 1957 Africans voted for the first time and filled many seats in the legislature with their own people. Pressure then began for self-rule. Her Majesty's government drafted a plan granting a gradual turning over of the reins to the Africans, with a proposed date of final independence some twenty years down the line. But subsequent events conspired to force Whitehall into making an abrupt reversal of that decision, much to the shock and chagrin of the white settlers, who felt that they had been betrayed and "sold out."

First, a savage civil war in the Belgian Congo in 1960 had sent whites fleeing by car and train. Many had poured into Kenya, panicking the settlers with the prospect of such a rebellion spreading across Africa. It was then, three years ago, that the Kenya whites had begun their sad exodus.

Next had come Jomo Kenyatta's unexpected release from prison, an event which London had promised *would never happen.* But the problem was, hostilities were starting to break out in Kenya again, and there was a Mau Mau feeling in the air. Her Majesty's government regretfully informed the settlers that there would be no backup with British military forces a second time, that it was best just to let the colony go.

And so the "devil," as he had been called, the "leader unto death and darkness," was suddenly a free man and an extremely popular one. African voters immediately put Jomo Kenyatta, who had become a symbol of *uhuru,* at the head of KANU, the new, powerful African political party. And upon his declaration that Kenya would soon be racially integrated—in schools, hotels, and restaurants—the exodus of whites was stepped up.

Further outbreaks of Mau Mau-like activities, plus increasing pressure from the African delegation that attended the Lancaster House conference, finally squeezed Her Majesty's government into reversing its policy of a multiracial constitution in Kenya, granting instead an African majority based on a one-man, one-vote system. The result was, in the last elections, to place Jomo Kenyatta at the head of the coalition government as Kenya's first prime minister.

Under such rule most whites refused to exist.

"Pardon me, Mrs. Treverton."

Mona looked up to see Mrs. Waddell, the governess, come in. Her round face was flushed, and she panted as if she had walked a distance. "She's gone off again," the woman said, referring to the ethereal, free-spirited Deborah.

Mona put the mail down and got up to make tea. This was how it was in the "new Kenya": houseboys demanding more pay for less work and quitting in the middle of the day when they felt like it, leaving their employers to make tea. Now that Jomo Kenyatta was in the prime minister's seat, Solomon and many like him had undergone strange personality changes. Solomon no longer took orders from Mona and frequently disregarded his duties on a whim. "In two months we're going to be equals, memsaab," he had said when he had turned in his long white kanzu and red vest. "You will be providing me with trousers from now on." No doubt he had gone into Nyeri this morning for a beer drink. Such was the state of Kenya today.

"Did you search down by the river?" Mona asked the governess.

"I did, Mrs. Treverton. Your daughter is nowhere to be found."

Mona scowled as she spooned out the tea. Until earlier this year she had not had to bother much about Deborah. The child had lived almost constantly in the girls' boarding school. But now that white schools were being threatened with racial integration and settlers were pulling their children out and thus closing the schools, Deborah had to receive her schooling at home.

And Mona didn't want her daughter at home.

"Have you any ideas where I should look, Mrs. Treverton?"

The title of Mrs. was the governess's choosing. Mona decided that it made Mrs. Waddell feel better because it lent an air of respectability to her job. Certainly she knew that Mona was not married and that her child was a bastard. The whole colony knew it.

Mona remembered little of the night of David's death. She was told afterward that she had briefly gone out of her mind and that Tim had found her up here, going through her mother's things, searching for something. Mona didn't remember Tim's making love to her; he never spoke of it and never gave any indication that he wished to try it a second time. When, three months later, Mona had discovered she was pregnant, she was stunned.

Tim had been upset by the news. He had made a gallant, mumbled proposal of marriage. To his infinite relief Mona had refused him, saying that as they weren't in love and that as neither was cut out for marriage, it was an unnecessary and impractical idea. She had carried the baby indifferently for the next six months and had then named her, as her own mother had named her Mona, for a character in a book. From the moment Aunt Grace placed the baby in her arms, Mona felt no love for it.

"I was that surprised!" Mrs. Waddell said.

Mona looked at her. The governess had been talking, but Mona hadn't been listening. No doubt it was another string of complaints. Mrs. Waddell seemed to feel it her duty to report to Mona the latest "incidents."

"There we were," she went on, "Gladys Ormsby and I, with our flat tire and stranded on the road, when along comes a truckful of Africans. Instead of helping us, as they would have done in former times, they shout, 'Get out of the way, white bitches!' "

Mona put the tea on the table, found some biscuits in a tin, and sat down with the governess.

"Can you imagine?" Mrs. Waddell said as she helped herself. "They're spending over a quarter of a million pounds to enlarge the LegCo building. The African members are demanding it. Well, I suppose hot air does take up a lot of room!"

Mona gazed out the window, at the sunlight on dusty flowers, the yellowed grass, the weeds. She had a hard enough time keeping an adequate number of field hands working on the coffee; there just wasn't enough in the budget to hire a proper gardener.

"Have you heard that Tom Westfall sold out? To Kikuyu no less! That's the end of *that* farm."

Mona knew what Mrs. Waddell was referring to. Because of the rapid changeover, with Africans grabbing up land and the Europeans making hasty retreats, the transition was proving disastrous for the farms.

When Jomo had announced that in order to divert a second Mau Mau, which was brewing, thirty thousand Africans were to be settled on white land before independence, which was three months away, two hundred white families throughout the Rift Valley had received payment from the British government and relinquished farms they had built with their own hands many years ago. The Africans had moved in with the speed of locusts.

"I've heard it is simply ruinous," Mrs. Waddell said. "They've got chickens on the mantelpieces and goats in the bedrooms! And nothing gets mended, of course. I passed by the Collier homestead last week—shocking. Poor Trudie's roses all trampled. Her vegetable garden completely shot. Windows broken, doors hanging off hinges. And a charcoal fire in the middle of her living room! Her heart would break if she saw it. But Trudy's in Rhodesia now and well out of it. I ask you, Mrs. Treverton, if it's this bad now, what will it be like *after* independence?"

Mona had no idea, but it was the major concern among those whites who were still in Kenya. Every day Africans who had once been servile and obsequious were growing bold and impudent. She heard of whites being forced off sidewalks and being called names, of having their livestock stolen and carted away in broad daylight. The Africans were suddenly a race gone mad. It was as if independence were a strong liquor. "This is *our* home now" was the general feeling. "And you whites might as well get out because we won't tolerate you anymore."

Was this the beautiful future David had envisioned for himself and Mona?

"In December," the governess said, "the British police are going to turn their authority over to the Africans. *Then* whom do we call when there's trouble?"

That was precisely why Alice Hopkins had sold her huge ranch in the Rift—the one she had rescued when she was only sixteen—and moved down to Australia. She had seen terrible days ahead, in which the Africans, free from the arm of British law, were going to go on an antiwhite rampage of revenge and retribution.

And now Tim, too, was going to join his sister on her new sheep farm.

"Sell up, Mona," he had said. "You won't survive. Bellatu hasn't made a profit in years. Let the wogs have it. Come down to Tasmania and live with Alice and me."

But Mona was not going to sell. If she were the last white in Kenya, she would never sell.

"Well, Mrs. Treverton," the governess said as she finished her tea and wished there were proper sandwiches to go with it, "I suppose I'd best tell you my own news now. Mr. Waddell and I have decided to go down to South Africa and live with our daughter. We've lived in Kenya for thirty years, you know. Our children were born here. We turned a wilderness into a paradise. We made crops grow where there was only rock-hard ground. We poured money and industry into this colony. But now we're no longer welcome. We've sold the farm to Africans. And I want to be gone before I see what they do to it."

Mona was not surprised. Mrs. Waddell was the third governess she had hired for Deborah in the last few months. Kenya was a sinking ship, and all hands were deserting.

"When will you be leaving?"

"In two weeks. Just wanted to give you fair warning, on account of your daughter."

When her employer said nothing more but lapsed into silence, Mrs. Waddell helped herself to another biscuit and gave a mental shrug. Mrs. Treverton was a strange duck, the governess thought, living here on this derelict old estate and fighting to keep it going when everyone who had eyes could see what a futile struggle it was. Mrs. Treverton couldn't get enough Africans to work for her because they all were demanding higher pay. The quality of her coffee had declined as a result, so that she didn't receive sufficient world trade prices. It was a mystery to Mrs. Waddell why Mona Treverton held on so tenaciously to a losing farm, living alone in this white elephant of a house, all by herself with no husband and a wild, bastard daughter, when there were droves of gullible Africans waiting to buy it from her.

If Mona chose to explain her position, she would have told Mrs. Waddell that she stayed because Bellatu was all she had left—the impartial, unjudging land. There were no people in Mona's solitary life; she had no friends, no one she cared about. Any love or compassion or devotion she had ever felt had died with David and their baby.

When Mona had awakened that next morning to be told about her strange flight to her parents' bedroom—her momentary insanity—she had discovered a cold pain in the middle of her chest. And it was a pain that she knew would always be there.

Mona did not recover from her grief as her aunt Grace had done after six months of mourning for James Donald. Mona's indomitable aunt had allowed herself half a year of deep grief; then she had picked herself up, squared her shoulders, and resumed command of her mission and its needy population. Grace had the enviable capacity for regenerating love, Mona thought, as a lizard does a new tail. But Mona's own capacity for loving, once cut off, would never come back. And without love, there could be no people in her life. Only the farm.

She suddenly understood why her mother had chosen suicide after Carlo Nobili's death.

Although Mona had not had the courage to take her own life, she had retreated into a kind of suicide nonetheless. She saw her aunt occasionally, and Geoffrey and Tim once in a long while, but Mona had withdrawn into a reclusive life, dedicating herself to the five thousand acres of soil and enfeebled coffee trees that had been left to her. The baby, Deborah, she had turned over to a nursemaid the day she was born, and Mona never touched her again. The child, she believed, had sprung from a sterile, almost perverse act and had no right to live.

But now Deborah was in the house because the schools were closing, and governesses did not stay long. Mona was suddenly faced with a very unpleasant situation.

"If you'll pardon my saying so," Mrs. Waddell said, "you'd do well to sell up and leave with the rest of us, Mrs. Treverton. Come December, this isn't going to be a healthy climate for anyone with white skin."

But Mona said, "I shall never sell," as she cleared the tea dishes. "I was born in Kenya; this is my home. My father did more for this country than a million Africans ever did. He *built* Kenya, Mrs. Waddell. I have more right to be in this country than those people out there who have done nothing more than live in mud huts all their lives."

Mona paused at the sink and then turned around. "In fact," she said quietly but with a light behind her dark eyes, "it is the Africans who should leave. They don't deserve this rich and beautiful land. They have done nothing to earn Kenya. They will only spoil it and let it go to ruin. When my father came here, they were living in huts made of cow dung and wearing animal skins. They were grubbing out a meager existence as they had for centuries, with no further ambition than tomorrow's beer drink. And they would still be living like that today if the whites had never come to Kenya. We planted farms and built dams and paved roads and gave them medicine and books! We have put Kenya on the bloody map, and *they are telling us to leave!*"

Mrs. Waddell stared at her employer. Those were the most words she had ever heard Mrs. Treverton say at one time. And with such emotion! Who would have thought it, in a person whom all the colony regarded as hard and unfeeling?

Suddenly the governess recalled something she had once heard years ago: a nasty bit of gossip involving Mona Treverton and an African. But not even Mrs. Waddell, who did cherish such unsavory tidbits now and then, could swallow that distasteful story. It was unthinkable—the daughter of the earl having it on with her Kikuyu manager!

But now, as she heard the bitterness in Mrs. Treverton's voice and saw the passion in her eyes, Mrs. Waddell realized that her employer harbored some deep, extraordinary hatred for the Africans, and so she wondered if that horrible little rumor had been true.

Finally the governess left, and Mona was alone again. She stood at the sink, clutching its edge as if to keep from drowning. The cold pain in her chest had come back. It rose and filled her throat. She couldn't breathe; she felt as if she were choking.

But she fought it down and was soon in control again. Nine years ago, right after David's death, these spells had alarmed Grace, who had run an electrocardiogram on her niece. But Mona's heart—her *physical* heart—was found to be in excellent health. The constant pain and episodes of breathlessness stemmed from a spiritual source that Grace's modern medicine could not touch.

"You must let yourself cry, Mona," Grace had said. "You're bottling it up, and that's not good."

But Mona had lost the ability to cry. When David died in her arms, she had retreated into a kind of gray shock that had continued to envelop her long after the dead had been buried and Mau Mau been brought to an end. After her night with Tim not one tear had been shed by Mona for the deaths of David and their baby.

Mona heard a sound overhead.

She looked up at the ceiling and listened.

There was another sound and the drone of muffled voices.

In her parents' bedroom!

Mona ran from the kitchen and up the stairs.

DEBORAH HAD LEARNED about locks and keys in school. It had been part of the lesson on tying shoes, pouring one's own milk, how to carry scissors safely. A few months ago, all alone in the house and investigating, Deborah had come across an old tarnished set of keys, hidden away in a cupboard. She had tried matching them to various locks, as Miss Naismith had taught her, and had managed to open the door of this fabulous fairy tale bedroom.

When Deborah first set eyes upon the canopy bed with its ruffles, the window seat crowded with satin pillows, the dusty vanity table cluttered with beautiful old perfume bottles, she had thought she had stumbled upon the secret tower of a fairy tale princess. But then Deborah had realized that no one lived here and that therefore, she must be free to explore its wonderful treasures.

She had found old sequined gowns and dresses made of lace and gauze and jeweled tiaras and feather boas. She had played with the dried cakes of mascara and lipstick that crumbled when she touched them. She had opened the bottles and had smelled the vestiges of exquisite perfumes. And she had wondered, her child's imagination conjuring up Rapunzel and Sleeping Beauty, what sort of princess had lived here.

Now she shared her secret room with Christopher Mathenge, her new best friend.

They were sitting on the floor and going through what Deborah called the "paper box." It was small and wooden and contained packets of old yellowed photographs, letters, greeting cards, mementos from occasions Deborah knew nothing about. Since she didn't know who any of the people in the pictures were, she made up names and stories for them.

"This is me," she said, showing one to Christopher. Deborah had chosen to identify with the little girl in the old-fashioned sun helmet and funny clothes, not realizing that she indeed shared a strong resemblance with her. The girl was sitting among trees next to a blond, sad-eyed woman who had a monkey in her lap. There was something about their faces that made Deborah stare for hours; they both looked so unhappy. On the back of the photograph was written "Rose and daughter, 1927."

"Oh!" Deborah said as she pulled a thin little book out of the box. "Here's one *you* can be! See? You even look like him!"

Christopher was surprised to see that what Deborah held out to him was a passbook, very like the one his mother had carried for years. He stared at the face in the photo.

"Who is it?" Deborah asked. "Can you read the name?"

Christopher was nonplussed. The man's name was David Mathenge.

"But that's *your* last name!" Deborah said. She didn't understand about last names, had no idea that she should not have the same surname as her mother's parents. Deborah knew nothing about marriage and fathers and how women's last names changed when they became wives. She assumed that her own situation was the way it was with all mothers and daughters.

Christopher couldn't take his eyes away from the photo. There was a resemblance, yes, but his fascination went further: The passbook gave the man's home as the Nyeri District, and his parents as Chief Kabiru Mathenge and Wachera Mathenge.

Christopher knew nothing about his own father—what his name was, who he had been, or when and why he had died. His mother always refused to talk about him. When she had told stories to Christopher and Sarah, first in the Kamiti camp, which Christopher barely remembered and where his sister was born, and then later in the Hola camp, where they lived for five years, his mother only ever told tales of his grandmother, the medicine woman, and of the chief who lived long ago, the first Mathenge.

But this man David . . .

"You can keep it if you like," Deborah said when she saw how Christopher held on to the passbook.

He carefully tucked it into the waistband of his shorts.

As Deborah reached into the drawer to pull out more treasure, the light from the open doorway was suddenly cut off.

MONA STARED IN disbelief.

This room which she had locked up nine years ago now stood open to the hallway light. Familiar objects, for so long put out of her mind seemed to loom up before her in stablike waves of memory. Her mother's vanity table, where Rose would sit for hours, ignoring her daughter while Njeri combed out her long platinum hair. Valentine's rhinoceros whip, hanging on the wall, the symbol of his totalitarian power over her and Bellatu. And the big canopy bed where generations of Trevertons had been conceived—Mona herself, in England, forty-five years ago, and Deborah, her daughter, the night David had died.

Mona looked down, stunned, at the barefoot little girl with tanned limbs and masses of black hair who now lifted her face up to the light like a nut-brown sunflower. "Hello, Mummy," the child said.

Mona couldn't speak. Nine years ago she had closed this door and turned the key in the lock, sealing inside all her unbearable memories and private demons. She had walked away from this terrible room with its dusty secrets, a woman free of the past, feeling safe as long as the devils were never let loose.

But now the room stood wide open and menacing, its security breached by a little girl who had been created only because David had died.

"How dare you!" Mona said.

A look of bewilderment crossed Deborah's face. "I was just showing my new friend—" was all she had a chance to say before her mother swooped down, seized her in a painful grip, and dragged her to her feet. Startled, Deborah cried out. When her mother started to slap her, she tried to protect herself with her free arm.

"No!" shouted Christopher in Swahili. "Stop!"

Mona looked up. The light from the hallway fell over the African boy. She stared at him. Her grip loosened on Deborah.

She frowned. "David?" she whispered.

And then memories flooded back—the older, more deeply buried ones: the burning surgery hut; the necklace from Uganda.

The room seemed to tilt. The cold pain returned to her chest, and it rose in her throat, choking her. She groped for the doorjamb.

Deborah, who stood rubbing her arm and trying not to cry, said, "This is my best friend, Mummy. His name is Christopher Mathenge, and he lives with the medicine woman who's his grandmother."

Mona couldn't breathe. She pressed her hand to her chest. *David's son!*

Christopher's wide, terrified eyes watched the woman in the doorway. She was looking at him in a strange way, her eyes filling with tears. When she took a step toward him, he retreated.

"David," she murmured.

He thought of the passbook in his waistband.

Mona reached out, and Christopher stumbled backward, bumping against one of the bedposts.

She came closer. The two children watched in fear and fascination, the way her arms went out to him, the tears streaming down her face. When she was within inches of the boy, Deborah and Christopher held their breath.

And then Deborah was astonished to see a tender smile come to her mother's face, a face the girl had only ever known as hard and unchanging.

"David's son," Mona said softly, a tone of wonder in her voice.

Christopher, pressed against the bedpost, steeled himself when her hands came up and took gentle hold of his face.

A marveling look came into Mona's tear-filled eyes as she studied those sweetly familiar lines: the furrow between the brows; the almond-shaped eyes; the forward slung jaw that was the legacy of Masai warriors. Christopher was still just a boy, but the man he would one day be could be seen. And, Mona saw, he was going to look very much like David.

"David's son," she said again with her sorrowful smile. "He lives in you. He is not dead after all . . ."

Christopher's heart raced as the woman came even nearer, her cool hands on his cheeks, until her face was inches from his.

Then she bent and kissed him very gently on the mouth.

When Mona drew back, her face seemed to collapse, and a sob escaped her throat.

She touched him one last time—to trace a fingertip along the crease from his nose to the corner of his mouth—then turned and ran from the room.

54

After all these years Geoffrey Donald still desired Mona Treverton. As they sped along the highway into the brilliant equatorial sun, the Land-Rover startling herds of zebra and antelope on the roadside, Geoffrey glanced frequently at the woman sitting next to him. Mona was in the front seat between Aunt Grace and him, her expression fixed behind enormous sunglasses. She had lost weight and grown pale in the past few weeks, for reasons unknown to Geoffrey, but he liked her that way. At forty-four Mona was just as appealing, he thought, as she had ever been.

His anger and bitterness toward her, spawned on the night of his father's death, had faded. The years had mended his grief and had allowed his old appetite for her to return, especially as his wife got plumper and more indolent with each passing year, since the birth of Terry, their last child. It was not, of course, as if Mona gave him any encouragement or even really seemed to be aware of him beyond a purely superficial, almost afterthought relationship. But that was part of what made her fascinating—her aloofness and unavailability. Geoffrey Donald was, at fifty-one, ruggedly lean and sunburned, with silver in his hair and a charm that appealed to his female clients. His conquests were too easy and many; he had become bored and jaded in the area of romance. But Mona's apparent uninterest and her nine years of celibacy made the chase suddenly fresh and exciting. When she had agreed to come along on this safari into the Masai wilderness, Geoffrey's blood had raced with renewed lust and hope.

He had a surprise for her at the end of the road.

They were heading for Kilima Simba Safari Camp, a lonely outpost nestled in an outcropping of rock about twenty miles from the base of Mount Kilimanjaro. It lay in the heart of the Masai Amboseli Game Reserve, a vast tract of wilderness owned and overseen by the Masai tribe, whose grazing land this was. The road along which Geoffrey now drove in the heat of the day, with Deborah and Terry bouncing around in the back of the Rover like sacks of grain, was barely more than a ribbon of dirt through flat, yellow savanna. In the distance, mauve and snow-capped, Mount Kilimanjaro rose to a cloudless sky. As far as the eye could see, there were no signs of civilization; flat-topped thorn trees dotted the landscape; impalas and bushbucks grazed among the grasses; giraffes loped in graceful insouciance; a pride of lions basked under a tree. This was one of the richest game areas in Africa, and Geoffrey Donald was going to capitalize on it.

"A game lodge!" he had explained to Mona. "Tents just aren't appealing to everyone. Few of my clients find the camp pleasurable after a day or two, what with cots and mosquitoes to deal with, and no proper toilet facilities. I tried to think of ways to improve things, to get more tourists out here, and then it came to me. A resort, right in the middle of the African bush!"

Only a handful of Geoffrey's friends thought the idea had any worth. Most thought it would fail, reminding him that tourism was going to vanish from Kenya after independence. "This won't be a safe place for whites," they said. "The whole world knows what savagery this country is going to descend to after Her Majesty's government pulls out."

But Geoffrey saw things differently. "Old Jomo isn't crazy or stupid," he argued. "He knows he needs us. Europeans still monopolize all the large corporations, the banks, the hotels in Kenya. He knows he has to keep us on and keep us happy if he expects to maintain a stable economy. Without us and our connections and our capital and know-how, Kenya would collapse like a house of cards, and the wogs know it!"

It was something that was starting to prove true. In the five months since Kenyatta had taken over as prime minister, none of the vengeful reprisals the settlers had feared had come to pass. Indeed, to everyone's surprise Kenyatta was calling for moderate policies and peaceful coexistence between the races, and he had demonstrated the sincerity of his words by initiating a partnership with the European Farmers Association.

Nonetheless, Geoffrey's friends argued, Kenya was not yet fully independent. British troops were still here. Wait until next month, they said, when the government was officially handed over to the Africans, *then* see what happened.

But Geoffrey was determined. Sensing the direction of the "wind of change," he had sold the Donald cattle ranch near Nanyuki and had set himself up in Nairobi as a tour agent. When not dividing his time between his luxurious Parklands residence and his house in Nyeri, where Ilse lived with little Terry, Geoffrey met his few intrepid vacationers at the airport and escorted them all over Kenya in a convoy of Land-Rovers.

Despite Mau Mau and settlers' fears about independence, tourists *were* starting to come to East Africa, but in a trickle. Geoffrey wanted to convert that trickle into a flood and therefore had been working on ways to make his safaris more alluring. Camps smacked too much of hardship, no matter how many Africans were employed to pitch the tents, cook gourmet meals, make the beds, or do the tourists' laundry. The romance wore off quickly, and few went home believing they had gotten their money's worth.

That was when he had hit upon the idea of a resort hotel out in the bush, a "safari lodge," he called it, the first of its kind anywhere, complete with proper bedrooms, a dining room, a polite and friendly staff, and a cocktail bar from which the lazy adventurer could watch the wildlife.

"A place where tourists can be clean and drunk and *safe*," he declared, "where they can feel like Allan Quatermain without being threatened by animals or natives. Sort of like being on the inside looking out. A lodge that's set far away from Nairobi and from where Mau Mau took place, far away from any hint of politics or hostilities. My clients will taste the Kenya of fifty years ago. They will experience it as our parents did, when it was primitive and unspoiled and when the white man enjoyed a life of graciousness and elegance. And they'll pay top money for the opportunity, I guarantee it."

Geoffrey had then set out on a scouting safari in which he explored every corner of Kenya, observed each patch with the eye of a tourist, felt the wind, followed the game, and talked with local headmen. He had settled upon Amboseli for its beauty and abundant game and had leased from the Masai the site upon which his tent camp now stood.

In the beginning of the new year construction on the hotel was going to start.

He couldn't wait to reach camp. He was going to install Mona in the tent next to his, and later tonight, while everyone else was asleep, he was going to pay her a special call.

With each bound and jolt of the Rover, as it hit holes and boulders, the two children in the back held on and screamed with delight. Deborah and Terry rode on the side benches, facing each other. The canvas sides were rolled up so that they sat in the full force of the wind as Terry's father pushed the car at top speed. Deborah's unruly black hair had escaped its rubber band and now flew about her head in stinging whips.

This was her first safari; she could hardly control her excitement. As the Rover plunged through zebra herds, scattering the horselike creatures and making them bark, Deborah laughed and clapped her hands. She turned this way and that on her seat, watching giraffes run alongside the Rover, seeing startled rhinos suddenly turn and trot off in a trail of dust. She couldn't take in enough of it: the hawks in the sky; the vultures riding air currents; the lions drowsing; the weaverbirds building nests in the thorn trees. She had never before seen so much wildlife, such an endless expanse of land and sky. It took her breath away. She had had no idea Africa was so *big*.

They also passed herds of domestic cattle and Masai men whose bodies were painted red all over, each standing on one foot. They leaned on their spears—tall, angular men with long, plaited hair and crimson *shukas* knotted over one shoulder, flapping in the breeze. When the Rovers sped by, they raised their hands in generous, full-arm salutes. Deborah and Terry waved back, thinking them terribly foreign and exciting compared with the Westernized Kikuyu among whom they lived, and then they waved at Uncle Tim and Uncle Ralph, who rode behind in the supply Rover.

Deborah envied her ten-year-old friend in an almost physical ache. Terry was *so lucky*. His father led the most thrilling life! And he took his son on safaris with him, now that the white school in Nyeri was closed and Terry was still too young for boarding school in Nairobi where his brothers and sisters were. Terry had been to Kilima Simba Safari Camp before, and he had gone leopard hunting with his father

Deborah wished Christopher and Sarah Mathenge could have come along, but when Deborah had asked her mother if she could invite them, she had received a dismissive silence.

Deborah decided that when she got back to Bellatu, she was going to tell her two new friends all about this wonderful adventure and give them some of the photographs she planned to take with her Box Brownie.

By the time they reached the camp, weary and hungry and covered in red dust, the sun was on the horizon. Geoffrey's resident staff, young Masai in khaki shorts and clean white shirts, welcomed the travelers as they stumbled to the ground and stretched aching limbs, and then began the hasty unloading of supplies and luggage.

Deborah held her arms out and spun in a circle. It was glorious! The biting air, the long shadows, the unimaginable silence that stretched all the way to the flat horizon. It was a world with no walls, a land with no orderly rows of trees, a wilderness promising surprises and adventure. And Mount Kilimanjaro, she decided, was a thousand times more beautiful than her old Mount Kenya! She wished again, more desperately than ever, that Christopher Mathenge were here to share it with her.

"You see," Geoffrey explained to the grown-ups as they strode over the uneven ground toward the tents, "part of my advertising campaign will be that this was once the site of a Hemingway encampment. Moreover, this was where the film *Snows of Kilimanjaro* was made and also parts of *King Solomon's Mines.* That native village we passed back there—those huts were props for the film. Now, over here, contiguous with these giant boulders, is where I plan to locate the main lodge. . . ."

Supper was no less than excellent, everyone decided, served by waiters in kanzus and white gloves, on china and silver, in the romantic light of a watercolor sunset. Because there is no twilight in equatorial Africa, lanterns were promptly lit, filling the compound with a comforting glow. The dining tent was huge, with three gauze walls enabling those within to enjoy the panoramic view without having to battle mosquitoes. As they went through the consommé, the gazelle cutlets and new potatoes in gravy, and the lemon sherbet, Geoffrey continued to enlighten his companions about his plans.

"I've several investors," he said, signaling for a second bottle of wine. "One of them is a famous disc jockey."

Grace looked up from her food. "What's a disc jockey?"

Ralph said, "An American," and everyone laughed.

Including Mona, who had suffered the eight-hour journey from Nyeri in silence. She had taken the short tour of the camp without speaking a word, had washed and freshened up in her tent, and had come to the dining tent for sundowners with the guarded expression on her face that everyone had come to know. But now, after a few glasses of wine and the intimacy of the group, she, too, felt the immenseness of the plains, the otherworldliness of the isolated savanna, and she was starting to drop her defenses.

Geoffrey was the first to notice.

"We'll have what I call 'game runs,' " Geoffrey said, lighting a cigarette and sitting back. As he heard the noise of the night—the constant din of crickets, the roar of lions near by—Geoffrey congratulated himself once again on what he considered an exceptionally wise move. By selling his father's cattle ranch to Africans who had been eager to buy, Geoffrey was able to invest in a venture that he was certain was going to turn a huge profit. If he was going to be a white in Kenya, he decided, then he wanted to be a *wealthy* white.

"We'll get the tourists up at dawn and trot them around in Rovers, looking for game to photograph, which is always very active and visible in the early-morning hours. Afterward it's back to the lodge for a big breakfast and a day spent around the swimming pool. In the late afternoon, when the animals are waking up and on the prowl, we trot the people out again on another game run in Rovers fitted with brandy and sandwiches. In the evening we'll require formal dress for the dining room and put on a good show with local Masai dancers."

"It certainly sounds appealing," his brother, Ralph, said. "If old Jomo keeps the country stable, there's no reason why we can't make a go of this."

Ralph had come back to Kenya the year before, when Uganda had achieved *its* independence. President Obote had decided that the British system of provinces was no longer needed in his country, so he had dismissed all white civil servants. Ralph Donald, who was still a bachelor at forty-eight, had been a provincial commissioner and had been given, as the local slang called it, the "golden bowler"—compensation for his years of service to the Crown. After briefly operating a control post for receiving convoys of white Belgian Congo refugees coming through Uganda, Ralph had come to Kenya to join his brother in the new tourist business.

Silver-haired and ruddy of complexion, a man who had built a reputation for himself as a crack elephant hunter, Ralph Donald was the second person at the dinner table who had an eye on Mona.

"The way I see it," he said now as he filled and lit his pipe, "with so many Europeans getting out of Kenya, we few who are left are going to rule the roost. There will literally be rich pickings for us. The wogs will look around themselves, realize they haven't a bloody notion of how to run a country, and they'll come running to us for help."

Grace, who had hardly touched her food, gave Ralph a look. It was inconceivable to her that this self-centered man with the haw-haw voice could be James's son. "What baffles me," she said, "is where the Africans are getting all the money to buy up white farms. I heard that the Norich-Hastings plantation went for an astronomical sum!"

"It's no mystery, Aunt Grace," Geoffrey said. "The money isn't African; it's British. When Her Majesty's government as good as abandoned us all here by saying it wouldn't send in another army if Mau Mau broke out a second time and *then* agreed to turn complete rule over to the blacks, it had to find a way to assuage its feelings of guilt and assist the very people it had betrayed. It's this way: Money from Britain goes through the World Bank, through African middlemen, and into settler hands. That settler, having unloaded his farm, packs up and goes back to England, taking his money with him. In some cases, I've heard, the money never even leaves England!"

Ralph said, "I'll wager the wogs haven't a clue to what's going on," and then looked at Mona. He was remembering the day, years ago, when she had come to Entebbe with her aunt to take his father home.

"If you will excuse me," Grace said as she stood, "I'm very tired and not used to such traveling."

Geoffrey rose with her, thinking that, for seventy-three, Grace had weathered the journey remarkably well. He said, "I'll call for an askari to accompany you to your tent. Never go about the camp at night without an escort. Animals do come into the area and some get quite aggressive."

"Will the children be all right alone in a tent?"

"Terry's camped here before. He'll see that Deborah is well taken care of."

When Grace was by herself, a few minutes later, she sighed and sat down on the bed. She had to give Geoffrey his due; these tents were luxurious. They reminded her of the ones Valentine had erected back in 1919, when she and Rose had arrived to find that the house had not yet been built.

So long ago, she thought. *So very long ago* . . .

Grace was thinking that tomorrow was James's birthday and that he would have been seventy-five.

As a lonely wind whistled through the canvas walls and sent the Coleman lanterns swaying, Grace prepared for bed. She didn't really know why she had come along on this trip, except perhaps that Geoffrey had so wanted her to see and approve of his new idea. Also, she had thought a spell away from the mission would do her good. It was years since she had had a proper holiday; this might give her time to think, to consider the proposal of the order of African nuns who wanted to take over the mission school. She and James had always talked of going on a proper safari together but somehow had never found the time. Now here she was with his two sons.

She picked up the book she had brought along to read—the latest from America, *A Ship of Fools.* Then she put it down, unable to concentrate. James was on her mind. He filled her every thought; he lived in her soul.

As she went to the tent flap and peered through the mosquito netting at the serene, moon-washed landscape, which looked deceptively sterile and devoid of life but which was very much alive with killing and death and procreation and life, Grace thought of her beloved James and wondered again, as she had thousands of times, what he had died for.

It was a strange, new world she lived in now, and she wasn't sure if James would care for it. She herself understood little of it.

Playing in Nairobi was an American film, *Dr. Strangelove,* which Geoffrey and Ilse had taken her to see. The whole world, it seemed to

Grace, was suddenly preoccupied with global nuclear annihilation. The radio seemed to play only American songs, sung by a new breed of people—someone named Joan Baez, who protested racial hatred and called for love and peace. The news was full of reports on civil rights demonstrations in Alabama; of riots and beatings; of two hundred thousand freedom marchers descending upon Washington. Young people were dancing something called the watusi; dissolute teenagers in Britain were growing their hair long and calling themselves mods and rockers. The world was rushing at a breathless rate—an American astronaut, Gordon Cooper, had just orbited the earth twenty-two times; Dr. Michael De Bakey in Texas was making history by opening up people's chests and operating directly on the heart.

And three days ago President Kennedy had been assassinated.

What has all that, Grace wondered as she gazed out at the placid, untouched African plains, *to do with this?*

And Kenya was caught up in its own breakneck race to become part of the bewildering, modern new world. Barely sixty years ago, Grace thought, these people were living in the Stone Age, with no alphabet, no concept of the wheel, not a clue to the mighty nations that loomed on the other side of the mountain. Now the Africans were driving automobiles and flying airplanes; African barristers wore white wigs in Nairobi's courts and spoke the Queen's English; Kenya women were discovering birth control and secretarial jobs. New words peppered the language, such as *uhuru,* "freedom," and *wananchi,* "the people." And Prime Minister Kenyatta had declared a new pronunciation for Kenya, saying that the *e* was to be a short one and that it was from now illegal to say "Keenya."

How strange it had seemed to Grace, back in 1957, to vote alongside Africans for the first time. And what a shock it had been to encounter old Mama Wachera at the voting place just this past June. They had looked at each other, and Grace had gone cold to the core. The chance encounter with the medicine woman had brought back the painful memory of the day after James's death. Mama Wachera had come to Grace's house to claim her son's body, and without a word she had thrown a bundle at Grace's feet. Numb from the terrible tragedy of the night before—James dying in her arms, Mona's baby dead, Mario, her houseboy, revealing himself as the oath giver—Grace had picked up that bundle and found it contained all of Mona's letters to David.

Grace possessed them still. Not knowing what to do with them, she had put them away against the day she would pass them along to Mona. That had been nine years ago. At first Mona had been too grief-stricken, Grace thought, to be given the letters. Later she had decided they would only open Mona's wounds. *Perhaps,* Grace thought now, *I should simply destroy them and lay that dark chapter to rest.*

She heard footsteps crunching over the dirt and then a voice calling softly, "Dr. T?"

It was Tim. He had always called her Dr. T. When he stepped into the light which spilled from her tent, he apologized for disturbing her and asked if he could speak with her.

"I guess what I've really come for is to say good-bye, Dr. T," he said as he sat down. "We're leaving next week."

"Yes," she said softly. "I know."

"Now that everything's wrapped up, no use in hanging around for Freedom Day. I don't think I care to see the Union Jack come down once and for all."

"Perhaps it won't be so bad."

Tim thought for a moment, twisting his hat in his hands. Then he said, "We do wish you would come with us, Dr. T. Alice's sheep farm is doing smashingly, and Tasmania is a beautiful place. Clean and quiet, if you know what I mean."

Grace smiled and shook her head. "Kenya is my home. I belong here. And here I shall stay."

"I don't expect I'll ever be coming back. I was born here, you know, but I feel like an outsider. 'Kenya for Kenyans' is what they're saying. Then what am I if not a Kenyan? I hope you'll be all right, Dr. T."

"I shall be fine, Tim. Besides, I won't be alone. I shall have Deborah."

Tim avoided meeting Grace's eyes. It was an uncomfortable subject for him—Deborah. Perhaps if, eight years ago, Mona had agreed to marry him . . .

But no. Tim wasn't the marrying kind. He needed his freedom, needed his special friendships, which did not include women. As for the child, well, Mona felt the same way: that Deborah was a mistake and an embarrassing reminder of a night they both preferred to forget.

"Before I go, Dr. T," he said quietly, staring down at the canvas floor, "there's something I want to tell you. I don't know, I just don't feel I can go to Australia without getting this off my chest. It's about the night the earl was killed."

Grace waited.

He finally looked up. "I was the bloke on the bicycle."

She stared at him.

"I didn't kill the earl, though! I don't mean to say that. What happened is, I couldn't sleep that night, so I went downstairs for a drink. I saw the earl out on the drive, getting into his car. I wondered what he was up to. When he drove off, I went outside and saw the bicycle. I decided to follow him. I saw the car up ahead turn onto the Kiganjo Road. He was going a lot faster than I could pedal, so it was some time before I caught up with him. I saw his car pulled over to the side, the motor still running. When I got close, I thought the earl had fallen asleep. He had had so much to drink, you know?"

"Yes, I know."

"I pulled up alongside and peered in. Then I thought maybe he was ill or something. So I got off the bike and slipped in the mud. That's why there was mud on the passenger seat. As soon as I saw the gun in his hand and the bullet wound in his head, I knew what had happened. Whoever did it must have gotten away just before I arrived. I didn't see anybody or hear anything. And then, because I was so scared, I threw the bicycle into the bush when a tire blew, and I ran all the way back to Bellatu."

"Why didn't you tell this to the police?"

"What good would it have done? I couldn't have told them who did it. And they'd have arrested me on suspicion of the earl's murder. Everyone knew we hated each other."

He looked at Grace and said softly, "I guess we'll never know who did it, will we?"

"No, I don't suppose we ever will. But I don't think it matters anymore. Almost everyone who was a part of it is dead. It's best forgotten."

"I'll say good night then, Dr. T. Geoffrey is taking us on one of his game runs in the morning!"

Grace held out her hand, and he took it. "Take care, Tim," she said. "And good luck."

IT WAS GEOFFREY'S experience that the most resisting of women eventually succumbed to the magic and enchantment of the African bush. He had countless clients who could vouch for as much. So when he walked through the dark to Mona's tent, recalling how animated she had become at dinner and the way her cheeks had burned, he had high hopes. That, and a chilled bottle of champagne.

Mona didn't seem at all surprised to see him at the doorway of her tent, sending his hopes even higher. But when she said, "I'm glad you came, Geoff. I have something to tell you," the tone in her voice caught him off guard.

"What is it?" he said as he opened the champagne. When he offered Mona a glass, she refused it.

"I've sold the farm, Geoffrey."

He looked at her. Then he sat down, stunned. "You can't mean it! The whole thing?"

"All five thousand acres."

"Good God, I thought you would never sell! What on earth changed your mind?"

She turned away. She had put off telling him the news until now because she knew it would result in a row. But there was almost no time left; he had to be told.

Nonetheless, she couldn't tell him the truth. That she had decided to sell the coffee estate because of a little boy.

After the day she had found Deborah and Christopher Mathenge in her parents' bedroom, Mona had wept as she had never wept before. She had taken to her bed and finally released all the tears and pain that she had sealed inside herself since the night of David's death. And then, once again in control, all tears having been shed, she faced the cold reality that she could not possibly continue to live at Bellatu and watch that boy grow up into a second David.

And so she had known that she must get away from Kenya forever, turn her back on the country of her birth, the only country she had ever known, and find a new place somewhere.

"You know that the farm has barely been making it, Geoff. After the crop failure in 1953, and the loss of most of my field help during Mau Mau, and then the wet year of 1956, when the rains lasted too long and the berries rotted on the trees—well, I just haven't been able to recover. So I sold to an Asian named Singh. He'll do something profitable with it, I'm sure."

"I can't believe it! Asians living in Bellatu!"

"I didn't sell him the house. I've kept that. After all, the house is Deborah's inheritance."

"That was a wise move. And I'll tell you something else, Mona. I'm glad you sold the farm. Now you can come and work for me. I'll be opening a posh office in Nairobi, and I want someone capable to run it for me."

"Oh, Geoffrey!" she said, turning around to face him. "What madness! Tourists! In Kenya! You've been out in the sun too long! Do you really think people will want to come here for holidays? Can't you see where Kenya is heading? Back to the jungle and the mud huts! The minute independence is declared, this country is going to disintegrate into anarchy, and your white skin won't be worth sixpence!"

He stared at her, at first taken aback by her outburst and then finally realizing what she was saying. "What do you mean," he said slowly, "that *my* white skin won't be worth sixpence? Where will *you* be?"

She sat down on the edge of the bed and looked at her hands. "I'm going to Australia with Tim."

"*What?*" Geoffrey shot to his feet. "You can't be serious!"

"I am serious, Geoff. Alice has asked me to come and live with her on her farm. Tim decided for himself months ago. We don't want to live in Kenya anymore."

"I don't believe it!" he shouted. "You're running off with that—that faggot!"

"Geoffrey, that's not fair!"

"Is it because of Deborah? After all, everyone knows she's his child."

"No, it's not because of Deborah. We're not going to get married or anything like that. The three of us will simply live and work together on the sheep farm. I'm done with men and husbands and all that grief. We'll just be a family, living in peace. It's what Tim and I want. I know you find this hard to believe, Geoffrey, but Deborah means nothing to me. In fact, I'm not taking her with me. I've arranged for her to live with Aunt Grace."

Geoffrey was shocked into silence. All of a sudden he was looking at a woman he didn't know, a woman he didn't care to know. Finally he said quietly, "I think that's monstrous."

"Think what you want, Geoff—"

"Damn it, Mona. How can you abandon her like that? Your own child! What kind of mother *are* you?"

"Don't you lecture me on duties and responsibilities, Geoffrey Donald. Stop and think for a minute what sort of *husband* you are. Why, the whole colony knows about your escapades with your female clients and with the wives of your clients! You used to be an honorable man, Geoffrey. What happened?"

"I don't know," he said softly. "I don't know what's happened to any of us. We've all changed."

He went to the tent door, the champagne bottle in his hand, and paused to look at Mona. They had grown up together; he had given her her first kiss. Her letters, in that lonely outpost in Palestine, had sustained him. Where *had* they gone wrong? What erroneous turning in their mutual road had brought them to this? "Good night," he said unhappily, and left.

Mona watched him go. She stood at the mosquito net and saw his silhouette blend in with the dark night until only his footsteps remained, and then those, too, faded.

She clutched the tent post as she listened to the roaring of lions in the bush nearby. They sounded so lonely, so sad, as if trying to find one another. Mona looked out at Kenya, her home, and thought of the little train, now a museum oddity, that had once chuffed through just such a night as this and the frightened countess giving birth in one of its carriages.

Finally Mona closed her eyes and whispered, *"Kwa heri,"* to Kenya. "Good-bye."

55

Mama Wachera eyed the beast warily.

Although it purred harmlessly now, it had roared up in a cloud of dirt and noise. It was enormous and menacing, and she didn't trust it.

"Come along, Mama," Dr. Mwai said as he held the car door open for her. "You will have the honor of riding in the front seat."

Christopher and Sarah were already sitting in the back, on either side of their mother.

Mama Wachera looked at the smiling face of this African dressed in a European business suit and wearing a gold watch and gold rings. She knew she must regard him with respect. He was a healer like herself, what was called a *medical* doctor, but he bore no resemblance to the healers of old. Where was his magic gourd, his Bag of Questions, his sacred staff adorned with goats' ears? Why was he not wearing the ceremonial headdress; where was the ritual paint on his face and arms; did he know the sacred songs and dances? The medicine woman couldn't help it, she felt a mild contempt for this man.

"Don't be afraid, Mama!" Wanjiru called merrily from inside the car. "It won't hurt you."

Afraid? Wachera had never been afraid in her life.

She drew herself up with dignity and approached the humming vehicle. For an instant past met present as her small dark body in its traditional beads and hides stood within the embrace of the open car door. Then she was inside and setting her gaze stoically through the windshield.

This was such a monumental occasion—Mama Wachera going to

Nairobi in a motorcar!—that villagers from across the river and people
from the mission had come to give her a sendoff. Today was Independence Day, and the Mathenges were going to attend the ceremonies
at Uhuru Stadium. The significance of this—that their beloved and
revered old medicine woman should be on hand to witness Kenya's
birth—was not lost on those gathered to see her off. When the car
started to move, everyone cheered and ran behind, shouting and waving.

Wachera's impulse, when the car began to roll, was to grab the edge
of the seat. But because it would have been undignified for her to show
fear in front of others, Mama Wachera sat calmly with her hands
resting in her lap. Her expression was serene as trees and huts went by,
but her heart raced to see the world move while she herself remained
seated!

"It will be all right, Mama," Wanjiru had tried to reassure her. "Dr.
Mwai owns a Mercedes, and he is a very good driver."

Such words meant nothing to Wachera, who had announced her
intention to walk all the way to Nairobi.

"But it would take weeks!" Wanjiru had cried. "In the car it's only
three hours."

Even so, Wachera wondered at the propriety of it. Walking was
honorable; it was what the ancestors had done. Riding on wheels was
a *mzungu* custom and therefore could not be African or respectable.

But she had no choice. If she wanted to go to the stadium and see
the Union Jack come down, she would have to ride in Dr. Mwai's car.

She thought of her grandchildren in the back seat; they were beside
themselves with excitement. Although Christopher and Sarah had
experienced army transport trucks, for them nothing compared to the
thrill of riding in a "Benzi." Eight-year-old Sarah could hardly keep still
in her new dress and shoes. Christopher sat close to the window and
waved to everyone, his smile as bright as the white shirt he wore with
his long pants. For their sakes Mama Wachera had agreed to ride in
Dr. Mwai's Benzi. And it warmed her now to hear them chatter and
giggle in the back seat, and it helped allay her fear of riding in a car.
The medicine woman lived for her two grandchildren. They were all
she had; she would do anything for them.

They drove past the large fenced field where, countless harvests ago, the sacred fig tree had stood and where elder Wachera had built her new homestead—long before the white man came. The field had been cleared by the bwana for his game played on horses, but it had been neglected now for years. Mama Wachera saw, in satisfaction, the handiwork of vengeful Ngai in the weeds and creepers and dead grass.

The Benzi moved past the iron gateway of the mission, and in the flicker of an eye the decades fell away. Wachera saw the woods again as they had been in her girlhood, and she saw Memsaab Daktari's first little hut, which was only four posts and a thatch roof. Now there were big stone buildings and paved pathways, and the forest had long since vanished.

Mama Wachera had not at first wanted to have her grandchildren attend this school—it was owned and operated by a Treverton—but Wanjiru had argued convincingly in favor of enrolling Sarah and Christopher in the white mission school. Had not she herself, Wanjiru asked her mother-in-law, gone to this school as a girl? And didn't David also study here and thereby go on to become an educated man? Besides, Wanjiru had added, all the teachers and pupils were African.

And so Christopher and Sarah attended the Grace Mission School, getting up every morning to eat maize porridge with their grandmother and then going off in their blue uniforms with their books tucked inside canvas bags.

"In the new Kenya," Wanjiru had assured her mother-in-law, "our children will be educated and free to pursue any career they wish. Christopher will make a fine doctor. He has his father's good mind and logic. And Sarah will have a future such as I could never even have dreamed of. When I went to school, girls were taught domestic service; we were trained to be wives. But my little Sarah can be anything she wants!"

The new Kenya, Mama Wachera thought in disdain. It was the *old* Kenya they must return to! Africans must look to the ways of the ancestors and reclaim the old customs and traditions, for there lay honor and pride, and the Children of Mumbi could be virtuous and righteous once again.

But there was no use arguing such matters with the headstrong Wanjiru. Seven years in prison, the medicine woman knew, had hardened her daughter-in-law, had planted an obsession in her heart, and had even made her forget how to show respect and deference to an elder!

Wachera knew what Wanjiru had gone through since her arrest nine years ago. She knew that Sarah had been conceived in rape and that she was therefore not a true Mathenge; Wachera knew also that Wanjiru had suffered other, unspoken abuses while in the detention camps and that these experiences had made her into an obstinate, intractable woman. And then, afterward, upon her release at last and suddenly out in an uncaring world, penniless and husbandless with two children, Wanjiru had endured the humiliation of begging for food, of doing menial labor for Europeans in order to feed her children. Wanjiru was a KRN—a Kenya registered nurse—a skilled and educated woman, but she could find no respectable jobs because the hospitals were run by whites who were afraid to hire ex-Mau Mau. For two years Wanjiru had lived in the Nairobi tenements with the thousands of other abandoned women, preserving her virtue and protecting her babies, until at last the Native Hospital had acquired an African administrator who not only was not afraid of an ex-Mau Mau but, in fact, admired Wanjiru for her activities as a freedom fighter. She was given a decent job at last.

That was when she had finally brought Christopher and Sarah to live with their grandmother. Wanjiru sent money every week, and food and clothing, and now, because of her recent promotion to senior matron, Wanjiru was making the intimate acquaintance of powerful, emerging men such as Dr. Mwai.

While Mama Wachera was overjoyed to have the children live with her and to know that her loneliness was at an end, and while she was grateful for the extra food Wanjiru sent—although she had no use for the shillings—Wachera was unhappy with the lack of harmony in their lives. They were never in agreement, the medicine woman and her son's wife, and Wanjiru insisted always on arguing to the bitter end. It would not have been so in the old days, when a grandmother's word was law!

The Benzi climbed the road that went up to the top of the ridge, and there Wachera saw the big house that had been built eighty-eight harvests ago. It was dark and boarded up now, and in a deplorable state.

Mama Wachera knew that the memsaab named Mona had sold the

ruined coffee farm to an Asian and had left Kenya for good. That had been wonderful news for the medicine woman, who saw in it part of her *thahu* being fulfilled; The whites were leaving Kikuyuland. It would only be a matter of time, she was certain, before the Asian gave up on the failed plantation and relinquished the land to the Children of Mumbi at last. But, to Wachera's chagrin, she learned that the memsaab had left her daughter, the grandchild of the cursed Bwana Lordy, in the care of Memsaab Daktari.

As the big house receded behind trees, Mama Wachera recalled when, for the first and last time in her life, she had visited Memsaab Daktari's house at the mission. It had been the morning after she had been told of her son's death. Wachera had gathered up the letters Memsaab Mona had been bringing to her and had delivered them at the feet of Memsaab Daktari. Wachera did not know what was in the letters, for she could not read, and she had no desire to know. With David's death, her bitterness toward and hatred of the whites had intensified. While the *wazungu* had gathered to mourn the killing of one of their own—the one called Bwana James—Wachera had retreated to her lonely hut to grieve by herself for the murder of her one and only child.

Then, when Christopher had come home one day with David's passbook and Wachera had seen the photograph, it had been like seeing David alive again and seeing also her beloved Kabiru Mathenge, who had died many years ago.

It was then that she had told her stunned daughter-in-law of David's part in Mau Mau, revealing that he was not, as Wanjiru had thought, a coward, but was, in fact, a hero of *uhuru*.

And it was to honor him, Mama Wachera decided now as the Benzi turned onto the main road and headed toward Nairobi, it was to pay homage to the spirits and memories of David Kabiru Mathenge and his father, Chief Kabiru Mathenge, that all Kenya was gathering today at Uhuru Stadium.

THE RECENTLY NAMED Kenyatta Avenue, formerly Lord Delamere Avenue, was lined with flags of all nations. For days prime ministers and heads of state from around the world had been arriving in Nairobi to attend the celebrations. The air was charged; roads were clogged with Kenyans of all tribes, who had walked for days from ancestral home- lands to witness the birth of their new state. Two hundred and fifty thousand poured into Uhuru Stadium, trailing along wives and children and goats, their many dialects and tribal tongues creating a deafening babel. President Obote of Uganda got stuck in the mud and had to walk from his Rolls-Royce to the royal box. The Duke of Edinburgh arrived fifty minutes late and had to push his way through a wildly excited mob that had swept aside police barriers. A gentle rain fell steadily on ladies in evening gowns and Masai in red *shukas*. Beer and oranges were consumed as the masses in the stands cheered the tribal dancers down in the arena, who put on show after show with drums and spears and skins. All the peoples of Kenya were represented, and the mob howled with chauvinistic frenzy. When a handful of freedom fighters ap- peared—the last of the Mau Mau who had been holding out in the forests—Jomo Kenyatta embraced them and tried to introduce them to the Duke of Edinburgh, who politely shook his head no.

Finally the much anticipated moment arrived. Just before midnight, on December 11, 1963, the Union Jack was solemnly brought down while the military band played "God Save the Queen," and the new red, black, and green Kenya flag went up. It fluttered in the spotlight, proudly displaying the Kenya coat of arms—a shield with two crossed spears—and the crowd burst into wild cheering. A royal salute to the Duke of Edinburgh came next, followed by the official handing over of the colors from the King's African Rifles to the Kenya Rifles. The old maroon fez was replaced by a black peaked cap; Kenya now had its own modern army.

Then Jomo Kenyatta rose on the dais, and the stadium fell silent. The old man was impressive in his somber European suit and tradi- tional beaded Kikuyu cap. His sharp, penetrating eyes swept over the thousands of Africans in the stands, and his voice rang out in the night. "Fellow countrymen, we must all work hard, with our hands, to save ourselves from poverty, ignorance, and disease. In the past we used to blame the Europeans for everything that went wrong. Now the govern- ment is ours. . . . You and I must work together to develop our country, to get education for our children, to have doctors, to build roads, to improve day-to-day essentials. This should be our work, in the spirit that I am going to ask you to echo, to shout aloud, to shatter the foundations of the past with the strength of our new purpose. . . ."

He paused, surveyed the crowd, then held out his arms and cried, *"Harambee! Harambee!"*

"Harambee!" shouted the audience. *"Harambee!"* people chanted in one voice. "Pull together!"

Smiling, Kenyatta turned to the duke and said, "When you get back to England, take our greetings to the Queen and tell her that we are still friends. It will be a friendship from the heart, more than what was there before."

The crowd went insane. Hats and gourds flew up in the air; people embraced one another. It was a roar, they all thought, that was the roar of a lion, a roar, they were certain, that must have been heard around the world.

And then, at last, with great solemnity and dignity, the Kenya military band struck the first chords of the new national anthem, and two hundred and fifty thousand people rose as one body.

As the sad, sweet strains rose into the rainy night, filling everyone with a kind of melancholy pride and a sense, for the first time in anyone's memory, of real African unity, this final stronghold of British imperialism, the last colonial corner to break away from the no longer powerful British Empire, moved into the modern age.

From where she stood, in a privileged box with Geoffrey Donald and other prominent white Nairobi businessmen, Grace Treverton looked around the packed stadium and realized she had never before seen so many Africans gathered together in one place. It overwhelmed her. It also chilled her far more than the rain did. For the first time Grace received a true understanding of what the African fight had been all about. She looked at the black, pride-filled faces and thought about the cloudy, uncertain future. She knew that there was still much anger and resentment in these African hearts. Would they, she wondered, ever truly be able to forget their ignominious past and the humiliation suffered at the hands of the colonists? These hearts were barely fifty years away from the savage hearts of their warrior fathers. Would they revert to barbarism and bloodlust once the law of Britain was gone from Kenya? Grace knew that these people were drunk with their new power and that they lusted for luxuries they naively imagined self-rule would bring. Remembering Mau Mau, she wondered how the remaining Kenya whites would fare should a second emergency break out. The next time there would be no British troops to protect them.

She looked at Kenyatta down on the dais. To everyone's immense surprise, his European wife, whom he had married back in England years ago, had flown out to join him and his two Kenyan wives as a gesture of interracial goodwill. Kenyatta made impressive speeches about restraint and tolerance. But would he be able to control his volatile population of six million if a second revolution broke out?

What, Grace wondered anxiously, was the future going to be like, starting tomorrow?

As the national anthem came to a close and the crowds started cheering again, eight-year-old Deborah clapped her hands and laughed. This was better than Christmas! She stood shivering in the cold night between Aunt Grace and Uncle Geoffrey, and saw, across the arena, in another specially reserved box, Christopher Mathenge standing with his sister and mother and grandmother.

Deborah caught his eye. She smiled at him.

And he smiled back.

PART
EIGHT
1973

56

A re you excited about going to California?" Sarah asked as she stirred the pot of melted wax.

Deborah, sitting at the base of a Cape chestnut with her knees drawn up and her back against its trunk, was going through a fashion magazine—the *Mademoiselle* college issue, which showed the latest in campus wear. She paused at a page that showed models dressed in long skirts and platform shoes; then she looked up at her friend. "It scares me, in a way, Sarah. California is so foreign, so far away!"

Sarah bent to examine the consistency of her wax. She sniffed it, then added a small chunk of beeswax to the pot. As it melted, she said, "I can't believe you took so long to make up your mind! If that scholarship had been offered to me, I would have snapped it up like that!"

Looking back down at the models smiling in young American confidence, Deborah felt her fears rise again. How could she possibly fit in with these sophisticated girls?

It had been a big decision to make, accepting the Uhuru scholarship. It meant being away from Kenya for three years—away from all her friends, away from Aunt Grace and their home at the mission, and, most of all, away from Sarah, who was like a sister to her. Moreover, Christopher was returning today after four years of studying in England. Deborah would have just enough time to say hello to him and then would have to say good-bye again.

Deborah envied Sarah. She was so self-assured, so confident, just like the models in the magazine. Sarah had always been brave; it was because of having been born in a detention camp, Sarah always said.

She wasn't afraid of anything, and she was always willing to take on any challenge. Her own school leaving, for example, had been typical of Sarah, a brave move that had so angered her mother, Wanjiru, that the two were not speaking. It had shocked Deborah, too, that Sarah should drop out of college after just one year. But her friend had explained with characteristic self-certainty, "Egerton has nothing more to offer me. I haven't the time to sit through its useless courses. I know what I want. Egerton can't give it to me, so by God, I'm going after it on my own."

Sarah had been referring to her ambition to be a fashion designer. Ever since she was a little girl, she had known that was what she was going to do. In secondary school Sarah had taken every art and design and sewing class offered. Then she had gone on to Egerton College at Njoro, where, under its home economics diploma program, one of the very few higher education courses open to Kenya women, she had studied the identification and care of fabrics, sewing by hand and by machine, pattern drafting, dressmaking, alterations, and finishing. When she saw that the second year of the course concentrated on nutrition and child rearing, she had left the school and come home to pursue her dream along another path.

She worked now for an Asian woman named Mrs. Dar in Nyeri, as an assistant seamstress. The pay was very low, the hours long, and the working conditions hard, but Mrs. Dar made exquisite dresses for the wives of wealthy businessmen in the district, and Sarah was learning everything she could from her. But that wasn't enough. Even though her hope was someday to own her own sewing machines, her own business with assistants of her own, Sarah dreamed of something greater: of designing a whole new look.

That was why she was down by the river with Deborah, stirring a pot of hot wax over a fire. Sarah had recently discovered batik, the art of dyeing cloth by using wax, and she had been experimenting with the process for days.

"I shall feel so out of place in California," Deborah said, laying aside the fashion magazine. "I shan't know anything. And I'm sure they all will be smarter than I."

Sarah straightened and put her hands on her hips. "What rot, Deb! How do you suppose you earned that scholarship? By being stupid? Out of fifteen hundred applicants, you won! And didn't Professor Muriuki say that California's gain was going to be Nairobi University's loss?"

Professor Muriuki, Deborah told herself, was just being kind. She had taken four courses with him in the past year at the University of Nairobi, and he liked her.

He had, however, gone on to concede that "I cannot deny that the level of education at the California university is superior to ours. You're wise to go there, Miss Treverton. When you come back to Kenya and attend medical school here, you will be head and shoulders above your fellow students."

The eighteen-year-old girls were enjoying the warm August sun and the peace of the river. Through the trees they heard the cries of children playing rugby on the polo field which Deborah's mother had turned over to Grace Mission when she left Kenya ten years ago. Nearby, a hundred feet from where the two girls sat by the river, a familiar cluster of huts stood in a bucolic setting amid flourishing maize and bean plots, a healthy herd of goats, and a full granary. That was where Sarah lived, with her aged grandmother, Mama Wachera, but in her own hut, which she had made comfortable with a carpet and proper chairs. There was a hut, too, for Wanjiru, where she stayed when she drove up from Nairobi to visit. The fourth hut was Christopher's. It had once been his father's *thingira*, bachelor hut; Christopher was going to stay in it whenever he was on holiday from medical school.

Thinking of Christopher, Deborah looked at her watch. His flight from London was scheduled to arrive that morning, and he was to be met by his mother and come up with her in her car.

The hour seemed late to Deborah. Where were they?

She hadn't slept the night before, had only barely slept all week, anticipating Christopher's return. What was it going to be like after these past four years? Even now her heart raced to think of his being home again, to imagine the long talks they would have. *Will he have changed much?* she wondered.

Sarah left her wax pot and went to inspect the squares of cloth spread out on large boulders. Each was in a stage of the dyeing process; each had been prepared differently. She examined them closely. "I think I've finally conquered the problem of crackling," she said, holding up a piece. "What do you think, Deb?"

Deborah studied the large square of muslin which Sarah held up. The design was of a woman and child—very basic and primitive—and the colors were earth tones. She liked the way the sunlight shone through it, revealing black veins of dye where the wax had broken. "It's beautiful."

Sarah laid it down and stepped back. "I'm not so sure."

"You've mastered the wax. The colors hardly run at all."

Sarah pursed her lips as she gazed at her handiwork.

She had taught herself batik through a lengthy process of trial and error, experimenting on leftover scraps, which she bought from Mrs. Dar with almost half her wages. The wax and dye, purchased at an Asian *duka* in Nyeri, ate up the rest of her pay so that Sarah was constantly without money. But it was worth it. She had mastered batik, and her fabrics were beautiful.

Still, there was something missing.

"I don't know, Deb," Sarah said as she sat on the grass next to her friend. She dug her bare feet into the red clay and watched the fish in the clear water. "It's not enough somehow."

Deborah, who was unartistic and therefore was impressed with her friend's achievement, said, "You'll be able to make lovely dresses with that cloth, Sarah. I know that if I had the money, I would buy one!"

Sarah smiled. Despite the fact that Deborah's last name was Treverton and that she owned the huge house up on the hill smack in the middle of Mr. Singh's coffee farm, and despite the fact that her aunt owned Grace Mission, Deborah had no money. That was because the house was practically worthless; it cost too much to live in and keep up, and no one wanted to buy it, surrounded as it was by Mr. Singh's coffee trees. And everyone knew that the mission had been run at a loss almost since its founding, because the school and hospital were free to those who couldn't afford to pay, and that any money Dr. Treverton had ever brought in she had put right back into the mission, keeping none for herself. In fact, it was rumored that if the Catholic nuns hadn't stepped in to help, some years back, the mission would have gone bankrupt. So Deborah Treverton was as penniless as Sarah Mathenge; it was one of the many things they had in common.

"Can you believe it!" Deborah said as she handed the magazine to her friend. "They're still wearing miniskirts in America!"

Sarah gazed at the models in envy. The wearing of a miniskirt was banned in Kenya. It was "improper and unladylike," the government said, "and provoked men to lust."

"I shall never fit in," Deborah said. "Not dressed like this!" She wore a simple cotton dress and sandals. Fine for rural Kenya, she thought, but entirely out of place on a sophisticated California college campus.

"You can wear anything you want in America these days," Sarah assured her. "Look here—mididresses, granny dresses, peasant dresses, velour pantsuits, blue jeans with rainbow patches. Even hot pants! The important thing to remember is this." She gave Deborah a significant look. "You'll be a top scholar and will come home with honors. Just as Professor Muriuki said."

Deborah prayed that it would be so. Her most urgent dream was to be the best possible doctor. To be just like Aunt Grace and follow in her footsteps.

"If only I had money!" Sarah said as she tossed a pebble into the water. "I *know* I could do better than Mrs. Dar! She's so conservative. She has no imagination. And she won't let me voice my opinions! Dr. Chandra's wife came in last week, and Mrs. Dar put her in the most unflattering *green.* I saw right away that she needed something in soft brown with maybe gold trim. And the way skirts hang on her! Deb, if I had the money, I could buy a sewing machine and go into business for myself. I could work right here, out of my own house. And after I had a few regular paying customers, I could purchase unbleached muslin in bulk and dye various pieces of it to suit particular clients."

"Those are lovely," Deborah said, nodding toward the batiks drying on the boulders.

Sarah seized a length that had been dyed in shades of red and orange and said, "Let me see how it looks on you."

Deborah laughed and said, *"Kangas* don't suit me, Sarah." But she stood and let her friend drape the stiff material around her.

Although Deborah was a *mzunga,* she was hardly much lighter than Sarah because she had spent her entire life in the fierce equatorial sun. While most whites in Kenya sought carefully to protect themselves from the strong rays on the equator, Deborah loved the feel of sunlight on her bare arms and face. That was not to say, however, that the two were similar in appearance. Although Deborah had short, curly black hair and dark eyes, she was still very European, whereas Sarah was strikingly African. She wore her hair in the new cornrow style, the many tight braids culminating in a fountain of hair on top of her head. The effect was to lengthen her already long neck and to crown the grace of her supple arms and slender body. Sarah Mathenge was exceptionally beautiful, Deborah thought, envying her friend's natural elegance and style.

"That looks jolly good on you, Deb," Sarah said, standing back and studying her work.

Deborah turned slowly in the sunlight, trying to catch her reflection in the river. Sarah had fixed the cloth around her in *kanga* fashion— crisscrossed over her breast and tied behind her neck.

Sarah's frown returned.

"What's the matter?" asked Deborah. "Don't you like it?"

"It's not what I want to achieve, Deb. It looks just so bloody ordinary." Sarah's expression grew thoughtful. "Do you remember a few years back, the Liverpool look? And then the Carnaby Street look? There's no Kenya look. No style that is uniquely East African."

"What about the *kanga?* I'd say that was uniquely East African."

And that was true. Having originated on the coast of Kenya in the nineteenth century, the large rectangles of brightly patterned cotton cloth, known as *kangas,* were worn all over East Africa and seen everywhere on women in the fields and in the marketplace. The *kanga* formed a simple dress by being wrapped around under the armpits and tucked in; sometimes it was knotted over one shoulder or tied behind the neck. It was used as a wraparound skirt, as a shawl, as a baby sling and coiled around the head as a turban. The *kanga* was a cheap, simple and easy-to-care-for form of clothing, and it suited the purpose of the African peasant woman. But Sarah wasn't going to design clothes for the *wananchi.*

"I'm thinking of the women who are working more and more in the cities, Deb. So many women are getting office jobs; they're learning to become secretaries and receptionists. Women are beginning to work in banks and businesses. They're even becoming lawyers now! They can't wear *kangas.* So what do they wear?" She pointed to *Mademoiselle.* "They buy cheap imitations of American and British styles!"

"Well, then," Deborah said, "you could design ready-to-wear dresses out of *kanga* cloth. Those would certainly be a new style and definitely Kenyan."

Sarah shook her head no, her large gold hoop earrings catching the sun. "I don't want to use *kanga* cloth. I loathe those horrible little sayings that are printed on them."

For reasons no one knew, a tradition had begun years ago among the makers of *kanga* cloth; a Swahili aphorism was printed on each length. Many of them were so old and obscure of origin that they made no sense: *Vidole vitano, kipi ni bora?* "Of five fingers, which is the best?" And most were trite: *Akili ni mali,* "Wits are wealth."

Sarah took the batik from Deborah and spread it out on the boulder. "I don't want to use cloth that's already made. I want to create a new fabric. Don't you see, Deb?" Sarah grew excited. "I want to create a *whole* new style. Not just fabric or not just a new dress but a whole new look. Something that says Kenya, a style that preserves and perpetuates African tradition! And something that women in Europe and America will want to wear."

"What will it look like?"

"I don't know yet." Sarah stared at the batiked fabric drying in the sun. She had experimented with color and design, but all she seemed able to come up with was an imitation of the *kanga.* "What *is* Kenyan?" she said. "Besides the *kanga,* I mean."

Deborah shrugged. "I haven't a notion."

"Do you know what I'm going to do, Deb? I'm going to take a look around this country of ours and see what the people are wearing."

"What a marvelous idea!"

"Think of all the tribes that haven't been Westernized, Deb. The Luo, the Kipsigis, the Turkana! They must still wear traditional dress. I'm going to study them. I'll draw them. They will be my inspiration, Deb. I'll find my Kenya look among the people themselves!"

"It sounds beautiful, Sarah. And you're the one to do it!"

"Oh, the things I could accomplish if only I had money!"

"Sarah!" Deborah cried. "I have a wonderful idea! I can sell some of the things in Bellatu! Then you can have all the money you need!"

But Sarah smiled and said, "No, Deb. You can't do that. You'll be moving into Bellatu after medical school. You don't want to live in a bare house!" She turned and walked down to the water's edge. "I'll come up with the money somehow. I know I will. And I shall get started in my own business."

"Yes, you will," Deborah said. "And when I am a doctor, I shall come to you for all my clothes!"

Sarah spun around and held out her arms. "And you'll send all your rich friends to me! I'll be so busy that I'll have fifty people working for me and everyone will be wearing my clothes!"

"You'll be the Rudy Gernreich of East Africa!"

Sarah laughed. "I'd rather be Mary Quant!"

"Who's Mary Quant?" came a masculine voice.

The two girls turned to see a young man striding down the grassy bank toward them. He wore dark slacks, a white shirt with the sleeves rolled up, and sunglasses. "Christopher!" they cried.

While Deborah held back, suddenly shy, Sarah ran to her brother and threw her arms around him. He picked her up and swung her in a circle. "You're back!" she cried.

"And you've grown up!" He put her down, and they laughed breathlessly. Then Christopher turned to Deborah. "Hello," he said.

"Hello, Christopher. Welcome home."

They stood in the speckled sunlight that came through the Cape chestnuts, looking at each other, each thinking that the four years had seemed an eternity while they were passing but now seemed as if they had gone in a wink. Christopher marveled at how Deborah had changed, from a tomboyish fourteen-year-old to this lovely young woman, while Deborah wondered where the awkward, gangly seventeen-year-old had gone to and who this handsome man was.

"You're taller," he said quietly.

"So are you."

There was another moment of silence; then Sarah said, "Where's Mother?"

"She's in your hut, complaining that there is no *ugali* for us and that your manners are atrocious."

Sarah looked up at the sky in a suffering gesture, then said, "I'll go look for Grandmother. I think she's in the village. Oh, Christopher!" She hugged him again. "I'm so glad you're home! Tell me it's for good, that you're here to stay."

He laughed. "I'm here to stay."

Sarah ran off through the trees, leaving Deborah and Christopher alone.

She couldn't believe he was actually standing before her, at long last—after four years of letters and Christmas phone calls, of missing her dear friend and childhood playmate, of growing up and finding her fondness turning into a woman's love, of experiencing strange, disturbing dreams about him, of yearning for him, of lying awake in her bed and no longer reliving their old adventures as she had once done, but fantasizing romantic encounters. In his absence Deborah had fallen in love with Christopher Mathenge, and now it made her unexpectedly shy.

"I missed you," she said.

"I missed you, too, Deb. I can't tell you what your letters meant to me." He took a few steps toward her, then stopped and looked out over the river. "There's no forest anymore."

Deborah looked across at the patchwork shambas that covered the hillside all the way up to the top of the opposite ridge. When she and Christopher had been children, the woods had come right down to the river. Then the new African government had allocated all that land to resettled Kikuyu, who had set about at once to clearing the forest for their fields. Now there were many huts—no longer round, but square, after *mzungu* fashion—still made of mud and dung and thatched with elephant grass. And there were a few battered automobiles along the intersecting dirt lanes.

She looked at Christopher and thought that he had changed, too. Where had those lean muscles come from, and those broad, square shoulders straining the fabric of his shirt? There was a fluidness in the way he stood; Deborah was reminded of the Masai *morani* who roamed the Amboseli plains, strikingly handsome youths, lithe and angular, who were haughty enough to regard themselves as the most beautiful race on earth. Christopher gave that impression, except that the arrogance was not there. He turned and smiled at her in a way no *moran* ever would.

"How was England?" she asked.

"Cold and rainy. I am glad to be back."

He spoke differently, too. The Kikuyu accent that had always colored his speech had been polished away. Christopher no longer mixed his *l*'s and *r*'s, as the Kikuyu did because their language did not contain an *r*. He spoke like the Oxford scholar that he was.

"How is your aunt?" he asked.

"She's fine. Working as hard as ever. I remind her that she's eighty-three and should take things easy. But Aunt Grace thinks the mission will fall apart if she retires."

"Perhaps it will."

Deborah stared at his sunglasses. She found a degree of relief in his wearing them; they protected her from his eyes.

"And your mother?" he asked. "What do you hear from her?"

Deborah had a memory. She was eight years old and at the Kilima Simba Safari Camp. She had to go to the bathroom and was passing by her mother's tent. A voice came from inside: "Deborah means nothing to me, Geoffrey. I've arranged for her to live with Aunt Grace."

"Mother rarely writes to us anymore," Deborah said, thinking of the latest perfunctory, impersonal letter. "But she says the sheep farm is doing well, and she continues to like Australia. Every Christmas she sends Aunt Grace and me woolen pullovers."

They fell silent again, Christopher behind his sunglasses, Deborah to look down at the river rushing over pebbles and moss. The August heat was unusual; it seemed to seep up from the ground and envelop them. Kikuyu cook fires filled the air with an acrid, smoky scent. Shouts came from the rugby field; the grinding of motors was heard up among Mr. Singh's coffee trees. A bee landed on Deborah's arm; she shooed it away.

Christopher looked around again, slowly turning, taking it all in, the countless farms that now covered the countryside. This had once been dense forest. Wars with the Masai had been fought here generations ago, his ancestors had worshiped the trees and wild animals, and more recently Mau Mau freedom fighters had found refuge here. Now all Christopher saw were patches of green laid out neatly over the red earth. Naked children tended goats and cows; mamas were bent, with their legs straight and knees locked, pulling weeds, harvesting vegetables. It was a peaceful, reassuring scene, and Christopher, in his four years of studying in England, had sorely missed it.

He looked at last at Deborah, who was standing in a shaft of sunlight, gazing down into the water just as she had the day he had first met her here, ten years ago.

He thought of the letters she had sent him—once a week for four years. He had kept them all.

At first, on the one hand homesick for Kenya but also excited by his Oxford adventure, Christopher had merely missed the gay companion of his youth, the fey little girl who had made his new life with his grandmother bearable. He had missed Deborah as he had missed Sarah and his mother, as he had missed his comrades on the rugby team.

But then, as the first school year came and went, and then another came along, and as Deborah's letters arrived faithfully each week, he had found himself looking forward to reading her words, to getting off by himself to be alone with the letter, to spend, for a spell, a few stolen moments with her, back in Kenya. His feelings for her had begun to change, it seemed, when her letters started to change. The childishness gradually faded from her writing, and a new maturity slowly emerged. She reported on important things—the government, world events, her dream of becoming a doctor—and asked him a thousand questions about himself, his school, his future plans. Deborah's letters were a direct link to Kenya; with them he never felt cut off from home. And he never felt cut off from her but indeed drawn closer with each one that came. She had come to mean so much more to him than before.

Voices rising in argument came from Sarah's hut.

"Oh, dear," Deborah said, "they're at it again. Your mother's terribly angry with Sarah. Did she tell you about it?"

"Yes. I was opposed to it at first, when Sarah wrote and said she had left Egerton College. But I know my sister. She'll find a way to get what she wants. My mother should know by now that it's no use arguing with Sarah."

"They're very much alike, aren't they?"

"I wonder where my grandmother is."

"She's gone to deliver a baby." Deborah felt self-conscious; she seemed compelled to talk, to fill the space between her and Christopher. "Mama Wachera has done very well since independence. People are reverting to traditional healing, and the old witch doctors, once they came out of hiding, have become quite prosperous. As is your grandmother."

Christopher grew thoughtful. He was going to be a doctor in four years, and he, too, intended to be prosperous.

"Christopher, I have something to tell you," she said quickly. "I didn't write to you about it. I wanted to tell you in person. I've been awarded an Uhuru scholarship to study in California."

She saw no reaction in him, only her twin reflections in the sunglasses. He was silent for a moment; then he said, "California. For how long?"

"Three years."

He was silent again, his eyes hidden behind the dark lenses. The world seemed to hold its breath. The river ran quietly; birds withheld their song in the trees. Then Christopher strode up to Deborah and put his hands on her bare arms. There was a sudden charge; they both felt it. Christopher tightened his hold as he looked down at her.

Deborah was his oldest and dearest friend. She had rescued him from boyhood loneliness and had drawn him into her circle of sunlight. Her letters had comforted him; he had looked forward to seeing her again. But now it was all different. Something had changed.

Deborah seemed suddenly so small and vulnerable.

"You must take care," he said urgently. "The world is a far, far bigger place than you can imagine. You know only Kenya, Deborah, and just a small bit of that—" He caught himself. He wanted to say more, to voice this strange, new emotion that had suddenly gripped him. He looked down at her, felt the warm skin beneath his hands, and thought *She is so innocent.*

He was rocked by a feeling of protectiveness, of wanting to gather her to him and shelter her from all the things he himself had discovered out in the world. Kenya was such a small, insulated country. And Deborah was the child of a rural, backward province. What did she know of life?

"I'll be all right," she said in bewilderment, overcome by the power of his touch, of the passion in his voice. What had happened to him? Where had this intensity come from?

Deborah reached up and removed the sunglasses. He was gazing down at her with eyes that, generations ago, had measured the progress of lion in tall, tawny grass. She was captured in that look; she felt energy pass from his hands into her arms. Christopher overwhelmed her. She was suddenly breathless.

"Deborah," he said quietly, holding her, "I won't tell you not to go. I haven't that right. You must go. You must become the best that you can be. But . . . promise me, Deborah, that—"

She waited. A warm breeze stirred the overhead branches. Sunlight moved on his handsome face.

"Promise you what?" she whispered, her heart racing. *Say it, Christopher. Please say it.*

But the words wouldn't come to him. It had happened too quickly, the sudden leap from loving Deborah Treverton as a friend to loving her as a woman. In an instant it seemed to Christopher that a terrifying threshold had been crossed—one which he had not seen coming, had not been aware of stepping over. He was unprepared for this sudden rush of desire, this unexpected, outrageous impulse to take her into his arms and kiss her. And more.

He didn't know how to say it. He thought of California, of the men there whom Deborah was going to meet, men who were like her—white. She would go away from Kenya, Christopher realized in fear, and she would never come back.

"Deborah," he said at last, "promise me that you will always remember Kenya is your home. Here is where you belong. Here is where your people are. Out there, in the world, you will be a stranger. You will be a curiosity, and you will be misunderstood. The world doesn't know us, Deborah; they don't know our ways, our dreams. In England I was treated as an oddity. I was engulfed by people eager to make my acquaintance, but I made not one friend. They cannot imagine what it is like to be Kenyan, how unique we are. They can hurt you, Deborah. And I don't want you to be hurt."

She was lost—in his eyes, in his hold. The strange, frightening world he spoke of no longer existed, only this patch of river and herself and Christopher.

"Promise me," he said in a tight voice, "that you will come back."

She could hardly speak. "I promise," she whispered. And when his hands left her arms and he turned abruptly away, she felt the sunshine go out of her life.

57

S arah was angry.
 After two weeks of searching Kenya for her "look," she had come to the terminus of the road here on the coast, and she was no nearer to the end of her quest than when she had first started.

As she walked the ancient streets of Malindi, an exotic, decaying town that had once been an Arab slave port, and took in the blinding white walls, the veiled women, the crowded markets and flowering mango trees, feeling as if she were walking through a century far in the past, Sarah's exasperation mounted.

She had begun her pursuit along Lake Victoria, where she had visited the Luo people. She had studied and sketched them—at work, in the market, over their cook fires—and had found that for the most part the men wore slacks or shorts, and the women wrapped *kangas* around themselves. She had gone next to the Masai and the Samburu people and she had found plain red *shukas,* either knotted over the shoulder or wrapped around under the armpits, on both men and women. Kamba and Taita women also wore *kangas,* sometimes even over a European dress or blouse and on their heads as scarves. Red seemed to be the dominant color, and that was due to Kenya's ocher soil; brown was also prevalent, particularly among people who still wore loincloths and capes made of soft leather. Here on the coast, with its strong Arab influence, Sarah found Muslim women dressed entirely in black, so completely veiled that only their eyes showed, and Asian women in bright saris imported from India. She had traveled the length and width of Kenya, her sketchpad was full, and the hoped-for inspiration had never come.

She wished Deborah could have come along with her. They could have made a holiday of it, driving Dr. Mwai's Benzi and visiting the countryside. It would have been a nice sendoff before Deborah went to America, and Deborah would have had advice or would have listened to Sarah's ideas. But there was a going-away party for her at Kilima Simba Safari Lodge in Amboseli, and Deborah had to attend. So she had gone off with Terry Donald, while Sarah had explained her problem to Dr. Mwai, who was sympathetic and had let her borrow his car.

Now the two weeks were up; the Benzi had to be returned. Sarah had been everywhere and seen everything, and she had nothing to show for it but a hundred uninspired drawings.

She sat on a bench that overlooked a broad sweep of white sand beach and lime green coral reefs, in the shade of a palm tree, and watched the hesitant progress of a group of Europeans as they explored the perimeter of an ancient, crumbling mosque.

Tourists, convinced of the stability of Kenyatta's government and reassured that there would be no more revolutions, were starting to pour into Kenya. New hotels were going up in Nairobi and here on the coast; luxurious game lodges were springing up in the bush; Volkswagen minibuses were taking to Kenya's roads, chasing game and stopping at villages for picture taking. They were even coming as far north as Nyeri, on their way to Treetops Hotel; once Sarah had caught some Americans trying to take Mama Wachera's picture outside her hut.

As Sarah observed the group climbing through the abandoned Muslim graveyard, searching for an entrance into the deserted mosque, she took in their polyester pantsuits, their blue jeans and T-shirts. And she thought: *Why should we be the imitators? Why should we want to look like Americans? Why can't they imitate us?*

She pictured again the young women of Nairobi, fresh out of secretarial college, walking smartly down the sidewalks in protective groups, confident, laughing, their hair proudly cornrowed as if to tell the world that they, like their country, were now liberated and independent. But they wore European styles, and poor imitations at that!

Paris once led the fashion field, Sarah told herself as she got up from the bench and began walking again. *Ten years ago it was England. And now it's America. When will it be Africa's turn?*

This was her first visit to the coast, and she felt almost as much a stranger here as tourists must. There was very little about Malindi that resembled the rest of Kenya. It was exceedingly old, having been founded by the Portuguese centuries ago. It had flourished under the rule of the sultan of Zanzibar. Malindi was like something out of the *Arabian Nights,* Sarah thought, with its old Arab bazaars, domes and minarets, narrow streets and pushcarts. Men sat around in long white robes, smoking bubbly pipes and drinking coffee out of tiny cups. The women were furtive black shapes sharply etched against whitewashed walls. On the beaches, palm trees leaned with the wind, their great green fronds nodding toward the ancient town. Out on the water among the coral reefs, fishermen steered their picturesque dhows, triangular white sails painted upon a deep blue sky.

Malindi was a beautiful and enchanting town full of mystique, Sarah thought. But it was hardly typical of Kenya.

As she strolled among hibiscus, frangipani, and bougainvillaea, through the busy charcoal and fish market, by the seedy-luxurious villas of the past rich, her sketchbook in hand, Sarah considered the Turkana people, whom she had observed in the north. With their precious camels, which they used not as beasts of burden but only for milking, with their men in their peculiar caps made of clay and ancestors' hair, and with their preoccupation with bodily ornamentation, they had seemed so alien to Sarah that she had thought they, too, were not typically Kenyan.

When she arrived at Birdland, a large ornithological zoo, she paused to gaze at an Asian family picnicking on the grass among tamarisk and flame trees. The father wore a European shirt and slacks and a turban on his head; the mother and grandmother wore saris of bright turquoise and lemon yellow; the children were in ordinary dresses and shorts. Quite possibly, Sarah knew, these were descendants of the original Asian workers who had been brought out from India to build the railway more than seventy years ago. No doubt these three generations enjoying lunch on the grass had been born and reared in Kenya. And yet, ironically, Sarah, like most Africans and whites, did not consider the Asians Kenyan.

Frustrated, she continued walking. She headed toward the beach, where afternoon winds were starting to ripple the creamy dunes and cast sunlight speckles on the green water. She felt her irritation verge upon despondence. Was there no one, she wondered, among all the tribes and peoples of this country, who was truly Kenyan? Even her own Kikuyu had abandoned tradition. The men had given up the *shuka* for trousers, and the women wore *kangas*.

Where, then, *was* Kenya's style?

She sat down on a low moss-covered wall and watched fishermen in their long white skirts haul in the day's catch. She smelled the salty perfume of the Indian Ocean, listened to the cries of sea gulls, felt the sun on her arms. *Kenyan sun,* she thought, *which shines equally upon us all.*

She opened her sketchpad and went through her drawings: of Masai warriors jumping; of a Kisii soapstone carver; of a Samburu herdsman leaning on his staff. Sarah had sketched the eyes of Muslim women peering shyly over black veils; she had captured a happy Tharaka bride wearing no fewer than two hundred belts of cowry shells; Pokot women danced on a page, breasts bare, loops of earrings standing out from their heads. Sarah had even drawn an African businessman hurrying down a Nairobi street, briefcase in hand. And here was the smiling doorman of the new Hilton Hotel. Finally, she came to the last sketches in her book: the new, young women of Nairobi in their fake American look, which clashed with their proud, intricate African hairstyles.

Sarah looked up from the sketchpad and wondered where, in all these sketches, was Kenya.

The warm wind was building up. It fluttered the pages of her pad. A thin veil of sand raced over the dunes. Palm fronds rustled and slapped against one another. Sarah shaded her eyes and squinted out over the green-to-blue water. The hour was growing late. She knew she should be getting back to Nairobi. And yet she couldn't move.

Sarah was suddenly, inexplicably fixed to the spot.

It was as if the rising tropical wind held her prisoner, as if the whispering palms were urging her to *stay, stay. . . .* She stared at the sky, at the breakers rolling through distant reefs, at the shifting dunes, and suddenly she wanted to draw.

Turning hastily to a fresh page, Sarah pulled a pencil from her purse and began sketching.

She was hardly conscious of doing it; the pencil seemed to move on its own. Her hand flew over the paper, depositing lines and curves and shapes. She outlined and shaded. Her eyes went from the pad to the vista, back to the pad, rapidly, while the scene slowly emerged on the sheet.

And when she was done, barely minutes later, Sarah blinked in amazement.

She had captured the ancient beach on paper. Not just its likeness, for any camera could do that, but its *spirit.* There was *life* in the sweeping lines and arcs; one could almost hear the crash of the waves, the calls of the gulls. The penciled water seemed to undulate. And even though it was only gray lead, there was color in the picture. Sarah could see it; she could feel it. And her heart began to race.

Turning to another blank page, she changed her position on the low wall and began to draft the pretty little mosque hidden a hundred feet away behind tamarisk trees. When that was done, she sketched the narrow street with its Arab latticework balconies. And when the soul of Malindi was committed to paper, she closed her eyes and pictured the Amboseli plains, where lions roamed and flat-topped thorn trees held up the sky. Her hands flew. Page after page went by. She brought out fresh pencils. The afternoon waned; Africa's winking twilight was nearly upon her. But still she sketched.

She drew the shoreline of expansive Lake Victoria and the peaks of Mount Kenya and Mount Kilimanjaro. Her mind's eye saw round huts and Masai manyattas and Turkana tents, and her hand put them on paper. She drew birds and animals; she breathed life into wildflowers. And then there were clouds, great herds of them, moving around a central, dazzling sun. Finally, sunsets and sunrises went into the sketchbook, and the way the Chania tumbled over its riverbed, and the smoke curling up from her grandmother's cook fire, and the local bus from Karatina taking women back from the market to their various farms.

When Sarah had filled every page down to the last one and there was no more room, and all her pencils were dull, and she realized in surprise that she now sat in the darkness of night, she felt a strange, almost frightening emotion wash over her.

In a revelation that was like a blow, she realized she had been looking in the *wrong places.* Here, in this dime-store sketchpad now clutched between her hands, was Kenya. The East African "style" was not, she knew now, suddenly, excitedly, in the way its people dressed, but in

East Africa itself. The Kenyan soul lay not in *shukas* or *kangas* but in its sun and grasses and red earth; in the smiles of its children; in the toil of its women; in the soaring of a hawk, the loping of a giraffe, the lanteen sails of dhows at sunset.

Sarah began to tremble. She sprang up from the wall and ran to Dr. Mwai's car, holding the precious sketchpad to her breast. She didn't see the dark little streets she sped down or the dusky women who peered in curiosity from windows. Sarah saw only vast yellow savannas and herds of elephant, the desolate deserts of the north and marches of camels, the glass and concrete skyscrapers rising up from Nairobi's slums. And she saw it all in the colors and shapes of the new fabric she was going to create.

Sarah Mathenge was going to give the world a Kenya look at last.

"SO LET ME tell you what this bloke does," Terry Donald said as he opened his third Tusker beer.

Deborah wasn't listening. Sitting with Terry in the observation lounge of Kilima Simba Safari Lodge, she was watching a lone bachelor elephant that had come to the watering hole to drink. The lodge was quiet now; all the guests were in their rooms, changing out of swimsuits and into cocktail clothes. At sunset, when a great show of animals appeared at the watering hole, a hundred tourist cameras were going to click.

"I've told you about Roddy McArthur, haven't I?" Terry said, trying to get her attention. He understood her distraction. She was leaving for America in two weeks. "Anyway," he went on, "what Roddy does when he hasn't any clients to take out hunting is, he goes off alone and bags the largest trophies he can find. He sells them to Swanson, the taxidermist in Nairobi, who processes them and keeps them hidden. Then, when Roddy does have clients, or some other bloke has clients who bag small trophies and are dissatisfied, the heads are switched by Swanson, on the quiet, you understand, and the clients go home happy with the big trophies they later boast they bagged themselves. Mind you, Deborah, I don't get into that. I think hunting should be kept an honest sport." He leaned over and tapped her on the shoulder. "Deborah?"

She looked at him. "Sorry, Terry. My mind was wandering again."

"I'll bet you're all packed and ready to go."

No, she wasn't. In fact, as the day for departure drew nearer, Deborah's reluctance to leave grew stronger.

It was because of Christopher.

She could not get out of her mind their reunion down by the river, three weeks ago. She lived it over and over, filling her every waking moment with the memory of seeing him standing there in the sun. Each time she pictured Christopher, she felt the desperate rush of sexual desire that was growing within her every day.

"You know, Deborah," Terry said, "I wish you'd let me take you out just once more before you go away for three years."

She regarded Terry Donald. He was twenty years old, lean and sunburned, and ruggedly handsome like his father, Geoffrey, and his grandfather, Sir James. And he had a passion for hunting. When he had received his restricted license three years ago, Terry had taken Deborah on her first hunting safari.

They had gone in Land-Rovers down to the Serengeti in Tanganyika. Because his license was restricted, Terry had not been able to hunt any of the Big Five—elephant, rhino, buffalo, lion, and leopard. But they had come upon an old lion that had had a porcupine quill stuck up its cheek, all the way into its head, and it had made it crazy, attacking innocent villagers. Terry had brought the dangerous beast down with a single, merciful shot and had been allowed, because of the service he had performed, to keep the skin.

Their second safari had been a year ago, just before Deborah had entered the University of Nairobi for her premed studies. Then she and Terry had gone into Uganda after elephant. After long, hot days of trekking through eight-foot-tall hyperenia grass, carrying heavy rifles, cartridge bags, and water bottles, of following tracks and droppings into dense forest and feeling sharp danger all around, they had found a small bull group with excellent tusks.

Terry had given Deborah the honor of the first shot; but she had frozen, and so he had killed the best of the herd and had supervised the subsequent hacking away of the tusks. When, in a gesture of extreme generosity, he offered the ivory to Deborah, she had turned away.

She had not been able since to convince him of her dislike of hunting and her disapproval of its being permitted in Kenya. Nor had Terry been able to make her see his side of it: that hunters performed a valuable service. They culled dangerously large herds, saved crops and villages from marauding rogues, and policed the poachers, who had cruel ways of killing the animals.

Deborah shook her head and sipped her ginger ale. "No, Terry. I shall never go on safari again except to *look* at the animals."

She wasn't even sure she approved of that because already new tracks were crisscrossing virgin wilderness as more and more tourists plunged across Kenya in search of game. Mightn't this human and gasoline invasion, she wondered, upset the delicate balance of nature? She had seen carloads of whooping and hollering tourists race after animals, causing zebras and antelope to stampede blindly. The holidaymakers drove their rented cars into the herds, breaking them up, unwittingly separating young from mothers, driving a group from its territory, tiring them out, weakening them for the predators lurking nearby. What thrill was there, Deborah wondered, in chasing poor beasts until they nearly dropped, just for the sake of a bit of film footage?

Worse, the tourists were photographing the people. She had seen busloads pull up to villages with cameras out. Masai herdsmen, offended, would draw their cloaks up over their heads and turn away. The women would try to drive the intruders off with angry shouts. Such ignorance, they thought. Such lack of respect. The Africans knew that these *wazungu* were here to photograph animals. Did this then mean that they regarded the villagers as animals also?

Deborah looked around the luxurious lodge. It had been the first of its kind in Kenya, and now there were many imitators, from the Uganda border to the coast. Geoffrey Donald owned three as well as his growing fleet of minibuses, the same ones that trucked the holiday-makers over Masai land. Kilima Simba Safari Lodge was serene, taste-ful, and elegant. The guests arrived in groups, were dropped off by their weary African drivers, and entertained for a day or two with native dancing, poolside ease, gourmet meals, and an ancient watering hole, right here under the balcony of the observation lounge, to which the animals had been coming for centuries. Signs posted all around on the bamboo walls cautioned the guests to be silent, so that the animals would not be driven away.

Tourists were starting to filter into the bar, wearing stiff new khakis which they had purchased in Nairobi and in which they looked nervously self-conscious. But it was all part of the Kenya adventure. They ordered drinks the bartender had never heard of—margaritas, Long Island iced teas—and browsed through the expensive boutique, where a pretty African girl sold clothes imported from America.

Deborah looked out at the African vista. She heard the land breathe; she felt cool tropical arms reach out to embrace her. Once again the rest of the world—that fearful place which Christopher had so gravely warned her about—seemed to vanish, and she was all alone with the red earth, the animals, and the distant mountains.

Christopher's voice echoed over the vast plains: *Kenya is your home. Here is where you belong.*

Deborah was suddenly forlorn. Three years seemed an eternity. How would she survive, cut off from the very land that sustained her? She would feel like a caged bird, deprived of the sky.

Do you love me, Christopher? she asked the silence that drifted down from snowcapped Kilimanjaro. *Do you love me as much as I love you? With a terrible aching to be held, to touch, to kiss? Or do you think of me as a sister? Do you love me in the way you love Sarah? Would you have held her the way you held me, and spoken to her the way you spoke to me, if she were the one going to America? Will you perish when I am gone away from you, Christopher, as surely I will?*

"Can I get you another drink, Deborah?" Terry asked.

If only Sarah were here, Deborah thought. She desperately needed to talk to her best friend; perhaps Sarah had the answer to the enigma that was her brother. But Sarah wouldn't have come to the lodge if Deborah had asked her; she was roaming Kenya in Dr. Mwai's car.

"No, thank you, Terry," she said as she stood. "I'm going to my room for a while."

"Are you all right, Deborah?"

"I'm fine. See you at the party."

Deborah hurried across the suspension bridge that joined the "native-style" rooms built on stilts to the main lodge, and once inside the room, she leaned against the closed door, gazed at the wilderness that stretched beyond her balcony, and silently cried, *Christopher!*

* * *

"ASANTE SANA," SARAH said to the friend who had given her a lift up from Nairobi. She waved him off, then headed down the trail that led from the top of the ridge to her grandmother's huts on the broad riverbank below. She had said good-bye to the friend with a smile, but the smile had been forced. Sarah was, in fact, furious, and as she neared Mama Wachera, who was working in her herb garden, she cursed again every banker in Nairobi.

They had turned down her request for a small business loan—every last one of them!

When the medicine woman looked up and saw her granddaughter, she laid aside her hoe and went to embrace the girl. "Welcome home, daughter," she said. "I have missed you."

The old woman felt small and frail in Sarah's arms. No one knew exactly how old Wachera was, but because of her girlhood memories— Wachera had already given birth to David, Christopher's father, when the Trevertons first arrived fifty-four years ago—it was estimated that the medicine woman was around eighty. Yet, despite her age and size, Mama Wachera was still a strong woman.

"Is Christopher here, Grandmother?" Sarah asked before she went to her hut to put away her suitcase and fetch two gourds of sugarcane beer.

"Your brother has not come back since the day he returned from across the water."

Sarah changed out of her good traveling dress and wrapped a *kanga* about herself. When she brought the beer out into the sunshine, she wondered, Why was Christopher still in Nairobi?

"He is disrespectful, Sarah," Mama Wachera said as she took the offered beer. "My grandson should be here with me. After all, soon he enters the school of healing, and then I shall never see him."

"I'm sure Christopher means no disrespect, Grandmother. He must have a lot to do, to prepare to enter medical school."

They sat on the earth outside Wachera's old hut, two African women, generations apart, drinking together in an ages-old ritual of feminine companionship and intimacy.

"Tell me," Mama Wachera said, "did you find what you went searching for?"

Sarah recounted for her grandmother the marvelous revelation she had experienced in Malindi and her wonderful plans for the future. But when she came to the part in her story about her attempts to secure some money in Nairobi, Sarah's voice grew bitter.

"It was humiliating, Grandmother. They made me feel as if I were begging. Collateral, they said! In order to get a loan, one must prove that one doesn't need it! I showed them my sketchpad and the batik I've made. I said, *'Here* is my collateral! My future is my collateral!' And then they asked if I had a husband or father who would sign for the loan. Then they told me to go away. Grandmother, how does a woman get started in business?"

Mama Wachera shook her head. It all was a mystery to her. Women were meant to raise babies and work on the shamba. The things her granddaughter spoke of were alien to her.

"Why such a dream, my child? You must find yourself a husband first. You are old enough to have children by now, and yet you have none."

Sarah drew designs in the dirt. The Nairobi experience had been harsh and eye-opening. Several of the bankers had refused even to talk to her, two had been plainly amused with her plan, and three had made sexual overtures. For certain favors, they intimated, perhaps a loan could be arranged. . . .

Sarah was frustrated.

All over East Africa women were becoming emancipated. They were entering higher schools and coming out as doctors and lawyers, even as architects and chemists. But such pursuits, she had decided, were sanctioned by men. Those women were being carefully ushered through male channels, under constant male guidance and authority. There was a kind of patronizing, paternalistic acceptance of women who put on the barrister's wig and attended court. They were still under the male thumb, no matter how liberated they thought themselves. But women who wanted to go into business for themselves were another breed. They demanded total independence, and then it became another matter.

"We're a threat to them," Sarah had tried to explain to her mother in Nairobi. "A woman owning her own business is truly a woman standing on her own two feet. No man above her, to make the final decisions. It frightens men. Plus we're competition for their own businesses. But I'm not going to let them stop me. I'll find a way of getting started somehow."

Sarah had gone to her mother on the thin hope of gaining some support, but Wanjiru was as against her daughter's plans as the bankers were. "Finish school," she said over and over. "Why do you think I sacrificed so much for you? Divorcing your father, living in the forest, and spending all those years in detention camps? It was so you could have a good education and make something of yourself."

"I don't want to live *your* dream, Mother. I want to live my own! Isn't that what freedom really means?"

On the quiet Sarah had approached Dr. Mwai, whom her mother lived with in the Karen District. But although he was sympathetic with her, he had said, "If I were to give you money, Sarah, your mother would never speak to me again. In this case I shall have to side with her."

"Grandmother," Sarah cried, "what am I going to do?"

Mama Wachera regarded her granddaughter, who was not a true Mathenge but whom the old woman loved nonetheless. "Why is it so important to you, child?"

"It's not only important to me, Grandmother. It's important to Kenya!"

Seeing that her grandmother didn't understand, Sarah went to her hut, took the sketchpad out of her suitcase, and returned with it.

"Look," she said, slowly turning the pages. "See how I've captured the soul of our people?"

Mama Wachera had never seen pictures before. Her eye was not trained to grasp and understand an image. But she did recognize certain pieces of jewelry—a Masai necklace, Embu earrings. She gazed at the baffling lines on the paper and tried to comprehend what the girl was feeling. Although Sarah's words were strange to the old woman, there was a language that Wachera did understand—the language of the spirit.

And she felt it now, as they sat in the sun and Sarah turned her pages and spoke excitedly about the fabrics she was going to create, the dresses she was going to design, the "style" she was going to give to her African sisters. Mama Wachera felt a youthful energy fly out of Sarah and enter her own ancient body.

"And for this you need money?" Wachera finally asked.

"Mrs. Dar has promised to sell me one of her old sewing machines. I shall then need to rent a small space in town—nothing much, but where there is electricity and a room to spread out and cut my fabrics."

Wachera shook her head. "I don't understand money. Why can't you trade with Mrs. Dar? You are welcome to whatever is in my garden. My maize field by the river is more plentiful than ever. Or perhaps she would prefer goats? I am a rich woman, Sarah. I own nearly a hundred goats!"

In exasperation the girl shot to her feet. Her grandmother lived in the past. Buying a sewing machine with goats! "I need proper money, Grandmother. Pounds and shillings. If I were to try to work for it and save it up, it would take me years. I need it now!"

Mama Wachera looked thoughtful. Then she said, "Perhaps you are looking in the wrong place, child. You should look to the soil for your answer."

Sarah fought to curb her impatience. Trying to talk to her grandmother was almost as bad as talking to her mother. Older people simply did not understand. They lived in the past! If only Deborah were back from Kilima Simba—*she* would understand.

Wachera slowly rose, retrieved her hoe, and said, "Come with me."

Sarah wanted to protest, but it would have been disrespectful. So she followed her grandmother down to the maize plot by the river.

"The Children of Mumbi have lived on the soil ever since the First Man and Woman," Mama Wachera explained as she led her granddaughter among the tall stalks. "We sprang from the soil. When we take an oath, we eat the soil to bind our spirit to our words. The land is precious, Daughter, you must never forget that."

When they reached the corner of the plot, Wachera bent and struck the earth that lay in the shade of tall banana plants. "When one forgets the old ways," she said as she broke the earth, "then all is lost. In the soil lies our answers."

Sarah gazed out at the river, feeling her annoyance rise. She was in no mood for a lesson in planting.

But when the hoe struck something, she was suddenly attentive.

Wachera bent at the waist, keeping her legs straight as if she were weeding or harvesting, and dug into the loose earth. When she brought out a large leather bag, Sarah stared in amazement.

"Here," Mama Wachera said, handing the bag to her granddaughter.

Baffled, Sarah quickly undid the drawstring and blinked down at the great hoard of silver coins in the bag. There must have been a hundred pounds' worth in there!

"Grandmother," she said, "where did you get this?"

"I have told you, Daughter, that I have no use for money. Every week for twenty harvests your mother sent money for your keep. I had no need of it, as I fed you and your brother with food from my own shamba. I did not need to buy medicines, as I made my own. And when the school insisted that I pay for your uniforms and books, I sent goats, which they accepted. I do not understand coins. But I kept them, knowing they contain power."

Sarah stared at the old woman a moment longer. Then she cried, "Grandmother!"

"Is this what you need? Will this make you happy, child?"

"*Very* happy, Grandmother!"

"Then it is yours."

Sarah hugged the old woman, then spun deliriously in a circle.

Wachera laughed and said, "What will you do now, Daughter?"

Sarah came to a standstill, her eyes shining. She knew exactly what she was going to do with the money. But she would have to hurry. There wasn't much time.

Deborah was leaving in two weeks.

58

G race removed her stethoscope and folded it into the pocket of her white lab coat. To the sister at the bedside, an African nun in the pale blue habit of her order, she said, "Watch him closely and report to me at once any change."

"Yes, Memsaab Daktari."

Grace took one last look at the boy's medical chart, then, absently rubbing her left arm, walked out of the children's ward.

As she followed the treelined street from the hospital to her house, Grace was greeted by many people: a priest hurrying to a baptism; student nurses clutching books; blue-robed Catholic nuns; patients in wheelchairs; visitors bringing flowers. Grace Mission was like a small town; it was a self-contained, self-sufficient community that filled every inch of its thirty acres. And it was said to be the largest mission in Africa.

Grace Treverton was still the director, but much of the running of the mission was in the hands of others, to whom she had, over the years, gradually relinquished authority. At eighty-three Grace could no longer do all the work herself, as she would like to.

Streetlights came on with the descent of night. People hurried to dining rooms, to evening classes, to vespers in the church. Grace slowly climbed the steps of her comfortable and familiar veranda and was glad to see, when she walked through the front door, that Deborah was back from Amboseli.

"Hello, Aunt Grace," Deborah said as they embraced. "You're just in time. I've made tea."

The inside of the house had changed little over the years. The furniture, now considered antique, was protected by slipcovers and antimacassars. Grace's enormous rolltop desk was as cluttered as ever with bills, orders, medical journals, communications from all over the world.

"How was Kilima Simba?" Grace asked as she accompanied her niece into the kitchen.

"As luxurious as ever! And so overbooked that they had to double up the guests in their rooms and still turn people away! Uncle Geoffrey said he's going to build a new lodge, right here in the Aberdares. To rival Treetops, he said."

Grace laughed and shook her head. "Now there is a man who could truly see into the future. Ten years ago we all said he was mad. Now he's one of the richest men in East Africa."

Although there had been some trouble in the early days of independence—the Kenya Army had revolted, some lawless people had tried to terrorize the whites—none of the serious, anticipated trouble, such as a second Mau Mau, had happened. Through hard work and cooperation, and the spirit of *harambee*, "pulling together," and under Jomo Kenyatta's strong leadership, Kenya had emerged united and prosperous, earning for itself the title of Jewel of Black Africa. Only time would tell if this stability was going to continue in these next ten years of *uhuru*.

As she buttered the scones and put the jam and clotted cream on the table, Grace studied her niece. Deborah was not her usually lively self tonight.

"Is everything all right?" she asked, sitting at the table. "Are you feeling okay, Deborah?"

The smile that came was a lifeless one. "I'm all right, Aunt Grace."

"But something is troubling you. Is it your trip to California?"

Deborah stared down into her tea.

"You're having second thoughts about going," Grace said gently, "aren't you?"

"Oh, Aunt Grace! I'm so confused! I know it's a marvelous opportunity for me and all, but—"

"It frightens you, is that it?"

Deborah chewed her lip.

"Is it something else then? You're not worried about me, are you?

We've been over that already. I want you to go. I shan't be lonely. And the three years will go quickly."

To eighteen-year-old Deborah three years sounded like three centuries.

Grace waited. In their years together, living more as mother and daughter than as aunt and niece, Deborah had always been able to come to Grace with her fears, her questions, her dreams. They had spent many nights by the fire, talking. Grace had told Deborah stories of the Trevertons, and the girl had listened raptly. There had never been any secrets between them—with the exception of the identity of Deborah's father, which Mona had made Grace promise to keep a secret. And with Mona's departure from Kenya and only her sporadic, impersonal letters to take her place, Deborah had no other family than her aunt. They were as close as two people could be; they lived for each other.

Finally Deborah said softly, "It's about Christopher."

"What about him?"

Deborah stirred her tea with the look of someone searching for the right words.

"You two haven't had a row, have you?" Grace asked. "Is that why he went off to Nairobi the day he got back from England?" She was remembering the little boy Deborah had brought home for tea one day, a boy whom Grace had recognized instantly as a reincarnation of David Mathenge. From that day until the day he left for Oxford, Deborah and Christopher had been inseparable.

"I don't know why he went to Nairobi, Aunt Grace. I don't know why he's staying away."

"Well, he isn't away now. You must patch up your quarrel tomorrow."

Deborah brought her head up. "What do you mean, he isn't away now? Is Christopher home?"

"I saw him this afternoon. He had his suitcase, and he was going into his hut."

"He's back!"

When Grace saw the look in her niece's eyes and heard the excitement in her voice, she suddenly understood.

"I have to see him," Deborah said, standing up. "I have to talk to him."

"Not now, Deborah. Wait until tomorrow."

"It can't wait, Aunt Grace. I have to know something. And I have to know it *now.*"

Grace shook her head. The impatience of youth! "What is so important that you have to run over there now?"

"Because," Deborah said softly, "I'm in love with him. And I need to know how he feels about me."

Grace was not surprised. *Twenty years ago,* she thought sadly, *your mother followed the same path. But you are lucky. Today there is no color bar. Mona and David were born too soon. Their love was doomed.*

"You shouldn't go to him now, Deborah. You should wait until morning."

"Why?"

"Because when an unmarried girl goes into a man's bachelor hut, she is there for only one reason. The Kikuyu call it *ngweko.* It's an old custom which the missionaries have tried to stamp out, but I'm sure it is still practiced secretly in many places."

"What is *ngweko?*"

"It's a form of courtship, with rules and taboos governing it. If you were to visit Christopher's hut tonight, Deborah, it would mean only one thing to anyone who saw you."

"I don't care what people think."

"Then consider what Christopher might think. Does he feel about you the way you do for him?"

"I don't know," Deborah said unhappily.

Grace laid a hand on the girl's arm and said gently, "I know what you are going through. I was in love myself, many years ago, and was just as troubled by it as you are now. But you must go slowly and carefully, Deborah. We have to live by certain rules. Christopher is just as governed by Kikuyu tradition as we are by our European morals. If you visit him in his bachelor hut, you risk spoiling your reputation. And he might lose respect for you. Wait until tomorrow. Invite him here for tea."

Grace rose up from the table and, massaging her arm, said, "I'd better get back to the children's ward. I'm watching a little boy who I fear has meningitis."

"Can't someone else watch him, Aunt Grace? You work too hard. You look tired."

Grace smiled reassuringly. "In fifty-four years, Deborah, except for those few occasions when I was away from the mission, I have never missed a night of making rounds. Don't worry about me, dear. You get some rest and think about your exciting trip to California."

When her aunt had gone, Deborah sat glumly by the cold fireplace, torn in indecision: to wait or to go to him now?

She looked around the living room. One wall was lined with books, many of them quite old, dating from Grace's early days in East Africa. Deborah went to them and scanned the titles. She found what she was looking for: *Facing Mount Kenya,* by Jomo Kenyatta.

A description of *ngweko* was on page 155.

SHE LAY AWAKE, listening to the night. The mission slept; the coffee plantation up on the hill was empty of workers and machines. Deborah was in the bed she had occupied for ten years, the same bed, in fact, that her mother had slept in during the emergency and in the very bedroom where David Mathenge and Sir James had died—although Deborah didn't know this. A wind was blowing, and there was a full moon. Patterns moved on the whitewashed walls of the bedroom: the crooked branches of jacaranda; the graceful wands of alder and poplar. The wind stirred the trees, and the shadows on the wall by Deborah's bed resembled an underwater scene. She felt as if she were floating among seaweed and ocean grasses that waved and swayed with deep oceanic currents. The silence, too, was like the silence of the sea.

She listened to the steady rhythm of her heart. She felt its pulse at her neck, in her fingertips, in her thighs. It was a cold night, but she felt hot. She kicked the blankets off. She lay stretched out on her back, staring up at the ceiling. The wind moaned. A cloud covered the moon, plunging her into darkness. Then the light came out again, and the world was bleached in an eerie glow.

Deborah couldn't sleep because she was thinking of what she had read in Kenyatta's book, his description of *ngweko.* "The Kikuyu do not kiss girls on the lips as Europeans do; therefore, ngweko, *fondling,* takes the place of kissing. The girl brings the boy his favorite food as a token of affection. The boy removes all his clothing. The girl removes her upper garment and retains her skirt. The lovers lie together facing each other, with their legs interwoven. They fondle each other and engage in love-making conversation. This is the enjoyment of *the warmth of the breast.*"

Deborah sighed with the wind.

From the living room came the soft chime of the mantel clock. It was midnight.

Finally, unable to lie in bed any longer, Deborah got up and quickly changed into a skirt and blouse. She crept past her aunt's bedroom and went into the kitchen, where she put together a basket of food—two bottles of Tusker beer, a wedge of cheese, and a whole spice cake, Christopher's favorite. She hesitated for only a moment at the back door—long enough to consider what she was about to do and to decide that she would gladly risk anything to know, before she went to America, how Christopher felt about her.

She knew there was no danger on the path that followed the river; the wild animals had long since vanished from this area and were now found only deep in the mountain forests.

Shivering, she walked through the moon-kissed wind. Deborah went around Mama Wachera's hut, which was dark and silent, past Sarah's, and came to the doorway of Christopher's.

She stared into the interior darkness in fear and rising excitement. She felt as if her body were part of the wind, as if she had come from the whispering trees, or as if the river had created her and delivered her here on a wave. She moved on a compulsion that she could not control, that she had no desire to control. When she called his name, the wind carried it away from her lips and up into the night. She waited for a lull. Then she said, "Christopher? May I come in?"

It seemed to her that an eon passed before he appeared suddenly out of the darkness—a tall, lean warrior dressed only in soccer shorts.

"Deborah!" he said.

"May I come in? It's cold out here."

He stared at her for a moment, then stepped aside.

The inside of the hut was familiar to Deborah; she and Christopher had played in it as children. The walls were made of sun-baked mud; the roof was a thatch of elephant grass. The only furniture was a bed, constructed of a wooden frame and leather webbing and covered with blankets.

"Deborah," he said again, "it's late. What are you doing here?"

She turned to face him. Moonglow spilled into the hut, delineating the contours of Christopher's long, muscled limbs. Deborah felt as if she were gazing upon a ghost from his past. *Give him a shield and a spear*, she thought.

"What are you doing here, Deb?" he said more quietly.

"Why did you go to Nairobi, Christopher? Why have you stayed away?"

His expression became troubled. He looked away.

"Are you angry with me?" she whispered.

"No, Deb! No . . ."

"Then why?"

"It was because—"

Her heart pounded. There was but a short distance between them. She knew she had only to raise her hand and she would touch him.

"It was such a shock, Deb," he said in a tight voice, "to come home after four years and find out that you are going to America. I thought it would be best if I stayed away until you were gone. That would have made your leaving more bearable."

"But you came back too soon. I don't leave until next week."

He looked at her, at the way the moonlight whitened her skin. "I know," he said. "I couldn't stay away any longer."

They listened to the wind whistle through the thatch overhead; they felt cold drafts play about their ankles. Finally Christopher said softly, "Why did you come here, Deb?"

She held out the basket.

"What is it?"

"Take it," she said.

He took the basket, and when he opened it and saw what it contained, he knew why she had come.

When Christopher didn't say anything, Deborah turned away from him. With her back to him, she removed her blouse and carefully set it aside. Then she went to the bed and lay down on it, on her side, facing him. She kept her arm modestly across her breasts; she trembled. "Is this the way?" she whispered.

Christopher gazed down at her for a moment, with the basket in his arms; then he set it aside, removed his shorts, and went to lie next to her.

They faced each other in the darkness. He moved her arm and placed his hand on her breast.

"If you tell me," she murmured, "not to go to America, then I won't go."

He laid a hand on her cheek; he moved his fingers through her hair. "I can't tell you that, Deb. But, God, I don't want you to go!" He took her into his arms and pressed his face against her neck. "I want you to marry me, Deb! I love you."

"Then I'll stay. I won't go to America."

He drew back and gently put his hand on her mouth. He looked at her in the silver light of the moon, which made her skin almost luminescent, and he was certain that he was dreaming. Surely Deborah wasn't in his arms at last, he wasn't holding her and making love to her as he had done so often in his dreams! But here she was, her firm body pressed against his, her naked breast warming his chest, her mouth lifting up, seeking his.

He kissed her. He put his hand on her thigh and slowly lifted her skirt.

"Yes," she whispered.

GRACE OPENED HER eyes and looked at the ceiling. The wind and the trees were forming strange shapes on the walls of her bedroom. She lay for a long time, thinking.

She had heard Deborah go out, and she knew where she was going. Grace had not tried to stop her; she knew it was futile to try to keep Deborah from Christopher. Deborah could not be kept from him, Grace knew, any more than her mother could have been kept from David, or her grandmother from her Italian duke. The Treverton women, she told herself, were very strong-minded when it came to love.

Grace, who had always been a good sleeper, couldn't understand why she was so wide-awake now. Perhaps it was because of Deborah; perhaps it was only because of the wind. Getting up and going into the kitchen to warm some milk, Grace thought about her niece, and she found herself curiously untroubled by what Deborah was doing. Christopher was a good man, Grace knew, and would not harm Deborah. If he loved her as much as Grace hoped he did, then they would be very happy together in this new, interracial Kenya.

What will Mona think, Grace wondered as she poured the milk, *when she hears about it?*

Grace suspected that Mona wouldn't care. She and Tim had washed their hands of their "mistake" years ago.

Realizing that the milk was not doing any good and that sleep, for some inexplicable reason, was eluding her tonight, Grace decided to pay a visit to the children's ward and look in on her suspected meningitis case.

She hugged her sweater about her as she hurried down the dark, deserted road. Strange to think that at one time this was all dense forest and that she could not have set out at night without a rifle or an askari. As she went up the steps of the hospital bungalow, Grace glanced up at the night sky. Strangely, the moon, because of clouds, was heart-shaped.

The ward was dimly lit, with a nurse at the desk at one end, and Sister Perpetua sitting at the boy's bedside. She wasn't surprised to see Memsaab Daktari suddenly appear. Dr. Treverton was known for her devotion to patients, and she sometimes held long vigils at their bedsides. After receiving a report on the child's condition, Grace told the nun to get herself some tea, that she would watch for a while.

As Grace settled into the chair that the sister had vacated, she realized that she had an upset stomach. *This is why I could not sleep.*

She thought of what she and Deborah had had for supper: veal cutlets with mashed potatoes and gravy.

It was too much for a woman her age, Grace decided, and reminded herself that she should draw up a modified diet.

She looked down at the sleeping face and thought of all the sleeping faces she had watched down through the years. Was it only yesterday that she had supervised the construction of four poles and a thatch roof? And then there was little Birdsong Cottage.

Grace rubbed her stomach. The upset was getting worse.

The wind seemed to be stirring up more than leaves and dust tonight; it was whipping up old, forgotten memories. Images came into Grace's mind, and the faces of people whose names she no longer knew.

She even saw Albert Schweitzer, whom she had visited in his jungle clinic years ago.

When the nausea grew and a mild perspiration suddenly came to her hands and face, Grace began to wonder if the food had somehow been tainted. Phoebe, her Meru cook, was normally quite fastidious in the kitchen. Grace hadn't had to worry about food since the days of Mario, who had been known to be lax.

Then her breath came short, and Grace's worry turned to alarm. This was more than an ordinary stomach upset.

Finally, when a sharp pain sprang from her chest and shot down her left arm, she knew.

Not yet! I still have so much to do—

She tried to stand but fell back into the chair, clutching her chest. She tried to call out, but she had no breath. She looked down the long ward at the desk at the end. The sisters weren't there.

"Help," she whispered.

Grace attempted to get to her feet, but the pain pressed her back down. It seemed to pin her to the chair, as if a spear had pierced her heart. The ward tilted and swam around her. She fought for air. An incredible weakness flooded her, as if her bones had suddenly melted. And the pain was immense.

She heard voices—distant and sounding tinny, as if played on an old Victrola.

"Che Che, can't you make these wagons go any faster?"

"Do you mean to tell me, Valentine, that the house isn't even built yet?"

"Grace, please meet Sir James Donald."

"Thahu! A curse upon you and your descendants until this land is returned to the Children of Mumbi!"

The pathetic scream of a young girl, Njeri, at the *irua* ceremony.

"Help me," Grace whispered again.

She clutched the arms of the chair. The pain seemed to be cleaving her in two. She imagined her heart bursting. *Not yet. Let me finish my work. . . .*

But her only company was voices from the past.

"I'm sorry to have to report that His Lordship drove out in his car sometime during the night and committed suicide with a pistol."

"I'm going to have a baby, Aunt Grace. David Mathenge's baby."

"We all must pull together in our new Kenya. Harambee! Harambee!"

Grace felt the light around her grow dim; darkness encroached upon the edges of her vision. She felt all feeling, except for the intense coronary pain, ebb from her body. She was helpless to move, helpless to call out. A strange, floating sensation engulfed her. And then Grace felt a worried, loving presence swirl around her, like a warm mist.

She bowed her head. "James" was the last word she spoke.

59

The eulogy was delivered in the chapel of Grace Mission, where, fifty-one years ago, Grace Treverton had marched up to the Reverend Thomas Masters, who had been sent by the Mission Society to take over her mission, and said, "I want you to leave, sir, and I don't want you ever to come back. You are an unlikable, narrow-minded, un-Christian man, and you are doing my people more harm than good. You may also report to your superiors in Suffolk that I no longer need their support."

No one attending the funeral today knew of that event; no one, except for a few non-English-speaking Kikuyu, had witnessed it. But it had been a monumental hour in Grace's life.

The Lord Mayor of Nairobi was telling the enormous crowd now of Dr. Grace Treverton's life, and although the dismissal of the self-righteous reverend was not numbered among Grace's achievements, many others were.

Deborah, her eyes red and swollen, sat in the front pew with Geoffrey and Ralph Donald. In the simple casket lay the woman whom Deborah had thought of as mother, a source of love and protection and understanding for as far back as she could recall. Although it caused her pain to do so, Deborah allowed herself to think of how Aunt Grace had so lovingly taken her in when Deborah's mother had left Kenya. A bedroom had been converted to suit a child; Grace had bought toys and dolls; she had read stories at night to an unhappy, abandoned Deborah, had played "tea set" with her, and listened to a little girl's fears and dreams. Deborah remembered her aunt's tenderness, the cool and gentle hand on her forehead during a bout of measles, her patience at teaching, her plainly spoken explanation of Deborah's confusing emergence into adolescence, her laughter that was sometimes so hard that tears ran down Grace's cheeks. And then there had been the days spent in the mission's various health facilities, Aunt Grace showing Deborah how to use a stethoscope, letting her attend the morning dispensary hours, placing her first hypodermic syringe in her hand, explaining vital signs, quietly instructing Deborah in the mysterious secrets of healing and medicine.

Aunt Grace had always been there for Deborah. It was impossible to imagine a world without her. Deborah felt a terrible emptiness within herself, the sudden, isolating loss of family.

We all must die someday, she tried to tell herself. And it was fitting that Grace had been found slumped in a chair at a patient's bedside. *She would have wanted it that way.*

But it was little consolation to Deborah.

When Grace went at last into the ground, in a special plot at the side of the chapel where a bronze monument to her would one day stand, Deborah threw the first handful of red Kenya earth onto the coffin. It made a lonely, thudding sound.

DEBORAH PLACED THE journal to one side and told herself that someday, when she was over her grief, she would open it. But right now she was too distraught to read her aunt's private words.

Wiping her eyes, once again, with a handkerchief, she wondered when the crying would stop. When would the awful pain of loss finally dissolve and she accept the finality of death? *We were going to work together, Aunt Grace. But now I shall be Memsaab Daktari.*

She was sitting in the center of the living room floor, warmed by the sunlight that streamed in through open windows and doors. Deborah had opened up the house to keep it light and cheery, as her aunt always had. And she was going through boxes of Grace's personal things, collected over the years. Grace Treverton, it appeared, hadn't been able to throw anything away. Deborah found photographs, receipts of purchases, faded greeting cards, letters from Sir James.

There was Aunt Grace's military medal, the Distinguished Service Cross in its velvet case, awarded to her for valor and bravery during World War I. Deborah came across a small ring which was perplexing in that it looked like a school ring, but that she had never seen her aunt wear. And here was the turquoise brooch Grace had valued so highly and with great sentiment. A "lucky stone" Grace had called it, which was supposed to fade when the luck was used. Deborah now pinned the brooch to her dress but returned the other precious mementos to Grace's jewelry box.

There were unexplainable curiosities among her aunt's things: an old and yellow clipping from a newspaper, announcing Grace's presence in British East Africa to a man named Jeremy Manning; a menu from the Norfolk Hotel; a pressed flower. There were letters from famous people—Eleanor Roosevelt, President Nehru—and crayoned cards signed with names written in childish scripts.

Grace had saved everything. It seemed to Deborah that every moment, every breath of her aunt's life had been carefully preserved in these boxes. And now they all belonged to Deborah.

Grace's house had also been left to her, to live in for as long as she wished. The mission, however, by prearrangement, had been left to the order of Catholic nuns, with the provision that Deborah be allowed to practice there upon completion of medical school. But Deborah didn't want to live in this house. She wanted to open up Bellatu again, to take the boards off the windows, pull the sheets off the furniture, and bring life into it, with Christopher, with their children. She would let the nuns have Grace's house.

A shadow suddenly appeared in the doorway.

Deborah looked up and saw Sarah standing there, a parcel in her hands.

"I'm sorry, Deb," she said softly. "I only just heard about your aunt. I've been working in Nairobi, and I didn't see any newspapers."

Deborah stood and went into Sarah's arms. They held each other for a moment. Then Sarah said, "Christopher told me. What a terrible shock for you. He also said you're not going to California, that the two of you are going to get married. It's too much, Deb. Such good news following such sad."

"I'm glad you're here, Sarah. It seems so strange, Aunt Grace being gone. I keep expecting her to walk through the door or to call me for tea. I can't imagine what it's going to be like living in this house all by myself. Will I ever get used to it, do you think?"

"We'll help you, Deb."

"I feel like an orphan. I have no family now. I feel so alone in the world."

"Christopher and I will be your family from now on."

"I'm glad you're here, Sarah."

"I came by to show you something. But I think I should come back another day."

"Please come in. Have tea with me."

They sat at the kitchen table, drinking Countess Treverton tea. Sarah did not unwrap her parcel right away. "Do you know, Deb, that my grandmother offered a Kikuyu prayer to Ngai for your aunt?"

Deborah was surprised. "I always thought they were archrivals. Your grandmother never liked any of us. She even cursed my grandfather once. Or so the rumors say."

"Still, she respected your aunt. They both were healers."

"What did you bring to show me, Sarah?" Deborah said, not wishing to talk about death anymore. "And what were you doing in Nairobi? Christopher said you had come up with some new designs while you were in Malindi."

Sarah took the parcel to the kitchen counter and opened it. When she was ready, she turned around and unfurled the cloth like a banner, holding it between her outstretched hands.

Deborah stared. "Sarah," she whispered.

"What do you think?"

Deborah was overwhelmed. This cloth was nothing like the batiks Sarah had made down by the river. This was a whole new creation, something that didn't exist, Deborah was certain, anywhere else on earth.

As her gaze traveled over the stunning colors, followed the shapes and curves and lines, she began to discern the swirling, blending themes: of a sunset melting into an aqua sea, which fanned out into green palm trees, which curved against the back of an African mother, who walked a red ribbon of road, which led to distant purple mountains, which were capped by silver snow.

"It's beautiful, Sarah! How on earth did you do it?"

"I've been working on it for nearly three weeks. You have no idea what went into this."

It made Deborah shiver. The pattern was hypnotic. The people were like the landscape, and the landscape resembled people. It was so African. So *Kenyan.*

"I want to make dresses out of it, Deb. I've even come up with a new design. Let me show you."

Sarah draped the fabric around herself; it fell in subtle folds so that the scenes were cleverly continuous. The dress would have wide sleeves, and it flared at the hem, which reached the floor. It was a simple cut, but elegant. It set off Sarah's glowing black skin, her crown of corn-rowed braids. "Do you think women will buy it?"

"Yes, Sarah. It's stunning."

Sarah carefully folded the cloth, wrapped it up in its brown paper, and said, "I went to the Maridadi fabrics plant in Nairobi, Deb. I showed them this cloth, and they said they can produce it for me if I have guaranteed orders for it. You see, I could never do this myself. One dress alone would take weeks. And I would have to charge so much that no one but a very few women would be able to afford it. But Maridadi can mass-produce the fabric on its machinery, and then I can sew the dresses. But I have to have guaranteed orders, Deb. I went to the dress shops in Nairobi, but they wouldn't make any guarantees. Do you have any ideas?"

Deborah tried to think. But all that came to her mind was *I wish Aunt Grace were here. She would have some advice.*

"What I was thinking," Sarah said, "is that maybe your uncle could sell my dresses in his lodges. You know, to tourists."

"Uncle Geoffrey?" Deborah pictured Kilima Simba Safari Lodge with its little boutique that sold dresses imported from Europe. Now that she thought of it, she recalled her uncle's complaining not too long ago about recent government restrictions on importation in order to bolster internal manufacture and economy. In fact, she realized now, he had spoken of either closing the boutique, which never made money, or converting it into a native crafts shop.

"Of course," Deborah said to Sarah, "your dresses would be perfect for my uncle's lodges. Tourists would love them."

"I hope so, Deb," Sarah said softly.

"I have to go to Nairobi tomorrow and let Professor Muriuki know that I'm turning down the scholarship. I'll see if Uncle Geoffrey is in his office. I'll show him your fabric."

"Thank you, Deb. I know this is a difficult time for you."

"I need to keep myself busy. It's what Aunt Grace would do. I shall sign up for classes at the university and get my life in order."

They walked to the front door, where scarlet and salmon-colored bougainvillaea shed rainbows of color in the afternoon sun.

"I'm glad you're not going to America, Deb. I'll be at home if you need me."

"I'll be back from Nairobi day after tomorrow. Please come by and keep me company. Maybe you'd like to move in with me for a little while. You could have one of the bedrooms for a sewing room."

"I would like that, Deb. Thank you." They embraced again. "I'm so glad you're going to marry Christopher. We'll be sisters."

Deborah watched her go, thinking that Sarah's step was so light and confident that she seemed hardly to touch the ground. Then Deborah turned back into the living room where the boxes awaited her.

Deborah didn't want to face them now; she wanted to put it off. Right after the funeral Christopher had said that he would meet her down by the river in their favorite spot. But it seemed to Deborah that she owed it to her aunt to perform this last duty, to leave nothing undone.

It was in the last box that she found the letters.

Strangely the envelopes were blank. When she opened one, she was surprised to see that there was no date and that it was headed "My beloved David . . ."

Deborah turned the letter over and read the signature.

Mona.

Her mother.

Deborah sat frozen in the sun, the love letter in her hand. She was remembering the day, ten years ago, when she and Christopher had sneaked into her grandparents' bedroom in Bellatu and had gone through the drawer of secret things. They had come across David Mathenge's passbook, which Christopher kept to this day.

She looked at the letter, at the rest of the bundle, and wondered again why that passbook should have been among her mother's things.

David Mathenge and my mother—lovers?

Spellbound, Deborah read the letters. There were no dates on any of them. "I shall give these letters to your mother," Mona had written.

"as you told me to do. And she will pass them on to you. It is my one solace in this terrible time that we are linked in this way."

Deborah was mystified. How had these letters come to be in her aunt's possession?

She continued to read. The words on the pale pink and blue paper, with the Treverton crest at the top, could not possibly have been written by her hard, unfeeling mother! These words of love and devotion had been written by a young woman full of life and passion; she had put to paper exactly how Deborah felt about Christopher.

Deborah's eyes filled with tears. What a terrible thing, to be separated from the man one loved, to be damned by society for loving a man of a different race.

She suddenly wanted her mother to be there in the living room, to talk with her, to go back over the years together and start anew. How different things could have been!

Deborah knew that David Mathenge had been killed during the emergency. But when or where was unknown to her. Just as her own father's death had never been explained to her. "He died before you were born" was all her mother would say.

Was my father, too, killed in the emergency? Deborah wondered, greatly puzzled. *Did my mother know him before or after she fell in love with David Mathenge?*

For the first time Deborah was suddenly curious about her father. She had always imagined him as some smiling, shadowy figure who had passed briefly through her mother's life. He had never married Mona; had he even really loved her?

Deborah continued to read the letters. Halfway through came the thunderbolt announcement of her mother's pregnancy. Deborah read quickly now. A baby girl was born; Mona named her Mumbi for the First Woman. She wrote to David about their beautiful "love child."

And then, mysteriously, the letters ended.

That must be when David was killed.

Deborah gathered the letters up and frowned over them. *What happened to that baby? Where is Mumbi now?*

Deborah's mother had never mentioned another child, nor had Aunt Grace. Had Mumbi been given away for adoption? Or had she, too, died?

Suddenly needing to know, Deborah stood up and looked around the living room, as if the answers were hidden there. She could write to her mother. But weeks would pass before a reply came. And then perhaps her mother wouldn't want to be reminded of that painful episode in her past and would not speak of it.

Who else would know? Uncle Geoffrey, maybe. But then, if he didn't, Deborah did not want to disclose her mother's secret.

Aunt Grace would have known, but she's no longer here.

Deborah went to the veranda and looked out. There was one other person who would know what became of that baby. After all, she was David's mother, and these letters had been given to her.

But it daunted Deborah to go to the medicine woman. She had always felt vaguely afraid of Mama Wachera, had always squirmed slightly beneath that masked gaze. But Wachera was, after all, Christopher's grandmother and soon, Deborah told herself, to be a relative through marriage.

And she would know what had happened to that baby.

As she followed the old worn path that lay between the playing field and the river, Deborah felt her grief slowly give way to excitement. Not alone after all! There was a chance that that child had lived and was alive today. Mumbi—a half sister!

Mama Wachera was at the homestead, wrapping sweet potatoes in leaves while a millet stew bubbled on the outside cook fire. Deborah approached her shyly, clearing her throat first and then murmuring traditional greetings of respect in Kikuyu. She spoke the language well; Christopher had taught her.

The old woman regarded her with a stony expression. There was no greeting in return, no offer of beer or food. Recognizing that she had been received with the height of Kikuyu rudeness, Deborah spoke quickly.

"Please, I have found these letters among my aunt's things. I need to know about them. You are the only person I can think of who can tell me."

The medicine woman's eyes flickered to the letters in Deborah's hands. "What do you want to know?"

"They were written to your son, David, by my mother. She tells him of a baby, a daughter named Mumbi. She would be my sister, and I want to know what happened to her. Do you know, Lady Wachera? Is Mumbi still alive?"

The old woman's gaze was steady as she said, "I know of no baby."

"It's here in these letters. My mother tells David that Mumbi is his daughter. No one ever spoke of that child to me. Surely you know what became of her. Please tell me."

"I know of no baby," Wachera said. "You are the only child to come from your mother's body."

Deborah tried to think of a better approach. Perhaps with Christopher's help—

"You are the only child to come from your mother's body," Wachera repeated.

"But there was *this* one," Deborah argued. "The one called—"

She stopped. She looked into the enigmatic eyes of the medicine woman.

Then Deborah looked down at the letters in her hand.

They bore no date. But she knew they had been written during the emergency.

I was born during the emergency. . . .

She looked at the medicine woman again. "What are you saying?" Deborah whispered, feeling suddenly cold and frightened. "What are you saying?"

Mama Wachera didn't speak.

"Tell me!" Deborah cried.

"Go away from here," the old woman finally said. "You are *thahu*. You are cursed."

Deborah stared at her in horror. "Am I—" she whispered. "Am *I* that baby?"

"Go away from here. Go away from this land where you do not belong. You are *thahu*. You are taboo."

"It can't be!"

"*Thahu!*" Wachera shouted. "You are a child of wickedness! And you have slept with your father's son!"

"*No!*" Deborah screamed. "You're wrong!"

She backed away. She stumbled. Then she turned and ran.

60

The four young black women stood with the ease and confidence of those who know who they are and where they are going. They wore their hair in the new Afro style, smoothly sculpted bouffants of tight black curls. Their dresses were made of brightly patterned Nigerian fabric and heavily embroidered in white silk thread at the sleeves and neckline. They wore enormous hoop earrings, and rows of copper bracelets, and necklaces made of iron and wood. They had names like Dara and Fatma and Rasheeda. They were chic, fast-talking, politically wise, and beautiful. And they had, a few weeks ago, cut Deborah Treverton out of their circle.

She watched them now, from across the enormous recreation room that was filled with Christmas partyers. Her eyes betrayed feelings of confusion, envy, and solitude. She had not intended any offense when she had tried to make friends with them, but there was an enormous gulf, Deborah had discovered, between her and these Afro-American women that could never be bridged. Her initial hope, that she had found something of Sarah in them, had been crushed back in September, when just two weeks after starting the new term at the California college, Deborah had petitioned to join them.

"Women Against Repression is a black women's group," said the one who called herself Rasheeda, although her real name was LaDonna. "Why do you want to join?"

It had been impossible for Deborah to put into words her feelings of loss, of needing to belong somewhere, of how they reminded her of Sarah, of how lonely she was in this bewildering new country.

America seemed as alien to Deborah as she imagined Kenya must have been for the first white people. She didn't understand the language, even though it was English, because slang prevailed, words like *bummer* and *freakout,* or saying "bad" when one meant "good." She couldn't sort out the complex social rules, which were so different from Kenyan rules. And she was nonplussed by the many layers of subcultures through which all Americans seemed easily to swim. Deborah was searching for her niche in this baffling new land that seemed to have a place for everyone, and so she had simply said, "Because I am black."

To her surprise they had accepted that. Even just one drop of black blood, they had explained, placed a person in the ranks of the oppressed. And they welcomed her, for a while, as their sister.

But black skin, Deborah soon learned, did not make Africans of them. Although they staunchly regarded themselves as such, Deborah had seen none of her Kikuyu friends among these aggressive, worldly-wise, man-hating women who spoke freely and, in Deborah's opinion, shockingly about abortion, sex, and the emasculation of the American Negro male. There was none of the African naiveté, the demure respect for elders, the feminine modesty in them that she was used to seeing in Sarah and her friends. These were angry women, and they fought a mutual enemy whom Deborah had, so far, not found as threatening as they so vocally claimed, the white male.

Still, she had tried to stay with them, to keep her place among them, because she needed a *place,* just as she needed to surround herself with a barrier to keep out the overwhelming waves of pain that lay just at the edge of a threatening shore.

She had left Kenya without saying good-bye to Christopher or Sarah.

Someone jostled past her, knocking her arm so that her Coke spilled. She backed up against the wall, to be as out of the way as possible while still being part of the crowd. Christmas music blared from overhead speakers; long tables groaned with food; the two fireplaces at either end of the hall were blazing, even though it was a warm, balmy Southern California evening and everyone was dressed in summer clothes.

Deborah pressed herself against the wall and watched the boisterous, happy, multifaceted mob with growing dizziness, as if she were watching a merry-go-round spinning faster and faster.

She wasn't used to crowds. Classes at the University of Nairobi had been small; student gatherings were always intimate. But this fast-paced campus overlooking the Pacific Ocean boasted a population of twenty thousand, and it seemed to Deborah that every single one of them was at this Christmas party tonight.

The crowds and speed of California life were only one of the many culture shocks Deborah had experienced since fleeing Kenya and seeking refuge here. There was so much that she didn't understand, and feared she never would—inside jokes and references which evoked responses from everyone else but which only left her baffled. She had once asked where the Twilight Zone was, and everyone had laughed. She didn't ask questions after that. Eventually she had discovered that much of the California way was derived from television, something which, in all her life, Deborah had never seen. She felt as if she had missed out on a wedge of history, as if she were some sort of Rip Van Winkle who had slept through a revolution. So much of what she observed and overheard seemed to be connected in some way to television or derived from it—language, mannerisms, jingles, even fashion and food. But more perplexing to her was that she had found, directly alongside this deep-rooted cultural anchor to television, a sweeping denial, by those same people, of ever watching it!

The four Afro-American women laughed suddenly. They stood at the nucleus of popularity, at ease with their blackness and their sense of superiority. The one who called herself Fatma—in reality, Frances Washington—was the one who had cut Deborah from their radius.

Fatma was the most militant of the group. She belonged to the Black Panthers and was a close friend of Angela Davis's. She gave speeches and spoke out against three centuries of racial abuse. "Why does the white man refer to us as though we were edible?" she had once cried at a meeting of sisters. "Read their novels! Listen to how they talk! Black women are described as cocoa-skinned, café au lait, chocolate, licorice, brown sugar. We are *black*. We are not pieces of food!" It was Fatma who had approached Deborah one day early in October, when Deborah had been a member of the group for only a short time, and asked her how she was able to finance herself through such an expensive school. Fatma, having assumed like everyone else that Deborah was from England, had been surprised to learn that she was from Kenya and that she had come to America on one of the university's Uhuru scholarships.

"But," Fatma had said, "those scholarships are meant for Africans!"

"I am African. I was born in Kenya."

"But that money was intended to go to a black student."

"I'm half black."

Not black enough, Fatma's look had said. "You know what I mean. That money was intended for our oppressed black brothers and sisters. Students who need our help."

"*I* need the help. I have no money, no family. And I did win it fairly. I competed against fifteen hundred others."

"You should have given it to a black sister."

"Why?"

"Because you have advantages that she does not."

"What advantages do I have?"

"You're white."

By that time Deborah's Kenya tan was mellowing to a dark gold, and her short, curly hair, growing out, was straightening. She realized then that the Afro-American women did not really regard her as a sister because she didn't have the necessary appearance. *But in my soul I am African!* she wanted to cry. *I am more African than any of you! My father was David Mathenge, the great Mau Mau freedom fighter!*

She watched them move now among the crowd with an arrogant self-confidence that seemed almost to be a dare. Ten years earlier these four might not have been admitted to this exclusive school; now everyone, it seemed to Deborah, in this age of sudden liberal consciousness, was anxious to curry their friendship.

She had gone to a small party at Dara's apartment, where the sisters, Deborah, and a few token whites had mingled in a kind of interracial ostentation. That was when Deborah had been introduced to California wine, had drunk too much of it, and had ended up by offending both camps with one of Aunt Grace's amusing stories about Mario. "She caught him in the kitchen one day, rolling meatballs against his bare chest and popping them into the pan!"

Deborah's laughter had quickly died when she saw the faces staring at her, the room silent except for *Hair* playing on the stereo.

Dara had said, "Why do you call him your houseboy?"

And Deborah had not known what to say.

"It seems to me," someone else said, "that Kenyan imperialists are no different from Rhodesians and South Africans. Racist bastards, all of them."

Deborah had wanted to explain that they had it all wrong, that Kenya wasn't like that. Well, her uncle Geoffrey was a racist, but her aunt Grace and many others never were, and it seemed to Deborah that there was a great deal less racial bigotry in Kenya than there was in this pretentious country where people changed their names and put on costumes and pretended to be friends for an evening because that was the current trend. She had felt herself become angry toward these Americans. She had wanted to tell the "sisters" that they weren't African at all but some ludicrous parody and that Sarah wouldn't recognize them as one of her own and that, if they but knew, they wouldn't be so eager to be "African" because that meant being under the thumb of a husband or father and working in the fields and having one baby after another and carrying loads on their backs like animals. Then she thought of Sarah and her beautiful fabric and her inability to get help to produce it, and she thought of Christopher and their home by the Chania River, and she had burst into tears, and that had been the end of her membership in the black women's movement.

But there were other groups on campus where she might find a home—associations that went by letters, such as SNCC and CORE, coalitions of young progressive whites who didn't seem to judge a person by skin color, clothes, or way of speaking. Deborah had sought their companionship as a panacea for her growing loneliness and sense of alienation. And that, too, had ended in disappointment.

"Hello," said a voice next to her.

Deborah turned to find herself looking into a smiling, bearded face. She had seen him around school; there were a thousand of him. He marched in antiwar parades, dodged the draft, and wondered how Nixon had gotten into office when he and ten million others insisted that they hadn't voted for him.

"Nice party, huh?"

Deborah forced a smile. He stood too close to her. She felt trapped. And the pain, which she carried with her everywhere like a small, dark jewel, was starting to grow.

"So," he said. "You a student here?"

"Yes."

"What's your major?"

"I'm in premed."

"No kidding. Philosophy myself, although I don't know what the heck I'll do with it. Premed, huh? Where are you going to go to medical school?"

"I don't know." *I'm living one day at a time.*

"I like your accent. You from England?"

"No. Kenya."

"No kidding! I had a cousin who went there with the Peace Corps. He didn't last long, though. Too filthy, he said. I didn't know there were any whites left in Kenya. Wasn't there a Zulu uprising there about twenty years ago?"

"Mau Mau," she said.

He shrugged. "Same difference. Hey, can I get you something to eat? They've got a far-out curry here that's not to be believed. Hey! Where are you going?"

Deborah fled through the crowd, found the double doors that opened onto the patio, and delivered herself into the warm California night.

She ran across the lawn and found a deserted bench. She sat on it, tears filling her eyes, and felt the dark gemstone of pain expand within her until it filled her body and began to cut with sharp facets. An alien night engulfed her; the soul of a land that was not her own moved stealthily about her, as if sizing her up, as if deciding whether or not to let her stay.

I must not love you, Christopher. I must never think of you in that way again. . . .

Finally Deborah let the tears fall. She cried as she had cried almost every day since leaving Kenya, since the day she had found her mother's letters. Deborah remembered little of what had followed. With Mama Wachera's words ringing in her ears, she had found her way back to the mission, where she had telephoned her aunt's solicitor. "I want to sign this house over to the nuns," she had told him. "And I want you to sell Bellatu as quickly as possible. I don't care what you get for it. And everything inside is to go with it. I am leaving Kenya, and I am never coming back."

She hadn't even spent that night at the mission; it was too haunted.

She had packed hastily and gone down to Nairobi, where, after a terrible night at the Norfolk Hotel, she had caught the first flight to Los Angeles. The school had granted her an early check-in into the dormitory. And there Deborah had spent a week in solitude and spiritual turmoil. School had begun after that, and Deborah had dived into a consuming schedule of new classes and studies.

She had tried to write letters to Christopher and Sarah. But she was unable to. Christopher must never know the truth. Incest was one of the worst and most condemning of Kikuyu taboos. It would haunt him for the rest of his life and bring him unhappiness.

Neither had she been able to write to Sarah. Deborah had left the fabric with Sister Perpetua, with instructions to return it to Sarah Mathenge, and Deborah had not seen her friend after that.

Someone was walking across the lawn in front of Deborah. She knew who it was. Pam Weston. Deborah hoped the young woman wouldn't see her sitting there alone on the bench and was relieved to see Pam join the crowd in the recreation hall.

Pam Weston had been one of Deborah's new liberal friends. "My God," she had declared in the dining commons one evening, "virginity is just a state of mind. Girls simply don't *save* themselves for marriage anymore. And any girl who does is deluding herself. She's allowing herself to be manipulated by male chauvinist tyranny."

Those words had been spoken three weeks ago, when Deborah had lingered over evening coffee with her new friends. They had been more easily accepting of her than the militant black women had been, but even so, they had their requirements for membership. "Any girl who still shaves her legs isn't liberated," Pam maintained, and the group agreed.

These were a strange breed of women to Deborah, who had never heard of women's liberation. News from overseas came late to Kenya and was reported in government-censored form. It had surprised these young women, who had thought by her accent that she was from England, to discover how ignorant she was. Deborah was unfamiliar with names such as Gloria Steinem and Betty Friedan and had no idea what male chauvinism was. Deborah seemed a paradox to them: on the one hand, white and articulate, educated and intelligent but, on the other, hopelessly naive and provincial.

"If you look at women's clothing throughout history," Pam Weston declared, "you see how enslaved we were. Corsets, whalebone stays, eighteen-inch waistlines! But at last women are waking up and dressing the way they want to. No longer will we let ourselves be at the mercy of male chauvinistic fashion designers!"

"My best friend," Deborah had ventured quietly, "is designing the most beautiful dresses. She even batiks her own fabric."

"I love batik!" declared the business major in a tie-dyed blouse. "I tried it once, but the colors kept running."

"Sarah taught herself how to do it. She's clever like that. Her fabrics are actually works of art. I wouldn't be surprised if she became famous someday."

"Would she make a dress for me?" the business major asked. "I would pay, of course."

"Well, Sarah isn't here. She's in Kenya."

"Oh, African batik. Even better!"

"What's your friend doing in Kenya?" asked Pam Weston. "Is she in the Peace Corps?"

"She lives there."

"The whites have exploited East Africa long enough," said a student of political science. "Your friend should leave Kenya to its own people."

"Well," said Deborah, "Sarah isn't white."

They all looked at Deborah. "Your best friend is black?" Pam Weston said. "Why didn't you say so in the first place? Or are you ashamed of that fact?"

Deborah closed her out. They simply didn't understand. In their eagerness to demonstrate their racial toleration, these liberal-thinking women perpetuated color consciousness. It had never occurred to Deborah to think of Sarah or Christopher as anything other than her friends, than as people.

It was then that she had realized she would never fit in. Neither accepted by the blacks nor understood by the whites, Deborah was condemned to roam a kind of racial limbo. American ways were not her ways; its history and dialects were alien. She was a woman without a race, without a country, and now, finally, without a family.

I can never go back to Kenya. I must never see Christopher again. Aunt Grace is gone. I am alone. I must make a life for myself here, among strangers, in a world I was not born into.

"Hi. Mind if I join you?"

Deborah looked up to see a young woman in a turtleneck and jeans. She seemed familiar.

"We're in physiology together," the young woman explained. "I've seen you in class. I'm Ann Parker. Can I sit with you?"

Deborah moved over.

"I don't know why I came to this party," Ann said. "It's just that the dorm is so empty and lonely. Everyone's gone home for the holidays. I'm not used to crowds."

Deborah smiled. "Neither am I."

"I come from a small town in the Midwest, so you know what I mean."

"Where is the Midwest?"

"Good question!" Ann laughed. "I sometimes wonder if I made a mistake coming to this school. This campus is bigger than the town I grew up in. It scares me sometimes."

"I know how you feel."

"I feel like shouting, 'Beam me up, Scottie!' "

"Scottie?"

Ann smiled. "I like your accent. Are you from England?"

Deborah saw the golden savannas of Amboseli and the Masai herdsmen silhouetted against the blue sky. She smelled the red earth and the smoke and the wildflowers along the Chania. She heard the tinkle of goats' bells and the shrill, rapid speech of Kikuyu women on their shambas. She felt the strong arms and warrior's body of the man she was forbidden to love.

"Yes, I'm from England," Deborah said as she checked her watch and allowed herself to think, for the last time, that at that very moment, on the other side of the world, the sun was rising over Mount Kenya.

PART NINE

The Present

61

Deborah stared down at the last entry in Grace's journal, dated
August 16, 1973.

"Deborah is in love with Christopher Mathenge," her aunt had
written. "And I believe he is with her. I cannot imagine anyone I would
rather have marry my Deborah, and I pray that I live long enough to
attend their wedding, so that I can give them my blessings for a long
and happy future together."

Those were the last words Grace had written in her book. She died
later that night.

Closing the journal and setting it down on the bed, Deborah un-
folded her aching legs and went to the window. When she parted the
drapes, bright, unexpected sunlight stabbed her eyes. Startled to discover that it was broad daylight, she quickly pulled the curtains closed.
Deborah realized she had read all night and through the morning, with
no awareness of time.

She turned away from the window and sank onto the bony little sofa
that completed her hotel room. Resting her feet on the coffee table,
she settled back and gazed at the ceiling. Beyond the door, sounds of
life filled the corridor: room service carts rattling by; porters calling to
one another in Swahili; the periodic ding of the elevators. From her
windows behind the sealed drapes, Nairobi delivered up its daytime
cacophony of traffic, car horns, people shouting in the street below.

Deborah hugged herself. Tears stood behind her eyes.

It was too much—her family story. She felt as if a deluge had washed
over her, as if she were swimming in a churning sea.

They had been there all this time, the answers she had once gone to Wachera for about that other baby, the love child of Mona and David. The answers had been in the journal all these years, spelled out in Grace's neat hand: "We lost four lives to Mau Mau that night—my beloved James; Mario, who had been with me since the beginning; David Mathenge; and the baby, trampled. . . ."

And then, two pages later: "Mona is pregnant again. She says it is Tim Hopkins's child, a mistake, that she had been out of her mind with grief and didn't know what she was doing."

Tears came to Deborah's eyes as the truth cut through to her soul. *I was not a love child after all. But a mistake.*

Deborah drew her legs up and hugged them to her. She bent her head and cried softly onto her knees.

There was a knock at her door.

She raised her head. When she heard the sound of keys in the lock, she jumped up and went to answer it.

A room steward stood in the hall with his cleaning cart and an armload of fresh towels. He smiled apologetically and used gestures to indicate that he wanted to clean her room.

"No, thank you," she said in English, then repeated it in Swahili when she saw that he didn't understand. He smiled again and bowed and pushed his cart away. Deborah searched for a Do Not Disturb sign, found one that read USISUMBUE, and hung it on the outside knob.

She leaned against the door and closed her eyes.

Why am I here? Why did I come?

The noise beyond her windows seemed to come through the glass in urgent waves. She heard Nairobi's call but wanted to ignore it. Suddenly she was afraid.

"You're afraid of something," a voice now whispered in her memory. Jonathan, six months ago, asking, "Why are you running from me? Is it me you're afraid of, Debbie, or are you just afraid of commitment?"

She pictured Jonathan Hayes, tried to conjure him up and make him come to life, body and soul, here in this room. She tried to imagine how he would be at this very moment, getting her to talk, drawing her feelings out, helping her through this twisted maze she had gotten herself lost in. There was solace in thinking about Jonathan, comfort in his imagined presence. But as a specter he was too tenuous. At the sound of loud voices from the corridor he vanished.

Deborah felt as if she were scattered in pieces all over the globe, half of them here in East Africa, the other half revolving purposelessly around Jonathan in San Francisco. Since her early days in California, fifteen years ago, when she had blindly fled a reality too strong for one so young and unforged to face, Deborah had led a piecemeal existence, tacking together an identity when and wherever she could. "Where exactly in Cheshire are you from, Dr. Treverton?" Jonathan had asked the afternoon they had met. Deborah was new to the staff, and she had been assigned to assist him in surgery. And to her own surprise, Deborah had found herself confessing that she was actually from Kenya, not from England.

Looking back, she knew what had prompted the unexpected honesty. It was Jonathan himself. There was something about him, in his large brown eyes, as soul-seeing and commiserating as a priest's, and in his confessional voice, a sort of HAL computer voice, she had thought when she first met him. Everyone felt that way about Dr. Jonathan Hayes. People took their loves and frights to him, and he listened with consummate patience.

That was not to say, however, Deborah had learned in their two years together, that he was a man to display his own heart upon his sleeve. Jonathan was not a demonstrative man. If he had feelings, they were carefully harnessed beneath an even-tempered, easygoing exterior. And that was why his sudden, impulsive kiss at the airport—when? yesterday? the day before?—had so startled her.

Deborah shivered and discovered that she was cold.

Her hair had long since dried, but she still wore only her bathrobe. But the decision of whether or not to get dressed was beyond her ability.

Christopher, she thought at last.

He was not her brother after all.

She had been fighting thinking about him; from the moment she had closed the journal, she had turned her back on what had to be faced. Now it made her feel as if the floor had suddenly dropped away from under her. She clutched the doorknob as if to keep from falling. The very thing she had worked so hard for fifteen years to deny suddenly no longer existed.

She was not David Mathenge's daughter. She did not belong to Kenya's black race.

It took her breath away. Deborah managed to leave the door and make her way into the bathroom. She stared at her reflection in the mirror, at a face she had examined a thousand times for traces of a bloodline she had believed for so long to be there. How often she had studied herself! Scrutinizing every eyelash, every line and fold of her face, searching for the African clues, while at the same time praying that they would never appear, so that no one could suspect.

She groped for the edge of the sink.

I ran for no reason. No crime was committed. I was free to love Christopher. I could have stayed.

The tears rose again. Deborah felt ensnared. Jonathan would have helped her to control herself if he were here; he would have shown her how to master her confusion. But Jonathan wasn't here. Just the mocking image of the white woman in the mirror.

She went to the bed and picked up the photographs: Valentine on a polo pony; Lady Rose, looking back over her shoulder; Aunt Grace as a young woman; four barefoot kids standing in the sun. Deborah now looked at the last three pictures.

In her hasty flight from Kenya so long ago she had only packed a few things—Grace's journal; the love letters; a handful of snapshots. She had wrapped them all in paper and string, and there they had stayed for fifteen years. Deborah didn't know what the remaining three photos were of or why she had chosen them, but as she held them up now she felt a strange longing come over her. A longing for the past.

There was Terry Donald, his right foot perched on the carcass of a rhino, his right hand holding a rifle. He was the image of the Donald men: attractive and virile, beaming with confidence and masculinity, sunburned and safari-weary, third-generation Kenya-born.

Deborah next looked at Sarah. She was young in this one, her hair not yet cornrowed, her smile still uncertain and girlish. Sarah was wearing a school uniform; there was a touching aura of innocence about her. The photo reminded Deborah of simpler days, better days.

The last was of Christopher, standing on the bank of the river in dappled sunlight, wearing dark slacks and a white shirt with the sleeves rolled up and collar open. He was wearing sunglasses. He was smiling. And he was so very, very handsome.

Deborah gazed at him in wonder. The taboo was lifted. She was free to love him again.

And then she thought: *What do I do now?*

She looked at the telephone on her nightstand. She remembered the mission, that the nuns were expecting her. *I should call them and tell them I'm here.*

But when her eye fell upon the blue telephone book, Deborah froze.

She stared at it in nameless fear. It was as if her safe and secure hotel room had suddenly been invaded. The closed drapes and locked door were meant to keep the threatening things out. But they were here, after all, in the room with her. In that dog-eared directory.

She reached for it. Thinking of all the people who might be contained in this book, people who were roadways into her past, Deborah felt a curious rush of excitement. It was like taking a journey.

She found a listing for the Donald Tour Agency.

Deborah had cut ties completely when she had fled Kenya. In fifteen years of carefully constructing a new life and a new persona for herself, she had set her face away from the familiar and loved names in Kenya. If she could not have Christopher, she had determined in her immaturity, then she would not have his country or anyone who lived in it. Along with the Mathenges, she had cut the Donalds out of her life.

A search through the phone book told her that Kilima Simba Safari Lodge was still operating in Amboseli; four more Donald lodges were also located throughout Kenya. She came across an advertisement. It showed a Volkswagen minibus gaudily painted in zebra stripes and a line that read "Donald Tours, with the largest fleet of safe buses and drivers in East Africa."

So. They were still here, and apparently prospering. The Donalds. Sprung from Sir James, the man her aunt had loved, whom Deborah had never known.

She was suddenly filled with a desire to see Terry again. And Uncle Geoffrey and Uncle Ralph. Now they seemed to Deborah to be more than just old friends; all of a sudden the Donalds were like family.

Family! she thought excitedly. After so long there was someone she could talk to about the old days, someone who knew her, who would *understand.*

Deborah was suddenly afraid to turn the pages of the phone book. It frightened her to think of seeing Christopher's name printed there, with a phone number. It would place him too close. She had but to pick up the phone and dial. . . .

Then she turned the pages. Her hands trembled. She stared down. There were many Mathenges listed; there must be nearly thirty of them. She ran her finger down the list. The Mathenges skipped from Barnabas to Ezekiel.

Deborah read the names again, more carefully. She went all the way down to the bottom and then started at the top again. But there was no Christopher among them.

Did that mean he wasn't in Kenya?

There were three Sarah Mathenges listed. But wouldn't Sarah have gotten married? Wouldn't her last name be different now?

Deborah was overcome. Jet lag combined with two days without sleep, plus eighteen hours since she had last eaten, were exacting their toll on her. Physical exhaustion joined with raw emotion to make Deborah feel somehow defeated. She laid the phone book aside and buried her face in her hands.

She felt caught between nowhere and nowhere, as if she were on a long journey and the train had let her off at a deserted station. She felt as if she must keep on going because she had come so far, but to what end?

Why, oh, why is Mama Wachera asking for me?

When the phone rang, she cried out.

She stared at it, panicked, thinking irrationally in her fatigue that those whom she had just looked up in the phone book had somehow been brought back to life and were now haunting her.

Then she sighed and picked it up. "Hello?"

"Debbie? Hello? Can you hear me?"

"Jonathan?" She listened to the crackle and roar of the long-distance line. "Jonathan! Is that you?"

"God, Debbie! I've been worried! When did you get in? Why didn't you call me?"

She looked at her travel clock on the nightstand. Was it possible that her plane had landed only fourteen hours ago? "I'm sorry, Jonathan. I was so tired. I fell asleep. . . ."

"Are you okay? You sound strange."

"It's a bad connection. And I'm jet-lagged. Are you all right, Jonathan?"

"I miss you."

"I miss you, too."

There was a pause, filled with the ebb and flow of overseas lines. "Debbie? Are you sure you're all right?" he asked again.

She clutched the phone. "I don't know, Jonathan. I'm so mixed up."

"Mixed up! About what? Debbie, what's going on? Have you seen the old woman yet? When are you coming home?"

Despite the spontaneous honesty Jonathan Hayes brought out in people, Deborah had never told him her buried secret—of the man she had thought was her brother, Christopher, whose hut she had gone to one night. That awful secret and the guilt it had laid upon her. How to begin to tell Jonathan of it now and somehow to explain her feelings of confusion now that she was back in Kenya?

"Debbie?"

"I'm sorry, Jonathan. I know I'm being emotional. But I've received a bit of a shock. I've found some things out. . . ."

"What are you talking about?"

He sounded so harsh, so unlike Jonathan. Deborah tried to hold on to him. "I'll be going up to Nyeri tomorrow," she said in a composed voice. "I'll rent a car and drive up to the mission. I'm going to try to get a room at the Outspan Hotel."

"So then you'll be leaving Kenya day after tomorrow?"

She couldn't answer.

"Debbie? When are you coming home?"

"I—I don't know, Jonathan. I can't say yet. I've decided to look up a few people. Friends—"

He fell silent. She tried to picture him. It must be very early in San Francisco, she realized. Jonathan had no doubt just gotten up to get ready for morning surgery. He would be in his running clothes; he would jog through Golden Gate Park for half an hour, take a hot shower, put on a sweatshirt and jeans, and go to the hospital. He'd have coffee and a bran muffin in the cafeteria and then go up to surgery and change into greens. Deborah suddenly, desperately wanted to be doing those prosaic things with him, as they did every morning, had done for the year they had been living together. Deborah wished herself back in San Francisco, in the fog and among the comforting familiarity of their daily ritual.

But she had come to Kenya, and she had to finish what she had started.

"I love you, Debbie," he said.

She started to cry. "I love you, too."

"Call me when you know your return flight."

"I will."

He paused again, as if waiting for her to say something. So Deborah said, "Have a good run this morning."

And he said, "I will. Good-bye, Debbie," and hung up.

Deborah kept her bathrobe on as she slipped between the sheets of her bed. She was both frightened and relieved to discover that when she turned out the light, the room was plunged into nearly total darkness. The heavy drapes did a good job of sealing out the sharp, equatorial sun. But they couldn't stop the incessant noise from penetrating the glass—the constant, urgent pulse of East Africa.

Deborah lay staring up into the blackness. She felt every ounce of strength seep out of her body. Her eyelids grew heavy. Her thoughts seemed to break loose from anchors and float up to the surface of her mind, where they drifted in a kind of lazy incoherence. She half dreamed, half remembered.

She went back two years, to the day she first started at St. Bartholomew's Hospital in San Francisco. She was thirty-one years old and fresh out of a six-year surgical residency. It was Deborah's first day on the new job. She was a real doctor at last and completely on her own. She changed into surgical greens in the nurses' locker room and then went to room 8, where she was to assist Dr. Jonathan Hayes on a gallbladder removal.

"Welcome to St. B's, Dr. Treverton," the circulating nurse said. "What size glove do you wear?"

"Six."

The nurse reached up into the glove cupboard, then said, "Oops, out of sixes," and left the room.

As Deborah stood looking around the operating room, which, since such facilities are universally the same, was familiar and yet unfamiliar, a tall, brown-eyed man came in, tying a mask behind his head.

"Hi," he said. "Where's our gas passer?"

"I don't know."

He smiled at Deborah through horn-rimmed glasses. The rest of his face was hidden behind the mask. "You must be new here," he said with a smile in his voice. "I'm Dr. Hayes. I'm told that I'm easy to work with, so I'm sure we'll get along just fine. I have a few idiosyncrasies that you should know about. I use *two* silk ties to tie off the cystic duct, and I like them both on one tonsil clamp. Please have that ready for me. Also, four-by-eights on sponge sticks. Can't stand those other little things. Have a lot of them lined up for me, please."

She stared at him. "Yes, Doctor."

Jonathan walked over to the back table, which was already set up with instruments and supplies. He looked it over and nodded. "Good, good. I see you've already anticipated me. Where's the Bacitracin? Be sure to have some on your table."

He went to the door, looked up and down the busy hallway, then said, "By the way, I have a new man assisting me this morning. A Dr. Treverton. So I'll be relying on your help extra specially, okay?" He gave her a wink. "Give me a holler when the patient arrives. I'll be in the doctors' lounge."

Deborah was still staring after him when a young woman came hurrying in, tying up her mask and smelling faintly of cigarette smoke. "Was that Hayes I just saw? Good, we can get this show on the road. You must be Dr. Treverton. I'm Carla. What's your glove size?"

Fifteen minutes later Jonathan Hayes was at the sinks, finishing his scrub. Deborah was at a sink behind him, also finishing up. He turned off the faucet and went across the hall into room 8, hands held upright, elbows dripping. Deborah came into the room as he was drying his arms. When the scrub nurse stepped up with his gown, he gave her a brief, puzzled look. And when he turned around for the circulator to tie it, he blinked at Deborah.

"Have you met Dr. Treverton, Dr. Hayes?" the scrub nurse said as she handed Deborah a sterile towel.

"Dr. Treverton?" he said. Then, suddenly realizing his mistake, he turned red.

"No," Deborah said with a soft laugh, "we haven't been introduced."

Then Jonathan also laughed, and they began the operation.

62

D eborah found herself staring at every man who came into the restaurant. Any one of them could be Christopher.

She was eating an enormous breakfast. Two hours earlier Deborah had awakened to discover that she had slept for fourteen hours; she was surprisingly refreshed and rested and also ravenous. A hot bath had restored her vitality, and now she was down in the Mara Restaurant, off the Hilton lobby, where green-uniformed hostesses with cornrowed hair escorted African businessmen to tables. While Deborah ate generously of croissants and English jam, slices of papaya and pineapple, and an omelet folded around mushrooms, onions, olives, ham, and cheese, she surreptitiously looked over every man who came in.

The majority were Africans in business suits or tailored tropical outfits of pale green or pale blue cotton. They carried briefcases, had gold rings and wristwatches, and shook hands with one another before sitting down to eat. They spoke a variety of dialects, and when Deborah listened in, she found that she understood much of the Swahili and Kikuyu.

Surely Christopher would not be in Kenya, she thought as she sipped her coffee, if he was not listed in the telephone directory. Then where was he? Why had he left?

He went in search of me, fifteen years ago, she thought.

But then Deborah realized that if that were the case, he would have gone to the college that had granted her the scholarship, and he would have found her.

Whatever he had done, wherever he had gone, Deborah knew that she could not leave Kenya without finding out what became of Christopher.

After breakfast she went to the main desk, where she settled her Hilton bill, asked for a reservation to be made at the Outspan, and ordered a car with a driver. When she was told that it would be some time before the car would arrive, Deborah looked around for a place to wait.

The lobby was monstrously busy. It appeared that several large groups of tourists were arriving and departing at the same time, causing a jam of people at the desk, a jam of luggage near the double glass doors, and a jam of safari vans at the curb. Harried tour guides shouted orders in English and Swahili, while weary travelers found seats on the many sofas that were arranged around the spacious lobby. Deborah had heard that tourism was big business in Kenya. She surmised that it must rank just after coffee and tea as its main source of income. *Thanks*, she thought as she made her way to the glass doors, *to men like Uncle Geoffrey.*

She paused on the front steps to catch her breath.

The light!

Deborah had forgotten how crisp and buoyant the light of Kenya was. It was as if the air weren't made up of oxygen but of something indescribably light, such as helium. Everything was so clear, so sharp. Colors seemed to be more colorful here than anywhere else; outlines and details seemed to stand out. Although the air smelled smoky and fumy, it was wondrously thin and fresh. This was one of the reasons, Deborah had read in her aunt's journal, why her grandfather, the earl of Treverton, had so fallen in love with East Africa.

Deborah liked that thought—that she shared something with the man who was responsible for her having been born in Kenya. It gave her a sense of inheritance, of family lineage.

She struck off in the direction of Joseph Gicheru Street, which had once been Lord Treverton Avenue, and came, a few minutes later, to Jomo Kenyatta Avenue, where she found herself standing in front of the main office of Donald Tours.

Deborah was hesitant to go inside.

So she retreated to the curb, where a tree, growing out of the cracked and buckled sidewalk, provided shade from the slicing sunlight. The doorway into the agency seemed like a doorway into her past. Uncle Geoffrey might be in there, in his seventies now but just as vigorous and robust, Deborah had no doubt, as ever. Or possibly Terry was in there, arranging a hunting safari. Was he married now? she wondered. Had he settled down, had children? Or was he possessed of the restless, adventurous spirit that was the legacy of his forefathers? Deborah recalled what her aunt had written in the journal, back in 1919: "Sir James tells me his father was one of the first men to explore the interior of British East Africa. He had hoped to achieve lasting fame and immortality by having something named for him, after the fashion of Stanley and Thompson. Sadly he was killed by an elephant before the realization of that dream."

Immortality, Deborah thought as she gazed up at the modern sign over the large plate glass window. The dream of that first, intrepid Donald had come true after all.

She went inside.

The door opened upon a tastefully decorated office with a counter, plush carpeting, and seats with magazine racks. When the door closed, the noise of Nairobi was shut out and Deborah heard soft music. A young woman looked up from a computer terminal and smiled. "May I help you?" she said.

Deborah looked around. Murals—panoramic views of the elegant Donald lodges and their breathtaking vistas—covered three walls. On the countertop was a display of glossy, colorful brochures, a separate one for each lodge, and of individual pamphlets describing a variety of tours. The young African woman was pretty and well dressed, and she wore an elaborate hairdo. The whole Donald operation, it seemed to Deborah, spelled prosperity and wealth.

"I would like to see Mr. Donald, please. Tell him that Deborah Treverton is here."

The young woman looked puzzled. "I beg your pardon?"

"Is Mr. Donald not here?"

"I'm sorry, madam. There is no Mr. Donald."

"This *is* the Donald Tours agency, isn't it? The one that owns Kilima Simba Lodge?"

"Yes, but there is no Mr. Donald here."

"You mean he's out on safari."

"We do not have a Mr. Donald."

"But—"

At that moment a woman appeared from behind the partition that separated the front office from the back. She was Asian, beautifully dressed in a bright red sari, her thick black hair drawn back in a bun. "You are looking for Mr. Donald, madam?" she said.

"Yes. I'm an old friend."

"I am so sorry," the woman said with a look that implied how truly sorry she was. "Mr. Donald died a few years ago."

"Oh. I didn't know. What about his brother, Ralph?"

"The other Mr. Donald is also dead. They were killed in a car accident on the Nanyuki Road."

"Killed! They were together when it happened?"

The woman nodded sadly. "It was the whole family, madam. Mrs. Donald, her grandchildren—"

Deborah held onto the counter. "I can't believe it."

"May I offer you a cup of tea? Perhaps you would like to speak to Mr. Mugambi."

Deborah felt numb. She heard herself say, "Who is Mr. Mugambi?"

"He owns this agency. Perhaps he—"

"No," Deborah said. "No, thank you." She hurried to the door. "Don't bother him with it. I was a friend of the family. Thank you. Thank you very much."

She fell in with the heavy pedestrian traffic on the sidewalk and let herself be carried along. A sick feeling swept over her—*killed together*—and when it subsided, she was left feeling hollow and empty. It was as if part of herself had died.

She walked for what seemed a long time, crossing busy streets, getting horns honked at her for stepping out without looking first to the right, mingling with African women walking smartly in high heels and fashionable dresses, passing cripples and beggars in rags, ignoring persistent young men who tried to sell her elephant hair bracelets and Kikuyu baskets, encountering tourists who walked nervously in groups with their arms linked. Deborah passed guards in uniform standing in the doorways of expensive shops; she passed tall prostitutes wearing huge gold loop earrings, and policemen in ill-matched uniforms, and women sitting on the ground with starving children in their arms. On the congested street Mercedes-Benz limousines went by, their smoked windows hiding the elite passengers inside; battered taxis fought for space; safari vans filled with tourists inched their way toward the city's exits; a bus so packed that people hung on to the sides chuffed by, a large sign on its side reading VIOLENCE AGAINST WOMEN . . . AGAINST THE LAW!

Deborah was aware of little. She was remembering her first night at Kilima Simba Safari Lodge, when it was just a tent camp in the wilderness and she had overheard her mother telling Uncle Geoffrey that she was going away with Tim Hopkins and that she didn't want to take her daughter with her. Deborah had cried that night in the tent she shared with Terry. And Terry, then only ten years old, had tried to comfort her in his boy's way.

Deborah finally came to a halt when she realized that she had wandered onto the campus of the University of Nairobi. Sixteen years ago she had taken classes here, from men like Professor Muriuki. When she came down the path and saw the Norfolk Hotel before her, she realized with a jolt that she must be walking where the old jail had stood and that it was therefore probably on this very spot that Arthur Treverton had been killed. That organized protest, described in Grace's journal, had been to voice the people's wish for an African university here in Kenya. By an ironic twist, the spot was today part of the University of Nairobi grounds.

Deborah went back to the Hilton.

The rental car had not yet arrived, so she went to the small newsstand and purchased a newspaper.

She looked in the windows of the shops that lined the Hilton arcade. Valuable antiquities were displayed behind glass: medieval Ethiopian Bibles; a centuries-old Arab camel saddle; iron candlesticks from the Congo; necklaces fashioned by the Toro of Uganda. Souvenir shops offered "genuine native crafts," postcards, guidebooks, and T-shirts bearing lions, hippos, thorn trees at sunset. The dress shops were chic and expensive and offered a wide range of "safari ensembles" that had not been in existence fifteen years ago.

Deborah paused before one window. A mannequin stood on display, wearing a stunning dress of unique African design. Deborah thought it looked familiar.

Suddenly excited, she went inside.

The price on the tag was written in shillings; Deborah translated it into an amount of more than four hundred dollars. She reached up and felt along the neckline for a label.

She found it. It read "Sarah Mathenge."

"May I be of assistance, madam?"

Deborah turned to meet the snobbish smile of the Asian saleswoman. She wore a lavendar sari, and her black hair was twisted in a long braid down her back.

"This dress," Deborah said, "it's made by Sarah Mathenge?"

"Yes, it is."

"Where was it made, do you know? Was it made in Nyeri?"

"No, please, madam. It was made here in Nairobi."

"How often does Sarah Mathenge come in here?"

The young woman frowned.

"What I mean is, do you know when you will be seeing her again?"

"I am sorry please, madam. I have never met Miss Mathenge."

"I'm an old friend of hers, you see. I would like to get in touch with her."

The frown dissolved into the superior smile once again. "Perhaps, please, you would be able to find her at Mathenge House? That is where her head offices are."

"Head offices!"

"Yes, please, at Mathenge House. You go out of the hotel just here, madam, and turn right. It is just across the street, next to the archives."

"Thank you! Thank you very much!"

Deborah hurried, and this time she was very much aware of the crowd on the sidewalk, because it impeded her.

Mathenge House!

Deborah had imagined that Sarah made her dresses at home up in Nyeri and took them from shop to shop. But head offices!

Deborah stopped at the curb and stared across the street at the building next to the National Archives. It was a tall modern building, at least seven stories, with an enormous sign on top that read MATH-ENGE HOUSE.

Deborah dashed through the traffic, walked quickly along the stores and small businesses that occupied the ground level of the building, found the entrance, which was guarded by an askari, and went inside.

A small foyer, smelling of pungent cleaning solution, contained a directory and two elevators. Reading the directory, Deborah was amazed to discover that the entire building was occupied by Sarah Mathenge Enterprises, Ltd.

She stepped into the elevator, pressed the top button, and thought the ride would take forever. But presently the doors rattled open upon a small reception area where a young African woman was typing and talking on the phone at the same time.

"I would like to see Sarah Mathenge, please," Deborah told her.

"I believe Miss Mathenge has gone for the day."

"But it's only morning. Please check."

The receptionist picked up the phone, pushed one of many buttons, and spoke in rapid-fire Swahili. She looked up at Deborah. "What is the name, please?"

"Deborah Treverton."

The receptionist repeated it into the phone, waited a moment, then hung up and said, "Miss Mathenge will be right out."

Deborah realized she was twisting the strap of her shoulder purse. What would Sarah be like after all these years? How would she receive Deborah? *Was she angry with me for disappearing, for abandoning her after promising to help place her dresses in Uncle Geoffrey's lodges? Is she angry with me still?*

"Deborah!"

She turned. A plain, unlabeled door led off the small reception area. A beautiful woman, a vision of color and elegance, stood there now.

Sarah came forward with her arms open. The two women embraced as comfortably and naturally as if they had parted only yesterday.

"Deborah!" Sarah said, stepping back. "I was hoping you would come and see me! I called the mission this morning. They said you had not arrived the night before last, as they had expected."

Deborah could hardly speak. This was still her old friend. Sarah had changed very little. Except that her dress, a creation of copper shades dramatically enhanced with blacks and purples, was something eighteen-year-old Sarah could never have worn. Her head was covered in a turban of the same fabric; she wore enormous copper earrings that rested on her shoulders, copper bracelets on both slender wrists. Deborah felt as if she had stepped back into their happy past.

"You knew I was coming to Kenya?" she asked.

"The mission contacted me three weeks ago, when my grandmother was admitted into the hospital there. The mother superior said that my grandmother was asking for you. They wondered if I knew where you were. I told them the name of the college in California that had granted you the scholarship."

"How did you know I had gone there?"

"Professor Muriuki told us. But I am so glad to see you! You haven't changed at all, Deb! Well, maybe a little. You look more mature, wiser. You caught me just in time. I have an appointment at the President's house in a little while."

"The President's house! The President of Kenya?"

"I'm Mrs. Moi's dressmaker." Sarah laughed and put her arm through Deborah's. "Come to my house with me, Deb. There's something I must scc to before I go to my appointment. And Mrs. Moi can keep me for hours! You and I can talk on the way."

A Mercedes-Benz was waiting at the curb, with a smiling African chauffeur holding the rear door open. As they got in, Sarah said with a laugh, "I'm a *wabenzi* now, Deb. What do you think of that?"

Deborah had never heard the term before, but she knew enough Swahili to know that *wa* means "people of."

"We're a whole new breed, Deb," Sarah said as the Mercedes fought for a space in traffic. "We who run Kenya are called members of the Benzi race. It's a term of insult which the common people like to call us. But don't be fooled, Deb. They also aspire to being *wabenzis!*"

They rode in silence for a few moments, sitting in the rich interior of the car, surrounded by the smell of fine leather, radio music blocking out Nairobi's rude noise. Deborah had to say, "I can't tell you how impressed I am with you, Sarah. You've come such a long way."

"I prefer not to think just how far I've come!" Sarah said with a hard laugh. "I leave the past in the past. And I see to it that bloody few people know about the miserable huts on the Chania River. But tell me about you, Deb. What made you run off like that? Why did you never write to us?"

Deborah spoke haltingly at the beginning, but as she told of the discovery of her mother's love letters to David and of wondering what had become of that love child, Deborah found the words coming quickly and with astonishing ease. When she came to the part about going to Wachera and what the old woman had said to her, Sarah turned sharply.

But Deborah added hurriedly, "No, Sarah. Christopher is not my brother. Wachera wanted me to believe that for some reason. But I *thought* he was, you see. And we had made love in his hut. I couldn't live with it. I was too immature. All I wanted was to run away and hide. I certainly couldn't go on living in Kenya. I was in love with my own brother! Or so I thought." She finished by telling Sarah the answers she had found in her aunt's journal, fifteen years too late.

"My grandmother," Sarah said, gazing out at Nairobi's slums, where the road turned to dust and buildings seemed to lean under the weight of poverty. "That foolish old woman. She always resented white people, was always waiting for them to leave Kenya. She had some mad dream that we all were going to return to the past once the white people were gone. I suppose she was trying to get rid of you in order to complete her daft curse."

The Mercedes was slowed by children playing in the street. Sarah leaned forward, slid open a window in the partition that separated the front seat from the back, and said to the driver in Swahili, "Hurry up, will you?"

When she sat back, she turned to Deborah and said, "So, did you become a doctor after all?"

"Yes."

"Are you married? Do you have children?"

"No and no."

Sarah's finely plucked eyebrows rose. "No children? Deb, a woman must have children."

They had left the center of the city, and now the Mercedes was moving down a treelined street in one of the wealthier districts. Behind high hedges and fences Deborah could see the tile rooftops of stately old houses. This was Parklands, one of Kenya's finest suburbs.

"And you, Sarah? Are you married?"

"One lesson I learned from my mother was not to be the slave of husband. I know what she suffered in the detention camp at the hands of men. I know how I was conceived. I learned from her how to use men the way they have always used women. I turned the tables, so to speak, and I find it rather refreshing. But I do have special friends. Like General Mazrui. Right now he's one of the most powerful men in East Africa, and it suits my needs to develop an intimate relationship with him."

Sarah looked at her watch and spoke impatiently to the driver again. "I'd like you to meet General Mazrui, Deb. I think you'll be very impressed with him. I'm giving a dinner party tonight for the French ambassador; that's why I have to stop at home. If I don't keep after my staff constantly, things never get done right. Will you come, Deb?"

"I'm going up to Nyeri in a little while. I have a room at the Outspan. And I don't know how much time your grandmother has left."

Sarah shrugged. "I haven't spoken to her in years. But you can give her my love if you want."

The chauffeur turned the car down a short drive. He stopped when he came to a chain link fence. There were warning signs posted in big bold letters: KALI DOGS! DO NOT GET OUT OF YOUR CAR! And then an askari, carrying a rifle, appeared from a small kiosk. When he saw the car, he unlocked the gate, rolled it back, and saluted his employer through.

As the drive curved around a large green lawn and flower garden Deborah's eyes widened. There were more guards, holding barking dogs on leashes. "Sarah!" she said. "You told me we were going to your house, not to the President's house!"

"This *is* my house," Sarah said as the Mercedes pulled up near the front door.

"It's like a fortress!" Deborah was looking at the fence topped with a curl of barbed wire. It appeared to go all the way around the property.

"Don't pretend that you don't live like this, too, Deb."

As Deborah gave Sarah a startled, quizzical look, the front door was opened by an elderly African in an old-fashioned long white kanzu. He was very proper and formal and even wore, to Deborah's surprise, white gloves.

The interior of Sarah's house took Deborah's breath away.

It was one of the old colonial mansions once used as retreats for aristocratic settlers, like Deborah's grandparents, when they came into Nairobi for Race Week. But there were no portraits of Queen Victoria or King George here, no regimental swords on the wall, no Union Jack, no animal heads, stuffed and mounted. It was as if, she thought, Sarah had taken a broom, swept out all evidence of colonial imperialism, and brought in . . . *Africa*.

Woven rugs covered polished red-tile floors; leather sofas were protected by blankets from India; rattan chairs were strewn with batiked cushions. Every inch of wall space was taken up with carefully hung African masks, carved and painted, some exceedingly old, representing the tribes and nations of the continent. Deborah recognized many of the artifacts displayed around the room: Samburu gourds, a Masai lion's mane headdress, Turkana dolls, a Pokot calabash, spears, shields, and baskets. It was like a museum.

"I realized about ten years ago," Sarah explained as she invited Deborah to sit, "that African culture was rapidly vanishing. So much was becoming forgotten; old skills were ceasing to be passed along; old ceremonies were being abandoned. So I started to collect certain items that I knew would someday be quite valuable."

Sarah said something to the elderly servant, then sat on a leather sofa and crossed her legs. But her posture was stiff; she appeared to be a woman on the move even when she was sitting still.

"It's a beautiful collection, Sarah."

"I've had it appraised. It's worth nearly a million shillings."

"Is that why you have guards and dogs?"

"Lord, no. I'd need those even if my house was empty. The guards and the dogs are there to keep the thugs out. But thanks to my special friendship with General Mazrui, I am quite safe here. Just to be sure, though, I pay a monthly *magendo* to the local police."

Deborah didn't understand. "Thugs?"

"Surely you have them in America!" Sarah said with a hard laugh. She glanced at her watch and then in the direction of the kitchen. "There's crime everywhere you go in the world, Deb. You know that. In Kenya we have our gangs of thugs. It's because of the high unemployment rate. The official figure is ninety percent unemployed. Nairobi is full of jobless, restless young men. You saw them?"

Deborah had seen them. They traveled in pairs or packs, fairly decently dressed youths full of education and energy with no place to go, no jobs to support them.

"They attack private residences," Sarah explained. "About twenty or thirty of them will single out a house and assault it in the middle of the night with clubs and battering rams. Only last week my neighbor next door was awakened by the sound of an attack. He managed to get his wife and children into a closet upstairs, where they waited while they heard the gang downstairs cleaning out their house."

"Couldn't he have called the police?"

"What good would that have done? The man simply refuses to pay *magendo.*"

"*Magendo?*"

Sarah rubbed her fingers together. "Bribe. Money is the only language that people understand these days. And money is the only way you can survive."

She clapped her hands sharply together and said, "What is taking that old fool so long? Simon! *Haraka!*"

The elderly servant in the kanzu appeared at that moment with a tea cart. Under Sarah's keenly watchful eye he poured from a silver samovar with all the finesse and flourish of a servant from the old days, and Deborah wondered if he had once worked for a British master. It also surprised her that Sarah had adopted that system.

As Sarah invited Deborah to help herself from the plates of sandwiches and biscuits, fruits and cheeses, she said, "How long will you be in Kenya, Deb?"

"I don't know. Until four days ago I hadn't even known I was coming!"

"What's your life like in California? Is your medical practice profitable?"

Just then a young girl in a maid's uniform came into the room and waited to be acknowledged. Seeing her, Sarah waved her over, said to Deborah, "Pardon me a moment," and looked at the sheet of paper the maid held out. "No, no," Sarah said with a trace of impatience. "Tell the cook I want cold cucumber soup, not leek! And the Cabernet Sauvignon instead of the Chardonnay."

Sarah spoke in Swahili, and Deborah listened. "The seating plan is all right, except for . . ." Sarah took a pencil from the maid and wrote on the paper. "Put Bishop Musumbi on the ambassador's right. Place General Mazrui here, next to the foreign secretary. And tell Simon the dancers are to be assembled and ready to perform at nine o'clock sharp."

When the maid was gone, Sarah turned back to Deborah with apologies. "If I don't keep right on top of them, things don't get done right. These girls from the country are so slow!"

Deborah found herself staring at her old friend. Was this sharp-edged Nairobi socialite the same Sarah who had once sat barefoot on the bank of the Chania, wishing for a miniskirt? Deborah felt the colonial mansion shift around her, as if it, too, were suddenly uncomfortable.

"Don't you ever get lonely, Sarah? Living in this big house all by yourself?"

"Lonely! Deb, I don't have time to be lonely! There is always something going on at my house—nearly every night. And the weekends are taken up with houseguests. And over the holidays, of course, my children visit."

"Children!"

"I have two boys and three girls. The boys are in school in England, and the girls are in Switzerland."

"But you said you never got married."

"How provincial of you, Deb! I thought you were a liberated woman. Marriage isn't necessary for a woman to have children. I wanted babies, not a husband. You know, Deb, the Kenya male is a very macho male. If ever I married one, I would be subservient to him. He could even take over my business! My children had five different fathers. That was the way I wanted it. And now they're receiving European educations. When they return to Kenya, they'll have assured places in the proper society."

Deborah looked down at her tea. Something was wrong. Sarah seemed so hard around the edges, so competitive. She talked about women's liberation and used words like *macho* and had reverted to a system of master and servant that she had once denounced. When Sarah had come through that plain doorway back at Mathenge House, Deborah had been overjoyed with relief to think that her old friend hadn't changed. But Deborah realized now, sadly, Sarah had changed. With each passing minute, the woman sitting across the room from her was slowly turning into a stranger.

In another room a telephone rang. Simon came in a moment later and murmured something to his mistress. She replied in Swahili, which Deborah could understand: "Tell them I am on my way."

But Deborah needed to know something first, before she left Sarah's house. "What happened?" she asked. "After I left? What did you do?"

"What could I do, Deb? I survived! At first I used my grandmother's money to buy Mrs. Dar's old sewing machine. I made a few dresses and took them around to the Nairobi shops. But when that money ran out"—she paused to replace her cup in its saucer, a graceful, measured gesture—"I had no choice but to go back to the Nairobi bankers who were willing to deal with me for certain 'favors.' And I found out after a while, Deb, that there was nothing to it. Such a bloody silly thing pride is!"

Sarah paused. She glanced at her watch, then continued. "I eventually became quite successful. I bought out smaller firms and reduced my competition. When I saw there was no profit in making dresses for the typical Nairobi secretary, I gave that up and went into designing originals, which brought me a lot more money. It was a very smart move for me." Sarah twisted the copper bracelets around and around on her wrist. "Now my dresses are sold all over the world. There's a shop in Beverly Hills that carries my line, and another on the Champs-Élysées in Paris."

"I'm happy for you," Deborah said quietly.

"And are you a success, Deb? I seem to recall you had a rather quaint idea of running your aunt's mission after she was gone. I hope you gave that up!"

"I'm in practice with another surgeon. We're doing well."

They fell silent, awkwardly, avoiding each other's eyes. Finally Deborah asked about Christopher. "He's doing well," Sarah said rather perfunctorily, and followed it by asking after Deborah's mother.

Deborah didn't tell her the truth: that she had felt so sick fifteen years ago, thinking that she had made love to her own brother—she had been so angry with her mother for having never told her the truth—that Deborah had written a terrible, hateful letter to her mother, venting all her sickness in it. Two weeks later she had received a reply in the mail, but Deborah had torn it up without reading it. After that several more letters came from Australia, all thrown away without being opened, until finally the letters stopped coming.

"Sarah," Deborah asked, "do you know why your grandmother is asking for me?"

"Haven't a notion. She probably wants to rattle some chicken bones at you or something." Sarah rose, graceful and stately, like a queen dismissing an audience. "I'm sorry, Deb. But I really must get going. You're sure about tonight?"

"I'm positive. I have to get up to Nyeri." At the door Deborah paused to look at this stranger who had once been like a sister to her. "Where is Christopher, Sarah? Do you ever hear from him?"

"Where is he? Let me see. What day is it today? I imagine he's at Ongata Rongai."

"You mean he's in Kenya?"

"Of course. Where else would he be?"

"I looked him up in the phone book—"

"He's listed under the name of his clinic, Wangari. My fool brother found Jesus a few years back, after his wife died. Now he is a lay preacher as well as a doctor. He does charity work among the Masai. As if they would ever be grateful! I've told him he's just wasting his time."

A silence descended; it seemed to roll out from behind the African masks, from under old tribal drums, from calabashes and elephant grass *irua* skirts. Deborah imagined the colonial house shifting again, as if it were as bewildered and lost as she, and the whispered footsteps of Sarah's many unseen servants seemed to be saying, *The past is dead, the past is dead. . . .*

63

Deborah's driver was a friendly young Somali named Abdi, who wore slacks and a Beach Boys T-shirt and, on his head, a white knitted cap indicating he was a Muslim who had made the pilgrimage to Mecca.

"Where do we go please, miss?" he asked as he placed her suitcase in the trunk of the small white Peugeot.

"To Nyeri. The Outspan Hotel." Deborah paused. Then she said, "I would like to stop first at Ongata Rongai. It's a Masai village. Do you know where it is?"

"Yes, please, miss."

It took them some time to inch their way through the traffic congestion and onto one of the major roads leading out of the city. Deborah rode in the back seat, looking out at Nairobi.

She wondered what the population numbered now; it seemed so much more crowded than when she had left. And she counted so few white faces in the ceaseless tide of pedestrians that she wondered how small a minority they were now.

Because of a traffic accident up ahead, they were stalled for some minutes on Harambee Avenue, in front of the Kenyatta Conference Center. Deborah was afforded a more careful look at the beautiful new edifice, and she saw what one didn't see on the postcards—the signs of neglect, the lack of repair and upkeep, the overall *seediness* of an otherwise remarkable piece of architecture. Here, as everywhere else in the city, she saw the street people: cripples; beggars; little girls holding starving babies. But on the other side of the fence, in the parking lot of the center, there were lines of shiny limousines.

Abdi took Haile Selassie Avenue and followed it to Ngong Road, which carried them eventually out of the dense city and into increasingly less developed, more rural countryside. Soon they entered Karen, a district of green farms, woodland, and houses of the wealthy. As they sped along roads of cracked and potholed tarmac, Deborah gazed at the old colonial houses they passed, set back behind protective trees, with high fences and guards in uniform.

Then there appeared the simple shambas, where women were bent over in toil. Once these vast acres had belonged to European farmers; now they were broken up into postage-stamp African holdings.

When they came upon a group of tourist minibuses parked at what appeared to be an undistinguished shamba, Deborah asked Abdi what it was.

He slowed the Peugeot and said, "Finch Hatton grave. You see *Out of Africa*, miss? You want to stop?"

"No. Keep driving, please."

She looked back at the tourists milling about with their cameras. The need for pilgrimages, Deborah thought, seemed to be a universal human trait.

The road dipped, traveled through forest, came out upon acres and acres of puny farms, through dilapidated villages, and past roadside "taverns," boxy structures made of tin and cardboard, where men sat in idle clusters with bottles in their hands.

Deborah questioned her inexplicable feelings of being in an alien land; it was as if she were in a country she had never visited before. Could she truly, in fifteen years, have forgotten the extent of Kenya's poverty, its brutally defined classes, its massive base population of women and children living on bare subsistence? Had fifteen years' absence painted a deceptive patina over the uglier realities of East Africa, as the guidebooks did?

She arrived at last at Ongata Rongai, a Masai village of ramshackle masonry and muddy paths. Facing the road was the "town center," typical of Kenya villages: crude cinder-block structures with tin roofs, painted in awful shades of turquoise and pink, one with a sign that read MATHARI SALOON & HOTEL, BUTCHER & ANIMAL FEEDS. Old men loitered around the dark doorways or sat in the dirt, their clothes little more than rags. The village itself was a haphazard cluster of rude structures, many without doors and windows, all oriented toward a stream bed, where cows stood in dung-filled water, which Masai women were drawing up into drinking gourds. Overall there was an atmosphere of defeat and despair.

As Abdi maneuvered the Peugeot past stone huts and the rusting hulks of abandoned autos, naked children followed, their faces covered with flies, their arms and legs like sticks, bellies bloated with hunger. They stared at the white woman in the car with eyes too big for their heads.

When Deborah found what she was looking for, she said, "Stop here, please."

After turning off the motor, Abdi got out and came around to open her door. But she shook her head. Puzzled, he got back behind the wheel and waited.

Deborah was staring at a plain stone building with a wooden cross on its iron roof. Parked in front was a Land-Rover with letters on its side that read WANGARI CLINIC. THE WORK OF THE LORD. Wangari, Sarah had told her, had been Christopher's wife's name.

She decided that he must be inside the building because the crowd waiting outside was facing a closed door. Deborah watched that door. She was afraid to blink as if that would make it vanish.

Finally the door opened. When she saw the man who came out, Deborah's heart jumped.

He hadn't changed, not at all. Christopher walked with the same loping grace of his youth; his body was still slender, his movements hinting of concealed masculine power. He wore blue jeans and a shirt; a stethoscope hung around his neck. When he turned, Deborah saw the glint of sunlight off the gold rim of his glasses.

The crowd surged forward at the sight of him. It was then that Deborah saw that all the children were carrying something. A few held bowls in their little hands; many clutched empty bottles; some, she noticed in surprise, were holding what looked like hubcaps. She discovered the reason for this in the next instant, when massive cook pots were brought out from the building and set on a long wooden table outside. The children lined up in a strangely quiet, orderly fashion, their mothers, nearly all carrying babies, standing respectfully off to one side.

And then, as a young African, who was sitting cross-legged in the dirt, struck up a chord on his guitar and started to sing, the feeding of the children began.

It was an eerie scene. There was no pushing, no competition, no greed. Just the wordless doling out of what looked like maize porridge into whatever container a child might have brought. While this was going on, with the servers singing along with the guitar player—a Swahili hymn which Deborah recognized—Christopher and a nurse began examining patients.

The nurse was African, young and pretty, and she, too, sang the hymn as she worked.

Abdi glanced in the rearview mirror at his passenger. "You want to go now?" he asked.

Deborah looked up. "I beg your pardon?"

Abdi tapped his wristwatch. "We go to Nyeri now, please, miss?"

She looked out the window again. She thought of getting out of the car, walking down to the clinic, and saying, "Hello, Christopher." But something held her back. She wasn't ready to face him just yet.

"Yes," she said. "We'll go to Nyeri now."

THE THIKA ROAD cut through a plain of piecemeal cultivation. Deborah glimpsed, at one point, a modest little mosque among acacia trees. Beyond lay homely factories: Kenya Breweries, Firestone Tires, paper mills, tanneries, and canneries. Some, strangely, appeared to have been abandoned.

Telephone and power lines followed the highway; there were Shell stations, and billboards saying, COKE IS IT! A sign advertising Embassy Kings cigarettes read SAFIRI KWA USALAMA, "Drive in peace." The highway was a river of cars—Audis, Mercedes, Peugeots. Many had I LOVE KENYA on the bumper. *Matatus,* nine-passenger vehicles crammed with perhaps twenty people or more, chugged by. Another roadside sign warned: BEWARE OF HOW YOU DRIVE: TWENTY-FIVE PEOPLE DIED HERE IN MAY 1985.

When Abdi unexpectedly steered the car off the highway and pulled into the parking lot of the Blue Posts Hotel, Deborah said, "Why are we stopping here?"

"Very historic place, miss. All tourists stop here."

She looked out at the old, squat building that was hardly a shadow of its former colonial glory. The Blue Posts had once been a resort for white settlers. Now there were signs advertising grilled chicken necks and barbecued goat ribs.

"I don't want to stop here," Deborah said. "Let's get on to Nyeri."

Abdi gave her a quizzical look, then shrugged and guided the car back onto the road. Periodically he glanced at his passenger in the rearview mirror.

He turned on the radio. There was a brief ad for Mona Lisa skin lightener, and then a Voice of Kenya newscaster was saying, "Our beloved president, the Honorable Daniel Arap Moi, today said that the government is striving to make health care available to all Kenyans by the year 2000."

Deborah pictured the village of Ongata Rongai, the starved, diseased children, the filth, the flies, and Christopher, trying to bring some hope, some relief from misery into their squalid lives. She thought of Sarah, riding through the strife-torn streets of Nairobi in her chauffeured Mercedes, and of the beggars sitting in the shade of the ostentatious and ill-kept Conference Center. It was almost as if, Deborah realized, two completely separate worlds occupied the same space.

She tapped Abdi on the shoulder and said, "If you don't mind," and pointed to the radio.

"Oh, pardon, please, miss." He turned it off, pulled a *miraa* leaf stem from his shirt pocket, and popped it into his mouth. Although *miraa* was considered a stimulant, Deborah knew that it was really a mood lifter, chewed by Kenyans to help them shoulder their problems.

The Peugeot sped past mile after mile of farmland. There were women in the fields and women walking along the roadside with enormous loads on their backs. Nearly all, Deborah noticed, were either pregnant or carried babies on their backs. Women stood at crossroads with children hanging on to their skirts; they trudged to and from local roadside vegetable stands. They were bent over in dirty ponds where cows stood, drawing up drinking water into their gourds, or they waited at bus stops for the already dangerously overcrowded *matatus*. Beyond the limits of Nairobi, Deborah realized, Kenya was a nation of women and children.

"Rains coming soon," Abdi said, breaking into her thoughts.

She looked at the blue sky. "How do you know?"

"Mamas in the fields, digging."

Deborah had forgotten. But now she remembered what reliable weathervanes the women on their shambas were. Even if there wasn't a cloud in the sky and the air didn't feel like rain, you still knew it was coming when the women got busy with the soil.

The rain is coming soon. How could she have forgotten that? As a child she had been acclimated to the rhythm of wet and dry periods and had grown up sensing the change even as these African women did. But Deborah had lost that intuition in California, where she had experienced her first real summers followed by brown and gold autumns, wintry Januaries, and floral springs.

What else have I lost? she wondered as she looked out at the fields of maize and tea.

The scene began to change, and Deborah's heart grew increasingly more anxious. The straight, flat highway narrowed and started to wind up through hills which were carpeted with squares of lush farmland. Now, too, as she drew closer to Mount Kenya, Deborah saw the dark rain clouds that were starting to spread across the sky.

"Be in Nyeri town soon, miss," Abdi said as he shifted gears to pass a Tusker beer truck.

They were delayed by a highway accident. As the Peugeot inched past the chaotic scene, Deborah looked at the policemen and uninterested ambulance attendants, while an enormous crowd of women and children had gathered to look at the impossible wreckage of four cars. She thought of Uncle Geoffrey and Uncle Ralph. *The whole family killed . . .*

Suddenly Deborah was reminded of another accident, a year ago, in San Francisco.

It was the opening night of the ballet. Baryshnikov was dancing, and the performance had been sold out for months. Jonathan, using his influence, had managed to obtain box seats and an invitation to the special banquet afterward. They had looked forward to it for weeks, and Deborah had bought an evening gown especially for it. Jonathan had picked her up at her apartment, and they had gotten as far as Mason and Powell when they saw the accident occur. A car went out of control on the rain-slicked road and crashed into a cable car.

As calmly as if organizing a picnic, Jonathan had taken over, triaging the injured from the dead, giving orders to the first-aiders on the scene, reassuring the victims, getting his tuxedo dirty, using his white scarf as a bandage, sorting out the chaos and panic for the police and paramedics, going to the hospital in one of the ambulances. Deborah had worked with him; between the two of them they had saved lives and stemmed hysteria. They missed the ballet and the banquet that night, and Deborah's gown was ruined. But she felt she had been more than generously compensated, for she had fallen in love that night with Jonathan.

On the outskirts of Nyeri they passed a girls' school. Deborah had attended it as a child. She wondered if Miss Tomlinson was still the stern headmistress and then remembered that the school must have been Africanized by now. A black woman would be in charge. Deborah strained to look as her car went by. The buildings and grounds looked neglected, and among the students out on the dusty playing fields, she saw not a single white face.

Finally, a large, faded sign loomed up over a dirt road: AFRICAN COFFEE COOPERATIVE, NYERI DISTRICT.

The old Treverton plantation.

"Please drive down there," she said. The dirt track followed the Chania River, which was flowing down a familiar ravine on their left.

When they came to the beginning of the farm, Deborah said, "Please stop here," and Abdi pulled the car over to the side. After the motor was turned off, an impressive silence engulfed them.

Deborah stared out the window. The plantation was exactly as she remembered it. Neat rows of coffee bushes, heavy now with green berries, covered five thousand acres of gently undulating landscape. To her right, on the horizon, Mount Kenya lifted from flat earth to a perfect peak, "like a Chinaman's hat," Grace had written in her journal. To Deborah's left was Bellatu, looking restored and remarkably vital.

Deborah got out of the car and walked a few paces over the red dirt. She turned her face away from the wind that portended rain and looked at the big house.

Who had bought it? Who lived there now?

Then she saw someone emerge from the front door and pause for a moment on the veranda. She was a Catholic nun dressed in the blue habit of the order that had taken over Grace Mission.

Was Bellatu a residence for sisters now? A convent perhaps?

Deborah turned and walked across the road. She stood upon a grassy ridge and looked across the wide ravine that cradled the Chania. It was completely deforested now; the land was shaved and scarred and laid out with humble shambas. She saw the square mud huts and the women toiling in the fields.

Forcing her eyes downward, Deborah saw the rugby field, which had once been a polo field, where two teams of African boys now played ball. She tried to imagine her grandfather, the dashing earl, on his pony, riding to a win.

Abutting the chain link fence was a modest homestead consisting of neat little vegetable plots, a pen for goats, and four square mud huts with tin roofs. There were women with babies down there, working the land. Deborah wondered who they were.

Finally she squinted at the slow-rolling Chania. She saw a ghost standing on the bank: young Christopher, his eyes hidden behind sunglasses. Phantom laughter—the laughter of a softer, more innocent Sarah—seemed to ring out over the water.

Deborah wanted to turn her back on the painful scene.

But she was rooted to the spot, to the red earth that her bare feet had known so well as a child. Deborah shivered. Her hair, clasped behind her neck and hanging straight down her back, was whipped up. It stung her cheeks. It flicked in front of her eyes. She pushed it away and continued to stand on the grassy ridge.

This land was still so beautiful, the air so crisp and pure and so full of the magic that had nurtured her at a tender age. Deborah felt like a little girl again, running free along the river, in love with Africa, her only company a family of colobus monkeys and a pair of otters. There had been no ugliness or poverty in that world; *that* Kenya had been sparkling and full of fantasy. And it was to that country Deborah had hoped to return, to find the beginning again and start over, hoping, along the way, to find herself as well.

But that Kenya seemed no longer to exist, and Deborah was beginning to wonder if it ever had. How then, if she could not start again at the starting point, was she going to find her roots, the clues that would help her be at peace with herself?

She looked lastly at the mission, where a dying old medicine woman lay.

64

To Deborah's surprise, the management of the Outspan Hotel put her in Paxtu Cottage, the last home of Lord Baden-Powell, founder of the Boy Scouts.

In this bungalow, consisting of bedroom, living room, two fireplaces, and two bathrooms, the Chief Scout had lived out his final years and had died. He was buried in Nyeri, in a grave facing Mount Kenya, in the same churchyard where Sir James Donald had been laid to rest. The hotel was filled to capacity, the manager had explained. Normally they let the Baden-Powell cottage stand empty, as it was a beloved national memorial. But there were no other rooms available. The manager's name was Mr. Che Che, and Deborah wondered if he was a descendant of that same Che Che who had guided her aunt's oxcarts up from Nairobi sixty-nine years ago.

Paxtu was set among sloping green lawns with a perimeter of forest. It was isolated and quiet, and Deborah was glad to have it. As the porter brought in her suitcase and opened the drapes for her, revealing a spacious veranda and a view of Mount Kenya, she scanned the historical photos and letters that were carefully preserved in frames on the walls. Baden-Powell had named this cottage after Pax, his ancestral home in England; Deborah wondered if he had borrowed the example of Bellatu, which was nearby.

Since it was now past lunchtime, and the great busloads of tourists had come, eaten, and gone off up the mountain for an overnight at Treetops, the dining room and view terrace were quiet and nearly deserted. Deborah took a seat at a table and gazed at Mount Kenya, whose charcoal peaks against gunmetal clouds seemed to mock her return to East Africa. A soft-spoken waiter in black trousers and white jacket brought her a pot of tea and pointed to a table set out with afternoon pastries and tea sandwiches.

Despite "Africanization" and "Kenyanization" as official government initiatives to obliterate colonial traces from the country, such traditions seemed to Deborah too deeply embedded. High tea, she had seen, was also served at the Hilton, and she didn't doubt that like many other British customs that were holdovers from the colonial days, afternoon tea and white-gloved waiters were going to stay.

"Bugger me if it isn't Deborah Treverton!"

She looked up, startled. A stranger was standing on the lawn, staring at her.

She stared back. Then she said, "Terry?"

He came up to her, hand outstretched.

"Terry?" she said again, incredulous. Deborah thought she was seeing a ghost. But the hand that clasped hers belonged to a man very much alive.

He pulled out a chair and sat down. "Is this ever a shock! I saw you sitting here and I thought, *Blow me if that woman doesn't look just like Deborah Treverton!* And then I thought, *It is her!*"

She continued to stare, speechless. He looked the same as she remembered him, except that there was an even stronger resemblance now to Uncle Geoffrey, in the sunburned face, the outrageous self-confidence. Terry Donald was quite an attractive man, Deborah found herself thinking, in his beige cotton shirt, olive green vest and shorts, and knee socks and boots. His dark brown hair was considerably lighter than she recalled, no doubt from years in the sun, and his eyes were bluer.

"God, Deb! I can't believe it's you! How long's it been?"

The waiter came up. *"Nataka tembo baridi, tafadhali,"* Terry said to him, ordering a beer.

"How come you never wrote, Deb? Did you just get here or have you been in Kenya long?"

"I thought you were dead" was all she could say.

He laughed. "Not bloody likely! Seriously, Deb. I seem to recall your saying something at your aunt's funeral about not going to America after all. And then the next day you were gone. What happened?"

She tried to remember. Grace's funeral. Deborah had decided not to accept the scholarship and must have told everyone. She forced a smile. "A woman's prerogative to change her mind. I went to California after all."

"Is this your first time back to Kenya?"

"Yes." She regarded him, still shocked. The memories he triggered! "Terry, I don't understand. I really thought you were dead. At the agency they said your family had been killed in a car accident."

His handsome smile faded. "Yes, they were."

Terry's beer came. He opened the bottle and poured it into a tall glass. Then he took out a cigarette and lit it with the lighter that hung in a leather pouch on a thong about his neck. He puffed, inhaled deeply, and then considerately turned his head away to blow the smoke. "Dad, Mum, Uncle Ralph, and my two sisters," he said, "all at one go. It happened on the bloody Nanyuki Road. They were on their way to the Safari Club. One of those bloody *matatus* bashed right into them, trying to pass another *matatu*. Twelve people in the other vehicle were killed." He released a short, bitter laugh. "What blows me is I was supposed to have been with them, but I had a flat tire on the way up from Nairobi, so they went off without me. I was on the road to the Safari Club when I came upon the accident. They were just being put into the ambulance."

"Oh, Terry, I'm so sorry."

"These bloody roads," he said, turning his glass around and around on the tabletop. "They don't maintain them, you know. The roads get worse every year. Soon there won't be any left."

"So you sold the agency?"

"Sold it! Not on your Nellie! Donald Tours is one of the most profitable operations in East Africa! Why would I sell it?"

"I went into the agency this morning and was told that a Mr. Mugambi now owned it."

"Oh, that." Terry reddened and laughed a little. "*I'm* Mr. Mugambi. I changed my name. It isn't Donald anymore."

"Why did you do that?"

He looked up from his beer and made a discreet search of the terrace. "Tell you what, Deb," he said quietly. "Are you busy right now? Why don't you come over to the house with me? I'd like you to meet my wife. My home is here in Nyeri; it's not far."

Deborah, following his line of sight, looked over her shoulder and saw two Africans in casual linen suits drinking tea at a corner table and talking softly. "Who are they?" she asked.

Terry tossed a shilling on the table and pushed his chair back. "Come on, love. My Rover's out front."

When they were alone on a path crossing the hotel grounds, Terry said, "Those men were from Special Branch. You've got to watch what you say in Kenya these days."

As the Rover pulled out onto the main road, Terry said, "So how did you get up here? You're not driving yourself, I hope!"

"I rented a car and driver. I gave him the rest of the day off."

"So what is this for you then? A holiday? Come back to see the old places? You'll find that an awful lot's changed. Oh, maybe not on the outside, but underneath Kenya has changed."

She grew pensive as they passed the church where Terry's grandfather, Sir James, was buried. His grandmother, Lucille, whom neither of them had known, was buried in Uganda, as was his aunt Gretchen. Was Terry, then, the last of the Donalds?

"Do you have children?" she asked, suddenly needing to know.

"I have a boy and a girl. But you didn't answer my question. What brought you to Kenya?"

"Do you remember Mama Wachera, the medicine woman who lived in that hut by the polo field?"

"That queer old bird! Yes, I remember her. Is she still alive? My God, but I'd swear she was the last holdout of the older generation!"

Deborah told him about the letter from the nuns.

"What do you suppose she wants with you?" Terry asked as the Rover bounced along the track.

"I have no idea. I plan to go to the mission in the morning and find out."

"Are you in Kenya to stay, Deb?" he asked, casting her a cautious sideways glance.

His question surprised her. And then suddenly she thought: Am I here to stay? "I don't know, Terry," she replied honestly.

They pulled up to a chain link fence where signs read HATARI! DANGER! KALI DOGS! STAY IN YOUR CAR AND HONK YOUR HORN.

"Even here?" Deborah said as an askari opened the gate for them.

"Crime is bad all over Kenya, Deb. And it's on the rise. It's the population problem, you see. Kenya has the highest birthrate in the world. Did you know that?"

"No, I didn't."

"There isn't enough land to support everyone, not enough jobs to go around. And it's becoming a nation of youngsters. You've seen them, no doubt, young Africans in Nairobi, with nothing to do. You wouldn't believe the scams that are pulled on innocent tourists! I'm forever warning my people not to have anything to do with strangers they meet up with. So many of my female clients have their purses stolen."

"Are the police ineffectual then?"

"Ineffectual! Only if you don't pay them enough *magendo*. But I have a better system for keeping my chaps honest. If any of my clients come up missing something, I simply put the word out that I'm calling in a witch doctor. It never fails. The next morning there it is, whatever was nicked, quietly restored to the owner."

"Is such superstition so prevalent still?"

"Worse than ever, I suspect."

They pulled into a dusty compound where surly dogs were rounded up by Africans. The house was very old; Deborah recognized the original pioneer construction of whitewashed mud walls and thatch roof. It was large, long, and low and sagging-looking, but it was in good repair and appeared to be neatly kept.

"I have three residences," Terry explained as they went inside. "One in Nairobi, another on the coast. But this is where I keep my family. It's the safest place. So far."

The inside was cool and dark, with a low-beamed ceiling and polished wooden floor, leather sofas, and animal trophies everywhere. An African wearing khaki trousers and pullover sweater was setting the table for tea.

"We'll have that in here, Augustus," Terry called to the man, then guided Deborah to the arrangement of sofas around the biggest fireplace she had ever seen.

When they were seated, Terry lit another cigarette and said, "So when did you leave, Deb? Fourteen, fifteen years ago? You haven't come back to the old Kenya you once knew. For one thing, the government's a joke! Look how it's trying to put a lid on the population growth. Women who have no husbands, which is to say just about all the women in the bloody country, receive some sort of financial support for each child they have. As a birth control measure Moi's government has said that from now on only the first *four* babies receive aid; any after that are on their own. Now what bloody good is that?"

The tea tray was set before them on a low coffee table. *"Asante sana,* Augustus," Terry said. Then he went on. "Foreign health agencies and medical missionaries are trying to push for birth control, but African men don't go for it. So the women, if they want it, practice it on the sly. If a man discovers his wife is taking the pill or using a diaphragm, he beats her senseless, and it's his right to do so."

Terry stamped out his cigarette and lifted a fresh smile to Deborah. "Christ! Listen to me! What sort of reunion is this? I can't tell you how good it is to see you, Deb! What's it been like, living in California?"

She told him about her life, but only superficially.

"This bloke you're going to marry, does he want to come and live in Kenya?"

"He's never been here. I don't know if he would like it."

As soon as she said it, Deborah realized something that hadn't occurred to her before: how little Jonathan knew of Kenya. *Then how can he possibly know* me? she wondered.

"Miriam's out at the moment, visiting her sister. But she'll be home soon. I want you to meet her."

"And the children?"

"They're both in school. Wait a mo," he said, and stood up. Terry took two photographs from the mantel and handed them to Deborah. "This is Richard. He's fourteen."

"He's a handsome boy," Deborah said, gazing at a younger version of Terry.

"And this is Lucy. She's eight."

Deborah stared. Lucy was African.

As if reading her thoughts, Terry sat down, lit another cigarette, and said, "Richard's mother was my first wife. We got a divorce when Richard was a baby. That was when I was just getting started in Dad's business. Anne couldn't abide my long absences out on safari. And she was jealous of my female clients. So she left me and married an exporter in Mombasa. Richard spends half the year with me, the other half with Anne."

"And Lucy?"

"She's my daughter by my second wife, Miriam."

"Kikuyu?"

Terry nodded and exhaled smoke. "In fact, it's my wife's last name that I took. Mugambi."

Deborah set the pictures down on the table. "Why?"

He shrugged. "For survival mostly. There's a squeeze on to get the whites out of Kenya. An awful lot of prejudice against European businesses. I won't go into the details, but I saw that it was in my best interest to hold the agency under an African name."

"I thought all that was over with years ago."

"Since Jomo's death, back in 1978, things haven't been too settled in Kenya. Of course, there are blokes who disagree with me. But I speak from personal experience. Take my son's education, for example."

Before he explained further, Terry called out for Augustus and, when the man appeared, told him in Swahili to bring a bottle of wine. "Special occasion," Terry said to Deborah with a smile. "It's Kenya papaya wine, and I doubt it holds a candle to your famous California wines, but it's the best we've got."

"You were telling me about Richard."

"At this moment he's at a boarding school in Naivasha. But he's fourteen, time to move up to a higher level. The hitch is, the school I want him to go to has been totally Africanized. The King George in Nairobi, remember? Now it's the Uhuru Academy. There's a new headmaster, an African who absolutely will not allow any white boys to attend. What buggers me is that's the school my father attended when he was a boy. In fact, my father was in the very first class, when the school opened back in 1926. There's a plaque out front, listing the names of the founding pupils. Geoffrey Donald is at the top of the list. And then I attended, of course, in 1967. But the school's closed now to whites. And what's worse, there isn't another secondary school in Kenya that will take white pupils."

"What will you do?"

"I have no choice but to send him to a boarding school in England. I can afford it, mind you, but it's the principle of the thing. Richard's never set foot in England. Blast it, Deb. His great-grandfather was born in Kenya!"

Augustus brought the wine and set it on the table with two stem glasses, then cleared away the tea things. Terry poured and handed Deborah a glass. She sipped it. The wine had a harsh, bitter taste.

"What do you do these days, Terry?" she asked softly, to defuse his clearly rising anger. "Do you still escort tours, or are you strictly administrative now?"

He laughed, lit another cigarette, and settled back with his wine. "I take out hunting safaris."

"I thought hunting was illegal here."

"Tanzania. It's legal there. I take Americans mostly."

She spoke with reserve. "Is it profitable?"

"You wouldn't believe how much so! I'm booked clear into 1991. When hunting was banned here, ten years ago, we hunters took off for other countries and looked for work. I did a lot of herd control in the Sudan. Culling, mostly, north of Juba on the Nile. The elephant population had got too big and was destroying the crops. Those tusks over there"—he pointed to a pair, taller than a man, standing on either side of a doorway—"came from an old rogue that had been wounded with a musket loader. He was totally crazed. Killed about thirty Dinka tribesmen. I took him out with a single shot and asked to be paid in tusks rather than in Sudanese pounds, which are worthless."

Terry tasted his wine. "Anyway, I'm doing a good business now in Tanzania. And getting paid in American dollars!"

"But isn't it illegal to import hunting trophies into the United States?"

"*Used* to be illegal. Jimmy Carter banned the importation of leopard, jaguar, and ivory. But the Reagan administration permits trophies that have been shot in countries where it is allowed. My clients are guaranteed one lion, one leopard, two buffalo, and two Grant's gazelles. I take them out for twenty-one days, provide them with camps and trackers, and they pay me thirty thousand dollars."

Deborah didn't say anything.

"I know you don't approve of hunting," Terry said quietly. "You never did. But we hunters serve a good purpose. We kept the poachers out of Kenya. We were the unofficial police force. When hunting was banned in 1977, the hunters moved out and the poachers moved in. They don't care how many they kill or in what manner. The result is the unremitting suffering and slaughter of game. Do you know there are only about five hundred rhinos left in Kenya?"

Deborah gazed at the photographs of Terry's children. "I'm glad you're doing well," she said softly. "I've so often wondered . . ."

"Yes, I'm doing well," Terry said as he refilled his glass and lit another cigarette. "But for how long? Kenya's a bloody unstable country, Deb. You're not blind. You've seen what conditions are. The Africans don't seem to know how to run things. Or else they don't give a damn, I haven't figured out which it is. At the top you've got a handful of sodding rich elitists who say sweet fuck-all to the twenty million who are slowly starving to death. Look at what they're doing to Mount Kenya. Cutting down all the trees with absolutely no planning whatever. They don't study the ecology; they don't replant; they don't think of the consequences of taking out entire forests. The rivers around here are starting to run dry because the mountains are becoming barren wastelands."

Terry shook his head. "Africans don't think of the future. They never have, not even in my grandfather's day. They use up all the resources and keep having babies. It doesn't occur to them to do something about tomorrow. Look at Kilima Simba, my father's old ranch. My grandfather had established a system of furrows bringing water from boreholes. But the Africans who live there now, on hundreds of little shambas, haven't maintained the furrows, and so now they've no water and their farms are turning to dust."

Terry regarded Deborah with intense blue eyes. "Kenya's a powder keg, Deb. A ticking time bomb. With its skyrocketing birthrate, the famine is going to get worse."

"I thought other nations were helping."

He stamped out his half-smoked Embassy King and poured some more wine. "You mean USA for Africa? How much of that money do you think made it down to the people, Deb? I've got it on good authority that less than ten percent of those millions of dollars, generously donated by Americans, went to feeding the people. The rest? Well, just count the Benzes in the government parking lots. There's going to be another revolution here someday, Deb. You mark my words. And it'll make Mau Mau look like a bloody picnic!"

"Then why do you stay, Terry?"

"Where am I going to go? This is my country, my home. Old Moi can stuff off if he thinks he's going to scare us out!"

Terry suddenly fell silent. He looked over his shoulder, in the direction of the kitchen, then said in a lowered voice, "I'll tell you, Deb. Come the next revolution, I'll be regarded as a bloody colonial—a scapegoat. Even though I've done everything I can—married a Kikuyu woman, changed my name—I'm ready to leave at the drop of a hat. And any white person who has any sense is prepared to do the same. I've been sending money to England, on the quiet. Bought a house in the Cotswolds. When the shit hits the fan, I'll take my kids out of here with just the clothes we stand in if necessary, and I'll start over in England. Survival, Deb, is what being Kenyan has taught me. And if you're smart, you won't entertain any thoughts of moving back here to live."

The dogs were suddenly barking in the yard. When Deborah looked out the window, she was surprised to see that night had fallen and that it was starting to rain.

"That'll be Miriam," Terry said, standing. "Please stay for supper, Deb. I promise not to be such a crepehanger. We have so much to catch up on!"

HE RETURNED HER to the Outspan a few hours later. And because it was three o'clock in the afternoon in San Francisco, Deborah decided to call Jonathan.

She tried their apartment first.

While she waited for the hotel operator to get back to her with the call, Deborah took a hot bath. And as she soaked, she reflected upon her evening with Terry, which had been both enlightening and terrifying. But rather than scare her off, as he had seemed determined to do, his doomsday words were working a curiously opposite effect on her. The more she heard about Kenya's troubles, the more Deborah felt a sense of responsibility to do something about them.

She was wrapping up in her bathrobe when a room steward came by to build a fire in her fireplace. As he worked, Deborah stood at the French doors which opened onto the veranda of her cottage, and she watched the light rain fall like silver dust in the glow from the windows. The gentle drizzle reminded her of another such cold and damp night, when a fire also crackled and the world beyond the windows was safely locked out. It was the night she and Jonathan had made love for the first time.

"I've shied away from serious relationships," Jonathan's soft-spoken voice had said, "until now."

Deborah, lying in his arms, staring at the leaping flames and feeling, for the first time, completely relaxed and at ease with a man, had listened to Jonathan open up, bit by bit, as he had not done so far in their yearlong friendship.

"Why didn't you marry her?" she asked, referring to the woman who had hurt him years ago. "What happened?"

It wasn't an easy subject for him to talk about; Deborah heard the hesitation, the discomfort, the carefully chosen words of a man confessing a secret pain perhaps for the first time. Deborah understood how he felt. Her own past lay safely concealed behind such unspoken confessions. Not even this man with whom she was falling in love knew of the crime committed in Christopher's hut, nor had she ever told him of the racial mix in her blood. It served no purpose, she believed, to parade her demons in public. Deborah had worked hard to bury the past; she had even invented falsehoods to explain away certain situations. Such as the problem of children. She would never have any because of her ancestry. It frightened her to think what an unpredictable grouping of her genes might produce. How could she chance to have a baby that was less white than its father? When would the hidden African part of her suddenly show itself and under what poorly timed circumstances? And so she had fabricated a medical history: "I can't have children. Endometriosis . . ." She had told it more than once—to Jonathan as well—so that she almost believed it herself.

Now, after months of working together in the operating room, of smiling at each other over the tops of green masks, of sharing private jokes, of fighting to save lives, of discussing the mutual benefits of going into medical practice together, now, after a missed evening at the ballet and two glorious hours in front of his fireplace, she and Jonathan had taken the next determining step. Having committed themselves to each other with their bodies, Jonathan was now paving the way toward the spiritual commitment—through the confession of secrets and hidden pasts.

"Why didn't you marry her?" Deborah had asked on that rainy night in San Francisco. "You were so close. The wedding was only a week away. What happened?"

And he had replied, in a voice so strained that Deborah heard the pain even all these years later, "Because I found out that she had done an unforgivable thing. She had done something that I cannot abide in a woman who supposedly loves a man. She had lied to me."

The ringing of the telephone startled her. Deborah turned away from the French doors and saw that she was alone. The steward had built the fire and discreetly left. And the telephone was ringing.

Jonathan!

She picked it up, suddenly wanting him, only to hear the hotel operator's voice saying, "I am sorry, madam. But there is no answer at this number. Shall I try later?"

She thought a moment. Their office was closed on Wednesday afternoons, but he might be in surgery. So she gave the man the number of their answering service. It could page him, tell him to call her.

There was no use standing by the phone; it took half an hour to get calls connected to California. So she went and sat on the sofa, curled her legs under her, and gazed into the fire.

On that other rainy night, a year ago, she had stared into the fire in Jonathan's fireplace, feeling a sort of numb shock at hearing what he had just said.

"It's a thing with me," he had gone on to explain, his voice growing relaxed now that he had eased into it, now that he felt comfortable and safe with Deborah. "All my life, ever since I can remember, I have detested lies. Perhaps it's because of my strict Catholic upbringing. I can forgive almost anything as long as a person is honest about it. But to tell me she loved me and to let me believe a lie, a lie which she later admitted she had no intention of ever correcting, I was beside myself with anger and pain."

"What was the lie?" Deborah had asked.

"It's not important. What's important is that knowing that I believed untruths, she was going to go to the altar with me. And knowing that the cloak of dishonesty covered us, she was ready to live a married life with me. It doesn't matter what the lie was, Debbie, only that she lied, and I found out from another source."

Deborah had closed her eyes and held tightly to him. *Yes, it does matter what the lie was,* she thought. *I must know if it was as big as mine.*

Her own lies had frightened her after that. Deborah had come close, that same evening, to telling Jonathan everything. But their relationship, having moved from the easygoing world of friends to the fragile, oh, so important plane of lovers, was too new, too breakable. *I'll wait,* she had told herself. *I'll tell him when it's safe.*

But it never got safe. Deborah discovered to her dismay that as their relationship grew stronger, as their love for each other deepened, as he suddenly became the most important thing in her life, her opportunity had slipped away. Until finally they had set the date for their wedding and she was going to stand at the altar with lies.

When the phone rang again, she looked at her watch. It had taken only five minutes.

"This is Dr. Treverton," she said to the answering service. "Can you page Dr. Hayes for me?"

"I'm sorry, Dr. Treverton. Dr. Hayes cannot be reached. Dr. Simonson is taking his calls."

"But do you know where Dr. Hayes is?"

"I'm sorry. I don't. Shall I page Dr. Simonson for you?"

She thought a moment. "No. No, thank you." And she hung up, deciding to try Jonathan again in the morning, when it would be night in San Francisco and he was sure to be in the apartment. She left a request with the front desk for an early wake-up call and drifted off into a troubled sleep.

65

I wonder if you remember me, Dr. Treverton," the mother superior said to Deborah as they walked along the lane leading to Grace House. "I was Sister Perpetua then. And I believe I was the last person to see your aunt alive."

"I remember you," Deborah said, marveling at the memories the walk from the gate was producing. Grace Mission had been her first home, the only childhood home she had really known. And it seemed wrong somehow that a nun in blue robes should be standing on that familiar veranda instead of a white-haired woman in white lab coat, with the ever-present stethoscope around her neck.

A bronze plaque was on the wall by the front door: GRACE HOUSE, EST. 1919. Deborah was surprised to find that the house was no longer lived in.

"We keep our administrative offices here," Mother Superior said, "and a small visitor center. You would be impressed to know how many people come from all over the world to visit the home of Dr. Grace Treverton."

The living room had been converted into a small museum, with glass cases and framed letters and photographs on the walls. Locked in a display case was Grace's war medal; next to it was the insignia of the Order of the British Empire, given to Grace by Queen Elizabeth in 1960, when she had been made a Dame. There was even an antique supply cabinet filled with old medical instruments, medicine bottles, and faded diagnostic notes.

Deborah paused before a photograph of Aunt Grace standing at the base of Treetops with Princess Elizabeth, in 1952, and her eyes misted over. It was as if Grace hadn't died at all but lived on.

"All this really belongs to you, Dr. Treverton," Mother Superior said. "After you had left for America, I found storage boxes full of keepsakes. I had thought you would be coming back for them. I even wrote to you in California. Did you not receive my letters?"

Deborah wordlessly shook her head. She had thrown those letters away—anything bearing a Kenya stamp—without opening them.

"And then we decided to share these things with the world. Of course, if you wish to take anything away with you, it is your right, Dr. Treverton."

Fifteen years ago Deborah had left Kenya with the only mementos she had wanted. Among them had been her aunt's turquoise brooch. Unfortunately that stone had been stolen from Deborah during her first year in medical school. A fellow student, one of the few other women in the class and an unhappy person, had admired the stone to the point of asking Deborah if she could buy it from her. When it came up missing, Deborah knew who had taken it but had no proof. The same girl dropped out of school a few weeks later and returned to her home up north in Washington. At the time Deborah had been upset over the stone's loss; as the years passed, however, she had come to accept the impermanence of all things—possessions, relationships— and had decided that the turquoise had been meant to be passed along.

Deborah turned to the kindly spoken nun, whose black face sharply contrasted with the white simple of her habit, and said, "These things do belong to the world, as you say. I have no need of them. May I see Mama Wachera now?"

As they crossed the lawn, Deborah said, "Do you know why she is asking for me, Mother Superior?"

The nun frowned slightly. "It was not an easy decision for me to make, sending for you, Dr. Treverton. Because you see, I am not sure she is asking for you. The poor woman is so terribly distraught. She came here on her own, you know. She appeared one day, very tired and in ill health—we estimate her age to be well over ninety—saying that the ancestors had instructed her to come here to die. She lapses into moments of lucidness, but most of the time she seems to be confused. Her mind moves to and from different points in time. Occasionally she will even wake up and asked for Kabiru Mathenge, her husband! But she has called out the Treverton name so many times, and she is so insistent on such occasions and so agitated as to require medication that

I thought a letter to you might help. I pray that once she has seen you, she will rest more easily."

Inside the bungalow they were greeted by a young nursing sister in a blue uniform and blue veil and taken to a bed at the end of the sunlit ward. Wachera was asleep, her dark head resting peacefully on the white pillow.

Deborah stared down at her, prepared to feel anger and bitterness toward this woman who had been so cruel to her. But strangely, all Deborah saw was an old woman, frail and unthreatening. She didn't remember Wachera's being so *small*. . . .

"She usually wakens later in the day," the young African nurse said. "Can we telephone you?"

"Please. I'll be at the Outspan."

"Let me offer you some tea, Dr. Treverton," the mother superior said. "We feel so honored to have you visit us."

Deborah talked for a while with Mother Superior, drinking Countess Treverton tea and discussing Mama Wachera.

"Her grandson visits her quite often," Perpetua said. "Dr. Mathenge is a good man. His wife died a few years ago. Did you know that?"

"Yes. But I don't know how she died."

"Malaria, it was. Just when we thought we had conquered it, now there's a new strain that is resistant to chloroquine. Dr. Mathenge is carrying on the work he and his wife both had been doing. We pray for him daily. Dr. Mathenge is taking healing and the Lord to the people of Kenya."

Afterward Deborah visited the eucalyptus glade, where the Sacrario Duca d'Alessandro was still maintained by an old caretaker, the light still burning inside. Deborah liked to think that her grandmother and the Italian duke dwelt in a kind of eternal, spiritual lovemaking.

THE RAIN WAS coming down hard by the time she returned to the Outspan Hotel. She went straight to her cottage, bypassing the dining room where lunch was being served. As she closed the door behind her, cutting off the wind and driving rain, and began to remove her damp sweater, Deborah received a shock.

"Jonathan!"

He rose from the sofa. "Hi, Debbie. I hope you don't mind. I told them I was your husband. A bribe got me the key to your room."

"Jonathan," she said again, "what are you doing here?"

"You sounded so strange on the phone the last time we talked that I got worried. I decided to come and find out what's going on."

66

Jonathan opened his arms to receive her.

But Deborah hesitated by the door. She hadn't planned to tell him so soon. She had wanted time, to think and to prepare. So she went to the phone and asked for room service. As she ordered salad, fruit, sandwiches, and tea, she kept her eye on Jonathan. He looked tired.

By the time Deborah had hung up and was removing her sweater, Jonathan was on his knees lighting a fire.

This was a familiar scene, one which they had enacted many times in their apartment on Nob Hill. Coming in out of fog or rain, shrugging out of wet clothes, Jonathan started the fire, Deborah made the tea, and then came the hours of warmth and coziness, just the two of them, talking quietly, reviewing the day—patients, surgery, plans for their new office. It was within such golden circles of firelight that their love for each other had grown and strengthened and bound them together.

But now the fire smelled wrong because the wood was foreign, and Jonathan kept his leather jacket on; the tea was brought by an African room steward, who served in silence while Deborah remained standing, ready with the five-shilling tip; and then, when she was alone with Jonathan again, she didn't go sit next to him on the sofa, sliding under his arm, curling her legs up and leaning into his body. She stood by the fireplace, looking at him, suddenly afraid.

"What's happened, Debbie?" he asked at last.

Deborah struggled for self-control. "Jonathan, I lied to you."

His expression didn't change.

"You asked me what a dying old African medicine woman was to me. I told you I didn't know. That was a lie. She's my grandmother."

He remained perfectly still, staring up at her.

"At least," she added, "I thought so at the time."

The fire cracked loudly, and a red-hot shower of sparks went up the chimney. Outside heavy rain had turned the day as dark as night. It pelted the veranda roof; it drenched the forest that grew at the bottom of the sloping lawn. Deborah went to the low table in front of the sofa and poured two cups of tea. But they remained untouched.

"Your grandmother?" Jonathan said. "An African woman?"

Deborah avoided his eyes. It was easier to stare into the fire. She sat at the other end of the sofa, maintaining a distance from him, and said, "I *thought* she was my grandmother. It was what she wanted me to believe. She was the reason I left Kenya."

Deborah's soft voice joined the whispers of fire and rain. She talked quietly, without emotion, leaving nothing out. Jonathan listened. He didn't move. He watched her tight profile, the fall of black hair down her back, untidy from the wind and rain. He listened to an incredible tale of Mau Mau freedom fighters and forbidden racial love, of childhood sweethearts, African and white, of a bachelor hut, of a funeral, of finding love letters, and of an old woman's curse. Jonathan was spellbound.

"I had my aunt's journal all these years," Deborah said as she came to the end of her story, "but I never read it. I opened it when I checked in at the Hilton in Nairobi. And that was when I found out"—she finally turned to Jonathan, her eyes unusually dark, the dilated pupils reflecting the fire's glow—"that Christopher is not my brother after all."

He met her straightforward gaze for a moment; then it was his turn to look away.

During her story a log had rolled off the fire, and it lay at the edge of the flames. Jonathan got up, took the poker, and maneuvered the log back onto the fire. Then he straightened and gazed at the portrait over the mantel, an elderly man with white mustache, wearing a Boy Scout uniform. Lord Baden-Powell, who had forsaken his comfortable life in England to live in the Kenya wilderness.

Jonathan was perplexed. What was it about this country that seemed to turn people's heads? What special magic made men give up lives of ease?

He turned and looked at Deborah. She sat on the edge of the sofa, tensed, as if ready to run. Her hands were clasped tightly before her; her face was drawn. He was familiar with that look. It came upon her when she stood by a patient in the intensive care unit. She would watch the monitors with singular passion.

"Why did you never tell me all this, Debbie?"

She looked up, her eyes full of pain. "I couldn't, Jonathan. I felt so ashamed. So . . . dirty. I just wanted to forget my past and start anew. I saw no point in dredging it up. I never intended to come back to Kenya."

"It wasn't a lie you told me," he said quietly. "All you did was keep an unpleasant memory a secret."

"But there's more. I thought I was part black, Jonathan. And I never told you that. I said I couldn't have children. That's not true. I didn't *want* to have children. I was terrified that my ancestry would show up."

"You could have told me all this, Debbie. You know that I don't give a damn about race or color."

"Yes, I know that now. But I wasn't sure about you at first, when we started dating. So I told you the same lie I had told others. That I had had endometriosis."

"But later, Debbie! When we realized we were in love, when we decided to get married. You could have told me then."

She bowed her head. "I was going to. And then you told me about Sharon, the woman you almost married. That she had lied to you."

Jonathan was thunderstruck. "You're blaming *me?* You're saying it's *my* fault that you perpetuated your lies?"

"No, Jonathan!"

"Christ, Debbie!" He turned away from the fireplace and walked to the French doors. Thrusting his hands into his pockets, he stared out at the gray rain.

"I was afraid," she said. "I was afraid that if I told you that I had lied, I would lose you."

"You thought our relationship was that tenuous?" he asked, looking at her reflection in the window pane. "You thought so little of me? You thought I was that shallow?"

"But Sharon—"

He spun around. "Debbie, that was seventeen years ago! I was twenty at the time! I was young and intolerant and an arrogant son of a bitch! Good God, I like to think I've changed since then. At least I thought I had. I thought that I was a reasonable man and that you saw that in me."

"But when you told me about her—"

"Debbie," he said, crossing the room and sitting next to her, "Sharon and I were two young, selfish people. The lies she told me were outrageous ones. They were intended to deceive, even to hurt me. But your lie, Debbie, was intended only to protect yourself and to protect me. Don't you see the difference?"

She mutely shook her head.

"Lord," he said softly, "you've got to know me better than that, Debbie. You've got to know that I love you too much to pass judgment on you because of your past. I wish you had told me about it long ago. I could have helped you come to terms with it."

"That's what I'm trying to do now, Jonathan. Coming back to Kenya has less to do with seeing Mama Wachera than it has to do with me finding out who I am. Reading Aunt Grace's journal has helped me a little. At least now I know my family's history. But I still have this . . . *rootless* feeling. I don't know where I belong."

He searched her face, saw the honesty in her eyes. He took her hands in his and said, "God, I love you, Debbie. I want to help you. I could tell on the phone. You didn't sound right. I got worried. So I canceled my surgery schedule and asked Simonson to take emergencies. All the way over here, on that damn jet, I kept trying to think what might be wrong. Lord knows this isn't what I expected. But at least it's not as bad as I had imagined."

When Deborah didn't say anything, he said, "Is there more?"

She nodded.

"What is it?"

"It's Kenya, Jonathan. I have this strong feeling that I must stay and help. In the past few days I've seen such poverty, such disease, people living in inhuman conditions. Except for a few caring individuals, like the nuns at the mission"—*and Christopher,* she thought, recalling how futile she had thought he looked, with his bag of medicines and all those desperate people—"no one seems to give a damn about all the suffering in this country. I feel this inexplicable pull at me, Jonathan.

To stay, to put my medical skills to use here, as Aunt Grace had done."

"People all over the world need our help, Debbie. Not just Kenya. What about our patients back in San Francisco? Are they any less in need of you because they're white and live in America?"

"Yes," she said earnestly. "Because they have more doctors and better facilities."

"What do those mean to Bobby Delaney?"

Deborah looked away.

Bobby Delaney was nine years old and fighting for his life in the hospital burn unit. He had been purposely set on fire by his mentally unstable mother, and Deborah was one of a team of physicians who were taking care of him. Having sustained third-degree burns over ninety percent of his body, Bobby now endured incredible pain and suffering, severe mental as well as physical trauma, living in a sterile bubble, where his only human contact was through rubber gloves, the only faces he saw, masked. For reasons no one knew, Bobby had singled out Dr. Debbie as his one friend. The way his eyes, in that poor, disfigured face, moved toward her each time she came in . . .

"You know he won't talk to anyone else," Jonathan said. "You know he lives for your visits. But there are others, too. All your patients are worthy of your care, Debbie."

"I don't know," she said slowly. "I feel so strange, so undecided. Where do I belong?"

"With me."

"I believe that, Jonathan. But at the same time . . ." She looked out at the Kenya rain. "I was born here. Don't I owe something to this country?"

"Listen, Debbie. We all have two lives: the one we're born into and the one we seek out and make for ourselves. I believe you're caught in between the two. You need to find your way out."

"I wish Aunt Grace were here. I could talk to her. She would help me."

"Let *me* help you, Debbie. We can find a way out together."

"How?"

"We can start by having me read the journal."

They made themselves comfortable on the sofa, Jonathan at one end, reading under a table lamp, Deborah curled up at the other end, pillows at her back. As Jonathan opened the old book to the first yellowed page, Deborah felt herself become lulled into a strange sense of complacency. There was something vaguely consoling about Jonathan's reading her aunt's words. She listened to the rain and closed her eyes.

THE RINGING TELEPHONE jarred her out of a deep, dreamless sleep.

Jonathan was up first, answering it. He hung up and said, "That was the mission. Mama Wachera is awake and asking for you, Debbie."

She stretched and rubbed her stiff neck. "What time is it?"

"It's late. I'm more than half done with the book." Jonathan hefted it in his hand. "The earl's just been found dead in his car. Quite a family you have here, Debbie!"

She reached for her sweater, which had dried by the fire, and said, "I hate to leave you, Jonathan."

"Don't worry. You just go and get things sorted out with the old woman. I'll still be here when you get back."

"I don't know how long I'll be."

He smiled and held up the book. "I have plenty of company."

At the door he held her and said quietly, "I want you to come home with me, Debbie. I want you to find what you're seeking here, come to terms with it, and then lay the past to rest. The future belongs to us, Debbie."

"Yes," she whispered, and kissed him.

DEBORAH REALIZED SHE was suddenly very nervous. As she followed the night nurse down the dimly lit ward, she felt her pulse quicken, her anxiousness mount.

Wachera was resting against pillows that had been built up to put her in a comfortable half-reclining position. Deborah saw that she was having trouble breathing. Dark brown eyes fixed on her and followed her as she came to the foot of the bed; they stayed on her as she came around and sat in a chair at the bedside.

"You . . ." Wachera said in a papery voice. "The memsaab. You came."

Deborah was surprised. She hadn't heard that word in years; it had been banned upon independence. But she also noticed that the medicine woman was not using it as a respectful term of address. *Which memsaab?* Deborah wondered. *Does she think I am my mother?*

"You came," the ancient voice continued. "So many harvests ago. With your wagons and your strange ways."

My grandmother!

"You were the only one among the *wazungu* who understood the Children of Mumbi. You brought medicine."

And then Deborah realized: *She thinks I'm Aunt Grace.*

"You sent for me, Mama Wachera," she said softly, bending close. "Why?"

"The ancestors . . ."

Wachera was speaking in Kikuyu, and Deborah was amazed at how easily she understood the words and then with what familiarity she herself now spoke it. "What about the ancestors, Mama?"

"I will be with them very soon now. I will return to the bosom of the First Mother. But I go with lies and *thahu* upon my soul."

Deborah grew tense. She watched the aged black face, still carved with dignity after nearly a century but looking strangely naked and vulnerable without the beaded headbands and great looped earrings that Wachera had always worn. Now she lay beneath white sheets in a plain hospital gown, her long, sinewy arms laid out on the pale blue blanket. Deborah wondered if the medicine woman knew how stripped she looked, how divested of authority and power.

"There was the last girl," Wachera said, her breathing labored. "I let her believe my grandson was her brother. It was a lie."

"I know that," Deborah said gently.

"So many sins . . ." the old woman said in such a wandering way that Deborah wondered if she was even aware of her presence at the bedside.

"My husband's daughter killed the bwana. I made her vow to keep silent while the bwana's wife stood before a council that was to decide if she should live or die."

Deborah didn't understand at first; then she realized that Wachera was speaking of the earl's murder. She recalled what she had read of it in her aunt's journal. Njeri. Rose's personal maid.

"How?" Deborah asked. "Mama Wachera, how did Njeri kill the bwana?"

"She heard him leave the big house. She left the memsaab's sleeping room and followed him. He went in the beast that rolls on wheels. He went to the glass house in the forest, and Njeri saw what he did to the stranger there. She held on to the beast and rode it through the night. The bwana's window was open. She stabbed him. It was just punishment. But she grew afraid. She shot him with his own weapon."

Deborah could picture it. The young African woman holding on to Valentine's car, perhaps crouched on the running board, waiting for an opportunity. Killing him because she feared for the life of her memsaab.

"For a woman to die with sins on her soul is very bad," Wachera said. "Her spirit is restless; she never sleeps. And she haunts the woods and dwells with the wild beasts. I, Wachera, desire peace."

She fell silent for a long time, her breathing becoming increasingly more strained, the flutter of pulse at her neck barely visible. Then she said, "The voices of the ancestors grow faint. With the coming of the white man, the ancestors began to depart Kikuyuland. To appease them, I fought the white man. But now that Kikuyuland is being restored to the Children of Mumbi, the ancestors will return."

Wachera drew in a deep, ragged breath. When she let it out, Deborah heard the familiar rattle of death. "The *thahu* is ended," the medicine woman said, "as I promised. The land belongs to the African again; the white man is gone."

Wachera looked at Deborah and seemed, for the first time, truly to see her. The wise old eyes became suddenly keen, and Wachera's mouth lifted in a brief, triumphant smile. "Memsaab Daktari," she whispered, "I have won."

And then she died.

Deborah remained for a while at the bedside. She had come to Kenya full of hatred for this woman who had driven her away; now she saw only the reposed face of an old woman whose death symbolized the death of a history.

When she finally stood up, Deborah's eye fell upon the crucifix over Wachera's bed. It was Jesus, hanging on his cross. But the figure was African. Deborah stared at it. She had never seen one before. When her aunt was still alive, all religious statues in the mission had been imported from Europe and were white. This black Jesus seemed to Deborah to be all wrong, almost blasphemous.

But then, as she looked again at the dark face against the hospital pillow and the rows of dark faces down the length of the sleeping ward, and as she thought of the African sisters in their blue habits, she realized that in her short time back at the mission she had seen no white faces.

And suddenly Deborah realized that the black Jesus was proper after all.

THE RAIN HAD stopped by the time she returned to her room at the Outspan. To her surprise Jonathan was getting ready to leave.

"Simonson called," he said. "I have to go. Bobby Delaney's body is rejecting the latest series of skin grafts. He has a rampant infection, and he's in critical condition. I'm going to Nairobi and make reservations on the first plane out. I want you to leave with me, Debbie. I'll wait for you at the airport."

He kissed her and then said, "You said you wished you could talk to your aunt. Open the journal where I've marked it. It might help. I love you, Debbie. And I'll be waiting."

When he had gone, she sat down on the sofa and picked up the journal. Jonathan had marked, she thought, a rather insignificant passage. It was dated 1920, and Grace had written about a letter she had received from her brother Harold, back at Bella Hill. But as Deborah read the passage now, more carefully and with a newer eye than when she had first read it, she began to see what Jonathan meant. Grace's elegant copperplate script read:

> *Another letter from Harold. He continues to persist in the notion that we cannot possibly be happy here in British East Africa and that we must soon return to Suffolk. His argument is the same old tired one that he used when he tried to dissuade me from leaving in the first place. "Suffolk is your home," he repeats like a parrot. "Here is where you belong. Here is where your people are, not among strangers who will only think you an intruder. They won't know your ways. They won't understand you."*

Deborah looked up from the journal and stared at the misty blue dawn breaking through the forest. These words sounded so familiar! Where, other than here, had she heard them before?

And then she remembered: Christopher, fifteen years ago, standing on the riverbank and saying, ". . . Always remember Kenya is your home. Here is where you belong. Out there, in the world, . . . you will be a curiosity, and you will be misunderstood. . . . Promise me that you will come back."

She looked down again at the journal:

I wrote at once to Harold and told him to abandon the subject once and for all. I have chosen British East Africa as my home, and here I shall stay. It is what I have chosen to do. If history had been peopled by the likes of Harold, where would we be today? If one never followed the call of the spirit or ventured into new worlds, how tiresome a place this would be! It is in the nature of the human to move on, to experiment, to look at the horizon and wonder what lies beyond it. When my time comes, I pray that I shall not be as ossified as my brother, that I shall have the courage to say to a future Treverton: Seek your destiny where your heart leads. Always remember and cherish the place of your birth, but then go your own way, as a child must leave its mother.

DEBORAH ASKED ABDI to wait at the entrance for her. She went first to the bronze memorial that stood at the side of the mission church, where, next to it, was Grace Treverton's grave. Deborah saw evidence of loving care in the small patch of ground; the nuns kept the grass weeded, the flowers neatly tended. The marker was simple—DR. GRACE TREVERTON, OBE, 1890–1973—but the monument was a tribute both to the artist who had cast it and to the woman it represented in such a lifelike way.

Deborah gazed up at the figure on the pedestal. She wore a long, old-fashioned skirt with high-buttoned shoes and a long-sleeved blouse with a brooch at her collar. Strangely, her head was bare. In one hand she held her sun helmet; in the other, a stethoscope. And she was eternally facing Mount Kenya.

Deborah stayed for a moment in the peace of the churchyard; then she continued on to Grace House.

"I was hoping to see you again," Mother Superior said, greeting her in the little museum. "I wanted to thank you for being with Wachera in her last moments. I've informed Dr. Mathenge of his grandmother's passing."

Deborah explained the reason for this morning's visit. "I've decided to take you up on your generous offer, Mother Superior, to take something from among my aunt's things."

"By all means. What would you like?"

Deborah walked to a display case. "This necklace. You see, it didn't belong to my aunt. It was my mother's. Someone very dear to her gave it to her many years ago."

"A beautiful piece," the nun said as she unlocked the case and withdrew the necklace. "Ethiopian, is it?"

"Ugandan. I'm going to write to my mother and let her know I have it."

At the door, as they were saying good-bye, the nun hesitated, as if there was something she wanted to say. "I was wondering, Dr. Treverton, if I might ask you something."

"Certainly. Ask me anything you like."

"You see, I was so unsure that I had done the right thing in writing to you, taking you away from your work and bringing you all these miles. *Was* it you Wachera was asking for?"

Deborah thought for a moment; then she smiled and said quietly, "Yes, it was."

DEBORAH HAD ASKED Abdi to drive her to Ongata Rongai, and so now they were parked in the same spot as before, a safe distance away from the cinder-block structure that served the Wangari Clinic's medical ministry. A large crowd was waiting patiently as the visiting doctor saw to them, one person at a time, with the aid of a nurse and the young man who played Swahili songs to God on his guitar.

Deborah got out of the car but stayed by it, watching Christopher as he worked.

The air was cool, breezy. Colorful *kangas*, hanging on a line in the small marketplace, fluttered like bright pennants. The smell of smoke mingled with the aromas of goat, cooked food, and animal dung. It was the smell, Deborah thought, of Kenya.

She watched Christopher take babies into his arms, examine them, and return them to mothers with sternly spoken instructions. She saw him look into the mouths and ears of old men and listen to the modestly uttered complaints of women. She saw him use instruments, apply bandages, inject needles, and press his stethoscope to emaciated chests. She watched how he smiled at times, frowned at others, but always maintained the dignified, authoritative doctor air that kept his patients in awe of him. And she watched how the pretty nurse at his side worked so well with him, anticipating him, sometimes laughing softly with him and the children. They prayed together with the people, and every so often a special look passed between the nurse and Christopher.

Deborah thought of Terry Donald's doomsday words about the end of the whites in Kenya; she recalled Mama Wachera's dying utterance; she pictured the black Jesus on the cross. But Deborah knew that the traces of colonial pioneers like her grandfather would never be totally erased from East Africa; the hand of the white man had left an indelible mark.

Because there it was, in the midst of that hope-seeking crowd, in the person of Dr. Christopher Mathenge. *He* was Grace Treverton's true, lasting legacy.

Kwa heri, Deborah's lips said, mouthing a silent good-bye.

Then she got back in the car and said to Abdi, "Take me to Jomo Kenyatta Airport, please. I'm going home."

ABOUT THE AUTHOR

BARBARA WOOD served as a surgical technician for ten years, specializing in neurosurgery at Santa Monica Hospital in California before turning her favorite hobby, writing, into a full-time occupation. She has written the successful novels *Domina*, *Vital Signs*, and *Soul Flame*. She lives in Riverside, California.